13 SHORT SCIENCE FICTION NOVELS

ABOUT THE EDITORS

ISAAC ASIMOV, one of America's great resources, has by now written more than 300 books. No other writer in history has published so much on such a wide variety of subjects, which range from science fiction and murder novels to books on history, the physical sciences, and Shakespeare. Born in the Soviet Union and raised in Brooklyn, he lives in New York City with his wife, electric typewriter, and word processor. He recently achieved best-seller status with both *Foundation's Edge*, the 1982 Hugo Award winner for Best Novel, and *The Robots of Dawn*.

MARTIN H. GREENBERG, who has been called "the king of anthologists," now has some 120 to his credit. He is also coeditor, with Bill Pronzini, of *Baker's Dozen: 13 Short Mystery Novels, Baker's Dozen: 13 Short Fantasy Novels*, and *Baker's Dozen: 13 Short Espionage Novels*. Greenberg is professor of regional analysis and political science at the University of Wisconsin–Green Bay, where he also teaches a course in the history of science fiction.

CHARLES G. WAUGH, a professor of psychology and mass communications at the University of Maine at Augusta, is a leading authority on science fiction and fantasy who has collaborated on more than 75 anthologies and single-author collections with Isaac Asimov, Martin H. Greenberg, and assorted colleagues.

13 SHORT SCIENCE FICTION NOVELS

PRESENTED BY ISAAC ASIMOV

Edited by
Isaac Asimov,
Martin H. Greenberg,
and Charles G. Waugh

With an Introduction by
Isaac Asimov

BONANZA BOOKS
New York

Grateful acknowledgment for permission to reprint material is hereby given to the following:
Profession by Isaac Asimov—Copyright ©1957 by Street and Smith Publications, Inc.; copyright © renewed 1985 by Nightfall, Inc. Reprinted by permission of the author.
Who Goes There? by John W. Campbell, Jr.—Copyright 1938 by Street and Smith Publications, Inc.; copyright © renewed 1966 by John W. Campbell, Jr. Reprinted by permission of the agents for the author's estate, the Scott Meredith Literary Agency, Inc., 845 Third Avenue, New York, NY 10022.
For I Am a Jealous People!—Copyright 1954 and copyright © renewed 1982 by Lester Del Rey. Reprinted by permission of the author and his agents, the Scott Meredith Literary Agency, Inc., 845 Third Avenue, New York, NY 10022.
The Mortal and the Monster by Gordon R. Dickson—Copyright ©1976 by Random House, Inc. Reprinted by permission of the author.
Time Safari—Copyright ©1981 by David Drake. Reprinted by permission of Kirby McCauley, Ltd.
In the Western Tradition—Copyright ©1981 by Phyllis Eisenstein. From *The Magazine of Fantasy and Science Fiction*. Reprinted by permission of the author.
The Alley Man by Philip José Farmer—Copyright ©1959 by Mercury Press, Inc. From *The Magazine of Fantasy and Science Fiction*. Reprinted by permission of the author and his agents, the Scott Meredith Literary Agency, Inc., 845 Third Avenue, New York, NY 10022.
The Sellers of the Dream by John Jakes—Copyright ©1963 by Galaxy Publishing Corporation. Reprinted by permission of the author.
The Moon Goddess and the Son by Donald Kingsbury—Copyright ©1979 by David Publications, Inc. and copyright ©1985 by 96114 Canada Ltd. Reprinted by permission of the Spectrum Literary Agency, Inc.
Enemy Mine by Barry Longyear—Copyright ©1979 by David Publications, Inc. From the September 1979 issue of *Isaac Asimov's Science Fiction Magazine*. Collected in *Manifest Destiny* by Barry Longyear; Berkeley, 1980. Reprinted by permission of Richard Curtis Associates, Inc.
Flash Crowd—Copyright ©1973 by Larry Niven. Reprinted by permission of Kirby McCauley, Ltd.
In the Problem Pit by Frederik Pohl—Copyright ©1973 by Mercury Press, Inc. From *The Magazine of Fantasy and Science Fiction*. Reprinted by permission of the author.
The Desert of Stolen Dreams by Robert Silverberg—Copyright ©1981 by Agberg, Ltd. Reprinted by permission of Agberg, Ltd.

This 1985 edition is published by Bonanza Books, distributed by Crown Publishers, Inc. by arrangement with Nightfall, Inc., Martin H. Greenberg and Charles G. Waugh.

Printed and bound in the United States of America

Library of Congress Cataloging in Publication Data
Main entry under title:

Baker's dozen.

1. Science fiction, American. I. Asimov, Isaac, 1920- . II. Greenberg, Martin Harry. III. Waugh, Charles.

PS648.S3B27 1985 813'.0876'08 85-3766
ISBN 0-517-476460

h g f e d c b a

CONTENTS

INTRODUCTION

ISAAC ASIMOV

Novellas

Fiction comes in different sizes, as do jars of pickles, boxes of candy, and many, many other things. In the case of fiction, however, the difference is not merely a matter of quantity. A large jar of pickles will contain more pickles than a small jar and that may well be all there is to it. A long piece of fiction, however, may be fundamentally different from a short piece in its nature as well as in its word-count.

To see what I mean, let's begin by presenting the different categories of fiction, together with my own notion of what the word-lengths ought to be:

1. Short-short story ..... 1,000 to 2,000 words
2. Short story .... 5,000 to 7,000 words
3. Novelette .... 10,000 to 20,000 words
4. Novella .... 30,000 to 50,000 words
5. Novel .... 70,000 words and up.

(Notice that the shorter the name of the category, the longer the piece of fiction, but that's just a coincidence.)

Of these, the most popular lengths are the short story and the novel. The short story has a single plot line and, ideally, every sentence ought to contribute to the development of the plot. There is no room for anything else. The advantage to this is that you can read the story at a sitting and, if it is a good story, you will sail smoothly along its length, going faster and faster, and ending up with a satisfying crash. In fact, you *must* read it at a sitting, for if you stop in the middle, you will start again cold and it simply loses the effect it ought to have.

The novel, on the other hand, mustn't have a single plot line to which everything else is subordinated. You can't keep things going that long without exhausting the reader long before you're done. Instead, the novel proceeds leisurely, and allows room for humor, for characterization, even for a bit of philosophizing. It also has its nooks and byways, so that there are subsidiary plots, side-actions, comic relief, and so on. A novel is too long to be read at a sitting and *shouldn't* be, for you need time to absorb the intricate structure, the point and counterpoint, the intertwining and blending of different courses of action.

What about the other categories? The short-short story is a still further sharpened short story. It pares away everything until there is nothing left but an arrow—a thin, straight story line bearing the point, which should be aimed right at your heart. It is very difficult to do well, and hard to take in quantity.

A novelette, on the other hand, is a long short story. It is fattened, so that you might have some characterization, some side-action, though not too much. It is a rather relaxing length for a writer for it gives him a bit of room to play around, without making too many demands on him for complexity.

A novella is sometimes referred to as a "short novel" and, to some extent, that is exactly what it is. It can have some of the complexity of the true novel, and ample room for characterization, but a writer must not let it run away with him. A novella differs from a novel in that the former may be read at a sitting if the reader is sufficiently caught up in it, so the writer must labor to make that possible by not cramming into it all the complexity of a novel.

The science fiction novella is a special case because for a quarter-century, American science fiction was hardly ever found anywhere but in magazines. Novels were so long that they had to be serialized in the magazines, something that had both advantages and disadvantages. Either way, there was no room for more than four or five novels per year in the magazines and there was no other way of publishing them. For a time, then, s. f. novels were few.

Magazine publishers liked to present their readers with variety, and would supply stories of different length—say, three novelettes, perhaps, and six short stories in each issue. Once in a while they would present a novella, giving readers the luxury of complexity, without having to risk the dangers of serialization.

Risk existed, nevertheless. A novella would take up a major portion of the magazine and reduce the total number of stories that could be presented. If a reader disliked one of the shorter stories, that would be a small fraction of the magazine and was tolerable. If he disliked a novella, however, that virtually ruined the issue for him, and he was quite likely to write a sizzling letter to the editor—and editors are sensitive to such things.

The result was that editors chose only those novellas that were sure-fire, so that, by and large, only well-established and experienced authors dared write them. They meant a lot of money (comparatively) if they sold, but a lot of wasted effort if they didn't. The result is that some of the best science fiction in existence is present in novellas.

Science fiction differs from other classifications of popular genre fiction in that it is extraordinarily rich in anthologies; and yet, those anthologies rarely take advantage of the many splendid novellas that exist. It is easy to see why. A novella absorbs a sizable percentage of the pages of an anthology, as it would the pages of a magazine, and most anthology editors feel nervous about placing so many words in a single basket.

Not we, however. We present you now with nothing ***but*** science fiction novellas—thirteen of them—a baker's dozen. They differ in subject matter, in style, in everything you can think of but quality. They are all skillfully written, cleverly constructed stories, with ingenious ideas, as you will have to admit, even if one or two of them should happen, for one reason or another, not to be entirely to your liking.

And you'll be getting your money's worth, for we might, in all truth, call them thirteen short novels—all in one book.

ISAAC ASIMOV

Profession

GEORGE PLATEN could not conceal the longing in his voice. It was too much to suppress. He said, "Tomorrow's the first of May. Olympics!"

He rolled over on his stomach and peered over the foot of his bed at his roommate. Didn't *he* feel it, too? Didn't *this* make some impression on him?

George's face was thin and had grown a trifle thinner in the nearly year and a half that he had been at the House. His figure was slight but the look in his blue eyes was as intense as it had ever been, and right now there was a trapped look in the way his fingers curled against the bedspread.

George's roommate looked up briefly from his book and took the opportunity to adjust the light-level of the stretch of wall near his chair. His name was Hali Omani and he was a Nigerian by birth. His dark brown skin and massive features seemed made for calmness, and mention of the Olympics did not move him.

He said, "I know, George."

George owed much to Hali's patience and kindness when it was needed, but even patience and kindness could be overdone. Was this a time to sit there like a statue built of some dark, warm wood?

George wondered if he himself would grow like that after ten years here and rejected the thought violently. No!

He said defiantly, "I think you've forgotten what May means."

The other said, "I remember very well what it means. It means nothing! You're the one who's forgotten that. May means nothing to you, George Platen, and," he added softly, "it means nothing to me, Hali Omani."

George said, "The ships are coming in for recruits. By June, thousands and thousands will leave with millions of men and women heading for any world you can name, and all that means nothing?"

"Less than nothing. What do you want me to do about it, anyway?" Omani ran his finger along a difficult passage in the book he was reading and his lips moved soundlessly.

George watched him. Damn it, he thought, yell, scream; you can do that much. Kick at me, do anything.

It was only that he wanted not to be so alone in his anger. He wanted not to be the only one so filled with resentment, not to be the only one dying a slow death.

It was better those first weeks when the Universe was a small shell of vague light and sound pressing down upon him. It was better before Omani had wavered into view and dragged him back to a life that wasn't worth living.

Omani! He was old! He was at least thirty. George thought: Will I be like that at thirty? Will I be like that in twelve years?

And because he was afraid he might be, he yelled at Omani, "Will you stop reading that fool book?"

Omani turned a page and read on a few words, then lifted his head with its skullcap of crisply curled hair and said, "What?"

"What good does it do you to read the book?" He stepped forward, snorted "More electronics," and slapped it out of Omani's hands.

Omani got up slowly and picked up the book. He smoothed a crumpled page without visible rancor. "Call it the satisfaction of curiosity," he said. "I understand a little of it today, perhaps a little more tomorrow. That's a victory in a way."

"A victory. What kind of a victory? Is that what satisfies you in life? To get to know enough to be a quarter of a Registered Electronician by the time you're sixty-five?"

"Perhaps by the time I'm thirty-five."

"And then who'll want you? Who'll use you? Where will you go?"

"No one. No one. Nowhere. I'll stay here and read other books."

"And that satisfies you? Tell me! You've dragged me to class. You've got me to reading and memorizing, too. For what! There's nothing in it that satisfies me."

"What good will it do you to deny yourself satisfaction?"

"It means I'll quit the whole farce. I'll do as I planned to do in the beginning before you dovey-lovied me out of it. I'm going to force them to—to——"

Omani put down his book. He let the other run down and then said, "To what, George?"

"To correct a miscarriage of justice. A frame-up. I'll get that Antonelli and force him to admit he—he——"

Omani shook his head. "Everyone who comes here insists it's a mistake. I thought you'd passed that stage."

"Don't call it a stage," said George violently. "In my case, it's a fact. I've told you——"

"You've told me, but in your heart you know no one made any mistake as far as you were concerned."

"Because no one will admit it? You think any of them would admit a mistake unless they were forced to?——Well, I'll force them."

It was May that was doing this to George; it was Olympics month. He felt it bring the old wildness back and he couldn't stop it. He didn't want to stop it. He had been in danger of forgetting.

He said, "I was going to be a Computer Programmer and I *can* be one. I could be one today, regardless of what they say analysis shows." He pounded his mattress. "They're wrong. They *must* be."

"The analysts are never wrong."

"They *must* be. Do you doubt my intelligence?"

"Intelligence hasn't one thing to do with it. Haven't you been told that often enough? Can't you understand that?"

George rolled away, lay on his back and stared somberly at the ceiling.

"What did you want to be, Hali?"

"I had no fixed plans. Hydroponicist would have suited me, I suppose."

"Did you think you could make it?"

"I wasn't sure."

George had never asked personal questions of Omani before. It struck him as queer, almost unnatural, that other people had had ambitions and ended here. Hydroponicist!

He said, "Did you think you'd make *this?*"

"No, but here I am just the same."

"And you're satisfied. Really, really satisfied. You're happy. You love it. You wouldn't be anywhere else."

Slowly, Omani got to his feet. Carefully, he began to unmake his bed. He said, "George, you're a hard case. You're knocking yourself out because you won't accept the facts about yourself. George, you're here in what you call the House, but I've never heard you give it its full title. Say it, George, say it. Then go to bed and sleep this off."

George gritted his teeth and showed them. He choked out, "No!"

"Then I will," said Omani, and he did. He shaped each syllable carefully.

George was bitterly ashamed at the sound of it. He turned his head away.

For most of the first eighteen years of his life, George Platen had headed firmly in one direction, that of Registered Computer Programmer. There were those in his crowd who spoke wisely of Spationautics, Refrigeration Technology, Transportation Control, and even Administration. But George held firm.

He argued relative merits as vigorously as any of them, and why not? Education Day loomed ahead of them and was the great fact of their existence. It approached steadily, as fixed and certain as the calendar—the first day of November of the year following one's eighteenth birthday.

After that day, there were other topics of conversation. One could discuss with others some detail of the profession, or the virtues of one's wife and children, or the fate of one's space-polo team, or one's experience in the Olympics. Before Education Day, however, there was only one topic that unfailingly and unwearyingly held everyone's interest, and that was Education Day.

"What are you going for? Think you'll make it? Heck, that's no good. Look at the records; quota's been cut. Logistics now——"

Or Hypermechanics now—— Or Communications now—— Or Gravitics now——

Especially Gravitics at the moment. Everyone had been talking about Gravitics in the few years just before George's Education Day because of the development of the Gravitic power engine.

Any world within ten light-years of a dwarf star, everyone said, would give its eyeteeth for any kind of Registered Gravitics Engineer.

The thought of that never bothered George. Sure it would; all the eyeteeth it could scare up. But George had also heard what had happened before in a newly developed technique. Rationalization and simplification followed in a flood. New models each year; new types of gravitic engines; new principles. Then all those eyeteeth gentlemen would find themselves out of date and superseded by later models with later educations. The first group would then have to settle down to unskilled labor or ship out to some backwoods world that wasn't quite caught up yet.

Now Computer Programmers were in steady demand year after year, century after century. The demand never reached wild peaks; there was never a howling bull market for Programmers; but the demand climbed steadily as new worlds opened up and as older worlds grew more complex.

He had argued with Stubby Trevelyan about that constantly. As best friends, their arguments had to be constant and vitriolic and, of course, neither ever persuaded or was persuaded.

But then Trevelyan had had a father who was a Registered Metallurgist and had actually served on one of the Outworlds, and a grandfather who had also been a Registered Metallurgist. He himself was intent on becoming a Registered Metallurgist almost as a matter of family right and was firmly convinced that any other profession was a shade less than respectable.

"There'll always be metal," he said, "and there's an accomplishment in molding alloys to specification and watching structures grow. Now what's a Programmer going to be doing. Sitting at a coder all day long, feeding some fool mile-long machine."

Even at sixteen, George had learned to be practical. He said simply, "There'll be a million Metallurgists put out along with you."

"Because it's good. A good profession. The best."

"But you get crowded out, Stubby. You can be way back in line. Any world can tape out its own Metallurgists, and the market for advanced Earth models isn't so big. And it's mostly the small worlds that want them. You know what percent of the turnout of Registered Metallurgists get tabbed for worlds with a Grade A rating. I looked it up. It's just 13.3 percent. That means you'll have seven chances in eight of being stuck in some world that just about has running water. You may even be stuck on Earth; 2.3 percent are."

Trevelyan said belligerently, "There's no disgrace in staying on Earth. Earth needs technicians, too. Good ones." His grandfather had been an Earth-bound Metallurgist, and Trevelyan lifted his finger to his upper lip and dabbed at an as yet nonexistent mustache.

George knew about Trevelyan's grandfather and, considering the Earth-bound position of his own ancestry, was in no mood to sneer. He said diplomatically, "No intellectual disgrace. Of course not. But it's nice to get into a Grade A world, isn't it?

"Now you take Programmers. Only the Grade A worlds have the kind of computers that really need first-class Programmers so they're the only ones in the market. And Programmer tapes are complicated and hardly any one fits. They need more Programmers than their own population can supply. It's just a matter of statistics. There's one first-class Programmer per million, say. A world needs twenty and has a population of ten million, they have to come to Earth for five to fifteen Programmers. Right?

"And you know how many Registered Computer Programmers went to Grade A planets last year? I'll tell you. Every last one. If you're a Programmer, you're a picked man. Yes, sir."

Trevelyan frowned. "If only one in a million makes it, what makes you think *you'll* make it?"

George said guardedly, "I'll make it."

He never dared tell anyone; not Trevelyan; not his parents; of exactly what he was doing that made him so confident. But he wasn't worried. He was simply confident (that was the worst of the memories he had in the hopeless days afterward). He was as blandly confident as the average eight-year-old kid approaching Reading Day—that childhood preview of Education Day.

Of course, Reading Day had been different. Partly, there was the simple fact of childhood. A boy of eight takes many extraordinary things in stride. One day you can't read and the next day you can. That's just the way things are. Like the sun shining.

And then not so much depended upon it. There were no recruiters just ahead, waiting and jostling for the lists and scores on the coming Olympics. A boy or girl who goes through the Reading Day is just someone who has ten more years of undifferentiated living upon Earth's crawling surface; just someone who returns to his family with one new ability.

By the time Education Day came, ten years later, George wasn't even sure of most of the details of his own Reading Day.

Most clearly of all, he remembered it to be a dismal September day with a mild rain falling. (September for Reading Day; November for Education Day; May for Olympics. They made nursery rhymes out of it.) George had dressed by the wall lights, with his parents far more excited than he himself was. His father was a Registered Pipe Fitter and had found his occupation on earth. This fact had always been a humiliation to him, although, of course, as anyone could see plainly, most of each generation must stay on Earth in the nature of things.

There had to be farmers and miners and even technicians on Earth. It was only the late-model, high-specialty professions that were in demand on the Outworlds, and only a few millions a year out of Earth's eight billion population could be exported. Every man and woman on Earth couldn't be among that group.

But every man and woman could hope that at least one of his children could be one, and Platen, Senior, was certainly no exception. It was obvious to him (and, to be sure, to others as well) that George was notably intelligent and quick-minded. He would be bound to do well and he would have to, as he was an only child. If George didn't end on an Outworld, they would have to wait for grandchildren before a next chance would come along, and that was too far in the future to be much consolation.

Reading Day would not prove much, of course, but it would be the only indication they would have before the big day itself. Every parent on Earth would be listening to the quality of reading when his child came home with it; listening for any particularly easy flow of words and building that into certain omens of the future. There were few families that didn't have at least one hopeful who, from Reading Day on, was the great hope because of the way he handled his trisyllabics.

Dimly, George was aware of the cause of his parents' tension, and if there was any anxiety in his young heart that drizzly morning, it was only the fear that his father's hopeful expression might fade out when he returned home with his reading.

The children met in the large assembly room of the town's Education hall. All over Earth, in millions of local halls, throughout that month, similar groups of children would be meeting. George felt depressed by the grayness of the room and by the other children, strained and stiff in unaccustomed finery.

Automatically, George did as all the rest of the children did. He found the small clique that represented the children on his floor of the apartment house and joined them.

Trevelyan, who lived immediately next door, still wore his hair childishly long and was years removed from the sideburns and thin, reddish mustache that he was to grow as soon as he was physiologically capable of it.

Trevelyan (to whom George was then known as Jaw-jee) said, "Bet you're scared."

"I am not," said George. Then, confidentially, "My folks got a hunk of printing up on the dresser in my room, and when I come home, I'm going to read it for them." (George's main suffering at the moment lay in the fact that he didn't quite know where to put his hands. He had been warned not to scratch his head or rub his ears or pick his nose or put his hands into his pockets. This eliminated almost every possibility.)

Trevelyan put *his* hands in his pockets and said, "My father isn't worried."

Trevelyan, Senior, had been a Metallurgist on Diporia for nearly seven years, which gave him a superior social status in his neighborhood even though he had retired and returned to Earth.

Earth discouraged these re-immigrants because of population problems, but a small trickle did return. For one thing the cost of living was lower on Earth, and what was a trifling annuity on Diporia, say, was a comfortable income on Earth. Besides, there were always men who found more satisfaction in displaying their success before the friends and scenes of their childhood than before all the rest of the Universe besides.

Trevelyan, Senior, further explained that if he stayed on Diporia, so would his children, and Diporia was a one-spaceship world. Back on Earth, his kids could end anywhere, even Novia.

Stubby Trevelyan had picked up that item early. Even before Reading Day, his conversation was based on the carelessly assumed fact that his ultimate home would be in Novia.

George, oppressed by thoughts of the other's future greatness and his own small-time contrast, was driven to belligerent defense at once.

"My father isn't worried either. He just wants to hear me read because he knows I'll be good. I suppose your father would just as soon not hear you because he knows you'll be all wrong."

"I will not be all wrong. Reading is *nothing*. On Novia, I'll *hire* people to read to me."

"Because *you* won't be able to read yourself, on account of you're *dumb!*"

"Then how come I'll be on Novia?"

And George, driven, made the great denial. "Who says you'll be on Novia? Bet you don't go anywhere."

Stubby Trevelyan reddened. "I won't be a Pipe Fitter like your old man."

"Take that back, you dumbhead."

"You take *that* back."

They stood nose to nose, not wanting to fight but relieved at having something familiar to do in this strange place. Furthermore, now that George had curled his hands into fists and lifted them before his face, the problem of what to do with his hands was, at least temporarily, solved. Other children gathered round excitedly.

But then it all ended when a woman's voice sounded loudly over the public address system. There was instant silence everywhere. George dropped his fists and forgot Trevelyan.

"Children," said the voice, "we are going to call out your names. As each child is called, he or she is to go to one of the men waiting along the side walls. Do you see them? They are wearing red uniforms so they will be easy to find. The girls will go to the right. The boys will go to the left. Now look about and see which man in red is nearest to you—''

George found his man at a glance and waited for his name to be called off. He had not been introduced before this to the sophistications of the alphabet, and the length of time it took to reach his own name grew disturbing.

The crowd of children thinned; little rivulets made their way to each of the red-clad guides.

When the name ''George Platen'' was finally called, his sense of relief was exceeded only by the feeling of pure gladness at the fact that Stubby Trevelyan still stood in his place, uncalled.

George shouted back over his shoulder as he left, ''Yay, Stubby, maybe they don't want you.''

That moment of gaiety quickly left. He was herded into a line and directed down corridors in the company of strange children. They all looked at one another, large-eyed and concerned, but beyond a snuffling, ''Quitcher pushing'' and ''Hey, watch out'' there was no conversation.

They were handed little slips of paper which they were told must remain with them. George stared at his curiously. Little black marks of different shapes. He knew it to be printing but how could anyone make words out of it? He couldn't imagine.

He was told to strip; he and four other boys who were all that now remained together. All the new clothes came shucking off and four eight-year-olds stood naked and small, shivering more out of embarrassment than cold. Medical technicians came past, probing them, testing them with odd instruments, pricking them for blood. Each took the little cards and made additional marks on them with little black rods that produced the marks, all neatly lined up, with great speed. George stared at the new marks, but they were no more comprehensible than the old. The children were ordered back into their clothes.

They sat on separate little chairs then and waited again. Names were called again and ''George Platen'' came third.

He moved into a large room, filled with frightening instruments with knobs and glassy panels in front. There was a desk in the very center, and behind it a man sat, his eyes on the papers piled before him.

He said, ''George Platen?''

''Yes, sir,'' said George in a shaky whisper. All this waiting and all this going here and there was making him nervous. He wished it were over.

The man behind the desk said, ''I am Dr. Lloyed, George. How are you?''

The doctor didn't look up as he spoke. It was as though he had said those words over and over again and didn't have to look up any more.

''I'm all right.''

''Are you afraid, George?''

"N—no, sir," said George, sounding afraid even in his own ears.

"That's good," said the doctor, "because there's nothing to be afraid of, you know. Let's see, George. It says here on your card that your father is named Peter and that he's a Registered Pipe Fitter and your mother is named Amy and is a Registered Home Technician. Is that right?"

"Y—yes, sir."

"And your birthday is February 13, and you had an ear infection about a year ago. Right?"

"Yes, sir."

"Do you know how I know all these things?"

"It's on the card, I think, sir."

"That's right." The doctor looked up at George for the first time and smiled. He showed even teeth and looked much younger than George's father. Some of George's nervousness vanished.

The doctor passed the card to George. "Do you know what all those things there mean, George?"

Although George knew he did not he was startled by the sudden request into looking at the card as though he might understand now through some sudden stroke of fate. But they were just marks as before and he passed the card back. "No, sir."

"Why not?"

George felt a sudden pang of suspicion concerning the sanity of this doctor. Didn't he know why not?

George said, "I can't read, sir."

"Would you like to read?"

"Yes, sir."

"Why, George?"

George stared, appalled. No one had ever asked him that. He had no answer. He said falteringly, "I don't know, sir."

"Printed information will direct you all through your life. There is so much you'll have to know even after Education Day. Cards like this one will tell you. Books will tell you. Television screens will tell you. Printing will tell you such useful things and such interesting things that not being able to read would be as bad as not being able to see. Do you understand?"

"Yes, sir."

"Are you afraid, George?"

"No, sir."

"Good. Now I'll tell you exactly what we'll do first. I'm going to put these wires on your forehead just over the corners of your eyes. They'll stick there but they won't hurt at all. Then, I'll turn on something that will make a buzz. It will sound funny and it may tickle you, but it won't hurt. Now if it does hurt, you tell me, and I'll turn it off right away, but it won't hurt. All right?"

George nodded and swallowed.

"Are you ready?"

George nodded. He closed his eyes while the doctor busied himself. His parents had explained this to him. They, too, had said it wouldn't hurt, but then there were always the older children. There were the ten- and twelve-year-olds who howled after the eight-year-olds waiting for Reading Day, "Watch out for the needle." There were the others who took you off in confidence and said, "They got to cut your head open. They use a sharp knife that big with a hook on it," and so on into horrifying details.

George had never believed them but he had had nightmares, and now closed his eyes and felt pure terror.

He didn't feel the wires at his temple. The buzz was a distant thing, and there was the sound of his own blood in his ears, ringing hollowly as though it and he were in a large cave. Slowly he chanced opening his eyes.

The doctor had his back to him. From one of the instruments a strip of paper unwound and was covered with a thin, wavy purple line. The doctor tore off pieces and put them into a slot in another machine. He did it over and over again. Each time a little piece of film came out, which the doctor looked at. Finally, he turned toward George with a queer frown between his eyes.

The buzzing stopped.

George said breathlessly, "Is it over?"

The doctor said, "Yes," but he was still frowning.

"Can I read now?" asked George. He felt no different.

The doctor said, "What?" then smiled very suddenly and briefly. He said, "It works fine, Geoge. You'll be reading in fifteen minutes. Now we're going to use another machine this time and it will take longer. I'm going to cover your whole head, and when I turn it on you won't be able to see or hear anything for a while, but it won't hurt. Just to make sure I'm going to give you a little switch to hold in your hand. If anything hurts, you press the little button and everything shuts off. All right?"

In later years, George was told that the little switch was strictly a dummy; that it was introduced solely for confidence. He never did know for sure, however, since he never pushed the button.

A large smoothly curved helmet with a rubbery inner lining was placed over his head and left there. Three or four little knobs seemed to grab at him and bite into his skull, but there was only a little pressure that faded. No pain.

The doctor's voice sounded dimly. "Everything all right, George?"

And then, with no real warning, a layer of thick felt closed down all about him. He was disembodied, there was no sensation, no universe, only himself and a distant murmur at the very ends of nothingness telling him something—telling him—telling him—

He strained to hear and understand but there was all that thick felt between.

Then the helmet was taken off his head, and the light was so bright that it hurt his eyes while the doctor's voice drummed at his ears.

The doctor said, "Here's your card, George. What does it say?"

George looked at his card again and gave out a strangled shout. The marks weren't just marks at all. They made up words. They were words just as clearly as though something were whispering them in his ears. He could *hear* them being whispered as he looked at them.

"What does it say, George?"

"It says—it says—'Platen, George. Born 13 February 6492 of Peter and Amy Platen in . . .' " He broke off.

"You can read, George," said the doctor. "It's all over."

"For good? I won't forget how?"

"Of course not." The doctor leaned over to shake hands gravely. "You will be taken home now."

It was days before George got over this new and great talent of his. He read for his father with such facility that Platen, Senior, wept and called relatives to tell the good news.

George walked about town, reading every scrap of printing he could find and wondering how it was that none of it had ever made sense to him before.

He tried to remember how it was not to be able to read and he couldn't. As far as his feeling about it was concerned, he had always been able to read. Always.

At eighteen, George was rather dark, of medium height, but thin enough to look taller. Trevelyan, who was scarcely an inch shorter, had a stockiness of build that made "Stubby" more than ever appropriate, but in this last year he had grown self-conscious. The nickname could no longer be used without reprisal. And since Trevelyan disapproved of his proper first name even more strongly, he was called Trevelyan or any decent variant of that. As though to prove his manhood further, he had most persistently grown a pair of sideburns and a bristly mustache.

He was sweating and nervous now, and George, who had himself grown out of "Jaw-jee" and into the curt monosyllabic gutterality of "George," was rather amused by that.

They were in the same large hall they had been in ten years before (and not since). It was as if a vague dream of the past had come to sudden reality. In the first few minutes George had been distinctly surprised at finding everything seem smaller and more cramped than his memory told him; then he made allowance for his own growth.

The crowd was smaller than it had been in childhood. It was exclusively male this time. The girls had another day assigned them.

Trevelyan leaned over to say, "Beats me the way they make you wait."

"Red tape," said George. "You can't avoid it."

Trevelyan said, "What makes *you* so damned tolerant about it?"

"I've got nothing to worry about."

"Oh, brother, you make me sick. I hope you end up Registered Manure Spreader just so I can see your face when you do." His somber eyes swept the crowd anxiously.

George looked about, too. It wasn't quite the system they used on the children. Matters went slower, and instructions had been given out at the start in print (an advantage over the pre-Readers). The names Platen and Trevelyan were well down the alphabet still, but this time the two knew it.

Young men came out of the education rooms, frowning and uncomfortable, picked up their clothes and belongings, then went off to analysis to learn the results.

Each, as he came out, would be surrounded by a clot of the thinning crowd. "How was it?" "How'd it feel?" "Whacha think ya made?" "Ya feel any different?"

Answers were vague and noncommittal.

George forced himself to remain out of those clots. You only raised your own blood pressure. Everyone said you stood the best chance if you remained calm. Even so, you could feel the palms of your hands grow cold. Funny that new tensions came with the years.

For instance, high-specialty professionals heading out for an Outworld were accompanied by a wife (or husband). It was important to keep the sex ratio in good balance on all worlds. And if you were going out to a Grade A world, what girl would refuse you? George had no specific girl in mind yet; he wanted none. Not now! Once he made Programmer; once he could add to his name, Registered Computer Programmer, he could take his pick, like a sultan in a harem. The thought excited him and he tried to put it away. Must stay calm.

Trevelyan muttered, "What's it all about anyway? First they say it works best if you're relaxed and at ease. Then they put you through this and make it impossible for you to be relaxed and at ease."

"Maybe that's the idea. They're separating the boys from the men to begin with. Take it easy, Trev."

"Shut up."

George's turn came. His name was not called. It appeared in glowing letters on the notice board.

He waved at Trevelyan. "Take it easy, Trev. Don't let it get you."

He was happy as he entered the testing chamber. Actually happy.

The man behind the desk said, "George Platen?"

For a fleeting instant there was a razor-sharp picture in George's mind of another man, ten years earlier, who had asked the same question, and it was almost as though this were the same man and he, George, had turned eight again as he stepped across the threshold.

But the man looked up and, of course, the face matched that of the sudden memory not at all. The nose was bulbous, the hair thin and stringy, and the chin wattled as though its owner had once been grossly overweight and had reduced.

The man behind the desk looked annoyed. "Well?"

George came to Earth. "I'm George Platen, sir."

"Say so, then. I'm Dr. Zachary Antonelli, and we're going to be intimately acquainted in a moment."

He stared at small strips of film, holding them up to the light owlishly.

George winced inwardly. Very hazily, he remembered that other doctor (he had forgotten the name) staring at such film. Could these be the same? The other doctor had frowned and this one was looking at him now as though he were angry.

His happiness was already just about gone.

Dr. Antonelli spread the pages of a thickish file out before him now and put the films carefully to one side. "It says here you want to be a Computer Programmer."

"Yes, doctor."

"Still do?"

"Yes, sir."

"It's a responsible and exacting position. Do you feel up to it?"

"Yes, sir."

"Most pre-Educates don't put down any specific profession. I believe they are afraid of queering it."

"I think that's right, sir."

"Aren't you afraid of that?"

"I might as well be honest, sir."

Dr. Antonelli nodded, but without any noticeable lightening of his expression. "Why do you want to be a Programmer?"

"It's a responsible and exacting position as you said, sir. It's an important job and an exciting one. I like it and I think I can do it."

Dr. Antonelli put the papers away, and looked at George sourly. He said, "How do you know you like it? Because you think you'll be snapped up by some Grade A planet?"

George thought uneasily: He's trying to rattle you. Stay calm and stay frank.

He said, "I think a Programmer has a good chance, sir, but even if I were left on Earth, I know I'd like it." (That was true enough. I'm not lying, thought George.)

"All right, how do you know?"

He asked it as though he knew there was no decent answer and George almost smiled. He had one.

He said, "I've been reading about Programming, sir."

"You've been *what?*" Now the doctor looked genuinely astonished and George took pleasure in that.

"Reading about it, sir. I bought a book on the subject and I've been studying it."

"A book for Registered Programmers?"

"Yes, sir."

"But you couldn't understand it."

"Not at first. I got other books on mathematics and electronics. I made out all I could. I still don't know much, but I know enough to know I like it and to know I can make it." (Even his parents never found that secret cache of books or knew why he spent so much time in his own room or exactly what happened to the sleep he missed.)

The doctor pulled at the loose skin under his chin. "What was your idea in doing that, son?"

"I wanted to make sure I would be interested, sir."

"Surely you know that being interested means nothing. You could be devoured by a subject and if the physical makeup of your brain makes it more efficient for you to be something else, something else you will be. You know that, don't you?"

"I've been told that," said George cautiously.

"Well, believe it. It's true."

George said nothing.

Dr. Antonelli said, "Or do you believe that studying some subject will bend the brain cells in that direction, like that other theory that a pregnant woman need only listen to great music persistently to make a composer of her child. Do you believe that?"

George flushed. That had certainly been in his mind. By forcing his intellect constantly in the desired direction, he had felt sure that he would be getting a head start. Most of his confidence had rested on exactly that point.

"I never—" he began, and found no way of finishing.

"Well, it isn't true. Good Lord, youngster, your brain pattern is fixed at birth. It can be altered by a blow hard enough to damage the cells or by a burst blood vessel or by a tumor or by a major infection—each time, of course, for the worse. But it certainly can't be affected by your thinking special thoughts." He stared at George thoughtfully, then said, "Who told you to do this?"

George, now thoroughly disturbed, swallowed and said, "No one, doctor. My own idea."

"Who knew you were doing it after you started?"

"No one. Doctor, I meant to do no wrong."

"Who said anything about wrong? Useless is what I would say. Why did you keep it to yourself?"

"I—I thought they'd laugh at me." (He thought abruptly of a recent exchange with Trevelyan. George had very cautiously broached the thought, as of something merely circulating distantly in the very outermost reaches of his mind, concerning the possibility of learning something by ladling it into the mind by hand, so to speak, in bits and pieces. Trevelyan had hooted, "George, you'll be tanning your own shoes next and weaving your own shirts." He had been thankful for his policy of secrecy.)

Dr. Antonelli shoved the bits of film he had first looked at from position to position in morose thought. Then he said, "Let's get you analyzed. This is getting me nowhere."

The wires went to George's temples. There was the buzzing. Again there came a sharp memory of ten years ago.

George's hands were clammy; his heart pounded. He should never have told the doctor about his secret reading.

It was his damned vanity, he told himself. He had wanted to show how enterprising he was, how full of initiative. Instead, he had showed himself superstitious and ignorant and aroused the hostility of the doctor. (He could tell the doctor hated him for a wise guy on the make.)

And now he had brought himself to such a state of nervousness, he was sure the analyzer would show nothing that made sense.

He wasn't aware of the moment when the wires were removed from his temples. The sight of the doctor, staring at him thoughtfully, blinked into his consciousness and that was that; the wires were gone. George dragged himself together with a tearing effort. He had quite given up his ambition to be a Programmer. In the space of ten minutes, it had all gone.

He said dismally, "I suppose no?"

"No what?"

"No Programmer?"

The doctor rubbed his nose and said, "You get your clothes and whatever belongs to you and go to room 15-C. Your files will be waiting for you there. So will my report."

George said in complete surprise, "Have I been Educated already? I thought this was just to—"

Dr. Antonelli stared down at his desk. "It will all be explained to you. You do as I say."

George felt something like panic. What was it they couldn't tell him? He wasn't fit for anything but Registered Laborer. They were going to prepare him for that; adjust him to it.

He was suddenly certain of it and he had to keep from screaming by main force.

He stumbled back to his place of waiting. Trevelyan was not there, a fact for which he would have been thankful if he had had enough self-possession to be meaningfully aware of his surroundings. Hardly anyone was left, in fact, and the few who were looked as though they might ask him questions were it not that they were too worn out by their tail-of-the-alphabet waiting to buck the fierce, hot look of anger and hate he cast at them.

What right had *they* to be technicians and he, himself, a Laborer? Laborer! He was *certain!*

He was led by a red-uniformed guide along the busy corridors lined with separate rooms each containing its groups, here two, there five: the Motor Mechanics, the Construction Engineers, the Agronomists— There were hundreds of specialized Professions and most of them would be represented in this small town by one or two anyway.

He hated them all just then: the Statisticians, the Accountants, the lesser breeds and the higher. He hated them because they owned their smug knowledge now, knew their fate, while he himself, empty still, had to face some kind of further red tape.

He reached 15-C, was ushered in and left in an empty room. For one moment, his spirits bounded. Surely, if this were the Labor classification room, there would be dozens of youngsters present.

A door sucked into its recess on the other side of a waist-high partition and an elderly, white-haired man stepped out. He smiled and showed even teeth that were obviously false, but his face was still ruddy and unlined and his voice had vigor.

He said, "Good evening, George. Our own sector has only one of you this time, I see."

"Only one?" said George blankly.

"Thousands over the Earth, of course. Thousands. You're not alone."

George felt exasperated. He said, "I don't understand, sir. What's my classification? What's happening?"

"Easy, son. You're all right. It could happen to anyone." He held out his hand and George took it mechanically. It was warm and it pressed George's hand firmly. "Sit down, son. I'm Sam Ellenford."

George nodded impatiently. "I want to know what's going on, sir."

"Of course. To begin with, you can't be a Computer Programmer, George. You've guessed that, I think."

"Yes, I have," said George bitterly. "What will I be, then?"

"That's the hard part to explain, George." He paused, then said with careful distinctness, "Nothing."

"*What!*"

"Nothing!"

"But what does that mean? Why can't you assign me a profession?"

"We have no choice in the matter, George. It's the structure of your mind that decides that."

George went a sallow yellow. His eyes bulged. "There's something wrong with my mind?"

"There's *something* about it. As far as professional classification is concerned, I suppose you can call it wrong."

"But why?"

Ellenford shrugged. "I'm sure you know how Earth runs its Educational program, George. Practically any human being can absorb practically any body of knowledge, but each individual brain pattern is better suited to receiving some types of knowledge than others. We try to match mind to knowledge as well as we can within the limits of the quota requirements for each profession."

George nodded. "Yes, I know."

"Every once in a while, George, we come up against a young man whose mind is not suited to receiving a superimposed knowledge of any sort."

"You mean I can't be Educated?"

"That is what I mean."

"But that's crazy. I'm intelligent. I can understand—" He looked helplessly about as though trying to find some way of proving that he had a functioning brain.

"Don't misunderstand me, please," said Ellenford gravely. "You're intelligent. There's no question about that. You're even above average in intelligence. Unfortunately that has nothing to do with whether the mind ought to be allowed to accept superimposed knowledge or not. In fact, it is almost always the intelligent person who comes here."

"You mean I can't even be a Registered Laborer?" babbled George. Suddenly even that was better than the blank that faced him. "What's there to know to be a Laborer?"

"Don't underestimate the Laborer, young man. There are dozens of subclassifications and each variety has its own corpus of fairly detailed knowledge. Do you think there's no skill in knowing the proper manner of lifting a weight? Besides, for the Laborer, we must select not only minds suited to it, but bodies as well. You're not the type, George, to last long as a Laborer."

George was conscious of his slight build. He said, "But I've never heard of anyone without a profession."

"There aren't many," conceded Ellenford. "And we protect them."

"Protect them?" George felt confusion and fright grow higher inside him.

"You're a ward of the planet, George. From the time you walked through that door, we've been in charge of you." And he smiled.

It was a fond smile. To George it seemed the smile of ownership; the smile of a grown man for a helpless child.

He said, "You mean, I'm going to be in prison?"

"Of course not. You will simply be with others of your kind."

Your kind. The words made a kind of thunder in George's ear.

Ellenford said, "You need special treatment. We'll take care of you."

To George's own horror, he burst into tears. Ellenford walked to the other end of the room and faced away as though in thought.

George fought to reduce the agonized weeping to sobs and then to strangle those. He thought of his father and mother, of his friends, of Trevelyan, of his own shame—

He said rebelliously, "I learned to read."

"Everyone with a whole mind can do that. We've never found exceptions. It is at this stage that we discover—exceptions. And when you learned to read, George, we were concerned about your mind pattern. Certain peculiarities were reported even then by the doctor in charge."

"Can't you try Educating me? You haven't even tried. I'm willing to take the risk."

"The law forbids us to do that, George. But look, it will not be bad. We will explain matters to your family so they will not be hurt. At the place to which you'll be taken, you'll be allowed privileges. We'll get you books and you can learn what you will."

"Dab knowledge in by hand," said George bitterly. "Shred by shred. Then, when I die I'll know enough to be a Registered Junior Office Boy, Paper-Clip Division."

"Yet I understand you've already been studying books."

George froze. He was struck devastatingly by sudden understanding. "That's it . . ."

"What's it?"

"That fellow Antonelli. He's knifing me."

"No, George. You're quite wrong."

"Don't tell me that." George was in an ecstasy of fury. "That lousy bastard is selling me out because he thought I was a little too wise for him. I read books and tried to get a head start toward programming. Well, what do you want to square things? Money? You won't get it. I'm getting out of here and when I finish broadcasting this—"

He was screaming.

Ellenford shook his head and touched a contact.

Two men entered on catfeet and got on either side of George. They pinned his arms to his sides. One of them used an air-spray hypodermic in the hollow of his right elbow and the hypnotic entered his vein and had an almost immediate effect.

His screams cut off and his head fell forward. His knees buckled and only the men on either side kept him erect as he slept.

They took care of George as they said they would; they were good to him and unfailingly kind—about the way, George thought, he himself would be to a sick kitten he had taken pity on.

They told him that he should sit up and take some interest in life; and then told him that most people who came there had the same attitude of despair at the beginning and that he would snap out of it.

He didn't even hear them.

Dr. Ellenford himself visited him to tell him that his parents had been informed that he was away on special assignment.

George muttered, "Do they know—"

Ellenford assured him at once, "We gave no details."

At first George had refused to eat. They fed him intravenously. They hid sharp objects and kept him under guard. Hali Omani came to be his roommate and his stolidity had a calming effect.

One day, out of sheer desperate boredom, George asked for a book. Omani, who himself read books constantly, looked up, smiling broadly. George almost withdrew the request then, rather than give any of them satisfaction, then thought: What do I care?

He didn't specify the book and Omani brought one on chemistry. It was in big print, with small words and many illustrations. It was for teen-agers. He threw the book violently against the wall.

That's what he would be always. A teen-ager all his life. A pre-Educate forever and special books would have to be written for him. He lay smoldering in bed, staring at the ceiling, and after an hour had passed, he got up sulkily, picked up the book, and began reading.

It took him a week to finish it and then he asked for another.

"Do you want to take the first one back?" asked Omani.

George frowned. There were things in the book he had not understood, yet he was not so lost to shame as to say so.

But Omani said, "Come to think of it, you'd better keep it. Books are meant to be read and reread."

It was that same day that he finally yielded to Omani's invitation that he tour the place. He dogged at the Nigerian's feet and took in his surroundings with quick hostile glances.

The place was no prison certainly. There were no walls, no locked doors, no guards. But it was a prison in that the inmates had no place to go outside.

It was somehow good to see others like himself by the dozen. It was so easy to believe himself to be the only one in the world so—maimed.

He mumbled, "How many people here anyway?"

"Two hundred and five, George, and this isn't the only place of the sort in the world. There are thousands."

Men looked up as he passed, wherever he went; in the gymnasium, along the tennis courts; through the library (he had never in his life imagined books could exist in such numbers; they were stacked, actually stacked, along long shelves). They stared at him curiously and he returned the looks savagely. At least *they* were no better than he; no call for *them* to look at him as though he were some sort of curiosity.

Most of them were in their twenties. George said suddenly, "What happens to the older ones?"

Omani said, "This place specializes in the younger ones." Then, as though he suddenly recognized an implication in George's question that he had missed earlier, he shook his head gravely and said, "They're not put out of the way, if that's what you mean. There are other Houses for older ones."

"Who cares?" mumbled George, who felt he was sounding too interested and in danger of slipping into surrender.

"You might. As you grow older, you will find yourself in a House with occupants of both sexes."

That surprised George somehow. "Women, too?"

"Of course. Do you suppose women are immune to this sort of thing?"

George thought of that with more interest and excitement than he had felt for anything since before that day when— He forced his thought away from that.

Omani stopped at the doorway of a room that contained a small closed-circuit television and a desk computer. Five or six men sat about the television. Omani said, "This is a classroom."

George said, "What's that?"

"The young men in there are being educated. Not," he added, quickly, "in the usual way."

"You mean they're cramming it in bit by bit."

"That's right. This is the way everyone did it in ancient times."

This was what they kept telling him since he had come to the House but what of it? Suppose there had been a day when mankind had not known the diatherm-oven. Did that mean he should be satisfied to eat meat raw in a world where others ate it cooked?

He said, "Why do they want to go through that bit-by-bit stuff?"

"To pass the time, George, and because they're curious."

"What good does it do them?"

"It makes them happier."

George carried that thought to bed with him.

The next day he said to Omani ungraciously, "Can you get me into a classroom where I can find out something about programming?"

Omani replied heartily, "Sure."

It was slow and he resented it. Why should someone have to explain something and explain it again? Why should he have to read and reread a passage, then stare at a mathematical relationship and not understand it at once? That wasn't how other people had to be.

Over and over again, he gave up. Once he refused to attend classes for a week.

But always he returned. The official in charge, who assigned reading, conducted the television demonstrations, and even explained difficult passages and concepts, never commented on the matter.

George was finally given a regular task in the gardens and took his turn in the various kitchen and cleaning details. This was represented to him as being an advance, but he wasn't fooled. The place might have been far more mechanized than it was, but they deliberately made work for the young men in order to give them the illusion of worthwhile occupation, of usefulness. George wasn't fooled.

They were even paid small sums of money out of which they could buy certain specified luxuries or which they could put aside for a problematical use in a problematical old age. George kept his money in an open jar, which he kept on a closet shelf. He had no idea how much he had accumulated. Nor did he care.

He made no real friends though he reached the stage where a civil good day was in order. He even stopped brooding (or almost stopped) on the miscarriage of justice that had placed him there. He would go weeks without dreaming of Antonelli, of his gross nose and wattled neck, of the leer with which he would push George into a boiling quicksand and hold him under, till he woke screaming with Omani bending over him in concern.

Omani said to him on a snowy day in February, "It's amazing how you're adjusting."

But that was February, the thirteenth to be exact, his nineteenth birthday. March came, then April, and with the approach of May he realized he hadn't adjusted at all.

The previous May had passed unregarded while George was still in his bed, drooping and ambitionless. This May was different.

All over Earth, George knew, Olympics would be taking place and young men would be competing, matching their skills against one another in the fight for a place on a new world. There would be the holiday atmosphere, the excitement, the news reports, the self-contained recruiting agents from the worlds beyond space, the glory of victory or the consolations of defeat.

How much of fiction dealt with these motifs; how much of his own boyhood excitement lay in following the events of Olympics from year to year; how many of his own plans—

George Platen could not conceal the longing in his voice. It was too much to suppress. He said, "Tomorrow's the first of May. Olympics!"

And that led to his first quarrel with Omani and to Omani's bitter enunciation of the exact name of the institution in which George found himself.

Omani gazed fixedly at George and said distinctly, "A House for the Feeble-minded."

George Platen flushed. Feeble-minded!

He rejected it desperately. He said in a monotone, "I'm leaving."

He said it on impulse. His conscious mind learned it first from the statement as he uttered it.

Omani, who had returned to his book, looked up. "What?"

George knew what he was saying now. He said it fiercely, "I'm leaving."

"That's ridiculous. Sit down, George, calm yourself."

"Oh, no. I'm here on a frame-up, I tell you. This doctor, Antonelli, took a dislike to me. It's the sense of power these petty bureaucrats have. Cross them and they wipe out your life with a stylus mark on some card file."

"Are you back to that?"

"And staying there till it's all straightened out. I'm going to get to Antonelli somehow, break him, force the truth out of him." George was breathing heavily and he felt feverish. Olympics month was here and he couldn't let it pass. If he did, it would be the final surrender and he would be lost for all time.

Omani threw his legs over the side of his bed and stood up. He was nearly six feet tall and the expression on his face gave him the look of a concerned Saint Bernard. He put his arm about George's shoulder, "If I hurt your feelings—"

George shrugged him off. "You just said what you thought was the truth, and I'm going to prove it isn't the truth, that's all. Why not? The door's open. There aren't any locks. No one ever said I couldn't leave. I'll just walk out."

"All right, but where will you go?"

"To the nearest air terminal, then to the nearest Olympics center. I've got money." He seized the open jar that held the wages he had put away. Some of the coins jangled to the floor.

"That will last you a week maybe. Then what?"

"By then I'll have things settled."

"By then you'll come crawling back here," said Omani earnestly, "with all the progress you've made to do over again. You're mad, George."

"Feeble-minded is the word you used before."

"Well, I'm sorry I did. Stay here, will you?"

"Are you going to try to stop me?"

Omani compressed his full lips. "No, I guess I won't. This is your business. If the only way you can learn is to buck the world and come back with blood on your face, go ahead.—Well, go ahead."

George was in the doorway now, looking back over his shoulder. "I'm going,"—he came back to pick up his pocket grooming set slowly—"I hope you don't object to my taking a few personal belongings."

Omani shrugged. He was in bed again reading, indifferent.

George lingered at the door again, but Omani didn't look up. George gritted his teeth, turned and walked rapidly down the empty corridor and out into the night-shrouded grounds.

He had expected to be stopped before leaving the grounds. He wasn't. He had stopped at an all-night diner to ask directions to an air terminal and expected the proprietor to call the police. That didn't happen. He summoned a skimmer to take him to the airport and the driver asked no questions.

Yet he felt no lift at that. He arrived at the airport sick at heart. He had not realized how the outer world would be. He was surrounded by professionals. The diner's proprietor had had his name inscribed on the plastic shell over the cash register. So and so, Registered Cook. The man in the skimmer had his license up, Registered Chauffeur. George felt the bareness of his name and experienced a kind of nakedness because of it; worse, he felt skinned. But no one challenged him. No one studied him suspiciously and demanded proof of professional rating.

George thought bitterly: Who would imagine any human being without one?

He bought a ticket to San Francisco on the 3 A.M. plane. No other plane for a sizable Olympics center was leaving before morning and he wanted to wait as little as possible. As it was, he sat huddled in the waiting room, watching for the police. They did not come.

He was in San Francisco before noon and the noise of the city struck him like a blow. This was the largest city he had ever seen and he had been used to silence and calm for a year and a half now.

Worse, it was Olympics month. He almost forgot his own predicament in his sudden awareness that some of the noise, excitement, confusion was due to that.

The Olympics boards were up at the airport for the benefit of the incoming travelers, and crowds jostled around each one. Each major profession had its own board. Each listed directions to the Olympics Hall where the contest for that day for that profession would be given; the individuals competing and their city of birth; the Outworld (if any) sponsoring it.

It was a completely stylized thing. George had read descriptions often enough in the newsprints and films, watched matches on television, and even witnessed a small Olympics in the Registered Butcher classification at the county seat. Even that, which had no conceivable Galactic implication (there was no Outworlder in attendance, of course) aroused excitement enough.

Partly, the excitement was caused simply by the fact of competition, partly by the spur of local pride (oh, when there was a home-town boy to cheer for, though he might be a complete stranger), and, of course, partly by betting. There was no way of stopping the last.

George found it difficult to approach the board. He found himself looking at the scurrying, avid onlookers in a new way.

There must have been a time when they themselves were Olympic material. What had *they* done? Nothing!

If they had been winners, they would be far out in the Galaxy somewhere, not stuck here on Earth. Whatever they were, their professions must have made them Earth-bait from the beginning; or else they had made themselves Earth-bait by inefficiency at whatever high-specialized professions they had had.

Now these failures stood about and speculated on the chances of newer and younger men. Vultures!

How he wished they were speculating on him.

He moved down the line of boards blankly, clinging to the outskirts of the groups about them. He had eaten breakfast on the strato and he wasn't hungry. He was afraid, though. He was in a big city during the confusion of the beginning of Olympics competition. That was protection, sure. The city was full of strangers. No one would question George. No one would care about George.

No one would care. Not even the House, thought George bitterly. They cared for him like a sick kitten, but if a sick kitten up and wanders off, well, too bad, what can you do?

And now that he was in San Francisco, what did he do? His thoughts struck blankly against a wall. See someone? Whom? How? Where would he even stay? The money he had left seemed pitiful.

The first shamefaced thought of going back came to him. He could go to the police— He shook his head violently as though arguing with a material adversary.

A word caught his eye on one of the boards, gleaming there: *Metallurgist*. In smaller letters, *nonferrous*. At the bottom of a long list of names, in flowing script, *sponsored by Novia*.

It induced painful memories: himself arguing with Trevelyan, so certain that he himself would be a Programmer, so certain that a Programmer was superior to a Metallurgist, so certain that he was following the right course, so certain that he was clever—

So clever that he had to boast to that small-minded, vindictive Antonelli. He had been so sure of himself that moment when he had been called and had left the nervous Trevelyan standing there, so cocksure.

George cried out in a short, incoherent high-pitched gasp. Someone turned to look at him, then hurried on. People brushed past impatiently pushing him this way and that. He remained staring at the board, open-mouthed.

It was as though the board had answered his thought. He was thinking "Trevelyan" so hard that it had seemed for a moment that of course the board would say "Trevelyan" back at him.

But that *was* Trevelyan, up there. And *Armand* Trevelyan (Stubby's hated first name; up in lights for everyone to see) and the right hometown. What's more, Trev had wanted Novia, aimed for Novia, insisted on Novia; and this competition was sponsored by Novia.

This had to be Trev; good old Trev. Almost without thinking, he noted the directions for getting to the place of competition and took his place in line for a skimmer.

Then he thought somberly: Trev made it. He wanted to be a Metallurgist, and he made it!

George felt colder, more alone than ever.

There was a line waiting to enter the hall. Apparently, Metallurgy Olympics was to be an exciting and closely fought one. At least, the illuminated sky sign above the hall said so, and the jostling crowd seemed to think so.

It would have been a rainy day, George thought, from the color of the sky, but San Francisco had drawn the shield across its breadth from bay to ocean. It was an expense to do so, of course, but all expenses were warranted where the comfort of Outworlders was concerned. They would be in town for the Olympics. They were heavy spenders. And for each recruit taken, there would be a fee both to Earth and to the local government from the planet sponsoring the Olympics. It paid to keep Outworlders in mind of a particular city as a pleasant place in which to spend Olympics time. San Francisco knew what it was doing.

George, lost in thought, was suddenly aware of a gentle pressure on his shoulder blade and a voice saying, "Are you in line here, young man?"

The line had moved up without George's having noticed the widening gap. He stepped forward hastily and muttered, "Sorry, sir."

There was the touch of two fingers on the elbow of his jacket and he looked about furtively.

The man behind him nodded cheerfully. He had iron-gray hair, and under his jacket he wore an old-fashioned sweater that buttoned down in front. He said, "I didn't mean to sound sarcastic."

"No offense."

"All right, then." He sounded cozily talkative. "I wasn't sure you might not simply be standing there, entangled with the line, so to speak, only by accident. I thought you might be a—"

"A what?" said George sharply.

"Why, a contestant, of course. You look young."

George turned away. He felt neither cozy nor talkative, and bitterly impatient with busybodies.

A thought struck him. Had an alarm been sent out for him? Was his description known, or his picture? Was Gray-hair behind him trying to get a good look at his face?

He hadn't seen any news reports. He craned his neck to see the moving strip of news headlines parading across one section of the city shield, somewhat lackluster against the gray of the cloudy afternoon sky. It was no use. He gave up at once. The headlines would never concern themselves with him. This was Olympics time and the only news worth headlining was the comparative scores of the winners and the trophies won by continents, nations, and cities.

It would go on like that for weeks, with scores calculated on a per capita basis and every city finding some way of calculating itself into a position of honor. His own town had once placed third in an Olympics covering Wiring Technician; third in the whole state. There was still a plaque saying so in Town Hall.

George hunched his head between his shoulders and shoved his hands in his pocket and decided that made him more noticeable. He relaxed and tried to look unconcerned, and felt no safer. He was in the lobby now, and no authoritative hand had yet been laid on his shoulder. He filed into the hall itself and moved as far forward as he could.

It was with an unpleasant shock that he noticed Gray-hair next to him. He looked away quickly and tried reasoning with himself. The man had been right behind him in line after all.

Gray-hair, beyond a brief and tentative smile, paid no attention to him and, besides, the Olympics was about to start. George rose in his seat to see if he could make out the position assigned to Trevelyan and at the moment that was all his concern.

The hall was moderate in size and shaped in the classical long oval, with the spectators in the two balconies running completely about the rim and the contestants in the linear trough down the center. The machines were set up, the progress boards above each bench were dark, except for the name and contest number of each man. The contestants themselves were on the scene, reading, talking together; one was checking his fingernails minutely. (It was, of course, considered bad form for any contestant to pay any attention to the problem before him until the instant of the starting signal.)

George studied the program sheet he found in the appropriate slot in the arm of his chair and found Trevelyan's name. His number was twelve and, to George's chagrin, that was at the wrong end of the hall. He could make out the figure of Contestant Twelve, standing with his hands in his pockets, back to his machine, and staring at the audience as though he were counting the house. George couldn't make out the face.

Still, that was Trev.

George sank back in his seat. He wondered if Trev would do well. He hoped, as a matter of conscious duty, that he would, and yet there was something within him that felt rebelliously resentful. George, professionless, here, watching. Trevelyan, Registered Metallurgist, Nonferrous, there, competing.

George wondered if Trevelyan had competed in his first year. Sometimes men did, if they felt particularly confident—or hurried. It involved a certain risk. However efficient the Educative process, a preliminary year on Earth ("oiling the stiff knowledge," as the expression went) insured a higher score.

If Trevelyan was repeating, maybe he wasn't doing so well. George felt ashamed that the thought pleased him just a bit.

He looked about. The stands were almost full. This would be a well-attended Olympics, which meant greater strain on the contestants—or greater drive, perhaps, depending on the individual.

Why Olympics, he thought suddenly? He had never known. Why was bread called bread?

Once he had asked his father: "Why do they call it Olympics, Dad?"

And his father had said: "Olympics means competition."

George had said: "Is when Stubby and I fight an Olympics, Dad?"

Platen, Senior, had said: "No. Olympics is a special kind of competition and don't ask silly questions. You'll know all you have to know when you get Educated."

George, back in the present, sighed and crowded down into his seat.

All you have to know!

Funny that the memory should be so clear now. "When you get Educated." No one ever said, "*If* you get Educated."

He always had asked silly questions, it seemed to him now. It was as though his mind had some instinctive foreknowledge of its inability to be Educated and had gone about asking questions in order to pick up scraps here and there as best it could.

And at the House they encouraged him to do so because they agreed with his mind's instinct. It was the only way.

He sat up suddenly. What the devil was he doing? Falling for that lie? Was it because Trev was there before him, an Educee, competing in the Olympics that he himself was surrendering?

He *wasn't* feeble-minded! *No!*

And the shout of denial in his mind was echoed by the sudden clamor in the audience as everyone got to his feet.

The box seat in the very center of one long side of the oval was filling with an entourage wearing the colors of Novia, and the word "Novia" went up above them on the main board.

Novia was a Grade A world with a large population and a thoroughly developed civilization, perhaps the best in the Galaxy. It was the kind of world that every Earthman wanted to live in someday; or, failing that, to see his children live in. (George remembered Trevelyan's insistence on Novia as a goal—and there he was competing for it.)

The lights went out in that section of the ceiling above the audience and so did the wall lights. The central trough, in which the contestants waited, became floodlit.

Again George tried to make out Trevelyan. Too far.

The clear, polished voice of the announced sounded. "Distinguished Novian sponsors. Ladies. Gentlemen. The Olympics competition for Metallurgist, Nonferrous, is about to begin. The contestants are—"

Carefully and conscientiously, he read off the list in the program. Names. Home towns. Educative years. Each name received its cheers, the San Franciscans among them receiving the loudest. When Trevelyan's name was reached, George surprised himself by shouting and waving madly. The gray-haired man next to him surprised him even more by cheering likewise.

George could not help but stare in astonishment and his neighbor leaned over to say (speaking loudly in order to be heard over the hubbub), "No one here from my home town; I'll root for yours. Someone you know?"

George shrank back. "No."

"I noticed you looking in that direction. Would you like to borrow my glasses?"

"No. Thank you." (Why didn't the old fool mind his own business?)

The announcer went on with other formal details concerning the serial number of the competition, the method of timing and scoring and so on. Finally, he approached the meat of the matter and the audience grew silent as it listened.

"Each contestant will be supplied with a bar of nonferrous alloy of unspecified composition. He will be required to sample and assay the bar, reporting all results correctly to four decimals in percent. All will utilize for this purpose a Beeman Microspectrograph, Model FX-2, each of which is, at the moment, not in working order."

There was an appreciative shout from the audience.

"Each contestant will be required to analyze the fault of his machine and correct it. Tools and spare parts are supplied. The spare part necessary may not be present, in which case it must be asked for, and time of delivery thereof will be deducted from final time. Are all contestants ready?"

The board above Contestant Five flashed a frantic red signal. Contestant Five ran off the floor and returned a moment later. The audience laughed good-naturedly.

"Are all contestants ready?"

The boards remained blank.

"Any questions?"

Still blank.

"You may begin."

There was, of course, no way anyone in the audience could tell how any contestant was progressing except for whatever notations went up on the notice board. But then, that didn't matter. Except for what professional Metallurgists there might be in the audience, none would understand anything about the contest professionally in any case. What was important was who won, who was second, who was third. For those who had bets on the standings (illegal, but unpreventable) that was all-important. Everything else might go hang.

George watched as eagerly as the rest, glancing from one contestant to the next, observing how this one had removed the cover from his microspectrograph with deft strokes of a small instrument; how that one was peering into the face of the thing; how still a third was setting his alloy bar into its holder; and how a fourth adjusted a vernier with such small touches that he seemed momentarily frozen.

Trevelyan was as absorbed as the rest. George had no way of telling how he was doing.

The notice board over Contestant Seventeen flashed: Focus plate out of adjustment.

The audience cheered wildly.

Contestant Seventeen might be right and he might, of course, be wrong. If the latter, he would have to correct his diagnosis later and lose time. Or he might never correct his diagnosis and be unable to complete his analysis or, worse still, end with a completely wrong analysis.

Never mind. For the moment, the audience cheered.

Other boards lit up. George watched for Board Twelve. That came on finally: "Sample holder off-center. New clamp depresser needed."

An attendant went running to him with a new part. If Trevelyan was wrong, it would mean useless delay. Nor would the time elapsed in waiting for the part be deducted. George found himself holding his breath.

Results were beginning to go up on Board Seventeen, in gleaming letters: aluminum, 41.2649; magnesium, 22.1914; copper, 10.1001.

Here and there, other boards began sprouting figures.

The audience was in bedlam.

George wondered how the contestants could work in such pandemonium, then wondered if that were not even a good thing. A first-class technician should work best under pressure.

Seventeen rose from his place as his board went red-rimmed to signify completion. Four was only two seconds behind him. Another, then another.

Trevelyan was still working, the minor constituents of his alloy bar still unreported. With nearly all contestants standing, Trevelyan finally rose, also. Then, tailing off, Five rose, and received an ironic cheer.

It wasn't over. Official announcements were naturally delayed. Time elapsed was something, but accuracy was just as important. And not all diagnoses were of equal difficulty. A dozen factors had to be weighed.

Finally, the announcer's voice sounded, "Winner in the time of four minutes and twelve seconds, diagnosis correct, analysis correct within an average of zero point seven parts per hundred thousand, Contestant Number—*Seventeen*, Henry Anton Schmidt of—"

What followed was drowned in the screaming. Number Eight was next and then Four, whose good time was spoiled by a five part in ten thousand error in the niobium figure. Twelve was never mentioned. He was an also-ran.

George made his way through the crowd to the Contestants' Door and found a large clot of humanity ahead of him. There would be weeping relatives (joy or sorrow, depending) to greet them, newsmen to interview the top-scorers, or the home-town boys, autograph hounds, publicity seekers and the just plain curious. Girls, too, who might hope to catch the eye of a top-scorer, almost certainly headed for Novia (or perhaps a low-scorer who needed cnosolation and had the cash to afford it).

George hung back. He saw no one he knew. With San Francisco so far from home, it seemed pretty safe to assume that there would be no relatives to condole with Trev on the spot.

Contestants emerged, smiling weakly, nodding at shouts of approval. Policemen kept the crowds far enough away to allow a lane for walking. Each high-scorer drew a portion of the crowd off with him, like a magnet pushing through a mound of iron filings.

When Trevelyan walked out, scarcely anyone was left. (George felt somehow that he had delayed coming out until just that had come to pass.) There was a cigarette in his dour mouth and he turned, eyes downcast, to walk off.

It was the first hint of home George had had in what was almost a year and a half and seemed almost a decade and a half. He was almost amazed that Trevelyan hadn't aged, that he was the same Trev he had last seen.

George sprang forward. "*Trev!*"

Trevelyan spun about, astonished. He stared at George and then his hand shot out. "George Platen, *what* the devil—"

And almost as soon as the look of pleasure had crossed his face, it left. His hand dropped before George had quite the chance of seizing it.

"Were you in there?" A curt jerk of Trev's head indicated the hall.

"I was."

"To see me?"

"Yes."

"Didn't do so well, did I?" He dropped his cigarette and stepped on it, staring off to the street, where the emerging crowd was slowly eddying and finding its way into skimmers, while new lines were forming for the next scheduled Olympics.

Trevelyan said heavily, "So what? It's only the second time I missed. Novia can go shove after the deal I got today. There are planets that would jump at me fast enough— But, listen, I haven't seen you since Education Day. Where did you go? Your folks said you were on special assignment but gave no details and you never wrote. You might have written."

"I should have," said George uneasily. "Anyway, I came to say I was sorry the way things went just now."

"Don't be," said Trevelyan. "I told you. Novia can go shove— At that I should have known. They've been saying for weeks that the Beeman machine would be used. All the wise money was on Beeman machines. The damned Education tapes they ran through me were for Henslers and who uses Henslers? The worlds in the Goman Cluster if you want to call them worlds. Wasn't *that* a nice deal they gave me?"

"Can't you complain to—"

"Don't be a fool. They'll tell me my brain was built for Henslers. Go argue. *Everything* went wrong. I was the only one who had to send out for a piece of equipment. Notice that?"

"They deducted the time for that, though."

"Sure, but I lost time wondering if I could be right in my diagnosis when I noticed there wasn't any clamp depressor in the parts they had supplied. They don't deduct for that. If it had been a Hensler, I would have *known* I was right. How could I match up then? The top winner was a San Franciscan. So were three of the next four. And the fifth guy was from Los Angeles. They get big-city Educational tapes. The best available. Beeman spectrographs and all. How do I compete with them? I came all the way out here just to get a chance at a Novian-sponsored Olympics in my classification and I might just as well have stayed home. I knew it, I tell you, and that settles it. Novia isn't the only chunk of rock in space. Of all the damned—"

He wasn't speaking to George. He wasn't speaking to anyone. He was just uncorked and frothing. George realized that.

George said, "If you knew in advance that the Beemans were going to be used, couldn't you have studied up on them?"

"They weren't in my tapes, I tell you."

"You could have read—books."

The last word had trailed off under Trevelyan's suddenly sharp look.

Trevelyan said, "Are you trying to make a big laugh out of this? You think this is funny? How do you expect me to read some book and try to memorize enough to match someone else who *knows*."

"I thought—"

"You try it. You try—" Then, suddenly, "What's your profession, by the way?" He sounded thoroughly hostile.

"Well—"

"Come on, now. If you're going to be a wise guy with me, let's see what you've done. You're still on Earth, I notice, so you're not a Computer Programmer and your special assignment can't be much."

George said, "Listen, Trev. I'm late for an appointment." He backed away, trying to smile.

"No, you don't." Trevelyan reached out fiercely, catching hold of George's jacket. "You answer my question. Why are you afraid to tell me? What is it with you? Don't come here rubbing a bad showing in my face, George, unless you can take it, too. Do you hear me?"

He was shaking George in frenzy and they were struggling and swaying across the floor, when the Voice of Doom struck George's ear in the form of a policeman's outraged call.

"All right now. *All* right. Break it up."

George's heart turned to lead and lurched sickeningly. The policeman would be taking names, asking to see identity cards, and George lacked one. He would be questioned and his lack of profession would show at once; and before Trevelyan, too, who ached with the pain of the drubbing he had taken and would spread the news back home as a salve for his own hurt feelings.

George couldn't stand that. He broke away from Trevelyan and made to run, but the policeman's heavy hand was on his shoulder. "Hold on, there. Let's see your identity card."

Trevelyan was fumbling for his, saying harshly. "I'm Armand Trevelyan, Metallurgist, Nonferrous. I was just competing in the Olympics. You better find out about him, though, officer."

George faced the two, lips dry and throat thickened past speech.

Another voice sounded, quiet, well-mannered. "Officer. One moment."

The policeman stepped back. "Yes, sir?"

"This young man is my guest. What is the trouble?"

George looked about in wild surprise. It was the gray-haired man who had been sitting next to him. Gray-hair nodded benignly at George.

Guest? Was he mad?

The policeman was saying, "These two were creating a disturbance, sir."

"Any criminal charges? Any damages?"

"No, sir."

"Well, then, I'll be responsible." He presented a small card to the policeman's view and the latter stepped back at once.

Trevelyan began indignantly. "Hold on, now—" but the policeman turned on him.

"All right now. Got any charges?"

"I just—"

"On your way. The rest of you—move on." A sizable crowd had gathered, which now, reluctantly, unknotted itself and raveled away.

George let himself be led to a skimmer but balked at entering.

He said, "Thank you, but I'm not your guest." (Could it be a ridiculous case of mistaken identity?)

But Gray-hair smiled and said, "You weren't but you are now. Let me introduce myself, I'm Ladislas Ingenescu, Registered Historian."

"But—"

"Come, you will come to no harm, I assure you. After all, I only wanted to spare you some trouble with a policeman."

"But why?"

"Do you want a reason? Well, then, say that we're honorary townsmates, you and I. We both shouted for the same man, remember, and we townspeople must stick together, even if the tie is only honorary. Eh?"

And George, completely unsure of this man, Ingenescu, and of himself as well, found himself inside the skimmer. Before he could make up his mind that he ought to get off again, they were off the ground.

He thought confusedly: The man has some status. The policeman deferred to him.

He was almost forgetting that his real purpose here in San Francisco was not to find Trevelyan but to find some person with enough influence to force a reappraisal of his own capacity of Education.

It could be that Ingenescu was such a man. And right in George's lap.

Everything could be working out fine—fine. Yet it sounded hollow in his thought. He was uneasy.

During the short skimmer-hop, Ingenescu kept up an even flow of small-talk, pointing out the landmarks of the city, reminiscing about past Olympics he had seen. George, who paid just enough attention to make vague sounds during the pauses, watched the route of flight anxiously.

Would they head for one of the shield-openings and leave the city altogether?

No, they headed downward, and George sighed his relief softly. He felt safer in the city.

The skimmer landed at the roof-entry of a hotel and, as he alighted, Ingenescu said, "I hope you'll eat dinner with me in my room?"

George said, "Yes," and grinned unaffectedly. He was just beginning to realize the gap left within him by missing lunch.

Ingenescu let George eat in silence. Night closed in and the wall lights went on automatically. (George thought: I've been on my own almost twenty-four hours.)

And then over the coffee, Ingenescu finally spoke again. He said, "You've been acting as though you think I intend you harm."

George reddened, put down his cup and tried to deny it, but the older man laughed and shook his head.

"It's so. I've been watching you closely since I first saw you and I think I know a great deal about you now."

George half rose in horror.

Ingenescu said, "But sit down. I only want to help you."

George sat down but his thoughts were in a whirl. If the old man knew who he was, why had he not left him to the policeman? On the other hand, why should he volunteer help?

Ingenescu said, "You want to know why I should want to help you? Oh, don't look alarmed. I can't read minds. It's just that my training enables me to judge the little reactions that give minds away, you see. Do you understand that?"

George shook his head.

Ingenescu said, "Consider my first sight of you. You were waiting in line to watch an Olympics, and your micro-reactions didn't match what you were doing. The expression of your face was wrong, the action of your hands was wrong. It meant that something, in general, was wrong, and the interesting thing was that, whatever it was, it was nothing common, nothing obvious. Perhaps, I thought, it was something of which your own conscious mind was unaware.

"I couldn't help but follow you, sit next to you. I followed you again when you left and eavesdropped on the conversation between your friend and yourself. After that, well, you were far too interesting an object of study—I'm sorry if that sounds cold-blooded—for me to allow you to be taken off by a policeman.—Now tell me, what is it that troubles you?"

George was in an agony of indecision. If this was a trap, why should it be such an indirect, roundabout one? And he *had* to turn to someone. He had come to the city to find help and here was help being offered. Perhaps what was wrong was that it was being offered. It came too easy.

Ingenescu said, "Of course, what you tell me as a Social Scientist is a privileged communication. Do you know what that means?"

"No, sir."

"It means, it would be dishonorable for me to repeat what you say to anyone for any purpose. Moreover no one has the legal right to compel me to repeat it."

George said, with sudden suspicion, "I thought you were a Historian."

"So I am."

"Just now you said you were a Social Scientist."

Ingenescu broke into loud laughter and apologized for it when he could talk. "I'm sorry, young man, I shouldn't laugh, and I wasn't really laughing at you. I was laughing at Earth and its emphasis on physical science, and the practical segments of it at that. I'll bet you can rattle off every subdivision of construction technology or mechanical engineering and yet you're a blank on social science."

"Well, then what *is* social science?"

"Social science studies groups of human beings and there are many high-specialized branches to it, just as there are to zoology, for instance. For instance, there are Culturists, who study the mechanics of cultures, their growth, development, and decay. Cultures," he added, forestalling a question, "are all the aspects of a way of life. For instance, it includes the way we make our living, the things we enjoy and believe, what we consider good and bad and so on. Do you understand?"

"I think I do."

"An Economist—not an Economic Statistician, now, but an Economist—specialized in the study of the way a culture supplies the bodily needs of its individual members. A Psychologist specializes in the individual member of a society and how he is affected by the society. A Futurist specializes in planning the future course of a society, and a Historian—That's where I come in, now."

"Yes, sir."

"A Historian specializes in the past development of our own society and of societies with other cultures."

George found himself interested. "Was it different in the past?"

"I should say it was. Until a thousand years ago, there was no Education, not what we call Education, at least."

George said, "I know. People learned in bits and pieces out of books."

"Why, how do you know this?"

"I've heard it said," George said cautiously. Then, "Is there any use in worrying about what's happened long ago? I mean, it's all done with, isn't it?"

"It's never done with, my boy. The past explains the present. For instance, why is our Educational system what it is?"

George stirred restlessly. The man kept bringing the subject back to that. He said snappishly, "Because it's best."

"Ah, but why is it best?" Now you listen to me for one moment and I'll explain. Then you can tell me if there is any use in history. Even before interstellar travel was developed—" He broke off at the look of complete astonishment on George's face. "Well, did you think we always had it?"

"I never gave it any thought, sir."

"I'm sure you didn't. But there was a time, four or five thousand years ago, when mankind was confined to the surface of Earth. Even then, his culture had grown quite technological and his numbers had increased to the point where any failure in technology would have meant mass starvation and disease. To maintain the technological level and advance it in the face of an increasing population, more and more technicians and scientists had to be trained, and yet, as science advanced, it took longer and longer to train them.

"As first interplanetary and then interstellar travel was developed, the problem grew more acute. In fact, actual colonization of extra-Solar planets was impossible for about fifteen hundred years because of a lack of properly trained men.

"The turning point came when the mechanics of the storage of knowledge within the brain was worked out. Once that had been done, it became possible to devise Educational tapes that would modify the mechanics in such a way as to place within the mind a body of knowledge ready-made so to speak. But you know about *that*.

"Once that was done, trained men could be turned out by the thousands and millions, and we could begin what someone has since called the 'Filling of the Universe.' There are now fifteen hundred inhabited planets in the Galaxy and there is no end in sight.

"Do you see all that is involved? Earth exports Education tapes for low-specialized professions and that keeps the Galactic culture unified. For instance, the Reading tapes insure a single language for all of us.—Don't look so surprised, other languages are possible, and in the past were used. Hundreds of them.

"Earth also exports high-specialized professionals and keeps its own population at an endurable level. Since they are shipped out in a balanced sex ratio, they act as self-reproductive units and help increase the populations on the Outworlds where an increase is needed. Furthermore, tapes and men are paid for in material which we much need and on which our economy depends. *Now* do you understand why our Education is the best way?"

"Yes, sir."

"Does it help you to understand, knowing that without it, interstellar colonization was impossible for fifteen hundred years?"

"Yes, sir."

"Then you see the uses of history." The Historian smiled. "And now I wonder if you see why I'm interested in you?"

George snapped out of time and space back to reality. Ingenescu, apparently, didn't talk aimlessly. All this lecture had been a device to attack him from a new angle.

He said, once again withdrawn, hesitating, "Why?"

"Social Scientists work with societies and societies are made up of people."

"All right."

"But people aren't machines. The professionals in physical science work with machines. There is only a limited amount to know about a machine and the professionals know it all. Furthermore, all machines of a given sort are just about alike so that there is nothing to interest them in any given individual machine. But people, ah— They are so complex and so different one from another that a Social Scientist never knows all there is to know or even a good part of what there is to know. To understand his own specialty, he must always be ready to study people; particularly unusual specimens."

"Like me," said George tonelessly.

"I shouldn't call you a specimen, I suppose, but you are unusual. You're worth studying, and if you will allow me that privilege then, in return, I will help you if you are in trouble and if I can."

There were pin wheels whirring in George's mind. —All this talk about people and colonization made possible by Education. It was as though caked thought within him were being broken up and strewn about mercilessly.

He said, "Let me think," and clamped his hands over his ears.

He took them away and said to the Historian, "Will you do something for me, sir?"

"If I can," said the Historian amiably.

"And everything I say in this room is a privileged communication. You said so."

"And I meant it."

"Then get me an interview with an Outworld official, with—with a Novian."

Ingenescu looked startled. "Well, now—"

"You can do it," said George earnestly. "You're an important official. I saw the policeman's look when you put that card in front of his eyes. If you refuse, I—I won't let you study me."

It sounded a silly threat in George's own ears, one without force. On Ingenescu, however, it seemed to have a strong effect.

He said, "That's an impossible condition. A Novian in Olympics month—"

"All right, then, get me a Novian on the phone and I'll make my own arrangements for an interview."

"Do you think you can?"

"I know I can. Wait and see."

Ingenescu stared at George thoughtfully and then reached for the visiphone.

George waited, half drunk with his new outlook on the whole problem and the sense of power it brought. It couldn't miss. It *couldn't* miss. He would be a Novian yet. He would leave Earth in triumph despite Antonelli and the whole crew of fools at the House for the (he almost laughed aloud) Feeble-minded.

George watched eagerly as the visiplate lit up. It would open up a window into a room of Novians, a window into a small patch of Novia transplanted to Earth. In twenty-four hours, he had accomplished that much.

There was a burst of laughter as the plate unmisted and sharpened, but for the moment no single head could be seen but rather the fast passing of the shadows of men and women, this way and that. A voice was heard, clear-worded over a background of babble. "Ingenescu? He wants me?"

Then there he was, staring out of the plate. A Novian. A genuine Novian. (George had not an atom of doubt. There was something completely

Outworldly about him. Nothing that could be completely defined, or even momentarily mistaken.)

He was swarthy in complexion with a dark wave of hair combed rigidly back from his forehead. He wore a thin black mustache and a pointed beard, just as dark, that scarcely reached below the lower limit of his narrow chin, but the rest of his face was so smooth that it looked as though it had been depilated permanently.

He was smiling. "Ladislas, this goes too far. We fully expect to be spied on, within reason, during our stay on Earth, but mind reading is out of bounds."

"Mind reading, Honorable?"

"Confess! You knew I was going to call this evening. You knew I was only waiting to finish this drink." His hand moved up into view and his eye peered through a small glass of a faintly violet liqueur. "I can't offer you one, I'm afraid."

George, out of range of Ingenescu's transmitter could not be seen by the Novian. He was relieved at that. He wanted time to compose himself and he needed it badly. It was as though he were made up exclusively of restless fingers, drumming, drumming—

But he was right. He hadn't miscalculated. Ingenescu *was* important. The Novian called him by his first name.

Good! Things worked well. What George had lost on Antonelli, he would make up, with advantage, on Ingenescu. And someday, when he was on his own at last, and could come back to Earth as powerful a Novian as this one who could negligently joke with Ingenescu's first name and be addressed as "Honorable" in turn—when he came back, he would settle with Antonelli. He had a year and a half to pay back and he—

He all but lost his balance on the brink of the enticing daydream and snapped back in sudden anxious realization that he was losing the thread of what was going on.

The Novian was saying, "—doesn't hold water. Novia has a civilization as complicated and advanced as Earth's. We're not Zeston, after all. It's ridiculous that we have to come here for individual technicians."

Ingenescu said soothingly, "Only for new models. There is never any certainty that new models will be needed. To buy the Educational tapes would cost you the same price as a thousand technicians and how do you know you would need that many?"

The Novian tossed off what remained of his drink and laughed. (It displeased George, somehow, that a Novian should be this frivolous. He wondered uneasily if perhaps the Novian ought not to have skipped that drink and even the one or two before that.)

The Novian said, "That's typical pious fraud, Ladislas. You know we can make use of all the late models we can get. I collected five Metallurgists this afternoon—"

"I know," said Ingenescu. "I was there."

"Watching me! Spying!" cried the Novian. "I'll tell you what it is. The new-model Metallurgists I got differed from the previous model only in knowing the use of Beeman Spectrographs. The tapes couldn't be modified that much, not that much" (he held up two fingers close together) "from last year's model. You introduce the new models only to *make* us buy and spend and come here hat in hand."

"We don't *make* you buy."

"No, but you sell late-model technicians to Landonum and so we have to keep pace. It's a merry-go-round you have us on, you pious Earthmen, but watch out, there may be an exit somewhere." There was a sharp edge to his laugh, and it ended sooner than it should have.

Ingenescu said, "In all honesty, I hope there is. Meanwhile, as to the purpose of my call—"

"That's right, *you* called. Oh, well, I've said my say and I suppose next year there'll be a new model of Metallurgist anyway for us to spend goods on, probably with a new gimmick for niobium assays and nothing else altered and the next year— But go on, what is it you want?"

"I have a young man here to whom I wish you to speak."

"Oh?" The Novian looked not completely pleased with that. "Concerning what?"

"I can't say. He hasn't told me. For that matter he hasn't even told me his name and profession."

The Novian frowned. "Then why take up my time?"

"He seems quite confident that you will be interested in what he has to say."

"I dare say."

"And," said Ingenescu, "as a favor to me."

The Novian shrugged. "Put him on and tell him to make it short."

Ingenescu stepped aside and whispered to George, "Address him as 'Honorable.' "

George swallowed with difficulty. This was it.

George felt himself going moist with perspiration. The thought had come so recently, yet it was in him now so certainly. The beginnings of it had come when he had spoken to Trevelyan, then everything had fermented and billowed into shape while Ingenescu had prattled, and then the Novian's own remarks had seemed to nail it all into place.

George said, "Honorable, I've come to show you the exit from the merry-go-round." Deliberately, he adopted the Novian's own metaphor.

The Novian stared at him gravely. "What merry-go-round?"

"You yourself mentioned it, Honorable. The merry-go-round that Novia is on when you come to Earth to—to get technicians." (He couldn't keep his teeth from chattering; from excitement, not fear.)

The Novian said, "You're trying to say that you know a way by which we can avoid patronizing Earth's mental supermarket. Is that it?"

"Yes, sir. You can control your own Educational system."

"Umm. Without tapes?"

"Y—yes, Honorable."

The Novian, without taking his eyes from George, called out, "Ingenescu, get into view."

The Historian moved to where he could be seen over George's shoulder.

The Novian said, "What is this? I don't seem to penetrate."

"I assure you solemnly," said Ingenescu, "that whatever this is it is being done on the young man's own initiative, Honorable. I have not inspired this. I have nothing to do with it."

"Well, then, what is the young man to you? Why do you call me on his behalf?"

Ingenescu said, "He is an object of study, Honorable. He has value to me and I humor him."

"What kind of value?"

"It's difficult to explain; a matter of my profession."

The Novian laughed shortly. "Well, to each his profession." He nodded to an invisible person or persons outside plate range. "There's a young man here, a protégé of Ingenescu or some such thing, who will explain to us how to Educate without tapes." He snapped his fingers, and another glass of pale liqueur appeared in his hand. "Well, young man?"

The faces on the plate were multiple now. Men and women, both, crammed in for a view of George, their faces molded into various shades of amusement and curiosity.

George tried to look disdainful. They were all, in their own ways, Novians as well as the Earthman, "studying" him as though he were a bug on a pin. Ingenescu was sitting in a corner, now, watching him owl-eyed.

Fools, he thought tensely, one and all. But they would have to understand. He would *make* them understand.

He said, "I was at the Metallurgist Olympics this afternoon."

"You, too?" said the Novian blandly. "It seems all Earth was there."

"No, Honorable, but I was. I had a friend who competed and who made out very badly because you were using the Beeman machines. His education had included only the Henslers, apparently an older model. You said the modification involved was slight." George held up two fingers close together in conscious mimicry of the other's previous gesture. "And my friend had known some time in advance that knowledge of the Beeman machines would be required."

"And what does that signify?"

"It was my friend's lifelong ambition to qualify for Novia. He already knew the Henslers. He had to know the Beemans to qualify and he knew that. To learn about the Beemans would have taken just a few more facts, a bit more data, a small amount of practice perhaps. With a life's ambition riding the scale, he might have managed this—"

"And where would he have obtained a tape for the additional facts and data? Or has Education become a private matter for home study here on Earth?"

There was dutiful laughter from the faces in the background.

George said, "That's why he didn't learn, Honorable. He thought he needed a tape. He wouldn't even try without one, no matter what the prize. He refused to try without a tape."

"Refused, eh? Probably the type of fellow who would refuse to fly without a skimmer." More laughter and the Novian thawed into a smile and said, "The fellow is amusing. Go on. I'll give you another few moments."

George said tensely, "Don't think this is a joke. Tapes are actually bad. They teach too much; they're too painless. A man who learns that way doesn't know how to learn any other way. He's frozen into whatever position he's been taped. Now if a person *weren't* given tapes but were forced to learn by hand, so to speak, from the start; why, then he'd get the habit of learning, and continue to learn. Isn't that reasonable? Once he has the habit well developed he can be given just a small amount of tape-knowledge, perhaps, to fill in gaps or fix details. Then he can make further progress on his own. You can make Beeman Metallurgists out of your own Hensler Metallurgists in that way and not have to come to Earth for new models."

The Novian nodded and sipped at his drink. "And where does everyone get knowledge without tapes? From interstellar vacuum?"

"From books. By studying the instruments themselves. By *thinking*."

"Books? How does one understand books without Education?"

Books are in words. Words can be understood for the most part. Specialized words can be explained by the technicians you already have."

"What about reading? Will you allow reading tapes?"

"Reading tapes are all right, I suppose, but there's no reason you can't learn to read the old way, too. At least in part."

The Novian said, "So that you can develop good habits from the start?"

"Yes, yes," George said gleefully. The man was beginning to understand.

"And what about mathematics?"

"That's the easiest of all, sir—Honorable. Mathematics is different from other technical subjects. It starts with certain simple principles and proceeds by steps. You can start with nothing and learn. It's practically designed for that. Then, once you know the proper types of mathematics, other technical books become quite understandable. Especially if you start with easy ones."

"Are there easy books?"

"Definitely. Even if there weren't, the technicians you now have can try to write easy books. Some of them might be able to put some of their knowledge into words and symbols."

"Good Lord," said the Novian to the men clustered about him. "The young devil has an answer for everything."

"I have. I have," shouted George. "Ask me."

"Have you tried learning from books yourself? Or is this just theory with you?"

George turned to look quickly at Ingenescu, but the Historian was passive. There was no sign of anything but gentle interest in his face.

George said, "I have."

"And do you find it works?"

"Yes, Honorable," said George eagerly. "Take me with you to Novia. I can set up a program and direct—"

"Wait, I have a few more questions. How long would it take, do you suppose, for you to become a Metallurgist capable of handling a Beeman machine, supposing you started from nothing and did not use Educational tapes?"

George hesitated. "Well—years, perhaps."

"Two years? Five? Ten?"

"I can't say, Honorable."

"Well, there's a vital question to which you have no answer, have you? Shall we say five years? Does that sound reasonable to you?"

"I suppose so."

"All right. We have a technician studying metallurgy according to this method of yours for five years. He's no good to us during that time, you'll admit, but he must be fed and housed and paid for all that time."

"But—"

"Let me finish. Then when he's done and can use the Beeman, five years have passed. Don't you suppose we'll have modified Beemans then which he *won't* be able to use?"

"But by then he'll be expert on learning. He could learn the new details necessary in a matter of days."

"So you say. And suppose this friend of yours, for instance, had studied up on Beemans on his own and managed to learn it; would he be as expert in its use as a competitor who had learned it off the tapes?"

"Maybe not—" began George.

"Ah," said the Novian.

"Wait, let *me* finish. Even if he doesn't know something as well, it's the ability to learn further that's important. He may be able to think up things, new things that no tape-Educated man would. You'll have a reservoir of original thinkers—"

"In your studying," said the Novian, "have you thought up any new things?"

"No, but I'm just one man and I haven't studied long—"

"Yes. —Well, ladies, gentlemen, have we been sufficiently amused?"

"Wait," cried George, in sudden panic. "I want to arrange a personal interview. There are things I can't explain over the visiphone. There are details—"

The Novian looked past George. "Ingenescu! I think I have done you your favor. Now, really, I have a heavy schedule tomorrow. Be well."

The screen went blank.

George's hands shot out toward the screen, as though in a wild impulse to shake life back into it. He cried out, "He didn't believe me. He didn't believe me."

Ingenescu said, "No, George. Did you really think he would?"

George scarcely heard him. "But why not? It's all true. It's all so much to his advantage. No risk. I and a few men to work with— A dozen men training for years would cost less than one technician. —He was drunk. Drunk! He didn't understand."

George looked about breathlessly. "How do I get to him? I've got to. This was wrong. Shouldn't have used the visiphone. I need time. Face to face. How do I—"

Ingenescu said, "He won't see you, George. And if he did, he wouldn't believe you."

"He will, I tell you. When he isn't drinking. He—" George turned squarely toward the Historian and his eyes widened. "Why do you call me George?"

"Isn't that your name? George Platen?"

"You know me?"

"All about you."

George was motionless except for the breath pumping his chest wall up and down.

Ingenescu said, "I want to help you, George. I told you that. I've been studying you and I want to help you."

George screamed, "I don't need help. I'm not feeble-minded. The whole world is, but I'm not." He whirled and dashed madly for the door.

He flung it open and two policemen roused themselves suddenly from their guard duty and seized him.

For all George's straining, he could feel the hypo-spray at the fleshy point just under the corner of his jaw, and that was it. The last thing he remembered was the face of Ingenescu, watching with gentle concern.

George opened his eyes to the whiteness of a ceiling. He remembered what had happened. He remembered it distantly as though it had happened to somebody else. He stared at the ceiling till the whiteness filled his eyes and washed his brain clean, leaving room, it seemed, for new thought and new ways of thinking.

He didn't know how long he lay there so, listening to the drift of his own thinking.

There was a voice in his ear. "Are you awake?"

And George heard his own moaning for the first time. Had he been moaning? He tried to turn his head.

The voice said, "Are you in pain, George?"

George whispered, "Funny. I was so anxious to leave Earth. I didn't understand."

"Do you know where you are?"

"Back in the—the House." George managed to turn. The voice belonged to Omani.

George said, "It's funny I didn't understand."

Omani smiled gently, "Sleep again—"

George slept.

And woke again. His mind was clear.

Omani sat at the bedside reading, but he put down the book as George's eyes opened.

George struggled to a sitting position. He said, "Hello."

"Are you hungry?"

"You bet." He stared at Omani curiously. "I was followed when I left, wasn't I?"

Omani nodded. "You were under observation at all times. We were going to maneuver you to Antonelli and let you discharge your aggressions. We felt that to be the only way you could make progress. Your emotions were clogging your advance."

George said, with a trace of embarrassment, "I was all wrong about him."

"It doesn't matter now. When you stopped to stare at the Metallurgy notice board at the airport, one of our agents reported back the list of names. You and I had talked about your past sufficiently so that I caught the significance of Trevelyan's name there. You asked for directions to the Olympics; there was the possibility that this might result in the kind of crisis we were hoping for; we sent Ladislas Ingenescu to the hall to meet you and take over."

"He's an important man in the government, isn't he?"

"Yes, he is."

"And you had him take over. It makes me sound important."

"You *are* important, George."

A thick stew had arrived, steaming, fragrant. George grinned wolfishly and pushed his sheets back to free his arms. Omani helped arrange the bed-table. For a while, George ate silently.

Then George said, "I woke up here once before just for a short time."

Omani said, "I know. I was here."

"Yes, I remember. You know, everything was changed. It was as though I was too tired to feel emotion. I wasn't angry any more. I could just think. It was as though I had been drugged to wipe out emotion."

"You weren't," said Omani. "Just sedation. You had rested."

"Well, anyway, it was all clear to me, as though I had known it all the time but wouldn't listen to myself. I thought: What was it I had wanted Novia to let me do? I had wanted to go to Novia and take a batch of un-Educated youngsters and teach them out of books. I had wanted to establish a House for the Feeble-minded—like here—and Earth already has them—many of them."

Omani's white teeth gleamed as he smiled. "The Institute of Higher Studies is the correct name for places like this."

"Now I see it," said George, "so easily I am amazed at my blindness before. After all, who invents the new instrument models that require new-model technicians? Who invented the Beeman spectrographs, for instance? A man called Beeman, I suppose, but he couldn't have been tape-Educated or how could he have made the advance?"

"Exactly."

"Or who makes Educational tapes? Special tape-making technicians? Then who makes the tapes to train *them*? More advanced technicians? Then who makes the tapes— You see what I mean. Somewhere there has to be an end. Somewhere there must be men and women with capacity for original thought."

"Yes, George."

George leaned back, stared over Omani's head, and for a moment there was the return of something like restlessness to his eyes.

"Why wasn't I told all this at the beginning?"

"Oh, if we could," said Omani, "the trouble it would save us. We can analyze a mind, George, and say this one will make an adequate architect and that one a good woodworker. We know of no way of detecting the capacity for original, creative thought. It is too subtle a thing. We have some rule-of-thumb methods that mark out individuals who may possibly or potentially have such a talent.

"On Reading Day, such individuals are reported. You were, for instance. Roughly speaking, the number so reported comes to one in ten thousand. By the time Education Day arrives, these individuals are checked again, and nine out of ten of them turn out to have been false alarms. Those who remain are sent to places like this."

George said, "Well, what's wrong with telling people that one out of—of a hundred thousand will end at places like these? Then it won't be such a shock to those who do."

"And those who don't? The ninety-nine thousand nine hundred and ninety-nine that don't? We can't have all those people considering themselves failures. They aim at the professions and one way or another they all make it. Everyone can place after his or her name: Registered something-or-other. In one fashion or another every individual has his or her place in society and this is necessary."

"But we?" said George. "The one in ten thousand exception?"

"You can't be told. That's exactly it. It's the final test. Even after we've thinned out the possibilities on Education Day, nine out of ten of those who come here are not quite the material of creative genius, and there's no way we can distinguish those nine from the tenth that we want by any form of machinery. The tenth one must tell us himself."

"How?"

"We bring you here to a House for the Feeble-minded and the man who won't accept that is the man we want. It's a method that can be cruel, but it works. It won't do to say to a man, 'You can create. Do so.' It is much safer to wait for a man to say, 'I can create, and I will do so whether you wish it or not.' There are ten thousand men like you, George, who support the advancing technology of fifteen hundred worlds. We can't allow ourselves to miss one recruit to that number or waste our efforts on one member who doesn't measure up."

George pushed his empty plate out of the way and lifted a cup of coffee to his lips.

"What about the people here who don't—measure up?"

"They are taped eventually and become our Social Scientists. Ingenescu is one. I am a Registered Psychologist. We are second echelon, so to speak."

George finished his coffee. He said, "I still wonder about one thing."

"What is that?"

George threw aside the sheet and stood up. "Why do they call them Olympics?"

JOHN W. CAMPBELL, JR.

Who Goes There?

1

THE PLACE stank. A queer, mingled stench that only the ice-buried cabins of an antarctic camp know, compounded of reeking human sweat, and the heavy, fish-oil stench of melted seal blubber. An overtone of liniment combatted the musty smell of sweat-and-snow-drenched furs. The acrid odor of burnt cooking fat, and the animal, not-unpleasant smell of dogs, diluted by time, hung in the air.

Lingering odors of machine oil contrasted sharply with the taint of harness dressing and leather. Yet, somehow, through all that reek of human beings and their associates—dogs, machines, and cooking—came another taint. It was a queer, neck-ruffling thing, a faintest suggestion of an odor alien among the smells of industry and life. And it was a life-smell. But it came from the thing that lay bound with cord and tarpaulin on the table, dripping slowly, methodically onto the heavy planks, dank and gaunt under the unshielded glare of the electric light.

Blair, the little bald-pated biologist of the expedition, twitched nervously at the wrappings, exposing clear, dark ice beneath and then pulling the tarpaulin back into place restlessly. His little birdlike motions of suppressed eagerness danced his shadow across the fringe of dingy gray underwear hanging from the low ceiling, the equatorial fringe of stiff, graying hair around his naked skull a comical halo about the shadow's head.

Commander Garry brushed aside the lax legs of a suit of underwear, and stepped toward the table. Slowly his eyes traced around the rings of men sardined into the Administration Building. His tall, stiff body straightened finally, and he nodded. "Thirty-seven. All here." His voice was low, yet carried the clear authority of the commander by nature, as well as by title.

"You know the outline of the story back of that find of the Secondary Pole Expedition. I have been conferring with Second-in-Command McReady, and Norris, as well as Blair and Dr. Copper. There is a difference of opinion, and because it involves the entire group, it is only just that the entire Expedition personnel act on it.

"I am going to ask McReady to give you the details of the story, because each of you has been too busy with his own work to follow closely the endeavors of the others. McReady?''

Moving from the smoke-blued background, McReady was a figure from some forgotten myth, a looming, bronze statue that held life, and walked. Six feet four inches he stood as he halted beside the table, and with a characteristic glance upward to assure himself of room under the low ceiling beams, straightened. His rough, clashingly orange windproof jacket he still had on, yet on his huge frame it did not seem misplaced. Even here, four feet beneath the drift-wind that droned across the antarctic waste above the ceiling, the cold of the frozen continent leaked in, and gave meaning to the harshness of the man. And he was bronze—his great red-bronze beard, the heavy hair that matched it. The gnarled, corded hands gripping, relaxing, gripping and relaxing on the table planks were bronze. Even the deep-sunken eyes beneath heavy brows were bronzed.

Age-resisting endurance of the metal spoke in the cragged heavy outlines of his face, and the mellow tones of the heavy voice. ''Norris and Blair agree on one thing; that animal we found was not—terrestrial in origin. Norris fears there may be danger in that; Blair says there is none.

''But I'll go back to how, and why we found it. To all that was known before we came here, it appeared that this point was exactly over the South Magnetic Pole of Earth. The compass does point straight down here, as you all know. The more delicate instruments of the physicists, instruments especially designed for this expedition and its study of the magnetic pole, detected a secondary effect, a secondary, less powerful magnetic influence about eighty miles southwest of here.

''The Secondary Magnetic Expedition went out to investigate it. There is no need for details. We found it, but it was not the huge meteorite mountain Norris had expected to find. Iron ore is magnetic, of course; iron more so—and certain special steels even more magnetic. From the surface indications, the secondary pole we found was small, so small that the magnetic effect it had was preposterous. No magnetic material conceivable could have that effect. Soundings through the ice indicated it was within one hundred feet of the glacier surface.

''I think you should know the structure of the place. There is a broad plateau, a level sweep that runs more than 150 miles due south from the Secondary Station, Van Wall says. He didn't have time or fuel to fly farther, but it was running smoothly due south then. Right there, where that buried thing was, there is an ice-drowned mountain ridge, a granite wall of unshakable strength that has dammed back the ice creeping from the south.

''And four hundred miles due south is the South Polar Plateau. You have asked me at various times why it gets warmer here when the wind rises, and most of you know. As a meteorologist I'd have staked my word that no wind could blow at −70 degrees; that no more than a five-mile wind could blow at −50; without causing warming due to friction with ground, snow and ice and the air itself.

''We camped there on the lip of that ice-drowned mountain range for twelve days. We dug our camp into the blue ice that formed the surface, and escaped most of it. But for twelve consecutive days the wind blew at forty-five miles an hour. It went as high as forty-eight, and fell to forty-one at times. The temperature was −63 degrees. It rose to −60 and fell to −68. It was meteorologically impossible, and it went on uninterruptedly for twelve days and twelve nights.

"Somewhere to the south, the frozen air of the South Polar Plateau slides down from that 18,000-foot bowl, down a mountatin pass, over a glacier, and starts north. There must be a funneling mountain chain that directs it, and sweeps it away for four hundred miles to hit that bald plateau where we found the secondary pole, and 350 miles farther north reaches the Antarctic Ocean.

"It's been frozen there since Antarctica froze twenty million years ago. There never has been a thaw there.

"Twenty million years ago Antarctica was beginning to freeze. We've investigated, though and built speculations. What we believe happened was about like this.

"Something came down out of space, a ship. We saw it there in the blue ice, a thing like a submarine without a conning tower or directive vanes, 280 feet long and 45 feet in diameter at its thickest.

"Eh, Van Wall? Space? Yes, but I'll explain that better later." McReady's voice went on.

"It came down from space, driven and lifted by forces men haven't discovered yet, and somehow—perhaps something went wrong then—it tangled with Earth's magnetic field. It came south here, out of control probably, circling the magnetic pole. That's a savage country there; but when Antarctica was still freezing, it must have been a thousand times more savage. There must have been blizzard snow, as well as drift, new snow falling as the continent glaciated. The swirl there must have been particularly bad, the wind hurling a solid blanket of white over the lip of that now-buried mountain.

"The ship struck solid granite head-on, and cracked up. Not every one of the passengers in it was killed, but the ship must have been ruined, her driving mechanism locked. It tangled with Earth's field, Norris believes. No thing made by intelligent beings can tangle with the dead immensity of a planet's natural forces and survive.

"One of its passengers stepped out. The wind we saw there never fell below forty-one, and the temperature never rose above −60. Then—the wind must have been stronger. And there was drift falling in a solid sheet. The *thing* was lost completely in ten paces." He paused for a moment, the deep steady voice giving way to the drone of wind overhead and the uneasy, malicious gurgling in the pipe of the galley stove.

Drift—a drift-wind was sweeping by overhead. Right now the snow picked up by the mumbling wind fled in level, blinding lines across the face of the buried camp. If a man stepped out of the tunnels that connected each of the camp buildings beneath the surface, he'd be lost in ten paces. Out there, the slim, black finger of the radio mast lifted three hundred feet into the air, and at its peak was the clear night sky. A sky of thin, whining wind rushing steadily from beyond to another beyond under the licking, curling mantle of the aurora. And off north, the horizon flamed with queer, angry colors of the midnight twilight. That was Spring three hundred feet above Antarctica.

At the surface—it was white death. Death of a needle-fingered cold driven before the wind, sucking heat from any warm thing. Cold—and white mist of endless, everlasting drift, the fine, fine particles of licking snow that obscured all things.

Kinner, the little scar-faced cook, winced. Five days ago he had stepped out to the surface to reach a cache of frozen beef. He had reached it, started back—and the drift-wind leapt out of the south. Cold, white death that streamed across the ground blinded him in twenty seconds. He stumbled on wildly in circles. It was half an hour before rope-guided men from below found him in the impenetrable murk.

It was easy for man—or *thing*—to get lost in ten paces.

"And the drift-wind then was probably more impenetrable than we know." McReady's voice snapped Kinner's mind back. Back to the welcome, dank warmth of the Ad Buiding. "The passenger of the ship wasn't prepared either, it appears. It froze within ten feet of the ship.

"We dug down to find the ship, and our tunnel happened to find the frozen—animal. Barclay's ice-ax struck its skull.

"When we saw what it was, Barclay went back to the tractor, started the fire up and when the steam pressure built, sent a call for Blair and Dr. Copper. Barclay himself was sick then. Stayed sick for three days, as a matter of fact.

"When Blair and Copper came, we cut out the animal in a block of ice, as you see, wrapped it and loaded it on the tractor for return here. We wanted to get into that ship.

"We reached the side and found the metal was something we didn't know. Our beryllium-bronze, non-magnetic tools wouldn't touch it. Barclay had some tool-steel on the tractor, and that wouldn't scratch it either. We made reasonable tests—even tried some acid from the batteries with no results.

"They must have had a passivating process to make magnesium metal resist acid that way, and the alloy must have been at least ninety-five percent magnesium. But we had no way of guessing that, so when we spotted the barely opened lock door, we cut around it. There was clear, hard ice inside the lock, where we couldn't reach it. Through the little crack we could look in and see that only metal and tools were in there, so we decided to loosen the ice with a bomb.

"We had decanite bombs and thermite. Thermite is the ice-softener; decanite might have shattered valuable things, where the thermite's heat would just loosen the ice. Dr. Copper, Norris and I placed a twenty-five-pound thermite bomb, wired it, and took the connector up the tunnel to the surface, where Blair had the steam tractor waiting. A hundred yards the other side of that granite wall we set off the thermite bomb.

"The magnesium metal of the ship caught of course. The glow of the bomb flared and died, then it began to flare again. We ran back to the tractor, and gradually the glare built up. From where we were we could see the whole ice-field illuminated from beneath with an unbearable light; the ship's shadow was a great, dark cone reaching off toward the north, where the twilight was just about gone. For a moment it lasted, and we counted three other shadow-things that might have been other—passengers—frozen there. Then the ice was crashing down and against the ship.

"That's why I told you about that place. The wind sweeping down from the pole was at our backs. Steam and hydrogen flame were torn away in white ice-fog; the flaming heat under the ice there was yanked away toward the Antarctic Ocean before it touched us. Otherwise we wouldn't have come back, even with the shelter of that granite ridge that stopped the light.

"Somehow in the blinding inferno we could see great hunched things—black bulks. They shed even the furious incandescence of the magnesium for a time. Those must have been the engines, we knew. Secrets going in blazing glory—secrets that might have given Man the planets. Mysterious things that could lift and hurl that ship—and had soaked in the force of the Earth's magnetic field. I saw Norris' mouth move, and ducked. I couldn't hear him.

"Insulation—something—gave way. All Earth's field they'd soaked up twenty million years before broke loose. The aurora in the sky above licked down, and the whole plateau there was bathed in cold fire that blanketed vision. The ice-ax in my hand got red hot, and hissed on the ice. Metal buttons on my clothes burned into me. And a flash of electric blue seared upward from beyond the granite wall.

"Then the walls of ice crashed down on it. For an instant it squealed the way dry ice does when it's pressed between metal.

"We were blind and groping in the dark for hours while our eyes recovered. We found every coil within a mile was fused rubbish, the dynamo and every radio set, the earphones and speakers. If we hadn't had the steam tractor, we wouldn't have gotten over to the Secondary Camp.

"Van Wall flew in from Big Magnet at sun-up, as you know. We came home as soon as possible. That is the history of—that." McReady's great bronze beard gestured toward the thing on the table.

2

Blair stirred uneasily, his little, bony fingers wriggling under the harsh light. Little brown freckles on his knuckles slid back and forth as the tendons under the skin twitched. He pulled aside a bit of the tarpaulin and looked impatiently at the dark ice-bound thing inside.

McReady's big body straightened somewhat. He'd ridden the rocking, jarring steam tractor forty miles that day, pushing on to Big Magnet here. Even his calm will had been pressed by the anxiety to mix again with humans. It was lone and quiet out there in Secondary Camp, where a wolf-wind howled down from the Pole. Wolf-wind howling in his sleep—winds droaning and the evil, unspeakable face of that monster leering up as he'd first seen it through clear, blue ice, with a bronze ice-ax buried in its skull.

The giant meteorologist spoke again. "The problem is this. Blair wants to examine the thing. Thaw it out and make micro slides of its tissues and so forth. Norris doesn't believe that is safe, and Blair does. Dr. Copper agrees pretty much with Blair. Norris is a physicist, of course, not a biologist. But he makes a point I think we should all hear. Blair has described the microscopic life-forms biologists find living, even in this cold and inhospitable place. They freeze every winter, and thaw every summer—for three months—and live.

"The point Norris makes is—they thaw, and live again. There must have been microscopic life associated with this creature. There is with every living thing we know. And Norris is afraid that we may release a plague—some germ disease unknown to Earth—if we thaw those microscopic things that have been frozen there for twenty million years.

"Blair admits that such micro-life might retain the power of living. Such unorganized things as individual cells can retain life for unknown periods, when solidly frozen. The beast itself is as dead as those frozen mammoths they find in Siberia. Organized, highly developed life-forms can't stand that treatment.

"But micro-life could. Norris suggests that we may release some disease-form that man, never having met it before, will be utterly defenseless against.

"Blair's answer is that there may be such still-living germs, but that Norris has the case reversed. They are utterly nonimmune to man. Our life-chemistry probably—"

"Probably!" The litle biologist's head lifted in a quick, birdlike motion. The halo of gray hair about his bald head ruffled as though angry. "Heh, one look—"

"I know," McReady acknowledged. "The thing is not Earthly. It does not seem likely that it can have a life-chemistry sufficiently like ours to make cross-infection remotely possible. I would say that there is no danger."

McReady looked toward Dr. Copper. The physician shook his head slowly. "None whatever," he asserted confidently. "Man cannot infect or be infected by germs that live in such comparatively close relatives as the snakes. And they are, I assure you," his clean-shaven face grimaced uneasily, "*much* nearer to us than—*that*."

Van Norris moved angrily. He was comparatively short in this gathering of big men, some five feet eight, and his stocky, powerful build tended to make him seem shorter. His black hair was crisp and hard, like short, steel wires, and his eyes were the gray of fractured steel. If McReady was a man of bronze, Norris was all steel. His movements, his thoughts, his whole bearing had the quick, hard impulse of a steel spring. His nerves were steel—hard, quick acting—swift corroding.

He was decided on his point now, and he lashed out in its defense with a characteristic quick, clipped flow of words. "Different chemistry be damned. That thing may be dead—or, by God, it may not—but I don't like it. Damn it, Blair, let them see the monstrosity you are petting over there. Let them see the foul thing and decide for themselves whether they want that thing thawed out in this camp.

"Thawed out, by the way. That's got to be thawed out in one of the shacks tonight, if it is thawed out. Somebody—who's watchman tonight? Magnetic—oh, Connant. Cosmic rays tonight. Well, you get to sit up with that twenty-million-year-old mummy of his. Unwrap it, Blair. How the hell can they tell what they are buying, if they can't see it? I may have a different chemistry. I don't care what else it has, but I know it has something I don't want. If you can judge by the look on its face—it isn't human so maybe you can't—it was annoyed when it froze. Annoyed, in fact, is just about as close an approximation of the way it felt, as crazy, mad, insane hatred. Neither one touches the subject.

"How the hell can these birds tell what they are voting on? They haven't seen those three red eyes and that blue hair like crawling worms. Crawling—damn, it's crawling there in the ice right now!

"Nothing Earth ever spawned had the unutterable sublimation of devastating wrath that thing let loose in its face when it looked around its frozen desolation twenty million years ago. Mad? It was mad clear through—searing, blistering mad!

"Hell, I've had bad dreams ever since I looked at those three red eyes. Nightmares. Dreaming the thing thawed out and came to life—that it wasn't dead, or even wholly unconscious all those twenty million years, but just slowed, waiting—waiting. You'll dream, too, while that damned thing that Earth wouldn't own is dripping, dripping in the Cosmos House tonight.

"And, Connant," Norris whipped toward the cosmic ray specialist, "won't you have fun sitting up all night in the quiet. Wind whining above—and that thing dripping—" he stopped for a moment, and looked around.

"I know. That's not science. But this is, it's psychology. You'll have nightmares for a year to come. Every night since I looked at that thing I've had 'em. That's why I hate it—sure I do—and don't want it around. Put it back where it came from and let it freeze for another twenty million years. I had some swell nightmares—that it wasn't made like we are—which is obvious—but of a different kind of flesh that it can really control. That it can change its shape, and look like a man—and wait to kill and eat—

"That's not a logical argument. I know it isn't. The thing isn't Earth-logic anyway.

"Maybe it has an alien body-chemistry, and maybe its bugs do have a different body-chemistry. A germ might not stand that, but, Blair and Copper, how about a virus? That's just an enzyme molecule, you've said. That wouldn't need anything but a protein molecule of any body to work on.

"And how are you so sure that, of the million varieties of microscopic life it may have, *none* of them are dangerous. How about diseases like hydrophobia—rabies—that attack any warmblooded creature, whatever its body-chemistry may be? And parrot fever? Have you a body like a parrot, Blair? And plain rot—gangrene—necrosis if you want? That isn't choosy about body-chemistry!"

Blair looked up from his puttering long enough to meet Norris' angry, gray eyes for an instant. "So far the only thing you have said this thing gave off that was catching was dreams. I'll go so far as to admit that." An impish, slightly malignant grin crossed the little man's seamed face. "I had some, too. So. It's dream-infectious. No doubt an exceedingly dangerous malady.

"So far as your other things go, you have a badly mistaken idea about viruses. In the first place, nobody has shown that the enzyme-molecule theory, and that alone, explains them. And in the second place, when you catch tobacco mosaic or wheat rust, let me know. A wheat plant is a lot nearer your body-chemistry than this other-world creature is.

"And your rabies is limited, strictly limited. You can't get it from, nor give it to, a wheat plant or a fish—which is a collateral descendant of a common ancestor of yours. Which this, Norris, is not." Blair nodded pleasantly toward the tarpaulined bulk on the table.

"Well, thaw the damned thing in a tub of formalin if you must. I've suggested that—"

"And I've said there would be no sense in it. You can't compromise. Why did you and Commander Garry come down here to study magnetism? Why weren't you content to stay at home? There's magnetic force enough in New York. I could no more study the life this thing once had from a formalin-pickled sample than you could get the information you wanted back in New York. And—if this one is to treated, *never in all time to come can there be a duplicate!* The race it came from must have passed away in the twenty million years it lay frozen, so that even if it came from Mars then, we'd never find its like. And—the ship is gone.

"There's only one way to do this—and that is the best possible way. It must be thawed slowly, carefully, and not in formalin."

Commander Garry stood forward again, and Norris stepped back muttering angrily. "I think Blair is right, gentlemen. What do you say?"

Connant grunted. "It sounds right to us, I think—only perhaps he ought to stand watch over it while it's thawing." He grinned ruefully, brushing a stray lock of ripe-cherry hair back from his forehead. "Swell idea, in fact—if he sits up with his jolly little corpse."

Garry smiled slightly. A general chuckle of agreement rippled over the group. "I should think any ghost it may have had would have starved to death if it hung around here that long, Connant," Garry suggested. "And you look capable of taking care of it. 'Iron-man' Connant ought to be able to take out any opposing players, still."

Connant shook himself uneasily. "I'm not worrying about ghosts. Let's see that thing. I—"

Eagerly Blair was stripping back the ropes. A single throw of the tarpaulin revealed the thing. The ice had melted somewhat in the heat of the room, and it was clear and blue as thick, good glass. It shone wet and sleek under the harsh light of the unshielded globe above.

The room stiffened abruptly. It was face up there on the plain, greasy planks of the table. The broken haft of the bronze ice-ax was still buried in the queer skull. Three mad, hate-filled eyes blazed up with a living fire, bright as fresh-spilled blood, from a face ringed with a writhing, loathsome nest of worms, blue, mobile worms that crawled where hair should grow—

Van Wall, six feet and two hundred pounds of ice-nerved pilot, gave a queer, strangled gasp, and butted, stumbled his way out to the corridor. Half the company broke for the doors. The others stumbled away from the table.

McReady stood at one end of the table watching them, his great body planted solid on his powerful legs. Norris from the opposite end glowered at the thing with smouldering hate. Outside the door, Garry was talking with half a dozen of the men at once.

Blair had a tack hammer. The ice that cased the thing *schluffed* crisply under its steel claw as it peeled from the thing it had cased for twenty thousand thousand years—

3

"I know you don't like the thing, Connant, but it just has to be thawed out right. You say leave it as it is till we get back to civilization. All right, I'll admit your argument that we could do a better and more complete job there is sound. But—how are we going to get this across the line? We have to take this through one temperate zone, the equatorial zone, and halfway through the other temperate zone before we get it to New York. You don't want to sit with it one night, but you suggest, then, that I hang its corpse in the freezer with the beef?" Blair looked up from his cautious chipping, his bald freckled skull nodding triumphantly.

Kinner, the stocky, scar-faced cook saved Connant the trouble of answering. "Hey, you listen, mister. You put that thing in the box with the meat, and by all the gods there ever were, I'll put you in to keep it company. You birds have brought everything movable in this camp in onto my mess tables here already, and I had to stand for that. But you go putting things like that in my meat box, or even my meat cache here, and you cook your own damn grub."

"But, Kinner, this is the only table in Big Magnet that's big enough to work on," Blair objected. "Everybody's explained that."

"Yeah, and everybody's brought everything in here. Clark brings his dogs every time there's a fight and sews them up on that table. Ralsen brings in his sledges. Hell, the only thing you haven't had on that table is the Boeing. And you'd 'a' had that in if you coulda figured a way to get it through the tunnels."

Commander Garry chuckled and grinned at Van Wall, the huge Chief Pilot. Van Wall's great blond beard twitched suspiciously as he nodded gravely to Kinner. "You're right, Kinner. The aviation department is the only one that treats you right."

"It does get crowded, Kinner," Garry acknowledged. "But I'm afraid we all find it that way at times. Not much privacy in an antarctic camp."

"Privacy? What the hell's that? You know, the thing that really made me weep, was when I saw Barclay marchin' through here chantin' 'The last lumber in the camp! The last lumber in the camp!' and carryin' it out to build that house on his tractor. Damn it, I missed that moon cut in the door he carried out more'n I missed the sun when it set. That wasn't just the last lumber Barclay was walkin' off with. He was carryin' off the last bit of privacy in this blasted place."

A grin rode even on Connant's heavy face as Kinner's perennial, good-natured grouch came up again. But it died away quickly as his dark, deepset eyes turned again to the red-eyed thing Blair was chipping from its cocoon of ice. A big hand ruffed his shoulder-length hair, and tugged at a twisted lock that fell behind his ear in a familiar gesture. "I know that cosmic ray shack's going to be too crowded if I have to sit up with that thing," he growled. "Why can't you go on chipping the ice away from around it—you can do that without anybody butting in, I assure you—and then hang the thing up over the power-plant boiler? That's warm enough. It'll thaw out a chicken, even a whole side of beef, in a few hours."

"I know," Blair protested, dropping the tack hammer to gesture more effectively with his bony, freckled fingers, his small body tense with eagerness, "but this is too important to take any chances. There never was a find like this; there never can be again. It's the only chance men will ever have, and it has to be done exactly right.

"Look, you know how the fish we caught down near the Ross Sea would freeze almost as soon as we got them on deck, and come to life again if we thawed them gently? Low forms of life aren't killed by quick freezing and slow thawing. We have—"

"Hey, for the love of Heaven—you mean that damned thing will come to life!" Connant yelled. "You get the damned thing— Let me at it! That's going to be in so many pieces—"

"No! *No,* you fool—"Blair jumped in front of Connant to protect his precious find. "No. just *low* forms of life. For Pete's sake let me finish. You can't thaw higher forms of life and have them come to. Wait a moment now—hold it! A fish can come to after freezing because it's so low a form of life that the individual cells of its body can revive, and that alone is enough to reestablish life. Any higher forms thawed out that way are dead. Though the individual cells revive, they die because there must be organization and cooperative effort to live. That cooperation cannot be reestablished. There is a sort of potential life in any uninjured, quick-frozen animal. But it can't—can't under any circumstances—become active life in higher animals. The higher animals are too complex, too delicate. This is an intelligent creature as high in its evolution as we are in ours. Perhaps higher. It is as dead as a frozen man would be."

"How do you know?" demanded Connant, hefting the ice-ax he had seized a moment before.

Commander Garry laid a restraining hand on his heavy shoulder. "Wait a minute, Connant. I want to get this straight. I agree that there is going to be no thawing of this thing if there is the remotest chance of its revival. I quite agree it is much too unpleasant to have alive, but I had no idea there was the remotest possibility."

Dr. Copper pulled his pipe from between his teeth and heaved his stocky, dark body from the bunk he had been sitting in. "Blair's being technical. That's dead. As dead as the mammoths they find frozen in Siberia. We have all sorts of proof that things don't live after being frozen—not even fish, generally speaking—and no proof that higher animal life can under any circumstances. What's the point, Blair?"

The little biologist shook himself. The little ruff of hair standing out around his bald pate waved in righteous anger. "The point is," he said in an injured tone, "that the individual cells might show the characteristics they had in life if it is properly thawed. A man's muscle cells live many hours after he has died. Just because they live, and a few things like hair and fingernail cells still live, you wouldn't accuse a corpse of being a zombie, or something.

"Now if I thaw this right, I may have a chance to determine what sort of world it's native to. We don't, and can't know by any other means, whether it came from Earth or Mars or Venus or from beyond the stars.

"And just because it looks unlike men, you don't have to accuse it of being evil, or vicious or something. Maybe that expresson on its face is its equivalent to a resignation to fate. White is the color of mourning to the Chinese. If men can have different customs, why can't a so-different race have different understandings of facial expressions?"

Connant laughed softly, mirthlessly. "Peaceful resignation! If that is the best it could do in the way of resignation, I should exceedingly dislike seeing it when it was looking mad. That face was never designed to express peace. It just didn't have any philosophical thoughts like peace in its make-up.

"I know it's your pet—but be sane about it. That thing grew up on evil, adolesced slowly roasting alive the local equivalent of kittens, and amused itself through maturity on new and ingenious torture."

"You haven't the slightest right to say that," snapped Blair. "How do you know the first thing about the meaning of a facial expression inherently inhuman? It may well have no human equivalent whatever. That is just a different development of Nature, another example of Nature's wonderful adaptability. Growing on another, perhaps harsher world, it has different form and features. But it is just as much a legitimate child of Nature as you are. You are displaying that childish human weakness of hating the different. On its own world it would probably class you as a fish-belly, white monstrosity with an insufficient number of eyes and a fungoid body pale and bloated with gas.

"Just because its nature is different, you haven't any right to say it's necessarily evil."

Norris burst out a single, explosive, "Haw!" He looked down at the thing. "May be that things from other worlds don't *have* to be evil just because they're different. But that thing *was!* Child of Nature, eh? Well, it was a hell of an evil Nature."

"Aw, will you mugs cut crabbing at each other and get the damned thing off my table?" Kinner growled. "And put a canvas over it. It looks indecent."

"Kinner's gone modest," jeered Connant.

Kinner slanted his eyes up to the big physicist. The scarred cheek twisted to join the line of his tight lips in a twisted grin. "All right, big boy, and what were you grousing about a minute ago? We can set the thing in a chair next to you tonight, if you want."

"I'm not afraid of its face," Connant snapped. "I don't like keeping a wake over its corpse particularly, but I'm going to do it."

Kinner's grin spread. "Uh-huh." He went off to the galley stove and shook down ashes vigorously, drowning the brittle chipping of the ice as Blair fell to work again.

4

"Cluck," reported the cosmic-ray counter, *"cluck-burrrp-cluck."*

Connant started and dropped his pencil.

"Damnation." The physicist looked toward the far corner, back at the Geiger counter on the table near that corner. And crawled under the desk at which he had been working to retrieve the pencil. He sat down at his work again, trying to make his writing more even. It tended to have jerks and quavers in it, in time with the abrupt proud-hen noises of the Geiger counter. The muted shoosh of the pressure lamp he was using for illumination, the mingled gargles and bugle calls of a dozen men sleeping down the corridor in Paradise House formed the background sounds for the irregular, clucking noises of the counter, the occasional rustle of falling coal in the copper-bellied stove. And a soft, steady *drip-drip-drip* from the thing in the corner.

Connant jerked a pack of cigarettes from his pocket, snapped it so that a cigarette protruded, and jabbed the cylinder into his mouth. The lighter failed to function, and he pawed angrily through the pile of papers in search of a match. He scratched the wheel of the lighter several times, dropped it with a curse and got up to pluck a hot coal from the stove with the coal tongs.

The lighter functioned instantly when he tried it on returning to the desk. The counter ripped out a series of chuckling guffaws as a burst of cosmic rays struck through to it. Connant turned to glower at it, and tried to concentrate on the interpretation of data collected during the past week. The weekly summary—

He gave up and yielded to curiosity, or nervousness. He lifted the pressure lamp from the desk and carried it over to the table in the corner. Then he returned to the stove and picked up the coal tongs. The beast had been thawing for nearly eighteen hours now. He poked at it with an unconscious caution; the flesh was no longer hard as armor plate, but had assumed a rubbery texture. It looked like wet, blue rubber glistening under droplets of water like little round jewels in the glare of the gasoline pressure lantern. Connant felt an unreasoning desire to pour the contents of the lamp's reservoir over the thing in its box and drop the cigarette into it. The three red eyes glared up at him sightlessly, the ruby eyeballs reflecting murky, smoky rays of light.

He realized vaguely that he had been looking at them for a very long time, even vaguely understood that they were no longer sightless. But it did not seem of importance, of no more importance than the labored, slow motion of the tentacular things that sprouted from the base of the scrawny, slowly pulsing neck.

Connant picked up the pressure lamp and returned to his chair. He sat down, staring at the pages of mathematics before him. The clucking of the counter was strangely less disturbing, the rustle of the coals in the stove no longer distracting.

The creak of the floorboards behind him didn't interrupt his thoughts as he went about his weekly report in an automatic manner, filling the columns of data and making brief, summarizing notes.

The creak of the floorboards sounded nearer.

5

Blair came up from the nightmare-haunted depths of sleep abruptly. Connant's face floated vaguely above him; for a moment it seemed a continuance of the wild horror of the dream. But Connant's face was angry, and a little frightened. "Blair—Blair you damned log, wake up."

"Uh-eh?" the little biologist rubbed his eyes, his bony, freckled finger crooked to a mutilated child-fist. From surrounding bunks other faces lifted to stare down at them.

Connant straightened up. "Get up—and get a lift on. Your damned animal's escaped."

"Escaped—what!" Chief Pilot Van Wall's bull voice roared out with a volume that shook the walls. Down the communicaton tunnels other voices yelled suddenly. The dozen inhabitants of Paradise House tumbled in abruptly, Barclay, stocky and bulbous in long woolen underwear, carrying a fire extinguisher.

"What the hell's the matter?" Barclay demanded.

"Your damned beast got loose. I fell asleep about twenty minutes ago, and when I woke up, the thing was gone. Hey, Doc, the hell you say those things can't come to life. Blair's blasted potential life developed a hell of a lot of potential and walked out on us."

Copper stared blankly. "It wasn't—Earthly," he sighed suddenly. "I—I guess Earthly laws don't apply."

"Well, it applied for leave of absence and took it. We've got to find it and capture it somehow." Connant swore bitterly, his deepset black eyes sullen and angry. "It's a wonder the hellish creature didn't eat me in my sleep."

Blair started back, his pale eyes suddenly fear-struck. "Maybe it di—er—uh—we'll have to find it."

"You find it. It's your pet. I've had all I want to do with it, sitting there for several hours with the counter clucking every few seconds, and you birds in here singing night-music. It's a wonder I got to sleep. I'm going through to the Ad Building."

"Commander Garry ducked through the doorway, pulling his belt tight. "You won't have to. Van's roar sounded like the Boeing taking off downwind. So it wasn't dead?"

"I didn't carry it off in my arms, I assure you," Connant snapped. "The last I saw, the split skull was oozing green goo, like a squashed caterpillar. Doc just said our laws don't work—it's unearthly. Well, it's an unearthly monster, with an unearthly disposition, judging by the face, wandering around with a split skull and brains oozing out." Norris and McReady appeared in the doorway, a doorway filling with other shivering men. "Has anybody seen it coming over here?" Norris asked innocently. "About four feet tall—three red eyes—brains oozing out— Hey, has anybody checked to make sure this isn't a cracked idea of humor? If it is, I think we'll unite in tying Blair's pet around Connant's neck like the ancient Mariner's albatross."

"It's no humor," Connant shivered. "Lord, I wish it were. I'd rather wear—" He stopped. A wild, weird howl shrieked through the corridors. The men stiffened abruptly and half turned.

"I think it's been located," Connant finished. His dark eyes shifted with a queer unease. He darted back to his bunk in Paradise House, to return almost immediately with a heavy .45 revolver and an ice-ax. He hefted both gently as he started for the corridor toward Dogtown.

"It blundered down the wrong corridor—and landed among the huskies. Listen—the dogs have broken their chains—"

The half-terrorized howl of the dog pack had changed to a wild hunting melee. The voices of the dogs thundered in the narrow corridors, and through them came a low rippling snarl of distilled hate. A shrill of pain, a dozen snarling yelps.

Connant broke for the door. Close behind him, McReady, then Barclay and Commander Garry came. Other men broke for the Ad Building, and weapons—the sledge house. Pomroy, in charge of Big Magnet's five cows, started down the corridor in the opposite direction—he had a six-foot-handled, long-tined pitchfork in mind.

Barclay slid to a halt, as McReady's giant bulk turned abruptly away from the tunnel leading to Dogtown, and vanished off at an angle. Uncertainly, the mechanician wavered a moment, the fire extinguisher in his hands, hesitating from one side to the other. Then he was racing after Connant's broad back. Whatever McReady had in mind, he could be trusted to make it work.

Connant stopped at the bend in the corridor. His breath hissed suddenly through his throat. "Great God—" The revolver exploded thunderously; three numbing, palpable waves of sound crashed through the confined corridors. Two more. The revolver dropped to the hard-packed snow of the trail, and Barclay saw the ice-ax shift into defensive position. Connant's powerful body blocked his vision, but beyond he heard something mewing, and, insanely, chuckling. The dogs were quieter; there was a deadly seriousness in their low snarls. Taloned feet scratched at hard-packed snow, broken chains were clinking and tangling.

Connant shifted abruptly, and Barclay could see what lay beyond. For a second he stood frozen, then his breath went out in a gusty curse. The Thing launched itself at Connant, the powerful arms of the man swung the ice-ax flat-side first at what might have been a head. It scrunched horribly, and the tattered flesh, ripped by a half-dozen savage huskies, leapt to its feet again. The red eyes blazed with an unearthly hatred, an unearthly, unkillable vitality.

Barclay turned the fire extinguisher on it; the blinding, blistering stream of chemical spray confused it, baffled it, together with the savage attacks of the huskies, not for long afraid of anything that did, or could live, and held it at bay.

McReady wedged men out of his way and drove down the narrow corridor packed with men unable to reach the scene. There was a sure foreplanned drive to McReady's attack. One of the giant blowtorches used in warming the plane's engines was in his bronzed hands. It roared gustily as he turned the corner and opened the valve. The mad mewing hissed louder. The dogs scrambled from the three-foot lance of blue-hot flame.

"Bar, get a power cable, run it in somehow. And a handle. We can electrocute this—monster, if I don't incinerate it." McReady spoke with an authority of planned action. Barclay turned down the long corridor to the power plant, but already before him Norris and Van Wall were racing down.

Barclay found the cable in the electrical cache in the tunnel wall. In a half minute he was hacking at it, walking back. Van Wall's voice rang out in warning shout of "Power!" as the emergency gasoline-powered dynamo thudded into action. Half a dozen other men were down there now; the coal, kindling were going into the firebox of the steam power plant. Norris, cursing in a low, deadly monotone, was working with quick, sure fingers on the other end of Barclay's cable, splicing a contactor into one of the power leads.

The dogs had fallen back when Barclay reached the corridor bend, fallen back before a furious monstrosity that glared from baleful red eyes, mewing in tapped hatred. The dogs were a semi-circle of red-dipped muzzles with a fringe of glistening white teeth, whining with a vicious eagerness that near matched the fury of the red eyes. McReady stood confidently alert at the corridor bend, the gustily muttering torch held loose and ready for action in his hands. He stepped aside without moving his eyes from the beast as Barclay came up. There was a slight, tight smile on his lean, bronzed face.

Norris' voice called down the corridor, and Barclay stepped forward. The cable was taped to the long handle of a snow shovel, the two conductors split and held eighteen inches apart by a scrap of lumber lashed at right angles across the far end of the handle. Bare copper conductors, charged with 220 volts, glinted in the light of pressure lamps. The Thing mewed and hated and dodged. McReady advanced to Barclay's side. The dogs beyond sensed the plan with the almost telepathic intelligence of trained huskies. Their whining grew shriller, softer, their mincing steps carried them nearer. Abruptly a huge night-black Alaskan leapt onto the trapped thing. It turned squalling, saber-clawed feet slashing.

Barclay leapt forward and jabbed. A weird, shrill scream rose and choked out. The smell of burnt flesh in the corridor intensified; greasy smoke curled up. The echoing pound of the gas-electric dynamo down the corridor became a slogging thud.

The red eyes clouded over in a stiffening, jerking travesty of a face. Armlike, leglike members quivered and jerked. The dogs leapt forward, and Barclay yanked back his shovel-handled weapon. The thing on the snow did not move as gleaming teeth ripped it open.

6

Garry looked about the crowded room. Thirty-two men, some tensed nervously standing against the wall, some uneasily relaxed, some sitting, most perforce standing as intimate as sardines. Thirty-two, plus the five engaged in sewing up wounded dogs, made thirty-seven, the total personnel.

Garry started speaking. "All right, I guess we're here. Some of you—three or four at most—saw what happened. All of you have seen that thing on the table, and can get a general idea. Anyone hasn't, I'll lift—" His hand strayed to the tarpaulin over the thing on the table. There was an acrid odor of singed flesh seeping out of it. The men stirred restlessly, hasty denials.

"It looks rather as though Charnauk isn't going to lead any more teams," Garry went on. "Blair wants to get at this thing, and make some more detailed examination. We want to know what happened, and make sure right now that this is permanently, totally dead. Right?"

Connant grinned. "Anybody that doesn't can sit up with it tonight."

"All right then, Blair, what can you say about it? What was it?" Garry turned to the little biologist.

"I wonder if we ever saw its natural form," Blair looked at the covered mass. "It may have been imitating the beings that built that ship—but I don't think it was. I think that was its true form. Those of us who were up near the bend saw the thing in action; the thing on the table is the result. When it got loose, apparently, it started looking around. Antarctica still frozen as it was ages ago when the creature first saw it—and froze. From my observations while it was thawing out, and the bits of tissue I cut and hardened then, I think it was native to a hotter planet than Earth. It couldn't, in its natural form, stand the temperature. There is no life-form on Earth that can live in Antarctica during the winter, but the best compromise is the dog. It found the dogs, and somehow got near enough to Charnauk to get him. The others smelled it—heard it—I don't know—anyway they went wild, and broke chains, and attacked it before it was finished. The thing we found was part Charnauk, queerly only half-dead, part Charnauk half-digested by the jellylike protoplasm of that creature, and part the remains of the thing we originally found, sort of melted down to the basic protoplasm.

"When the dogs attacked it, it turned into the best fighting thing it could think of. Some other-world beast apparently."

"Turned," snapped Garry. "How?"

"Every living thing is made up of jelly—protoplasm and minute, sub-microscopic things called nuclei, which control the bulk, the protoplasm. This thing was just a modification of that same worldwide plan of Nature; cells made up of protoplasm, controlled by infinitely tinier nuclei. You physicists might compare it—an individual cell of any living thing—with an atom; the bulk of the atom, the space-filling part, is made up of the electron orbits but the character of the thing is determined by the atomic nucleus.

"This isn't wildly beyond what we already know. It's just a modification we haven't seen before. It's as natural, as logical, as any other manifestation of life. It obeys exactly the same laws. The cells are made of protoplasm, their character determined by the nucleus.

"Only, in this creature, the cell nuclei can control those cells *at will*. It digested Charnauk, and as it digested, studied every cell of his tissue, and shaped its own cells to imitate them exactly. Parts of it—parts that had time to finish changing—are dog-cells. But they don't have dog-cell nuclei." Blair lifted a fraction of the tarpaulin. A torn dog's leg, with stiff gray fur protruded. "That, for instance, isn't dog at all; it's imitation. Some parts I'm uncertain about; the nucleus was hiding itself, covering up with dog-cell imitation nucleus. In time, not even a microscope would have shown the difference."

"Suppose," asked Norris bitterly, "it had had lots of time?"

"Then it would have been a dog. The other dogs would have accepted it. We would have accepted it. I don't think anything would have distinguished it, not microscope, nor X-ray, nor any other means. This is a member of a supremely intelligent race, a race that has learned the deepest secrets of biology, and turned them to its use."

"What was it planning to do?" Barclay looked at the humped tarpaulin.

Blair grinned unpleasantly. The wavering halo of thin hair round his bald pate wavered in a stir of air. "Take over the world, I imagine."

"Take over the world! Just it, all by itself?" Connant gasped. "Set itself up as a lone dictator?"

"No," Blair shook his head. The scalpel he had been fumbling in his bony fingers dropped; he bent to pick it up, so that his face was hidden as he spoke. "It would become the population of the world."

"Become—populate the world? Does it reproduce asexually?"

Blair shook his head and gulped. "It's—it doesn't have to. It weighed eighty-five pounds. Charnauk weighed about ninety. It would have become Charnauk, and had eighty-five pounds left, to become—oh, Jack for instance, or Chinook. It can imitate anything—that is, become anything. If it had reached the Antarctic Sea, it would have become a seal, maybe two seals. They might have attacked a killer whale, and become either killers, or a herd of seals. Or maybe it would have caught an albatross, or a skua gull, and flown to South America."

Norris cursed softly. "And every time it digested something, and imitated it—"

"It would have had its original bulk left, to start again," Blair finished. "Nothing would kill it. It has no natural enemies, because it becomes whatever it wants to. If a killer whale attacked it, it would become a killer whale. If it was an albatross, and an eagle attacked it, it would become an eagle. Lord, it might become a female eagle. Go back—build a nest and lay eggs!"

"Are you sure that thing from hell is dead?" Dr. Copper asked softly.

"Yes, thank Heaven," the little biologist gasped. "After they drove the dogs off, I stood there poking Bar's electrocution thing into it for five minutes. It's dead and—cooked."

"Then we can only give thanks that this is Antarctica, where there is not one, single solitary living thing for it to imitate, except these animals in camp.''

''Us,'' Blair giggled. ''It can imitate us. Dogs can't make four hundred miles to the sea; there's no food. There aren't any skua gulls to imitate at this season. There aren't any penguins this far inland. There's nothing that can reach the sea from this point—except us. We've got brains. We can do it. Don't you see—*it's got to imitate us—it's got to be one of us—that's the only way it can fly an airplane—fly a plane for two hours, and rule—be—all Earth's inhabitants*. A world for the taking—*if it imitates us!*

''It didn't know yet. It hadn't had a chance to learn. It was rushed—hurried—took the thing nearest its own size. Look—I'm Pandora! I opened the box! And the only hope that can come out is—that nothing can come out. You didn't see me. I did it. I fixed it. I smashed every magneto. Not a plane can fly. Nothing can fly.'' Blair giggled and lay down on the floor crying.

Chief Pilot Van Wall made for the door. His feet were fading echoes in the corridors as Dr. Copper bent unhurriedly over the little man on the floor. From his office at the end of the room he brought something and injected a solution into Blair's arm. ''He might come out of it when he wakes up,'' he sighed, rising. McReady helped him lift the biologist onto a nearby bunk. ''It all depends on whether we can convince him that thing is dead.''

Van Wall ducked into the shack, brushing his heavy blond beard absently. ''I didn't think a biologist would do a thing like that up thoroughly. He missed the spares in the second cache. It's all right. I smashed them.''

Commander Garry nodded. ''I was wondering about the radio.''

Dr. Copper snorted. ''You don't think it can leak out on a radio wave do you? You'd have five rescue attempts in the next three months if you stop the broadcasts. The thing to do is talk loud and not make a sound. Now I wonder—''

McReady loooked speculatively at the doctor. ''It might be like an infectious disease. Everthing that drank any of its blood—''

Copper shook his head. ''Blair missed something. Imitate it may, but it has, to a certain extent, its own body chemistry, its own metabolism. If it didn't, it would become a dog—and be a dog and nothing more. It has to be an imitation dog. Therefore you can detect it by serum tests. And its chemistry, since it comes from another world, must be so wholly radically different that a few cells, such as gained by drops of blood, would be treated as disease germs by the dog, or human body.''

''Blood—would one of those imitations bleed?'' Norris demanded.

''Surely. Nothing mystic about blood. Muscle is about 90% water; blood differs only in having a couple percent more water, and less connective tissue. They'd bleed all right,'' Copper assured him.

Blair sat up in his bunk suddenly. ''Connant—where's Connant?''

The physicist moved over toward the little biologist. ''Here I am. What do you want?''

"Are you?" giggled Blair. He lapsed back into the bunk contorted with silent laughter.

Connant looked at him blankly. "Huh? Am I what?"

"*Are* you there?" Blair burst into gales of laughter. "*Are* you Connant? The beast wanted to be *man*—not a dog—"

7

Dr. Copper rose wearily from the bunk, and washed the hypodermic carefully. The little tinkles it made seemed loud in the packed room, now that Blair's gurgling laughter had finally quieted. Copper looked toward Garry and shook his head slowly. "Hopeless, I'm afraid. I don't think we can ever convince him the thing is dead now."

Norris laughed uncertainly. "I'm not sure you can convince me. Oh, damn you, McReady."

"McReady?" Commander Garry turned to look from Norris to McReady curiously.

"The nightmares," Norris explained. "He had a theory about the nightmares we had at the Secondary Station after finding that thing."

"And that was?" Garry looked at McReady levelly.

Norris answered for him, jerkily, uneasily. "That the creature wasn't dead, had a sort of enormously slowed existence, an existence that permitted it, nonetheless, to be vaguely aware of the passing of time, of our coming, after endless years. I had a dream it could imitate things."

"Well," Copper grunted, "it can."

"Don't be an ass," Norris snapped. "That's not what's bothering me. In the dream it could read minds, read thoughts and ideas and mannerisms."

"What's so bad about that? It seems to be worrying you more than the thought of the joy we're going to have with a madman in an antarctic camp." Copper nodded toward Blair's sleeping form.

McReady shook his great head slowly. "You know that Connant is Connant, because he not merely looks like Connant—which we're beginning to believe that beast might be able to do—but he thinks like Connant, moves himself around as Connant does. That takes more than merely a body that looks like him; that takes Connant's own mind, and thoughts and mannerisms. Therefore, though you know that the thing might make itself *look* like Connant, you aren't much bothered, because you know it has a mind from another world, a totally unhuman mind, that couldn't possibly react and think and talk like a man we know, and do it so well as to fool us for a moment. The idea of the creature imitating one of us is fascinating, but unreal, because it is too completely unhuman to deceive us. It doesn't have a human mind."

"As I said before," Norris repeated, looking steadily at McReady, "you can say the damnedest things at the damnedest times. Will you be so good as to finish that thought—one way or the other?"

Kinner, the scar-faced expedition cook, had been standing near Connant. Suddenly he moved down the length of the crowded room toward his familiar galley. He shook the ashes from the galley stove noisily.

"It would do it no good," said Dr. Copper, softly as though thinking out loud, "to merely look like something it was trying to imitate; it would have to understand its feelings, its reactions, It *is* unhuman; it has powers of imitation beyond any conception of man. A good actor, by training himself, can imitate another man, another man's mannerisms, well enough to fool most people. Of course no actor could imitate so perfectly as to deceive men who had been living with the imitated one in the complete lack of privacy of an antarctic camp. That would take a superhuman skill."

"Oh, you've got the bug, too?" Norris cursed softly.

Connant, standing alone at one end of the room, looked about him wildly, his face white. A gentle eddying of the men had crowded them slowly down toward the other end of the room, so that he stood quite alone. "My God, will you two Jeremiahs shut up?" Connant's voice shook. "What am I? Some kind of a microscopic specimen you're dissecting? Some unpleasant worm you're discussing in the third person?"

"McReady looked up at him; his slowly twisting hands stopped for a moment. "Having a lovely time. Wish you were here. Signed: Everybody.

"Connant, if you think you're having a hell of a time, just move over on the other end for a while. You've got one thing we haven't; you know what the answer is. I'll tell you this, right now you're the most feared and respected man in Big Magnet."

"Lord, I wish you could see your eyes," Connant gasped. "Stop staring, will you! What the hell are you going to do? Have you any suggestions, Dr. Copper?" Commander Garry asked steadily. "The present situation is impossible."

"Oh, is it?" Connant snapped. "Come over here and look at that crowd. By Heaven, they look exactly like that gang of huskies around the corridor bend. Benning, will you stop hefting that damned ice-ax?"

The coppery blade rang on the floor as the aviation mechanic nervously dropped it. He bent over and picked it up instantly, hefting it slowly, turning it in his hands, his brown eyes moving jerkily about the room.

Copper sat down on the bunk beside Blair. The wood creaked noisily in the room. Far down a corridor, a dog yelped in pain, and the dog drivers' tense voices floated softly back. "Microscopic examination," said the doctor thoughtfully, "would be useless, as Blair pointed out. Considerable time has passed. However, serum tests would be definitive."

"Serum tests? What do you mean exactly?" Commander Garry asked.

"If I had a rabbit that had been injected with human blood—a poison to rabbits, of course, as is the blood of any animal save that of another rabbit—and the injections continued in increasing doses for some time, the rabbit would be human-immune. If a small quantity of its blood were drawn off, allowed to separate in a test tube, and to the clear serum, a bit of human blood were added, there would be a visible reaction, proving the blood was human. If cow, or dog blood were added—or any protein material other than that one thing, human blood—no reaction would take place. That would prove definitely."

"Can you suggest where I might catch a rabbit for you, Doc?" Norris asked. "That is, nearer than Australia; we don't want to waste time going that far."

"I know there aren't any rabbits in Antarctica," Copper nodded, "but that is simply the usual animal. Any animal except man will do. A dog for instance. But it will take several days, and due to the greater size of the animal, considerable blood. Two of us will have to contribute."

"Would I do?" Garry asked.

"That will make two," Copper nodded. "I'll get to work on it right away."

"What about Connant in the meantime," Kinner demanded. "I'm going out that door and head for the Ross Sea before I cook for him."

"He may be human—" Copper started.

Connant burst in a flood of curses. "Human! *May* be human, you damned sawbones! What in hell do you think I am?"

"A monster," Copper snapped sharply. "Now shut up and listen." Connant's face drained of color and he sat down heavily as the indictment was put in words. "Until we know—you know as well as we do that we have reason to question that fact, and only you know how that question is to be answered—we may reasonably be expected to lock you up. If you are—unhuman—you're a lot more dangerous than poor Blair there, and I'm going to see that he's locked up thoroughly. I expect that his next stage will be a violent desire to kill you, all the dogs, and probably all of us. When he wakes, he will be convinced we're all unhuman, and nothing in the planet will ever change his conviction. It would be kinder to let him die, but we can't do that, of course. He's going in one shack, and you can stay in Cosmos House with your cosmic ray apparatus. Which is about what you'd do anyway. I've got to fix up a couple of dogs."

Connant nodded bitterly. "I'm human. Hurry that test. Your eyes—Lord, I wish you could see your eyes staring—"

Commander Garry watched anxiously as Clark, the dog-handler, held the big brown Alaskan husky, while Copper began the injection treatment. The dog was not anxious to cooperate; the needle was painful, and already he'd experienced considerable needle work that morning. Five stitches held closed a slash that ran from his shoulder, across the ribs, halfway down his body. One long fang was broken off short; the missing part was to be found half buried in the shoulder bone of the monstrous thing on the table in the Ad Building.

''How long will that take?'' Garry asked, pressing his arm gently. It was sore from the prick of the needle Dr. Copper had used to withdraw blood.

Copper shrugged. ''I don't know, to be frank. I know that general method. I've used it on rabbits. But I haven't experimented with dogs. They're big, clumsy animals to work with; naturally rabbits are preferable, and serve ordinarily. In civilized places you can buy a stock of human-immune rabbits from suppliers, and not many investigators take the trouble to prepare their own.''

''What do they want with them back there?'' Clark asked.

''Criminology is one large field. A says he didn't murder B, but that the blood on his shirt came from killing a chicken. The State makes a test, then it's up to A to explain how it is the blood reacts on human-immune rabbits, but not on chicken-immunes.''

''What are we going to do with Blair in the meantime?'' Garry asked wearily. ''It's all right to let him sleep where he is for a while, but when he wakes up—''

''Barclay and Bennington are fitting some bolts on the door of Cosmos House,'' Copper replied grimly. ''Connant's acting like a gentleman. I think perhaps the way the other men look at him makes him rather want privacy. Lord knows, heretofore we've all of us individually prayed for a little privacy.''

Clark laughed brittlely. ''Not any more, thank you. The more the merrier.''

''Blair,'' Copper went on, ''will also have to have privacy—and locks. He's going to have a pretty definite plan in mind when he wakes up. Ever hear the old story of how to stop hoof-and-mouth disease in cattle?''

Clark and Garry shook their heads silently.

''If there isn't any hoof-and-mouth disease, there won't be any hoof-and-mouth disease,'' Copper explained. ''You get rid of it by killing every animal that's been near the diseased animal. Blair's a biologist, and knows that story. He's afraid of this thing we loosed. The answer is probably pretty clear in his mind now. Kill everybody and everything in this camp before a skua gull or a wandering albatross coming in with the spring chances out this way and—catches the disease.''

Clark's lips curled in a twisted grin. ''Sounds logical to me. If things get too bad—maybe we'd better let Blair get loose. It would save us committing suicide. We might also make something of a vow that if things get bad, we see that that does happen.''

Copper laughed softly. ''The last man alive in Big Magnet—wouldn't be a man,'' he pointed out. ''Somebody's got to kill those—creatures that don't desire to kill themselves, you know. We don't have enough thermite to do it all at once, and the decanite explosive wouldn't help much. I have an idea that even small pieces of one of those beings would be self-sufficient.''

''If,'' said Garry thoughtfully, ''they can modify their protoplasm at will, won't they simply modify themselves to birds and fly away? They can read all about birds, and imitate their structure without even meeting them. Or imitate, perhaps, birds of their home planet."

Copper shook his head, and helped Clark to free the dog. "Man studied birds for centuries, trying to learn how to make a machine to fly like them. He never did do the trick; his final success came when he broke away entirely and tried new methods. Knowing the general idea, and knowing the detailed structure of wing and bone and nerve-tissue is something far, far different. And as for otherworld birds; perhaps, in fact very probably, the atmospheric conditions here are so vastly different that their birds couldn't fly. Perhaps, even, the being came from a planet like Mars with such a thin atmosphere that there were no birds."

Barclay came into the building, trailing a length of airplane control cable. "It's finished, Doc. Cosmos House can't be opened from the inside. Now where do we put Blair?"

Copper looked toward Garry. "There wasn't any biology building. I don't know where we can isolate him."

"How about East Cache?" Garry said after a moment's thought. "Will Blair be able to look after himself—or need attention?"

"He'll be capable enough. We'll be the ones to watch out," Copper assured him grimly. "Take a stove, a couple of bags of coal, necessary supplies and a few tools to fix it up. Nobody's been out there since last fall, have they?"

"Garry shook his head. "If he gets noisy—I thought that might be a good idea."

Barclay hefted the tools he was carrying and looked up at Garry. "If the muttering he's doing now is any sign, he's going to sing away the night hours. And we won't like his song."

"What's he saying?" Copper asked.

Barclay shook his head. "I didn't care to listen much. You can if you want to. But I gathered that the blasted idiot had all the dreams McReady had, and a few more. He slept beside the thing when we stopped on the trail coming in from Secondary Magnetic, remember. He dreamt the thing was alive, and dreamt more details. And—damn his soul—knew it wasn't all dream, or had reason to. He knew it had telepathic powers that were stirring vaguely, and that it could not only read minds, but project thoughts. They weren't dreams, you see. They were stray thoughts that thing was broadcasting, the way Blair's broadcasting his thoughts now—a sort of telepathic muttering in its sleep. That's why he knew so much about its powers. I guess you and I, Doc, weren't so sensitive—if you want to believe in telepathy."

"I have to," Copper sighed. "Dr. Rhine of Duke University has shown that it exists, shown that some are much more sensitive than others."

"Well, if you want to learn a lot of details, go listen in on Blair's broadcast. He's driven most of the boys out of the Ad Building; Kinner's rattling pans like coal going down a chute. When he can't rattle a pan, he shakes ashes.

"By the way, Commander, what are we going to do this spring, now the planes are out of it?"

"Garry sighed. "I'm afraid our expedition is going to be a loss. We cannot divide our strength now."

"It won't be a loss—if we continue to live, and come out of this," Copper promised him. "The find we've made, if we can get it under control, is important enough. The cosmic ray data, magnetic work, and atmospheric work won't be greatly hindered."

"Garry laughed mirthlessly. "I was just thinking of the radio broadcasts. Telling half the world about the wonderful results of our exploration flights, trying to fool men like Byrd and Ellsworth back home there that we're doing something."

Copper nodded gravely. "They'll know something's wrong. But men like that have judgment enough to know we wouldn't do tricks without some sort of reason, and will wait for our return to judge us. I think it comes to this: men who know enough to recognize our deception will wait for our return. Men who haven't discretion and faith enough to wait will not have the experience to detect any fraud. We know enough of the conditions here to put through a good bluff."

"Just so they don't send 'rescue' expeditions," Garry prayed. "When—if—we're ever ready to come out, we'll have to send word to Captain Forsythe to bring a stock of magnetos with him when he comes down. But—never mind that."

"You mean if we don't come out?" asked Barclay. "I was wondering if a nice running account of an eruption or an earthquake via radio—with a swell windup by using a stick of decanite under the microphone—would help. Nothing, of course, will entirely keep people out. One of those swell, melodramatic 'last-man-alive-scenes' might make 'em go easy though."

Garry smiled with genuine humor. "Is everybody in camp trying to figure that out, too?"

Copper laughed. "What do you think, Garry? We're confident we can win out. But not too easy about it, I guess."

Clark grinned up from the dog he was petting into calmness. "Confident, did you say, Doc?"

8

Blair moved restlessly around the small shack. His eyes jerked and quivered in vague, fleeting glances at the four men with him; Barclay, six feet tall and weighing over 190 pounds; McReady, a bronze giant of a man;

Dr. Copper, short, squatly powerful; and Benning, five feet ten of wiry strength.

Blair was huddled up against the far wall of the East Cache cabin, his gear piled in the middle of the floor beside the heating stove, forming an island between him and the four men. His bony hands clenched and fluttered, terrified. His pale eyes wavered uneasily as his bald, freckled head darted about in birdlike motion.

"I don't want anybody coming here. I'll cook my own food," he snapped nervously. "Kinner may be human now, but I don't believe it. I'm going to get out of here, but I'm not going to eat any food you send me. I want cans. Sealed cans."

"OK, Blair, we'll bring 'em tonight," Barclay promised. "You've got coal, and the fire's started. I'll make a last—" Barclay started forward.

Blair instantly scurried to the farthest corner. "Get out! Keep away from me, you monster!" the little biologist shrieked, and tried to claw his way through the wall of the shack. "Keep away from me—keep away—I won't be absorbed—I won't be—"

Barclay relaxed and moved back. Dr. Copper shook his head. "Leave him alone, Bar. It's easier for him to fix the thing himself. Wel'll have to fix the door, I think—"

The four men let themselves out. Efficiently, Benning and Barclay fell to work. There were no locks in Antarctica; there wasn't enough privacy to make them needed. But powerful screws had been driven in each side of the door frame, and the spare aviation control cable, immensely strong, woven steel wire, was rapidly caught between them and drawn taut. Barclay went to work with a drill and a key-hole saw. Presently he had a trap cut in the door through which goods could be passed without unlashing the entrance. Three powerful hinges from a stock crate, two hasps and a pair of three-inch cotter pins made it proof against opening from the other side.

Blair moved about restlessly inside. He was dragging something over to the door with with panting gasps, and muttering frantic curses. Barclay opened the hatch and glanced in, Dr. Copper peering over his shoulder. Blair had moved the heavy bunk against the door. It could not be opened without his cooperation now.

"Don't know but what the poor man's right at that," McReady sighed. "If he gets loose, it is his avowed intention to kill each and all of us as quickly as possible, which is something we don't agree with. But we've something on our side of that door that is worse than a homicidal maniac. If one or the other has to get loose, I think I'll come up and undo these lashings here.

Barclay grinned. "You let me know, and I'll show you how to get these off fast. Let's go back."

The sun was painting the northern horizon in multicolored rainbows still, though it was two hours below the horizon. The field of drift swept off to the north, sparkling under its flaming colors in a million reflected glories. Low mounds of rounded white on the northern horizon showed the Magnet

Range was barely awash above the sweeping drift. Little eddies of wind-lifted snow swirled away from their skis as they set out toward the main encampment two miles away. The spidery finger of the broadcast radiator lifted a gaunt black needle against the white of the Antarctic continent. The snow under their skis was like fine sand, hard and gritty.

"Spring," said Benning bitterly, "is come. Ain't we got fun! And I've been looking forward to getting away from this blasted hole in the ice."

"I wouldn't try it now, if I were you." Barclay grunted. "Guys that set out from here in the next few days are going to be marvelously unpopular."

"How is your dog getting along, Dr. Copper?" McReady asked. "Any results yet?"

"In thirty hours? I wish there were. I gave him an injection of my blood today. But I imagine another five days will be needed. I don't know certainly enough to stop sooner."

"I've been wondering—if Connant were—changed, would he have warned us so soon after the animal escaped? Wouldn't he have waited long enough for it to have a real chance to fix itself? Until we woke up naturally?" McReady asked slowly.

"The thing is selfish. You didn't think it looked as though it were possessed of a store of the higher justices, did you?" Dr. Copper pointed out. "Every part of it is all of it, every part of it is all for itself, I imagine. If Connant were changed, to save his skin, he'd have to—but Connant's feelings aren't changed; they're imitated perfectly, or they're his own. Naturally, the imitation, imitating perfectly Connant's feelings would do exactly what Connant would do."

"Say, couldn't Norris or Vane give Connant some kind of a test? If the thing is brighter than men, it might know more physics than Connant should, and they'd catch it out," Barclay suggested.

Copper shook his head wearily. "Not if it reads minds. You can't plan a trap for it. Vane suggested that last night. He hoped it would answer some of the questions of physics he'd like to know answers to."

"This expedition-of-four idea is going to make life happy." Benning looked at his companion. "Each of us with an eye on the other to make sure he doesn't do something—peculiar. Man, aren't we going to be a trusting bunch! Each man eyeing his neighbors with the grandest exhibition of faith and trust—I'm beginning to know what Connant meant by 'I wish you could see your eyes.' Every now and then we all have it, I guess. One of you looks around with a sort of 'I-wonder-if-the other-*three*-are-looking.' Incidentally, I'm not excepting myself."

"So far as we know, the animal is dead, with a slight question as to Connant. No other is suspected," McReady stated slowly. "The 'always-four' order is merely a precautionary measure."

"I'm waiting for Garry to make it four-in-a-bunk," Barclay sighed. "I thought I didn't have any privacy before, but since that order—"

9

None watched more tensely than Connant. A little sterile glass test tube, half filled with straw-colored fluid. One—two—three—four—five drops of the clear solution Dr. Copper had prepared from the drops of blood from Connant's arm. The tube was shaken carefully, then set in a beaker of clear, warm water. The thermometer read blood heat, a little thermostat clicked noisily, and the electric hotplate began to glow as the lights flickered slightly. Then—little white flecks of precipitation were forming, snowing down in the clear straw-colored fluid. "Lord," said Connant. He dropped heavily into a bunk, crying like a baby. "Six days—" Connant sobbed, "six days in there—wondering if that damned test would lie—"

Garry moved over silently, and slipped his arm across the physicist's back.

"It couldn't lie," Dr. Copper said. "The dog was human-immune—and the serum reacted."

"He's—all right?" Norris gasped. "Then—the animal is dead—dead forever?"

"He is human," Copper spoke definitely, "and the animal is dead."

Kinner burst out laughing, laughing hysterically. McReady turned toward him and slapped his face with a methodical one-two, one-two action. The cook laughed, gulped, cried a moment, and sat up rubbing his cheeks, mumbling his thanks vaguely. "I was scared. Lord, I was scared—"

Norris laughed brittlely. "You think we weren't, you ape? You think maybe Connant wasn't?"

The Ad Building stirred with a sudden rejuvenation. Voices laughed, the men clustering around Connant spoke with unnecessarily loud voices, jittery, nervous voices relievedly friendly again. Somebody called out a suggestion, and a dozen started for their skis. Blair, Blair might recover—Dr. Copper fussed with his test tubes in nervous relief, trying solutions. The party of relief for Blair's shack started out the door, skis clapping noisily. Down the corridor, the dogs set up a quick yelping howl as the air of excited relief reached them.

Dr. Copper fussed with his tubes. McReady noticed him first, sitting on the edge of the bunk, with two precipitin-whitened test tubes of straw-colored fluid, his face whiter than the stuff in the tubes, silent tears slipping down from horror-widened eyes.

McReady felt a cold knife of fear pierce through his heart and freeze in his breast. Dr. Copper looked up. "Garry," he called hoarsely. "Garry, for God's sake, come here."

Commander Garry walked toward him sharply. Silence clapped down on the Ad Building. Connant looked up, rose stiffly from his seat.

"Garry—tissue from the monster—precipitates, too. It proves nothing.

Nothing—but the dog was monster-immune too. That *one of the two contributing blood—one of us two,* you and I, Garry—*one of us is a monster.*''

10

''Bar, call back those men before they tell Blair,'' McReady said quietly. Barclay went to the door; faintly his shouts came back to the tensely silent men in the room. Then he was back.

''They're coming,'' he said. ''I didn't tell them why. Just that Dr. Copper said not to go.''

''McReady,'' Garry sighed, ''you're in command now. May God help you. I cannot.''

The bronzed giant nodded slowly, his deep eyes on Commander Garry.

''I may be the one,'' Garry added. ''I know I'm not, but I cannot prove it to you in any way. Dr. Copper's test has broken down. The fact that he showed it was useless, when it was to the advantage of the monster to have that uselessness not known, would seem to prove he was human.''

Copper rocked back and forth slowly on the bunk. ''I know I'm human. I can't prove it either. One of us two is a liar, for that test cannot lie, and it says one of us is. I gave proof that the test was wrong, which seems to prove I'm human, and now Garry has given that argument which proves me human—which he, as the monster, should not do. Round and round and round and round and—''

Dr. Copper's head, then his neck and shoulders began circling slowly in time to the words. Suddenly he was lying back on the bunk, roaring with laughter. ''It doesn't have to prove *one* of us is a monster! It doesn't have to prove that at all! Ho-ho. If we're *all* monsters it works the same—we're all monsters—all of us—Connant and Garry and I—and all of you.''

''McReady,'' Van Wall, the blond-bearded Chief Pilot, called softly, ''you were on the way to an M.D. when you took up meteorology, weren't you? Can you make some kind of test?''

McReady went over to Copper slowly, took the hypodermic from his hand, and washed it carefully in ninety-five percent alcohol. Garry sat on the bunk edge with wooden face, watching Copper and McReady expressionlessly. ''What Copper said is possible,'' McReady sighed. ''Van, will you help here? Thanks.'' The filled needle jabbed into Copper's thigh. The man's laughter did not stop, but slowly faded into sobs, then sound sleep as the morphia took hold.

McReady turned again. The men who had started for Blair stood at the far end of the room, skis dripping snow, their faces as white as their skis.

Connant had a lighted cigarette in each hand; one he was puffing absently, and staring at the floor. The heat of the one in his left hand attracted him and he stared at it and the one in the other hand stupidly for a moment. He dropped down and crushed it under his heel slowly.

"Dr. Copper," McReady repeated, "could be right. I know I'm human—but of course can't prove it. I'll repeat the test for my own information. Any of you others who wish to may do the same."

Two minutes later, McReady held a test tube with white precipitin settling slowly from straw-colored serum. "It reacts to human blood too, so they aren't both monsters."

"I didn't think they were," Van Wall sighed. "That wouldn't suit the monster either; we could have destroyed them if we knew. Why hasn't the monster destroyed us, do you suppose? It seems to be loose."

McReady snorted. Then laughed softly. "Elementary, my dear Watson. The monster wants to have life-forms available. It cannot animate a dead body, apparently. It is just waiting—waiting until the best opportunities come. We who remain human, it is holding in reserve."

Kinner shuddered violently. "Hey. Hey, Mac. Mac, would I know if I was a monster? Would I know if the monster had already got me? Oh Lord, I may be a monster already."

"You'd know," McReady answered.

"But we wouldn't," Norris laughed shortly, half hysterically.

McReady looked at the vial of serum remaining. "There's one thing this damned stuff is good for, at that," he said thoughtfully. "Clark, will you and Van help me? The rest of the gang better stick together here. Keep an eye on each other," he said bitterly. "See that you don't get into mischief, shall we say?"

McReady started down the tunnel toward Dogtown, with Clark and Van Wall behind him. "You need more serum?" Clark asked.

McReady shook his head. "Tests. There's four cows and a bull, and nearly seventy dogs down there. This stuff reacts only to human blood and—monsters."

11

McReady came back to the Ad Building and went silently to the wash stand. Clark and Van Wall joined him a moment later. Clark's lips had developed a tic, jerking into sudden, unexpected sneers.

"What did you do?" Connant exploded suddenly. "More immunizing?"

Clark snickered, and stopped with a hiccough. "Immunizing. Haw! Immune all right."

"That monster," said Van Wall steadily, "is quite logical. Our immune dog was quite all right, and we drew a little more serum for the tests. But we won't take any more."

"Can't—can't you use one man's blood on another dog—" Norris began.

"There aren't," said McReady softly, "any more dogs. Nor cattle, I might add."

"No more dogs?" Benning sat down slowly.

"They're very nasty when they start changing," Van Wall said precisely. "But slow. That electrocution iron you made up, Barclay, is very fast. There is only one dog left—our immune. The monster left that for us, so we could play with our little test. The rest—" He shrugged and dried his hands.

"The cattle—" gulped Kinner.

"Also. Reacted very nicely. They look funny as hell when they start melting. The beast hasn't any quick escape, when it's tied in dog chains, or halters, and it had to be to imitate."

Kinner stood up slowly. His eyes darted around the room, and came to rest horribly quivering on a tin bucket in the galley. Slowly, step by step, he retreated toward the door, his mouth opening and closing silently, like a fish out of water.

"The milk—" he gasped. "I milked 'em an hour ago—" His voice broke into a scream as he dived through the door. He was out on the ice cap without windproof or heavy clothing.

Van Wall looked after him for a moment thoughtfully. "He's probably hopelessly mad," he said at length, "but he might be a monster escaping. He hasn't skis. Take a blow torch—in case."

The physical motion of the chase helped them; something that needed doing. Three of the other men were quietly being sick. Norris was lying flat on his back, his face greenish, looking steadily at the bottom of the bunk above him.

"Mac, how long have the—cows been not-cows—"

McReady shrugged his shoulders hopelessly. He went over to the milk bucket, and with his little tube of serum went to work on it. The milk clouded it, making certainty difficult. Finally he dropped the test tube in the stand, and shook his head. "It tests negatively. Which means either they were cows then, or that, being perfect imitation, they gave perfectly good milk."

Copper stirred restlessly in his sleep and gave a gurgling cross between a snore and a laugh. Silent eyes fastened on him. "Would morphia—a monster—" somebody started to ask.

"Lord knows," McReady shrugged. "It affects every Earthly animal I know of."

Connant suddenly raised his head. "Mac! The dogs must have swallowed pieces of the monster, and the pieces destroyed them! The dogs were where the monster resided. I was locked up. Doesn't that prove—"

Van Wall shook his head. "Sorry. Proves nothing about what you are, only proves what you didn't do."

"It doesn't do that," McReady sighed. "We are helpless because we don't know enough, and so jittery we don't think straight. Locked up! Ever watch a white corpuscle of the blood go through the wall of a blood vessel? No? It sticks out a pseudopod. And there it is—on the far side of the wall."

"Oh," said Van Wall unhappily. "The cattle tried to melt down, didn't they? They could have melted down—become just a threat of stuff and leaked under a door to re-collect on the other side. Ropes—no—no, that wouldn't do it. They couldn't live in a sealed tank or—"

"If," said McReady, "you shoot it through the heart, and it doesn't die, it's a monster. That's the best test I can think of, offhand."

"No dogs," said Garry quietly, "and no cattle. It has to imitate men now. And locking up doesn't do any good. Your test might work, Mac, but I'm afraid it would be hard on the men."

12

Clark looked up from the galley stove as Van Wall, Barclay, McReady, and Benning came in, brushing the drift from their clothes. The other men jammed into the Ad Building continued studiously to do as they were doing, playing chess, poker, reading. Ralsen was fixing a sledge on the table; Vane and Norris had their heads together over magnetic data, while Harvey read tables in a low voice.

Dr. Copper snored softly on the bunk. Garry was working with Dutton over a sheaf of radio messages on the corner of Dutton's bunk and a small fraction of the radio table. Connant was using most of the table for cosmic ray sheets.

Quite plainly through the corridor, despite two closed doors, they could hear Kinner's voice. Clark banged a kettle onto the galley stove and beckoned McReady silently. The meteorologist went over to him.

"I don't mind the cooking so damn much," Clark said nervously, "but isn't there some way to stop that bird? We all agreed that it would be safe to move him into Cosmos House."

"Kinner?" McReady nodded toward the door. "I'm afraid not. I can dope him, I suppose, but we don't have an unlimited supply of morphia, and he's not in danger of losing his mind. Just hysterical."

"Well, we're in danger of losing ours. You've been out for an hour and a half. That's been going on steadily ever since, and it was going for two hours before. There's a limit, you know."

Garry wandered over slowly, apologetically. For an instant, McReady caught the feral spark of fear—horror—in Clark's eyes, and knew at the same instant it was in his own. Garry—Garry or Copper—was certainly a monster.

"If you could stop that, I think it would be a sound policy, Mac," Garry spoke quietly. "There are—tensions enough in this room. We agreed that it would be safe for Kinner in there, because everyone else in camp is under constant eyeing." Garry shivered slightly. "And try, try in God's name, to find some test that will work." McReady sighed. "Watched or unwatched, everyone's tense. Blair's jammed the trap so it won't open now. Says he's got food enough, and keeps screaming 'Go away, go away—you're monsters. I won't be absorbed. I won't. I'll tell men when they come. Go away.' So—we went away."

"There's no other test?" Garry pleaded.

McReady shrugged his shoulders. "Copper was perfectly right. The serum test could be absolutely definitive if it hadn't been—contaminated. But that's the only dog left, and he's fixed now."

"Chemicals? Chemical tests?"

McReady shook his head. "Our chemistry isn't that good. I tried the microscope you know."

Garry nodded. "Monster-dog and real dog were identical. But—you've got to go on. What are we going to do after dinner?"

Van Wall had joined them quietly. "Rotation sleeping. Half the crowd sleep; half stay awake. I wonder how many of us are monsters? All the dogs were. We thought we were safe, but somehow it got Copper—or you." Van Wall's eyes flashed uneasily. "It may have gotten every one of you—all of you but myself may be wondering, looking. No, that's not possible. You'd just spring then, I'd be helpless. We humans must somehow have the greater numbers now. But—" he stopped.

McReady laughed shortly. "You're doing what Norris complained of in me. Leaving it hanging. 'But if one more is changed—that may shift the balance of power.' It doesn't fight. I don't think it ever fights. It must be a peaceable thing, in its own—inimitable—way. It never had to, because it always gained its end otherwise."

Van Wall's mouth twisted in a sickly grin. "You're suggesting then, that perhaps it already *has* the greater numbers, but is just waiting—waiting, all of them—all of you, for all I know—waiting till I, the last human, drop my wariness in sleep. Mac, did you notice their eyes, all looking at us."

Garry sighed. "You haven't been sitting here for four straight hours, while all their eyes silently weighed the information that one of us two, Copper or I, is a monster certainly—perhaps both of us."

Clark repeated his request. "Will you stop that bird's noise? He's driving me nuts. Make him tone down anyway."

"Still praying?" McReady asked.

"Still praying," Clark groaned. "He hasn't stopped for a second. I don't mind his praying if it relieves him, but he yells, he sings psalms and hymns and shouts prayers. He thinks God can't hear well way down here."

"Maybe he can't," Barclay grunted. "Or he'd have done something about this thing loosed from hell."

"Somebody's going to try that test you mentioned, if you don't stop him," Clark stated grimly. "I think a cleaver in the head would be as positive a test as a bullet in the heart."

"Go ahead with the food. I'll see what I can do. There may be something in the cabinets." McReady moved wearily toward the corner Copper had used as his dispensary. Three tall cabinets of rough boards, two locked, were the repositories of the camp's medical supplies. Twelve years ago, McReady had graduated, had started for an internship, and been diverted to meteorology. Copper was a picked man, a man who knew his profession thoroughly and modernly. More than half the drugs available were totally unfamiliar to McReady; many of the others he had forgotten. There was no huge medical library here, no series of journals available to learn the things he had forgotten, the elementary, simple things to Copper, things that did not merit inclusion in the small library he had been forced to content himself with. Books are heavy, and every ounce of supplies had been freighted in by air.

McReady picked a barbiturate hopefully. Barclay and Van Wall went with him. One man never went anywhere alone in Big Magnet.

Ralsen had his sledge put away, and the physicists had moved off the table, the poker game broken up when they got back. Clark was putting out the food. The click of spoons and the muffled sounds of eating were the only sign of life in the room. There were no words spoken as the three returned; simply all eyes focused on them questioningly while the jaws moved methodically.

McReady stiffened suddenly. Kinner was screeching out a hymn in a hoarse, cracked voice. He looked wearily at Van Wall with a twisted grin and shook his head. "Uh-uh."

Van Wall cursed bitterly, and sat down at the table. "We'll just plumb have to take that till his voice wears out. He can't yell like that forever."

"He's got a brass throat and a cast-iron larynx," Norris declared savagely. "Then we could be hopeful, and suggest he's one of our friends. In that case he could go on renewing his throat till doomsday."

Silence clamped down. For twenty minutes they ate without a word. Then Connant jumped up with an angry violence. "You sit as still as a bunch of graven images. You don't say a word, but oh, Lord, what expressive eyes you've got. They roll around like a bunch of glass marbles spilling down a table. They wink and blink and stare—and whisper things. Can you guys look somewhere else for a change, please?

"Listen, Mac, you're in charge here. Let's run movies for the rest of the night. We've been saving those reels to make 'em last. Last for what? Who is it's going to see those last reels, eh? Let's see 'em while we can, and look at something other than each other."

"Sound idea, Connant. I, for one, am quite willing to change this in any way I can."

"Turn the sound up loud, Dutton. Maybe you can drown out the hymns," Clark suggested.

"But don't," Norris said softly, "don't turn off the lights altogether."

"The lights will be out." McReady shook his head. "We'll show all the cartoon movies we have. You won't mind seeing the old cartoons will you?"

"Goody, goody—a moom-pitcher show. I'm just in the mood." McReady turned to look at the speaker, a lean, lanky New Englander, by the name of Caldwell. Caldwell was stuffing his pipe slowly, a sour eye cocked up to McReady.

The bronze giant was forced to laugh. "OK, Bart, you win. Maybe we aren't quite in the mood for Popeye and trick ducks, but it's something."

"Let's play Classifications," Caldwell suggested slowly. "Or maybe you call it Guggenheim. You draw lines on a piece of paper, and put down classes of things—like animals, you know. One for 'H' and one for 'U' and so on. Like 'Human' and 'Unknown' for instance. I think that would be a hell of a lot better game. Classification, I sort of figure, is what we need right now a lot more than movies. Maybe somebody's got a pencil that he can draw lines with, draw lines between the 'U' animals and the 'H' animals for instance."

"McReady's trying to find that kind of a pencil," Van Wall answered quietly, "but, we've got three kinds of animals here, you know. One that begins with 'M.' We don't want any more."

"Mad ones, you mean. Uh-huh. Clark, I'll help you with those pots so we can get our little peep show going." Caldwell got up slowly.

Dutton and Barclay and Benning, in charge of the projector and sound mechanism arrangements, went about their job silently, while the Ad Building was cleared and the dishes and pans disposed of. McReady drifted over toward Van Wall slowly, and leaned back in the bunk beside him. "I've been wondering, Van," he said with a wry grin, "whether or not to report my ideas in advance. I forgot the 'U animal' as Caldwell named it, could read minds. I've a vague idea of something that might work. It's too vague to bother with, though. Go ahead with your show, while I try to figure out the logic of the thing. I'll take this bunk."

Van Wall glanced up, and nodded. The movie screen would be practically on a line with this bunk, hence making the pictures least distracting here, because least intelligible. "Perhaps you should tell us what you have in mind. As it is, only the unknowns know what you plan. You might be—unknown before you got it into operation."

"Won't take long, if I get it figured out right. But I don't want any more all-but-the-test-dog-monsters things. We better move Copper into this bunk directly above me. He won't be watching the screen either." McReady nodded toward Copper's gently snoring bulk. Garry helped them lift and move the doctor.

McReady leaned back against the bunk, and sank into a trance, almost, of concentration, trying to calculate chances, operations, methods. He was scarcely aware as the others distributed themselves silently, and the screen lit up. Vaguely Kinner's hectic, shouted prayers and his rasping hymn-singing annoyed him till the sound accompaniment started. The lights were turned out, but the large, light-colored areas of the screen reflected enough light for ready visibility. It made men's eyes sparkle as they moved restlessly. Kinner was still praying, shouting, his voice a raucous accompaniment to the mechanical sound. Dutton stepped up the amplification.

So long had the voice been going on, that only vaguely at first was McReady aware that something seemed missing. Lying as he was, just across the narrow room from the corridor leading to Cosmos House, Kinner's voice had reached him fairly clearly, despite the sound accompaniment of the pictures. It struck him abruptly that it had stopped.

"Dutton, cut that sound," McReady called as he sat up abruptly. The pictures flickered a moment, soundless and strangely futile in the sudden, deep silence. The rising wind on the surface above bubbled melancholy tears of sound down the stove pipes. "Kinner's stopped," McReady said softly.

"For God's sake start that sound then; he may have stopped to listen," Norris snapped.

McReady rose and went down the corridor. Barclay and Van Wall left their places at the far end of the room to follow him. The flickers bulged and twisted on the back of Barclay's gray underwear as he crossed the still-functioning beam of the projector. Dutton snapped on the lights, and the pictures vanished.

Norris stood at the door as McReady had asked. Garry sat down quietly in the bunk nearest the door, forcing Clark to make room for him. Most of the others had stayed exactly where they were. Only Connant walked slowly up and down the room, in steady, unvarying rhythm.

"If you're going to do that, Connant," Clark spat, "we can get along without you altogether, whether you're human or not. Will you stop that damned rhythm?"

"Sorry." The physicist sat down in a bunk, and watched his toes thoughtfully. It was almost five minutes, five ages, while the wind made the only sound, before McReady appeared at the door.

"Well," he announced, "haven't got enough grief here already. Somebody's tried to help us out. Kinner has a knife in his throat, which was why he stopped singing, probably. We've got monsters, madmen and murderers. Any more 'M's' you can think of, Caldwell? If there are, we'll probably have 'em before long."

13

"Is Blair loose?" someone asked.

"Blair is not loose. Or he flew in. If there's any doubt about where our gentle helper came from—this may clear it up." Van Wall held a foot-long, thin-bladed knife in a cloth. The wooden handle was half burnt, charred with the peculiar pattern of the top of the galley stove.

Clark stared at it. "I did that this afternoon. I forgot the damn thing and left it on the stove."

Van Wall nodded "I smelled it, if you remember. I knew the knife came from the galley."

"I wonder," said Benning, looking around at the party warily, "how many more monsters have we? If somebody could slip out of his place, go back of the screen to the galley and then down to the Cosmos House and back—he did come back, didn't he? Yes—everybody's here. Well, if one of the gang could do all that—"

"Maybe a monster did it," Garry suggested quietly.

"There's that possibility."

"The monster, as you pointed out today, has only men left to imitate. Would he decrease his—supply, shall we say?" Van Wall pointed out. "No, we just have a plain, ordinary louse, a murderer to deal with. Ordinarily we'd call him an 'inhuman murderer' I suppose, but we have to distinguish now. We have inhuman murderers, and now we have human murderers. Or one at least."

"There's one less human," Norris said softly. "Maybe the monsters have the balance of power now."

"Never mind that," McReady sighed and turned to Barclay. "Bar, will you get your electric gadget? I'm going to make certain—"

Barclay turned down the corridor to get the pronged electrocuter, while McReady and Van Wall went back toward Cosmos House. Barclay followed them in some thirty seconds.

The corridor to Cosmos House twisted, as did nearly all corridors in Big Magnet, and Norris stood at the entrance again. But they heard, rather muffled, McReady's sudden shout. There was a savage flurry of blows, dull *ch-thunk, shluff* sounds. "Bar—Bar—" And a curious, savage mewing scream, silenced before even quick-moving Norris had reached the bend.

Kinner—or what had been Kinner—lay on the floor, cut half in two by the great knife McReady had had. The meteorologist stood against the wall, the knife dripping red in this hand. Van Wall was stirring vaguely on the floor, moaning, his hand half-consciously rubbing at his jaw. Barclay, an unutterable savage gleam in his eyes, was methodically leaning on the pronged weapon in his hand, jabbing—jabbing, jabbing.

Kinner's arms had developed a queer, scaly fur, and the flesh had twisted. The fingers had shortened, the hand rounded, the fingernails become three-inch long things of dull red horn, keened to steel-hard, razor-sharp talons.

McReady raised his head, looked at the knife in his hand and dropped it. "Well, whoever did it can speak up now. He was an inhuman murderer at that—in that he murdered an inhuman. I swear by all that's holy, Kinner was a lifeless corpse on the floor here when we arrived. But when It found we were going to jab It with the power—It changed."

Norris stared unsteadily. "Oh, Lord, those things can act. Ye gods—sitting in here for hours, mouthing prayers to a God it hated! Shouting hymns in a cracked voice—hymns about a Church it never knew. Driving us mad with its ceaseless howling—

"Well. Speak up, whoever did it. You didn't know it, but you did the camp a favor. And I want to know how in blazes you got out of the room without anyone seeing you. It might help in guarding ourselves."

"His screaming—his singing. Even the sound projector couldn't drown it." Clark shivered. "It was a monster."

"Oh," said Van Wall in sudden comprehension. "You *were* sitting right next to the door, weren't you? And almost behind the projection screen already."

Clark nodded dumbly. "He—it's quiet now. It's a dead—Mac, your test's no damn good. It was dead anyway, monster or man, it was dead."

McReady chuckled softly. "Boys, meet Clark, the only one we know is human! Meet Clark, the one who proves he's human by trying to commit murder—and failing. Will the rest of you please refrain from trying to prove you're human for a while? I think we may have another test."

"A test!" Connant snapped joyfully, then his face sagged in dissappointment. "I suppose it's another either-way-you-want-it."

"No," said McReady steadily. "Look sharp and be careful. Come into the Ad Building. Barclay, bring your electrocuter. And somebody—Dutton—stand with Barclay to make sure he does it. Watch every neighbor, for by the Hell these monsters came from, I've got something, and they know it. They're going to get dangerous!"

The group tensed abruptly. An air of crushing menace entered into every man's body, sharply they looked at each other. More keenly than ever before—*is that man next to me an inhuman monster?*

"What is it?" Garry asked, as they stood again in the main room. "How long will it take?"

"I don't know, exactly," said McReady, his voice brittle with angry determination. "But I *know* it will work, and no two ways about it. It depends on a basic quality of the *monsters*, not on us. *'Kinner'* just convinced me." He stood heavy and solid in bronzed immobility, completely sure of himself again at last.

"This," said Barclay, hefting the wooden-handled weapon tipped with its two sharp-pointed, conductors, "is going to be rather necessary, I take it. Is the power plant assured?"

Dutton nodded sharply. "The automatic stoker bin is full. The gas power plant is on standby. Van Wall and I set it for the movie operation—and we've checked it over rather carefully several times, you know. Anything those wires touch, dies," he assured them grimly. "*I* know that."

Dr. Copper stirred vaguely in his bunk, rubbed his eyes with fumbling hand. He sat up slowly, blinked his eyes blurred with sleep and drugs, widened with an unutterable horror of drug-ridden nightmares. "Garry," he mumbled, "Garry—listen. Selfish—from hell they came, and hellish shellfish—I mean self— Do I? What do I mean?" He sank back in his bunk, and snored softly.

McReady looked at him thoughtfully. "We'll know presently," he nodded slowly. "But selfish is what you mean, all right. You may have thought of that, half sleeping, dreaming there. I didn't stop to think what dreams you might be having. But that's all right. Selfish is the word. They must be, you see." He turned to the men in the cabin, tense, silent men staring with wolfish eyes each at his neighbor. "Selfish, and as Dr. Copper said—*every part is a whole*. Every piece is self-sufficient, an animal in itself.

"That, and one other thing, tell the story. There's nothing mysterious about blood; it's just as normal a body tissue as a piece of muscle, or a piece of liver. But it hasn't so much connective tissue, though it has millions, billions of life-cells."

McReady's great bronze beard ruffled in a grim smile. "This is satisfying, in a way. I'm pretty sure we humans still outnumber you—others. Others standing here. And we have what you, your otherworld race, evidently doesn't. Not an imitated, but a bred-in-the-bone instinct, a driving, unquenchable fire that's genuine. We'll fight, fight with a ferocity you may attempt to imitate, but you'll never equal! We're human. We're real. You're imitations, false to the core of your every cell."

"All right. It's a showdown now. *You* know. You, with your mind reading. You've lifted the idea from my brain. You can't do a thing about it.

"Standing here—

"Let it pass. Blood is tissue. They have to bleed; if they don't bleed when cut, then by heaven, they're phoney from hell! If they bleed—then that blood, separated from them, is an individual—*a newly formed individual in its own right, just as they—split, all of them, from one original—are individuals!*

"Get it, Van? See the answer, Bar?"

Van Wall laughed very softly. "The blood—the blood will not obey. It's a new individual, with all the desire to protect its own life that the original—the main mass from which it was split—has. The *blood* will live—and try to crawl away from a hot needle, say!"

McReady picked up the scalpel from the table. From the cabinet, he took a rack of test tubes, a tiny alcohol lamp, and a length of platinum wire set in a little glass rod. A smile of grim satisfaction rode his lips. For a moment he glanced up at those around him. Barclay and Dutton moved toward him slowly, the wooden-handled electric instrument alert.

"Dutton," said McReady, "suppose you stand over by the splice there where you've connected that in. Just make sure no—thing pulls it loose."

Dutton moved away. "Now, Van, suppose you be first on this."

White-faced, Van Wall stepped forward. With a delicate precision, McReady cut a vein in the base of his thumb. Van Wall winced slightly, then held steady as a half inch of bright blood collected in the tube. McReady put the tube in the rack, gave Van Wall a bit of alum, and indicated the iodine bottle.

Van Wall stood motionlessly watching. McReady heated the platinum wire in the alcohol lamp flame, then dipped it into the tube. It hissed softly. Five times he repeated the test. "Human, I'd say," McReady sighed, and straightened. "As yet, my theory hasn't been actually proven—but I have hopes. I have hopes.

"Don't, by the way, get too interested in this. We have with us some unwelcome ones, no doubt. Van, will you relieve Barclay at the switch? Thanks. OK, Barclay, and may I say I hope you stay with us? You're a damned good guy."

Barclay grinned uncertainly; winced under the keen edge of the scalpel. Presently, smiling widely, he retrieved his long-handled weapon.

"Mr. Samuel Dutt—*Bar!*"

The tensity was released in that second. Whatever of hell the monsters may have had within them, the men in that instant matched. Barclay had no chance to move his weapon, as a score of men poured down on the thing that had seemed Dutton. It mewed, and spat, and tried to grow fangs—and was a hundred broken, torn pieces. Without knives, or any weapon save the brute-given strength of a staff of picked men, the thing was crushed, rent.

Slowly, they picked themselves up, their eyes smouldering, very quiet in their motions. A curious wrinkling of their lips betrayed a species of nervousness.

Barclay went over with the electric weapon. Things smouldered and stank. The caustic acid Van Wall dropped on each spilled drop of blood gave out tickling, cough-provoking fumes.

McReady grinned, his deepset eyes alight and dancng. "Maybe," he said softly, "I underrated man's abilities when I said nothing human could have the ferocity in the eyes of that thing we found. I wish we could have the opportunity to treat in a more befitting manner these things. Something with boiling oil, or melted lead in it, or maybe slow roasting in the power boiler. When I think what a man Dutton was—

"Never mind. My theory is confirmed by—by one who knew? Well, Van Wall and Barclay are proven. I think, then, that I'll try to show you what I already know. That I, too, am human." McReady swished the scalpel in absolute alcohol, burned it off the metal blade, and cut the base of his thumb expertly.

Twenty seconds later he looked up from the desk at the waiting men. There were more grins out there now, friendly grins, yet withal, something else in the eyes.

"Connant," McReady laughed softly, "was right. The huskies watching that thing in the corridor had nothing on you. Wonder why we think only the wolf blood has the right to ferocity? Maybe on spontaneous viciousness a wolf takes tops, but after these seven days—abandon all hope, ye wolves who enter here!

"Maybe we can save time. Connant, would you step for—"

Again Barclay was too slow. There were more grins, less tensity still, when Barclay and Van Wall finished their work.

Garry spoke in a low, bitter voice. "Connant was one of the finest men we had here—and five minutes ago I'd have sworn he was a man. Those damnable things are more than imitation." Garry shuddered and sat back in his bunk.

And thirty seconds later, Garry's blood shrank from the hot platinum wire, and struggled to escape the tube, struggled as frantically as a suddenly feral, red-eyed, dissolving imitation of Garry struggled to dodge the snake-tongue weapon Barclay advanced at him, white-faced and sweating. The Thing in the test tube screamed with a tiny, tinny voice as McReady dropped it into the glowing coal of the galley stove.

14

"The last of it?" Dr. Copper looked down from his bunk with bloodshot, saddened eyes. "Fourteen of them—"

McReady nodded shortly. "In some ways—if only we could have permanently prevented their spreading—I'd like to have even the imitations back. Commander Garry—Connant—Dutton—Clark—"

"Where are they taking those things?" Copper nodded to the stretcher Barclay and Norris were carrying out.

"Outside. Outside on the ice, where they've got fifteen smashed crates, half a ton of coal, and presently will add ten gallons of kerosene. We've dumped acid on every spilled drop, every torn fragment. We're going to incinerate those."

"Sounds like a good plan." Copper nodded wearily. "I wonder, you haven't said whether Blair—"

McReady started a second time. "Even a madman. It imitated Kinner and his praying hysteria—" McReady turned toward Van Wall at the long table. "Van, we've got to make an expedition to Blair's shack."

Van looked up sharply, the frown of worry faded for an instant in surprised remembrance. Then he rose, nodded. "Barclay better go along. He applied the lashings, and may figure how to get in without frightening Blair too much."

Three quarters of an hour, through −37° cold, while the aurora curtain bellied overhead. The twilight was nearly twelve hours long, flaming in the north on snow like white, crystalline sand under their skis. A five-mile wind piled it in drift-lines pointing off to the northwest. Three quarters of an hour to reach the snow-buried shack. No smoke came from the little shack, and the men hastened.

"Blair!" Barclay roared into the wind and when he was still a hundred yards away. "Blair!"

"Shut up," said McReady softly. "And hurry. He may be trying a lone hike. If we have to go after him—no planes, the tractors disabled—"

"Would a monster have the stamina a man has?"

"A broken leg wouldn't stop it for more than a minute," McReady pointed out.

Barclay gasped suddenly and pointed aloft. Dim in the twilit sky, a winged thing circled in curves of indescribable grace and ease. Great white wings tipped gently, and the bird swept over them in silent curiosity. "Albatross—" Barclay said softly. "First of the season, and wandering way inland for some reason. If a monster's loose—"

Norris bent down on the ice, and tore hurriedly at his heavy, windproof clothing. He straightened, his coat flapping open, a grim blue-metaled weapon in his hand. It roared a challenge to the white silence of Antarctica.

The thing in the air screamed hoarsely. Its great wings worked frantically as a dozen feathers floated down from its tail. Norris fired again. The bird was moving swiftly now, but in an almost straight line of retreat. It screamed again, more feathers dropped, and with beating wings it soared behind a ridge of pressure ice, to vanish.

Norris hurried after the other. "It won't come back," he panted.

Barclay cautioned him to silence, pointing. A curiously, fiercely blue light beat out from the cracks of the shack's door. A very low, soft humming sounded inside, a low, soft humming and a clink and click of tools, the very sounds somehow bearing a message of frantic haste.

McReady's face paled. "Lord help us if that thing has—" He grabbed Barclay's shoulder, and made snipping motions with his fingers, pointing toward the lacing of control cables that held the door.

Barclay drew the wire cutters from his pocket, and kneeled soundlessly at the door. The snap and twang of cut wires made an unbearable racket in the utter quiet of the Antarctic hush. There was only that strange, sweetly soft hum from within the shack, and the queerly, hecticly clipped clicking clicking and rattling of tools to drown their noises.

McReady peered through a crack in the door. His breath sucked in huskily and his great fingers clamped cruelly on Barclay's shoulder. The meteorologist backed down. "It isn't," he explained very softly, "Blair. It's kneeling on something on the bunk—something that keeps lifting. Whatever it's working on is a thing like a knapsack—and it lifts."

"All at once," Barclay said grimly. "No. Norris, hang back, and get that iron of yours out. It may have—weapons."

Together, Barclay's powerful body and McReady's giant strength struck the door. Inside, the bunk jammed against the door, screeched madly, and crackled into kindling. The door flung down from broken hinges, the patched lumber of the doorpost dropping inward.

Like a blue rubber ball, a Thing bounded up. One of its four tentacle-like arms looped out like a striking snake. In a seven-tentacled hand a six-inch pencil of winking, shining metal glinted and swung upward to face them. Its line-thin lips twitched back from snake-fangs in a grin of hate, red eyes blazing.

Norris' revolver thundered in the confined space. The hate-washed face twitched in agony, the looping tentacle snatched back. The silvery thing in its hand a smashed ruin of metal, the seven-tentacled hand became a mass of mangled flesh oozing greenish-yellow ichor. The revolver thundered three times more. Dark holes drilled each of the three eyes before Norris hurled the empty weapon against its face.

The Thing screamed in feral hate, a lashing tentacle wiping at blinded eyes. For a moment it crawled on the floor, savage tentacles lashing out, the body twitching. Then it staggered up again, blinded eyes working, boiling hideously, the crushed flesh sloughing away in sodden gobbets.

Barclay lurched to his feet and dove forward with an ice-ax. The flat of the weighty thing crushed against the side of the head. Again the unkillable monster went down. The tentacles lashed out, and suddenly Barclay fell to his feet in the grip of a living, livid rope. The thing dissolved as he held it, a white-hot band that ate into the flesh of his hands like living fire. Frantically he tore the stuff from him, held his hands where they could not be reached. The blind Thing felt and ripped at the tough, heavy, windproof cloth, seeking flesh—flesh it could convert—

The huge blowtorch McReady had brought coughed solemnly. Abruptly it rumbled disapproval throatily. Then it laughed gurglingly, and thrust out a blue-white, three-foot tongue. The Thing on the floor shrieked, flailed out blindly with tentacles that writhed and withered in the bubbling wrath of the blowtorch. It crawled and turned on the floor, it shrieked and hobbled madly, but always McReady held the blowtorch on the face, the dead eyes burning and bubbling uselessly. Frantically the Thing crawled and howled.

A tentacle sprouted a savage talon—and crisped in the flame. Steadily McReady moved with a planned, grim campaign. Helpless, maddened, the Thing retreated from the grunting torch, the caressing licking tongue. For a moment it rebelled, squalling in inhuman hatred at the touch of the icy snow. Then it fell back before the charring breath of the torch, the stench of its flesh bathing it. Hopelessly it retreated—on and on across the Antarctic snow. The bitter wind swept over it, twisting the torch-tongue; vainly it flopped, a trail of oily, stinking smoke bubbling away from it—

McReady walked back toward the shack silently. Barclay met him at the door. "No more?" the giant meteorologist asked grimly.

Barclay shook his head. "No more. It didn't split?"

"It had other things to think about," McReady assured him. "When I left it, it was a glowing coal. What was it doing?"

Norris laughed shortly. "Wise boys, we are. Smash magnetos, so planes won't work. Rip the boiler tubing out of the tractors. And leave that Thing alone for a week in this shack. Alone and undisturbed."

McReady looked in at the shack more carefully. The air, despite the ripped door, was hot and humid. On a table at the far end of the room rested a thing of coiled wires and small magnets, glass tubing and radio tubes. At the center a block of rough stone rested. From the center of the block came the light that flooded the place, the fiercely blue light bluer than the glare of an electric arc and from it came the sweetly soft hum. Off to one side was another mechanism of crystal glass, blown with an incredible neatness and delicacy, metal plates and a queer, shimmery sphere of insubstantiality.

"What is that?" McReady moved nearer.

Norris grunted. "Leave it for investigation. But I can guess pretty well. That's atomic power. That stuff to the left—that's a neat little thing for doing what men have been trying to do with hundred-ton cyclotrons and so forth. It separates neutrons from heavy water, which he was getting from the surrounding ice."

"Where did he get all—oh. Of course. A monster couldn't be locked in—or out. He's been through the apparatus caches." McReady stared at the apparatus. "Lord, what minds that race must have—"

"The shimmery sphere—I think it's a sphere of pure force. Neutrons can pass through any matter, and he wanted a supply reservoir of neutrons. Just project neutrons against silica—calcium—beryllium—almost anything, and the atomic energy is released. That thing is the atomic generator."

McReady plucked a thermometer from his coat. "It's 120° in here, despite the open door. Our clothes have kept the heat out to an extent, but I'm sweating now."

Norris nodded. "The light's cold. I found that. But it gives off heat to warm the place through that coil. He had all the power in the world. He could keep it warm and pleasant, as his race thought of warmth and pleasantness. Did you notice the light, the color of it?"

McReady nodded. "Beyond the stars is the answer. From beyond the stars. From a hotter planet that circled a brighter, bluer sun they came."

McReady glanced out the door toward the blasted, smoke-stained trail that flipped and wandered blindly off across the drift. "There won't be any more coming. I guess. Sheer accident it landed here, and that was twenty million years ago.What did it do all that for?" He nodded toward the apparatus.

Barclay laughed softly. "Did you notice what it was working on when we came? Look." He pointed toward the ceiling of the shack.

Like a knapsack made of flattened coffee tins, with dangling cloth straps and leather belts, the mechanism clung to the ceiling. A tiny, glaring heart of supernal flame burned in it, yet burned through the ceiling's wood without scorching it. Barclay walked over to it, grasped two of the dangling straps in his hands, and pulled it down with an effort. He strapped it about his body.

A slight jump carried him in a weirdly slow arc across the room.

"Antigravity," Norris nodded. "Yes, we had 'em stopped, with no planes, and no birds. The birds hadn't come—but it had coffee tins and radio parts, and glass and the machine ship at night. And a week—a whole week—all to itself. America is a single jump—with antigravity powered by the atomic energy of matter.

"We had 'em stopped. Another half hour—it was just tightening these straps on the device so it could wear it—and we'd have stayed in Antarctica, and shot down any moving thing that came from the rest of the world."

"The albatross—" McReady said softly. "Do you suppose—"

"With this thing almost finished? With that death weapon it held in its hand?

"No, by the grace of God, who evidently does hear very well, even down here, and the margin of half an hour, we keep our world, and the planets of the system, too. Antigravity, you know, and atomic power. Because They came from another sun, a star beyond the stars. *They* came from a world with a bluer sun."

LESTER DEL REY

For I Am a Jealous People!

1

. . . the keepers of the house shall tremble, and the strong men shall bow themselves . . . and the doors shall be shut in the streets, when the sound of the grinding is low . . . they shall be afraid of that which is high, and fears shall be in the way, and the almond tree shall flourish . . . because man goeth to his long home, and the mourners go about the streets . . .

ECCLESIASTES, XII, 3-5.

THERE WAS the continuous shrieking thunder of an alien rocket overhead as the Reverend Amos Strong stepped back into the pulpit. He straightened his square, thin shoulders slightly, and the gaunt hollows in his cheeks deepened. For a moment he hesitated, while his dark eyes turned upwards under bushy, grizzled brows. Then he moved forward, placing the torn envelope and telegram on the lectern with his notes. The blue-veined hand and knobby wrist that projected from the shiny black serge of his sleeve hardly trembled.

His eyes turned toward the pew where his wife was not. Ruth would not be there this time. She had read the message before sending it on to him. Now she could not be expected. It seemed strange to him. She hadn't missed service since Richard was born nearly thirty years ago.

The sound hissed its way into silence over the horizon, and Amos stepped forward, gripping the rickety lectern with both hands. He straightened and forced into his voice the resonance and calm it needed.

"I have just received word that my son was killed in the battle of the moon," he told the puzzled congregation. He lifted his voice, and the resonance in it deepened. "I had asked, if it were possible, that this cup might pass from me. Nevertheless, not as I will, Lord, but as Thou wilt."

He turned from their shocked faces, closing his ears to the sympathetic cry of others who had suffered. The church had been built when Wesley was twice its present size, but the troubles that had hit the people had driven them into the worn old building until it was nearly filled. He pulled his notes to him, forcing his mind from his own loss to the work that had filled his life.

"The text today is drawn from Genesis," he told them. "Chapter seventeen, seventh verse; and chapter twenty-six, fourth verse. The promise which God made to Abraham and to Isaac." He read from the Bible before him, turning the pages unerringly at the first try.

"And I will establish my covenant between me and thee and thy seed after thee in their generations for an everlasting covenant, to be a God unto thee, and to thy seed after thee."

"And I will make thy seed to multiply as the stars of heaven, and will give unto thy seed all these countries, and in thy seed shall all the nations of the earth be blessed."

He had memorized most of his sermon, no longer counting on inspiration to guide him as it had once done. He began smoothly, hearing his own words in snatches as he drew the obvious and comforting answer to their uncertainty. God had promised man the earth as an everlasting covenant. Why then should men be afraid or lose faith because alien monsters had swarmed down out of the emptiness between the stars to try man's faith? As in the days of bondage in Egypt or captivity in Babylon, there would always be trials and times when the fainthearted should waver, but the eventual outcome was clearly promised.

He had delivered a sermon from the same text in his former parish of Clyde when the government had first begun building its base on the moon, drawing heavily in that case from the reference to the stars of heaven to quiet the doubts of those who felt that man had no business in space. It was then that Richard had announced his commission in the lunar colony, using Amos' own words to defend his refusal to enter the ministry. It had been the last he saw of the boy.

He had used the text one other time, over forty years before, but the reason was lost, together with the passion that had won him fame as a boy evangelist. He could remember the sermon only because of the shock on the bearded face of his father when he had misquoted a phrase. It was one of his few clear memories of the period before his voice changed and his evangelism came to an abrupt end.

He had tried to recapture his inspiration after ordination, bitterly resenting the countless intrusions of marriage and fatherhood on his spiritual forces. But at last he had recognized that God no longer intended him to be a modern Peter the Hermit, and resigned himself to the work he could do. Now he was back in the parish where he had first begun; and if he could no longer fire the souls of his flock, he could at least help somewhat with his memorized rationalizations for the horror of the alien invasion.

Another ship thundered overhead, nearly drowning his words. Six months before, the great ships had exploded out of space and had dropped carefully to the moon, to attack the forces there. In another month, they had begun forays against Earth itself. And now, while the world haggled and struggled to unite against them, they were setting up bases all over and conquering the world mile by mile.

Amos saw the faces below him turn up, furious and uncertain. He raised his voice over the thunder, and finished hastily, moving quickly through the end of the service.

He hesitated as the congregation stirred. The ritual was over and his words were said, but there had been no real service. Slowly, as if by themselves, his lips opened, and he heard his voice quoting the Twenty-Seventh Psalm. "The Lord is my light and my salvation; whom shall I fear?"

His voice was soft, but he could feel the reaction of the congregation as the surprisingly timely words registered. "Though an host should encamp against me, my heart shall not fear: though war should rise against me, in this will I be confident." The air seemed to quiver, as it had done long ago when God had seemed to hold direct communion with him, and there was no sound from the pews when he finished. "Wait on the Lord: be of good courage, and he shall strengthen thine heart: wait, I say, on the Lord."

The warmth of that mystic glow lingered as he stepped quietly from the pulpit. Then there was the sound of motorcycles outside, and a pounding on the door. The feeling vanished.

Someone stood up and sudden light began pouring in from outdoors. There was a breath of the hot, droughty physical world with its warning of another dust storm, and a scattering of grasshoppers on the steps to remind the people of the earlier damage to their crops. Amos could see the bitterness flood back over them in tangible waves, even before they noticed the short, plump figure of Dr. Alan Miller.

"Amos! Did you hear?" He was wheezing as if he had been running. "Just came over the radio while you were in here gabbling."

He was cut off by the sound of more motorcycles. They swept down the single main street of Wesley, heading west. The riders were all in military uniform, carrying weapons and going at top speed. Dust erupted behind them, and Doc began coughing and swearing. In the last few years, he had grown more and more outspoken about his atheism; when Amos had first known him, during his first pastorate, the man had at least shown some respect for the religion of others.

"All right," Amos said sharply. "You're in the house of God, Doc. What came over the radio?"

Doc caught himself and choked back his coughing fit. "Sorry. But damn it, man, the aliens have landed in Clyde, only fifty miles away. They've set up a base there! That's what all those rockets going over meant."

There was a sick gasp from the people who had heard, and a buzz as the news was passed back to others.

Amos hardly noticed the commotion. It had been Clyde where he had served before coming here again. He was trying to picture the alien ships dropping down, scouring the town ahead of them with gas and bullets. The grocer on the corner with his nine children, the lame deacon who had served there, the two Aimes sisters with their horde of dogs and cats and their constant crusade against younger sinners. He tried to picture the green-skinned, humanoid aliens moving through the town, invading the church, desecrating the altar! And there was Anne Seyton, who had been Richard's sweetheart, though of another faith. . . .

"What about the garrison nearby?" a heavy farmer yelled over the crowd. "I had a boy there, and he told me they could handle any ships when they were landing! Shell their tubes when they were coming down——"

Doc shook his head. "Half an hour before the landing, there was a cyclone up there. It took the roof off the main building and wrecked the whole training garrison."

"Jim!" The big man screamed out the name, and began dragging his frail wife behind him, out toward his car. "If they got Jim——"

Others started to rush after him, but another procession of motorcycles stopped them. This time they were traveling slower, and a group of tanks was rolling behind them. The rear tank drew abreast, slowed, and stopped, while a dirty-faced man in an untidy major's uniform stuck his head out.

"You folks get under cover! Ain't you heard the news? Go home and stick to your radios, before a snake plane starts potshooting the bunch of you for fun. The snakes'll be heading straight over here if they're after Topeka, like it looks!" He jerked back down and began swearing at someone inside. The tank jerked to a start and began heading away toward Clyde.

There had been enough news of the sport of the alien planes in the papers. The people melted from the church. Amos tried to stop them for at least a short prayer and to give them time to collect their thoughts, but gave up after the first wave shoved him aside. A minute later, he was standing alone with Doc Miller.

"Better get home, Amos," Doc suggested. "My car's half a block down. Suppose I give you a lift?"

Amos nodded wearily. His bones felt dry and brittle, and there was a dust in his mouth thicker than that in the air. He felt old and, for the first time, almost useless. He followed the doctor quietly, welcoming the chance to ride the six short blocks to the little house the parish furnished him.

A car of ancient age and worse repair rattled toward them as they reached Doc's auto. It stopped, and a man in dirty overalls leaned out, his face working jerkily. "Are you prepared, brothers? Are you saved? Armageddon has come, as the Book foretold. Get right with God, brothers! The end of the world as foretold is at hand, amen!"

"Where does the Bible foretell alien races around other suns?" Doc shot at him.

The man blinked, frowned, and yelled something about sinners burning forever in hell before he started his rickety car again. Amos sighed. Now, with the rise of their troubles, fanatics would spring up to cry doom and false gospel more than ever, to the harm of all honest religion. He had never decided whether they were somehow useful to God or whether they were inspired by the forces of Satan.

"In my Father's house are many mansions," he quoted to Doc, as they started up the street. "It's quite possibly an allegorical reference to other worlds in the heavens."

Doc grimaced, and shrugged. Then he sighed and dropped one hand from the wheel onto Amos' knee. "I heard about Dick, Amos. I'm sorry. The first baby I ever delivered—and the handsomest!" He sighed again, staring toward Clyde as Amos found no words to answer. "I don't get it. Why can't we drop atom bombs on them? What happened to the moon base's missiles?"

Amos got out at the unpainted house where he lived, taking Doc's hand silently and nodding his thanks.

He would have to organize his thoughts this afternoon. When night fell and the people could move about without the danger of being shot at by chance alien planes, the church bell would summon them, and they would need spiritual guidance. If he could help them to stop trying to understand God, and to accept Him. . . .

There had been that moment in the church when God had seemed to enfold him and the congregation in warmth—the old feeling of true fulfillment. Maybe, now in the hour of its greatest need, some measure of inspiration had returned.

He found Ruth setting the table. Her small, quiet body moved as efficiently as ever, though her face was puffy and her eyes were red. "I'm sorry I couldn't make it, Amos. But right after the telegram, Anne Seyton came. She'd heard—before we did. And——"

The television set was on, showing headlines from the *Kansas City Star*, and he saw there was no need to tell her the news. He put a hand on one of hers. "God has only taken what he gave, Ruth. We were blessed with Richard for thirty years."

"I'm all right." She pulled away and turned toward the kitchen, her back frozen in a line of taut misery. "Didn't you hear what I said? Anne's here. Dick's wife! They were married before he left, secretly—right after you talked with him about the difference in religion. You'd better see her, Amos. She knows about her people in Clyde."

He watched his wife go. The slam of the outside door underlined the word. He'd never forbidden the marriage; he had only warned the boy, so much like Ruth. He hesitated, and finally turned toward the tiny, second bedroom. There was a muffled answer to his knock, and the lock clicked rustily.

"Anne?" he said. The room was darkened, but he could see her blond head and the thin, almost unfeminine lines of her figure. He put out a hand and felt her thin fingers in his palm. As she turned toward the weak light, he saw no sign of tears, but her hand shook with her dry shudders. "Anne, Ruth has just told me that God has given us a daughter—"

"God!" She spat the word out harshly, while the hand jerked back.

"God, Reverend Strong? Whose God? The one who sends meteorites against Dick's base, plagues of insects, and drought against our farms? The God who uses tornadoes to make it easy for the snakes to land? That God, Reverend Strong? Dick gave you a daughter, and he's dead! Dead!"

Amos backed out of the room. He had learned to stand the faint mockery with which Doc pronounced the name of the Lord, but this was something that set his skin into goose-pimples and caught at his throat. Anne had been of a different faith, but she had always seemed religious before.

It was probably only hysteria. He turned toward the kitchen door to call Ruth and send her in to the girl.

Overhead, the staccato bleating of a ram-jet cut through the air in a sound he had never heard. But the radio description fitted in perfectly. It could be no Earth ship!

Then there was another and another, until they blended together into a steady drone.

And over it came the sudden firing of a heavy gun, while a series of rapid thuds came from the garden behind the house.

Amos stumbled toward the back door. "Ruth!" he cried.

There was another burst of shots. Ruth was crumpling before he could get to the doorway.

2

My God, my God, why hast thou forsaken me? . . . I am poured out like water, and all my bones are out of joint: my heart is like wax; it is melted in the midst of my bowels. My strength is dried up like a potsherd; and my tongue cleaveth to my jaws; and thou hast brought me into the dust of death.

PSALMS, XXII, I, 14, 15.

There were no more shots as he ran to gather her into his arms. The last of the alien delta planes had gone over, heading for Topeka or whatever city they were attacking.

Ruth was still alive. One of the ugly slugs had caught her in the abdomen, ripping away part of the side, and it was bleeding horribly. But he felt her heart still beating, and she moaned faintly. Then as he put her on the couch, she opened her eyes briefly, saw him, and tried to smile. Her lips moved, and he dropped his head to hear.

"I'm sorry, Amos. Foolish. Nuisance. Sorry."

Her eyes closed, but she smiled again after he bent to kiss her lips. "Glad now. Waited so long."

Anne stood in the doorway, staring unbelievingly. But as Amos stood up, she unfroze and darted to the medicine cabinet, to come back and begin snipping away the ruined dress and trying to staunch the flow of blood.

Amos reached blindly for the phone. He mumbled something to the operator, and a minute later to Doc Miller. He'd been afraid that the doctor would still be out. He had a feeling that Doc had promised to come, but could remember no words.

The flow of blood outside the wound had been stopped, but Ruth was white, even to her lips. Anne forced him back to a chair, her fingers gentle on his arm.

"I'm sorry, Father Strong. I—I——"

He stood up and went over to stand beside Ruth, letting his eyes turn toward the half-set table. There was a smell of something burning in the air, and he went out to the old wood-burning stove to pull the pans off and drop them into the sink. Anne followed, but he hardly saw her, until he heard her begin to cry softly. There were tears this time.

"The ways of God are not the ways of man, Anne," he said, and the words released a flood of his own emotions. He dropped tiredly to a chair, his hands falling limply onto his lap. He dropped his head against the table, feeling the weakness and uncertainty of age. "We love the carnal form and our hearts are broken when it is gone. Only God can know all of any of us or count the tangled threads of all our lives. It isn't good to hate God!"

She dropped beside him. "I don't, Father Strong. I never did." He couldn't be sure of the honesty of it, but he made no effort to question her, and she sighed. "Mother Ruth isn't dead yet!"

He was saved from any answer by the door being slammed open as Doc Miller came rushing in. The plump little man took one quick look at Ruth, and was beside her, reaching for plasma and his equipment. He handed the plasma bottle to Anne, and began working carefully.

"There's a chance," he said finally. "If she were younger or stronger, I'd say there was an excellent chance. But now, since you believe in it, you'd better do some fancy praying."

"I've been praying," Amos told him, realizing that it was true. The prayers had begun inside his head at the first shot, and they had never ceased.

They moved her gently, couch and all, into the bedroom where the blinds could be drawn, and where the other sounds of the house couldn't reach her. Doc gave Anne a shot of something and sent her into the other room. He turned to Amos, but didn't insist when the minister shook his head.

"I'll stay here, Amos," he said. "With her. Until we know, or I get another call. The switchboard girl knows where I am."

He went into the bedroom and closed the door. Amos stood in the center of the living room, his head bowed, for long minutes.

The sound of the television brought him back. Topeka was off the air, but another station was showing scenes of destruction.

Hospitals and schools seemed to be their chief targets. The gas had accounted for a number of deaths, though those could have been prevented if instructions had been followed. But now the incendiaries were causing the greatest damage.

And the aliens had gotten at least as rough treatment as they had meted out. Of the forty that had been counted, twenty-nine were certainly down.

"I wonder if they're saying prayers to God for their dead?" Doc asked. "Or doesn't your God extend his mercy to races other than man?"

Amos shook his head slowly. It was a new question to him. But there could be only one answer. "God rules the entire universe, Doc. But these evil beings surely offer him no worship!"

"Are you sure? They're pretty human!"

Amos looked back to the screen, where one of the alien corpses could be seen briefly. They did look almost human, though squat and heavily muscled. Their skin was green and they wore no clothes. There was no nose, aside from two orifices under their curiously flat ears that quivered as if in breathing. But they were human enough to pass for deformed men, if they were worked on by good make-up men.

They were creatures of God, just as he was! And as such, could he deny them? Then his mind recoiled, remembering the atrocities they had committed, the tortures that had been reported, and the utter savagery so out of keeping with their inconceivably advanced ships. They were things of evil who had denied their birthright as part of God's domain. For evil, there could be only hatred. And from evil, how could there be worship of anything but the powers of darkness?

The thought of worship triggered his mind into an awareness of his need to prepare a sermon for the evening. It would have to be something simple; both he and his congregation were in no mood for rationalizations. Tonight he would have to serve God through their emotions. The thought frightened him. He tried to cling for strength to the brief moment of glory he had felt in the morning, but even that seemed far away.

There was the wail of a siren outside, rising to an ear-shattering crescendo, and the muffled sound of a loud-speaker driven beyond its normal operating level.

He stood up at last and moved out onto the porch with Doc as the tank came by. It was limping on treads that seemed to be about to fall apart, and the amplifier and speakers were mounted crudely on top. It pushed down the street, repeating its message over and over.

"Get out of town! Everybody clear out! This is an order to evacuate! The snakes are coming! Human forces have been forced to retreat to regroup. The snakes are heading this way, heading toward Topeka. They are looting and killing as they go. Get out of town! Everybody clear out!"

It paused, and another voice blared out, sounding like that of the major who had stopped before. "Get the hell out, all of you! Get out while you've still got your skins outside of you. We been licked. Shut up, Blake! We've had the holy living pants beat off us, and we're going back to momma. Get out, scram, vamoose! The snakes are coming! Beat it!"

It staggered down the street, rumbling its message, and now other stragglers began following it—men in cars, piled up like cattle; men in carts of any kind, drawn by horses. Then another amplifier sounded from one of the wagons.

"Stay under cover until night! Then get out! The snakes won't be here at once. Keep cool. Evacuate in order, and under cover of darkness. We're holing up ourselves when we get to a safe place. This is your last warning. Stay under cover now, and evacuate as soon as it's dark."

There was a bleating from the sky, and alien planes began dipping down. Doc pulled Amos back into the house, but not before he saw men being cut to ribbons by shots that seemed to fume and burst into fire as they hit. Some of the men on the retreat made cover. When the planes were gone, they came out and began regrouping, leaving the dead and hauling the wounded with them.

"Those men need me!" Amos protested.

"So does Ruth," Doc told him. "Besides, we're too old, Amos. We'd only get in the way. They have their own doctors and chaplains, probably. They're risking their lives to save us, damn it—they've piled all their worst cases there and left them to warn us and to decoy the planes away from the rest who are probably sneaking back through the woods and fields. They'd hate your guts for wasting what they're trying to do. I've been listening to one of the local stations, and it's pretty bad."

He turned on his heel and went back to the bedroom. The television program tardily began issuing evacuation orders to all citizens along the road from Clyde to Topeka, together with instructions. For some reason, the aliens seemed not to spot small objects in movement at night, and all orders were to wait until then.

Doc came out again, and Amos looked up at him, feeling his head bursting, but with one clear idea fixed in it. "Ruth can't be moved, can she, Doc?"

"No, Amos." Doc sighed. "But it won't matter. You'd better go in to her now. She seems to be coming to. I'll wake the girl and get her ready."

Amos went into the bedroom as quietly as he could, but there was no need for silence. Ruth was already conscious, as if some awareness of her approaching death had forced her to use the last few minutes of her life. She put out a frail hand timidly to him. Her voice was weak, but clear.

"Amos, I know. And I don't mind now, except for you. But there's something I had to ask you. Amos, do you——?"

He dropped beside her when her voice faltered, wanting to bury his head against her, but not daring to lose the few remaining moments of her sight. He fought the words out of the depths of his mind, and then realized it would take more than words. He bent over and kissed her again, as he had first kissed her so many years ago.

"I've always loved you, Ruth," he said. "I still do love you."

She sighed and relaxed. "Then I won't be jealous of God any more, Amos. I had to know."

Her hand reached up weakly, to find his hair and run through it. She smiled, the worn lines of her face softening. Her voice was soft and almost young. "And forsaking all others, cleave only unto thee——"

The last syllable whispered out, and the hand dropped.

Amos dropped his head at last, and a single sob choked out of him. He folded her hands tenderly, with the worn, cheap wedding ring uppermost, and arose slowly with his head bowed.

"Then shall the dust return to the earth as it was; and the spirit shall return unto God who gave it. Father, I thank thee for this moment with her. Bless her, O Lord, and keep her for me."

He nodded to Doc and Anne. The girl looked sick and sat staring at him with eyes that mixed shock and pity.

"You'll need some money, Anne," he told her as Doc went into the bedroom. "I don't have much, but there's a little——"

She drew back, choking, and shook her head. "I've got enough, Reverend Strong. I'll make out. Doctor Miller has told me to take his car. But what about you?"

"There's still work to be done," he said. "I haven't even written my sermon. And the people who are giving up their homes will need comfort. In such hours as these, we all need God to sustain us."

She stumbled to her feet and into the bedroom after Miller. Amos opened his old desk and reached for pencil and paper.

3

The wicked have drawn out the sword, and have bent their bow, to cast down the poor and needy, and to slay such as be of upright conversation.

I have seen the wicked in great power, and spreading himself like a green bay tree.

PSALMS, XXXVII, 14, 35.

Darkness was just beginning to fall when they helped Anne out into the doctor's car, making sure that the tank was full. She was quiet, and had recovered herself, but avoided Amos whenever possible. She turned at last to Doc Miller.

"What are you going to do? I should have asked before, but——"

"Don't worry about me, girl," he told her, his voice as hearty as when he was telling an old man he still had forty years to live. "I've got other ways. The switchboard girl is going to be one of the last to leave, and I'm driving her in her car. You go ahead, the way we mapped it out. And pick up anyone else you find on the way. It's safe; it's still too early for men to start turning to looting, rape, or robbery. They'll think of that a little later."

She held out a hand to him, and climbed in. At the last minute, she pressed Amos' hand briefly. Then she stepped on the accelerator and the car took off down the street at its top speed.

"She hates me," Amos said. "She loves men too much and God too little to understand."

"And maybe you love your God too much to understand that you love men, Amos. Don't worry, she'll figure it out. The next time you see her, she'll feel different. I'll see you later."

Doc swung off toward the telephone office, carrying his bag. Amos watched him, puzzled as always at anyone who could so fervently deny God and yet could live up to every commandment of the Lord except worship. They had been friends for a long time, while the parish stopped fretting about it and took it for granted, yet the riddle was no nearer solution.

There was the sound of a great rocket landing, and the smaller stutterings of the peculiar alien ram-jets. The ships passed directly overhead, yet there was no shooting this time.

Amos faced the bedroom window for a moment, and then turned toward the church. He opened it, throwing the doors wide. There was no sign of the sexton, but he had rung the bell in the tower often enough before. He took off his worn coat and grabbed the rope.

It was hard work, and his hands were soft. Once it had been a pleasure, but now his blood seemed too thin to suck up the needed oxygen. The shirt stuck wetly to his back, and he felt giddy when he finished.

Almost at once, the telephone in his little office began jangling nervously. He staggered to it, panting as he lifted it, to hear the voice of Nellie, shrill with fright. "Reverend, what's up? Why's the bell ringing?"

"For prayer meeting, of course," he told her. "What else?"

"Tonight? Well, I'll be——" She hung up.

He lighted a few candles and put them on the altar, where their glow could be seen from the dark street, but where no light would shine upwards for alien eyes. Then he sat down to wait, wondering what was keeping the organist.

There were hushed calls from the street and nervous cries. A car started, to be followed by another. Then a group took off at once. He went to the door, partly for the slightly cooler air. All along the street, men were moving out their possessions and loading up, while others took off. They waved to him, but hurried on by. He heard telephones begin to ring, but if Nellie was passing on some urgent word, she had forgotten him.

He turned back to the altar, kneeling before it. There was no articulate prayer in his mind. He simply clasped his gnarled fingers together and rested on his knee, looking up at the outward symbol of his life. Outside the sounds went on, blending together. It did not matter whether anyone chose to use the church tonight. It was open, as the house of God must always be in times of stress. He had long since stopped trying to force religion on those not ready for it.

And slowly, the strains of the day began to weave themselves into the pattern of his life. He had learned to accept; from the death of his baby daughter on, he had found no way to end the pain that seemed so much a part of life. But he could bury it behind the world of his devotion, and meet whatever his lot was to be without anger at the will of the Lord. Now again, he accepted things as they were ordered.

There was a step behind him. He turned, not bothering to rise, and saw the dressmaker, Angela Anduccini, hesitating at the door. She had never entered, though she had lived in Wesley since she was eighteen. She crossed herself doubtfully, and waited.

He stood up. "Come in, Angela. This is the house of God, and all His daughters are welcome."

There was a dark, tight fear in her eyes as she glanced back to the street. "I thought—maybe the organ——"

He opened it for her and found the switch. He started to explain the controls, but the smile on her lips warned him that it was unnecessary. Her calloused fingers ran over the stops, and she began playing, softly as if to herself. He went back to one of the pews, listening. For two years he had blamed the organ, but now he knew that there was no fault with the instrument, but only with its player before. The music was sometimes strange for his church, but he liked it.

A couple who had moved into the old Surrey farm beyond the town came in, holding hands, as if holding each other up. And a minute later, Buzz Williams stumbled in and tried to tiptoe down the aisle to where Amos sat. Since his parents had died, he'd been the town problem. Now he was half-drunk, though without his usual boisterousness.

"I ain't got no car and I been drinking," he whispered. "Can I stay here till maybe somebody comes or something?"

Amos sighed, motioning Buzz to a seat where the boy's eyes had centered. Somewhere, there must be a car for the four waifs who had remembered God when everything else had failed them. If one of the young couple could drive, and he could locate some kind of a vehicle, it was his duty to see that they were sent to safety.

Abruptly, the haven of the church and the music came to an end, leaving him back in the real world—a curiously unreal world now.

He was heading down the steps, trying to remember whether the Jameson boy had taken his flivver, when a panel truck pulled up in front of the church. Doc Miller got out, wheezing as he squeezed through the door.

He took in the situation at a glance. "Only four strays, Amos? I thought we might have to pack them in." He headed for Buzz. "I've got a car outside, Buzz. Gather up the rest of this flock and get going!"

"I been drinking," Buzz said, his face reddening hotly.

"Okay, you've been drinking. At least you know it, and there's no traffic problem. Head for Salina and hold it under forty and you'll be all right." Doc swept little Angela Anduccini from the organ and herded her out, while Buzz collected the couple. "Get going, all of you!"

They got, with Buzz enthroned behind the wheel and Angela beside him. The town was dead. Amos closed the organ and began shutting the doors to the church.

"I've got a farm tractor up the street for us, Amos," Doc said at last. "I almost ran out of tricks. There were more fools than you'd think who thought they could hide out right here. At that, I probably missed some. Well, the tractor's nothing elegant, but it can take those back roads. We'd better get going."

Amos shook his head. He had never thought it out, but the decision had been in his mind from the beginning. Ruth still lay waiting a decent burial. He could no more leave her now than when she was alive. "You'll have to go alone, Doc."

"I figured." The doctor sighed, wiping the sweat from his forehead. ". . . I'd remember to my dying day that believers have more courage than an atheist! No sale, Amos. It isn't sensible, but that's how I feel. We'd better put out the candles, I guess."

Amos snuffed them reluctantly, wondering how he could persuade the other to leave. His ears had already caught the faint sounds of shooting; the aliens were on their way.

The uncertain thumping of a laboring motor sounded from the street, to wheeze to silence. There was a shout, a pause, and the motor caught again. It might have run for ten seconds before it backfired, and was still.

Doc opened one of the doors. In the middle of the street, a man was pushing an ancient car while his wife steered. But it refused to start again. He grabbed for tools, threw up the hood, and began a frantic search for the trouble.

"If you can drive a tractor, there's one half a block down," Doc called out.

The man looked up, snapped one quick glance behind him, and pulled the woman hastily out of the car. In almost no time, the heavy roar of the tractor sounded. The man revved it up to full throttle and tore off down the road, leaving Doc and Amos stranded. The sounds of the aliens were clearer now, and there was some light coming from beyond the bend of the street.

There was no place to hide. They found a window where the paint on the imitation stained glass was loose, and peeled it back enough for a peephole. The advance scouts of the aliens were already within view. They were dashing from house to house. Behind them, they left something that sent up clouds of glowing smoke that seemed to have no fire connected to their brilliance. At least, no buildings were burning.

Just as the main group of aliens came into view, the door of one house burst open. A scrawny man leaped out, with his fat wife and fatter daughter behind him. They raced up the street, tearing at their clothes and scratching frantically at their reddened skin.

Shots sounded. All three jerked, but went racing on. More shots sounded. At first, Amos thought it was incredibly bad shooting. Then he realized that it was even more unbelievably good marksmanship. The aliens were shooting at the hands first, then moving up the arms methodically, wasting no chance for torture.

For the first time in years, Amos felt fear and anger curdle solidly in his stomach. He stood up, feeling his shoulders square back and his head come up as he moved toward the door. His lips were moving in words that he only half understood. "Arise, O Lord; O God, lift up thine hand; forget not the humble. Wherefore doth the wicked condemn God? He hath said in his heart, Thou wilt not requite it. Thou hast seen it, for thou beholdest mischief and spite, to requite it with thy hand: the poor committeth himself unto thee; thou art the helper of the fatherless. Break thou the arm of the wicked and the evil ones; seek out their wickedness till thou find none. . . ."

"Stop it, Amos!" Doc's voice rasped harshly in his ear. "Don't be a fool! And you're misquoting that last verse!"

It cut through the fog of his anger. He knew that Doc had deliberately reminded him of his father, but the trick worked, and the memory of his father's anger at misquotations replaced his cold fury. "We can't let that go on!"

Then he saw it was over. They had used up their targets. But there was the sight of another wretch, unrecognizable in half of his skin. . . .

Doc's voice was as sick as he felt. "We can't do anything, Amos. I can't understand a race smart enough to build star ships and still going in for this. But it's good for our side, in the long run. While our armies are organizing, they're wasting time on this. And it makes resistance tougher, too."

The aliens didn't confine their sport to humans. They worked just as busily on a huge old tomcat they found. And all the corpses were being loaded onto a big wagon pulled by twenty of the creatures.

The aliens obviously had some knowledge of human behavior. At first they had passed up all stores, and had concentrated on living quarters. The scouts had passed on by the church without a second glance. But they moved into a butcher shop at once, to come out again, carrying meat which was piled on the wagon with the corpses.

Now a group was assembling before the church, pointing up toward the steeple where the bell was. Two of them shoved up a mortar of some sort. It was pointed quickly and a load was dropped in. There was a muffled explosion, and the bell rang sharply, its pieces rattling down the roof and into the yard below.

Another shoved the mortar into a new position, aiming it straight for the door of the church. Doc yanked Amos down between two pews. "They don't like churches, damn it! A fine spot we picked. Watch out for splinters!"

The door smashed in and a heavy object struck the altar, ruining it and ricocheting onto the organ. Amos groaned at the sound it made.

There was no further activity when they slipped back to their peepholes. The aliens were on the march again, moving along slowly. In spite of the delta planes, they seemed to have no motorized ground vehicles, and the wagon moved on under the power of the twenty green-skinned things, coming directly in front of the church.

Amos stared at it in the flickering light from the big torches burning in the hands of some of the aliens. Most of the corpses were strangers to him. A few he knew. And then his eyes picked out the twisted, distorted upper part of Ruth's body, her face empty in death's relaxation.

He stood up wearily, and this time Doc made no effort to stop him. He walked down a line of pews and around the wreck of one of the doors. Outside the church, the air was still hot and dry, but he drew a long breath into his lungs. The front of the church was in the shadows, and no aliens seemed to be watching him.

He moved down the stone steps. His legs were firm now. His heart was pounding heavily, but the clot of feelings that rested leadenly in his stomach had no fear left in it. Nor was there any anger left, nor any purpose.

He saw the aliens stop and stare at him, while a jabbering began among them.

He moved forward with the measured tread that had led him to his wedding the first time. He came to the wagon, and put his hand out, lifting one of Ruth's dead-limp arms back across her body.

"This is my wife," he told the staring aliens quietly. "I am taking her home with me."

He reached up and began trying to move the other bodies away from her. Without surprise, he saw Doc's arms moving up to help him, while a steady stream of whispered profanity came from the man's lips.

He hadn't expected to succeed. He had expected nothing.

Abruptly, a dozen of the aliens leaped for the two men. Amos let them overpower him without resistance. For a second, Doc struggled, and then he too relaxed while the aliens bound them and tossed them onto the wagon.

4

He hath bent his bow like an enemy: he stood with his right hand as an adversary, and slew all that were pleasant to the eye in the tabernacle of the daughter of Zion: he poured out his fury like fire.

The Lord was as an enemy: he hath swallowed up Israel, he hath

> *swallowed up all her palaces: he hath destroyed his strong holds, and hath increased in the daughter of Judah mourning and lamentation.*
> *The Lord hath cast off his altar, he hath abhorred his sanctuary, he hath given up into the hand of the enemy the walls of her palaces; they have made a noise in the house of the Lord, as in the day of a solemn feast.*
>
> LAMENTATIONS, II, 4, 5, 7.

Amos' first reaction was one of dismay at the ruin of his only good suit. He struggled briefly on the substance under him, trying to find a better spot. A minister's suit might be old, but he could never profane the altar with such stains as these. Then some sense of the ridiculousness of his worry reached his mind, and he relaxed as best he could.

He had done what he had to do, and it was too late to regret it. He could only accept the consequences of it now, as he had learned to accept everything else God had seen fit to send him. He had never been a man of courage, but the strength of God had sustained him through as much as most men had to bear. It would sustain him further.

Doc was facing him, having flopped around to lie facing toward him. Now the doctor's lips twisted into a crooked grin. "I guess we're in for it now. But it won't last forever, and maybe we're old enough to die fast. At least, once we're dead, we won't know it, so there's no sense being afraid of dying."

If it was meant to provoke him into argument, it failed. Amos considered it a completely hopeless philosophy, but it was better than none, probably. His own faith in the hereafter left something to be desired; he was sure of immortality and the existence of heaven and hell, but he had never been able to picture either to his own satisfaction.

The wagon had been swung around and was now being pulled up the street, back toward Clyde. Amos tried to take his mind off the physical discomforts of the ride by watching the houses, counting them to his own. They drew near it finally, but it was Doc who spotted the important fact. He groaned. "My car!"

Amos strained his eyes, staring into the shadows through the glare of the torches. Doc's car stood at the side of the house, with the door open! Someone must have told Anne that he hadn't left, and she'd swung back around the alien horde to save him!

He began a prayer that they might pass on without the car being noticed, and it seemed at first that they would. Then there was a sudden cry from the house, and he saw her face briefly at a front window. She must have seen Doc and himself lying on the wagon!

He opened his mouth to risk a warning, but it was too late. The door swung back, and she was standing on the front steps, lifting Richard's rifle to her shoulder. Amos' heart seemed to hesitate with the tension of his body. The aliens still hadn't noticed. If she'd only wait . . .

The rifle cracked. Either by luck or some skill he hadn't suspected, one of the aliens dropped. She was running forward now, throwing another cartridge into the barrel. The gun barked again, and an alien fell to the ground, bleating horribly.

There was no attempt at torture this time, at least. The leading alien jerked out a tubelike affair from a scabbard at his side and a single sharp explosion sounded. Anne jerked backward as the heavy slug hit her forehead, the rifle spinning from her dead hands.

The wounded alien was trying frantically to crawl away. Two of his fellows began working on him mercilessly, with as little feeling as if he had been a human. His body followed that of Anne toward the front of the wagon, just beyond Amos' limited view.

She hadn't seemed hysterical this time, Amos thought wearily. It had been her tendency to near hysteria that had led to his advising Richard to wait, not the difference in faith. Now he was sorry he'd had no chance to understand her better.

Doc sighed, and there was a peculiar pride under the thickness of his voice. "Man," he said, "has one virtue which is impossible to any omnipotent force like your God. He can be brave. He can be brave beyond sanity, for another man or for an idea. Amos, I pity your God if man ever makes war on Him!"

Amos flinched, but the blasphemy aroused only a shadow of his normal reaction. His mind seemed numbed. He lay back, watching black clouds scudding across the sky almost too rapidly. It looked unnatural, and he remembered how often the accounts had mentioned a tremendous storm that had wrecked or hampered the efforts of human troops. Maybe a counteract had begun, and this was part of the alien defense. If they had some method of weather control, it was probable. The moonlight was already blotted out by the clouds.

Half a mile further on, there was a shout from the aliens, and a big tractor chugged into view, badly driven by one of the aliens, who had obviously only partly mastered the human machine. With a great deal of trial and error, it was backed into position and coupled to the wagon. Then it began churning along at nearly thirty miles an hour, while the big wagon bucked and bounced behind. From then on, the ride was physical hell. Even Doc groaned at some of the bumps, though his bones had three times more padding than Amos'.

Mercifully, they slowed when they reached Clyde. Amos wiped the blood off his bitten lip and managed to wriggle to a position where most of the bruises were on his upper side. There was a flood of brilliant lights beyond the town where the alien rockets stood, and he could see a group of nonhuman machines busy unloading the great ships. But the drivers of the machines looked totally unlike the other aliens.

One of the alien trucks swung past them, and he had a clear view of the creature steering it. It bore no resemblance to humanity. There was a conelike trunk, covered with a fine white down, ending in four thick stalks to serve as legs. From its broadest point, four sinuous limbs spread out to the truck controls. There was no head, but only eight small tentacles waving above it.

He saw a few others, always in control of machines, and no machines being handled by the green-skinned people as they passed through the ghost city that had been Clyde. Apparently there were two races allied against humanity, which explained why such barbarians could come in space ships. The green ones must be simply the fighters, while the downy cones were the technicians. From their behavior, though, the pilots of the planes must be recruited from the fighters.

Clyde had grown since he had been there, unlike most of the towns about. There was a new supermarket just down the street from Amos' former church, and the tractor jolted to a stop in front of it. Aliens swarmed out and began carrying the loot from the wagon into its big food lockers, while two others lifted Doc and Amos.

But they weren't destined for the comparatively merciful death of freezing in the lockers. The aliens threw them into a little cell that had once apparently been a cashier's cage, barred from floor to ceiling. It made a fairly efficient jail, and the lock that clicked shut as the door closed behind them was too heavy to be broken.

There was already one occupant—a medium-built young man whom Amos finally recognized as Smithton, the Clyde dentist. His shoulders were shaking with sporadic sobs as he sat huddled in one corner. He looked at the two arrivals without seeing them. "But I surrendered," he whispered. "I'm a prisoner of war. They can't do it. I surrendered——"

A fatter-than-usual alien, wearing the only clothes Amos had seen on any of them, came waddling up to the cage, staring in at them, and the dentist wailed off into silence. The alien drew up his robe about his chest and scratched his rump against a counter without taking his eyes off them. "Humans," he said in a grating voice, but without an accent, "are peculiar. No standardization."

"I'll be damned!" Doc swore. "English!"

The alien studied them with what might have been surprise, lifting his ears. "Is the gift of tongues so unusual, then? Many of the priests of the Lord God Almighty speak all the human languages. It's a common miracle, not like levitation."

"Fine. Then maybe you'll tell us what we're being held for?" Doc suggested.

The priest shrugged. "Food, of course. The *grethi* eat any kind of meat—even our people—but we have to examine the laws to find whether you're permitted. If you are, we'll need freshly killed specimens to sample, so we're waiting with you."

"You mean you're attacking us for *food?*"

The priest grunted harshly. "No! We're on a holy mission to exterminate you. The Lord commanded us to go down to Earth where abominations existed and to leave no living creature under your sun."

He turned and waddled out of the store, taking the single remaining torch with him, leaving only the dim light of the moon and reflections from further away.

Amos dropped onto a stool inside the cage. "They had to lock us in a new building instead of one I know," he said. "If it had been the church, we might have had a chance."

"How?" Doc asked sharply.

Amos tried to describe the passage through the big, unfinished basement under the church, reached through a trap door. Years before, a group of teen-agers had built a sixty-foot tunnel into it and had used it for a private club until the passage had been discovered and bricked over from outside. The earth would be soft around the bricks, however. Beyond, the outer end of the tunnel opened in a wooded section, which led to a drainage ditch that in turn connected with the Republican River. From the church, they could have moved to the stream and slipped down that without being seen, unlike most of the other sections of the town.

Doc's fingers were trembling on the lock when Amos finished. "If we could get the two hundred feet to the church—— They don't know much about us, Amos, if they lock us in where the lock screws are on our side. Well, we'll have to chance it."

Amos' own fingers shook as he felt the screwheads. He could see what looked like a back door to the store. If they could come out into the alley that had once been there, they could follow it nearly to the church—and then the trees around that building would cut off most of the light. It would be a poor chance. But was it chance? It seemed more like the hand of God to him.

"More like the carelessness of the aliens to me," Doc objected. "It would probably be a lot less complicated in most other places, the way they light the town. Knock the bottom out of the money drawer and break off two slats. I've got a quarter that fits these screws."

Smithton fumbled with the drawer, praying now—a childhood prayer for going to sleep. But he succeeded in getting two slats Doc could place the quarter between.

It was rough going, with more slipping than turning of the screws, but the lock had been meant to keep outsiders out, not cashiers in. Three of the screws came loose, and the lock rotated on the fourth until they could force the cage open.

Doc stopped and pulled Smithton to him. "Follow me, and do what I do. No talking, no making a separate break, or I'll break your neck. All right!"

The back door was locked, but on the inside. They opened it to a backyard filled with garbage. The alley wasn't as dark as it should have been, since open lots beyond let some light come through. They hugged what shadows they could until they reached the church hedge. There they groped along, lining themselves up with the side office door. There was no sign of aliens.

Amos broke ahead of the others, being more familiar with the church. It wasn't until he had reached the door that he realized it could have been locked; it had been kept that way part of the time. He grabbed the handle and forced it back—to find it open!

For a second, he stopped to thank the Lord for their luck. Then the others were with him, crowding into the little kitchen where social suppers were prepared. He'd always hated those functions, but now he blessed them for a hiding place that gave them time to find their way.

There were sounds in the church, and odors, but none that seemed familiar to Amos. Something made the back hairs of his neck prickle. He took off his shoes and tied them around his neck, and the others followed suit.

The trap door lay down a small hall, across in front of the altar, and in the private office on the other side.

They were safer together than separated, particularly since Smithton was with them. Amos leaned back against the kitchen wall to catch his breath. His heart seemed to have a ring of needled pain around it, and his throat was so dry that he had to fight desperately against gagging. There was water here, but he couldn't risk rummaging across the room to the sink.

He was praying for strength, less for himself than the others. Long since, he had resigned himself to die. If God willed his death, he was ready; all he had were dead and probably mutilated, and he had succeeded only in dragging those who tried to help him into mortal danger. He was old, and his body was already treading its way to death. He could live for probably twenty more years, but aside from his work, there was nothing to live for—and even in that, he had been only a mediocre failure. But he was still responsible for Doc Miller, and even for Smithton now.

He squeezed his eyes together and squinted around the doorway. There was some light in the hall that led toward the altar, but he could see no one, and there were drapes that gave a shadow from which they could spy the rest of their way. He moved to it softly, and felt the others come up behind him.

He bent forward, parting the drapes a trifle. They were perhaps twenty feet in front of the altar, on the right side. He spotted the wreckage that had once stood as an altar. Then he frowned as he saw evidence of earth piled up into a mound of odd shape.

He drew the cloth back further, surprised at the curiosity in him, as he had been surprised repeatedly by the changes taking place in himself.

There were two elaborately robed priests kneeling in the center of the chapel. But his eye barely noticed them before it was attracted to what stood in front of the new altar.

A box of wood rested on an earthenware platform. On it were four marks which his eyes recognized as unfamiliar, but which his mind twisted into a sequence from the alphabets he had learned, unpronounceable yet compelling. And above the box was a veil, behind which Something shone brightly without light.

In his mind, a surge of power pulsed, making patterns that might almost have been words through his thoughts—words like the words Moses once had heard—words that Amos, heartsick, knew. . . .

"I AM THAT I AM, who brought those out of bondage from Egypt and who wrote upon the wall before Belshazzar, MENE, MENE, TEKEL, UPHARSIN, as it shall be writ large upon the Earth, from this day forth. For I have said unto the seed of Mikhtchah, thou art my chosen people and I shall exalt thee above all the races under the heavens!"

5

And it was given unto him to make war with the saints, and to overcome them: and power was given him over all kindreds, and tongues, and nations.

He that leadeth into captivity shall go into captivity: he that killeth with the sword must be killed with the sword.

REVELATIONS, XIII, 7, 10.

The seed of Mikhtchah. The seed of the invaders. . . .

There was no time and all time, then. Amos felt his heart stop, but the blood pounded through his arteries with a vigor it had lacked for decades. He felt Ruth's hand in his, stirring with returning life, and knew she had never existed. Beside him, he saw Doc Miller's hair turn snow-white and knew that it was so, though there was no way he could see Doc from his position.

He felt the wrath of the Presence rest upon him, weighing his every thought from his birth to his certain death, where he ceased completely and went on forever, and yet he knew that the Light behind the veil was unaware of him, but was receptive only to the two Mikhtchah priests who knelt, praying.

All of that was with but a portion of his mind so small that he could not locate it, though his total mind encompassed all time and space, and that which was neither; yet each part of his perceptions occupied all of his mind that had been or ever could be, save only the present, which somehow was a concept not yet solved by the One before him.

He saw a strange man on a low mountain, receiving tablets of stone that weighed only a pennyweight, engraved with a script that all could read. And he knew the man, but refused to believe it, since the garments were not those of his mental image, and the clean-cut face fitted better with the strange headpiece than with the language the man spoke.

He saw every prayer of his life tabulated. But nowhere was there the mantle of divine warmth which he had felt as a boy and had almost felt again the morning before. And there was a stirring of unease at his thought, mixed with wrath; yet while the thought was in his mind, nothing could touch him.

Each of those things was untrue, because he could find no understanding of that which was true.

It ended as abruptly as it had begun, either a microsecond or a million subjective years after. It left him numbed, but newly alive. And it left him dead as no man had ever been hopelessly dead before.

He knew only that before him was the Lord God Almighty, He who had made a covenant with Abraham, with Isaac, and with Jacob, and with their seed. And he knew that the covenant was ended. Mankind had been rejected, while God now was on the side of the enemies of Abraham's seed, the enemies of all the nations of earth.

Even that was too much for a human mind no longer in touch with the Presence, and only a shadow of it remained.

Beside him, Amos heard Doc Miller begin breathing again, brushing the white hair back from his forehead wonderingly as he muttered a single word, "God!"

One of the Mikhtchah priests looked up, his eyes turning about; there had been a glazed look on his face; but it was changing.

Then Smithton screamed! His open mouth poured out a steady, unwavering screaming, while his lungs panted in and out. His eyes opened, staring horribly. Like a wooden doll on strings, the man stood up and walked forward. He avoided the draperies and headed for the Light behind the veil. Abruptly, the Light was gone, but Smithton walked toward it as steadily as before. He stopped before the falling veil, and the scream cut off sharply.

Doc had jerked silently to his feet, tugging Amos up behind him. The minister lifted himself, but he knew there was no place to go. It was up to the will of God now . . . Or. . . .

Smithton turned on one heel precisely. His face was rigid and without expression, yet completely mad. He walked mechanically forward toward the two priests. They sprawled aside at the last second, holding two obviously human-made automatics, but making no effort to use them. Smithton walked on toward the open door at the front of the church.

He reached the steps, with the two priests staring after him. His feet lifted from the first step to the second and then he was on the sidewalk.

The two priests fired!

Smithton jerked, halted, and suddenly cried out in a voice of normal, rational agony. His legs kicked frantically under him and he ducked out of the sight of the doorway, his faltering steps sounding further and further away. He was dead—the Mikhtchah marksmanship had been as good as it seemed always to be—but still moving, though slower and slower, as if some extra charge of life were draining out like a battery running down.

The priests exchanged quick glances and then darted after him, crying out as they dashed around the door into the night. Abruptly, a single head and hand appeared again, to snap a shot at the draperies from which Smithton had come. Amos forced himself to stand still, while his imagination supplied the jolt of lead in his stomach. The bullet hit the draperies, and something else.

The priest hesitated, and was gone again.

Amos broke into a run across the chapel and into the hall at the other side of the altar. He heard the faint sound of Doc's feet behind him.

The trap door was still there, unintentionally concealed under carpeting. He forced it up and dropped through it into the four-foot depth of the uncompleted basement, making room for Doc. They crouched together as he lowered the trap and began feeling his way through the blackness toward the other end of the basement. It had been five years since he had been down there, and then only once for a quick inspection of the work of the boys who had dug the tunnel.

He thought he had missed it at first, and began groping for the small entrance. It might have caved in, for that matter. Then, two feet away, his hand found the hole and he drew Doc after him.

It was cramped, and bits of dirt had fallen in places and had to be dug out of the way. Part of the distance was covered on their stomachs. They found the bricked-up wall ahead of them and began digging around it with their bare hands. It took another ten minutes, while distant sounds of wild yelling from the Mikhtchah reached them faintly. They broke through at last with bleeding hands, not bothering to check for aliens near. They reached a safer distance in the woods, caught their breath, and went on.

The biggest danger lay in the drainage trench, which was low in several places. But luck was with them, and those spots lay in the shadow.

Then the little Republican River lay in front of them, and there was a flatbottom boat nearby.

Moments later, they were floating down the stream, resting their aching lungs, while the boat needed only a trifling guidance. It was still night, with only the light from the moon, and there was little danger of pursuit by the alien planes. Amos could just see Doc's face as the man fumbled for a cigarette.

He lighted it and exhaled deeply. "All right, Amos—you were right, and God exists. But damn it, I don't feel any better for knowing that. I can't see how God helps me—nor even how He's doing the Mikhtchah much good. What do they get out of it, beyond a few miracles with the weather? They're just doing God's dirty work."

"They get the Earth, I suppose—if they want it," Amos said doubtfully. He wasn't sure they did. Nor could he see how the other aliens tied into the scheme; if he had known the answers, they were gone now. "Doc, you're still an atheist, though you now know God is."

The plump man chuckled bitterly. "I'm afraid you're right. But at least I'm myself. You can't be, Amos. You've spent your whole life on the gamble that God is right and that you must serve him—when the only way you could serve was to help mankind. What do you do now? God is automatically right—but everything you've ever believed makes Him completely wrong, and you can only serve Him by betraying your people. What kind of ethics will work for you now?"

Amos shook his head wearily, hiding his face in his hands. The same problem had been fighting its way through his own thoughts. His first reaction had been to acknowledge his allegiance to God without question; sixty years of conditioned thought lay behind that. Yet now he could not accept such a decision. As a man, he could not bow to what he believed completely evil, and the Mikhtchah were evil by every definition he knew.

Could he tell people the facts, and take away what faith they had in any purpose in life? Could he go over to the enemy, who didn't even want him, except for their feeding experiments? Or could he encourage people to fight with the old words that God was with them—when he knew the words were false, and their resistance might doom them to eternal hellfire for opposing God?

It hit him then that he could remember nothing clearly about the case of a hereafter—either for or against it. What happened to a people when God deserted them? Were they only deserted in their physical form, and still free to win their spiritual salvation? Or were they completely lost? Did they cease to have souls that could survive? Or were those souls automatically consigned to hell, however noble they might be?

No question had been answered for him. He knew that God existed, but he had known that before. He knew nothing now beyond that. He did not even know when God had placed the Mikhtchah before humanity. It seemed unlikely that it was as recent as his own youth. Yet otherwise, how could he account for the strange spiritual glow he had felt as an evangelist?

"There's only one rational answer," he said at last. "It doesn't make any difference what I decide! I'm only one man."

"So was Columbus when he swore the world was round. And he didn't have the look on his face you've had since we saw God, Amos! I know what the Bible means when it says Moses' face shone after he came down from the mountain, until he had to cover it with a veil. If I'm right, God help mankind if you decide wrong!"

Doc tossed the cigarette over the side and lighted another, and Amos was shocked to see that the man's hands were shaking. The doctor shrugged, and his tone fell back to normal. "I wish we knew more. You've always thought almost exclusively in terms of the Old Testament and a few snatches of Revelations—like a lot of men who became evangelists. I've never really thought about God—I couldn't accept Him, so I dismissed Him. Maybe that's why we got the view of Him we did. I wish I knew where Jesus fits in, for instance. There's too much missing. Too many imponderables and hiatuses. We have only two facts, and we can't understand either. There is a manifestation of God which has touched both Mikhtchah and mankind; and He has stated now that he plans to wipe out mankind. We'll have to stick to that."

Amos made one more attempt to deny the problem that was facing him. "Suppose God is only testing man again, as He did so often before?"

"Testing?" Doc rolled the word on his tongue, and seemed to spit it out. The strange white hair seemed to make him older, and the absence of mockery in his voice left him almost a stranger. "Amos, the Hebrews worked like the devil to get Canaan; after forty years of wandering around a few square miles God suddenly told them this was the land—and then they had to take it by the same methods men have always used to conquer a country. The miracles didn't really decide anything. They got out of Babylon because the old prophets were slaving night and day to hold them together as one people, and because they managed to sweat it out until they finally got a break. In our own time, they've done the same things to get Israel, and with no miracles! It seems to me God took it away, but they had to get it back by themselves. I don't think much of that kind of a test in this case."

Amos could feel all his values slipping and spinning. He realized that he was holding himself together only because of Doc; otherwise, his mind would have reached for madness, like any intelligence forced to solve the insoluble. He could no longer comprehend himself, let alone God. And the feeling crept into his thoughts that God couldn't wholly understand Himself, either.

"Can a creation defy anything great enough to create it, Doc? And should it, if it can?"

"Most kids have to," Doc said. He shook his head. "It's your problem. All I can do is point a few things out. And maybe it won't matter, at that. We're still a long ways inside Mikhtchah territory, and it's getting along toward daylight."

The boat drifted on, while Amos tried to straighten out his thoughts and grew more deeply tangled in a web of confusion. What could any man who worshipped devoutly do if he found his God was opposed to all else he had ever believed to be good?

A version of Kant's categorical imperative crept into his mind; somebody had once quoted it to him—probably Doc. "So act as to treat humanity, whether in thine own person or in that of any other, in every case as an end withal, never as a means only." Was God now treating man as an end, or simply as a means to some purpose, in which man had failed? And had man ever seriously treated God as an end, rather than as a means to spiritual immortality and a quietus to the fear of death?

"We're being followed!" Doc whispered suddenly. He pointed back, and Amos could see a faint light shining around a curve in the stream. "Look—there's a building over there. When the boat touches shallow water, run for it!"

He bent to the oars, and a moment later they touched bottom and were over the side, sending the boat back into the current. The building was a hundred feet back from the bank, and they scrambled madly toward it. Even in the faint moonlight, they could see that the building was a wreck, long since abandoned. Doc went in through one of the broken windows, dragging Amos behind him.

Through a chink in the walls, they could see another boat heading down the stream, lighted by a torch and carrying two Mikhtchah. One rowed, while the other sat in the prow with a gun, staring ahead. They rowed on past.

"We'll have to hole up here," Doc decided. "It'll be light in half an hour. Maybe they won't think of searching a ruin like this."

They found rickety steps, and stretched out on the bare floor of a huge upstairs closet. Amos groaned as he tried to find a position in which he could get some rest. Then, surprisingly, he was asleep.

He woke once with traces of daylight coming into the closet, to hear sounds of heavy gunfire not far away. He was just drifting back to sleep when hail began cracking furiously down on the roof. When it passed, the gunfire was stilled.

Doc woke him when it was turning dark. There was nothing to eat, and Amos' stomach was sick with hunger. His body ached in every joint, and walking was pure torture. Doc glanced up at the stars, seemed to decide on a course, and struck out. He was wheezing and groaning in a way that indicated he shared Amos' feelings.

But he found enough energy to begin the discussion again. "I keep wondering what Smithton saw, Amos? It wasn't what we saw. And what about the legends of war in heaven? Wasn't there a big battle there once, in which Lucifer almost won? Maybe Lucifer simply stands for some other race God cast off?"

"Lucifer was Satan, the spirit of evil. He tried to take over God's domain."

"Mmm. I've read somewhere that we have only the account of the victor, which is apt to be pretty biased history. How do we know the real issues? Or the true outcome? At least he thought he had a chance, and he apparently knew what he was fighting."

The effort of walking made speech difficult. Amos shrugged, and let the conversation die. But his own mind ground on.

If God was all-powerful and all-knowing, why had He let them spy upon Him? Or was He all-powerful over a race He had dismissed? Could it make any difference to God what man might try to do, now that He had condemned him? Was the Presence they had seen the whole of God—or only one manifestation of Him?

His legs moved on woodenly, numbed to fatigue and slow from hunger, while his head churned with his basic problem. Where was his duty now? With God or against Him?

They found food in a deserted house, and began preparing it by the hooded light of a lantern, while they listened to the news from a small battery radio that had been left behind. It was a hopeless account of alien landings and human retreats, yet given without the tone of despair they should have expected. They were halfway through the meal before they discovered the reason.

"Flash!" the radio announced. "Word has just been come through from the Denver area. A second atomic missile, piloted by a suicide crew, has fallen successfully! The alien base has been wiped out, and every ship is ruined. It is now clear that the trouble with earlier bombing attempts lay in the detonating mechanism. This is being investigated, while more volunteers are being trained to replace this undependable part of the bomb. Both missiles carrying suicide bombers have succeeded. Captive aliens of both races are being questioned in Denver now, but the same religious fanaticism found in Portland seems to make communication difficult."

It went back to reporting alien landings, while Doc and Amos stared at each other. It was too much to absorb at once.

Amos groped in his mind, trying to dig out something that might tie in the success of human bombers, where automatic machinery was miraculously stalled, with the reaction of God to his thoughts of the glow he had felt in his early days. Something about man. . . .

"They can be beaten!" Doc said in a harsh whisper.

Amos sighed as they began to get up to continue the impossible trek. "Maybe. We know God was at Clyde. Can we be sure He was at the other places to stop the bombs by His miracles?"

They slogged on through the night, cutting across country in the dim light, where every footstep was twice as hard. Amos turned it over, trying to use the new information for whatever decision he must reach. If men could overcome those opposed to them, even for a time. . . .

It brought him no closer to an answer.

The beginnings of dawn found them in a woods. Doc managed to heave Amos up a tree, where he could survey the surrounding terrain. There was a house beyond the edge of the woods, but it would take dangerous minutes to reach it. They debated, and then headed on.

They were just emerging from the woods when the sound of an alien plane began its stuttering shriek. Doc turned and headed back to where Amos was behind him. Then he stopped. "Too late! He's seen something. Gotta have a target!"

His arms swept out, shoving Amos violently back under the nearest tree. He swung and began racing across the clearing, his fat legs pumping furiously as he covered the ground in straining leaps. Amos tried to lift himself where he had fallen, but it was too late.

There was the drumming of gunfire and the earth erupted around Doc. He lurched and dropped, to twitch and lie still.

The plane swept over, while Amos disentangled himself from a root. It was gone as he broke free. Doc had given it a target, and the pilot was satisfied, apparently.

He was still alive as Amos dropped beside him. Two of the shots had hit, but he managed to grin as he lifted himself on one elbow. It was only a matter of minutes, however, and there was no help possible. Amos found one of Doc's cigarettes and lighted it with fumbling hands.

"Thanks," Doc wheezed after taking a heavy drag on it. He started to cough, but suppressed it, his face twisting in agony. His words came in an irregular rhythm, but he held his voice level. "I guess I'm going to hell, Amos, since I never did repent—if there is a hell! And I hope there is! I hope it's filled with the soul of every poor damned human being who died in less than perfect grace. Because I'm going to find some way——"

He straightened suddenly, coughing and fighting for breath. Then he found one final source of strength and met Amos' eyes, a trace of his old cynical smile on his face.

"——some way to open a recruiting station!" he finished. He dropped back, letting all the fight go out of his body. A few seconds later, he was dead.

6

. . . Thou shalt have no other peoples before me . . . Thou shalt make unto them no covenant against me. . . . Thou shalt not foreswear thyself to them, nor serve them . . . for I am a jealous people . . .

EXULTATIONS, XII, 2-4.

Amos lay through the day in the house to which he had dragged Doc's body. He did not even look for food. For the first time in his life since his mother had died when he was five, he had no shield against his grief. There was no hard core of acceptance that it was God's will to hide his loss at Doc's death. And with the realization of that, all the other losses hit at him as if they had been no older than the death of Doc.

He sat with his grief and his newly sharpened hatred, staring toward Clyde. Once, during the day, he slept. He awakened to a sense of tremendous sound and shaking of the earth, but all was quiet when he finally became conscious. It was nearly night, and time to leave.

For a moment, he hesitated. It would be easier to huddle here, beside his dead, and let whatever would happen come to him. But within him was a sense of duty that drove him on. In the back of his mind, something stirred, telling him he still had work to do.

He found part of a stale loaf of bread and some hard cheese and started out, munching on them. It was still too light to move safely, but he was going through woods again, and he heard no alien planes. When it grew darker, he turned to the side roads that led in the direction of Wesley.

In his mind was the knowledge that he had to return there. His church lay there; if the human fighters had pushed the aliens back, his people might be there. If not, it was from there that he would have to follow them.

His thoughts were too deep for conscious expression, and too numbed with exhaustion. His legs moved on steadily. One of his shoes had begun to wear through, and his feet were covered with blisters, but he went grimly on. It was his duty to lead his people, now that the aliens were here, as he had led them in easier times. His thinking had progressed no further.

He holed up in a barn that morning, avoiding the house because of the mutilated things that lay on the doorstep where the aliens had left them. And this time he slept with the soundness of complete fatigue, but he awoke to find one fist clenched and extended toward Clyde. He had been dreaming that he was Job, and that God had left him sitting unanswered on his boils until he died, while mutilated corpses moaned around him, asking for leadership he would not give.

It was nearly dawn before he realized that he should have found himself some kind of a car. He had seen none, but there might have been one abandoned somewhere. Doc could probably have found one. It was too late to bother, then. He had come to the outskirts of a tiny town, and started to head beyond it, before realizing that all the towns must have been well searched by now. He turned down the small street, looking for a store where he could find food.

There was a small grocery with a door partly ajar. Amos pushed it open, to the clanging of a bell. Almost immediately, a dog began barking, and a human voice came sharply from the back.

"Down, Shep! Just a minute, I'm a-coming." A door to the rear opened, and a bent old man emerged, carrying a kerosene lamp. "Darned electric's off again! Good thing I stayed. Told them I had to mind my store, but they wanted me to get with them. Had to hide out in the old well. Darned nonsense about——"

He stopped, his eyes blinking behind thick lenses, and his mouth dropped open. He swallowed, and his voice was startled and shrill. *"Mister, who are you?"*

"A man who just escaped from the aliens," Amos told him. He hadn't realized the shocking appearance he must present by now. "One in need of food and a chance to rest until night. But I'm afraid I have no money on me."

The old man tore his eyes away slowly, seeming to shiver. Then he nodded, and pointed to the back. "Never turned nobody away hungry yet," he said, but the words seemed automatic.

An old dog backed slowly under a couch as Amos entered. The man put the lamp down and headed into a tiny kitchen to begin preparing food. Amos reached for the lamp and blew it out. "There really are aliens—worse than you heard," he said.

The old man bristled, met his eyes, and then nodded slowly. "If *you* say so. Only it don't seem logical God would let things like that run around in a decent state like Kansas."

He shoved a plate of eggs onto the table, and Amos pulled it to him, swallowing a mouthful eagerly. He reached for a second, and stopped. Something was violently wrong, suddenly. His stomach heaved, the room began to spin, and his forehead was cold and wet with sweat. He gripped the edge of the table, trying to keep from falling. Then he felt himself being dragged to a cot. He tried to protest, but his body was shaking with ague, and the words that spilled out were senseless. He felt the cot under him, and waves of sick blackness spilled over him.

It was the smell of cooking food that awakened him finally, and he sat up with a feeling that too much time had passed. The old man came back from the kitchen, studying him. "You sure were sick, Mister. Guess you ain't used to going without decent food and rest. Feeling okay?"

Amos nodded. He felt a little unsteady, but it was passing.

He pulled on the clothes that had been somewhat cleaned for him, and found his way to the table. "What day is it?"

"Saturday, evening," the other answered. "At least the way I figure. Here, eat that and get some coffee in you." He watched until Amos began on the food, and then dropped to a stool to begin cleaning an old rifle and loading it. "You said a lot of things. They true?"

For a second, Amos hesitated. Then he nodded, unable to lie to his benefactor. "I'm afraid so."

"Yeah, I figured so, somehow, looking at you." The old man sighed. "Well, I hope you make wherever you're going."

"What about you?" Amos asked.

The old man sighed, running his hands along the rifle. "I ain't leaving my store for any bunch of aliens. And if the Lord I been doing my duty by all my life decides to put Himself on the wrong side, well, maybe He'll win. But it'll be over my dead body!"

Nothing Amos could say would change his mind. He sat on the front step of the store, the rifle on his lap and the dog at his side, as Amos headed down the street in the starlight.

The minister felt surprisingly better after the first half mile. Rest and food, combined with crude treatment of his sores and blisters, had helped. But the voice inside him was driving him harder now, and the picture of the old man seemed to lend it added strength. He struck out at the fastest pace he could hope to maintain, leaving the town behind and heading down the road that the old man had said led to Wesley.

It was just after midnight that he saw the lights of a group of cars or trucks moving along another road. He had no idea whether they were driven by men or aliens, but he kept steadily on. There were sounds of traffic another time on a road that crossed the small one he followed. But he knew now he was approaching Wesley, and speeded up his pace.

When the first light came, he made no effort to seek shelter. He stared at the land around him, stripped by grasshoppers that could have been killed off if men had worked as hard at ending the insects as they had at their bickerings and wars. He saw the dry, arid land, drifting into dust, and turning a fertile country into a nightmare. Men could put a stop to that.

It had been no act of God that had caused this ruin, but man's own follies. And without help from God, man might set it right in time.

God had deserted men. But mankind hadn't halted. On his own, man had made a path to the moon and had unlocked the atom. He'd found a means, out of his raw courage, to use those bombs against the aliens when miracles were used against him. He had done everything but conquer himself—and he could do that, if he were given time.

Amos saw a truck stop at the crossroads ahead and halted, but the driver was human. He saw the open door and quickened his step toward it. "I'm bound for Wesley!"

"Sure." The driver helped him into the seat. "I'm going back for more supplies myself. You sure look as if you need treatment at the aid station there. I thought we'd rounded up all you strays. Most of them came in right after we sent out the word on Clyde."

"You've taken it?" Amos asked.

The other nodded wearily. "We took it. Got 'em with a bomb, like sitting ducks, then we've been mopping up since. Not many aliens left."

They were nearing the outskirts of Wesley, and Amos pointed to his own house. "If you'll let me off there——"

"Look, I got orders to bring all strays to the aid station," the driver began firmly. Then he swung and faced Amos. For a second, he hesitated. Finally, he nodded quietly. "Sure. Glad to help you."

Amos found the water still running. He bathed slowly. Somewhere, he felt his decision had been made, though he was still unsure of what it was. He climbed from the tub at last, and began dressing. There was no suit that was proper, but he found clean clothes. His face in the mirror looked back at him, haggard and bearded, as he reached for the razor.

Then he stopped as he encountered the reflection of his eyes. A shock ran over him, and he backed away a step. They were eyes foreign to everything in him. He had seen a shadow of what lay in them only once, in the eyes of a great evangelist; and this was a hundred times stronger. He tore his glance away to find himself shivering, and avoided them all through the shaving. Oddly, though, there was a strange satisfaction in what he had seen. He was beginning to understand why the old man had believed him, and why the truck driver had obeyed him.

Most of Wesley had returned, and there were soldiers on the streets. As he approached the church, he saw the first-aid station, hectic with business. And a camera crew was near it, taking shots for television of those who had managed to escape from alien territory after the bombing.

A few people called to him, but he went on until he reached the church steps. The door was still in ruins and the bell was gone. Amos stood quietly waiting, his mind focusing slowly as he stared at the people who were just beginning to recognize him and to spread hasty words from mouth to mouth. Then he saw little Angela Anduccini, and motioned for her to come to him. She hesitated briefly, before following him inside and to the organ.

The little Hammond still functioned. Amos climbed to the pulpit, hearing the old familiar creak of the boards. He put his hands on the lectern, seeing the heavy knuckles and blue veins of age as he opened the Bible and made ready for his Sunday-morning congregation. He straightened his shoulders and turned to face the pews, waiting as they came in.

There were only a few at first. Then more and more came, some from old habit, some from curiosity, and many only because they had heard that he had been captured in person, probably. The camera crew came to the back and set up their machines, flooding him with bright lights and adjusting their telelens. He smiled on them, nodding.

He knew his decision now. It had been made in pieces and tatters. It had come from Kant, who had spent his life looking for a basic ethical principle, and had boiled it down in his statement that men must be treated as ends, not as means. It had been distilled from Doc's final challenge, and the old man sitting in his doorway.

There could be no words with which to give his message to those who waited. No orator had ever possessed such a command of language. But men with rude speech and limited use of what they had had fired the world before. Moses had come down from a mountain with a face that shone, and had overcome the objections of a stiff-necked people. Peter the Hermit had preached a thankless crusade to all of Europe, without radio or television. It was more than words or voice.

He looked down at them when the church was filled and the organ hushed.

"My text for today," he announced, and the murmurs below him hushed as his voice reached out to the pews. "Ye shall know the truth and the truth shall make men free!"

He stopped for a moment, studying them, feeling the decision in his mind, and knowing he could make no other. The need of him lay here, among those he had always tried to serve while believing he was serving God through them. He was facing them as an end, not as a means, and he found it good.

Nor could he lie to them now, and deceive them with false hopes. They would need all the facts if they were to make an end to their bickerings and to unite themselves in the final struggle for the fullness of their potential glory.

"I have come back from captivity among the aliens," he began. "I have seen the hordes who have no desire but to erase the memory of man from the dust of the earth that bore him. I have stood at the altar of their God. I have heard the voice of God proclaim that He is also our God, and that He has cast us out. I have believed Him, as I believe Him now."

He felt the strange, intangible something that was greater than words or oratory flow out of him, as it had never flowed in his envied younger days. He watched the shock and the doubt arise and disappear slowly as he went on, giving them the story and the honest doubts he still had. He could never know many things, or even whether the God worshipped on the altar was wholly the same God who had been in the hearts of men for a hundred generations. No man could understand enough. They were entitled to all his doubts, as well as to all that he knew.

He paused at last, in the utter stillness of the chapel. He straightened and smiled down at them, drawing the smile out of some reserve that had lain dormant since he had first tasted inspiration as a boy. He saw a few smiles answer him, and then more—uncertain, doubtful smiles that grew more sure as they spread.

"God has ended the ancient covenants and declared Himself an enemy of all mankind," Amos said, and the chapel seemed to roll with his voice. "I say this to you: He has found a worthy opponent."

GORDON R. DICKSON

The Mortal and the Monster

THAT SUMMER more activity took place upon the shores of the loch and more boats appeared on its waters than at any time in memory. Among them was even one of the sort of boats that went underwater. It moved around in the loch slowly, diving quite deep at times. From the boats, swimmers with various gear about them descended on lines—but not so deep—swam around blindly for a while, and then returned to the surface.

Brought word of all this in her cave, First Mother worried and speculated on disaster. First Uncle, though equally concerned, was less fearful. He pointed out that the Family had survived here for thousands of years; and that it could not all end in a single year—or a single day.

Indeed, the warm months of summer passed one by one with no real disturbance to their way of life.

Suddenly fall came. One night, the first snow filled the air briefly above the loch. The Youngest danced on the surface in the darkness, sticking out her tongue to taste the cold flakes. Then the snow ceased, the sky cleared for an hour, and the banks could be seen gleaming white under a high and watery moon. But the clouds covered the moon again; and because of the relative warmth of the loch water nearby, in the morning, when the sun rose, the shores were once more green.

With dawn, boats began coming and going on the loch again and the Family went deep, out of sight. In spite of this precaution, trouble struck from one of these craft shortly before noon. First Uncle was warming the eggs on the loch bottom in the hatchhole, a neatly cleaned shallow depression scooped out by Second Mother, near Glen Urquhart, when something heavy and round descended on a long line, landing just outside the hole and raising an almost-invisible puff of silt in the blackness of the deep, icy water. The line tightened and began to drag the heavy thing about.

First Uncle had his huge length coiled about the clutch of eggs, making a dome of his body and enclosing them between the smooth skin of his underside and the cleaned lakebed. Fresh, hot blood pulsed to the under-surface of his smooth skin, keeping the water warm in the enclosed area. He dared not leave the clutch to chill in the cold loch, so he sent a furious signal for Second Mother, who, hearing that her eggs were in danger, came swiftly from her feeding. The Youngest heard also and swam up as fast as she could in mingled alarm and excitement.

She reached the hatchhold just in time to find Second Mother coiling herself around the eggs, her belly skin already beginning to radiate heat from the warm blood that was being shunted to its surface. Released from his duties, First Uncle shot up through the dark, peaty water like a sixty-foot missile, up along the hanging line, with the Youngest close behind him.

They could see nothing for more than a few feet because of the murkiness. But neither First Uncle nor the Youngest relied much on the sense of sight, which was used primarily for protection on the surface of the loch, in any case. Besides, First Uncle was already beginning to lose his vision with age, so he seldom went to the surface nowadays, preferring to do his breathing in caves, where it was safer. The Youngest had asked him once if he did not miss the sunlight, even the misty and often cloud-dulled sunlight of the open sky over the loch, with its instinctive pull at ancestral memories of the ocean, retold in the legends. No, he had told her, he had grown beyond such things. But she found it hard to believe him; for in her, the yearning for the mysterious and fascinating world above the waters was still strong. The Family had no word for it. If they did, they might have called her a romantic.

Now through the pressure-sensitive cells in the cheek areas of her narrow head, she picked up the movements of a creature no more than six feet in length. Carrying some long, narrow made thing, the intruder was above them, though descending rapidly, parallel to the line.

"Stay back," First Uncle signaled her sharply; and, suddenly fearful, she lagged behind. From the vibrations she felt, their visitor could only be one of the upright animals from the world above that walked about on its hind legs and used "made" things. There was an ancient taboo about touching one of these creatures.

The Youngest hung back, then, continuing to rise through the water at a more normal pace.

Above her, through her cheek cells, she felt and interpreted the turbulence that came from First Uncle's movements. He flashed up, level with the descending animal, and with one swirl of his massive body snapped the taut descending line. The animal was sent tumbling—untouched by First Uncle's bulk (according to the taboo), but stunned and buffeted and thrust aside by the water-blow like a leaf in a sudden gust of wind when autumn sends the dry tears of the trees drifting down upon the shore waters of the loch.

The thing the animal had carried, as well as the lower half of the broken line, began to sink to the bottom. The top of the line trailed aimlessly. Soon the upright animal, hanging limp in the water, was drifting rapidly away from it. First Uncle, satisfied that he had protected the location of the hatchhole for the moment, at least—though later in the day they would move the eggs to a new location, anyway, as a safety precaution—turned and headed back down to release Second Mother once more to her feeding.

Still fearful, but fascinated by the drifting figure, the Youngest rose timidly through the water on an angle that gradually brought her close to it. She extended her small head on its long, graceful neck to feel about it from close range with her pressure-sensitive cheek cells. Here, within inches of the floating form, she could read minute differences, even in its surface textures. It seemed to be encased in an unnatural outer skin—one of those skins the creatures wore which were not actually theirs—made of some material that soaked up the loch water. This soaked-up water was evidently heated by the interior temperature of the creature, much as members of the Family could warm their belly skins with shunted blood, which protected the animal's body inside by cutting down the otherwise too-rapid radiation of its heat into the cold liquid of the loch.

The Youngest noticed something bulky and hard on the creature's head, in front, where the eyes and mouth were. Attached to the back was a larger, doubled something, also hard and almost a third as long as the creature itself. the Youngest had never before seen a diver's wetsuit, swim mask, and air tanks with pressure regulator, but she had heard them described by her elders. First Mother had once watched from a safe distance while a creature so equipped had maneuvered below the surface of the loch, and she had concluded that the things he wore were devices to enable him to swim underwater without breathing as often as his kind seemed to need to, ordinarily.

Only this one was not swimming. He was drifting away with an underwater current of the loch, rising slowly as he traveled toward its south end. If he continued like this, he would come to the surface near the center of the loch. By that time the afternoon would be over. It would be dark.

Clearly, he had been damaged. The blow of the water that had been slammed at him by the body of First Uncle had hurt him in some way. But he was still alive. The Youngest knew this, because she could feel through her cheek cells the slowed beating of his heart and the movement of gases and fluids in his body. Occasionally, a small thread of bubbles came from his head to drift surfaceward.

It was a puzzle to her where he carried such a reservoir of air. She herself could contain enough oxygen for six hours without breathing, but only a portion of that was in gaseous form in her lungs. Most was held in pure form, saturating special tissues throughout her body.

Nonetheless, for the moment the creature seemed to have more than enough air stored about him; and he still lived. However, it could not be good for him to be drifting like this into the open loch with night coming on. Particularly is he was hurt, he would be needing some place safe out in the air, just as members of the family did when they were old or sick. These upright creatures, the Youngest knew, were slow and feeble swimmers. Not one of them could have fed himself, as she did, by chasing and catching the fish of the loch; and very often when one fell into the water at any distance from the shore, he would struggle only a little while and then die.

This one would die also, in spite of the things fastened to him, if he stayed in the water. The thought raised a sadness in her. There was so much death. In any century, out of perhaps five clutches of a dozen eggs to a clutch, only one embryo might live to hatch. The legends claimed that once, when the Family had lived in the sea, matters had been different. But now, one survivor out of several clutches was the most to be hoped for. A hatchling who survived would be just about the size of this creature, the Youngest thought, though of course not with his funny shape. Nevertheless, watching him was a little like watching a new hatchling, knowing it would die.

It was an unhappy thought. But there was nothing to be done. Even if the diver were on the surface now, the chances were small that his own People could locate him.

Struck by a thought, the Youngest went up to look around. The situation was as she had guessed. No boats were close by. The nearest was the one from which the diver had descended; but it was still anchored close to the location of the hatchhole, nearly half a mile from where she and the creature now were.

Clearly, those still aboard thought to find him near where they had lost him. The Youngest went back down, and found him still drifting, now not more than thirty feet below the surface, but rising only gradually.

Her emotions stirred as she looked at him. He was not a cold life-form like the salmons, eels, and other fishes on which the Family fed. He was warm—as she was—and if the legends were all true, there had been a time and a place on the wide oceans where one of his ancestors and one of her ancestors might have looked at each other, equal and unafraid, in the open air and the sunlight.

So, it seemed wrong to let him just drift and die like this. He had shown the courage to go down into the depths of the loch, this small, frail thing. And such courage required some recognition from one of the Family, like herself. After all, it was loyalty and courage that had kept the Family going all these centuries: their loyalty to each other and the courage to conserve their strength and go on, hoping that someday the ice would come once more, the land would sink, and they would be set free into the seas again. Then surviving hatchlings would once more be numerous, and the Family would begin to grow again into what the legends had once called them, a "True People." Anyone who believed in loyalty and courage, the Youngest told herself, ought to respect those qualities wherever she found them—even in one of the upright creatures.

He should not simply be left to die. It was a daring thought, that she might interfere. . . .

She felt her own heart beating more rapidly as she followed him through the water, her cheek cells only inches from his dangling shape. After all, there was the taboo. But perhaps, if she could somehow help him without actually touching him . . . ?

"Him," of course, should not include the "made" things about him. But even if she could move him by these made parts alone, where could she take him?

Back to where the others of his kind still searched for him?

No, that was not only a deliberate flouting of the taboo but was very dangerous. Behind the taboo was the command to avoid letting any of his kind know about the Family. To take him back was to deliberately risk that kind of exposure for her People. She would die before doing that. The Family had existed all these centuries only because each member of it was faithful to the legends, to the duties, and to the taboos.

But, after all, she thought, it wasn't that she was actually going to break the taboo. She was only going to do something that went around the edge of it, because the diver had shown courage and because it was not his fault that he had happened to drop his heavy thing right beside the hatchhole. If he had dropped it anyplace else in the loch, he could have gone up and down its cable all summer and the Family members would merely have avoided that area.

What he needed, she decided, was a place out of the water where he could recover. She could take him to one of the banks of the loch. She rose to the surface again and looked around.

What she saw made her hesitate. In the darkening afternoon, the headlights of the cars moving up and down the roadways on each side of the loch were still visible in unusual numbers. From Fort Augustus at the south end of the loch to Castle Ness at the north, she saw more headlights about than ever before at this time of year, especially congregating by St. Ninian's, where the diver's boat was docked, nights.

No, it was too risky, trying to take him ashore. But she knew of a cave, too small by Family standards for any of the older adults, south of Urquhart Castle. The diver had gone down over the hatchhole, which had been constructed by Second Mother in the mouth of Urquhard Glen, close by St. Ninian's; and he had been drifting south ever since. Now he was below Castle Urquhart and almost level with the cave. It was a good, small cave for an animal his size, with edge of rock that was dry above the water at this time of year; and during the day even a little light would filter through cracks where tree roots from above had penetrated its rocky roof.

The Youngest could bring him there quite easily. she hesitated again, but then extended her head toward the air tanks on his back, took the tanks in her jaws, and began to carry him in the direction of the cave.

As she had expected, it was empty. This late in the day there was no light inside; but since, underwater, her cheek cells reported accurately on conditions about her and, above water, she had her memory, which was ultimately reliable, she brought him—still unconscious—to the ledge at the back of the cave and reared her head a good eight feet out of the water to lift him up on it. As she set him down softly on the bare rock, one of his legs brushed her neck, and a thrill of icy horror ran through the warm interior of her body.

Now she had done it! She had broken the taboo. Panic seized her.

She turned and plunged back into the water, out through the entrance to the cave and into the open loch. The taboo had never been broken before, as far as she knew—never. Suddenly she was terribly frightened. She headed at top speed for the hatchhole. All she wanted was to find Second Mother, or the Uncle, or anyone, and confess what she had done, so that they could tell her that the situation was not irreparable, not a signal marking an end of everything for them all.

Halfway to the hatchhole, however, she woke to the fact that it had already been abandoned. She turned immediately and began to range the loch bottom southward, her instinct and training counseling her that First Uncle and Second Mother would have gone in that direction, south toward Inverfarigaig, to set up a new hatchhole.

As she swam, however, her panic began to lessen and guilt moved in to take its place. How could she tell them? She almost wept inside herself. Here it was not many months ago that they had talked about how she was beginning to look and think like an adult; and she had behaved as thoughtlessly as if she was still the near-hatchling she had been thirty years ago.

Level with Castle Kitchie, she sensed the new location and homed in on it, finding it already set up off the mouth of the stream which flowed past that castle into the loch. The bed of the loch about the new hatchhole had been neatly swept and the saucer-shaped depression dug, in which Second Mother now lay warming the eggs. First Uncle was close by enough to feel the Youngest arrive, and he swept in to speak to her as she halted above Second Mother.

"Where did you go after I broke the line?" he demanded before she herself could signal.

"I wanted to see what would happen to the diver," she signaled back. "Did you need me? I would have come back, but you and Second Mother were both there."

"We had to move right away," Second Mother signaled. She was agitated. "It was frightening!"

"They dropped another line," First Uncle said, "with a thing on it that they pulled back and forth as if to find the first one they dropped. I thought it not wise to break a second one. One break could be a chance happening. Two, and even small animals might wonder."

"But we couldn't keep the hole there with the thing dragging back and forth near the eggs," explained Second Mother. "So we took them and moved without waiting to make the new hole here, first. The Uncle and I carried them, searching as we went. If you'd been here, you could have held half of them while I made the hole by myself, the way I wanted it. But you weren't. We would have sent for First Mother to come from her cave and help us, but neither one of us wanted to risk carrying the eggs about so much. So we had to work together here while still holding the eggs."

"Forgive me," said the Youngest. She wished she were dead.

"You're young," said Second Mother. "Next time you'll be wiser. But you do know that one of the earliest legends says the eggs should be moved only with the utmost care until hatching time; and you know we think that may be one reason so few hatch."

"If none hatch now," said First Uncle to the Youngest, less forgiving than Second Mother, even though they were not his eggs, "you'll remember this and consider that maybe you're to blame."

"Yes," mourned the Youngest.

She had a sudden, frightening vision of this one and all Second Mother's future clutches failing to hatch and she herself proving unable to lay when her time came. It was almost unheard of that a female of the Family should be barren, but a legend said that such a thing did occasionally happen. In her mind's eye she held a terrible picture of First Mother long dead, First Uncle and Second Mother grown old and feeble, unable to stir out of their caves, and she herself—the last of her line—dying alone, with no one to curl about her to warm or comfort her.

She had intended, when she caught up with the other two members of the Family, to tell them everything about what she had done with the diver. But she could not bring herself to it now. Her confession stuck in her mind. If it turned out that the clutch had been harmed by her inattention while she had actually been breaking the taboo with one of the very animals who had threatened the clutch in the first place. . . .

She should have considered more carefully. But, of course, she was still too ignorant and irresponsible. First Uncle and Second Mother were the wise ones. First Mother, also, of course; but she was now too old to see a clutch of eggs through to hatching stage by herself alone, or with just the help of someone presently as callow and untrustworthy as the Youngest.

"Can I— It's dark now," she signaled. "Can I go to feed, now? Is it all right to go?"

"Of course," said Second Mother, who switched her signaling to First Uncle. "You're too hard sometimes. She's still only half grown."

The Youngest felt even worse, intercepting that. She slunk off through the underwater, wishing something terrible could happen to her so that when the older ones did find out what she had done they would feel pity for her, insted of hating her. For a while she played with mental images of what this might involve. One of the boats on the surface could get her tangled in their lines in such a way that she could not get free. Then they would tow her to shore, and since she was so tangled in the line she could not get up to the surface, and since she had not breathed for many hours, she would drown on the way. Or perhaps the boat that could go underwater would find her and start chasing her and turn out to be much faster than any of them had ever suspected. It might even catch her and ram her and kill her.

By the time she had run through a number of these dark scenarios, she had begun almost automatically to hunt, for the time was in fact well past her usual second feeding period and she was hungry. As she realized this, her hunt became serious. Gradually she filled herself with salmon; and as she did so, she began to feel better. For all her bulk, she was swifter than any fish in the loch. The wide swim-paddle at the end of each of her four limbs could turn her instantly; and with her long neck and relatively small head outstretched, the streamlining of even her twenty-eight-foot body parted the waters she displaced with an absolute minimum of resistance. Last, and most important of all, was the great engine of her enormously powerful, lashing tail: that was the real drive behind her ability to flash above the loch bottom at speeds of up to fifty knots.

She was, in fact, beautifully designed to lead the life she led, designed by evolution over the generations from that early land-dwelling, omnivorous early mammal that was her ancestor. Actually, she was herself a member of the mammalian sub-class prototheria, a large and distant cousin of monotremes like the platypus and the echidna. Her cretaceous forebears had drifted over and become practicing carnivores in the process of readapting to life in the sea.

She did not know this herself, of course. The legends of the Family were incredibly ancient, passed down by the letter-perfect memories of the individual generations; but they actually were not true memories of what had been, but merely deductions about the past gradually evolved as her People had acquired communication and intelligence. In many ways, the Youngest was very like a human savage: a member of a Stone Age tribe where elaborate ritual and custom directed every action of her life except for a small area of individual freedom. And in that area of individual freedom she was as prone to ignorance and misjudgments about the world beyond the waters of her loch as any Stone Age human primitive was in dealing with the technological world beyond his familiar few square miles of jungle.

Because of this—and because she was young and healthy—by the time she had filled herself with salmon, the exercise of hunting her dinner had burned off a good deal of her feelings of shame and guilt. She saw, or thought she saw, more clearly that her real fault was in not staying close to the hatchhole after the first incident. The diver's leg touching her neck had been entirely accidental; and besides, the diver had been unconscious and unaware of her presence at that time. So no harm could have been done. Essentially, the taboo was still unbroken. But she must learn to stay on guard as the adults did, to anticipate additional trouble, once some had put in an appearance, and to hold herself ready at all times.

She resolved to do so. She made a solemn promise to herself not to forget the hatchhole again—ever.

Her stomach was full. Emboldened by the freedom of the night-empty waters above, for the loch was always clear of boats after sundown, she swam to the surface, emerging only a couple of hundred yards from shore. Lying there, she watched the unusual number of lights from cars still driving on the roads that skirted the loch.

But suddenly her attention was distracted from them. The clouds overhead had evidently cleared, some time since. Now it was a clear, frosty night and more than half the sky was glowing and melting with the northern lights. She floated, watching them. So beautiful, she thought, so beautiful. Her mind evoked pictures of all the Family who must have lain and watched the lights like this since time began, drifting in the arctic seas or resting on some skerry or ocean rock where only birds walked. The desire to see all the wide skies and seas of all the world swept over her like a physical hunger.

It was no use, however, The mountains had risen and they held the Family here, now. Blocked off from its primary dream, her hunger for adventure turned to a more possible goal. The temptation came to go and investigate the loch-going "made" things from which her diver had descended.

She found herself up near Dores, but she turned and went back down opposite St. Ninian's. The dock to which this particular boat was customarily moored was actually a mile below the village and had no illumination. But the boat had a cabin on its deck, amidships, and through the square windows lights now glowed. Their glow was different from that of the lights shown by the cars. The Youngest noted this difference without being able to account for it, not understanding that the headlights she had been watching were electric, but the illumination she now saw shining out of the cabin windows of the large, flat-hulled boat before her came from gas lanterns. She heard sounds coming from inside the cabin.

Curious, the Youngest approached the boat from the darkness of the lake, her had now lifted a god six feet out of the water so that she could look over the side railing. Two large, awkward-looking shapes rested on the broad deck in front of the cabin—one just in front, the other right up in the bow with its far end overhanging the water. Four more shapes, like the one in the bow but smaller, were spaced along the sides of the foredeck, two to a side. The Youngest slid through the little waves until she was barely a couple of dozen feet from the side of the boat. At that moment, two men came out of the cabin, strode onto the deck, and stopped by the shape just in front of the cabin.

The Youngest, though she knew she could not be seen against the dark expanse of the loch, instinctively sank down until only her head was above water. The two men stood, almost overhead, and spoke to each other.

Their voices had a strangely slow, sonorous ring to the ears of Youngest, who was used to hearing sound waves traveling through the water at four times the speed they moved in air. She did understand, of course, that they were engaged in meaningful communication, much as she and the others of the Family were when they signaled each other. This much her People had learned about the upright animals: they communicated by making sounds. A few of these sounds—the *"Ness"* sound, which, like the other sound, *"loch"* seemed to refer to the water in which the Family lived—were by now familiar. But she recognized no such noises among those made by the two above her; in fact, it would have been surprising if she had, for while the language was the one she was used to hearing, the accent of one of the two was Caribbean English, different enough from that of those living in the vicinity of the loch to make what she heard completely unintelligible.

". . . poor bastard," the other voice said.

"Man, you forget that 'poor bastard' talk, I tell you! He knew what he doing when he go down that line. He know what a temperature like that mean. A reading like that big enough for a blue whale. He just want the glory—he all alone swimming down with a speargun to drug that great beast. It the newspaper headlines, man; that's what he after!"

"Gives me the creeps, anyway. Think we'll ever fish up the sensor head?"

"You kidding. Lucky we find *him*. No, we use the spare, like I say, starting early tomorrow. And I mean it, early!"

"I don't like it. I tell you, he's got to have relatives who'll want to know why we didn't stop after we lost him. It's his boat. It's his equipment. They'll ask who gave us permission to go on spending money they got coming, with him dead."

"You pay me some heed. We've got to try to find him, that's only right. We use the equipment we got—what else we got to use? Never mind his rich relatives. They just like him. He don't never give no damn for you or me or what it cost him, this expedition. He was born with money and all he want to do is write the book about how he an adventurer. We know what we hunt be down there, now. We capture it, then everybody happy. And you and me, we get what's in the contract, the five thousand extra apiece for taking it. Otherwise we don't get nothing—you back to that machine shop, me to the whaling, with the pockets empty. We out in the cold then, you recall that!"

"All right."

"You damn right, it all right. Starting tomorrow sunup."

"I said *all right!*" The voice paused for a second before going on. "But I'm telling you one thing. If we run into it, you better get it fast with a drug spear; because I'm not waiting. If I see it, I'm getting on the harpoon gun."

The other voice laughed.

"That's why he never let you near the gun when we out before. But I don't care. Contract, it say alive or dead we get what he promise us. Come on now, up the inn and have us food and drink."

"I want a drink! Christ, this water's empty after dark, with that law about no fishing after sundown. Anything could be out there!"

"Anything is. Come on, mon."

The Youngest heard the sound of their footsteps backing off the boat and moving away down the dock until they became inaudible within the night of the land.

Left alone, she lifted her head gradually out of the water once more and cautiously examined everything before her: big boat and small ones nearby, dock and shore. There was no sound or other indication of anything living. Slowly, she once more approached the craft the two had just left and craned her neck over its side.

The large shape in front of the cabin was box-like like the boat, but smaller and without any apertures in it. Its top sloped from the side facing the bow of the craft to the opposite side. On that sloping face she saw circles of some material that, although as hard as the rest of the object, still had a subtly different texture when she pressed her cheek cells directly against them. Farther down from these, which were in fact the glass faces of meters, was a raised plate with grooves in it. The Youngest would not have understood what the grooves meant, even if she had had enough light to see them plainly; and even if their sense could have been translated to her, the words "caloric sensor" would have meant nothing to her.

A few seconds later, she was, however, puzzled to discover on the deck beside this object another shape which her memory insisted was an exact duplicate of the heavy round thing that had been dropped to the loch bed beside the old hatchhole. She felt all over it carefully with her cheek cells, but discovered nothing beyond the dimensions of its almost plumb-bob shape and the fact that a line was attached to it in the same way a line had been attached to the other. In this case, the line was one end of a heavy coil that had a farther end connected to the box-like shape with the sloping top.

Baffled by this discovery, the Youngest moved forward to examine the strange object in the bow of the boat with its end overhanging the water. This one had a shape that was hard to understand. It was more complex, made up of a number of smaller shapes both round and boxy. Essentially, however, it looked like a mound with something long and narrow set on top of it, such as a piece of waterlogged tree from which the limbs had long since dropped off. The four smaller things like it, spaced two on each side of the foredeck, were not quite like the big one, but they were enough alike so that she ignored them in favor of examining the large one. Feeling around the end of the object that extended over the bow of the boat and hovered above the water, the Youngest discovered the log shape rotated at a touch and even tilted up and down with the mound beneath it as a balance point. On further investigation, she found that the log shape was hollow at the water end and was projecting beyond the hooks the animals often let down into the water with little dead fish or other things attached, to try to catch the larger fish of the loch. This end, however, was attached not to a curved length of metal, but to a straight metal rod lying loosely in the hollow log space. To the rod part, behind the barbed head, was joined the end of another heavy coil of line wound about a round thing on the deck. This line was much thicker than the one attached to the box with the sloping top. Experimentally, she tested it with her teeth. It gave—but did not cut when she closed her jaws on it—then sprang back, apparently unharmed, when she let it go.

All very interesting, but puzzling—as well it might be. A harpoon gun and spearguns with heads designed to inject a powerful tranquilizing drug on impact were completely outside the reasonable dimensions of the world as the Youngest knew it. The heat-sensing equipment that had been used to locate First Uncle's huge body as it lay on the loch bed warming the eggs was closer to being something she could understand. She and the rest of the Family used heat sensing themselves to locate and identify one another, though their natural abilities were nowhere near as sensitive as those of the instrument she had examined on the foredeck. At any rate, for now, she merely dismissed from her mind the question of what these things were. Perhaps, she thought, the upright animals simply liked to have odd shapes of "made" things around them. That notion reminded her of her diver; and she felt a sudden, deep curiosity about him, a desire to see if he had yet recovered and found his way out of the cave to shore.

She backed off from the dock and turned toward the south end of the loch, not specifically heading for the cave where she had left him but traveling in that general direction and turning over in her head the idea that perhaps she might take one more look at the cave. But she would not be drawn into the same sort of irresponsibility she had fallen prey to earlier in the day, when she had taken him to the cave! Not twice would she concern herself with one of the animals when she was needed by others of the Family. She decided, instead, to go check on Second Mother and the new hatchhole.

When she got to the hole, however, she found that Second Mother had no present need of her. The older female, tired from the exacting events of the day and heavy from feeding later than her usual time—for she had been too nervous, at first, to leave the eggs in First Uncle's care and so had not finished her feeding period until well after dark—was half asleep. She only untucked her head from the coil she had made of her body around and above the eggs long enough to make sure that the Youngest had not brought warning of some new threat. Reassured, she coiled up tightly again about the clutch and closed her eyes.

The Youngest gazed at her with a touch of envy. It must be a nice feeling, she thought, to shut out everything but yourself and your eggs. There was plainly nothing that Youngest was wanted for, here—and she had never felt less like sleeping herself. The night was full of mysteries and excitements. She headed once more north, up the lake.

She had not deliberately picked a direction, but suddenly she realized that unconsciously she was once more heading toward the cave where she had left the diver. She felt a strange sense of freedom. Second Mother was sleeping with her eggs. First Uncle by this time would have his heavy bulk curled up in his favorite cave and his head on its long neck resting on a ledge at the water's edge, so that he had the best of both the worlds of air and loch at the same time. The Youngest had the loch to herself, with neither Family nor animals to worry about. It was all hers, from Fort Augustus clear to Castle Ness.

The thought gave her a sense of power. Abruptly, she decided that there was no reason at all why she should not go see what had happened to the diver. She turned directly toward the cave, putting on speed.

At the last moment, however, she decided to enter the cave quietly. If he was really recovered and alert, she might want to leave again without being noticed. Like a cloud shadow moving silently across the surface of the waves, she slid through the underwater entrance of the cave, invisible in the blackness, her cheek cells reassuring her that there was no moving body in the water inside.

Once within, she paused again to check for heat radiation that would betray a living body in the water even if it was being held perfectly still. But she felt no heat. Satisfied, she lifted her head silently from the water inside the cave and approached the rock ledge where she had left him.

Her hearing told that he was still here, though her eyes were as useless in this total darkness as his must be. Gradually, that same, sensitive hearing filled in the image of his presence for her.

He still lay on the ledge, apparently on his side. She could hear the almost rhythmic scraping of a sort of metal clip he wore on the right side of his belt. It was scratching against the rock as he made steady, small movements. He must have come to enough to take off his head-things and back-things, however, for she heard no scraping from these. His breathing was rapid and hoarse, almost a panting. Slowly, sound by sound, she built up a picture of him, there in the dark. He was curled up in a tight ball, shivering.

The understanding that he was lying, trembling from the cold, struck the Youngest in her most vulnerable area. Like all the Family, she had vivid memories of what it had been like to be a hatchling. As eggs, the clutch was kept in open water with as high an oxygen content as possible until the moment for hatching came close. Then they were swiftly transported to one of the caves so that they would emerge from their shell into the land and air environment that their warm-blooded, air-breathing ancestry required. And a hatchling could not drown on a cave ledge. But, although he or she was protected there from the water, a hatchling was still vulnerable to the cold; and the caves were now warmer than the water—which was snow-fed from the mountains most of the year. Furthermore, the hatchling would not develop the layers of blubber-like fat that insulated an adult of the Family for several years. The life of someone like the Youngest began with the sharp sensations of cold as a newborn, and ended the same way, when aged body processes were no longer able to generate enough interior heat to keep the great hulk going. The first instinct of the hatchling was to huddle close to the warm belly skin of the adult on guard. And the first instinct of the adult was to warm the small, new life.

She stood in the shallow water of the cave, irresolute. The taboo, and everything that she had ever known, argued fiercely in her against any contact with the upright animal. But this one had already made a breach in her cosmos, had already been promoted from an "it" to a "he" in her thoughts; and her instincts cried out as strongly as her teachings, against letting him chill there on the cold stone ledge when she had within her the heat to warm him.

It was a short, hard, internal struggle; but her instincts won. After all, she rationalized, it was she who had brought him here to tremble in the cold. The fact that by doing so she had saved his life was beside the point.

Completely hidden in the psychological machinery that moved her toward him now was the lack in her life that was the result of being the last, solitary child of her kind. From the moment of hatching on, she had never had a playmate, never known anyone with whom she could share the adventures of growing up. An unconscious part of her was desperately hungry for a friend, a toy, anything that could be completely and exclusively hers, apart from the adult world that encompassed everything around her.

Slowly, silently, she slipped out of the water and up onto the ledge and flowed around his shaking form. She did not quite dare to touch him; but she built walls about him and a roof over him out of her body, the inward-facing skin of which was already beginning to pulse with hot blood pumped from deep within her.

Either dulled by his semi-consciousness or else too wrapped up in his own misery to notice, the creature showed no awareness that she was there. Not until the warmth began to be felt did he instinctively relax the tight ball of his body and, opening out, touch her—not merely with his wetsuit-encased body, but with his unprotected hands and forehead.

The Youngest shuddered all through her length at that first contact. But before she could withdraw, his own reflexes operated. His chilling body felt warmth and did not stop to ask its source. Automatically, he huddled close against the surfaces he touched.

The Youngest bowed her head. It was too late. It was done.

This was no momentary, unconscious contact. She could feel his shivering directly now through her own skin surface. Nothing remained but to accept what had happened. She folded herself close about him, covering as much of his small, cold trembling body as possible with her own warm surface, just as she would have if he had been a new hatchling who suffered from the chill. He gave a quavering sigh of relief and pressed close against her.

Gradually he warmed and his trembling stopped. Long before that, he had fallen into a deep torpor-like slumber. She could hear the near-snores of his heavy breathing.

Grown bolder by contact with him and abandoning herself to an affection for him, she explored his slumbering shape with her sensitive cheek cells.

He had no true swim paddles, of course—she already knew this about the upright animals. But she had never guessed how delicate and intricate were the several-times split appendages that he possessed on his upper limbs where swim paddles might have been. His body was very narrow, its skeleton hardly clothed in flesh. Now that she knew that his kind were as vulnerable to cold as new hatchlings, she did not wonder that it should be so with them: they had hardly anything over their bones to protect them from the temperature of the water and air. No wonder they covered themselves with non-living skins.

His head was not long at all, but quite round. His mouth was small and his jaws flat, so that he would be able to take only very small bites of things. There was a sort of protuberance above the mouth and a pair of eyes, side by side. Around the mouth and below the eyes his skin was full of tiny, sharp points; and on the top of his head was a strange, springy mat of very fine filaments. The Youngest rested the cells of her right cheek for a moment on the filaments, finding a strange inner warmth and pleasure in the touch of them. It was a completely inexplicable pleasure, for the legends had forgotten what old, primitive parts of her brain remembered: a time when her ancestors on land had worn fur and known the feel of it in their close body contacts.

Wrapped up in the subconscious evocation of ancient companionship, she lay in the darkness spinning impossible fantasies in which she would be able to keep him. He could live in this cave, she thought, and she would catch salmon—since that was what his kind, with their hooks and filaments, seemed most to search for—to bring to him for food. If he wanted "made" things about him, she could probably visit docks and suchlike about the loch and find some to bring here to him. When he got to know her better, since he had the things that let him hold his breath underwater, they could venture out into the loch together. Of course, once that time was reached, she would have to tell Second Mother and First Uncle about him. No doubt it would disturb them greatly, the fact that the taboo had been broken; but once they had met him underwater, and seen how sensible and friendly he was—how wise, even, for a small animal like himself. . . .

Even as she lay dreaming these dreams, however, a sane part of her mind was still on duty. Realistically, she knew that what she was thinking was nonsense. Centuries of legend, duty, and taboo were not to be upset in a few days by any combination of accidents. Nor, even if no problem arose from the Family side, could she really expect him to live in a cave, forsaking his own species. His kind needed light as well as air. They needed the freedom to come and go on shore. Even if she could manage to keep him with her in the cave for a while, eventually the time would come when he would yearn for the land under his feet and the open sky overhead, at one and the same time. No, her imaginings could never be; and, because she knew this, when her internal time sense warned her that the night was nearly over, she silently uncoiled from around him and slipped back into the water, leaving the cave before the first light, which filtered in past the tree roots in the cave roof, could let him see who it was that had kept him alive through the hours of darkness.

Left uncovered on the ledge but warm again, he slept heavily on, unaware.

Out in the waters of the loch, in the pre-dawn gloom, the Youngest felt fatigue for the first time. She could easily go twenty-four hours without sleep; but this twenty-four hours just past had been emotionally charged ones. She had an irresistible urge to find one of the caves she favored herself and to lose herself in slumber. She shook it off. Before anything else, she must check with Second Mother.

Going swiftly to the new hatchhole, she found Second Mother fully awake, alert, and eager to talk to her. Evidently Second Mother had awakened early and spent some time thinking.

"You're young," she signaled the Youngest, "far too young to share the duty of guarding a clutch of eggs, even with someone as wise as your First Uncle. Happily, there's no problem physically. You're mature enough so that milk would come, if a hatchling should try to nurse from you. But, sensibly, you're still far too young to take on this sort of responsibility. Nonetheless, if something should happen to me, there would only be you and the Uncle to see this clutch to the hatching point. Therefore, we have to think of the possibility that you might have to take over for me."

"No. No, I couldn't," said the Youngest.

"You may have to. It's still only a remote possibility; but I should have taken it into consideration before. Since there're only the four of us, if anything happened to one of us, the remaining would have to see the eggs through to hatching. You and I could do it, I'm not worried about that situation. But with a clutch there must be a mother. Your uncle can be everything but that, and First Mother is really too old. Somehow, we must make you ready before your time to take on that duty."

"If you say so. . . ." said the Youngest, unhappily.

"Our situation says so. Now, all you need to know, really, is told in the legends. But knowing them and understanding them are two different things. . . ."

Then Second Mother launched into a retelling of the long chain of stories associated with the subject of eggs and hatchlings. The Youngest, of course, had heard them all before. More than that, she had them stored, signal by signal, in her memory as perfectly as had Second Mother herself. But she understood that Second Mother wanted her not only to recall each of these packages of stored wisdom, but to think about what was stated in them. Also—so much wiser had she already become in twenty-four hours—she realized that the events of yesterday had suddenly shocked Second Mother, giving her a feeling of helplessness should the upright animals ever really chance to stumble upon the hatchhole. For she could never abandon her eggs, and if she stayed with them the best she could hope for would be to give herself up to the land-dwellers in hope that this would satisfy them and they would look no further.

It was hard to try and ponder the legends, sleepy as the Youngest was, but she tried her best; and when at last Second Mother turned her loose, she swam groggily off to the nearest cave and curled up. It was not broad-enough daylight for her early feeding period, but she was too tired to think of food. In seconds, she was sleeping almost as deeply as the diver had been when she left him.

She came awake suddenly and was in motion almost before her eyes were open. First Uncle's signal of alarm was ringing all through the loch. She plunged from her cave into the outer waters. Vibrations told her that he and Second Mother were headed north, down the deep center of the loch as fast as they could travel, carrying the clutch of eggs. She drove on to join them, sending ahead her own signal that she was coming.

"Quick! Oh, quick!" signaled Second Mother.

Unencumbered, she began to converge on them at double their speed. Even in this moment her training paid off. She shot through the water, barely fifty feet above the bed of the loch, like a dolphin in the salt sea; and her perfect shape and smooth skin caused no turbulence at all to drag at her passage and slow her down.

She caught up with them halfway between Inverfarigaig and Dores and took her half of the eggs from Second Mother, leaving the older female free to find a new hatchhole. Unburdened, Second Mother leaped ahead and began to range the loch bed in search of a safe place.

"What happened?" signaled Youngest.

"Again!" First Uncle answered. "They dropped another 'made' thing, just like the first, almost in the hatchhole this time!" he told her.

Second Mother had been warming the eggs. Luckily he had been close. He had swept in; but not daring to break the line a second time for fear of giving clear evidence of the Family, he had simply scooped a hole in the loch bed, pushed the thing in, buried it and pressed down hard on the loch bed material with which he had covered it. He had buried it deeply enough so that the animals above were pulling up on their line with caution, for fear that they themselves might break it. Eventually, they would get it loose. Until then, the Family had a little time in which to find another location for the eggs.

A massive shape loomed suddenly out of the peaty darkness, facing them. It was First Mother, roused from her cave by the emergency.

"I can still carry eggs. Give them here, and you go back," she ordered First Uncle. "Find out what's being done with that 'made' thing you buried and what's going on with those creatures. Two hatchholes stumbled on in two days is too much for chance."

First Uncle swirled about and headed back.

The Youngest slowed down. First Mother was still tremendously powerful, of course, more so than any of them; but she no longer had the energy reserves to move at the speed at which First Uncle and the Youngest had been traveling. Youngest felt a surge of admiration for First Mother, battling the chill of the open loch water and the infirmities of her age to give help now, when the Family needed it.

"Here! this way!" Second Mother called.

They turned sharply toward the east bank of the loch and homed in on Second Mother's signal. She had found a good place for a new hatchhole. True, it was not near the mouth of a stream; but the loch bed was clean and this was one of the few spots where the rocky slope underwater from the shore angled backward when it reached a depth below four hundred feet, so that the loch at this point was actually in under the rock and had a roof overhead. Here, there was no way that a "made" thing could be dropped down on a line to come anywere close to the hatchhole.

When First Mother and the Youngest got there, Second Mother was already at work making and cleaning the hole. The hole had barely been finished and Second Mother settled down with the clutch under her, when First Uncle arrived.

"They have their 'made' thing back," he reported. "They pulled on its line with little, repeated jerkings until they loosened it from its bed, and then they lifted it back up."

He told how he had followed it up through the water until he was just under the "made" thing and rode on the loch surface. Holding himself there, hidden by the thing itself, he had listened, trying to make sense out of what the animals were doing, from what he could hear.

They had made a great deal of noise after they hoisted the thing back on board. They had moved it around a good deal and done things with it, before finally leaving it alone and starting back toward the dock near St. Ninian's. First Uncle had followed them until he was sure that was where they were headed; then he had come to find the new hatchhole and the rest of the Family.

After he was done signaling, they all waited for First Mother to respond, since she was the oldest and wisest. She lay thinking for some moments.

"They didn't drop the 'made' thing down into the water again, you say?" she asked at last.

"No," signaled First Uncle.

"And none of them went down into the water, themselves?"

"No."

"It's very strange," said First Mother. "All we know is that they've twice almost found the hatchhole. All I can guess is that this isn't a chance thing, but that they're acting with some purpose. They may not be searching for our eggs, but they seem to be searching for *something*."

The Youngest felt a sudden chilling inside her. But First Mother was already signaling directly to First Uncle.

"From now on, you should watch them, whenever the thing in which they move about the loch surface isn't touching shore. If you need help, the Youngest can help you. If they show any signs of coming close to here, we must move the eggs immediately. I'll come out twice a day to relieve Second Mother for her feeding, so that you can be free to do that watching. No"—she signaled sharply before they could object—"I *will* do this. I can go for some days warming the eggs for two short periods a day, before I'll be out of strength; and this effort of mine is needed. The eggs *should* be safe here, but if it proves that the creatures have some means of finding them, wherever the hatchhole is placed in the open loch, we'll have to move the clutch into the caves."

Second Mother cried out in protest.

"I know," First Mother said, "the legends counsel against ever taking the eggs into the caves until time for hatching. But we may have no choice."

"My eggs will die!" wept Second Mother.

"They're your eggs, and the decision to take them inside has to be yours," said First Mother. "But they won't live if the animals find them. In the caves there may be a chance of life for them. Besides, our duty as a Family is to survive. It's the Family we have to think of, not a single clutch of eggs or a single individual. If worse comes to worst and it turns out we're not safe from the animals even in the caves, we'll try the journey of the Lost Father from Loch Morar before we'll let ourselves all be killed off."

"What Lost Father?" the Youngest demanded. "No one ever told me a legend about a Lost Father from Loch Morar. What's Loch Morar?"

"It's not a legend usually told to those too young to have full wisdom," said First Mother. "But these are new and dangerous times. Loch Morar is a loch a long way from here, and some of our People were also left there when the ice went and the land rose. They were of our People, but a different Family."

"But what about a Lost Father?" the Youngest persisted, because First Mother had stopped talking as if she would say no more about it. "How could a Father be lost?"

"He was lost to Loch Morar," First Mother explained, "because he grew old and died here in Loch Ness."

"But how did he get here?"

"He couldn't, that's the point," said First Uncle, grumpily. "There are legends *and* legends. That's why some are not told to young ones until they've matured enough to understand. The journey the Lost Father's supposed to have made is impossible. Tell it to some youngster and he or she's just as likely to try and duplicate it."

"But you said we might try it!" The Youngest appealed to First Mother.

"Only if there were no other alternative," First Mother answered. "I'd try flying out over the mountains if that was the only alternative left, because it's our duty to keep trying to survive as a Family as long as we're alive. So, as a last resort, we'd try the journey of the Lost Father, even though as the Uncle says, it's impossible."

"Why? Tell me what it was. You've already begun to tell me. Shouldn't I know all of it?"

"I suppose. . . ." said First Mother, wearily. "Very well. Loch Morar isn't surrounded by mountains as we are here. It's even fairly close to the sea, so that if a good way could be found for such as us to travel over dry land, members of the People living there might be able to go home to the sea we all recall by the legends. Well, this legend says that there once was a Father in Loch Morar who dreamed all his life of leading his Family home to the sea. But we've grown too heavy nowadays to travel any distance overland, normally. One winter day, when a new snow had just fallen, the legend says this Father discovered a way of traveling on land that worked."

In sparse sentences, First Mother rehearsed the legend to a fascinated Youngest. It told that the snow provided a slippery surface over which the great bodies of the People could slide under the impetus of the same powerful tail muscles that drove them through the water, their swim paddles acting as rudders—or brakes—on downslopes. Actually, what the legend described was a way of swimming on land. Loch Ness never froze and First Mother therefore had no knowledge of ice-skating, so she could not explain that what the legend spoke of was the same principle that makes a steel ice blade glide over ice—the weight upon it causing the ice to melt under the sharp edge of the blade so that, effectively, it slides on a cushion of water. With the People, their ability to shunt a controlled amount of warmth to the skin in contact with the ice and snow did the same thing.

In the legend, the Father who discovered this tried to take his Family from Loch Morar back to the sea, but they were all afraid to try going, except for him. So he went alone and found his way to the ocean more easily than he had thought possible. He spent some years in the sea, but found it lonely and came back to land to return to Loch Morar. However, though it was winter, he could not find enough snow along the route he had taken to the sea in order to get back to Loch Morar. He hunted northward for a snow-covered route inland, north past the isle of Sleat, past Glenelg; and finally under Benn Attow, he found a snow route that led him ultimately to Glen Moriston and into Loch Ness.

He went as far back south through Loch Ness as he could go, even trying some distance down what is now the southern part of the Caledonian Canal before he became convinced that the route back to Loch Morar by that way would be too long and hazardous to be practical. He decided to return to the sea and wait for snow to make him a way over his original route to Morar.

But, meanwhile, he had become needed in Loch Ness and grown fond of the Family there. He wished to take them with him to the sea. The others, however, were afraid to try the long overland journey; and while they hesitated and put off going, he grew too old to lead them; and so they never did go. Nevertheless, the legend told of his route and, memories being what they were among the People, no member of the Family in Loch Ness, after First Mother had finished telling the legend to the Youngest, could have retraced the Lost Father's steps exactly.

"I don't think we should wait," the Youngest said, eagerly, when First Mother was through. "I think we should go now—I mean, as soon as we get a snow on the banks of the loch so that we can travel. Once we're away from the loch, there'll be snow all the time, because it's ony the warmth of the loch that keeps the snow off around here. Then we could all go home to the sea, where we belong, away from the animals and their 'made' things. Most of the eggs laid there would hatch—"

"I told you so," First Uncle interrupted, speaking to First Mother. "Didn't I tell you so?"

"And what about my eggs now?" said Second Mother.

"We'll try something like that only if the animals start to destroy us," First Mother said to the Youngest with finality. "Not before. If it comes to that, Second Mother's present clutch of eggs will be lost, anyway. Otherwise, we'd never leave them, you should know that. Now, I'll go back to the cave and rest until late feeding period for Second Mother."

She went off. First Uncle also went off, to make sure that the animals had really gone to the dock and were still there. The Youngest, after asking Second Mother if there was any way she could be useful and being told there was none, went off to her delayed first feeding period.

She was indeed hungry, with the ravenous hunger of youth. But once she had taken the edge off her appetite, an uneasy feeling began to grow inside her, and not even stuffing herself with rich-fleshed salmon made it go away.

What was bothering her, she finally admitted to herself, was the sudden, cold thought that had intruded on her when First Mother had said that the creatures seemed to be searching for something. The Youngest was very much afraid she knew what they were searching for. It was their fellow, the diver she had taken to the cave. If she had not done anything, they would have found his body before this; but because she had saved him, they were still looking; and because he was in a cave, they could not find him. So they would keep on searching, and sooner or later they would come close to the new hatchhole; and then Second Mother would take the clutch into one of the caves, and the eggs would die, and it would be her own fault, the Youngest's fault alone.

She was crying inside. She did not dare cry out loud because the others would hear and want to know what was troubling her. She was ashamed to tell them what she had done. Somehow, she must put things right herself, without telling them—at least until some later time, when it would be all over and unimportant.

The diver must go back to his own people—if he had not already.

She turned and swam toward the cave, making sure to approach it from deep in the loch. Through the entrance of the cave, she stood up out of the water; and he was still there.

Enough light was filtering in through the ceiling cracks of the cave to make a sort of dim twilight inside. She saw him plainly—and he saw her.

She had forgotten that he would have no idea of what she looked like. He had been sitting up on the rock ledge; but when her head and its long neck rose out of the water, he stared and then scrambled back—as far back from her as he could get, to the rock wall of the cave behind the ledge. He stood pressed against it, still staring at her, his mouth open in a soundless circle.

She paused, irresolute. She had never intended to frighten him. She had forgotten that he might consider her at all frightening. All her foolish imaginings of keeping him here in the cave and of swimming with him in the loch crumbled before the bitter reality of his terror at the sight of her. Of course, he had had no idea of who had been coiled about him in the dark. He had only known that something large had been bringing the warmth of life back into him. But surely he would make the connection, now that he saw her?

She waited.

He did not seem to be making it. He simply stayed where he was, as if paralyzed by her presence. She felt an exasperation with him rising inside her. According to the legends, his kind had at least a share of intelligence, possibly even some aspect of wisdom, although that was doubtful. But now, crouched against the back of the cave, he looked like nothing more than another wild animal—like one of the otters, strayed from nearby streams, she had occasionally encountered in these caves. And as with such an otter, for all its small size ready to scratch or bite, she felt a caution about approaching him.

Nevertheless, something had to be done. At any moment now, the others like him would be out on the loch in their "made" things, once more hunting for him and threatening to rediscover the hatchhole.

Cautiously, slowly, so as not to send him into a fighting reflex, she approached the ledge and crept up on it sideways, making an arc of her body and moving in until she half surrounded him, an arm's length from him. She was ready to pull back at the first sign of a hostile move, but no action was triggered in him. He merely stayed where he was, pressing against the rock wall as if he would like to step through it, his eyes fixed on her and his jaws still in the half-open position. Settled about him, however, she shunted blood into her skin area and began to radiate heat.

It took a little while for him to feel the warmth coming from her and some little while more to understand what she was trying to tell him. But then, gradually, his tense body relaxed. He slipped down the rock against which he was pressed and ended up sitting, gazing at her with a different shape to his eyes and mouth.

He made some noises with his mouth. These conveyed no sense to the Youngest, of course, but she thought that at least they did not sound like unfriendly noises.

"So now you know who I am," she signaled, although she knew perfectly well he could not understand her. "Now, you've got to swim out of here and go back on the land. Go back to your People."

She had corrected herself instinctively on the last term. She had been about to say "go back to the other animals"; but something inside her dictated the change—which was foolish, because he would not know the difference, anyway.

He straightened against the wall and stood up. Suddenly, he reached out an upper limb toward her.

She flinched from his touch instinctively, then braced herself to stay put. If she wanted him not to be afraid of her, she would have to show him the same fearlessness. Even the otters, if left alone, would calm down somewhat, though they would take the first opportunity to skip past and escape from the cave where they had been found.

She held still, accordingly. The divided ends of his limb touched her and rubbed lightly over her skin. It was not an unpleasant feeling, but she did not like it. It had been different when he was helpless and had touched her unconsciously.

She now swung her head down close to watch him and had the satisfaction of seeing him start when her own eyes and jaws came within a foot or so of his. He pulled his limbs back quickly, and made more noises. They were still not angry noises, though, and this fact, together with his quick withdrawal, gave her an impression that he was trying to be conciliatory, even friendly.

Well, at least she had his attention. She turned, backed off the ledge into the water, then reached up with her nose and pushed toward him the "made" things he originally had had attached to his back and head. Then, turning, she ducked under the water, swam out of the cave into the loch, and waited just under the surface for him to follow.

He did not.

She waited for more than enough time for him to reattach his things and make up his mind to follow, then she swam back inside. To her disgust, he was now sitting down again and his "made" things were still unattached to him.

She came sharply up to the edge of the rock and tumbled the two things literally on top of him.

"Put them on!" she signaled. "Put them on, you stupid animal!"

He stared at her and made noises with his mouth. He stood up and moved his upper limbs about in the air. But he made no move to pick up the "made" things at his feet. Angrily, she shoved them against his lower limb ends once more.

He stopped making noises and merely looked at her. Slowly, although she could not define all of the changes that signaled it to her, an alteration of manner seemed to take place in him. The position of his upright body changed subtly. The noises he was making changed; they became slower and more separate, one from another. He bent down and picked up the larger of the things, the one that he had had attached to his back; but he did not put it on.

Instead, he held it up in the air before him as if drawing her attention to it. He turned it over in the air and shook it slightly, then held it in that position some more. He rapped it with the curled-over sections of one of his limb ends, so that it rang with a hollow sound from both its doubled parts. Then he put it down on the ledge again and pushed it from him with one of his lower limb ends.

The Youngest stared at him, puzzled, but nonetheless hopeful for the first time. At last he seemed to be trying to communicate something to her, even though what he was doing right now seemed to make no sense. Could it be that this was some sort of game the upright animals played with their "made" things; and he either wanted to play it, or wanted her to play it with him, before he would put the things on and get in the water? When she was much younger, she had played with things herself—interesting pieces of rock or waterlogged material she found on the loch bed, or flotsam she had encountered on the surface at night, when it was safe to spend time in the open.

No, on second thought that explanation hardly seemed likely. If it was a game he wanted to play with her, it was more reasonable for him to push the things at her instead of just pushing the bigger one away and ignoring it. She watched him baffled. Now he had picked up the larger thing again and was repeating his actions, exactly.

The creature went through the same motions several more times, eventually picking up and putting the smaller "made" things about his head and muzzle, but still shaking and pushing away the larger thing. Eventually he made a louder noise which, for the first time, sounded really angry; threw the larger thing to one end of the ledge; and went off to sit down at the far end of the ledge, his back to her.

Still puzzled, the Youngest stretched her neck up over the ledge to feel the rejected "made" thing again with her cheek cells. It was still an enigmatic, cold, hard, double-shaped object that made no sense to her. What he's doing can't be playing, she thought. Not that he was playing at the last, there. And besides, he doesn't act as if he liked it and liked to play with it, he's acting as if he hated it—

Illumination came to her, abruptly.

"Of course!" she signaled at him.

But of course the signal did not even register on him. He still sat with his back to her.

What he had been trying to tell her, she suddenly realized, was that for some reason the "made " thing was no good for him any longer. Whether he had used it to play with, to comfort himself, or, as she had originally guessed, it had something to do with making it possible for him to stay underwater, for some reason it was now no good for that purpose.

The thought that it might indeed be something to help him stay underwater suddenly fitted in her mind with the fact that he no longer considered it any good. She sat back on her tail, mentally berating herself for being so foolish. Of course, that was what he had been trying to tell her. It would not help him stay underwater anymore; and to get out of the cave he had to go underwater—not very far, of course, but still a small distance.

On the other hand, how was he to know it was only a small distance? He had been unconscious when she had brought him here.

Now that she had worked out what she thought he had been trying to tell her, she was up against a new puzzle. By what means was she to get across to him that she had understood?

She thought about this for a time, then picked up the thing in her teeth and threw it herself against the rock wall at the back of the ledge.

He turned around, evidently alerted by the sounds it made. She stretched out her neck, picked up the thing, brought it back to the water edge of the ledge, and then threw it at the wall again.

Then she looked at him.

He made sounds with his mouth and turned all the way around. Was it possible he had understood, she wondered? But he made no further moves, just sat there. She picked up and threw the "made" thing a couple of more times; then she paused once again to see what he might do.

He stood, hesitating, then inched forward to where the thing had fallen, picked up and threw it himself. But he threw it, as she had thrown it—at the rock wall behind the ledge.

The Youngest felt triumph. They were finally signaling each other—after a fashion.

But now where did they go from here? She wanted to ask him if there was anything they could do about the "made" thing being useless, but she couldn't think how to act that question out.

He, however, evidently had something in mind. He went to the edge of the rock shelf, knelt down and placed one of his multi-divided limb ends flat on the water surface, but with its inward-grasping surface upward. Then he moved it across the surface of the water so that the outer surface, or back, of it was in the water but the inner surface was still dry.

She stared at him. Once more he was doing something incomprehensible. He repeated the gesture several more times, but still it conveyed no meaning to her. He gave up, finally, and sat for a few minutes looking at her; then he got up, went back to the rock wall, turned around, walked once more to the edge of the ledge, and sat down.

Then he held up one of his upper limb ends with all but two of the divisions curled up. The two that were not curled up he pointed downward, and lowered them until their ends rested on the rock ledge. Then, pivoting first on the end of one of the divisions, then on the other, he moved the limb end back toward the wall as far as he could stretch, then turned it around and moved it forward again to the water's edge, where he folded up the two extended divisions, and held the limb end still.

He did this again. And again.

The Youngest concentrated. There was some meaning here; but with all the attention she could bring to bear on it, she still failed to see what it was. This was even harder than extracting wisdom from the legends. As she watched, he got up once more, walked back to the rock wall, came forward again and sat down. He did this twice.

Then he did the limb-end, two-division-movement thing twice.

Then he walked again, three times.

Then he did the limb-end thing three more times—

Understanding suddenly burst upon the Youngest. He was trying to make some comparison between his walking to the back of the ledge and forward again, and moving his limb ends in that odd fashion, first backward and then forward. The two divisions, with their little joints, moved much like his two lower limbs when he walked on them. It was extremely interesting to take part of your body and make it act like your whole body, doing something. Youngest wished that her swim paddles had divisions on the ends, like his, so she could try it.

She was becoming fascinated with the diver all over again. She had almost forgotten the threat to the eggs that others like him posed as long as he stayed hidden in this cave. Her conscience caught her up sharply. She should check right now and see if things were all right with the Family. She turned to leave, and then checked herself. She wanted to reassure him that she was coming back.

For a second only she was baffled for a means to do this; then she remembered that she had already left the cave once, thinking he would follow her, and then come back when she had given up on his doing so. If he saw her go and come several times, he should expect that she would go on returning, even though the interval might vary.

She turned and dived out through the hole into the loch, paused for a minute or two, then went back in. She did this two more times before leaving the cave finally. He had given her no real sign that he understood what she was trying to convey, but he had already showed signs of that intelligence the legends credited his species with. Hopefully, he would figure it out. If he did not—well, since she was going back anyway, the only harm would be that he might worry a bit about being abandoned there.

She surfaced briefly, in the center of the loch, to see if many of the "made" things were abroad on it today. But none were in sight and there was little or no sign of activity on the banks. The sky was heavy with dark, low-lying clouds; and the hint of snow, heavy snow, was in the sharp air. She thought again of the journey of the Lost Father of Loch Morar, and of the sea it could take them to—their safe home, the sea. They should go. They should go without waiting. If only she could convince them to go. . . .

She dropped by the hatchhole, found First Mother warming the eggs while Second Mother was off feeding, and heard from First Mother that the craft had not left its place on shore all day. Discussing this problem almost as equals with First Mother—of whom she had always been very much in awe—emboldened the Youngest to the point where she shyly suggested she might try warming the clutch herself, occasionally, so as to relieve First Mother from these twice-daily stints, which must end by draining her strength and killing her.

"It would be up to Second Mother, in any case," First Mother answered, "but you're still really too small to be sure of giving adequate warmth to a full clutch. In an emergency, of course, you shouldn't hesitate to do your best with the eggs, but I don't think we're quite that desperate, yet."

Having signaled this, however, First Mother apparently softened.

"Besides," she said, "the time to be young and free of responsibilities is short enough. Enjoy it while you can. With the Family reduced to the four of us and this clutch, you'll have a hard enough adulthood, even if Second Mother manages to produce as many as two hatchlings out of the five or six clutches she can still have before her laying days are over. The odds of hatching females over males are four to one; but still, it could be that she might produce only a couple of males—and then everything would be up to you. So, use your time in your own way while it's still yours to use. But keep alert. If you're called, come immediately!"

The Youngest promised that she would. She left First Mother and went to find First Uncle, who was keeping watch in the neighborhood of the dock to which the craft was moored. When she found him, he was hanging in the loch about thirty feet deep and about a hundred feet offshore from the craft, using his sensitive hearing to keep track of what was happening in the craft and on the dock.

"I'm glad you're here," he signaled to the Youngest when she arrived. "It's time for my second feeding; and I think there're none of the animals on the 'made' thing, right now. But it wouldn't hurt to keep a watch, anyway. Do you want to stay here and listen while I go and feed?"

Actually, Youngest was not too anxious to do so. Her plan had been to check with the Uncle, then do some feeding herself and get back to her diver while daylight was still coming into his cave. But she could hardly explain that to First Uncle.

"Of course," she said. "I'll stay here until you get back."

"Good," said the Uncle; and went off.

Left with nothing to do but listen and think, the Youngest hung in the water. Her imagination, which really required very little to start it working, had recaptured the notion of making friends with the diver. It was not so important, really, that he had gotten a look at her. Over the centuries a number of incidents had occurred in which members of the Family were seen briefly by one or more of the animals, and no bad results had come from those sightings. But it was important that the land-dwellers not realize there was a true Family. If she could just convince the diver that she was the last and only one of her People, it might be quite safe to see him from time to time—of course, only when he was alone and when they were in a safe place of her choosing, since though he might be trustworthy, his fellows who had twice threatened the hatchhole clearly were not.

The new excitement about getting to know him had come from starting to be able to "talk" with him. If she and he kept at it, they could probably work out ways to tell all sorts of things to each other eventually.

That thought reminded her that she had not yet figured out why it was important to him that she understand that moving his divided limb ends in a certain way could stand for his walking. He must have had some reason for showing her that. Maybe it was connected with his earlier moving of his limb ends over the surface of the water?

Before she had a chance to ponder the possible connection, a sound from above, reaching down through the water, alerted her to the fact that some of the creatures were once more coming out onto the dock. She drifted in closer, and heard the sounds move to the end of the dock and onto the craft.

Apparently, they were bringing something heavy aboard, because along with the noise of their lower limb ends on the structure came the thumping and rumbling of something which ended at last—to judge from the sounds—somewhere up on the forward deck where she had examined the box with the sloping top and the other "made" thing in the bow.

Following this, she heard some more sounds moving from the foredeck area into the cabin.

A little recklessly, the Youngest drifted in until she was almost under the craft and only about fifteen feet below the surface, and so verified that it was, indeed, in that part of the boat where the box with the sloping box stood that most of the activity was going on. Then the noise in that area slowed down and stopped, and she heard the sound of the animals walking back off the craft, down the dock and ashore. Things became once more silent.

First Uncle had not yet returned. The Youngest wrestled with her conscience. She had not been specifically told not to risk coming up to the surface near the dock; but she knew that was simply because it had not occurred to any of the older members of the Family that she would be daring enough to do such a thing. Of course, she had never told any of them how she had examined the foredeck of the craft once before. But now, having already done so, she had a hard time convincing herself it was too risky to do again. After all, hadn't she heard the animals leave the area? No matter how quiet one of them might try to be, her hearing was good enough to pick up little sounds of his presence, if he was still aboard.

In the end, she gave in to temptation—which is not to say she moved without taking every precaution. She drifted in, underwater, so slowly and quietly that a little crowd of curious minnows formed around her. Approaching the foredeck from the loch side of the craft, she stayed well underwater until she was right up against the hill. Touching it, she hung in the water, listening. When she still heard nothing, she lifted her head quickly, just enough for a glimpse over the side; then she ducked back under again and shot away and down to a safe distance.

Eighty feet deep and a hundred feet offshore, she paused to consider what she had seen.

Her memory, like that of everyone in the Family, was essentially photographic when she concentrated on remembering, as she had during her brief look over the side of the craft. But being able to recall exactly what she had looked at was not the same thing as realizing its import. In this case, what she had been looking for was what had just been brought aboard. By comparing what she had just seen with what she had observed on her night visit earlier, she had hoped to pick out any addition to the "made" things she had noted then.

At first glance, no difference had seemed visible. She noticed the box with the sloping top and the thing in the bow with the barbed rod inside. A number of other, smaller things were about the deck, too, some of which she had examined briefly the time before and some that she had barely noticed. Familiar were several of the doubled things like the one the diver had thrown from him in order to open up communicatons between them at first. Largely unfamiliar were a number of smaller boxes, some round things, other things that were combinations of round and angular shapes, and a sort of tall open frame, upright and holding several rods with barbed ends like the ones which the thing in the bow contained.

She puzzled over the assortment of things—and then without warning an answer came. But provokingly, as often happened with her, it was not the answer to the question she now had, but to an earlier one.

It had suddenly struck her that the diver's actions in rejecting the "made" thing he had worn on his back, and all his original signals to her, might mean that for some reason it was not the one he wanted, or needed, in order to leave the cave. Why there should be that kind of difference between it and these things left her baffled. The one with him now in the cave had been the right one; but maybe it was not the right one, today. Perhaps—she had a sudden inspiration—"made" things could die like animals or fish, or even like People, and the one he now had was dead. In any case, maybe what he needed was another of that particular kind of thing.

Perhaps this insight had come from the fact that several of these same "made" things were on the deck; and also, there was obviously only one diver, since First Uncle had not reported any of the other animals going down into the water. She was immediatley tempted to go and get another one of the things, so that she could take it back to the diver. If he put it on, that means she was right. Even if he did not, she might learn something by the way he handled it.

If it had been daring to take one look at the deck, it was inconceivably so to return now and actually try to take something from it. Her sense of duty struggled with her inclinations but slowly was overwhelmed. After all, she knew now—knew positively—that none of the animals were aboard the boat and none could have come aboard in the last few minutes because she was still close enough to hear them. But if she went, she would have to hurry if she was going to do it before the Uncle got back and forbade any such action.

She swam back to the craft in a rush, came to the surface beside it, rose in the water, craned her neck far enough inboard to snatch up one of the things in her teeth and escape with it.

A few seconds later, she had it two hundred feet down on the bed of the loch and was burying it in silt. Three minutes later she was back on station watching the craft, calmly enough but with her heart beating fast. Happily, there was still no sign of First Uncle's return.

Her heartbeat slowed. She went back to puzzling over what it was on the foredeck that could be the thing she had heard the creatures bring aboard. Of course, she now had three memory images of the area to compare. . . .

Recognition came.

There *was* a discrepancy between the last two mental images and the first one, a discrepancy about one of the "made" things to which she had devoted close attention, that first time.

The difference was the line attached to the box with the sloping top. It was not the same line at all. It was a drum of other line at least twice as thick as the one which had connected the heavy thing and the box previously—almost as thick as the thick line connecting the barbed rod to the thing in the bow that contained it. Clearly, the animals of the craft had tried to make sure that they would run no danger of losing their drop-weight if it became buried again. Possibly they had foolishly hoped that it was so strong that not even First Uncle could break it as he had the first.

That meant they were not going to give up. Here was clear evidence they were going to go on searching for their diver. She *must* get him back to them as soon as possible.

She began to swim restlessly, to and fro in the underwater, anxious to see the Uncle return so that she could tell him what had been done.

He came not long afterward, although it seemed to her that she had waited and worried for a considerable time before he appeared. When she told him about the new line, he was concerned enough by the information so that he barely reprimanded her for taking the risk of going in close to the craft.

"I must tell First Mother, right away—He checked himself and looked up through the twenty or so feet of water that covered them. "No, there're only a few more hours of daylight left. I need to think, anyway. I'll stay on guard here until dark, then I'll go see First Mother in her cave. Youngest, for right now don't say anything to Second Mother, or even to First Mother if you happen to talk to her. I'll tell both of them myself after I've had time to think about it."

"Then I can go now?" asked the Youngest, almost standing on her tail in the underwater in her eagerness to be off.

"Yes, yes," signaled the Uncle.

The Youngest turned and dove toward the spot where she had buried the "made" thing she had taken and about which she had been careful to say nothing to First Uncle. She had no time to explain about the diver now, and any mention of the thing would bring demands for a full explanation from her elders. Five minutes later, the thing in her teeth, she was splitting the water in the direction of the cave where she had left the diver.

She had never meant to leave him alone this long. An irrational fear grew in her that something had happened to him in the time she had been gone. Perhaps he started chilling again and had lost too much warmth, like one of the old ones, and was now dead. If he was dead, would the other animals be satisfied just to have his body back? But she did not want to think of him dead: He was not a bad little animal, in spite of his acting in such an ugly fashion when he had seen her for the first time. She should have realized that in the daylight, seeing her as he had without warning for the first time—

The thought of daylight reminded her that First Uncle had talked about there being only a few hours of it left. Surely there must be more than that. The day could not have gone so quickly.

She took a quick slant up to the surface to check. No, she was right. There must be at least four hours yet before the sun would sink below the mountains. However, in his own way the Uncle had been right, also, because the clouds were very heavy now. It would be too dark to see much, even long before actual nightfall. Snow was certain by dark, possibly even before. As she floated for a moment with her head and neck out of water, a few of the first wandering flakes came down the wind and touched her right cheek cells with tiny, cold fingers.

She dived again. It would indeed be a heavy snowfall; the Family could start out tonight on their way to the sea, if only they wantd to. It might even be possible to carry the eggs, distributed among the four of them, just two or three carried pressed between a swim paddle and warm body skin. First Mother might tire easily; but after the first night, when they had gotten well away from the loch, and with new snow falling to cover their footsteps, they could go by short stages. There would be no danger that the others would run out of heat or strength. Even the Youngest, small as she was, had fat reserves for a couple of months without eating and with ordinary activity. The Lost Father had made it to Loch Ness from the sea in a week or so.

If only they would go now. If only she were old enough and wise enough to convince them to go. For just a moment she gave herself over to a dream of their great sea home, of the People grown strong again, patrolling in their great squadrons past the white-gleaming ice berg or under the tropic stars. Most of the eggs of every clutch would hatch, then. The hatchlings would have the beaches of all the empty islands of the world to hatch on. Later, in the sea, they would grow up strong and safe, with their mighty elders around to guard them from anything that moved in the salt waters. In their last years, the old ones would bask under the hot sun in warm, hidden places and never need to chill again. The sea. That was where they belonged. Where they must go home to, someday. And that day should be soon. . . .

The Youngest was almost to the cave now. She brought her thoughts, with a wrench, back to the diver. Alive or dead, he too must go back—to his own kind. Fervently, she hoped that she was right about another "made" thing being what he needed before he would swim out of the cave. If not, if he just threw this one away as he had the other one, then she had no choice. She would simply have to pick him up in her teeth and carry him out of the cave without it. Of course, she must be careful to hold him so that he could not reach her to scratch or bite; and she must get his head back above water as soon as they got out of the cave into the open loch, so that he would not drown.

By the time she had gotten this far in her thinking, she was at the cave. Ducking inside, she exploded up through the surface of the water within. The diver was seated with his back against the cave wall, looking haggard and savage. He was getting quite dark-colored around the jaws, now. The little points he had there seemed to be growing. She dumped the new "made" thing at his feet.

For a moment he merely stared down at it, stupidly. Then he fumbled the object up into his arms and did something to it with those active little divided sections of his two upper limb ends. A hissing sound came from the thing that made her start back, warily. So, the "made" things were alive, after all!

The diver was busy attaching to himself the curious things he had worn when she had first found him—with the exception that the new thing she had brought him, rather than its old counterpart, was going on his back. Abruptly, though, he stopped, his head-thing still not on and still in the process of putting on the paddle-like things that attached to his lower limb ends. He got up and came forward to the edge of the water, looking at her.

He had changed again. From the moment he had gotten the new thing to make the hissing noise, he had gone into yet a different way of standing and acting. Now he came within limb reach of her and stared at her so self-assuredly that she almost felt she was the animal trapped in a cave and he was free. Then he crouched down by the water and once more began to make motions with his upper limbs and limb ends.

First, he made the on-top-of-the-water sliding motion with the back of one limb end that she now began to understand must mean the craft he had gone overboard from. Once she made the connection it was obvious: the craft, like his hand, was in the water only with its underside. Its top side was dry and in the air. As she watched, he circled his "craft" limb end around in the water and brought it back to touch the ledge. Then, with his other limb end, he "walked" two of its divisions up to the "craft" and continued to "walk" them onto it.

She stared. He was apparently signaling something about his getting on the craft. But why?

However, now he was doing something else. He lifted his walking-self limb end off the "craft" and put it standing on its two stiff divisions, back on the ledge. Then he moved the "craft" out over the water, away from the ledge, and held it there. Next, to her surprise, he "walked" his other limb end right off the ledge into the water. Still "walking" so that he churned the still surface of the cave water to a slight roughness, he moved that limb end slowly to the unmoving "craft." When the "walking" limb end reached the "craft," it once more stepped up onto it.

The diver now pulled his upper limbs back, sat crouched on the ledge, and looked at the Youngest for a long moment. Then he made the same signals again. He did it a third time, and she began to understand. He was showing himself swimming to his craft. Of course, he had no idea how far he actually was from it, here in the cave—an unreasonable distance for as weak a swimmer as one of his kind was.

But now he was signaling yet something else. His "walking" limb end stood at the water's edge. His other limb end was not merely on the water, but in it, below the surface. As she watched, a single one of that other limb end's divisions rose through the surface and stood, slightly crooked, so that its upper joint was almost at right angles to the part sticking through the surface. Seeing her gaze on this part of him, the diver began to move that solitary joint through the water in the direction its crooked top was pointing. He brought it in this fashion all the way to the rock ledge and halted it opposite the "walking" limb end standing there.

He held both limb ends still in position and looked at her, as if waiting for a sign of understanding.

She gazed back, once more at a loss. The joint sticking up out of the water was like nothing in her memory but the limb of a waterlogged tree, its top more or less looking at the "walking" limb end that stood for the diver. But if the "walking" limb end was *he—?* Suddenly she understood. The division protruding from the water signalized *her!*

To show she understood, she backed off from the ledge, crouched down in the shallow water of the cave until nothing but her upper neck and head protruded from the water, and then—trying to look as much like his crooked division as possible—approached him on the ledge.

He made noises. There was no way of being sure, of course, but she felt she was beginning to read the tone of some of the sounds he made; and these latest sounds, she was convinced, sounded pleased and satisfied.

He tried something else.

He made the "walking" shape on the ledge, then added something. In addition to the two limb-end divisions standing on the rock, he unfolded another—a short, thick division, one at the edge of that particular limb end, and moved it in circular fashion, horizontally. Then he stood up on the ledge himself and swung one of his upper limbs at full length, in similar, circular fashion. He did this several times.

In no way could she imitate that kind of gesture, though she comprehended immediately that the movement of the extra, short division above the "walking" form was supposed to indicate him standing and swinging his upper limb like now. She merely stayed as she was and waited to see what he would do next.

He got down by the water, made the "craft" shape, "swam" his "walking" shape to it, climbed the "walking" shape up on the "craft," then had the "walking" shape turn and make the upper-limb swinging motion.

The Youngest watched, puzzled, but caught up in this strange game of communication she and the diver had found to play together. Evidently he wanted to go back to his craft, get on it, and then wave his upper limb like that, for some reason. It made no sense so far—but he was already doing something more.

He now had the "walking" shape standing on the ledge, making the upper-limb swinging motion, and he was showing the crooked division that she was approaching through the water.

That was easy: he wanted her to come to the ledge when he swung his upper limb.

Sure enough, after a couple of demonstrations of the last shape signals, he stood up on the ledge and swung his arm. Agreeably, she went out in the water, crouched down, and approached the ledge. He made pleased noises. This was all rather ridiculous, she thought, but enjoyable nonetheless. She was standing half her length out from the edge, where she had stopped, and was trying to think of a body signal she could give that would make him swim to her, when she noticed that he was going on to further signals.

He had his "walking" shape standing on the "craft" shape, in the water out from the ledge, and signaling "Come." But then he took his "walking" shape away from the "craft" shape, put it under the water a little distance off, and came up with it as the "her" shape. He showed the "her" shape approaching the "craft" shape with her neck and head out of water.

She was to come to his craft? In response to his "Come" signal?

No!

She was so furious with him for suggesting such a thing that she had no trouble at all thinking of a way to convey her reaction. Turning around, she plunged underwater, down through the cave entrance and out into the loch. Her first impulse was to flash off and leave him there to do whatever he wanted—stay forever, go back to his kind, or engage in any other nonsensical activity his small head could dream up. Did he think she had no wisdom at all? To suggest that she come right up to his craft with her head and neck out of water when he signaled—as if there had never been a taboo against her People having anything to do with his! He must not understand her in the slightest degree.

Common sense caught up with her, halted her, and turned her about not far from the cave mouth. Going off like this would do her no good—more, it would do the Family no good. On the other hand, she could not bring herself to go back into the cave, now. She hung in the water, undecided, unable to conquer the conscience that would not let her swim off, but also unable to make herself re-enter.

Vibrations from the water in the cave solved her problem. He had evidently put on the "made" thing she had brought him and was coming out. She stayed where she was, reading the vibrations.

He came to the mouth of the cave and swam slowly, straight up, to the surface. Level with him, but far enough away to be out of sight in the murky water, the Youngest rose, too. He lifted his head at last into the open air and looked around him.

He's looking for me, thought the Youngest, with a sense of satisfaction that he would see no sign of her and would assume she had left him for good. Now, go ashore and go back to your own kind, she commanded in her thoughts.

But he did not go ashore, though shore was only a matter of feet from him. Instead, he pulled his head underwater once more and began to swim back down.

She almost exploded with exasperaton. He was headed toward the cave mouth! He was going back inside!

"You stupid animal!" she signaled to him. "*Go ashore!*"

But of course he did not even perceive the signal, let alone understand it. Losing all patience, the Youngest swooped down upon him, hauled him to the surface once more, and let him go.

For a second he merely floated there, motionless, and she felt a sudden fear that she had brought him up through the water too swiftly. She knew of some small fish that spent all their time down in the deepest parts of the loch, and if you brought one of them too quickly up the nine hundred feet or so to the surface, it twitched and died, even though it had been carried gently. Sometimes part of the insides of these fish bulged out through their mouths and gill slits after they were brought up quickly.

After a second, the diver moved and looked at her.

Concerned for him, she had stayed on the surface with him, her head just barely out of the water. Now he saw her. He kicked with the "made" paddles on his lower limbs to raise himself partly out of the water and, a little awkwardly, with his upper limb ends made the signal of him swimming to his craft.

She did not respond. He did it several more times, but she stayed stubbornly non-communicative. It was bad enough that she had let him see her again after his unthinkable suggestion.

He gave up making signals. Ignoring the shore close at hand, he turned from her and began to swim slowly south and out into the center of the loch.

He was going in the wrong direction if he was thinking of swimming all the way to his craft. And after his signaling it was pretty clear that this was what he had in mind. Let him find out his mistake for himself, the Youngest thought, coldly.

But she found that she could not go through with that. Angrily, she shot after him, caught the thing on his back with her teeth, and, lifting him by it enough so that his head was just above the surface, began to swim with him in the right direction.

She went slowly—according to her own ideas of speed—but even so a noticeable bow wave built up before him. She lifted him a little higher out of the water to be on the safe side; but she did not go any faster: perhaps he could not endure too much speed. As it was, the clumsy shape of his small body hung about with "made" things was creating surprising turbulence for its size. It was a good thing the present hatchhole (and, therefore, First Mother's current resting cave and the area in which First Uncle and Second Mother would do their feeding) was as distant as they were; otherwise First Uncle, at least, would certainly have been alarmed by the vibrations and have come to investigate.

It was also a good thing that the day was as dark as it was, with its late hour and the snow that was now beginning to fall with some seriousness; otherwise she would not have wanted to travel this distance on the surface in daylight. But the snow was now so general that both shores were lost to sight in its white, whirling multitudes of flakes, and certainly no animal on shore would be able to see her and the diver out here.

There was privacy and freedom, being hidden by the snow like this—like the freedom she felt on dark nights when the whole loch was free of the animals and all hers. If only it could be this way all the time. To live free and happy was so good. Under conditions like these, she could not even fear or dislike the animals, other than her diver, who were a threat to the Family.

At the same time, she remained firm in her belief that the Family should go, now. None of the others had ever before told her that any of the legends were untrustworthy, and she did not believe that the one about the Lost Father was so. It was not that that legend was untrustworthy, but that they had grown conservative with age and feared to leave the loch; while she, who was still young, still dared to try great things for possibly great rewards.

She had never admitted it to the older ones, but one midwinter day when she had been very young and quite small—barely old enough to be allowed to swim around in the loch by herself—she had ventured up one of the streams flowing into the loch. It was a stream far too shallow for an adult of the Family; and some distance up it, she found several otters playing on an ice slide they had made. She had joined them, sliding along with them for half a day without ever being seen by any upright animal. She remembered this all very well, particularly her scrambling around on the snow to get to the head of the slide; and that she had used her tail muscles to skid herself along on her warm belly surface, just as the Lost Father had described.

If she could get the others to slip ashore long enough to try the snowy loch banks before day-warmth combined with loch-warmth to clear them of the white stuff . . . But even as she thought this, she knew they would never agree to try. They would not even consider the journey home to the sea until, as First Mother said, it became clear that that was the only alternative to extinction at the hands of the upright animals.

It was a fact, and she must face it. But maybe she could think of some way to make plain to them that the animals had, indeed, become that dangerous. For the first time, it occurred to her that her association with the diver could turn out to be something that would help them all. Perhaps, through him, she could gain evidence about his kind that would convince the rest of the Family that they should leave the loch.

It was an exciting thought. It would do no disservice to him to use him in that fashion, because clearly he was different from others of his kind: he had realized that not only was she warm as he was, but as intelligent or more so than he. He would have no interest in being a danger to her People, and might even cooperate—if she could make him understand what she wanted—in convincing the Family of the dangers his own race posed to them. Testimony from one of the animals directly would be an argument to convince even First Uncle.

For no particular reason, she suddenly remembered how he had instinctively huddled against her when he had discovered her warming him. The memory roused a feeling of tenderness in her. She found herself wishing there were some way she could signal that feeling to him. But they were almost to his craft, now. It and the dock were beginning to be visible—dark shapes lost in the dancing white—with the dimmer dark shapes of trees and other things ashore behind them.

Now that they were close enough to see a shore, the falling snow did not seem so thick, nor so all-enclosing as it had out in the middle of the loch. But there was still a privacy to the world it created, a feeling of security. Even sounds seemed to be hushed.

Through the water, Youngest could feel vibrations from the craft. At least one, possibly two, of the other animals were aboard it. As soon as she was close enough to be sure her diver could see the craft, she let go of the thing on his back and sank abruptly to about twenty feet below the surface, where she hung and waited, checking the vibrations of his movements to make sure he made it safely to his destination.

At first, when she let him go, he trod water where he was and turned around and around as if searching for her. He pushed himself up in the water and made the "Come" signal several times; but she refused to respond. Finally, he turned and swam to the edge of the craft.

He climbed on board very slowly, making so little noise that the two in the cabin evidently did not hear him. Surprisingly, he did not seem in any hurry to join them or to let them know he was back.

The Youngest rose to just under the surface and lifted her head above to see what he was doing. He was still standing on the foredeck, where he had climbed aboard, not moving. Now, as she watched, he walked heavily forward to the bow and stood beside the "made" thing there, gazing out in her direction.

He lifted his arm as if to make the "Come" signal, then dropped it to his side.

The Youngest knew that in absolutely no way could he make out the small portion of her head above the waves, with the snow coming down the way it was and day drawing swiftly to its dark close. She stared at him. She noticed something weary and sad about the way he stood. I should leave now, she thought. But she did not move. With the other two animals still unaware in the cabin, and the snow continuing to fall, there seemed to be no reason to hurry off. She would miss him, she told herself, feeling a sudden pang of loss. Looking at him, it came to her suddenly that from the way he was acting he might well miss her, too.

Watching, she remembered how he had half lifted his limb as if to signal and then dropped it again. Maybe his limb is tired, she thought.

A sudden impulse took her. I'll go in close, underwater, and lift my head high for just a moment, she thought, so he can see me. He'll know then that I haven't left him for good. He already understands I wouldn't come on board that thing of his under any circumstance. Maybe if he sees me again for a second, now, he'll understand that if he gets back in the water and swims to me, we can go on learning signals from each other. Then, maybe, someday, we'll know enough signals together so that he can convince the older ones to leave.

Even as she thought this, she was drifting in, underwater, until she was only twenty feet from the craft. She rose suddenly and lifted her head and neck clear of the water.

For a long second, she saw he was staring right at her but not responding. Then she realized that he might not be seeing her, after all, just staring blindly out at the loch and the snow. She moved a little sideways to attract his attention, and saw his head move. Then he *was* seeing her? Then why didn't he do something?

She wondered if something was wrong with him. After all, he had been gone for nearly two days from his own People and must have missed at least a couple of his feeding periods in that time. Concern impelled her to a closer look at him. She began to drift in toward the boat.

He jerked upright suddenly and swung an upper limb at her.

But he was swinging it all wrong. It was not the "Come" signal he was making, at all. It was more like the "Come" signal in reverse—as if he was pushing her back and away from him. Puzzled, and even a little hurt, because the way he was acting reminded her of how he had acted when he first saw her in the cave and did not know she had been with him earlier, the Youngest moved in even closer.

He flung both his upper limbs furiously at her in that new, "rejecting" motion and shouted at her—a loud, angry noise. Behind him, came an explosion of different noise from inside the cabin, and the other two animals burst out onto the deck. Her diver turned, making noises, waving both his limbs at them the way he had just waved them at her. The Youngest, who had been about to duck down below the safety of the loch surface, stopped. Maybe this was some new signal he wanted her to learn, one that had some reference to his two companions?

But the others were making noises back at him. The taller one ran to one of the "made" things that were like, but smaller than, the one in the bow of the boat. The diver shouted again, but the tall one ignored him, only seizing one end of the thing he had run to and pulling that end around toward him. The Youngest watched, fascinated, as the other end of the "made" thing swung to point at her.

Then the diver made a very large angry noise, turned, and seized the end of the largest "made" thing before him in the bow of the boat.

Frightened suddenly, for it had finally sunk in that for some reason he had been signaling her to get away, she turned and dived. Then, as she did so, she realized that she had turned, not away from, but into line with, the outer end of the thing in the bow of the craft.

She caught a flicker of movement, almost too fast to see, from the thing's hollow outer end. Immediately, the loudest sound she had ever heard exploded around her, and a tremendous blow struck her behind her left shoulder as she entered the underwater.

She signaled for help instinctively, in shock and fear, plunging for the deep bottom of the loch. From far off, a moment later, came the answer of First Uncle. Blindly, she turned to flee to him.

As she did, she thought to look and see what had happened to her. Swinging her head around, she saw a long, but shallow, gash across her shoulder and down her side. Relief surged in her. It was not even painful yet, though it might be later; but it was nothing to cripple her, or even to slow her down.

How could her diver have done such a thing to her? The thought was checked almost as soon as it was born—by the basic honesty of her training. *He* had not done this. *She* had done it, by diving into the path of the barbed rod cast from the thing in the bow. If she had not done that, it would have missed her entirely.

But why should he make the thing throw the barbed rod at all? She had thought he had come to like her, as she liked him.

Abruptly, comprehension came; and it felt as if her heart leaped in her. For all at once it was perfectly clear what he had been trying to do. She should have had more faith in him. She halted her flight toward the Uncle and turned back toward the boat.

Just below it, she found what she wanted. The barbed rod, still leaving a taste of her blood in the water, was hanging point down from its line, in about two hundred feet of water. It was being drawn back up, slowly but steadily.

She surged in close to it, and her jaws clamped on the line she had tried to bite before and found resistant. But now she was serious in her intent to sever it. Her jaws scissored and her teeth ripped at it, though she was careful to rise with the line and put no strain upon it that would warn the animals above about what she was doing. The tough strands began to part under her assault.

Just above her, the sound of animal noises now came clearly through the water: her diver and the others making sounds at each other.

"... I tell you we're through!" It was her diver speaking. "It's over. I don't care what you saw. It's my boat. I paid for it; and I'm quitting."

"It not *your* boat, man. It a boat belong to the company, the company that belong all three of us. We got contracts."

"I'll pay off your damned contracts."

"There's more to this than money, now. We know that great beast in there, now. We get our contract money, and maybe a lot more, going on the TV telling how we catch it and bring it in. No, man, you don't stop us now."

"I say, it's my boat. I'll get a lawyer and court order—"

"You do that. You get a lawyer and a judge and a pretty court order, and we'll give you the boat. You do that. Until then, it belong to the company and it keep after that beast."

She heard the sound of footsteps—her diver's footsteps, she could tell, after all this time of seeing him walk his lower limbs—leaving the boat deck, stepping onto the dock, going away.

The line was almost parted. She and the barbed rod were only about forty feet below the boat.

"What'd you have to do that for?" That was the voice of the third creature. "He'll do that! He'll get a lawyer and take the boat and we won't even get our minimum pay. Whyn't you let him pay us off, the way he said?"

"Hush, you fooking fool. How long you think it take him get a lawyer, a judge, and a writ? Four days, maybe five—"

The line parted. She caught the barbed rod in her jaws as it started to sink. the ragged end of the line lifted and vanished above her.

"—and meanwhile, you and me, we go hunting with this boat. We know the beast there, now. We know what to look for. We find it in four, five day, easy."

"But even if we get it, he'll just take it away from us again with his lawyer—"

"I tell you, no. We'll get ourselves a lawyer, also. This company formed to take the beast; and he got to admit he tried to call off the hunt. And we both seen what he do. He've fired that harpoon gun to scare it off, so I can't get it with the drug lance and capture it. We testify to that, we got him—Ah!"

"What is it?"

"What is it? You got no eyes, man? The harpoon gone. It in that beast after all, being carried around. We don't need no four, five days, I tell you now. That be a good long piece of steel, and we got the locators to find metal like that. We hunt that beast and bring it in tomorrow. Tomorrow, man, I promise you! It not going to go too fast, too far, with that harpoon."

But he could not see below the snow and the black surface of the water. The Youngest was already moving very fast indeed through the deep loch to meet the approaching First Uncle. In her jaws she carried the harpoon, and on her back she bore the wound it had made. The elders could have no doubt, now, about the intentions of the upright animals (other than her diver) and their ability to destroy the Family.

They must call First Mother, and this time there would be no hesitation. She would see the harpoon and the wound and decide for them all. Tonight they would leave by the route of the Lost Father, while the snow was still thick on the banks of the loch. They might have to leave the eggs behind, after all; but if so, Second Mother could have more clutches, and maybe later they would even find a way ashore again to Loch Morar and meet others of their own People at last.

But, in any case, they would go now to live free in the sea; and in the sea most of Second Mother's future eggs would hatch and the Family would grow numerous and strong again.

She could see them in her mind's eye, now. They would leave the loch by the mouth of Glen Moriston—First Mother, Second Mother, First Uncle, herself—and take to the snow-covered banks when the water became too shallow. . . .

They would travel steadily into the mountains, and the new snow falling behind them would hide the marks of their going from the eyes of the animals. They would pass by deserted ways through the silent rocks to the ocean. They would come at last to its endless waters, to the shining bergs of the north and the endless warmth of the Equator sun. The ocean, their home, was welcoming them back, at last. There would be no more doubt, no more fear or waiting. They were going home to the sea . . . they were going home to the sea. . . .

DAVID DRAKE

Time Safari

THE TYRANNOSAUR'S bellow made everyone jump except Vickers, the guide. The beast's nostrils flared, sucking in the odor of the light helicopter and the humans aboard it. It stalked forward.

"The largest land predator that ever lived," whispered one of the clients.

"A lot of people think that," said Vickers in what most of the rest thought was agreement.

There was nothing in the graceful advance of the tyrannosaur to suggest its ten ton mass, until its tail side-swiped a flower-trunked cycad. The tree was six inches thick at the point of impact, and it sheared at that point without time to bend.

"Oh dear," the female photographer said. Her brother's grip on the chair arms was giving him leverage to push its cushion against the steel backplate.

The tyrannosaur's strides shifted the weight of its deep torso, counterbalanced by the swinging of its neck and tail. At each end of the head's arcs, the beast's eyes glared alternately at its prey. Except for the size, the watchers could have been observing a grackle on the lawn; but it was a grackle seen from a june-bug's perspective.

"Goddam, he won't hold still!" snarled Salmes, the old-money client, the know-it-all. Vickers smiled. The tyrannosaur chose that movement to pause and bellow again. It was now a dozen feet from the helicopter, a single claw-tipped stride. If the blasting sound left one able, it was an ideal time to admire the beauty of the beast's four-foot head. Its teeth were irregular in length and placement, providing in sum a pair of yellowish, four-inch deep, saws. They fit together too loosely to shear; but with the power of the tyrannosaur's jaw muscles driving them, they could tear the flesh from any creature on Earth—in any age.

The beast's tongue was like a crocodile's, attached for its full length to the floor of its mouth. Deep blue with purple veins, it had a floral appearance. The tongue was without sensory purpose and existed only to help by rhythmic flexions to ram chunks of meat down the predator's throat. The beast's head scales were the size of little fingernails, somewhat finer than those of the torso. Their coloration was consistent—a base of green nearing black, blurred by rosettes of a much lighter, yellowish, hue. Against that background, the tyrannosaur's eyes stood out like needlepoints dripping blood.

"They don't always give you that pause," Vickers said aloud. "Sometimes they come—"

The tyrannosaur lunged forward. Its lower jaw, half-opened during its bugling challenge, dropped to full gape. Someone shouted. The action blurred as the hologram dissolved a foot or two from the arc of clients.

Vickers thumbed up the molding lights. He walked to the front of the conference room, holding the remote control with which the hotel had provided him. The six clients viewed him with varied expressions. The brother and sister photographers, dentists named McPherson, whispered in obvious delight. They were best able to appreciate the quality of the hologram and to judge their own ability to duplicate it. Any fear they had felt during the presentation was buried in their technical enthusiasm afterward.

The two individual gunners were a general contractor named Mears and Brewer, a meat-packing magnate. Brewer was a short man whose full moustache and balding head made him a caricature of a Victorian industrialist. He loosened his collar and massaged his flushed throat with his thumb and index finger. Mears, built like an All-Pro linebacker after twenty years of retirement, was frowning. He still gripped the chair arms in a way that threatened the plastic. Those were normal reactions to one of Vickers' pre-hunt presentations. It meant the clients had learned the necessity of care in a way no words or still photos could have taught them. Conversely, that familiarity made them less likely to freeze when they faced the real thing.

The presentations unfortunately did not have any useful effect on people like the Salmes. Or at least on Jonathan Salmes, blond and big but with the look of a movie star, not a football player. Money and leisure could not make Salmes younger, but they made him look considerably less than his real age of forty years. His face was now set in its habitual pattern of affected boredom. As not infrequently happens, the affectation created its own reality and robbed Salmes of whatever pleasure three generations of oil money might otherwise have brought him.

Adrienne Salmes was as blond and as perfectly preserved as her husband, but she had absorbed the presentation without interest. Time safaris were the property of wealth alone, and she had all the trapping of that wealth. Re-emitted light made her dress—and its wearer—the magnet of all eyes in a dim room, and her silver lame wristlet responded to voice commands with a digital display. That sort of money could buy beauty like Adrienne Salmes'; but it could not buy the inbred assurance with which she wore that beauty. She forestalled any tendency the guide might have had to think that her personality stopped with the skin by asking, ''Mr. Vickers, would you have waited to see if the tyrannosaurus would stop, or would you have shot while it was still at some distance from the helicopter?''

''Umm?'' said Vickers in surprise. ''Oh, wait, I suppose. If he doesn't stop, there's still time for a shot; and your guide, whether that's me or Dieter, will be backing you. That's a good question.'' He cleared his throat. ''And that brings up an important point,'' he went on. ''We don't shoot large carnivores on foot. Mostly, the shooting platform—the helicopter—won't be dropping as low as it was for the pictures, either. For these holos I was sitting beside the photographer, sweating blood the whole time that nothing would go wrong. If the bird had stuttered or the pilot hadn't timed it just right, I'd have had just about enough time to try for a brain shot. Anywhere else and we'd have been in that fellow's gut faster'n you could swallow a sardine.'' He smiled. It made him look less like a bank clerk, more like a bank robber. ''Three sardines,'' he corrected himself.

''If you used a man-sized rifle, you'd have been a damned sight better off,'' offered Jonathan Salmes. He had one ankle crossed on the other knee, and his chair reclined at a 45° angle.

Vickers looked at the client. They were about of an age, though the guide was several inches shorter and not as heavily built. ''Yes, well,'' he said. ''That's a thing I need to talk about. Rifles.'' He ran a hand through his light brown hair.

''Yeah, I couldn't figure that either,'' said Mears. ''I mean, I read the stuff you sent, about big-bores not being important.'' The contractor frowned. ''I don't figure that. I mean, God almighty, as big as one of those mothers is, I wouldn't feel overgunned with a one-oh-five howitzer . . . and I sure don't think my .458 Magnum's any too big.''

''Right, right,'' Vickers said, nodding his head. His discomfort at facing a group of humans was obvious. ''A .458's fine if you can handle it—and I'm sure you can. I'm sure any of you can,'' he added, raising his eyes and sweeping the group again. ''What I said, what I meant, was that size isn't important, penetration and bullet placement are what's important. The .458 penetrates fine—with solids—I hope to God all of you know to bring solids, not soft-nosed bullets. If you're not comfortable with that much recoil, though, you're liable to flinch. And that means you'll miss, even at the ranges we shoot dinos at. A wounded dino running around, anywhere up to a hundred tons of him, and that's when things get messy. You and everybody around is better off with you holding a gun that doesn't make you flinch.''

''That's all balls, you know,'' Salmes remarked conversationally. He glanced around at the other clients. ''If you're man enough, I'll tell you what to carry.'' He looked at Vickers, apparently expecting an attempt to silence him. The guide eyed him with a somewhat bemused expression. ''A .500 Salmes, that's what,'' the big client asserted loudly. ''It was designed for me specially by Marquart and Wells, gun and bullets both. It uses shortened fifty-caliber machinegun cases, loaded to give twelve thousand foot-pounds of energy. That's enough to knock a tyrannosaurus right flat on his ass. It's the only gun that you'll be safe with on a hunt like this." He nodded toward Vickers to put a period to his statement.

"Yes, well," Vickers repeated. His expression shifted, hardening. He suddenly wore the visage that an animal might have glimpsed over the sights of his rifle. "Does anybody else feel that they need a—a *gun* like that to bring down anything they'll see on this safari?"

No one nodded to the question when it was put that way. Adrienne Salmes smiled. She was a tall woman, as tall as Vickers himself was.

"Okay, then," the guide said. "I guess I can skip the lesson to basic physics. Mr. Salmes, if you can handle your rifle, that's all that matters to me. If you can't handle it, you've still got time to get something useful instead. Now—"

"Now wait a goddamned minute!" Salmes said, his foot thumping to the floor. His face had flushed under its even tan. "Just what do you mean by that crack? You're going to teach *me* physics?"

"I don't think Mr. Vickers—" began Miss McPherson.

"I want an explanation!" Salmes demanded.

"All right, no problem," said Vickers. He rubbed his forehead and winced in concentration. "What you're talking about," he said to the floor, "is kinetic energy. That's a function of the square of the velocity. Well and good, but it won't knock anything down. What knocks things down is momentum, that's weight times velocity, not velocity squared. Anything that the bullet knocks down, the butt of the rifle would knock down by recoiling—which is why I encourage clients to carry something they can handle." He raised his eyes and pinned Salmes with them. "I've never yet had a client who weighed twelve thousand pounds, Mr. Salmes. And so I'm always tempted to tell people who talk about 'knock-down power' that they're full to the eyes."

Mrs. Salmes giggled. The other clients did not, but all the faces save Salmes' own bore more-than-hinted smiles. Vickers suspected that the handsome blond man had gotten on everyone else's nerves in the bar before the guide had opened the conference suite.

Salmes purpled to the point of an explosion. The guide glanced down again and raised his hand before saying, "Look, all other things being equal, I'd sooner hit a dino—or a man—with a big bullet than a little one. But if you put the bullet in the brain or the heart, it really doesn't matter much how big it is. And especially with a dino, if you put the bullet anywhere else, it's not going to do much good at all."

"Look," said Brewer, hunching forward and spreading his hands palms down, "I don't flinch, and I got a .378 Weatherby that's got penetration up the ass. But—" he turned his hands over and over again as he looked at them—"I'm not Annie Oakley, you know. If I have to hit a brain the size of a walnut with a four-foot skull around it—well, I may as well take a camera myself instead of the gun. I'll have *something* to show people that way."

Salmes snorted—which could have gotten him one of Brewer's big, capable fists in the face, Vickers thought. "That's another good question," the guide said. "Very good. Well. Brain shots are great if you know where to put them. I attached charts of a lot of the common dinos with the material I sent out, look them over and decide if you want to try.

"Thing is," he continued, "taking the top off a dino's heart'll drop it in a couple hundred yards. They don't charge when they're heart-shot, they just run till they fall. And we shoot from up close, as close as ten yards. They don't take any notice of you, the big ones, you could touch them if you wanted. You just need enough distance to be able to pick your shot. You see—" he gestured toward Brewer with both index fingers—"you won't have any problem hitting a heart the size of a bushel basket from thirty feet away. Brains—well, skin hunters have been killing crocs with brain shots for a century. Crocodile brains are just as small as a tyrannosaur's, and the skulls are just as big. Back where we're going, there were some that were a damn sight bigger than tyrannosaurs. But don't feel you have to. And anyway, it'd spoil your trophy if you brain-shot some of the small-headed kind."

Brewer cleared his throat. "Hey," he said, "I'd like to go back to something you said before. About using the helicopter."

"Right, the shooting platform," Vickers agreed.

"Look," said the meat-packer, "I mean . . . well, that's sort of like shooting wolves from a plane, isn't it? I mean, not, well, Christ . . . not sporting, is it?"

Vickers shrugged. "I won't argue with you," he said, "and you don't have to use the platform if you don't want to. But it's the only way you can be allowed to shoot the big carnosaurs. I'm sorry, that's just how it is." He leaned forward and spoke more intensely, popping the fingers of his left hand against his right palm. "It's as sporting as shooting tigers from an elephant-back, I guess, or shooting lions over a butchered cow. The head looks just as big over your mantle. And there's no sport at all for me to tell my bosses how one of my clients was eaten. They aren't bad, the big dinos, people aren't in their scale so they'll pretty much ignore you. Wound one and it's kitty bar the door. These aren't plant eaters, primed to run if there's trouble. These are carnivores we're talking about, animals that spend most of their waking lives killing or looking for something to kill. They *will* connect the noise of a shot with the pain, and they *will* go after whoever made the noise."

The guide paused and drew back. More calmly he concluded, "So carnosaurs you'll hunt from the platform. Or not at all."

"Well, what happens if they come to us?" Salmes demanded with recovered belligerence. "Right up to the camp, say? You can't keep us from shooting then."

"I guess this is a good time to discuss arrangements for the camp," Vickers said, approaching the question indirectly. "There's four of us staff with the safari, two guides—that's me and Dieter Jost—and two pilots. One pilot, one guide, and one client—one of you—go up in the platform every day. You'll each have two chances to bag a big carnosaur. They're territorial and not too thick on the ground, but there's almost certain to be at least one tyrannosaur and a pack of gorgosaurs in practical range. The other guide takes out the rest of the clients on foot, well, on motorized wagons you could say, ponies we call them. And the pilot who isn't flying the platform doubles as camp guard. He's got a heavy machinegun—" the guide smiled—"a Russian .51 cal. Courtesy of your hosts for the tour, the Israeli government. It'll stop dinos and light tanks without a bit of bother."

Vickers' face lost its crinkling of humor. "If there's any shooting to be done from the camp," he continued, "that's what does it. Unless Dieter or me specifically tell you otherwise. We're not going to have the intrusion vehicle trampled by a herd of dinos that somebody spooked right into it. If something happens to the intrusion vehicle, we don't go home." Vickers smiled again. "That might be okay with me, but I don't think any of the rest of you want to have to explain to the others how you stuck them in the Cretaceous."

"That would be a paradox, wouldn't it, Mr. Vickers?" Miss McPherson said. "That is, uh, human beings living in the Cretaceous? So it couldn't happen. Not that I'd want any chances taken with the vehicle, of course."

Vickers shrugged with genuine disinterest. "Ma'am, if you want to talk about paradox, you need Dr. Galil and his team. So far as I understand it, though, if there's not a change in the future, then there's no paradox; and if there *is* a change, then there's no paradox either because the change—well, the change is reality then."

Mr. McPherson leaned forward with a frown. "Well, surely two bodies—the same body—can't exist simultaneously," he insisted. If he and his sister had been bored with the discussion of firearms, then they had recovered their interest with mention of the mechanics of time transport.

"Sure they can," the guide said with the asperity of someone who had been asked the same question too often. He waved his hand back and forth as if erasing the thought from a chalk board. "They do. Every person, every gun or can of food, contains at least some atoms that were around in the Cretaceous—or the Pre-Cambrian, for that matter. It doesn't matter to the atoms whether they call themselves Henry Vickers or the third redwood from the big rock. . . ." He paused. "There's just one rule that I've heard for true from people who know," he continued at last. "If you travel into the future, you travel as energy. And you don't come back at all."

Mears paled and looked at the ceiling. People got squeamish about the damnedest things, thought Vickers. Being converted into energy . . . or being eaten . . . or being drowned in dark water lighted only by the dying radiance of your mind—but he broke away from that thought, a little sweat on his forehead with the strain of it. He continued aloud, ''There's no danger for us, heading back into the far past. But the intrusion vehicle can't be calibrated closer than 5,000 years plus or minus so far. The, the research side—'' he had almost said ''the military side,'' knowing the two were synonymous; knowing also that the Israeli government disapproved intensely of statements to that effect—''was trying for the recent past—'' 1948, but that was another thing you didn't admit you knew—''and they put a man into the future instead. After Dr. Galil had worked out the math, they moved the lab and cleared a quarter-mile section of Tel Aviv around the old site. They figure the poor bastard will show up sometime in the next few thousand years . . . and nobody better be sharing the area when he does.''

Vickers frowned at himself. ''Well, that's probably more than the, the government wants me to say about the technical side,'' he said. ''And anyway, I'm not the one to ask. Let's get back to the business itself—which I do know something about.''

''You've said that this presentation and the written material are all yours,'' Adrienne Salmes said with a wave of her hand. ''I'd like to know why.''

Vickers blinked at the unexpected question. He looked from Mrs. Salmes to the other clients, all of them but her husband staring back at him with interest. The guide laughed. ''I like my job,'' he said. ''A century ago, I'd have been hiking through Africa with a Mauser, selling ivory every year or so when I came in from the bush.'' He rubbed his left cheekbone where a disk of shiny skin remained from a boil of twenty years before. ''That sort of life was gone before I was born,'' he went on. ''What I have is the closest thing there is to it now.''

Adrienne Salmes was nodding. Mr. McPherson put his own puzzled frown into words and said, ''I don't see what that has to do with, well, you holding these sessions, though.''

''It's like this,'' Vickers said, watching his fingers tent and flatten against each other. ''They pay me, the government does, a very good salary that I personally don't have much use for.'' Jonathan Salmes snorted, but the guide ignored him. ''I use it to make my job easier,'' he went on, ''by sending the clients all the data *I've* found useful in the five years I've been travelling back to the Cretaceous . . . and elsewhere, but mostly the Cretaceous. Because if people go back with only what they hear in the advertising or from folks who need to make a buck or a name with their stories, they'll have problems when they see the real thing. Which means problems for me. So a month before each safari, I rent a suite in New York or Frankfurt or wherever the hell seems reasonable, and I offer to give a presentation to the clients. Nobody has to come, but most people do.'' He scanned the group. ''All of you did, for instance. It makes life easier for me.''

He cleared his throat. ''Well, in another way, we're here to make life easier for you,'' he went on. ''I've brought along holos of the standard game animals you'll be seeing.'' He dimmed the lights and stepped toward the back of the room. ''First the sauropods, the big long-necks. The most impressive things you'll see in the Cretaceous, but a disappointing trophy because of the small heads. . . .''

''All right, ladies and gentlemen,'' said Dieter Jost. Vickers always left the junior guide responsible for the social chores when both of them were present. ''Please line up here along the wall until the Doctor Galil directs us onto the vehicle.''

The members of Cretaceous Safari 87 backed against the hangar wall, their weapons or cameras in their hands. The guides and the two pilots, Washman and Brady, watched the clients rather than the crew preparing the intrusion vehicle. You could never tell what sort of mistake a tensed-up layman would make with a loaded weapon in his or her hands.

In case the clients were not laymen at all, there were four guards seated in a balcony-height alcove in the opposite wall. They wore civilian clothes, but the submachineguns they carried were just as military as their ID cards. The Israelis were, of all people, alert to the chance that a commando raid would be aimed at an intrusion vehicle and its technical staff. For that reason, the installation was in an urban setting from which there could be no quick escape; and its corridors and rooms, including the gaping hangar itself, were better guarded than the Defense Ministry had been during the most recent shooting war.

Dr. Galil and his staff were only occasionally visible to the group on the floor of the hangar. The intrusion vehicle rested on four braced girders twenty feet high. On its underside, a cylindrical probe was repeatedly blurring and reappearing. The technicians received data from the probe on instruments plugged into various sockets on the vehicle. Eighty million years in the past, the cylinder was sampling its surroundings on a score of wavelengths. When necessary, Dr. Galil himself changed control settings. Despite that care, there was no certainty of the surface over which the travellers would appear—or how far or under it they would appear. The long legs gave the intrusion vehicle a margin that might otherwise have been achieved by a longer drop than anything aboard would have survived.

''Well, this is it, hey?'' said Jonathan Salmes, speaking to Don Washman. To do so, Salmes had to talk through his wife, who ignored him in turn. ''A chance to hunt the most dangerous damned creatures ever to walk the Earth!'' Salmes' hands, evenly tanned like every other inch of exposed skin on him, tightened still further on the beautiful bolt-action rifle he carried.

Washman's smile went no further than Adrienne Salmes. The pilot was a big man also. The 40 mm grenade launcher he held looked like a sawed-off shotgun with him for scale. ''Gee, Mr. Salmes,'' he said in false surprise. ''People our age all had a chance to learn the most dangerous game on Earth popped out of a spider hole with an AK-47 in its hands. All the *men* did, at least.''

Vickers scowled. ''Don,'' he said. But Washman was a pilot, not a PR man. Besides, Salmes had coming anything of the sort he got.

Adrienne Salmes turned to Washman and laughed.

A heavy-set man climbed down from the intrusion vehicle and strolled across the concrete floor toward the waiting group. Like the guards, he wore an ordinary business suit. He kept his hands in his pants pockets. ''Good evening, ladies and sirs,'' he said in accented English. ''I am Mr. Stern; you might say, the company manager. I trust the preparations for your tour have been satisfactory?'' He eyed Dieter, then Vickers, his face wearing only a bland smile.

''All present and accounted for,'' said Dieter in German. At his side, Mears nodded enthusiastically.

''By God,'' said Jonathan Salmes with recovered vigor, ''I just want this gizmo to pop out right in front of a tyrannosaurus rex. Then I'll pop *him*, and I'll double your fees for a bonus!''

Don Washman smirked, but Vickers' scowl was for better reason than that. ''Ah, Mr. Salmes,'' the guide said, ''I believe Mr. Brewer drew first shot of the insertion. Fire discipline is something we *do* have to insist on.''

''Naw, that's okay,'' said Brewer unexpectedly. He looked sheepishly at Vickers, then looked away. ''We made an agreement on that,'' he added. ''I don't mind paying for something I want; but I don't mind selling something I don't need, either, you see?''

''In any case,'' said Stern, ''even the genius of Dr. Galil cannot guarantee to place you in front of a suitable dinosaur. I must admit to some apprehension, in fact, that some day we will land an intrusion vehicle in mid-ocean.'' He gestured both elbows outward, like wings flapping. ''Ah, this is a magnificent machine; but not, I fear, very precise.'' He smiled.

''Not precise enough to . . . put a battalion of paratroops in the courtyard of the Temple in 70 AD, you mean?'' suggested Adrienne Salmes with a trace of a smile herself.

Vickers' gut sucked in. Stern's first glance was to check the position of the guards. The slightly seedy good-fellowship he had projected was gone. ''Ah, you Americans,'' Stern said in a voice that was itself a warning. ''Always making jokes about the impossible. But you must understand that in a small and threatened country like ours, there are some jokes one does not make.'' His smile now had no humor. Adrienne Salmes returned it with a wintry one of her own. If anyone had believed her question was chance rather than a deliberate goad, the smile disabused them.

Atop the intrusion vehicle, an indicator began buzzing in a continuous rhythm. It was not a loud sound. The high ceiling of the hangar drank it almost completely. The staff personnel looked up sharply. Stern nodded again to Vickers and began to walk toward a ground-level exit. He was whistling under his breath. After a moment, a pudgy man stepped to the edge of the vehicle and looked down. He had a white moustache and a fringe of hair as crinkled as rock wool. "I believe we are ready, gentlemen," he said.

Dieter nodded. "We're on the way, then, Dr. Galil," he replied to the older man. Turning back to the safari group, he went on, "Stay in line, please. Hold the handrail with one hand as you mount the steps, and do be very careful to keep your weapons vertical. Accidents happen, you know." Dieter gave a brief nod of emphasis and led the way. The flight of metal steps stretched in a steep diagonal between two of the vehicle's legs. Vickers brought up the rear of the line, unhurried but feeling the tingle at the base of the neck which always preceded time travel with him. It amused Vickers to find himself trying to look past the two men directly in front of him to watch Adrienne Salmes as she mounted the stairs. The woman wore a baggy suit like the rest of them, rip-stopped Kelprin which would shed water and still breathe with 80% efficiency. On her the mottled coveralls had an interest which time safari clients, male or female, could rarely bring to such garments.

The floor of the intrusion vehicle was perforated steel from which much of the anti-slip coating had been worn. Where the metal was bare, it had a delicate patina of rust. In the center of the twenty-foot square, the safari's gear was neatly piled. The largest single item was the 500-gallon bladder of kerosene, fuel both for the turbine of the shooting platform and the diesel engines of the ponies. There was some dehydrated food, though the bulk of the group's diet would be the meat they shot. Vickers had warned the clients that anyone who could not stomach the idea of eating dinosaur should bring his own alternative. It was the idea that caused some people problems—the meat itself was fine. Each client was allowed a half-cubic meter chest for personal possessions. Ultimately they would either be abandoned in the Cretaceous or count against the owner's volume for trophies.

The intrusion vehicle was surrounded by a waist-high railing, hinged to flop down out of the way during loading and unloading. The space between the rail and the gear in the center was the passenger area. This open walkway was a comfortable four feet wide at the moment. On return, with the vehicle packed with trophies, there would be only standing room. Ceratopsian skulls, easily the most impressive of the High Cretaceous trophies, could run eight feet long with a height and width in proportion.

On insertion, it was quite conceivable that the vehicle would indeed appear in the midst of a pack of gorgosaurs. That was not something the staff talked about; but the care they took positioning themselves and the other gunners before insertion was not mere form. "Mr. McPherson," Dieter said, "Mr. Mears, if you will kindly come around with me to Side Three—that's across from the stairs here. Do not please touch the red control panel as you pass it."

"Ah, can't Charles and I stay together?" Mary McPherson asked. Both of the dentists carried motion cameras with the lenses set at the 50 mm minimum separation. A wider spread could improve hologram quality; but it might prove impossibly awkward under the conditions obtaining just after insertion.

"For the moment," Vickers said, "I'd like you on Side One with me, Miss McPherson. That puts two guns on each side; and it's just during insertion."

Boots clanking on the metal stairs, the safari group mounted the vehicle. Four members of Dr. Galil's team had climbed down already. They stood in a row beside the steps like a guard of honor in lab smocks. Galil himself waited beside the vertical control panel at the head of the stairs. The red panel was the only portion of the vehicle which looked more in keeping with a laboratory than a mineshaft. Even so, its armored casing was a far cry from the festooned breadboards that typically marked experimental machinery.

Not that anyone suggested to the clients that the machinery was as surely experimental as a 1940 radar set.

Dr. Galil shook hands with each member of the group, staff and clients alike. Vickers shifted his modified Garand rifle into the crook of his left arm and took the scientist's hand. "Henry, I pray you God-speed and a safe return," Galil said in English. His grip was firm.

"God's for afterwards, Shlomo," the guide said. "You'll bring us back, you and your boys. That's what I have faith in."

Dr. Galil squeezed Vickers' hand again. He walked quickly down the steps. The hangar lights dimmed as the big room emptied of everything but the intrusion vehicle and its cargo. Vickers took a deep breath and unlocked the T-handled switch in the center of the control panel. He glanced to either side. Miss McPherson was to his left, Mrs. Salmes to his right.

Adrienne Salmes smiled back. "Did you put me with you because you think you can't trust a woman's shooting?" she asked.

Vickers cleared his throat. "No," he lied. More loudly, he added, "We are about to make our insertion. Everyone please grip the rail with your free hand. Don't let your rifles or cameras project more than two feet beyond the railing, though." He threw the switch. A blue light on the hangar ceiling began to pulse slowly, one beat per second. Vickers' belly drew in again. At the tenth pulse, the light and the hangar disappeared together. There was an instant of sensory blurring. Some compared the sensation of time travel to falling, others to immersion in vacuum. To Vickers, it was always a blast of heat. Then the heat was real and the sun glared down through a haze thick enough to shift the orb far into the red. The intrusion vehicle lurched in a walloping spray. Ooze and reeds sloshed sideways to replace those scalloped out of the slough and transported to the hangar in Tel Aviv. The vehicle settled almost to the full depth of its legs.

"Christ on a crutch!" snarled Don Washman, hidden from Vickers by the piled gear. "Tell us it's a grassy clearing and drop us in a pissing swamp! Next time it'll be a kelp bed!" In a different voice he added, "Target."

All of Vickers' muscles had frozen when he thought they were about to drown. They were safe after all, though, and he turned to see the first dinosaur of the safari.

It was a duckbill—though the head looked more like that of a sheep than a duck. Jaw muscles and nasal passages filled the hollows of the snout which early restorations had left bare. The dinosaur had been dashing through the low pines fringing the slough when the crash and slap of the insertion caused it to rear up and attempt to stop. Reeds and water sprayed in a miniature echo of the commotion the vehicle itself had made.

The firm soil of the shore was only ten feet from the vehicle, roughly parallel to Side Four. The duckbill halted, almost in front of Washman and Jonathan Salmes. Scrabbling for traction in muck covered by two feet of water, the beast tried to reverse direction. The pilot leveled his grenade launcher but did not fire. Vickers stepped to the corner where he could see the target. It lacked the crests that made many similar species excellent trophies, but it was still two tons at point-blank range and the first dino the clients had seen in the flesh. "Go ahead," he said to Salmes. "It's yours."

The duckbill lunged back toward the shore, swinging the splayed toes of its right foot onto solid ground. Salmes' rifle slammed. It had an integral muzzle brake to help reduce recoil by redirecting muzzle gases sideways. The muzzle blast was redirected as well, a palpable shock in the thick air. The duckbill lurched, skidding nose-first through a tree. Its long hind legs bunched under it while the stubby forelegs braced to help the beast rise. If it could get to the well-beaten trail by which it had approached the slough, it would disappear.

"Good, good," said Vickers. His voice was tinny in his own ears because of the muzzle blast. "Now finish it with another one at the base of the tail." Fired from such short range, Salmes' bullet could be expected to range through the duckbill's body. It was certain to rip enough blood vessels to let the beast's life out quickly, and it might also break the spine.

The second shot did not come. The duckbill regained its feet. There was a rusty splotch of blood against the brown-patterned hide of its left shoulder. Vickers risked a look away from the shore to see what was the matter with Salmes. The client had a glazed expression on his face. His big rifle was raised, but its butt did not appear to be solidly resting on his shoulder. Don Washman wore a disgusted look. Beyond both gunners, Mr. McPherson knelt and shot holo tape of the beast leaping back toward the trees.

"Shoot, for Chrissake!" Vickers shouted.

Salmes' rifle boomed again. A triple jet of smoke flashed from the bore and muzzle brake. Salmes cried out as the stock hit him. The bullet missed even the fringe of ten-foot pine trees. The duckbill disappeared into them.

Vickers carefully did not look at Salmes—or Adrienne Salmes, standing immediately behind the guide with her rifle ready to shoot if directed. She had snickered after her husband's second shot. "First we'll find a dry campsite and move the gear," Vickers started to say.

The forest edge exploded as the duckbill burst back through it in the midst of a pack of dromaeosaurs.

In the first flaring confusion, there seemed to be a score of the smaller carnivores. In fact, there were only five—but that was quite enough. One had the duckbill by the throat and was wrapping forelegs around the herbivore's torso to keep from being shaken loose. The rest of the pack circled the central pair with the avidity of participants in a gang rape. Though the carnivores were bipedal, they bore a talon on each hind foot that was a sickle in size and lethality. Kicking from one leg, the hooting dromaeosaurs slashed through the duckbill's belly hide. Soft, pink coils of intestine spilled out into the water.

One of the half-ton carnivores cocked its head at the group on the intrusion vehicle. The men on Side Four were already spattered with the duckbill's blood. "Take 'em," Vickers said. He punched a steel-cored bullet through the nearest dromaeosaur's skull, just behind its eyes.

Washman and Adrienne Salmes fired while Vickers' cartridge case was still in the air. The pilot's grenade launcher chugged rather than banging, but the explosion of its projectile against the chest of a carnivore was loud even to ears numbed by the muzzle blasts of Salmes' rifle. The grenade was a caseless shaped charge which could be used point-blank without endangering the firer with fragments. Even so, the concussion from less than twenty feet rocked everyone on the near side of the vehicle. There was a red flash and a mist of pureed dinosaur. A foreleg, torn off at the shoulder, sailed straight into the air. Two of the dromaeosaurs bolted away from the blast, disappearing among the trees in flat arcs and sprays of dirt and pine straw.

Vickers' target had fallen where it stood. All four limbs jerked like those of a pithed frog. The dromaeosaur Adrienne Salmes had shot dropped momentarily, then sprang to its feet again. The tall woman worked the bolt of her rifle smoothly without taking the butt from her shoulder. The grenade explosion did not appear to have disconcerted her. The guide, poised to finish the beast, hesitated. Adrienne shot again and the dino's limbs splayed. Its dark green hide showed clearly the red and white rosette between the shoulders where the second bullet had broken its spine.

Dieter Jost leaned past Mr. McPherson and put a uranium penetrator through the brain of the duckbill, ending its pain. All four of the drowned dinosaurs continued to twitch.

"Jesus," said Don Washman quietly as he closed the breech on a grenade cartridge.

Although he had only fired once, Henry Vickers replaced the 20-round magazine of his Garand with a fresh one from his belt pouch. "Mr. McPherson," he said, "I hope you got good pictures, because I swear that's the most excitement I've had in a long time in this business."

Dieter had moved back to watch the slough with Steve Brady. Most of the clients crowded to Side Four to get a better view of the Cretaceous and its denizens. Adrienne Salmes had not moved from where she stood beside Vickers. She thumbed a second cartridge into the magazine of her rifle and closed the breech. "Still doubt I can shoot?" she asked with a smile.

"Heart and spine," the guide said. "No, I guess you can back me up any day of the week. I tell you, dromaeosaurs aren't as impressive as some of the larger carnivores, but they're just as dangerous." He looked more carefully at her rifle, a Schultz and Larsen with no ornamentation but the superb craftsmanship that had gone into its production. "Say, nice," Vickers said. "In .358 Norma?"

The blonde woman smiled with pleasure. "It's the same rifle I've used for everything from whitetails to elephant," she said. "I'd planned to bring something bigger, but after what you said, I had five hundred bullets cast from bronze and loaded at the factory for me. Johnnie—" she glanced at her husband, now loudly describing how he had shot the duckbill to the other clients. "Well," Adrienne continued quietly, "I'm the hunter in the household, not him. I told him he was crazy to have a cannon like that built, but he listens to me as badly as he listens to everyone else."

"That may be a problem," Vickers muttered. More loudly, he said, "All right, I think it's time to start setting up camp on top of this ridge. Around now, it's asking for trouble to be any closer than a hundred yards to the water, especially with this much meat nearby. After Steve and I get the ponies assembled, we'll need everybody's help to load them. Until then, just try not to get in the way."

Sometimes working with his hands helped Vickers solve problems caused by the human side of his safaris. It did not seem to do so on this occasion. Of course, a client who was both arrogant and gun-shy was a particularly nasty problem.

But Vickers was irritated to realize that it also bothered him that Don Washman and Mrs. Salmes seemed to be getting along very well together.

The campfire that evening provided an aura of human existence more important than the light of its banked coals. The clients had gone to sleep—or at least to their tents. That the Salmes at least were not asleep was evident from the sound of an argument. The double walls of the tents cut sound penetration considerably, but there were limits. Steve Brady shoved another log on the fire and said, "Damn, but I swear that chainsaw gets heavier every time I use it. Do you suppose the Israelis designed them to be air-dropped without parachutes?"

"You want a high horsepower-to-weight ratio, you don't use a diesel," agreed Dieter Jost with a shrug. "If you want a common fuel supply for everything and need diesel efficiency for the ponies, though—well, you get a heavy chainsaw."

"Can't imagine why she ever married him," Don Washman said. "Beef like that's a dime a dozen. Why, you know he didn't even have balls enough to chamber a third round? He's scared to death of that gun, scared almost to touch it now."

"Yeah," agreed Vickers, working a patch into the slot of his cleaning rod, "but the question's what to do about it. I don't have any good answers, God knows."

"Do?" Washman repeated. "Well, hell, leave him, of course. She's got money of her own—"

Brady broke into snorting laughter. Dieter grimaced and said, "Don, I do not think it is any business of ours how our clients live. The Salmes are adults and can no doubt solve their own problems." He pursed his lips. The fire threw the shadow of his bushy moustache misshapenly against his cheeks. "As for our problem, Henry, why don't we offer him the use of the camp gun? The .375? I think Mr. Salmes' difficulty is in precisely the same category as the more usual forms of mechanical breakdown or guns falling into the river."

"Fine with me if you can talk him into it," Vickers said dubiously, "but I wouldn't say Salmes is the sort to take a well-meant suggestion." He nodded toward the tent. The couple within seemed to be shouting simultaneously. "Or any other kind of suggestion," he added.

"Things would sure be simpler if they didn't allow booze on safaris," Brady said.

"Things would be simpler for us if our employers paid us to sleep all day and drink schnapps," said Dieter Jost. He tugged a lock of hair absently. "That does not comport well with economic realities, however. And so long as each of our clients has paid fifty thousand American dollars for the privilege of spending two weeks in the Cretaceous, it is unrealistic to assume that the staff will be treated as anything but the hired help. If drunken clients make the job more difficult, then that is simply one of the discomforts of the job. Like loading gear in the heat, or tracking down an animal that a client has wounded. It is easier for our employers, Mr. Stern and those above him, to hire new staff members than it would be to impose their underlings' view on persons of the sort who take time safaris."

"Moshe Cohn was head guide when I made my first insertion," said Vickers aloud. His cleaning rod rested on his lap beside the Garand, but he had not run it through the bore yet. "He told a client—a Texan, it was a US safari that time too—that he'd be better off to slack up a little on his drinking while he was in the field. The client was generally too stiff to see a dino, much less shoot one." The guide's forefinger tapped the breech of his rifle as he recalled the scene. "He said to Moshe, 'Jew-boy, you sound just like my third wife. One more word and I'll whip you with my belt, just like I did her.' Moshe broke his hand on the Texan's jaw. When we got back, the government—the Israeli but very pragmatic government—fired Moshe and denied him compensation for his hand. Ten days in the field with broken bones, remember." Vickers paused, then went on. "That taught me the rules. So far, I've been willing to live by them."

Don Washman laughed. "Right, when you hit a client, use your gunstock," he said and opened another beer.

Technically Steve Brady had the first watch, even though all four staff members were up. The alarm panel was facing Steve when it beeped, therefore. "Jesus!" the stubby, long-haired pilot blurted when he saw the magnitude of the signal fluorescing on the display. "Down the trail—must be a herd of something!"

Don Washman upset his fresh beer as he ran to the spade grips of the heavy machine-gun. It was in the center of the camp, on ground slightly higher than its immediate surroundings but by no means high enough to give the weapon an unbroken field of fire. The staff had sawed clear a campsite along the game trail leading down to the intrusion vehicle two hundred yards away. Assuming that animals were most likely to enter the area by the trail, Dieter had sited the tents on the other side of the gun. The next day they could assemble the six-foot high tower for the gun, but time had been too short to finish that the first night.

While the other staff members crouched over weapons, Vickers darted to the three occupied tents. The sensor loop that encircled the camp 100 yards out could pick up very delicate impacts and relay them to the display screen. This signal, however, was already shaking the ground. Miss McPherson poked her head out of the tent she shared with her brother. "What—" the dentist began.

The file of huge ceratopsians rumbled into sight on their way to the water to drink. They were torosaurs or a species equally large. In the dim glow of the fire, they looked more like machines than anything alive. Their beaks and the tips of their triple horns had a black glint like raku ware, and they averaged twice the size of elephants.

The tent that Mears and Brewer shared shuddered as both clients tried to force their way through the opening simultaneously. Vickers lifted the muzzles of their rifles skyward as he had been waiting to do. "No shooting now," he cried over the thunder of the dinosaurs. "In the morning we'll follow them up."

Adrienne Salmes slipped out of her tent before Vickers could reach over and take her rifle. It was pointed safely upward anyway. Despite the hour-long argument she had been engaged in, the blonde woman looked calm and alert. She looked breath-takingly beautiful as well—and wore only her rifle. "If you can wait a moment for my firepower," she said to Vickers without embarrassment, "I'll throw some clothes on." The guide nodded.

The bony frills at the back of the ceratopsians' skulls extended their heads to well over the height of a man. Less for protection than for muscle attachment, the frills locked the beasts' heads firmly to their shoulders. The bulging jaw muscles that they anchored enabled the ceratopsians to literally shear hardwood the thickness of a man's thigh. The last thing a safari needed was a herd of such monsters being stampeded through the camp. A beast wounded by a shot ill-aimed in the darkness could lead to just that result.

Mears and Brewer were staring at the rapid procession in wonder. The left eye of each torosaur glinted in the firelight. "Mother o' God, what a trophy!" Brewer said.

"Best in the world," Vickers agreed. "You'll go back with one, never fear." He looked at the McPhersons to his other side. The dentists were clutching their holo cameras, which were almost useless under the light conditions. "And you'll get your fill too," Vickers said. "The trip isn't cheap, but I've never yet guided a client who didn't think he'd gotten more than he bargained for." Though a drunken SOB like Jonathan Salmes might spoil that record, he added silently.

Adrienne Salmes re-emerged from her tent, wearing her coveralls and boots. Mears and Brewer had been so focused on the herd of torosaurs that the guide doubted the men had noticed her previous display. She was carrying a sleeping bag in addition to her rifle. Vickers raised an eyebrow. Adrienne nodded back at the tent. "Screaming beauty seems to have passed out," she said, "but I'm damned if I'll stay in the tent with him. Going on about his shoulder, for God's sake, and expecting sympathy from *me*. Is it all right if I doss down in the open?"

The ceratopsians were sporting in the water, making as much noise as the Waikiki surf. Vickers smiled. "They could eat tree trunks and drink mud," he said, as if he had not heard the client's question. "And I still meet people who think mammals are better adapted for survival than dinos were." He turned to Adrienne Salmes. "It's all right, so long as you stay out of the gun's way," he said, "but you'll wash away if it rains. And we're bound to get at least one real gully-washer while we're here."

"Hell, there's an easy answer to that," said Don Washman. He had strolled over to the tents when it became clear no predators had followed the torosaurs. "One of us is on watch all night, right? So there's always a slot open in the staff tents. Let noble hunter there sleep by himself, Hank. And she shoots well enough to be a pro, so let her stay dry with us too." He gave his engaging smile.

The other clients were listening with interest. "Maybe if Mr. McPherson wants to trade—" Vickers began in a neutral voice.

Adrienne Salmes hushed him with a grimace. "I'm a big girl now, Mr. Vickers," she snapped, "and I think I'm paying enough to make my own decisions. Don, if you'll show me the tent, I'll resume getting the sleep I've been assured I'll need in the morning."

Washman beamed. "Let's see," he said, "Steve's got watch at the moment, so I suppose you're my tentmate till I go on at four in the morning. . . ."

They walked toward the tent. Dieter, standing near the fire with his rifle cradled, looked from them to Vickers. Vickers shrugged. He was thinking about Moshe Cohn again.

"Platform to Mobile One," crackled the speaker of the unit clipped to Vickers' epaulet. Vickers threw the last of the clamps that locked the two ponies into a single, articulated vehicle. "Go ahead, Dieter," he said.

"Henry, the torosaurs must have run all night after they left the water," the other guide announced through the heavy static. "They're a good fifteen klicks west of camp. But there's a sauropod burn just three klicks south and close to the river. Do you want me to drop a marker?''

Vickers frowned. "Yeah, go ahead," he decided. He glanced at but did not really see the four clients, festooned with gear, who awaited his order to board the ponies. "Any sign of carnosaurs?"

"Negative," Dieter replied, "but we're still looking. I spotted what looked like a fresh kill when we were tracking the torosaurs. If we don't get any action here, I'll carry Miss McPherson back to that and see what we can stir up."

"Good hunting, Dieter," Vickers said. "We'll go take a look at your sauropods. Mobile One out." Again his eyes touched the clients. He appeared startled to see them intent on him. "All right," he said, "if you'll all board the lead pony. The other's along for trophies—sauropods this time, we'll get you the ceratopsians another day. Just pull down the jump seats."

The guide seated himself behind the tiller bar and clipped his rifle into its brackets. His clients stepped over the pony's low sides. The vehicle was the shape of an aluminum casket, scaled up by a half. A small diesel engine rode over the rear axle. Though the engine was heavily muffled, the valves sang trills which blended with the natural sounds of the landscape. Awnings were pleated into trays at either end of the vehicle, but for today the trees would be sun-screen enough.

Don Washman waved. He had strung a tarp from four trees at the edge of the clearing. In that shade he was pinning together the steel framework of the gun tower. The alarm and his grenade launcher sat beside him.

"Take care," Vickers called.

"You take care," the pilot responded with a broad grin. "Maybe I can lose the yo-yo and then we're all better off." He jerked his head toward the tent which still held Jonathan Salmes. Dieter had tried to arouse Salmes for breakfast. Because Vickers was sawing at the time, no one but Dieter himself heard what the client shouted. Dieter, who had served in at least three armies and was used to being cursed, had backed out of the tent with a white face. Vickers had shut down the saw, but the other guide had shaken his head. "Best to let him sleep, I think," he said.

Remembering the night before, Vickers wished that it was Brady and not Washman who had the guard that day. Oh, well. "Hold on," he said aloud. He put the pony into gear.

Just west of the crest on which they had set up camp, the height and separation of the trees increased markedly. Small pines and cycads were replaced by conifers that shot over one hundred feet in the air. Everything east of the ridgeline was in the floodplain, where the river drowned tree roots with a regularity that limited survival to the smaller, faster-growing varieties. The thick-barked monsters through which Vickers now guided the ponies were centuries old already. Barring lightning or tornado, they would not change appreciably over further centuries. They were the food of the great sauropods.

The forest was open enough to permit the pony to run at over 15 mph, close to its top speed with the load. The saplings and pale, broad-leafed ferns which competed for the dim light were easily brushed aside. Animal life was sparse, but as the pony skirted a fallen log, a turkey-sized coelurosaur sprang up with a large beetle in its jaws. Mears' .458 boomed. There was an echo-chamber effect from the log which boosted the muzzle blast to a near equal for that of the Salmes' .500. Everyone on the pony jumped—Vickers more than the rest because he had not seen the client level his rifle. The dinosaur darted away, giving a flick of its gray-feathered tail as it disappeared around a trunk.

"Ah, don't shoot without warning," the guide said, loudly but without looking around. "It's too easy to wound something that you should have had backup for. Besides, we should be pretty close to the sauropods—and they make much better targets."

Even as Vickers spoke, the forest ahead of them brightened. The upper branches still remained, but all the limbs had been stripped below the level of sixty feet. One tree had been pushed over. It had fallen to a 45° angle before being caught and supported by the branches of neighboring giants. The matted needles were strewn with fresh blankets of sauropod droppings. They had a green, faintly Christmasy scent. Vickers stopped the vehicle and turned to his clients. "We're getting very close," he said, "and there'll be plenty of shooting for everybody in just a moment. But there's also a chance of a pack of carnosaurs nearby for the same reason that we are. Keep your eyes open as we approach—and for *God's* sake don't shoot until I've said to." His eyes scanned the forest again and returned to Adrienne Salmes. A momentary remembrance of her the night before, a nude Artemis with rifle instead of bow, made him smile. "Mrs. Salmes," he said, "would you watch behind us, please? Carnivores are likely to strike up a burn as we did . . . and I can't watch behind us myself."

Adrienne grinned. "Why Mr. Vickers, I think you've just apologized for doubting I could shoot," she said. She turned and faced back over the towed pony, left arm through the sling of her rifle in order to brace the weapon firmly when she shot.

Vickers eased forward the hand throttle. They were past the marker beacon Dieter had dropped from the shooting platform. The responder tab on the guide's wrist had pulsed from green to red and was now lapsing back into fire-orange; he cut it off absently. The sound of the dinosaurs were audible to him now: the rumble of their huge intestines; the slow crackle of branches being stripped of their needles, cones, and bark by the sauropods' teeth; and occasional cooing calls which the clients, if they heard them over the ringing of the diesel, probably mistook for those of unseen forest birds.

The others did not see the sauropods even when Vickers cut the motor off. They were titanosaurs or a similar species, only middling huge for their sub-order. Vickers pointed. Mears, Brewer, and McPherson followed the line of the guide's arm, frowning. "It's all right now, Mrs. Salmes,"

Vickers said softly. "The dinos will warn us if predators get near." Adrienne Salmes faced around as well.

"Oh, Jesus Christ," someone whispered as he realized what Vickers was pointing out. It was incredible, even to the guide, how completely a score or more of thirty-ton animals could blend into an open forest. In part, it may have been that human minds were not used to interpreting as animals objects which weighed as much as loaded semis. Once recognized, the vast expanses of russet and black hide were as obvious as inkblot pictures which someone else has described.

Silently and without direction, McPherson stepped from the pony and spread the lenses of his camera. Vickers nodded to the others. "They won't pay attention to a normal voice," he said—in a quieter than normal voice. "Try to avoid sudden movements, though. They may think it's a warning signal of some kind." He cleared his throat. "I want each of you to mark a target—"

"That one!" whispered Mears urgently, a boy in the toystore, afraid his aunt will renege on her promise of a gift unless he acts at once. The big contractor was pointing at the nearest of the sauropods, a moderate-sized female only thirty feet away.

"Fine, but wait," the guide said firmly. "I'll position each of you. When I call 'fire,' go ahead—but only then. They won't attack anything our size, but they might step on one of us if they were startled at the wrong time. That big, they don't have to be hostile to be dangerous."

The nearby female, which had been browsing on limbs twenty feet high, suddenly stepped closer to a tree and reared up on her hind legs. She anchored herself to the trunk with her forefeet, each armed with a single long claw. It shredded bark as it gripped. With the grace and power of a derrick, the titanosaur's head swung to a high branch, closed, dragged along it for several yards. It left only bare wood behind.

With his left hand, Vickers aimed a pen-sized laser pointer. A red dot sprang out on the chest of the oblivious titanosaur. "There's your aiming point," the guide said. "If she settles back down before I give the signal, just hit her at the top of the shoulder."

Mears nodded, his eyes intent on the dinosaur.

Vickers moved Brewer five yards away, with a broadside shot at a large male. McPherson stood beside him, using a pan-head still camera on the six sauropods visible within a stone's throw. The dentist's hands were trembling with excitement.

Vickers took Adrienne Salmes slightly to the side, to within twenty yards of another male. He chose the location with an eye on the rest of the herd. Sauropods had a tendency to bolt straight ahead if aroused.

"Why does this one have bright red markings behind its eyes?" Adrienne asked.

"First time I ever saw it," the guide said with a shrug. "Maybe some professor can tell you when you get back with the head." He did not bother to gesture with the laser. "Ready?" he asked.

She nodded and aimed.

"Fire!"

The three gunners volleyed raggedly. The thick tree trunks acted as baffles, blurring the sharpness of the reports. The gunfire had the same feeling of muffled desecration as farts echoing in a cathedral. The red-flashed titanosaur began striding forward. Adrienne Salmes worked her bolt and fired again. A wounded animal gave a warning call, so loud and low-pitched that the humans' bowels trembled. Mrs. Salmes fired again. The titanosaur was a flickering picture in a magic lantern formed by open patches between six-foot tree boles. The huntress began to run after her disappearing prey.

Vickers grabbed her shoulder, halting her with an ease that belied his slender build. She turned on him in fury. "I won't let a wounded animal go!" she screamed.

"It won't go far," Vickers said. He released her. "We'll follow as soon as it's safe." He gestured, taking in the bellowing, mountainous forms padding in all directions among the even larger trees. "They'll circle in a moment. Then it'll be safe for things our size to move," he said.

Russet motion ceased, though the tidal bellowing of over a dozen sauropods continued. Brewer had lowered his rifle and was rubbing his shoulder with his left hand. "Let's get everybody together," the guide suggested, "and go finish off some trophies."

Brewer's expression was awed as they approached. "It really did fall," he said. "It was so big, I couldn't believe. . . . But I shot it where you said and it just ran into the tree." He waved. "And I kept shooting and it fell."

The haunches of the titanosaur were twice the height of a man, even with the beast belly-down in the loam. McPherson pointed at the great scars in the earth beneath the sauropod's tail. "It kept trying to move," he said in amazement. "Even though there was a tree in the way. It was kicking away, trying to get a purchase, and I thought the *tree* was going to go over. But it did. The, the dinosaur. And I have a tape of all of it!"

Mears, closest to the bellowing giants, was just as enthusiastic. "Like a shooting gallery!" he said, "but the tin ducks're the size of houses. God Almighty! I only brought one box of ammo with me. I shot off every last slug! God Almighty!"

The titanosaurs had quieted somewhat, but they were still making an odd series of sounds. The noises ranged from bird calls as before, to something like the venting of high-pressure steam. Vickers nodded and began walking toward the sounds. He had caught Adrienne Salmes' scowl of distaste at the contractor's recital. If the guide agreed, it was still not his business to say so.

The herd was larger than Vickers had estimated. Forty of the sauropods were in a circle facing outwards around a forest giant, which was so much bigger than its neighbors that it had cleared a considerable area. Several of the beasts were rearing up. They flailed the air with clawed forefeet and emitted the penetrating steam-jet hiss that seemed so incongruous from a living being. Mears raised his rifle with a convulsed look on his face before he remembered that he had no ammunition left.

McPherson was already rolling tape. "Have you reloaded?" the guide asked, looking from Salmes to Brewer. The blonde woman nodded curtly while the meat packer fumbled in the side pocket of his coveralls.

"I don't see the one I hit," Adrienne Salmes said. Her face was tight.

"Don't worry," the guide said quietly. "It's down, it couldn't have made it this far the way you hit it. It's the ones that weren't heart-shot that we're dealing with now."

"That's not my responsibility," she snapped.

"It's no duty you owe to me," Vickers agreed, "or to anything human."

Brewer snicked his bolt home. Vickers' laser touched the center of the chest of a roaring titanosaur. Orange pulmonary blood splashed its tiny head like a shroud. "On the word, Mr. Brewer," he said, "if you would."

Adrienne said, "All right." She did not look at Vickers.

Across the circle, eighty yards away, a large male was trying to lick its belly. Its long neck strained, but it was not flexible enough to reach the wound. The laser pointer touched below the left eye. "There?" the guide asked.

Adrienne nodded and braced herself, legs splayed. Her arms, sling, and upper body made a web of interlocking triangles.

The guide swung his own weapon onto the third of the wounded animals. "All right," he said.

Adrienne's Schultz and Larsen cracked. The light went out of the gut-shot sauropod's eye. Undirected, the rest of the great living machine began slowly to collapse where it stood. Brewer was firing, oblivious of his bruised shoulder in the excitement. Vickers put three rounds into the base of his own target's throat. Its head and neck were weaving too randomly to trust a shot at them.

Either the muzzle blasts or the sight of three more of their number sagging to the ground routed the herd. Their necks swung around like compass needles to iron. With near simultaneity, all the surviving titanosaurs drifted away from the guns. Their tails were held high off the ground.

Adrienne Salmes lowered her rifle. "God Almighty, let me use that!" Mears begged, reaching out for the weapon. "I'll pay you—"

"Touch me and I'll shove this up your bum, you bloody butcher!" the blonde woman snarled.

The contractor's fist balled. He caught himself, however, even before he realized that the muzzle of the .358 had tilted in line with his throat.

"The river isn't that far away," said Vickers, pointing in the direction the sauropods had run. "We'll follow in the pony—it's a sight worth seeing. And taping," he added.

The undergrowth slowed the hunters after they recrossed the ridgeline, but the titanosaurs were still clearly evident. Their heads and even hips rocked above the lower vegetation that sloped toward the river. The herd, despite its size and numbers, had done surprisingly little damage to its rush to the water. The pony repeatedly had to swing aside from three-inch saplings which had sprung back when the last of the titanosaurs had passed.

But the beasts themselves were slowed by the very mechanics of their size. Their twelve-foot strides were ponderously slow even under the goad of panic. The tensile strength of the sauropods' thigh bones simply was not equal to the acceleration of the beasts' mass to more than what would be a fast walk in a man. The hunters reached a rocky spur over the mudflats fringing the water just as the leading titanosaurs splashed into the stream 150 yards away. The far bank of the river was lost in haze. The sauropods continued to advance without reference to the change in medium. Where a moment before they had been belly-deep in reeds, now they were belly-deep in brown water that was calm except for the wakes of their passage. When the water grew deeper, the procession sank slowly. The beasts farthest away, in mid-stream over a quarter mile out, were floating necks and tails while the forefeet propelled them by kicking down into the bottom muck.

"Don't they hide underwater and snorkel through their necks?" Brewer asked. Then he yipped in surprise as his hand touched the barrel of his Weatherby. The metal was hot enough to burn from strings of rapid fire and the Cretaceous sunlight.

Vickers nodded. He had heard the question often before. "Submarines breathe through tubes because the tubes are steel and the water pressure doesn't crush them," he explained. "Sauropods don't have armored gullets, and their lungs aren't diesel engines inside a steel pressure hull. Physics again. Besides, they float—the only way they could sink would be to grab a rock."

As Vickers spoke, the last titanosaur in the line sank.

"Well, I'll be damned!" the guide blurted.

The sauropod surfaced again a moment later. It blew water from its lungs as it gave the distress cry that had followed the shooting earlier.

The mild current of the river had bent the line of titanosaurs into a slight curve. The leaders were already disappearing into the haze. None of the other beasts even bothered to look back to see the cause of the bellowing. No doubt they already knew.

The stricken titanosaur sank again. It rolled partly onto its left side as it went under the surface this time. It was still bellowing, wreathing its head in a golden spray as it disappeared.

"I think," said Adrienne Salmes dryly, "that this time the rock grabbed the dinosaur."

Vickers grunted in reply. He was focusing his binoculars on the struggle.

Instead of rising vertically, the sauropod rolled completely over sideways. Clinging to the herbivore's left foreleg as it broke surface was something black and huge and as foul as a tumor. The linked beasts submerged again in an explosion of spray. Vickers lowered the binoculars, shivering. They were not common, even less commonly seen. Great and terrible as they were, they were also widely hated. For them to sun themselves on mudbanks as their descendants did would have been to court death by the horns and claws of land animals equally large. But in their own element, in the still, murky waters, they were lords without peer.

"Christ Almighty," Mears said, "was that a whale?"

"A crocodile," the guide replied, staring at the roiling water. "Enough like what you'd find in the Nile or the Congo that you couldn't tell the difference by a picture. Except for the size." He paused, then continued, "The science staff will be glad to hear about this. They always wondered if they preyed on the big sauropods too. It seems that they preyed on *any* goddam thing in the water."

"I'd swear it was bigger than the tyrannosaurus you showed us," Adrienne Salmes observed, lowering her own binoculars.

Vickers shrugged. "As long, at least. Probably heavier. I looked at a skull, a fossil in London . . . I don't know how I'd get one back as a trophy. . . . It was six feet long, which was impressive; and three feet wide, which was incredible, a carnivore with jaws three feet *wide*. Tyrannosaurs don't compare, no. Maybe whales do, Mr. Mears. But nothing else I know of."

There were no longer any titanosaurs visible. The herd had curved off down-stream, past the intrusion vehicle and the hunting camp. They were lost against the haze and the distant shoreline by now. The water still stirred where the last of them had gone down, but by now the struggles must have been the thrashings of the sauropod's autonomic nervous system. The teeth of the crocodile were six inches long; but they were meant only to hold, not to kill. The water killed, drowning a thirty-ton sauropod as implacably as it would any lesser creature anchored to the bottom by the crocodile's weight.

"We'd best take our trophies," Vickers said at last. No one in the world knew his fear of drowning, no one but himself. "The smell'll bring a pack of gorgosaurs soon, maybe even a tyrannosaur. I don't want that now, not with us on the ground."

The guide rubbed his forehead with the back of his left hand, setting his bush hat back in place carefully. "The ponies convert to boats," he said, patting the aluminum side. "The tread blocks can be rotated so they work like little paddle wheels." He paused as he swung the tiller bar into a tight circle. "I guess you see why we don't use them for boats in the Cretaceous," he added at last. "And why we didn't keep our camp down on the intrusion vehicle."

Vickers was even quieter than his wont for the rest of the morning.

The shooting platform had returned before the ponies did, the second of them dripping with blood from the titanosaur heads. Two heads had Mears' tags on them, though the contractor had finished none of the beasts he had wounded. The best head among those he had sprayed would have been the one the guide had directed Adrienne Salmes to kill—with a bullet through the skull that destroyed all trophy value.

There were no game laws in the Cretaceous, but the line between hunters and butchers was the same as in every other age.

The McPhersons greeted each other with mutual enthusiasm. Their conversation was technical and as unintelligible to non-photographers as the conversation of any other specialists. Jonathan Salmes was sitting on a camp stool, surly but alert. He did not greet the returning party, but he watched the unloading of the trophies with undisguised interest. The right side of his face was puffy.

"We've found a tyrannosaur," Dieter called as he and the pilots joined Vickers. That was good news, but there was obvious tension among the other members of the staff. Brady carried a spray gun loaded with antiseptic sealer. A thorough coating would prevent decay for almost a month, ample time to get the heads to proper taxidermists.

When Dieter was sure that all the clients were out of earshot, he said in a low voice, "Don has something to tell you, Henry."

"Eh?" prompted Vickers. He set one of the sauropod heads on the spraying frame instead of looking at the pilot.

"I had to clobber Salmes," Washman said, lifting out the red-flashed trophy. "He was off his head—I'm not sure he even remembers. There was a mixed herd of duckbills came down the trail. He came haring out of his tent with that gun of his. He didn't shoot, though, he started chasing them down the trail." The pilot straightened and shrugged. Steve Brady began pumping the spray gun. The pungent mist drifted downwind beyond the gaping heads. "I grabbed him. I mean, who knows what might be following a duckbill? When he swung that rifle at me, I had to knock him out for his own good. Like a drowning man." Washman shrugged again. "His gun wasn't even loaded, you know?"

"Don, run the ponies down to the water and mop them out, will you?" Vickers said. The pilot jumped onto the leading vehicle and spun them off down the trail. The two guides walked a little to the side, their rifles slung, while Brady finished sealing the trophies. "It's going to have to be reported, you know," Vickers said. "Whether Salmes does or not."

"You or I might have done the same thing," Dieter replied.

"I'm not denying that," the senior guide snapped. "But it has to be reported."

The two men stood in silence, looking out at a forest filled with sounds that were subtly wrong. At last Dieter said, "Salmes goes up in the platform with you and Don tomorrow, doesn't he?"

Vickers agreed noncommitally.

"Maybe you ought to go with Steve instead," Dieter suggested. He looked at Vickers. "Just for the day, you know."

"Washman just flies us," Vickers said with a shake of his head. "I'm the one that's in contact with the client. And Don's as good as pilots come."

"That he is," the other guide agreed, "that he is. But he is not a piece of furniture. You are treating him as a piece of furniture."

Vickers clapped his companion on the shoulder. "Come on," he said, "Salmes'll be fine when he gets his tyrannosaur. What we ought to be worrying about is three more for the others. If Salmes goes home with a big boy and the rest have to settle for less—well, it says no guarantees in the contracts, but you know the kind of complaints the company gets. That's the kind of problem we're paid to deal with. If they wanted shrinks instead of guides, they'd have hired somebody else."

Dieter laughed half-heartedly. "Let us see what we can arrange for lunch," he said. "At the moment, I am more interested in sauropod steak than I am in the carnivores that we compete with."

"Damn, the beacon cut out again!" Washman snarled. There was no need of an intercom system; the shooting platform operated with only an intake whine which was no impediment to normal speech. The silence was both a boon to coordination and a help in not alarming the prey. It did, however, mean that the client was necessarily aware of any technical glitches. When the client was Jonathan Salmes—

"God damn, you're not going to put *me* on that way!" the big man blazed. He had his color back and with it all his previous temper. Not that the bruise over his right cheekbone would have helped. "One of the others paid you to save the big one for them, didn't they?" he demanded. "By God, I'll bet it was my wife! And I'll bet it wasn't money either, the—"

"Take us up to a thousand feet," Vickers said sharply. "We'll locate the kill visually if the marker isn't working. Eighty tons of sauropod shouldn't be hard to spot."

"Hang on, there it's on again," said the pilot. The shooting platform veered slightly as he corrected their course. Vickers and Salmes stood clutching the rail of the suspended lower deck which served as landing gear as well. Don Washman was seated above them at the controls, with the fuel tank balancing his mass behind. The air intake and exhaust extended far beyond the turbine itself to permit the baffling required for silent running. The shooting platform was as fragile as a dragonfly; and it was, in its way, just as efficient a predator.

By good luck, the tyrannosaur had made its skill on the edge of a large area of brush rather than high forest. The platform's concentric-shaft rotors kept blade length short. Still, though it was possible to maneuver beneath the forest canopy, it was a dangerous and nerve-wracking business to do so. Washman circled the kill at 200 feet, high enough that he did not need to allow for trees beneath him. Though the primary airflow from the rotors was downward, the odor of tens of tons of meat dead in the sun still reached the men above. The guide tried to ignore it with his usual partial success. Salmes only wrinkled his nose and said, "Whew, what a pong." Then, "Where is it? The tyrannosaurus?"

That the big killer was still nearby was obvious from the types of scavengers on the sauropod. Several varieties of the smaller coelurosaurs scrambled over the corpse like harbor rats on a drowned man. None of the species weighed more than a few hundred pounds. A considerable flock of pterosaurs joined and squabbled with the coelurosaurs, wings tented and toothless beaks stabbing out like shears. There were none of the large carnivores around the kill—and that implied that something was keeping them away.

"Want me to go down close to wake him up?" Washman asked.

The guide licked his lips. "I guess you'll have to," he said. "There was always a chance that a pterodactyl would be sucked into the turbine when you hovered over a kill. The thought of dropping into a big carnosaur's lap that way kept some guides awake at night. Vickers looked at his client and added, "Mr. Salmes, we're just going to bring the tyrannosaur out of wherever it's lying up in the forest. After we get it into the open, we'll maneuver to give you the best shot. All right?"

Salmes grunted. His hands were tight on his beautifully finished rifle. He had refused Dieter's offer of the less-bruising camp gun with a scorn that was no less grating for being what all the staff had expected.

Washman dropped them vertically instead of falling in a less wrenching spiral. He flared the blades with a gentle hand, however, feathering the platform's descent into a hover without jarring the gunners. They were less than thirty feet in the air. Pterosaurs, more sensitive to moving air than the earth-bound scavengers, squealed and hunched their wings. The ones on the ground could not take off because the downdraft anchored them. The pilot watched carefully the few still circling above them.

"He's—" Vickers began, and with his word the tyrannosaur strode into the sunlight. Its bellow was intended to chase away the shooting platform. The machine trembled as the sound induced sympathetic vibrations in its rotor blades. Coelurosaurs scattered. The cries of the pterosaurs turned to blind panic as the downdraft continued to frustrate their attempts to rise. The huge predator took another step forward. Salmes raised his rifle. The guide cursed under his breath but did not attempt to stop him.

At that, it should have been an easy shot. The tyrannosaur was within thirty feet of the platform and less than ten feet below them. All it required was that Salmes aim past the large head as it swung to counterweight a stride and rake down through the thorax. Perhaps the angle caused him to shoot high, perhaps he flinched. Vickers, watching the carnosaur over his own sights, heard the big rifle crash. The tyrannosaur strode forward untouched, halving the distance between it and the platform.

"Take us up!" the guide shouted. If it had not been a rare trophy, he might have fired himself and announced that he had "put in a bullet to finish the beast". There were three other gunners who wanted a tyrannosaur, though; if Salmes took this one back, it would be after he had shot it or everyone else had an equal prize.

Salmes was livid. He gripped the bolt handle, but he had not extracted the empty case. "God damn you!" he screamed. "You made it wobble to throw me off! You son of a bitch, you robbed me!"

"Mr. Salmes—" Vickers said. The tyrannosaur was now astride the body of its prey, cocking its head to see the shooting platform fifty feet above it.

"By God, you want another chance?" Washman demanded in a loud voice. The platform plunged down at a steep angle. The floor grating blurred the sight of the carnosaur's mottled hide. Its upturned eye gleamed like a strobe-lit ruby.

"Jesus *Christ!*" Vickers shouted. "Take us the hell up, Washman!"

The plaform steadied, pillow soft, with its floor fifteen feet from the ground and less than twenty from the tyrannosaur. Standing on the sauropod's corpse, the great predator was eye to eye with Vickers and his client. The beast bellowed again as it lunged. The impulse of its clawed left leg rolled the sauropod's torso.

Salmes screamed and threw his rifle to the grating. The guide leveled his Garand. He was no longer cursing Washman. All of his being was focused on what would be his last shot if he missed it. Before he could fire, however, the shooting platform slewed sideways. Then they were out of the path of the charging dinosaur and beginning to circle with a safe thirty feet of altitude. Below them, the tyrannosaur clawed dirt as it tried to follow.

Salmes was crying uncontrollably.

"Ah, want me to hold it here for a shot?" Washman asked nervously.

"We'll go on back to the camp, Don," the guide said. "We'll talk there, all right?"

"Whatever you say."

Halfway back, Vickers remembered he had not dropped another marker to replace the one that was malfunctioning. God knew, that was the least of his problems.

"You know," Brewer said as he forked torosaur steaks onto the platter, "it tastes more like buffalo than beef; but if we could get some breeding stock back, I'd by God find a market for it!"

Everyone seemed to be concentrating on their meat—good, if pale and lean in comparison with feed-lot steer. "Ah," Vickers said, keeping his voice nonchalant. He looked down at the table instead of the people sitting around it. "Ah, Dieter and I were talking. . . . We'll bunk outside tonight. The, ah, the rest of that pack of dromaeosaurs chased some duckbills through the camp this morning, Steve thinks. So just for safety's sake, we'll both be out of the tent. . . . So, ah, Mrs. Salmes—"

Everyone froze. Jonathan Salmes was turning red. His wife had a forkful of steak poised halfway to her mouth and her eyebrows were rising. The guide swallowed, his eyes still fixed on his plate, and plowed on. "That is, you can have your own tent. Ah, to sleep in."

"Thank you," Adrienne Salmes said coolly, "but I'm quite satisfied with the present arrangements."

Dieter had refused to become involved in this, saying that interfering in the domestic affairs of the Salmes was useless at best. Vickers was sweating now, wishing that there was something to shoot instead of nine pairs of human eyes fixed on him. "Ah," he repeated, "Mrs. Salmes—"

"Mr. Vickers," she overrode him, "who I choose to sleep with—in any sense of the term—is none of your business. Anyone's business," she added with a sharp glance across the table at her husband.

Jonathan Salmes stood up, spilling his coffee cup. His hand closed on his fork; each of the four staff members made unobtrusive preparations. Cursing, Salmes flung the fork down and stalked back to his tent.

The others eased. Vickers muttered, "Christ." Then, "Sorry, Dieter, I. . . ." The thing that bothered him most about the whole incident was that he was unsure whether he would have said anything at all had it been Miss McPherson in Don's bed instead of someone he himself found attractive. Christ. . . .

"Mr. Vickers?" Adrienne Salmes said in a mild voice.

"Umm?" His steak had gotten cold. With Brewer cutting and broiling the meat, the insertion group was eating better than Vickers could ever remember.

"I believe Mr. Brady is scheduled to take me up in the platform tomorrow?"

"Yeah, that's right," Vickers agreed, chewing very slowly.

"I doubt my—husband—will be going out again tomorrow," the blonde woman continued with a nod toward his tent. "Under the circumstances, I think it might be better if Mr. Brady were left behind here at the camp. Instead of Don."

"Steve?" Dieter asked.

Brady shrugged. "Sure, I don't need the flying time. But say—I'm not going to finish ditching around the tents by myself. I've got blisters from today."

"All right," said Dieter. "Henry, you and Don—" no one was looking directly at Washman, who was blushing in embarrassment he had damned well brought on himself—"will take Mrs. Salmes up after the tyrannosaur tomorrow." Vickers and Brady both nodded. "The rest of us will wait here to see if the duckbills come through again as they have become accustomed. Steve, I will help you dig. And if the duckbills have become coy, we will ride down the river margin a little later in the morning and find them. Perhaps Mr. Salmes will feel like going with us by then."

Thank God for Dieter, Vickers thought as he munched another bite of his steak. He could always be counted on to turn an impossible social situation into a smoothly functioning one. There would be no trouble tomorrow after all.

The bulging heads of three torosaurs lay between the gun tower and the fire. There the flames and the guard's presence would keep away the small mammals that foraged in the night. As Miss McPherson followed her brother to their tent, she paused and fingered one of the brow horns of the largest trophy. The tip of the horn was on a level with the dentist's eyes, even though the skull lay on the ground. "They're so huge, so . . . powerful," she said. "And for them to fall when you shoot at them, so many of them falling and running. . . . I could never understand men who, well, who shot animals. But with so many of them everywhere—it's as if you were throwing rocks at the windows of an abandoned house, isn't it? It doesn't seem to hurt anything, and it's . . . an attractive feeling."

"Mary!" objected her brother, shadowed by the great heads.

"Oh, I don't mean I'm sorry that I didn't bring a gun," continued Mary McPherson calmly, her fingers continuing to stroke the smooth black horn. "No, I'm glad I didn't. Because if I had had a gun available this morning, I'm quite sure I would have used it. And after we return, I suppose I would regret that. I suppose." She walked off toward the tent. The rhythms of her low-voiced argument with her brother could be heard until the flaps were zipped.

"Dieter tells me they bagged sixteen torosaurs today," Vickers said. "Even though the intrusion vehicle hasn't room for more than one per client." Only Washman, who had the watch, and Adrienne Salmes were still at the campfire with him.

"*I* bagged one," the woman said with an emphatic flick of her cigar. "Jack Brewer shot five: and I sincerely hope that idiot Mears hit no more than ten, because that's all Dieter and I managed to finish off for him." She had unpinned her hair as soon as she came in from the field. In the firelight it rolled across her shoulders like molten amber.

"Dieter said that too," Vickers agreed. He stood, feeling older than usual. "That's why I said 'they'." He turned and began to walk back to the tent where Dieter was already asleep. There had been no point in going through with the charade of sleeping under the stars—overcast, actually—since the dromaeosaurs were daylight predators. They were as unlikely to appear in the camp after dark as the Pope was to speak at a KKK rally.

To the guide's surprise—and to Don Washman's—Adrienne rustled to her feet and followed. "Mr. Vickers," she said, "might I speak to you for a moment, please?"

Vickers looked at her. As the staff members did, and unlike the other clients, the blonde woman carried her weapon with her at all times. "All right," he said. They walked by instinct to the shooting platform, standing thirty feet away at the end of the arc of tents. The torosaur heads were monstrous silhouettes against the fire's orange glow. "Would it bother you as much if I were a man?" she asked bluntly.

"Anything that makes my job harder bothers me," Vickers said in half-truth. "You and Don are making my job harder. That's all."

Adrienne stubbed out her small cigar on the platform's rail. She scattered the remnants of the tobacco on the rocky soil. "Balls," she said distinctly. "Mr. Vickers—Henry, for Christ's sake—my husband was going to be impossible no matter what. He's here because I was going on a time safari and he was afraid to look less of a man than his wife was. Which he is. But he was going to be terrified of his rifle, he was going to pack his trunk with Scotch, and he was going to be a complete prick because that's the way he is."

"Mrs. Salmes—"

"Adrienne, and let me finish. I didn't marry Jonathan for his money—my family has just as much as his does. I won't claim it was a love match, but we . . . we seemed to make a good pair. A matched set, if you will. He won't divorce me—" her dimly-glimpsed index finger forestalled another attempt by the guide to break in—"because he correctly believes I'd tell the judge and the world that he couldn't get it up on our wedding night. Among other things. I haven't divorced him because I've never felt a need to. There are times that it's been marvelously useful to point out that 'I *do* after all have a husband, dearest. . . .' "

"This is none of my business, Mrs. Salmes—"

"Adrienne!"

"Adrienne, dammit!" Vickers burst out. "It's none of my business, but I'm going to say it anyway. You don't have anything to prove. That's fine, we all should be that way. But most of my clients have a lot to prove, to themselves and to the world. Or they wouldn't be down here in the Cretaceous. It makes them dangerous, because they're out of normal society and they may not be the men they hoped they were after all. And your husband is very God damned dangerous, Adrienne. Take my word for it."

"Well, it's not *my* fault," the woman said.

"Fault?" the guide snapped. "Fault? Is it a pusher's fault that kids OD on skag? You're goddamn right it's your fault! It's the fault of everybody involved who doesn't make it better, and you're sure not making it better. Look, you wouldn't treat a gun that way—and your husband is a human being!"

Adrienne frowned in surprise. There was none of the anger Vickers had expected in her voice when she said, "So are you, Henry. You shouldn't try so hard to hide the fact."

Abruptly, the guide strode toward his tent. Adrienne Salmes watched him go. She took out another cigar, paused, and walked carefully back to the fire where Washman waited with the alarm panel. The pilot looked up with concern. Adrienne sat beside him and shook her hair loose. "Here you go, Don sweetest," she said, extending her cigar. "Why don't you light it for me? It's one of the things you do so well."

Washman kissed her. She returned it, tonguing his lips; but when his hand moved to the zipper of her coveralls, she forced it away. "That's enough until you go off guard duty, dearest,'' she said. She giggled. ''Well—almost enough.''

Jonathan Salmes hunched in the shadow of the nearest torosaur head. He listened, pressing his fists to his temples. After several more minutes, he moved in a half-crouch to the shooting platform. In his pocket was a six-inch wooden peg, smooth and close-grained. It was whittled from a root he had worried from the ground with his fingers. Stepping carefully so that his boots did not scrunch on the metal rungs, Salmes mounted the ladder to the pilot's seat. He paused there, his khaki coveralls strained, white face reflecting the flames. The couple near the fire did not look up. The pilot was murmuring something, but his voice was pitched too low to hear . . . and the words might have been unintelligible anyway, given the circumstances.

Jonathan Salmes shuddered also. He moved with a slick grace that belied the terror and disgust frozen on his face. He slipped the dense peg from his pocket. Stretching his right arm out full length while he gripped the rotor shaft left-handed, Salmes forced the peg down between two of the angled blades of the stator. When he was finished, he scrambled back down the ladder. He did not look at his wife and the pilot again, but his ears could not escape Adrienne's contented giggle.

''Hank, she just isn't handling right this morning,'' Don Washman said. ''I'm going to have to blow the fuel lines out when we get back. Must've gotten some trash in the fuel transferring from the bladder to the cans to the tank. Wish to hell we could fuel the bird directly, but I'm damned if I'm going to set down on the intrusion vehicle where it's sitting now.''

Vickers glanced down at the treetops and scowled. ''Do you think we ought to abort?'' he asked. He had not noticed any difference in the flight to that point. Now he imagined they were moving slower and nearer the ground than was usual, and both the rush of air and the muted turbine whine took on sinister notes.

''Oh . . . ,'' the pilot said. ''Well, she's a lot more likely to clear herself than get worse—the crud sinks to the bottom of the tank and gets sucked up first. It'll be okay. I mean, she's just a little sluggish, is all.''

The guide nodded. ''M—'' he began. After his outburst of the night before, he was as embarrassed around Adrienne Salmes as a boy at his first dance. ''Ah, Adrienne, what do you think?''

The blonde woman smiled brightly, both for the question and the way it was framed. ''Oh, if Don's willing to go on, there's no question,'' she said. ''You know I'd gladly walk if it were the only way to get a tyrannosaurus, Henry—if you'd let me, I mean. We both know that when we go back in today, I've had my last chance at a big carnosaur until you've rotated through all your clients again. Including my husband.''

''We'll get you a tyrannosaur,'' Vickers said.

Adrienne edged slightly closer to the guide. She said softly, ''Henry, I want you to know that when we get back I'm going to give Johnnie a divorce.''

Vickers turned away as if slapped. ''That's none of my business,'' he said. ''I—I'm sorry for what I said last night.''

''Sorry?'' the woman repeated in a voice that barely carried over the wind noise. ''For making me see that I shouldn't make a doormat of . . . someone who used to be important to me? Don't be sorry.'' After a pause, she continued, ''When I ran for Congress. . . . God I was young! I offended it must have been everybody in the world, much less the district. But Johnnie was fantastic. I owe what votes I got to hands he shook for me.''

''I had no right to talk,'' Vickers said. By forcing himself, he managed to look the blonde woman in the eyes.

Adrienne smiled and touched his hand where it lay on the forestock of his rifle. ''Henry,'' she said, ''I'm not perfect, and the world's not going to be perfect either. But I can stop trying to make it actively worse.''

Vickers looked at the woman's hand. After a moment, he rotated his own to hold it. ''You've spent your life being the best man around,'' he said, as calm as he would be in the instant of shooting. ''I think you've got it in you to be the best person around instead. I'm not the one to talk . . . but I think I'd be more comfortable around people if more of them were the way you could be.''

With a final squeeze, Vickers released Adrienne's hand. During the remainder of the fifteen-minute flight, he concentrated on the ground below. He almost forgot Washman's concern about the engine.

Dieter Jost flicked a last spadeful of gritty soil from the drainage ditch and paused. Steve Brady gave him a thumbs-up signal from the gun tower where he sat. ''Another six inches, peon,'' he called to the guide. ''You need to sweat some.''

''Fah,'' said Dieter, laughing. ''If it needs to be deeper, the rain will wash it deeper—not so?'' He dug the spade into the ground and began walking over to the table. They had found a cache of sauropod eggs the day before. With the aid of torosaur loin and freeze-dried spices from his kit, Brewer had turned one of them into a delicious omelet. Brewer, Mears, and the McPhersons were just finishing. Dieter, who had risen early to finish ditching the tents, had worked up quite an appetite.

''Hey!'' Brady called. Then, louder, ''Hey! Mr. Salmes, that's not safe! Come back here, please!''

The guide's automatic rifle leaned against the gun tower. He picked it up. Jonathan Salmes was carrying his own rifle and walking at a deliberate pace down the trail to the water. He did not look around when the guard shouted. The other clients were staring in various stages of concern. Cradling his weapon, Dieter trotted after Salmes. Brady, standing on the six-foot tower, began to rotate the heavy machinegun. He stopped when he realized what he was doing.

The guide reached Salmes only fifty yards from the center of the camp, still in sight of the others. He put a hand on the blond man's shoulder and said, "Now, Mr. Salmes—"

Salmes spun like a mousetrap snapping. His face was white. He rang his heavy rifle off Dieter's skull with enough force to tear the stock out of his hands. The guide dropped as if brainshot. Salmes backed away from the fallen man. Then he turned and shambled out of sight among the trees.

"God damn!" Steve Brady said, blinking in surprise. Then he thought of something even more frightening. He unslung his grenade launcher and jumped to the ground without bothering to use the ladder. "If that bastard gets to the intrusion vehicle—" he said aloud, and there was no need for him to finish the statement.

Brady vaulted the guide's body without bothering to look at the injury. The best thing he could do for Dieter now was to keep him from being stranded in the Cretaceous. Brady's hobnails skidded where pine needles overlay rock, but he kept his footing. As the trail twisted around an exceptionally large tree, Brady caught sight of the client again. Salmes was not really running; or rather, he was moving like a man who had run almost to the point of death.

"Salmes, God damn you!" Brady called. He raised the grenade launcher. Two dromaeosaurs burst from opposite sides of the trail where they lay ambushed. Their attention had been on Salmes; but when the guard shouted, they converged on him.

The leftward dromaeosaur launched itself toward its prey in a flat, twenty-foot leap. Only the fact that Brady had his weapon aimed permitted him to disintegrate the beast's head with a point-blank shot. Death did nothing to prevent the beast from disemboweling Brady reflexively. The two mutilated bodies were thrashing in a tangle of blood and intestines as the remaining clients hurtled around the tree. They skidded to a halt. Mr. McPherson, who held Salmes' rifle—his sister had snatched up Dieter's FN a step ahead of him—began to vomit. Neither Salmes nor the other dromaeosaur were visible.

Jonathan Salmes had in fact squelched across the mud and up the ramp of the intrusion vehicle. He had unscrewed the safety cage from the return switch and had his hand poised on the lever. Something clanged on the ramp behind him.

Salmes turned. The dromaeosaur, panicked by the grenade blast that pulped its companion's head, was already in the air. Salmes screamed and threw the switch. The dromaeosaur flung him back against the fuel bladder. As everything around it blurred, the predator picked Salmes up with its forelegs and began methodically to kick him to pieces with its right hind foot. The dinosaur was still in the process of doing so when the submachineguns of the startled guards raked it to death with equal thoroughness.

The broad ribs of the sauropod thrust up from a body cavity that had been cleared of most of its flesh. There was probably another meal on the haunches, even for a beast of the tyrannosaur's voracity. If Adrienne missed the trophy this morning, however, Vickers would have to shoot another herbivore in the vicinity in order to anchor the prize for the next client.

Not that there was much chance that the blonde woman was going to miss.

Adrienne held her rifle with both hands, slanted across her chest. Her hip was braced against the guardrail as she scanned the forest edge. If she had any concern for her balance, it was not evident.

"Okay, down to sixty," Don Washman said, barely enough height to clear the scrub oaks that humped over lower brush in the clearing. The lack of grasses gave the unforested areas of the Cretaceous an open aspect from high altitude. Lower down, the spikes and wooden fingers reached out like a hedge of spears.

The tyrannosaur strode from the pines with a hacking challenge.

"Christ, he's looking for us," the pilot said. The carnosaur slammed aside the ribs of its kill like bowling pins. Its nostrils were flared, and the sound it made was strikingly different from the familiar bellows of earlier occasions.

"Yeah, that's its territorial call," Vickers agreed. "It seems to have decided that we're another tyrannosaur. It's not just talking, it wants our blood."

"S'pose Salmes really hit it yesterday?" Washman asked.

Vickers shook his head absently. "No," he said, "but the way you put the platform in its face after it'd warned us off. . . . Only a tyrannosaur would challenge another tyrannosaur that way. They don't have much brain, but they've got lots of instinctive responses; and the response we've triggered is, well . . . a good one to give us a shot. You ready, Adrienne?"

"Tell me when," the blonde woman said curtly. Washman was swinging the platform in loose figure-8s about 150 yards distant from the carnosaur. They could not circle at their present altitude because they were too low to clear the conifer backdrop. Adrienne aimed the Schultz and Larsen when the beast was on her side of the platform, raising the muzzle again each time the pilot swung onto the rear loop of the figure.

"Don, see if you can draw him out from the woods a little farther," the guide said, squinting past the barrel of his Garand. "I'd like us to have plenty of time to nail him before he can go to ground in the trees."

"Ah, Hank . . . ," the pilot began. Then he went on, "Oh, hell, just don't blow your shots. That's all I ask." He put the controls over and wicked up. There was a noticeable lag before the turbine responded to the demand for increased power. The section of root slapped as it vibrated from the stator and shot into the rotors spinning at near-maximum velocity.

"If you'll stand over here, Mis—Adrienne," Vickers said, stepping to the back rail of the platform. The client followed with brittle quickness. "When I say shoot," Vickers continued, "aim at the middle of the chest."

Washman had put the platform in an arc toward the tyrannosaur. The big carnivore lunged forward with a series of choppy grunts like an automatic cannon. The pilot rotated the platform on its axis, a maneuver he had carried out a thousand times before. This time the vehicle dipped. It was a sickening, falling-elevator feeling to the two gunners and a heart-stopping terror to the man at the controls who realized it was not caused by clumsiness. The platform began to stagger away from the dinosaur, following the planned hyperbola but lower and slower than intended.

"Nail him," Vickers said calmly, sighting his green-mottled sternum for the backup shot.

Partial disintegration of the turbine preceded the shot by so little that the two seemed a single event. Both gunners were thrown back from the rail. Something whizzed through the side of the turbine and left a jagged rent in the housing. Adrienne Salmes' bullet struck the tyrannosaur in the lower belly.

"Hang on!" Don Washman shouted needlessly. "I'm going to try—"

He pulled the platform into another arc, clawing for altitude. To get back to camp they had to climb over the pine forest that lay between. No one knew better than the pilot how hopeless that chance was. Several of the turbine blades had separated from the hub. Most of the rest were brushes of boron fiber now, their casing matrices destroyed by the peg or harmonics induced by the imbalance. But Washman had to try, and in any case they were curving around the wounded tyrannosaur while it was still—

The whole drive unit tore itself free of the rest of the shooting platform. Part of it spun for a moment with the rotor shafts before sailing off in a direction of its own. Had it not been for the oak tree in their path, the vehicle might have smashed into the ground from fifty feet and killed everyone aboard. On the other hand, Don Washman just might have been able to get enough lift from the auto-rotating blades to set them down on an even keel. Branches snagged the mesh floor of the platform and the vehicle nosed over into the treetop.

They were all shouting, but the din of bursting metal and branches overwhelmed mere human noise. Vickers held the railing with one hand and the collar of his client's garment with the other. Both of the rifles were gone. The platform continued to tilt until the floor would have been vertical had it not been so crumpled. Adrienne Salmes was supported entirely by the guide. "For God's sake!" she screamed. "Let go or we'll go over *with* it!"

Vickers' face was red with the impossible strain. He forced his eyes down, feeling as if even that minuscule added effort would cause his body to tear. Adrienne was right. They were better off dropping onto a lower branch—or even to the ground forty feet below—than they would be somersaulting down in the midst of jagged metal. The platform was continuing to settle as branches popped. Vickers let go of the blonde woman. Screaming at the sudden release of half the load, he loosed his other hand from the rail.

The guide's eyes were shut in a pain reflex. His chest hit a branch at an angle that saved his ribs but took off a plate-sized swatch of skin without harming his tunic's tough fabric. Adrienne, further out on the same branch, seized him by the collar and armpit. Both her feet were locked around the branch. She took the strain until the guide's overstressed muscles allowed him to get a leg up. The branch swayed, but the tough oak held.

Don Washman was strapped into his seat. Now he was staring straight down and struggling with the jammed release catch. Vickers reached for the folding knife he carried in a belt pouch. He could not reach the pilot, though. "Don, cut the strap!" he shouted.

A large branch split. The platform tumbled outward and down, striking on the top of the rotor shafts. The impact smashed the lightly-built aircraft into a tangle reeking of kerosene. Don Washman was still caught in the middle of it.

The limb on which Vickers and Adrienne Salmes balanced was swaying in harmony with the whole tree. When the thrashing stopped, the guide sat up and eyed the trunk. He held his arms crossed tightly over his chest, each hand squeezing the opposite shoulder as if to reknit muscles which felt as if they had been pulled apart. Nothing was moving in the wreckage below. Vickers crawled to the crotch. He held on firmly while he stepped to a branch three feet lower down.

"Henry," Adrienne Salmes said.

"Just wait, I've got to get him out," Vickers said. He swung down to a limb directly beneath him, trying not to wince when his shoulders fell below the level of his supporting hands.

"Henry!" the blonde woman repeated more urgently. "The tyrannosaur!"

Vickers jerked his head around. He could see nothing but patterns of light and the leaves that surrounded him. He realized that the woman had been speaking from fear, not because she actually saw anything. There was no likelihood that the carnosaur would wander away from its kill, even to pursue a rival. Adrienne, who did not understand the beast's instincts, in her fear imagined it charging toward them. The guide let himself down from the branch on which he sat, falling the last five feet to the ground.

Adrienne thought Vickers must have struck his head during the crash. From her vantage point, thirty feet in the air and well outboard on the limb that supported her, she had an excellent view of the tyrannosaur. Only low brush separated it from the tree in which they had crashed. The beast had stood for a moment at the point Washman lifted the platform in his effort to escape. Now it was ramping like a creature from heraldry, balanced on one leg with its torso high and the other hind leg kicking out at nothing. At first she did not understand; then she saw that each time the foot drew back, it caressed the wounded belly.

Suddenly the big carnivore stopped rubbing itself. It had been facing away from the tree at a 30° angle. Now it turned toward the woman, awesome even at three hundred yards. It began to stalk forward. Its head swung low as usual, but after each few strides the beast paused. The back raised, the neck stretched upward, and now Adrienne could see that the nostrils were spreading. A leaf, dislodged when Vickers scrambled to the ground, was drifting down. The light breeze angled it toward the oncoming dinosaur.

Vickers cut through one of the lower cross-straps holding Washman five feet in the air with his seat above him. The pilot was alive but unconscious. The guide reached up for the remaining strap, his free hand and forearm braced against the pilot's chest to keep him from dropping on his face.

"Henry, for God's sake!" the woman above him shouted. "It's only a hundred yards away!"

Vickers stared at the wall of brush, his lips drawn back in a snarl. "Where are the guns? Can you see the guns?"

"I can't see them! Get back, for God's sake!"

The guide cursed and slashed through the strap. To take Washman's weight, he dropped his knife and bent. Grunting, Vickers manhandled the pilot into position for a fireman's carry.

The tyrannosaur had lowered its head again. Adrienne Salmes stared at the predator, then down at Vickers staggering under the pilot's weight. She fumbled out one of her small cigars, lit it, and dropped the gold-chased lighter back into her pocket. Then she scrambled to the bole and began to descend. The bark tore the skin beneath her coveralls and from the palms of both hands.

From the lowest branch, head-height for the stooping Vickers, Adrienne cried, "Here!" and tried to snatch Washman from the guide's back. The pilot was too heavy. Vickers thrust his shoulders upward. Between them, they slung Washman onto the branch. His arms and legs hung down to either side and his face was pressed cruelly into the bark.

The tyrannosaur crashed through the woody undergrowth twenty feet away. It stank of death, even against the mild breeze. The dead sauropod, of course, rotting between the four-inch teeth and smeared greasily over the killer's head and breast . . . but beyond the carrion odor was a tangible sharpness filling the mouths of guide and client as the brush parted.

Vickers had no chance of getting higher into the oak than the jaws could pick him off. Instead he turned, wishing that he had been able to keep at least his knife for this moment. Adrienne Salmes dragged on her cigar, stood, and flung the glowing cylinder into the wreckage of the platform. "Henry!" she cried, and she bent back down with her hand out to Vickers.

One stride put the tyrannosaur into the midst of the up-ended platform. As flimsy as the metal was, its edges were sharp and they clung instead of springing back the way splintered branches would. The beast's powerful legs had pistoned it through dense brush without slowing. It could still have dragged the wreckage forward through the one remaining step that would have ended the three humans. Instead, it drew back with a startled snort and tried to nuzzle its feet clear.

The kerosene bloomed into a sluggish red blaze. The tyrannosaur's distended nostrils *whuffed* in a double lungful of the soot-laden smoke that rolled from the peaks of the flames. The beast squealed and kicked in berserk fury, scattering fire-wrapped metal. Its rigid tail slashed the brush, fanning the flames toward the oak. Deeply-indented leaves shrivelled like hands closing. Vickers forgot about trying to climb. He rolled Don Washman off the branch again, holding him by the armpits. The pilot's feet fell as they would. "While we've got a chance!" the guide cried, knowing that the brush fire would suffocate them in the treetop even if the flames themselves did not climb so high.

Adrienne Salmes jumped down. Each of them wrapped one of the pilot's arms around their shoulders. They began to stumble through the brush, the backs of their necks prickling with the heat of the fire.

The tyrannosaur was snarling in unexampled rage. Fire was familiar to a creature which had lived a century among forests and lightning. Being caught in the midst of a blaze was something else again. The beast would not run while the platform still tangled its feet, and the powerful kicks that shredded the binding metal also scattered the flames. When at last the great killer broke free, it did so from the heart of an amoeba a hundred yards in diameter crackling in the brush. Adrienne and the guide were struggling into the forest when they heard the tyrannosaur give its challenge again. It sounded far away.

"I don't suppose there's any way we could retrieve the rifles," Adrienne said as Vickers put another stick on their fire. It was a human touch in the Cretaceous night. Besides, the guide was chilly. They had used his coveralls to improvise a stretcher for Washman, thrusting a pruned sapling up each leg and out the corresponding sleeve. They had not used the pilot's own garment for fear that being stripped would accelerate the effects of shock. Washman was breathing stertorously and had not regained consciousness since the crash.

"Well, I couldn't tell about yours," Vickers said with a wry smile, "but even with the brush popping I'm pretty sure I heard the magazine of mine go off. I'd feel happier if we had it along, that's for sure."

"I'm going to miss that Schultz and Larsen," the woman said. She took out a cigar, looked at it, and slipped it back into her pocket. "Slickest action they ever put on a rifle. Well, I suppose I can find another when we get back."

They had found the saplings growing in a sauropod burn. Fortunately, Adrienne had retained her sheath knife, a monster with a saw-backed, eight-inch blade that Vickers had thought a joke—until it became their only tool. The knife and the cigarette lighter, he reminded himself. Resiny wood cracked, pitching sparks beyond the circle they had cleared in the fallen needles. The woman immediately stood and kicked the spreading flames back in toward the center.

"You saved my life," Vickers said, looking into the fire. "With that cigar. You were thinking a lot better than I was, and that's the only reason I'm not in a carnosaur's belly."

Adrienne sat down beside the guide. After a moment, he met her eyes. She said, "You could have left Don and gotten back safely yourself."

"I could have been a goddam politician!" Vickers snapped, "but that wasn't a way I wanted to live my life." He relaxed and shook his head. "Sorry," he said. She laughed and squeezed his bare knee above the abrasion. "Besides," Vickers went on, "I'm not sure it would have worked. The damned tyrannosaur was obviously tracking us by scent. Most of what we know about the big carnivores started a minute or two before they were killed. They . . . I don't mean dinos're smart. But their instincts are a lot more efficient than you'd think if you hadn't watched them."

Adrienne Salmes nodded. "A computer isn't smart either, but that doesn't keep it from solving problems."

"Exactly," Vickers said, "exactly. And if the problem that tyrannosaur was trying to solve was us—well, I'm just as glad the fire wiped out our scent. We've got a long hike tomorrow lugging Don."

"What bothers me," the blonde woman said carefully, "is the fact it could find us easily enough if it tried. Look, we can't be very far from the camp, not at the platform's speed. Why don't we push on now instead of waiting for daylight?"

Vickers glanced down at the responder on his wrist, tuned to the beacon in the center of the camp. "Five or six miles," he said. "Not too bad, even with Don. But I think we're better off here than stumbling into camp in the dark. The smell of the trophies is going to keep packs of the smaller predators around it. They're active in the dark, and they've got damned sharp teeth."

Adrienne chuckled, startling away some of the red eyes ringing their fire. Vickers had whittled a branch into a whippy cudgel with an eye toward bagging a mammal or two for dinner, but both he and his client were too thirsty to feel much hunger as yet. "Well," she said, "we have to find something else to do till daybreak, then—and I'm too keyed up to sleep." She touched Vickers' thigh again.

All the surrounding eyes vanished when a dinosaur grunted.

It could have been a smaller creature, even an herbivore; but that would not have made it harmless. In the event, it was precisely what they feared it was when the savage noise filled the forest: the tyrannosaur hunting them and very close.

The fire was of branches and four-foot lengths of sapling they had broken after notching with the knife. Vickers' face lost all expression. He grabbed the unburned end of a billet and turned toward the sound. "No!" Adrienne cried. "Spread the fire in a line—it won't follow us through a fire again!"

It was the difference between no good chance and no chance at all. Vickers scuffed a bootload of coals out into the heaped pine needles and ran into the night with his brand. The lowest branches of the pines were dead and dry, light-starved by the foliage nearer the sky. The resin-sizzling torch caught them and they flared up behind the guide. Half-burned twigs that fell to the forest floor flickered among the matted needles. Vickers already was twenty yards from their original campsite when he remembered Don Washman still lay helpless beside it.

The dozen little fires Vickers had set, and the similar line Adrienne Salmes had ignited on the other side of the campfire, were already beginning to grow and merge. The guide turned and saw the flames nearing Washman's feet, though not—thank God—his head. That was when the tyrannosaur stepped into view. In the firelight it was hard to tell the mottled camouflage natural to its hide from the cracked and blistered areas left by the earlier blaze. Vickers cursed and hurled his torch. It spun end over end, falling short of its intended target.

The tyrannosaur had been advancing with its head hung low. It was still fifteen feet high at the hips. In the flickering light, it bulked even larger than the ten tons it objectively weighed. Adrienne looked absurd and tiny as she leaped forward to meet the creature with a pine torch. Behind her the flames were spreading, but they were unlikely to form a barrier to the beast until they formed a continuous line. That was seconds or a minute away, despite the fact that the fuel was either dry or soaking with pitch.

Adrienne slashed her brand in a figure-8 like a child with a sparkler. Confused by the glare and stench of the resinous flames, the carnosaur reared back and took only a half step forward—onto the torch Vickers had thrown.

The guide grabbed up the poles at Washman's head. He dragged the pilot away from the fire like a pony hauling a travois. When the tyrannosaur screeched, Vickers dropped the stretcher again and turned, certain he would see the beast striding easily through the curtain of fire. Instead it was backing away, its great head slashing out to either side as if expecting to find a tangible opponent there. The blonde woman threw her torch at the dinosaur. Then, with her arms shielding her face, she leaped across the fire. She would have run into the bole of a tree had Vickers not caught her as she blundered past. "It's all right!" he shouted. "It's turned! Get the other end of the stretcher."

Spattering pitch had pocked but not fully ignited Adrienne's garments. The tears furrowing the soot on her cheeks were partly the result of irritants in the flames. "It'll be back," she said. "You know it will."

"I'll have a rifle in my hands the next time I see it," the guide said. "This is one dino that won't be a matter of business to shoot."

The alarm awakened the camp. Then muzzle flashes lit the white faces of the clients when the first dinosaur trotted down the trail. Even the grenade launcher could not divert the monsters. After a long time, the gunfire slackened. Then Miss McPherson returned with additional ammunition.

Somewhat later, the shooting stopped for good.

If he had not been moving in a stupor, the noise of the scavengers would have warned Vickers. As it was, he pushed out of the trees and into a slaughteryard teeming with vermin on a scale with the carcasses they gorged on. Only when Mears cried out did the guide realize they were back in the camp. The four clients were squeezed together on top of the machinegun tower.

Vickers was too shocked to curse. He set down his end of the stretcher abruptly. The other end was already on the ground. "Henry, do you want the knife?" Adrienne asked. He shook his head without turning around.

There were at least a dozen torosaurs sprawled on the northern quadrant of the camp, along the trail. They were more like hills than anything that had been alive, but explosive bullets from the 12.7 mm machinegun had opened them up like chainsaws. The clients were shouting and waving rifles in the air from the low tower. Vickers, only fifty feet away, could not hear them because of the clatter of the scavengers. There were well over one hundred tons of carrion in the clearing. Literally thousands of lesser creatures had swarmed out of the skies and the forest to take advantage.

"Lesser" did not mean "little" in the Cretaceous.

Vickers swallowed. "Can you carry Don alone if I lead the way?" he asked. "We've got to get to the others to find out what happened."

"I'll manage," the woman said. Then, "You know, they must have fired off all their ammunition. That's why they're huddled there beside—"

"I know what they goddam did!" the guide snarled. "I also know, that if there's one goddam round left, we've got a chance to sort things out!" Neither of them voiced the corollary. They had heard the tyrannosaur challenge the dawn an hour earlier. Just before they burst into the clearing, they had heard a second call; and it was much closer.

Adrienne knelt, locking one of the pilot's arms over her shoulders. She straightened at the knees, lifting her burden with her. Washman's muscles were slack. "That's something I owe my husband for," Adrienne gasped. "Practice moving drunks. When I was young and a fool."

Vickers held one of the stretcher poles like a quarterstaff. He knew how he must look in his underwear. That bothered him obscurely almost as much as the coming gauntlet of carrion-eaters did.

A white-furred pterosaur with folded, twenty-foot wings struck at the humans as they maneuvered between two looming carcasses. Vickers slapped away the red, chisel-like beak with his staff. Then he prodded the great carrion-eater again for good measure as Adrienne staggered around it. The guide began to laugh.

"What the hell's so funny?" she demanded.

"If there's an intrusion vehicle back there," Vickers said, "which there probably isn't or these sheep wouldn't be here now, maybe I'll send everybody home without me. That way I don't have to explain to Stern what went wrong."

"That's a hell of a joke!" Adrienne snapped.

"Who's joking?"

Because of the huge quantity of food, the scavengers were feeding without much squabbling. The three humans slipped through the mass, challenged only by the long-necked pterosaur. Fragile despite its size, the great gliding creature defended its personal space with an intensity that was its only road to survival. Met with equal force, it backed away of necessity.

Dieter Jost lay under the gun tower, slightly protected by the legs and crossbraces. He was mumbling in German and his eyes did not focus. Vickers took the pilot's weight to set him by the ladder. Mears hopped down and began shrieking at Adrienne Salmes, "God damn you, your crazy husband took the time machine back without us, you bitch!"

Vickers straightened and slapped the contractor with a blow that released all the frustrations that had been building. Mears stumbled against the tower, turned back with his fists bunched, and stopped. The blonde woman's knife was almost touching his ribs.

"Where's Steve?" the guide asked loudly. He was massaging his right palm with his left as if working a piece of clay between them.

Miss McPherson jumped to the ground. In the darkness the tower had drawn them. Since both boxes of 12.7 mm ammunition had been sluiced into the night, it was obviously irrational to stay on a platform that would not reach a tyrannosaur's knee . . . but human reason is in short supply in a darkened forest. "One of the dinosaurs killed him," the older woman blurted. "We, we tried to keep Mr. Jost safe with us, but we ran out of bullets and, and, the last hour has been—"

Brewer had a cut above his right eyebrow. He looked shell-shocked but not on the edge of hysteria as his three companions were. "When it was light enough to search," he said, "I got your ammo out. I thought it might work in his—" he gestured toward Dieter beneath him—"rifle. Close but no cigar." The meat packer's fingers traced the line which a piece of bursting cartridge case had drawn across his scalp.

"Well, we put the fear of God into 'em," Mears asserted sullenly. "They've been afraid to come close even though we're out of ammo now. But how d'we get *out* of here, I want to know!"

"We don't," Vickers said flatly. "If the intrusion vehicle's gone, we are well and truly screwed. Because there's never yet been an insertion within a hundred years of another insertion. But we've got a closer problem than that, because—"

The tyrannosaur drowned all other sounds with its roar.

Vickers stepped into the nearer of the ponies without changing expression. The engine caught when he pushed the starter. "Adrienne," he said, "get the rest of them down to the slough—Don and Dieter in the pony. Fast. If I don't come back, you're on your own."

Adrienne jumped in front of the vehicle. "We'll both go."

"God damn it, *move!*" the guide shouted. "We don't have time!"

"We don't know which of us it's tracking!" the woman shouted back. "I've got to come along!"

Vickers nodded curtly. "Brewer," he called over his shoulder, "get everybody else out of here before a pack of carnosaurs arrives and you're in the middle of it." He engaged the pony's torque converter while the blonde woman was barely over the side. As they spun out southward from the camp, the guide shouted, "Don't leave Don and Dieter behind, or so help me—"

"How fast can it charge?" Adrienne asked as they bounced over a root to avoid a tangle of berry bushes.

"Fast," Vickers said bluntly. "I figure if we can reach the sauropods we killed the other day, we've got a chance, though."

They were jouncing too badly for Adrienne to stay in a seat. She squatted behind Vickers and hung onto the sides. "If you think the meat's going to draw it off, won't it stop in the camp?" she asked.

"Not that," said the guide, slamming over the tiller to skirt a ravine jeweled with flecks of quartz. "I'm betting there'll be gorgosaurs there by now, feeding. That's how we'd have gotten carnosaur heads for the other gunners, you see. The best chance I can see is half a dozen gorgosaurs'll take care of even *our* problem."

"They'll take care of us too, won't they?" the woman objected.

"Got a better idea?"

The smell of the rotting corpses would have guided them the last quarter mile even without the marker. The tyrannosaur's own kill had been several days riper, but the sheer mass of the five titanosaurs together more than equalled the effect. The nearest of the bodies lay with its spine toward the approaching pony in a shaft of sunlight through the browsed-away top cover. Vickers throttled back with a curse. "If there's nothing here," he said, "then we may as well bend over and kiss our asses goo—"

A carnosaur raised its gory head over the carrion. It had been buried to its withers in the sauropod's chest, bolting bucket-loads of lung tissue. Its original color would have been in doubt had not a second killer stalked into sight. The gorgosaurs wore black stripes over fields of dirty sand color, and their tongues were as red as their bloody teeth. Each of the pair was as heavy as a large automobile, and they were as viciously lethal as leopards, pound for pound.

"All right," Vickers said quietly. He steered to the side of the waiting pair, giving the diesel a little more fuel. Three more gorgosaurs strode watchfully out of the forest. They were in an arc facing the pony. The nearest of them was only thirty feet away. Their breath rasped like leather pistons. The guide slowed again, almost to a stop. He swung the tiller away.

One of the gorgosaurs snarled and charged. Both humans shouted, but the killer's target was the tyrannosaur that burst out of the forest behind the pony. Vickers rolled the throttle wide open, sending the vehicle between two of the lesser carnivores. Instead of snapping or bluffing, the tyrannosaur strode through the gorgosaur that had tried to meet it. The striped carnosaur spun to the ground with its legs flailing. Pine straw sprayed as it hit.

"It's still coming!" Adrienne warned. Vickers hunched as if that could coax more speed out of the little engine. The four gorgosaurs still able to run had scattered to either side. The fifth threshed on the ground, its back broken by an impact the tyrannosaur had scarcely noted. At another time the pack might have faced down their single opponent. Now the wounded tyrannosaur was infuriated beyond questions of challenge and territory.

"Henry, the river," the woman said. Vickers did not change direction, running parallel to the unseen bank. "Henry," she said again, trying to steady herself close to his ear because she did not want to shout, not for this, "we've done everything else we could. We have to try this."

A branch lashed Vickers across the face. His tears streamed across the red brand it left on his cheek. He turned as abruptly as the pony's narrow axles allowed. They plunged to the right, over the ridgeline and into the thick-set younger trees that bordered the water. Then they were through that belt, both of them bleeding from the whipping branches. Reeds and mud were roostering up from all four wheels. The pony's aluminum belly began to lift. Their speed dropped as the treads started to act as paddles automatically.

"Oh dear God, he's stopping, he's stopping," Adrienne whimpered. Vickers looked over his shoulder. There was nothing to dodge now that they were afloat, only the mile of haze and water that they would never manage to cross. The tyrannosaur had paused where the pines gave way to reeds, laterite soil to mud. It stood splay-legged, turning first one eye, then the other, to the escaping humans. The bloody sun jeweled its pupils.

"If he doesn't follow—" Vickers said.

The tyrannosaur stepped forward inexorably. The muddy water slapped as the feet slashed through it. Then the narrow keel of the breastbone cut the water as well. The tyrannosaur's back sank to a line of knobs on the surface, kinking horizontally as the hind legs thrust the beast toward its prey. The carnosaur moved much more quickly in the water than did the vehicle it pursued. The beast was fifty yards away, now, and there was no way to evade it.

They were far enough out into the stream that Vickers could see the other pony winking on the bank a half mile distant. Brewer had managed to get them out of the charnel house they had made of the camp, at least. "Give me your knife," Vickers said. Twenty feet away, the ruby eye of the carnosaur glazed and cleared as its nicitating membrane wiped away the spray.

"Get your own damned knife!" Adrienne said. She half-rose, estimating that if she jumped straight over the stern she would not overset the pony.

Vickers saw the water beneath them darken, blacken. The pony quivered. There was no wake, but the tons of death slanting up from beneath raised a slick on the surface. They were still above the crocodile's vast haunches when its teeth closed on the tyrannosaur.

The suction of the tyrannosaur going under halted the pony as if it had struck a wall. Then the water rose and slapped them forward. Vickers' hand kept Adrienne from pitching out an instant after she had lost the need to do so. They drew away from the battle in the silt-golden water, fifty yards, one hundred. Vickers cut off the engine. "The current'll take us to the others," he explained. "And without the paddles we won't attract as much attention."

Adrienne was trying to resheathe her knife. Finally she held the leather with one hand and slipped the knife in with her fingers on the blade as if threading a needle. She looked at Vickers. "I didn't think that would work," she said. "Or it would work a minute after we were . . . gone."

The guide managed to laugh. "Might still happen," he said, nodding at the disturbed water. "Off-hand, though, I'd say the 'largest land predator of all time' just met something bigger." He sobered. "God, I hope we don't meet its mate. I don't want to drown. I really don't."

Water spewed skyward near the other pony. At first Vickers thought one of the clients had managed to detonate a grenade and blow them all to hell. "My God," Adrienne whispered. "You said they couldn't. . . ."

At the distance they were from it, only the gross lines of the intrusion vehicle could be identified. A pair of machineguns had been welded onto the frame, and there appeared to be a considerable party of uniformed men aboard. "I don't understand it either," Vickers said, "but I know where to ask." He reached for the starter.

Adrienne caught his arm. He looked back in surprise. "If it was safer to drift with the current before, it's still safer," she said. She pointed at the subsiding froth from which the tyrannosaur had never re-emerged. "We're halfway already. And besides, it gives us some time—" she put her hand on Vickers' shoulder—"for what I had in mind last night at the campfire."

"They're watching us with binoculars!" the guide sputtered, trying to break away from the kiss.

"They can all sit in a circle and play with themselves," the blonde woman said. "We've earned this."

Vickers held himself rigid for a moment. Then he reached out and began to spread the pony's front awning with one hand.

The secretary wore a uniform and a pistol. When he nodded, Vickers opened the door. Stern sat at the metal desk. Dr. Galil was to his right and the only other occupant of the room. Vickers sat gingerly on one of the two empty chairs.

"I'm not going to debrief you," Stern said. "Others have done that. Rather, I am going to tell you certain things. They are confidential. Utterly confidential. You understand that."

"Yes," Vickers said. Stern's office was not in the Ministry of Culture and Tourism; but then, Vickers had never expected that it would be.

"Dr. Galil," Stern continued, and the cherubic scientist beamed like a Christmas ornament, "located the insertion party by homing on the alpha waves of one of the members of it. You, to be precise. Frankly, we were all amazed at this breakthrough; it is not a technique we would have tested if there had been any alternative available."

Vickers licked his lips. "I thought you were going to fire me," he said flatly.

"Would it bother you if we did?" Stern riposted.

"Yes." The guide paused. The fear was greater now that he had voiced it. He had slept very little during the week since the curtailed safari had returned. "It—the job . . . suits me. Even dealing with the clients, I can do it. For having the rest."

Stern nodded. Galil whispered to him, then looked back at Vickers. "We wish to experiment with this effect," Stern continued aloud. "Future rescues—or resupplies—may depend on it. There are other reasons as well." He cleared his throat.

"There is the danger that we will not be able to consistently repeat the operation," Dr. Galil broke in. "That the person will be marooned, you see. For there must of course be a brain so that we will have a brain wave to locate. Thus we need a volunteer."

"You want a base line," Vickers said in response to what he had not been told. "You want to refine your calibration so that you can drop a man—or men—or tanks—at a precise time. And if your base line is in the Cretaceous instead of the present, you don't have the problem of closing off another block each time somebody is inserted into the future before you get the technique down pat."

Stern grew very still. "Do you volunteer?" he asked.

Vickers nodded. "Sure. Even if I thought you'd let me leave here alive if I didn't, I'd volunteer. For that. I should have thought of the—the research potential—myself. I'd have blackmailed you into sending me."

The entryway door opened unexpectedly. "I already did that, Henry," said Adrienne Salmes. "Though I wouldn't say their arms had to be twisted very hard." She stepped past Vickers and laid the small receiver on Stern's desk beside the sending unit. "I decided it was time to come in."

"You arranged this for me?" Vickers asked in amazement.

"I arranged it for us," Adrienne replied, seating herself on the empty chair. "I'm not entirely sure that I want to retire to the Cretaceous. But—" she looked sharply at Stern—"I'm quite sure that I don't want to live in the world our friends here will shape if they do gain complete ability to manipulate the past. At least in the Cretaceous, we know what the rules are."

Vickers stood. "Shlomo," he said shaking Dr. Galil's hand, "you haven't failed before, and I don't see you failing now. We won't be marooned. Though it might be better if we were." He turned to the man behind the desk. "Mr. Stern," he said, "you've got your volunteers. I—we—we'll get you a list of the supplies we'll need."

Adrienne touched his arm. "This will work, you know," she said. She took no notice of the others in the room. "Like the crocodile."

"Tell me in a year's time that it *has* worked," Vickers said.

And she did.

PHYLLIS EISENSTEIN

In the Western Tradition

IT WAS obvious from his reaction that Holland had never bought time on the Bubble before. He could scarcely sit still in his chair. "That's him! That's him!" he shouted. He was grinning like a child on Christmas morning, surrounded by toys.

I knew how he felt. I would never forget my own first assignment, and my first view of the man I sought. Holland knew his quarry from photographs; I had only stone likenesses to guide me. Yet I knew him immediately, though the statues had been idealized, youthful, flawless. That was back in the beginning, when almost all of us were involved in the Life of Jesus Project based in Istanbul. I was assigned to the western branch—the less important one, I thought. But my hands started to shake when I saw my man in the Forum, shaking as hard as if I were seeing Jesus himself, and they kept shaking while I brought his face closer and closer, close enough that he could have spit in my eye if he had not been just an image in the Bubble. Augustus Caesar, dead two thousand years, was in that moment as real to me as any of my fellow Bubble operators, and the most significant man in history. Yes, I knew how Dr. Frederick Holland felt. And no matter how often I sat at the console, or even just watched another operator at work, I still experienced a strong echo of that initial thrill every time I saw the Bubble spring into being from nothingness in a small, bare room. For I knew that within its confines the dead would walk again. Holland had known that, I supposed, on an intellectual level; now he knew it as I did, in his soul.

I sat behind him, a casual visitor to his enterprise. I was there because I never tired of watching the Bubble and because Alison and I would be going out to dinner as soon as she finished her shift. To my left, she played on the computer and gave Holland what he had paid for—Ellsworth, Kansas, August 18, 1873:

Wyatt Earp took a seat under the wooden awning that shaded Beebe's General Store from the scorching afternoon sun. He tipped the chair back against the weathered clapboard wall and surveyed the street from beneath the wide brim of his dark hat. Beyond him, the town stretched hot and dusty to the railroad tracks, and in the distance, long-horned cattle could be seen moving sluggishly as they grazed on an endless expanse of prairie grass.

Earp turned his face toward us; gaunt, hollow-cheeked, he appeared to be in his early twenties, not yet the legend he would become in Dodge and Tombstone. His eyes focused briefly on something we could not see.

"Shall I turn the viewpoint and catch what he's looking at?" Alison asked.

Holland shook his head violently. "No, stay where you are. We can check that out in another session."

A muffled uproar heralded the appearance of two men: they burst from a doorway down the street, shouting curses over their shoulders.

"The Thompsons," said Holland. "Ben and Bill."

They crossed the square at a run and entered a two-story building whose sun-bleached sign said GRAND CENTRAL HOTEL.

Earp rose from his chair, tall and loose-limbed, and stepped into the doorway of Beebe's, flattening himself against the jamb. Up and down the street, people peered out of other doorways, roused by the clamor but unwilling to come out into the sunlight. Quick footsteps sounded nearby, hard heels on the boards of the sidwalk; a man materialized from nothing directly in front of the console, his back to us. He was short and stocky, and the sleeves of his white shirt were rolled up over thick gray-haired forearms. He wore a sweat-stained vest.

"Whitney," said Holland.

Whitney stopped by Earp. "What's going on?" he asked.

Earp shook his head.

"Now Logan," whispered Holland.

More footsteps, very fast this time, and a young man—scarcely more than a boy, really—appeared abruptly to clutch at Whitney's arm. "I ran to find you as soon as it happened, sheriff." He was breathing hard, and his dark hair was plastered in wet points against his forehead. "Bill Thompson got nasty drunk, and John Sterling gave him the flat of his hand across the mouth. When Bill invited John to get a gun and meet him ouside, John hit him again and knocked him out of his seat. Then Bill and Ben ran after their guns."

Whitney turned, fists on his hips, and I could see the glint of the metal star on his vest.

By this time the Thompsons had returned to the street with gunbelts, shotgun, and rifle and were standing behind a hay wagon, shouting threats toward the saloon.

"All right," said Whitney. "We can't have this." He started across the street toward the wagon.

"You keep out of this, sheriff!" shouted a Thompson. "We don't want to hurt you."

"Don't be foolish, Ben," Whitney replied.

"You tell that to Sterling!" said Ben, and he shook a fist toward the saloon door, adding a string of profanities for Sterling's benefit.

Whitney went into the saloon.

Several people from the interior of the store crowded its doorway, craning over Earp's shoulder, trying for a good view of the excitement without exposing themselves to danger. Holland pointed to them one by one, relishing their names as if they were fine wines. "Stacey. Anderson. McDonald. And there's Beebe himself in the apron."

Alison leaned forward, elbows coming to rest among the telltales, fingers interlacing beneath her chin. "Logan's the young one, the one who brought the news?"

Holland nodded. "Jimmy Logan. The Blacksmith's son. Hangs around the saloons too much for his father's taste."

She smiled. "You've really done your homework."

"I know every man, woman, and child who impinged on Wyatt Earp's life."

"Must be quite a crowd," murmured Alison.

"Ah—he's coming back now."

Whitney strode down the sidewalk like a man very sure of himself. At Beebe's he waved as if clearing the air of flies. "You can all go about your business; there won't be any gunplay out here today. Sterling's gone out the back way, gone clear out of town."

"I didn't take Sterling for a coward," said young Logan.

The sheriff shook his head. "It wasn't his idea. He was ready to come out shooting, but he had some friends with better sense, and they wouldn't let him. Now everything is just fine, nothing to worry about. I'm going to treat the Thompson boys to a couple of drinks at Brennan's, and that'll be the end of it."

With some muttering, those who had been Beebe's customers drifted back inside while Whitney approached the Thompsons with his offer. Up and down the street, the rest of the audience melted away, too. Earp settled back into his chair, and Jimmy Logan leaned against the wall beside him.

"They've got this town treed good," said Logan. He was looking toward Brennan's.

Earp gazed out into the street. "Why'd you go for the sheriff? I hear he's not much use with a gun. Marshal, now—he's a man with a reputation."

"I knew the sheriff would be in his store. It was close-by."

Earp shook his head. "A man should be a full-time peace officer, not half merchant and half sheriff. Job's too hard in a town like this any other way."

"You're sure right about that." They lapsed into silence, each surveying the street in his own way. As the minutes passed, I found myself restless. Alison's shift had only about an hour to go, and I began to wonder if anything significant would happen in that time. Holland, however, seemed to find every swirl of dust in that scorching summer day fascinating. He had one elbow balanced on the edge of the console now, fist tight against his mouth; the outside of that hand almost brushed the insubstantial edge of the Bubble. He looked like he wanted to reach out and touch Earp. I thought he might be the kind that would try to enter the Bubble space to get closer to his subject, in spite of the standard warning. I had worked with one of those once—in his enthusiasm, he kept edging into the Bubble itself and blotting out sections of the scene with the interference generated by his own body. But as the minutes passed, Holland sat, obviously yearning but able to restrain himself.

Alison, too, seemed to have found some sort of fascination in the vision of two men doing nothing; she hadn't moved since speaking to Holland. My own restless shuffling sounded loud in the quiet room, and I was glad when Whitney finally came out of Brennan's, striding noisily.

He turned toward us and crossed the few meters that separated him from Earp and Logan. He stopped, smiling, self-satisfied. "They've calmed down a bit. They're inside with a bunch of Texas men."

Earp looked up at him. "Did you take their guns away from them?"

"No, they wouldn't stand for that."

Before Earp could comment further, Bill Thompson stepped out of the saloon, shotgun in his hands. "I'll get me a sheriff if I don't get anyone else!" he shouted.

Whitney turned to face him just as Thompson fired both barrels. At point-blank range, the blast caught the hapless sheriff full in the chest. The sound of the shot, earsplitting in such close quarters, rocked Alison and me back in our chairs; my pulse lurched wildly, while her knee slammed the underside of the console, and she clutched it, growling curses. Holland, evidently expecting the shot, was unruffled.

Whitney had fallen back into Earp's arms. Above the pounding of my heart I heard him gasp, "I'm done. Get me home."

Thompson had run back into the saloon. But there were hundreds of other people in the street now, most of them with drawn guns, and more were gushing from the hotels, the stores, the saloons with every passing moment. At last both Thompsons strode out of Brennan's, guns waving from one side to the other, and walked to the nearest rail where horses were hitched.

"Those are their friends," said Holland, pointing to a group that was gathering in front of the Grand Central Hotel. "Peshaur, Pierce, Kane, Good—"

"All right," said Alison, one hand still massaging her knee. "You don't have to name them all. I just work here."

Holland threw her an injured glance, then sighed. "Sorry. Still, you have to know some of them, for future reference."

"They can't *all* be important."

"That depends on how many times my grant is renewed."

Alison shook her head. "I won't remember most of them. Not from a single session."

"Very well," said Holland. "I'll try to keep to the crucial ones."

The sheriff had friends, too, it turned out, inside Beebe's. They bore his barely breathing body off. Earp and Logan backed into the doorway once more. Within a couple of minutes, a third face peeped out between them.

"Morco," said Holland. "Deputy marshal."

The deputy elbowed Logan aside and peered into the street. The Thompsons were facing the other way, engrossed in their guns.

"Jump out and get them now," Earp said to Morco.

Morco shook his head. "Those fellows across the street might get me."

"You'd get both Thompsons first."

"Not me, friend."

An expression of disgust passed over Earp's face.

Bill Thompson rode out of town, and Ben Thompson covered his retreat by stalking up and down the street with half a hundred armed men at his back. One of them fired his gun into the air and crowed, "I'll give a thousand dollars to anybody who'll knock off another lawman!"

Holland chuckled then. "Watch this next piece of frontier bravery. Here comes the mayor." Appearing from our side of the Bubble, the mayor edged along the wall of Beebe's as if magnetized to it. He slid into the doorway, crowding Logan and Earp. "And there's the marshal—that new face just behind Logan. He came in the back way."

"You've really picked the center of the action, Dr. Holland," said Alison.

He hushed her with a sharp gesture, and we spent the next few minutes listening to the mayor try, unsuccessfully, to talk the marshal and his deputy into arresting Ben Thompson. At the end of his tether, the mayor himself shouted at Thompson to lay down his arms and submit to arrest. But the mayor did not dare go out into the street to say that, and Thompson's only answer was some colorful profanity.

Earp had been silent since he suggested that Morco take action. Now he folded his arms across his chest and said to the harried mayor, "Nice police force you've got."

The mayor, whose face was red enough to explode, said, "Who the hell are you?"

Earp shrugged. "Just a looker-on."

"Well, don't talk so goddamned much. You haven't even got a gun."

Earp, wearing dark trousers and a long-sleeved white shirt with soft collar and string tie, looked more like a frontier schoolteacher than a gunfighter. "It's none of my business," he said slowly, "but if it was, I'd get me a gun and arrest Ben Thompson."

"Don't pay any attention to that kid," said the marshal.

The mayor looked the marshal in the face and said, "You're fired, Norton. You, too, Morco." He snatched the marshal's badge from Norton's shirt and turned to Earp. "I'll make this your business," he said. "You're marshal of Ellsworth. Here's your badge. Go into Beebe's and get some guns. I order you to arrest Ben Thompson."

Earp took the badge and went inside.

''Follow him!'' said Holland.

Alison's hands moved over the console; the viewpoint swung sideways to center on the doorway and swoop inside past the mayor, past the ex-marshal and his deputy and Logan, their bodies melting away at the edges of the Bubble like mist at sunrise.

The interior of the store was dim compared to the sun-scorched plaza. Without breaking stride, Earp turned to his left, to the firearms counter, where he requested second-hand forty-fives, holsters, and cartridges. Beebe himself hurried over to help with the selection and to watch the new marshal examine the weapons, load them, settle them on hips. Our viewpoint wheeled to float above Beebe's shoulder as Earp returned to the door and the store owner followed, then swept on past when the latter stopped with his customers at the threshold. Earp went out to the street alone save for our invisible, unknowable presence.

Fifty meters away, Thompson spotted his new adversary as soon as Earp stepped off the sidewalk. The shotgun muzzle swerved to point toward him as he began to close that gap with a slow, steady gait.

''What do you want, Wyatt?'' shouted Thompson.

Until that moment, I had not realized they were acquainted with each other. I wondered how much Thompson knew about Earp, how much there was to know at this early date.

''I want you, Ben,'' said Earp.

''I'd rather talk than fight,'' said Thompson. Whatever their relationship, he clearly did not think Earp insane for facing him down in that Ellsworth street.

''I'll get you either way, Ben,'' said Earp. He kept walking.

''Wait a minute. What do you want me to do?

''Throw your shotgun into the road, put up your hands, and tell your friends to stay out of this play.'' He was less than ten meters from Thompson.

Close up, Thompson was ugly, bloated from too much drinking, and powerfully built. He looked belligerent. Earp looked cool. I had to admire him; how many men could appear so calm while facing a loaded shotgun? And then there were all those other half-drunk cowboys in Thompson's entourage, including the one who had offered the reward for the lawman. I began to understand the making of a legend.

''Will you stop and let me talk to you?'' shouted Thompson.

Earp halted. He still had not drawn a gun.

''What are you going to do with me?'' Thompson asked.

''Kill you or take you to jail.''

''Deputy Brown's over there by the depot with a rifle,'' Thompson said, tilting his head in the appropriate direction. ''The minute I give up my guns he'll cut loose at me.''

Earp said, ''If he does, I'll give you back your guns and we'll shoot it out with him. As long as you're my prisoner, the man that gets you will have to get me.''

Thompson hesitated.

''Come on. Throw down your gun or make your fight.''

Thompson threw down the gun. ''You win.'' He raised his hands above his head. ''I'm all yours.''

Now Earp's right hand went to his hip, touched the butt of the weapon there, but still he did not draw. With his left hand he pointed toward Thompson's supporters, swinging his arm wide to encompass them all. ''Get back, all of you! Move!''

They moved, and Earp took his prisoner's shotgun and gunbelts and marched him through the throng to the courthouse. Some of Thompson's friends attempted to storm the court, but Earp drove them out and locked the door.

The arraignment was swift. ''What's the charge?'' said the judge.

The mayor was there, and the peace officers who had been fired, but now that they were sealed into a room with Thompson—a room surrounded by his supporters, who could be heard shouting through the thin walls—none of them had any suggestions to make.

''How about accessory to murder?'' offered Earp.

The judge looked to the mayor. ''How about it?''

The mayor frowned, hesitating, and finally said, ''Well, your honor, in my opinion, Ben Thompson here could be charged with . . . disturbing the peace.''

''Guilty!'' said the judge. ''Twenty-five-dollar fine.''

Thompson grinned and peeled two bills from a roll of greenbacks. He slapped them down before the judge. ''Do I get my guns back now?''

''Certainly,'' said the judge. ''You have paid your fine, and the marshal will restore any property he may have taken from you.''

As Thompson started to strap a gunbelt on, Earp caught his arm. ''Listen to me, Ben,'' he said. ''Court or no court, don't you put those guns on here. You carry them straight to the Grand Central, and don't so much as stop to say hello to anybody on the way. I'll be watching you. Keep moving till you're out of my sight. After that, whatever you do is your own business.''

Earp watched Thompson walk into the waiting crowd, which engulfed him and moved en masse toward the hotel. When Thompson was completely lost to sight, he turned to the mayor, plucking the badge from his shirt, unbuckling the gunbelts from his hips. ''I don't need these any more,'' he said.

The mayor stared at him, his hands receiving the items like coat hooks. ''Don't you want to be marshal of Ellsworth?''

''I do not.''

''We'll pay you a hundred and twenty-five dollars a month.''

Earp looked him in the eye. ''Ellsworth figures lawmen at twenty-five dollars a head. That's too cheap for me.'' He turned and walked out of the courthouse, down the street which no longer swarmed with armed men. We followed him for some minutes, but he only went into a hotel—not the Grand Central—for some dinner. He was just being served his steak when Holland's time ran out.

Alison hit the finish button and the Bubble collapsed into itself like a deflating balloon, dwindling to a spot of light before winking out. Without it, the room beyond the console was bare and lonely.

''All right,'' said Alison, swiveling her chair to face Holland. ''I'm impressed.''

''He was quite a man,'' said Holland. ''Now, where do I get the tape?''

''At the records office. Down the hall to your left.''

He rose from his chair and offered her his hand. ''Thank you very much for all your efforts. I'm very grateful that the company assigned me one of its best operators.''

She smiled. ''I'll see you tomorrow.''

''Yes.'' He hurried out, obviously eager to lay his hands on the tape and live the whole experience again.

Alison turned to me, still smiling, and shook her head. ''Sometimes I think the ones who just sit there with their mouths shut the whole time are the best clients of all, even if they don't offer any cues.''

I laughed as I reached out for her. ''He's in love with his subject matter.'' I pulled her onto my lap.''Almost as much as I'm in love with you.''

She slide her arms around my neck and touched my forehead with her lips. ''Don't we have a 1900 dinner reservation?'' she murmured.

''Uh-huh.'' She was warm, and soft in all the right places. I could have sat there for an hour, just holding her.

''And Myra's due on shift in about five minutes.''

I gave her a last squeeze. ''You must be hungry.''

''Dying,'' she said. ''Nothing like a little simulated fresh air to give a person an appetite.''

''It wasjust the look of that huge steak, I know. They don't make them like that any more. Or at least they don't serve them like that.''

''And a good thing, too,'' she said, extricating herself from my embrace. ''That was grass-fed beef, and I'm sure it tasted terrible by modern standards. Let's go get our dinner.''

We passed Myra on the way out; she was one of the two other operators who used Alison's Bubble. She had a sour-faced old woman in tow—a woman I had seen so often that I was beginning to wonder when her grant would run out. She was studying the Plains Indians, and I was sure she must have enough information to write a dozen books by now. Hers was one of the longest ongoing projects in the Kansas City Center, and Myra had been complaining lately that the whole thing was starting to bore her. I had never had that experience myself. All of my assignments had been fascinating;

perhaps that was the luck of the draw or just a reflection of my attitude toward time viewing. Time viewing, after all, had given me everything I wanted—the endlessly marvelous past, a fat salary, and Alison.

She and I had been living together for about a year just then, sharing an apartment in one of Kansas City's plushest high-rises. The place suited us well—it was full of creature comforts, of deep-cushioned chairs and thick carpeting, and of the personal things of our lives, the music we loved and the souvenirs of our work. We stayed there during most of our free time, relaxing together, content with each other's company. We had the money to do anything, go anywhere, but that never mattered. The only thing we ever spent it on was good food; and because neither of us cared much for cooking, we went out for almost every meal.

That evening we visited one of our favorite restaurants. We were dressed plainly compared to the other patrons, wearing our work clothes while other diners wore furs and jewels, but the manager was accustomed to that and did not even raise an eyebrow. His place was frequented by Bubble operators, and that only boosted its reputation.

We ordered wine, lobster, pâté. Alison had a weakness for Maine lobster; there were not many places in Kansas City that served it.

"I thought you'd be having steak," I said, "after seeing it in the Bubble."

She shook her head. "The more I thought about it, the less appetizing it seemed. Earp probably ate it every day of his life. He probably never tasted lobster. Why should I limit myself to his menu? I can have steak anyplace. The famous Kansas City Steak."

I had to laugh. "People in New England probably care as little about lobster."

"Ah, yes," she murmured. "One never appreciates what's available at home."

We stopped for a swim after that, in the pool on the fortieth floor of our building. Ordinary people would probably have taken in a show instead, but Bubble operators rarely found the artificial life of either the theatre or the holomovies attractive—they spent their days with the reality of the past, live people instead of actors, and if that moved more slowly than professional entertainment, it was still too similar for the other to be diverting.

We went to bed early, and to sleep somewhat later. Alison seemed distracted while we made love, and quickly tired, but I put that down to an irritating session with a new client; I had had the same experience myself often enough. Clients—invariably Ph.D.s in some variety of history or anthropology—would sit still for a short time, patient at first while the operator worked the Bubble back to the appropriate time period, patient still while the Bubble swept through space to locate the precise spot requested. Only when the process began to drag out did they become restless; only when they began to realize that pinpointing events in time and space was not a simple matter, that it took a practiced and delicate hand and a great deal more patience than they ever thought existed, did they start to show their annoyance. Some clients merely became tense and twitchy as their sessions stretched toward Finish and they saw nothing that they were searching for. Others became sarcastic, making snide comments on the ability of the operator. Some became abusive. One client—back in the early days, just after the Jesus Project was finally geared down to ordinary proportions, when we had trained enough operators that a few could be spared for other parts of the world and other projects—actually tried to strangle me for, as he put it, delaying him unconscionably. Fortunately, the intercom to the maintenance office was open as usual, and about ten seconds after I yelled for help, three technicians erupted into the room and pulled him off me. He was gabbling about me wasting his grant money as they dragged him out. The company refunded his grant money and barred him from further use of the Bubble.

Alison had never had quite so bad an experience—I was something of a showpiece among the operators, the guy everyone pointed to when new operators asked if there was anything else to know about handling clients. But she knew her share of petty irritants. No matter how well an operator worked, the clients were hardly ever satisfied. Ultimately, they always thought there was something else they could have seen. And they were probably right. Especially in the case of tracing historical figures, there was always far more to a person's life than could be viewed in a few hours, even a few hundred hours, in the Bubble.

Alison had been an operator almost as long as I, though I had known her only two years when we moved in together. She had come out of the Paris office, one of the earliest set up after the experimental Bubble in Los Angeles and the first commercial office in Istanbul. She had been kept busy with the Romans and the Vikings there until the Kansas City office opened and needed some experienced operators. When that finally happened, there was considerable maneuvering among the company staff, mostly people trying to avoid the Kansas City assignment; they pleaded that it was an out-of-the way place without much intrinsic interest, not like Istanbul, Paris, or even Los Angeles. But it was a good central location as long as the Bubble was limited in range to about 1500 kilometers—superior to Chicago, which would have pleased some operators better as a base. The result of all the maneuvering was that only the operators with the most interest in the job itself went to Kansas City, those who got pleasure from time viewing almost to the exclusion of outside concerns. We prided ourselves on being the best, the cream. Alison, Myra, and I, and half a dozen others.

There was no lack of work for us, certainly. Pre-Columbian culture studies swept up most of the viewing slots at first, though Vanderbilt University did put in a big, successful bid for the Civil War period as soon as the office was announced. Having a relatively small grant, Holland had been forced to wait a long time for his opportunity to study Wyatt Earp.

On the day after I watched Alison's first session with Holland, the holos appeared in our apartment. It was a common practice among operators to surround themselves with pictures of the current assignment—people, genre scenes, anything typical of the period, anything attractive to the eye. We kept in the mood of the assignment that way, kept our minds working on it even in off-duty hours. In some ways, we were never off duty, because there were always calculations to be made, procedures to be planned, suggestions to be formulated. Few of the scholars who used the Bubble understood its techniques or its limitations, nor did they often even know exactly what they wanted from it. Part of the Bubble operator's job was to show them what could be discovered with the device. Too many users wanted to know *why* things happened in addition to the events themselves. And they fumed that they couldn't walk right into the Bubble and ask questions of the people there. "Anthropology without informants" was what one of my clients called it—valuable, of course, but not enough for some researchers. Two clients out of three would moan that they wished the company sold time travel instead of time viewing.

Myself, I was glad enough that it was just viewing. The complexities of actually going to the past made my mind spin every time I considered them. I was happy to sit at the console, safe in the world I understood, guiding people through the museum of the past, where everything was locked away behind the invisible walls of the Bubble, tamper-proof and secure.

Not all of the operators agreed with me, of course. Some of them surrounded themselves with so many holos of the past that their homes seemed to *be* there instead of in the Twenty-first Century. Myra usually turned entire walls of her place into scenes from her current project—for example, endless vistas of the Great Plains, complete with buffalo herds and Indian villages. When we sat in her living room during that period, it was like being camped on the prairie. Other operators were less extreme, like Alison and me, with a few holos from the current project plus a few well-loved shots from previous ones. In my bedroom there was a full-length, life-sized portrait of Augustus Caesar standing in the Forum, just as I had seen him that first time. Alison's room had a dragon-prowed Viking ship, one-quarter size, but still large enough to span an entire wall, and the waves beneath it lapped gently at its wooden sides; she said the motion soothed her when she was thinking.

The day after her first meeting with Holland, she put up holos of the main street of Ellsworth and of Earp, Whitney, Logan, the Thompsons—almost everyone we had seen in the Bubble, some full body shots, some just faces. She put them in her own room, scattered them on the three walls not occupied by the dragon ship; we had agreed when we moved in together that we would each fill our rooms with whatever we wanted and that the common rooms—living room, dining room, kitchen—would be decorated by consultation. The result of that was that our bedrooms were crowded with memorabilia but the other three rooms held only furniture and drapes and a few music tapes that we both liked.

From the doorway, I looked around her walls. "They mostly seem to need baths," I said.

She nodded, still adjusting placement of the pictures. "Except Earp and Whitney. And Logan, I think—he bathes frequently, but smithing is dirty work. Lots of soot."

I glanced at Whitney's face. "I suppose you won't be seeing much more of the sheriff." I pointed at him.

"Some," she said. "I've seen him die from two viewpoints already. Holland says we'll try at least one more."

"How many times can you watch a man be shot?"

"It's Earp he's interested in, not Whitney. He thinks by watching this scene closely enough, he'll be able to figure out why Earp goes after Thompson in the face of all that opposition." She grinned at me. "He wants to read the man's mind."

"I take it nobody knows why Earp did it."

"There are a couple of books, each with its own interpretation, but Holland says they're both based on interviews with Earp when he was an old man. He suspects eighty-year-old Earp of either embroidery or forgetfulness." She shrugged. "I don't think he knew why he did it. He just did it. He was crazy."

"Wyatt Earp crazy? The greatest legend of the West?" She started to step back to see the effect of her adjustment of the holos, and I eased myself behind her so that she ended up in my arms. I locked my hands over her navel. "What a cruel thing to think," I murmured, nuzzling her neck.

"He has that penetrating look of madness in his eye," she said. She covered my hands with her own. "He has restless eyes, as if he thinks someone might be after him."

I chuckled against her hair. "That's the piercing gaze of the lone scout you're criticizing, you know."

"And he's thin—the nervous type that eats and eats but never gains weight. You saw the meal he ordered."

"He's the calmest person I ever saw. The way he faced that Thompson fellow, with the mob behind him. . . ."

"A suicidal impulse." She ticked items off on her fingers, pressing one after the other against my hand. "Suicide prone. Paranoid. Megalomaniacal."

"Megalomaniacal? How so?"

"No one but a megalomaniac would have thought he could face down all those armed men and get out alive."

"That's not consistent with the suicidal part of your diagnosis."

She shrugged. "I'm looking at all the options."

I had to laugh. "Have you discussed any of this with Dr. Holland?"

"No. I don't think he'd want to hear it. Earp is his hero—pure, good, the epitome of courage. Sort of larger than life. And, anyway, why should I offer my theories? He's not paying me for psychiatric services." She turned her head to look at me sidelong. "Besides . . . an operator should always try to maintain a tranquil relationship with the client."

"You think Dr. Holland would try to do something unpleasant if you told him you thought Earp was insane?"

She pivoted in my embrace and slid her arms up around my neck. "Who knows," she replied. "I don't know how crazy *he* is yet."

"We're all crazy somehow," I said. "Me, for example—I'm crazy about you."

"That's good to know," shc whispered.

We spent the rest of that night in her bedroom, surrounded by Ellsworth, Kansas, and its incongruous partner, the Viking ship.

My own project of the period was as routine as any had ever been—the endless trek along the Oregon Trail. There were thousands of stories in those covered wagons, most of which I never saw completed, for they passed beyond range of our equipment at the Snake River in Idaho, just before the last leg of their journey. Still, I thought their history, in a dramatic sense, had been pretty well covered by a multitude of classic movies I had seen as a child. So I didn't much mind it being cut short for me. My client, of course, didn't see things that way, and she would be finishing her research in Los Angeles, where she could view the other end of the Trail.

I had been living with several holos of covered wagons, dusty mules, and poke-bonneted women for some time on the day that Alison installed her new pictures, and it was shortly after that that I decided to get rid of them and bring back some old favorites. I had steeped myself in the period long enough, I thought, that I no longer needed visual inspiration; I just *knew* what to do every day, almost without conscious effort. That was a common experience among operators during extended projects.

I dumped the holos and surrounded Augustus with other successes. There had been failures, of course—certain historical figures who could not be found no matter what I tried, leading me to believe that either they were entirely mythical or that my clients' literary researches were less than perfect—but there were few operators who liked to keep records of *that* sort. Nothing was more frustrating, and more ulcer-making, than searching time and space for someone or something that wasn't there.

The central office had those records, of course—and the failures would go before the upper echelons of the company during the semiannual employee evaluation. So far, though, no operator had ever been fired for lack of success. There were just too few of us to go around, and training was, at that time, too long and expensive a procedure to waste on anyone without considerable potential. The bad risks were weeded out early, and most operators had a strong sense of having found their life's work. I know I did.

Not long after I got rid of my Oregon Trail holos, Alison added to her Earp collection. She and Holland had moved on to Wichita, and a new set of faces replaced the citizens of Ellsworth. Earp was more mature, I saw, but gaunt as ever, and I thought there were five pictures of him on the wall until Alison explained that two were of his brothers Morgan and Virgil. Only someone who had seen them often, alive, in motion, could have told them apart.

I also recognized another face, though at first I couldn't place it.

"Jimmy Logan, the blacksmith's boy, remember?" said Alison. 'He followed Earp to Wichita. Hero-worship, I think. Wants to be his deputy, but Earp says he's too young."

Logan looked older than before, had gained some weight, just enough to give him a mature physique. But he still had a boy's face, and I could see why Earp had said what he did.

"One less new name to memorize," Alison said, crossing her arms over her breasts. "Sometimes I suspect Holland can't possibly have any living friends—his mind can't have room for their names."

I had to smile at her. "Maybe he has holos of his living friends on his walls, just to remind him of them."

She laughed.

With the lights low, we couldn't see all those eyes looking down at us. When I was new at time viewing, that had made me feel strange—dead people watching my sleep. Now, it was nothing, and I slept well beneath them, perhaps better than if the walls had been bare. There was a kind of childish security in knowing that the shadows in the room held only familiar things. I even dreamed about my holos, night spent as my days were, perhaps even a touch more vividly. In my dreams I was often inside the Bubble instead of sitting at the console. Alison would smile when I told her that. She said she didn't dream about that sort of thing at all.

About a week after she and Holland began work on Wichita, the Viking ship vanished from the fourth wall, replaced by more shots of people. Alison's room was crowded with pictures now, every available centimeter, a kaleidoscope of pictures. She made no attempt at pattern, or at any illusion of reality; they were just scattered randomly, like a crowd pressing close to the bed. Her room had become a scrapbook.

Then she started spending her independent time in the period.

Most operators ran uninterrupted six-hour shifts, each trio assigned to a console arranging its own flexible schedule. The remaining time was, theoretically, reserved for maintenance, but in practice the machines rarely needed more than brief routine servicing. That left a couple of extra hours per day on each console. The company could have sold that time, of course, no matter how inconveniently placed the slots were, but early in its history it established a different policy: operators were required to sign up for those odd hours, every operator taking at least one of those slots every week, to practice search techniques. In the Kansas City Center, at least, no one had to be told to take a turn in independent study, and we all had pet private projects going that were important only to us. The company oversaw it all but generally looked the other way when an operator used independent time to make certain kinds of profit in the outside world. More than one operator had earned a minor scholarly reputation on independent work; even I had published a paper on the Indian Wars. Others just played at their consoles, watching famous sporting events or entertainments of the past. In the Paris office, according to Alison, the most popular independent study was viewing the great Elizabethan plays as they had been originally performed, with Shakespeare himself sometimes appearing onstage. Some of us would have liked to view more recent events, the great baseball and football games, and the Olympics of the middle and late Twentieth Century—but the Bubble failed us there. The 93.675 years immediately before our own were closed to the Bubble, too near to focus. That was an explanation the Company had to give out tiresomely often, especially to the various governments of the world, which wanted to spy on each other from the vantage of yesterday.

I really didn't mind the loss of ninety-three-odd years. Like most operators, I was fascinated by the remote past, by the worlds that were so different from the one that had encompassed my life before I discovered the Company. There was no single period that drew me; I moved from one to another as whim took me—which was typical. Ordinarily, an operator chose an area of independent study because of something he had seen during his regular work, something at a tangent to the client's desires but intriguing to the operator.

As Alison had chosen the period of Earp.

I became aware of her new interest when she signed a tape out of records and brought it home to project in her room. Projection required that she move a wall of holos, and for that she requested my help. I thought it was amusing that we didn't stack the holos but moved them to the ceiling, where she could see them from the bed. I had always thought of the ceiling as sacred blank territory, but Alison didn't want to discard any of the pictures. She asked me if I wanted to view the tape, knowing that I would demur. I rarely viewed tapes myself, only when necessary for the job, because their reality was so much less than that in the Bubble; they were not two-dimensional, but they seemed flat to me. I left her there, propped on a mound of pillows on the bed, and I went out to the living room to listen to a little music.

She didn't come out that evening and didn't invite me in. I never knew when she stopped viewing the tape. Rather than disturb her, I went to bed in my own room, alone. We had an agreement about that, too—we respected each other's privacy.

She brought another tape home the following evening. And the one after that. She said they related to Holland's investigations, that she was doing extra preparation for some difficult searches. Alison had always been diligent that way. She came back to my bed on the fourth night, and I was certainly glad to welcome her; I decided that she was working just a little too hard on Dr. Holland's project—a little too hard for my taste. But I didn't say anything. It was her job, she loved it, and this project wouldn't last forever. Holland's grant had to run out someday.

So for a time I didn't see much of Alison, though we shared the apartment and similar work schedules. But when I did see her, it was wonderful, fresh, as if we had just discovered each other, as if she were trying to make up for having so little time for me. There was an extra measure of passion in her lovemaking, and of unpredictability, for I would never know when she was going to creep into my bed in the middle of the night—after staying up that long—and wake me in the best possible way. It was fresh, and frustrating, and a little silly, and at last I tired of it and found myself looking forward impatiently to return to the old, settled relationship.

But I saw less and less of her, and what I did see began to be moody and morose, as if there were something nagging at her. I thought I recognized those symptoms—the signs of a project going sour, the goals not realized, seeming farther and farther away every day, or completely unrealizable. Better, I decided, not to discuss that possibility with her; I knew how oppressive such discussions could be. I saw Holland a couple of times in the corridors of the company building, and he seemed buoyant. He hardly noticed me, probably didn't recall me from that first day. The contrast between his and Alison's attitudes didn't seem odd to me; often the operator was the first to suspect that something was going bad, while the client was still wrapped up in evaluating earlier achievements.

Then her wardrobe changed.

Alison had never been much interested in clothes. Normally she wore jeans and a tee shirt and sneakers just this side of worn out. Now she traded the jeans for dark slacks, the tee shirt for man-cut long-sleeved white, the sneakers for boots. It was an unfamiliar style, not particularly attractive, except that Alison was wearing it. She never needed beautiful clothes in order to look beautiful. I didn't care that she wore something different. Except that it was . . . different. The change in wardrobe seemed to betoken some other change in her. She was . . . brisker, somehow. With me, at least. She didn't seem to have any time at all these days. There was pressure on her, of Holland's making or her own, I couldn't be sure which. Perhaps, I thought, his grant was running out and he was transmitting the pressure he was feeling to her. I found myself hoping that his grant would run out *very* soon.

Then she stayed away from our apartment all night.

It had happened before, always work. There was no reason for me to think it was anything else this time. When I saw her the next day, she didn't talk about it. She was in too much of a rush.

I hadn't wanted to believe it, but I couldn't resist the feeling that something was coming between us. The way Holland looked at me in the corridor, that look of complete disinterest . . . could it have been him? The new wardrobe nagged at my mind. Holland didn't dress that way, of course; he was just a typical, somewhat conservative academic type, subdued colors and patterns, his clothing ten or fifteen years behind the current fashions in their cut. But Earp dressed that way, and other men of the period—Sunday clothes, they called them, clothes of the leisure time. Alison wouldn't wear a hoop skirt and a poke bonnet, of course, but she might immerse herself in the masculine fashions of the day to be more in harmony with Holland's fascination.

I told myself not to be jealous. Holland was considerably older than Alison and I and, to my eyes, not particularly attractive. I didn't know if he was attached to someone else. But he wasn't a Kansas City resident, and so he would have to leave eventually. If it was Holland indeed, I could weather that. Alison and I had too much going for us for any outsider to pry us apart. I told myself that when she was out a second night, when I had lost track of how many nights it had been since we had made love.

I went shopping for myself. I figured that two could play this game, and so I bought myself a pair of dark slacks and some boots and a soft white shirt of the proper style. I even bought a string tie and did it up the way Earp did his. And then I checked at records to see when Alison was scheduled for her next independent stint; I was going to surprise her with my new outfit and see if I could get a laugh out of her. We had always laughed together, before Holland.

Records revealed that she had been spending an unusual amount of time in independent work. She had traded with the other operators assigned to her console, amassed a considerable number of extra hours, and spent them all viewing the period between 1873 and 1885. She had also signed out tapes of everything she had viewed independently and had claimed a projection room for replaying them. There were no records of how often she had used the projection room, just that she had access to it full-time. I thought about those rooms, with their wide, plush couches—perfect for meeting . . . close friends. I wondered if she had viewed any of the tapes in that room, or if she had done something else entirely there.

I had always been honest with Alison. I had thought she would be honest with me. I was sure there was something wrong now between us. And I wanted to bridge the gap before it became too wide. I didn't want to lose Alison. I didn't think I had done anything that would cause her to stop loving me. But maybe I hadn't done enough to keep her wanting to love me. All I could think of was Holland. What did he have to offer that was better? How could he possibly love her more than I did? He hardly knew her.

I went to the door of her projection room when she should have been there. It was locked. Somehow, I couldn't bring myself to ring the call bell. It wouldn't have been fair to disturb whatever she was doing in there. I stood by the door awhile, hoping she would come out on her own, hoping *someone* would come out, but at last I gave up. I told myself I was too hungry to wait for her. But when I got to the restaurant, everything on the menu looked like dust; I could hardly choke down the light salad that was all I ordered.

Finally, she changed shifts.

We had always arranged our shifts to more or less coincide, since the first day we decided to live together. No—before that, back when we first realized that we had something special. Each of us had settled into an arrangement with the other two operators of our consoles, and except for a few brief, temporary readjustments, everyone had been satisfied. Now I found a note taped to my bedroom door:

> MYRA IS ON A NEW PROJECT AND HAS ASKED ME TO SWITCH SHIFTS WITH HER FOR THE DURATION
>
> LOVE, ALLISON

I stared at the word LOVE. In spite of its presence, the note felt cold and impersonal. In other days, she would have told me herself, in bed, in an apologetic tone. She and Myra were very close, they did each other favors often. Myra always had a good reason for asking Alison to take her shift. It never lasted long. But . . . for the duration?

Because Alison obviously didn't want to discuss the matter with me in person, I called Myra—she was at home at the same times I was now, while Alison was not.

"You can't imagine how glad I was to get rid of that old prune!" she said almost as soon as I could say hello. "She's taking a vacation, and with any luck, I won't be available when she comes back, and she'll have to drive another operator crazy!"

"Yes," I said. "I'd heard from Alison that you had a new project. Some problem with the scheduling, wasn't there? Was it a local academic with a teaching conflict?"

Myra's expression was puzzled. "No, just the usual out-of-towner. From Dallas this time. Why do you ask?"

"Well, I was wondering . . . why you switched shifts with Alison."

She frowned a little. "Why, that was Alison's idea. She did it to stay in synch with you, didn't she?"

"I haven't changed."

"No?"

"No."

Her eyebrows rose slowly. "Are you and Alison . . . having problems?"

I said, "I don't know. How long is your new project going to last?"

"Awhile. A few weeks maybe. It doesn't look like anything monumental. Maybe she just wants a change. A vacation."

"From me?"

"Well, any relationship can get. . . ." She shrugged. "Claustrophobic." She leaned forward. "Is she talking about moving out?"

"She isn't talking at all. I haven't seen her in days."

"Maybe you should leave her alone for a while. Let her work through whatever it is that's bothering her."

"I don't think I have a choice on that. We may be living in the same apartment, but we don't seem to be living in the same world any more."

"Oh, Barry . . . I'm sorry." She spread her hands in helplessness. "Maybe it's just the job. She's been looking tired lately. Maybe she just doesn't have the energy left for her private life. After her current project is over, you two should take a long vacation, get away from the company, from the Bubble, from the pressure. Just the two of you."

"If it's still the two of us by then."

"Take it easy, Barry. Maybe it will all blow over, whatever it is."

I tried to smile at her, but my lips felt very stiff. "I hope so," I said. "Thanks, Myra. See you tomorrow." I broke the connection, and her face vanished from the viewscreen, but I couldn't get her expression of sympathy out of my mind. How did I look to her, I wondered, that provoked that expression? I went to the bathroom mirror and stared at myself for a while. I hadn't examined my own face so carefully in a long time; in the morning when I got ready for work, it was all business—the hair, the comb, the chin, the depilator. I never looked at my eyes. Now I saw they were bloodshot, as if I hadn't slept well in a long time. For the rest, it could have been misery or anger; I felt them both lapping over me, fighting with each other for supremacy. I wanted to break the mirror.

The apartment felt so empty with Alison gone. So cold. I stood before her door, that blank, familiar territory. We respected each other's privacy; I knew it would not be locked; I knew Alison would never have dreamed that I might go in without her permission. I touched the smooth panel with the flat of my hand. What did I expect to find? The walls covered with pictures of Holland? Or everything packed up, ready to be removed, a trunk standing in the middle of the floor? Or . . . nothing—an empty room, already divested of all the individuality that was Alison?

I slid the panel aside.

At first glance, the room appeared to be in its ordinary condition, much as I had seen it last, with holos on three walls and the ceiling, the fourth wall blank for projection. Scenes and people of the Classic West surrounded me, and Alison's bed and belongings were in their usual places. She wasn't moving out, at least. Then something began to nag at me and I turned slowly to take in all the pictures, to look at what they were, not just at the whole kaleidoscopic effect.

There was only one man on the walls of that room. In a hundred different poses, a hundred different sets of clothing, full body shots and portraits, profiles and frontal views, with mustache and clean-shaven, at a dozen different ages, but still, unmistakably, the same man. I knew him, I was sure of that, but it took me a few moments to place him. For me, he would never have stood out from a crowd, but I had seen him in the Bubble and I had seen him before on that wall. His name came at last—Jimmy Logan, the blacksmith's boy, the one who hero-worshipped Wyatt Earp. In one of the holos, a full-length shot, life-sized, he appeared to be about thirty years old, and he wore a marshal's star on his long-sleeved white shirt.

I sat down on the bed. In my periods of greatest devotion to Augustus Caesar, I had never been so immersed in him. It was overwhelming, stifling, claustrophobic. I lay back, and there he was on the ceiling, inescapable; he had his shirt off in the most central shot, hot sun pouring down on him, and the beads of sweat on his shoulders and chest glistened, giving him the appearance of being covered with oil. I rolled over, burying my face in her pillow to escape him. The pillow smelled faintly of her shampoo, and I wondered when the last time was that she had slept here. A glass half-full of water sat on the bedside table, the inside surface of the lower part covered with bubbles. Stale. Was it yesterday that she had drunk from that glass, or last week?

Behind the glass was a stack of tapes, coded with the company's emblem. The recording dates were all recent. These, I thought, were what she had been spending some of her spare time with. I dimmed the overhead lights and slipped one into her projector.

A dusty street materialized upon the blank wall. The sun was low, shadows long, few people walking anywhere in sight. The street looked vaguely familiar; it might have been Ellsworth, or any one of a hundred similar Western cowtowns of the period. I half expected to see Wyatt Earp stride through the field of view. Instead, Jimmy Logan entered it, Logan in his mid-twenties, I judged, walking with a sure stride down the street. The center of town was behind him. He was passing into a more residential sector, an area of clapboard houses surrounded by burnt-out gardens and white picket fences. He stopped to unlatch the gate at one of the houses, to step through it and latch it once more behind him. He hurried up the walk, climbed three steps and pulled the front door open without knocking. I guessed that it was his own house and he had come home for supper.

I swooped in behind him and found that more than supper was waiting inside for him. She was about his age, rather prim-looking in the tradition of the time, hair pulled back in a tight knot, dress high at the neck and long-sleeved, falling to the floor. Still, she was rather pretty and quite nicely built, and she gave him a very warm welcome. When her hand touched the back of his neck, I saw that she wore a wedding ring. They kissed for quite a long time, and the tape went on afterward, following lovingly close as they went into the bedroom and undressed each other and eased to the bed. From their intensity, I supposed that they hadn't been married long. Alison had caught everything, had recorded an excellent piece of erotica. I found myself reacting very strongly to it.

And wondering how she reacted.

I scanned the other tapes at high speed. They were all different, yet all fundamentally alike. Not that they were *all* erotic not overtly. A few just showed him moving, chopping wood, riding a horse, working in his father's forge. Still, there was an erotic element to them all, a physical element. When I had seen the lot, I had a very fine awareness of his body, of the play of muscles, the style of walk and posture, the little habitual gestures. And I knew I would never again have any trouble recognizing him. If he had been alive, if he had walked into the company's offices, I could have greeted him by name.

And I didn't know who he was.

I knew, of course, that he was Logan, but who was Logan? What was his place in history? Why was Alison so fascinated by him?

I put everything back as I had found it, smoothed the bed. When she came home . . . if she came home, she wouldn't be able to tell I had breached her privacy. I felt guilty about doing it, but glad. Out in the living room, I put in a call to the Encyclopedia Britannica, requested all their information on James Logan of Ellsworth, Kansas, approximate birth year 1853.

They had no listing for him.

He wasn't important, at least not that our contemporary culture knew. I thought that he must be important just to Dr. Frederick Holland.

So I waited until Alison was off shift and called Dr. Holland, taking a chance that he and she would not be together at his place. I was at work by then and didn't know if Alison had gone home. Records gave me Holland's number at the guest house. He was bright, polite, not rushed as if he had company. He didn't seem to recognize my name or face.

"Just some checking on behalf of records, Dr. Holland," I said. "We just want to confirm that some of your time has been devoted to an intensive study of one James Logan."

Holland looked puzzled. "Don't you people know what I'm studying?"

"We have a listing for Wyatt Earp, Dr. Holland, but you seem to have expanded your researches to include this other person."

"Is that wrong? Is that not allowed? I thought the fee covered whatever researches I chose to make."

"It does, Dr. Holland, it does. We only want to keep our records organized for purposes of cross-referencing. Someone else has requested materials on James Logan, and to avoid duplication of effort we would appreciate knowing how much of his life you intend to examine."

Holland shook his head. "Very little," he said. "If someone else is investigating him, they won't profit by *my* studies. Who is it, anyway?"

"I'm sorry, Dr. Holland, but we can't give out that information. Would you please tell me approximately how many hours of work you have spent or intend to spend on James Logan? An estimate."

"Well, none on him *per se*. I suppose he's appeared in an hour or two of my viewing so far, but just as a bystander. I don't expect to see him at all in the future."

"Thank you for your time, Dr. Holland. Sorry to have disturbed you."

"Not at all," he said. "I'm sorry I couldn't be more help."

I snapped off the connection.

Unless Holland was lying, Logan was Alison's own project. Unless he was lying. Perhaps the lack of recognition was just a sham, and he knew perfectly well that I was Alison's lover. Ex-lover? Still, I had called unexpectedly; he hadn't had time to prepare camouflage for his reactions. And the more I saw of him the less likely he seemed as a reasonable replacement for me. Of course, I couldn't be objective on that. I was rapidly discovering that I couldn't be objective on anything where Alison was concerned.

I had tried calling her during her off-shift, at work, at home. Her line had a block on my personal code; she wasn't accepting my calls. It seemed absurd—we lived together, but I didn't see her, couldn't talk to her. Part of that was my own doing, and I decided the time had come to ring at the door of her projection room, even if it meant disturbing her privacy.

I traded shifts with one of my co-workers, putting myself back in synch with Alison. Now I had time to spend in trying to touch her. It took me quite a while to get up the courage to ring. I kept telling myself that the truth couldn't possibly be worse than what I imagined.

I rang.

At first there was no answer, and I thought perhaps she wasn't inside. Like every room of the building, it was totally soundproofed. So I couldn't tell if it was occupied by pressing my ear against the panel, though I did that anyway. I rang again. And as I waited, while the occasional company personnel passed by and looked at me curiously, I began to think that she was inside all right, watching erotic tapes with Holland. I hadn't bothered to check on him. And then I didn't care. I rang again, a long, long ring, my finger pressed against the call button until the nail reddened.

The door opened.

Alison wore her new clothes, or perhaps they were her only clothes now. The soft white shirt, the dark trousers, the boots made her look like someone else, someone I didn't know. She wore her hair tied back now, too, with a thin ribbon, not loose about her shoulders any more.

"Oh," she said. "Hello." She leaned against the door, as if to block my way inside and my view of it.

"May I come in?"

"Why?" she said.

"I hope I'm not disturbing you too much."

"Some," she said.

"I'd like to talk to you. Please. If not now . . . then maybe I can make an appointment?" I tried to smile at that suggestion, but my mouth didn't want to cooperate.

She sighed heavily. "All right. Come in." She stood aside, holding the door with both hands, like a shield.

There was no one else in the room. It was a very bare little room, with minimum comforts. A thick rug. A couch in the center of the floor. A four-way projector, for displaying tapes on all the walls simultaneously. Alison walked to one end of the couch and stood there, waiting for me.

"Sit down," she said.

I sat, but she remained standing, I thought so that she could go back to the door any time she wanted and hold it open for my exit.

"Well?" she said.

I tried to smile again, but the effort was too much for me. I patted the cushion beside me. "Come here?"

She shook her head. "I don't have time for a long discussion."

I said, "Alison, what's wrong?"

"I'm just busy."

I leaned toward her. "You know what I mean. What's wrong with us? What's happened?"

She half turned away, looked down at the carpet. "Let it go, Barry. I don't want to talk about it."

"Let it go?" I stood up, took a step and reached for her, but she backed off, just beyond my grasp, "Alison, I love you."

She crossed her arms over her breasts. "Let's not play tag, Barry. Just leave me alone."

"Have you . . . changed your feelings about me?" The words caught in my throat, and I thought for a moment that they would choke me. Then I realized that the sensation was tears held back. I didn't want to cry in front of her; my pride wouldn't allow that.

"Do you want me to move out?" she said.

"No!"

"I don't want to. It's a lot of trouble." She spoke so casually, so effortlessly, while for me every word was like pulling knives from my belly.

"Alison," I began.

She walked over to the door and opened it for me, as I had known she would. "You'd better go. I'm very busy."

I couldn't move for a moment. Watching her walk—no, *stride* was the word to describe it—jarred me. Clothes, manner, even walk, this was a new Alison indeed. She didn't even stand the way she used to. Her step was longer now, harder, though maybe that was a result of the hard high heels on those boots, like the boots that Earp and Logan and Whitney had worn, the boots that hammered so hard on wooden sidewalks. She walked like the men of Ellsworth, Kansas, those men whose natural habitat included dusty, unpaved streets and wide prairie pounded flat by the hooves of buffalo. And she stood as they did, legs wide, hips canted as if a pair of forty-fives rode on them.

Standing by the couch, I felt as though time itself had come between us, as if some strange avatar of a man dead a century had come out of the Bubble to stand in Alison's place. I sagged. I, a mere mortal of the Twenty-first Century—what did I have in common with this creature from the past? I shook my head sharply. No, I told myself, this was just Alison, no matter how deeply she had immersed herself in vanished days. Perhaps, I thought, too deeply. I glanced sidelong at the projector, at the tapes racked in its holders. Four were in playing position; Alison had probably been running them one at a time, but I had only to touch a button to show them all simultaneously. A serious breach of operator etiquette.

"What's been keeping you so busy?" I asked softly, and my finger stabbed the button.

"No!" shouted Alison.

But it was too late. I saw what she had been seeing until she opened the door for me.

Four walls of Logan was too much for me. My head spun.

Logan in the dusty street, star on his chest, facing down a waiting gunman, tension evident in his straining stance. Logan with chest bared and running sweat in his father's forge, muscles glistening with the ruddy light of the coals. Logan making love to his wife in the bed I had seen once before. Logan by a brook, lying on green grass, obviously far from Ellsworth, and with him someone other than his wife, laughing, holding her arms out to him.

Alison reached the projector then and punched the OFF button. "Get out," she said, her face white with anger, her eyes hard. But she was so close as we both stood by the projector that I couldn't help encircling her with my arms, pressing her against me. She turned her face away from my kiss and tried to push me away; for a moment I held her tight, my lips against her hair, and at least she smelled like the old Alison. She hadn't changed her shampoo.

She broke free. "Out," she said, her hands making fists at her hips, and I could have sworn that if those forty-fives had been there she would have drawn on me. I had seen that kind of anger before, in the Bubble.

I didn't move. "What's going on, Alison?" I whispered. "What are you doing in here? Making tapes for public consumption? Or maybe just . . . for private?"

"What I do in here is none of your business."

I shook my head slowly. "What have I done, Alison? We used to confide in each other. We used to trust each other. We used to . . . love each other."

"I don't love you any more," she said. "Now leave me alone."

The words were like bricks dropping on my head, but instead of being beaten down, I felt myself drawing the strength of fury from them. "Who is it then?" I shouted. "Who is it? Holland?"

"No, it isn't Holland. It isn't anyone. Now will you leave before everbody on the floor comes running to see what the shouting's about?" She pointed peremptorily toward the door.

I went to the door, but I kicked it shut instead of going out. "He isn't worth it," I said, turning back to her, my voice a bit more under control "He'll bore you out of your mind!"

"I told you I'm not interested in Holland," she said. "And I'm not interested in continuing this conversation."

"Who, then?" I demanded. "Who are you making these tapes for? Who are you going to enjoy these choice bits of erotica with? Is it someone I know?"

"It isn't anyone," said Alison. "And even if it were, you have no right to ask who."

"I have the right to know who the competition is. I have a right to know what he's doing for you that I haven't done."

She turned away. "Go home, Barry. It's over, that's all. Since you feel this way, I'll move out as soon as I can find a new place."

"I don't want you to move out, Alison!"

"Well, what *do* you want?"

"I want . . . to understand." I took a step toward her and held my hands out, pleading. "What have I done wrong?"

She sighed. "Nothing, Barry. Nothing at all. I'm just . . . not interested any more. You're going to have to accept that."

"Then what are you interested in?" I looked at the projector. "This? Watching dead people make love? When you can have someone live and warm?"

"I'd rather not discuss it."

"What kind of replacement is that for me? Am I so . . . repulsive?"

"You're not repulsive, Barry."

I eased up behind her, touched her shoulders tentatively. "I've changed my schedule, Alison; we're back in synch. Why don't we go out for dinner and then home? Or whatever you want. I'll do whatever you want. Anything." I squeezed her shoulders with stiff finger, trying to be gentle, knowing that I was too tense to be so. "Come home, darling. Please come home."

She shook her head.

"I'll wait for you, till you're finished with whatever it is that you're doing. You can't stay here around the clock. You've got to eat, to sleep. It's all so much more pleasant with a warm body nearby. I won't even talk if you don't want me to."

Again, she shook her head.

"Alison, please."

"Barry," she said quietly, "I would rather stay here with him than go anywhere with you."

"With *him?* Who?"

"Jim Logan."

I glanced at the projector. "You'd rather watch a dead man than spend any time with me."

"Please don't take it as an insult."

"No?" I swung her around to face me. "How else can I take it?"

"He's fresh, Barry. He's different. He fascinates me."

"I can see that."

"I can watch him for hours. He's struggling to move from one world to another. His father want him to be a blacksmith, but he wants to be a peace officer. He has a very strong sense of right and wrong. And courage. Barry, I've never seen such courage."

"And his body isn't bad, either," I said. "Which do you watch more—the body or the courage?"

She shook her head. "You don't understand. He fulfills my highest expectations. I couldn't expect more from a human being than I see in him."

"There was Earp."

She dismissed him with a wave of her hand. "Earp wasn't the wonderful person legend would have him."

"And this guy is wonderful. It just makes you go all warm inside to watch him be so terrific."

She pushed away from me. "I knew I couldn't discuss it with you."

I stared at her for a long moment. At last I said, "Alison, do you have a crush on this guy?"

She stared back at me, her lips a thin, white line. "Don't be silly," she said.

I looked her up and down, slowly, and everything I had seen and heard since she opened the door began to make a sort of bizarre sense to me. "I think you're acting like a teenager in love with an entertainment idol. Only this . . . this one isn't even accessible through the stage door. You'll never touch him, Alison. You'll never even get close enough to find out if he has bad breath."

"That's nonsense."

"Then tell me who's really taking up your time. Tell me that I'm wrong, that it's a live person edging me out. I'd rather believe that, Alison."

"Barry, you're wrong on both counts. Look—you have your hobbies, your favorite historical people. I remember very clearly all those stories you used to tell about Augustus. I didn't accuse you of having a crush on him."

"This is different! I didn't trade time with my fellow operators to spend all my waking hours following his life. I didn't tape his orgies for later replay. I didn't wear a toga."

"So I traded a few hours; so what?" Her brows knit. "You've been checking up on me."

I nodded. "I'm fascinated by *you*, Alison."

"I don't think I care for that level of curiosity."

"I missed you. I was jealous. Isn't it understandable?"

She strode to the projector, pulled out one of the four tapes and inserted a replacement from the stach in one of the holders. She hit the ON button, and Logan flashed onto one of the walls, life-sized, standing spraddle-legged on the empty prairie, one hand raised before him holding a gun. He was shooting slow and steady at something—a target, I guessed, beyond the edge of the picture. He wore no hat, and a sharp wind ruffled his hair, his shirt collar. He made a striking figure against the endless expanse of prairie and cloudless sky.

"All right," said Alison, not looking at me but at the image on the wall. "There's your competition. Now get out of here. Or I'll call for help and have you thrown out. I signed out this room, and you haven't any right in it without my approval."

"Alison," I said. "This is all wrong."

"I'll be out of thc apartment as soon as I can manage it."

"You don't have to move. I want you to stay."

"I don't want to stay," she said.

"Alison . . . he's dead. He's dust."

"Get out!"

I felt my whole body slump, my legs carry me toward the door without any conscious volition on my part. I touched the panel with my fist before opening it. "I love you," I said. "I'll wait this thing out."

"Goodbye."

I closed the door softly behind me, leaned against the wall beside it. Then I just slid down to the floor and sat with my knees up, my head pillowed on my arms, and I wept. I didn't care who saw me. Several people passed in the ensuing minutes, most of them operators I had known for years, and each one of them asked if I needed any help. I did, but none they could give. At last I got tired of hearing their offers and staggered away. I locked myself in a bathroom for a while, and eventually I was empty enough to go home.

Alison moved out three days later. I wasn't home when it happened; she took a day off while I was on shift, and she cleaned her room out so thoroughly that it looked as if no one had ever lived there. When I got home I discovered her bedroom door ajar and went in and stood in the bare room for a time, not thinking anything at all. It was like our relationship had never been. Even the music collection, when I looked through it later to put something on the system, was missing the recordings she had selected. As I sat and listened to one of my own choices—I didn't really know which one—I couldn't help wondering if Holland had been angry at missing a day with the Bubble.

The next afternoon, Myra was sympathetic, everyone was sympathetic, though not all were verbal about it. Everyone knew that Alison had left me. But Myra assured me that she hadn't moved in with anyone else; she had taken a small place near the company building. I guessed that Myra thought she was being kind to me, to tell me that, and I didn't have the heart to explain that I would have been happier the other way, any other way.

I called Alison a couple of times in the following weeks, after Myra gave me her number, but her line was blocked to my code as before. I didn't know what I would say anyway; I just wanted to see her face. I didn't see her at work at all, though she was still there. I wondered briefly if her next step would be to transfer to another office, but then I realized that only in Kansas City could she watch Logan—he was out of range anywhere else. I was assuming, of course, that he spent his whole life in Kansas. After a while I thought she might transfer when she had tracked his life to some point where he moved to another base's range. Earp had done it, gone to California eventually, as Holland would have to do if he wanted to follow his quarry all the way.

I realized I didn't know very much about Logan. But Alison's interest in him was mesmeric. I *wanted* to know. I wanted to understand her fixation. So in my independent time I began to study him. If the records people thought it was strange that two operators were spending a lot of time in the same milieu, they never said anything, even when I, like Alison, traded away my future independent time to other operators willing to give up their present allotments.

I can't say I grew fond of him, though his wife was very pretty. The other woman I had seen him with on Alison's tape turned out to be a second wife, acquired after the first one died in childbirth. He was a very moral person, this Logan—never gambled, rarely drank, sent his children to Sunday school. His contemporaries considered him a pillar of the community. He moved back to Ellsworth soon after Earp left Wichita for Dodge, becoming its marshal in 1876. The town was past its days of glory then, but still a rowdy place, and there was plenty of work for a man with a fast gun hand and more courage than I could comprehend. I didn't compare to him there. I had seen a lot of guns pointed in my direction in the Bubble, and my mouth had gone dry at every one of them, though the bullets couldn't touch me; I probably would have fainted at the same sight in reality. Or at best, frozen. I had the wrong reactions to be a frontier gunfighter. I knew she compared me to him and found me lacking. But how well would James Logan function in the Kansas City of the Twenty-First Century, where the skills he had spent so many years honing would be useless? He wouldn't even be able to function as a contemporary law officer now that the police no longer carried guns.

I worked forward through Logan's life, watched his children grow, watched the trees that shaded his white clapboard house rise up and up till the street beneath them was moist with shade instead of dusty in the summer. Ellsworth aged, too, softened, settled down to quiet anonymity. In 1889 he and the family moved west to Colorado, where the town of Lamar needed a marshal. Life was more exciting for him there. He seemed to thrive on excitement, to be restless when things were quiet.

And then he disappeared.

The standard procedure for a quick Bubble survey of the life of a historical figure involved a delicate and almost intuitive use of the device. The operator had to guess where people were going, how long they would be there, when they would return. The operator had to skim through events at a speed that made them virtually incomprehensible to the layman, halting the process by some instinct that sensed significance. It took a long time to develop that instinct, but every good operator had it. I established my baselines immediately—the house Logan lived in, the marshal's office. I saw him pass in and out of them like a wraith, almost insubstantial against the long-lasting solidity of the walls and furnishing. I could run through the days of his life in the minutes of my own. Sometimes I lost track of him and had to retrace laboriously—when he escorted a prisoner to the next state, when he took a posse out after stage robbers, whenever he left the town for an extended period of time. Then, the process of following him had to slow enormously, and sometimes I didn't bother, merely returning to the house trusting that he would come back there eventually and I could take him up again.

I did that this time. I didn't know why he vanished, but I stationed my view in the bedroom, sure that he would return to the room where his wife slept fitfully every night he was away.

He didn't.

After going through a dozen stages of worry, his wife persuaded the mayor to send a search party out for him—which was when I learned that he had gone to check on some rumors of cattle rustling among outlying ranches. I backtracked to the day he left and followed him.

I watched him die.

At that point I had spent months on Logan, and I had had enough. Alison was right about him, completely right. I could see how attractive he was—charming, handsome, with all the qualities that his era valued. And in addition there was that touch of sadness about him, especially after he lost his first wife—just a touch of vulnerability to make the rest all that more endearing. And I was tired of watching such a paragon.

Alison, however, was not. Records showed that her use of the Bubble was still as heavy as ever in the period between 1873 and 1885. She kept returning to certain time segments, replaying them. She could have taped them, of course, probably had, but I could easily understand her desire to see them in the Bubble instead—the near-reality of the Bubble. She was selecting from his life, the high points, the cream. But not after 1885.

Out of curiosity, I turned in the last 1885 date myself. That turned out to be the day that Logan was shot by a drunken cowboy, shot from behind, from cover—a practice that occurred more often than admirers of the Classic West would have liked to believe. It was not a serious wound by modern standards, but in a world without antibiotics it came close to claiming his life. He was bedridden for a long time, but he recovered well under his wife's diligent care.

She was avoiding the shooting, the period of convalescence, the life afterward. Even though that life wasn't very different from the one he had led before. He hadn't let the shooting faze him.

I thought . . . maybe . . . he had come too close to death for her taste—his mortality had suddenly become too real. And I thought, too, that maybe now I had a way to pull her away from him and back to me. One last attempt, I told myself, now that she'd had some time to herself. I was hoping that, perhaps, she was beginning to get lonely for someone real. She still lived alone, and according to Myra, there was no one in her life. No one, at least, but Holland, whose grant had been renewed because of Alison's excellent work. I hated Holland by that time because he was seeing her, even if in a professional capacity. Holland; unattractive as he looked to me, he was still real and available for whenever she wanted reality. And Alison, even the new strange Alison, must have provoked some kind of reaction in him. Unless he was as fixated on Earp as she was on Logan. It was possible. I no longer knew what to believe, what to scoff at. Even my own clients seemed to have unnatural interests in their subjects. I found myself in a mental prison, and I had to escape somehow, and take Alison with me.

I taped about twenty minutes of James Logan, and with that tape I went to Alison's apartment. She had given up on the projection room after moving out of our place; she didn't need that extreme of privacy any more, didn't have to concern herself with the annoyance of encountering me in the kitchen or living room at home. I knew her door wouldn't respond to my code, though I tried it anyway. And I knew she wasn't there, but she was due soon, her shift having just ended. I waited for her, waited a long time. She must have gone someplace else before coming home, perhaps to dinner. I waited. She arrived at last, alone as I expected, alone for an evening with *him*.

She saw me when she stepped out of the elevator. She stood stock still and stared at me.

"Hello, Alison," I said. "It's been . . . a long time."

"Whatever you want," she said, "I haven't got it."

I shook my head. "I have something to show you."

"Another time, Barry. Catch me at work." I blocked her way to the door, but she elbowed me aside—harder than necessary—to open it.

"Please let me come in, Alison. It won't take long. Just a few minutes."

"I'm very tired," she said. "I'm going to take a bath and go to bed. I don't want any company." She stepped across the threshold, turned, and started to slide the portal shut in my face.

I leaned into the opening, blocking the door's closure. "Please."

"I don't want to see you, Barry. Now, go away or I'll call the police."

"Oh, Alison, it can't be *that* bad between us."

She looked at me rather sadly. "I don't know what you expect me to do, Barry. I'm really sorry, but it's all over. Why can't you understand that?"

I said, "Alison, have you changed so much . . . ?"

"These things happen all the time. Look at how many men Myra has run through."

"Myra is Myra, and you're you."

"And you're you, and I've had enough of it. Barry, don't try to recapture something that's gone. Can't we part friends? Can't we just . . . part?"

I put one hand on the door. "You're not being very friendly, Alison."

"You're being pushy."

"I haven't bothered you lately."

"You've tried to call."

"Why not? I'm still interested."

"And I'm not. So why don't you go home and get a good night's sleep instead of standing in my doorway?"

I pulled the tape out of my pocket, held it up. "I have something to show you. It won't take long."

She sighed, shifted her weight from one leg to the other and put one hand on her hip. "How long? That's a two-hour tape."

"Not full," I said. "Maybe fifteen minutes. Twenty at most."

"Of what?"

"You have to see it."

"Why?"

"Because I'll keep bothering you until you do."

"There are ways of dealing with that kind of harassment, Barry."

"Just view the tape. After that . . . I'll let the next move be up to you."

"It's not going to change my mind. I don't care what it is."

"Afterward . . . if you still want me to leave, I'll go. I promise."

"You're betting a lot on this tape," she said eyeing it suspiciously. "What is it?"

"You can find out right now."

She pursed her lips, then sighed so heavily that her shoulders heaved. She stepped aside. "All right. Come in. But I'm just doing this because you promised. I trust you, Barry—I trust you'll keep that promise. If you don't. . . ."

"I will."

This was Alison's apartment, no compromise with another human being; as soon as I entered, my eyes were assaulted with Logan—Logan on the living room walls, Logan visible through the bedroom door, even in the kitchen. Alison went into the bedroom to fetch the projector, which she placed on a low table beside the living room sofa.

"You sit here," she said, indicating the sofa. She seated herself in a chair some distance away. "You can project over here." She pointed to the wall facing the chair, the only wall with a large blank space.

I nodded, slipped the tape into the slot and flicked the machine on.

I heard her sharply indrawn breath as Logan bloomed into view; he was on horseback, riding among rolling hills near a wide river. He was heading westward, and beyond him we could see the lowering sun above mountains purple with distance.

Alison gripped the arms of her chair with white-knuckled fingers. "What *is* this?" she demanded.

"You said you'd watch."

She pushed herself deeper into the chair, and I could see the flexion of her jaw where the teeth were grinding. "All right," she murmured. "All right."

As Logan topped the next rise, we were behind him and saw what he saw—a cabin set well back from the river. A thin plume of smoke drifted from the chimney. Logan rode down to it, tethered his horse at the rail before the front porch, climbed the two steps to the door and knocked loudly. The panel swung open, and he entered, with us at his back. He was hardly a pace past the threshold when someone who had been concealed to one side of the aperture struck him over the head with a club. He fell without a sound and lay still upon the floor. The two men—the assailant and the one who had opened the door—picked him up by the shoulders and the heels and carried him outside. There, they draped him across his horse, and while one of them led the animal, the other steadied the unconscious body on the saddle. They walked toward the river.

I watched Alison. She was tense, but she never spared a glance for me; once she had begun to concentrate on Logan, she didn't seem to notice anything else. Her eyes were wide, staring, and her expression was stark.

At the riverbank, the two men pulled Logan's limp body from the horse, and between them they hauled it inot the stream until the brisk current swirled about their waists. Then they held his head underwater for a long, long time before letting go of him. He sank.

The rest of the tape was disjointed, jumping forward in time, skimming the surface of the river until the body washed ashore, bloated, scarcely recognizable. In fast motion we watched it decompose, watched buzzards pick the carcass, watched the skeleton separate into a scatter of bones as the last ligaments gave way. Dust alternated with snow in covering the remains, and before the tape ended they had disappeared from view.

Alison stood up when it was over, when the wall was blank once more. "Get out," she said in a low, tight voice.

I looked at her for a long moment, looked at the white face and wide eyes, at the fists working convulsively at her sides. "Don't you see?" I said softly. "He's dead. He's dust. Before you were born he was dust. If you love a man like that, you might as well be dead yourself."

She reached the projector in two strides, pulled the tape out and dashed it against the floor. "Get out of here!" she shouted.

I tried to pull her into my arms, but she struggled. "Alison, you're warm and alive! How can you waste yourself on him?"

She glared up into my face, her fingers curling into my shirt front till the fabric cut into the back of my neck. "Murderer!" she said. "Murderer!" And then she yanked me sideways, and suddenly we were on the floor, rolling over and over, and she was all nails and sharp knees and kicking feet. She went for my eyes, my throat, my groin, but I twisted and freed myself somehow, staggered to my feet. I felt my face bleeding, and the numb places scattered over my body where bruises would rise soon.

"Alison," I gasped, "*time* killed him, not *me*!"

She lay on the floor, her fists striking the rug in a slow, steady beat. "Murderer," she moaned. She turned her head gradually, till her tear-streaked face was visible. Her eyes seemed to look past me, unfocused. "Get out before I kill you." There were no tears in her voice, but there was something that chilled me.

"All right," I said, "I'll go. But I want you to know that I love you. I did this today because I love you. I hope . . . someday you'll understand that."

She was still beating on the rug when I left.

For three days I nursed my bruises, calling in sick to work. Finally, I had to go in, with a spray bandage covering the gashes on my cheeks. My client was sympathetic when I explained that I had fallen down a flight of stairs. Some of my fellow operators looked at me curiously, but none made any comment; they were much too engrossed in a more vital topic of conversation: Dr. Frederick Holland. As I came off shift, word of his complaints was buzzing through records. A crowd of workers was gathered about the counter there, discussing him. Myra, who was due on shift in a couple of minutes, took me aside as soon as she saw me.

"Maybe you could sub for her, Barry—double shift until she comes back. You must know more about his project than anybody else here. He's furious, threatening to sue, and the front office is giving us all a hard time."

"Threatening to sue? What's going on?"

"It's Alison. She's gone. She hasn't come in to work for three days, and nobody knows where she is or when she'll be back."

"She didn't call in?"

"She didn't *anything*. Her line rings forever, nobody answers the door, and her mail is piling up."

I clutched at her arms. "Maybe something's wrong! Have you called the police?"

"The police?" She frowned. "You think it might be that bad?"

I didn't know what to think. I didn't know what crazy ideas could have gone through Alison's mind after I left that day. "You'd better call them. They'll have to break in. I'll wait for them there. You want to come with me?"

"I can't. I'm on duty."

"Isn't this more important? She's your friend."

"You'll be there," she said. "What good will two of us do?"

"I don't know. I don't know." I let go of her. "I'll let you know what we find out." I started for the door at a run.

She called after me, "Will you take her shift?"

"Ask me later!"

She started to say something else, but the door cut her voice off as it slid shut behind me.

The police took their time. I paced the corridor outside her apartment for what seemed like hours before they finally arrived. They waved a warrant at me when I began babbling about the delay—"You don't get these things in five minutes, you know," they said. Then they asked for my company ID, to prove that I really was one of her co-workers, that I had some legitimate business witnessing the procedure. They asked me a lot of questions, too, and found out that she and I were former lovers and had had an argument three days before. One of them stood very close to me after that, while his partner rang the bell for a long time before unscrambling the lock.

We went inside. The apartment was just as I remembered it. The police did not seem to pay much attention to the pictures of Logan everywhere. They searched very thoroughly—rooms, closets, even under the bed. When they started on the bureau drawers and the kitchen cabinets, I began to wonder if they expected to find pieces of Alison hidden everywhere. But they found nothing—no blood, no sign of a struggle, and no Alison.

They were obviously disgusted, with the search and with me.

"Maybe she just went home to her mother," one of them suggested.

"She's an orphan," I said.

"Well, maybe she has a favorite aunt." They ushered me out and relocked the door. "People have been known to leave home for a few days, you know, even without telling anybody where they were going. Maybe she just wanted to get away. Maybe from you. You work together, don't you?"

I shook my head. "Just in the same building. We don't see each other much any more."

"Okay, maybe she just wanted to get out of that building, even out of the town. A little vacation. Why don't you wait a few more days—she'll probably turn up." He looked at me hard then. "But don't go anywhere we can't find you easily until she comes back, hmm?"

"I didn't do anything to her," I said.

"Looks like she did something to you."

I nodded. "It was a bad argument. Short, but bad. When I left she was very upset. She could have done . . . anything."

"For example?"

I clenched my teeth. "Suicide?"

The officers looked at each other, then back at me. "Well, we'll keep that in mind. Now I'd suggest that you go home and get yourself some rest."

"You're not . . . going to take me in?"

"For what? Meeting us at an empty apartment? Having a scratched face? Go home." He shook his head slowly. "Let me tell you, I've seen people gone four, five months and then they come back safe and sound. Drives their families crazy, and the families drive us crazy. You want to file a missing-person report? She has to be gone at least a month for that."

My hands gripped each other tightly. "She might have drowned herself."

"Oh? What makes you think that?"

"She . . . worked with someone who drowned. She was very despondent over his death."

"Well, we haven't had any reports of drownings lately. Of course, if she threw herself in the river, she *might* not have been found yet. She normally carries identification, doesn't she?"

"Yes."

"All right, we'll look into it. But there's really no point in worrying. She'll probably turn up when she's good and ready."

We went downstairs in the elevator together and they watched me walk to the tram and catch my line before they got into their vehicle.

I had made myself a murder suspect, but I didn't care. I felt drained. Where was she? What had she done? I tried to put myself in her place that night after I had left. I tried to feel what she must have felt. Fury? Hate? Despair? I tried to feel that I had seen someone I loved die. It didn't seem difficult. She had lost someone. I had lost her. What next?

Kansas City fled by as I leaned against the tram window, and I hardly saw it. I saw Ellsworth instead, in my mind's eye, and Logan stalking the streets with a star on his chest and a pair of forty-fives on his hips. Kansas City was cool with November, but Ellsworth was dust summer, always would be for me, since the first day Holland and Alison had worked together.

And then I knew where Alison had gone.

When I got home I checked out the Kansas air schedules and called in my reservation for the next hop to Salina. The computer answered my query on Alison: she had taken the same route the morning after I left her.

At Salina I rented a vehicle and drove west on old Route 140. The new highway, the rental agent told me, was restricted to wheeled traffic and very crowded. This road was in poor repair, but it was virtually deserted, and my hovercraft made good time over the cracked pavement. In less than an hour I was in Ellsworth, seat of Ellsworth County, population 2000.

Foolishly, I had expected to recognize the town. But a century and a half had erased the old village, and this Ellsworth could have been any county seat of the Great Plains—courthouse in the town square, traffic circle around that, streets extending grid-fashion from that center. The latest vehicles were parked at the curbs, both hovercraft and ground cars, not a horse in sight. And the dust had been laid by the damp November breeze. Citizens walked casually in the cool morning, dressed like anyone in Kansas City, and no one packed a gun, not even the traffic cop stationed by the stoplight in front of the courthouse.

I parked by a meter, fed it my credit card for the eight-hour maximum, then started my stroll around town. I really didn't know where to begin. I was disoriented, trying to figure out where old street had run; there was a Main Street on one side of the courthouse, but I couldn't connect that with Ellsworth's old Main Street, nor the courthouse with the old court building. There was no necessity for either of them to occupy the old sites, except perhaps human lethargy. So I just wandered, spiraling outward from the courthouse, thinking that eventually I'd find the place where the Logan house had been. Alison, I thought, would most likely be there.

I walked for hours. The sun reached its zenith and began to sink. I must have covered every street in town, some twice, and everywhere I walked people looked at me, the stranger. But none of them was Alison. At last I realized that I was very hungry, and I stepped into a bar for a sandwich. The town had only two restaurants—lunch counters, really—and by that time both of them were closed. The bartender served me a hamburger and a beer, and though he looked at me rather pointedly, he didn't ask any questions.

I asked him: "Is there a hotel in town?"

"Motel," he replied, flicking a thumb toward the south. "On the big highway."

"Any others?"

"No, just the one. Nice place, though. Clean. Truckers stop there."

"Thanks." I finished my beer and paid for the meal. I left him a big tip. One motel in town—where else could Alison be?

I took the hovercraft over to the highway, and there the place was, just beyond the foot of the exit ramp, without any name but MOTEL in medium-sized letters on the roof. I counted twelve units and five vehicles; they had room for me. I didn't ask about Alison when I checked in. I didn't want the owner suspicious, and I didn't want her to tell Alison that someone was looking for her. But I glimpsed a familiar signature in the motel's records—she was there all right. In my room I settled down in a reasonably comfortable chair by the window, the heavy drapes barely twitched aside to give me a view of the parking lot. Anyone walking from the town would be visible to me, too, though I didn't think Alison would be walking that sort of distance.

A couple of big rigs pulled in just after dark, their headlights flashing across the building like searchlights. Sometime later, more exhausted than I realized from the long day's activities, I fell asleep. I woke in the chair when one of the rigs revved its engine at first light.

I was cramped and stiff from sleeping in the chair, especially my legs. I had been doing my traveling by Bubble for a lot of years, and that and riding the tramways of Kansas City had not prepared me for tramping all over Ellsworth. In the bathroom, I splashed some water in my face and set the coffeemaker for a couple of cups. If Alison had come in as late as I suspected, she would still be sleeping and I would catch her as she left. I waited by the window, sipping my coffee.

I didn't recognize her at first. She stepped out of a unit somewhere to my left and climbed into a small hovercraft. She was wearing a groundsweeping dress of some heavy black material, with long sleeves and a high neck. Covering her head and shoulders was a black veil pulled back from her face for driving. She gunned the hovercraft and swung out of the parking lot, heading for town. I scrambled to follow her. By the time I was in my own vehicle, she was no more than a swirl of kicked-up dust in the distance.

She drove all the way through town, turning west at the courthouse, onto a road as old and decrepit as the one I had taken from Salina. Not far beyond the town limits, the land rose gently. At the crest of the rise, stark amid the endless stubble of harvested wheat fields, a parcel of land was surrounded by a spike-topped wrought-iron fence. The gate, replete with curlicue vines and leaves of age-darkened iron, stood wide open in the morning sunlight. As I eased my hovercraft into the small lot before the gate, I saw the gravestones, row on neat row, and the browning grass that cloaked them.

Alison was inside already, delicately picking her way among the graves, her long skirt lifted in front. She seemed extraordinarily slim in black, fragile, swaying a little as the prairie wind gusted against her. She stopped at a far corner of the cemetery and sat down on a stone bench.

It was an old place, maybe Ellsworth's original Boot Hill. Some of the markers were so weathered that their inscriptions were illegible. Those I could make out spanned the Twentieth Century, reached back into the Nineteenth, forward into the Twenty-First. A few were sharp-cut in their newness. None was exceptionally elaborate, none taller than my waist—it was not a place of ostentatious grief, that cemetery. It was just a spot where the dead were laid with some respect. Aside from Alison and me, it had no other visitors that November morning.

Slowly, I walked up behind her. Over her shoulder I read the inscription on the marker at her feet.

SACRED TO THE MEMORY OF
JAMES LOGAN
1853–1890
REST IN PEACE

It was very new. The space in front of it, however, was flat and completely overgrown with grass. If a grave lay there, it was not a recent one.

"Hello, Alison," I said.

She started at my words, her back straightening, but she didn't turn to look at me. "Good guess," she said.

"An operator has to know how to find people."

Her hands were folded in her lap, and the veil had fallen over her face, dark, shadowing her features. In old Ellsworth they would have called her dress widow's weeds.

"May I sit down?" I asked.

"Do what you like."

I sat on the very edge of the bench, an arm's length between us. "He's not buried here," I said.

"No."

"Who is?"

"Nobody. Does it matter?"

I gestured toward the marker. "You put up the stone."

She nodded almost imperceptibly. Behind the veil, I couldn't read her expression. She said, "His mother would have wanted it."

"Are you . . . going to try to recover the remains?"

She tilted her head, seemed to be looking down at her hands. "Not much point in that, is there? It's just bones."

I nodded. "Don't you think you should come back to Kansas City now? You've done . . . all that could be expected here."

"He spent most of his life here. This was his home. This is where I belong."

"You can't mean that, Alison. What about your work, your friends? What about your contract with the company?"

"Let them sue me. I don't care."

"Of course you do. You love your work. I know it. You can't give it up to . . . to bury yourself in this backwater."

She turned her face toward me, but the veil was a barrier between us, keeping her thoughts from me. "You don't understand me at all," she said. "And you don't know when you're not wanted. You are intruding upon my grief. I would appreciate it if you would go away."

"Grief over someone you never knew, Alison? What kind of grief is that?"

"A kind you obviously will never know."

"I know the other kind of grief."

"Fine. Go back to Kansas City and practice it there."

"Alison . . . Dr. Holland wants you to come back."

She let a moment of silence pass, and then she laughed a choking laugh, half a sob. "Holland. How I wish I had never met him! How I wish it!"

"Then . . . you would never have seen Logan."

"No," she said, looking at the gravestone. "Never." Then she bent forward a little and raised her hands to her face, pressing the veil against her cheeks. Her shoulders trembled, and I couldn't help reaching a hand toward her. But she shrugged off my comfort and slid to the far end of the bench. "He's dead," she murmured. "And I'm dead, too. Why won't you let me rest in peace?"

"Oh, Alison . . . come home. You're not going to find peace in this cemetery."

"I don't want to talk to you any more, Barry."

I stood up slowly. "All right. I'll go. I just want you to remember that if you ever need me, I'll always be there."

Her back toward me, she straightened up, shaking her head, the veil moving gently about her shoulders. "No," she murmured. "Nobody can make that kind of promise. You'll die someday. Everbody dies."

"Oh, Alison. . . ." I half lifted my hands toward her, but no words would come. What could I say? That, yes, we all die someday—James Logan, Augustus Caesar, and me . . . and that emotions die as well, eventually—love, hate, even grief. I knew she didn't want to listen. So I consoled myself with that knowledge instead of offering it to her, and I turned away and trudged back to the cemetery gate.

That night I was back in Kansas City. In the morning, I added Alison's shift to my own, tolerated Holland's indignation and gave him his money's worth. Earp was in Tombstone now, the hearing that followed the gunfight at the O.K. Corral behind him, one brother crippled, another dead. Soon he would be leaving for a new life in California, and Holland would have to move on, too, if he wanted to follow his subject. He was already foreseeing difficulties for the period that Earp would be spending in Alaska—it was out of range of all the company offices. He badgered me for information about new branches to be opened, obviously hoping for Seattle or Vancouver, and he was angry when I told him that all I knew about was the one in Tokyo.

He was gone by the time Alison came back.

I had known she would, known it in my soul. She was an operator first, like Myra, like me. Nothing could make us quit. Nothing.

She didn't speak to me. I passed her in the corridor a few times, but she just looked through me, walking briskly, as if to some important meeting.

She transferred to the Tokyo office as soon as it opened—looking for a new challenge, Myra said. Shortly afterward, I returned to Istanbul. To Imperial Rome. Someone needed an expert on Augustus Caesar.

PHILIP JOSÉ FARMER

The Alley Man

"THE MAN from the puzzle factory was here this morning," said Gummy, "While you was out fishin."

She dropped the piece of wiremesh she was trying to tie with string over a hole in the rusty window screen. Cursing, grunting like a hog in a wallow, she leaned over and picked it up. Straightening, she slapped viciously at her bare shoulder.

"Figurin skeeters! Must be a million outside, all tryin to get away from the burnin garbage."

"Puzzle factory?" said Deena. She turned away from the battered kerosene-burning stove over which she was frying sliced potatoes and perch and bullheads caught in the Illinois River, half a mile away.

"Yeah!" snarled Gummy. "You heard Old Man say it. Nuthouse. Booby hatch. So . . . this cat from the puzzle factory was named John Elkins. He gave Old Man all those tests when they had im locked up last year. He's the skinny little guy with a moustache 'n never lookin you in the eye 'n grinnin like a skunk eatin a shirt. The cat who took Old Man's hat away from him 'n wun't give it back to him until Old Man promised to be good. Remember now?"

Deena, tall, skinny, clad only in a white terrycloth bathrobe, looked like a surprised and severed head stuck on a pike. The great purple birthmark on her cheek and neck stood out hideously against her paling skin.

"Are they going to send him back to the State hospital?" she asked.

Gummy, looking at herself in the cracked full-length mirror nailed to the wall, laughed and showed her two teeth. Her frizzy hair was a yellow brown, chopped short. Her little blue eyes were set far back in tunnels beneath two protruding ridges of bone; her nose was very long, enormously wide, and tipped with a brokenveined bulb. Her chin was not there, and her head bent forward in a permanent crook. She was dressed only in a dirty once-white slip that came to her swollen knees. When she laughed, her huge breasts, resting on her distended belly quivered like bowls of fermented cream. From her expression, it was evident that she was not displeased with what she saw in the broken glass.

Again she laughed. "Naw, they din't come to haul him away. Elkins just wanted to interduce this chick he had with him. A cute little brunette with big brown eyes behint real thick glasses. She looked just like a collidge girl, 'n she was. This chick has got a B.M. or something in sexology . . ."

"Psychology?"

"Maybe it was societyology. . . "

"Sociology?"

"Umm. Maybe. Anyway, this foureyed chick is doin a study for a foundation. She wants to ride aroun with Old Man, see how he collects his junk, what alleys he goes up 'n down, what his, uh, habit patterns is, 'n learn what kinda bringing up he had . . ."

"Old Man'd never do it!" burst out Deena. "You know he can't stand the idea of being watched by a False Folker!"

"Umm. Maybe. Anyway, I tell em Old Man's not goin to like their slummin on him, 'n they say quick they're not slummin, it's for science. 'N they'll pay him for his trouble. They got a grant from the foundation. So I say maybe that'd make Old Man take another look at the color of the beer, 'n they left the house . . ."

"You *allowed* them in the house? Did you hide the birdcage?"

"Why hide it? His hat wasn't in it."

Deena turned back to frying her fish, but over her shoulder she said, "I don't think Old Man'll agree to the idea, do you? It's rather degrading."

"You *kiddin?* Who's lower'n Old Man? A snake's belly, maybe. Sure, he'll agree. He'll have a eye for the foureyed chick, sure."

"Don't be absurd," said Deena. "He's a dirty stinking one-armed middle-aged man, the ugliest man in the world."

"Yeah, it's the uglies he's got, for sure. 'N he smells like a goat that fell in a outhouse. But it's the smell that gets em. It got me, it got you, it got a whole stewpotfull a others, includin that high-society dame he used to collect junk off of . . ."

"Shut up!" spat Deena. "This girl must be a highly refined and intelligent girl. She'd regard Old Man as some sort of ape."

"You know them apes," said Gummy, and she went to the ancient refrigerator and took out a cold quart of beer.

Six quarts of beer later, Old Man had still not come home. The fish had grown cold and greasy, and the big July moon had risen. Deena, like a long lean dirty-white nervous alley cat on top of a backyard fence, patrolled back and forth across the shanty. Gummy sat on the bench made of crates and hunched over her bottle. Finally, she lurched to her feet and turned on the battered set. But, hearing a rattling and pounding of a loose motor in the distance, she turned it off.

The banging and popping became a roar just outside the door. Abruptly, there was a mighty wheeze, like an old rusty robot coughing with double pneumonia in its iron lungs. Then, silence.

But not for long. As the two women stood paralyzed, listening apprehensively, they heard a voice like the rumble of distant thunder.

Take it easy, kid.''

Another voice, soft, drowsy, mumbling.

''Where . . . we?''

The voice like thunder, ''Home, sweet home, where we rest our dome.''

Violent coughing.

''It's this smoke from the burnin' garbage, kid. Enough to make a maggot puke, ain't it? Lookit! The smoke's risin t'wards the full moon like the ghosts a men so rotten even their spirits're carrin the contamination with em. Hey, li'l chick, you din't know Old Man knew them big words like contamination, didja? That's what livin on the city dump does for you. I hear that word all a time from the big shots that come down inspectin the stink here so they kin get away from the stink a City Hall. I ain't no illiterate. I got a TV set. Hor, hor, hor!''

There was a pause, and the two women knew he was bending his knees and tilting his torso backwards so he could look up at the sky.

''Ah, you lovely lovely moon, bride a The Old Guy In The Sky! Some day to come, rum-a-dum-a-dum, one day I sear it, Old Woman a The Old Guy In The Sky, if you help me find the longlost headpiece a King Paley that I and my fathers been lookin' for for fifty thousand years, so help me, Old Man Paley'll spread the freshly spilled blood a a virgin a the False Folkers out across the ground for you, so you kin lay down in it like a red carpet or a new red dress and wrap it aroun you. And then you won't have to crinkle up your lovely shinin nose at me and spit your silver spit on me. Old Man promises that, just as sure as his good arm is holdin a daughter a one a the Falsers, a virgin, I think, and bringin her to his home, however humble it be, so we shall see . . .''

''Stone out a his head,'' whispered Gummy.

''My God, he's bringin a girl in here!'' said Deena. ''*The* girl!''

''Not the *collidge* kid?''

''Does the idiot want to get lynched?''

The man outside bellowed, ''Hey, you wimmen, get off your fat asses and open the door 'fore I kick it in! Old Man's home with a fistfull a dollars, a armful a sleepin lamb, and a gutfull a beer! Home like a conquerin hero and wants service like one, too!''

Suddenly unfreezing, Deena opened the door.

Out of the darkness and into the light shuffled something so squat and blocky it seemed more a tree trunk come to life than a man. It stopped, and the eyes under the huge black homburg hat blinked glazedly. Even the big hat could not hide the peculiar lengthened-out breadloaf shape of the skull. The forehead was abnormally low; over the eyes were bulging arches of bone. These were tufted with eyebrows like Spanish moss that made even more cavelike the hollows in which the little blue eyes lurked. Its nose was very long and very wide and flaring-nostrilled. The lips were thin but pushed out by the shoving jaws beneath them. Its chin was absent, and head and shoulders joined almost without intervention from a neck, or so it seemed. A corkscrew forest of rusty-red hairs sprouted from its open shirt front.

Over his shoulder, held by a hand wide and knobbly as a coral branch, hung the slight figure of a young woman. He shuffled into the room in an odd bent-kneed gait, walking on the sides of his thick-soled engineer's boots. Suddenly, he stopped again, sniffed deeply, and smiled, exposing teeth thick and yellow, dedicated to biting.

"Jeez, that smells good. It takes the old garbage stink right off. Gummy! You been sprinklin yourself with that perfume I found in a ash heap up on the bluffs?"

Gummy, giggling, looked coy.

Deena said, sharply, "Don't be a fool, Gummy. He's trying to butter you up so you'll forget he's bringing this girl home."

Old Man Paley laughed hoarsely and lowered the snoring girl upon an Army cot. There she sprawled out with her skirt around her hips. Gummy cackled, but Deena hurried to pull the skirt down and also to remove the girl's thick shellrimmed glasses.

"Lord," she said, "how did this happen? What'd you do to her?"

"Nothin," he growled, suddenly sullen.

He took a quart of beer from the refrigerator, bit down on the cap with teeth thick and chipped as ancient gravestones, and tore it off. Up went the bottle, forward went his knees, back went his torso as he leaned away from the bottle, and down went the amber liquid, gurgle, gurgle, glub. He belched, then roared. "There I was, Old Man Paley, mindin' my own figurin business, packin a bunch a papers and magazines I found, and here comes a blue fifty-one Ford sedan with Elkins, the doctor jerk from the puzzle factory. And this little foureyed chick here, Dorothy Singer. And . . ."

"Yes," said Deena. "We know who they are, but we didn't know they went after you."

"Who asked you? Who's tellin this story? Anyway, they tole me what they wanted. And I was gonna say no, but this little collidge broad says if I'll sign a paper that'll agree to let her travel around with me and even stay in our house a couple a evenins, with us actin natural, she'll pay me fifty dollars. I says yes! Old Guy In The Sky! That's a hundred and fifty quarts a beer! I got principles, but they're washed away in a roarin foamin flood of beer.

"I says yes, and the cute little runt give me the paper to sign, then advances me ten bucks and says I'll get the rest seven days from now.Ten dollars in my pocket! So she climbs up into the seat a my truck. And then this figurin Elkins parks his Ford and he says he thinks he ought to go with us to check on if everything's gonna be O.K.

"He's not foolin Old Man. He's after Little Miss Foureyes. Everytime he looks at her, the lovejuice runs out a his eyes. So, I collect junk for a couple a hours, talkin all the time. And she is scared a me at first because

I'm so figurin ugly and strange. But after a while she busts out laughin. Then I pulls the truck up in the alley back a Jack's Tavern on Ames Street. She asks me what I'm doin. I says I'm stoppin for a beer, just as I do every day. And she says she could stand one, too. So . . ."

"You actually went inside with her?" asked Deena.

"Naw. I was gonna try, but I started gettin the shakes. And I hadda tell her I coun't do it. She asks me why. I say I don't know. Ever since I quit bein a kid, I kin't. So she says I got a . . . something like a fresh flower, what is it?"

"Neurosis?" said Deena.

"Yeah. Only I call it a taboo. So Elkins and the little broad go into Jack's and get a cold six-pack, and bring it out, and we're off . . . "

"So?"

"So we go from place to place, though always stayin in alleys, and she thinks it's funnier'n hell gettin loaded in the backs a taverns. Then I get to seein double and don't care no more and I'm over my fraidies, so we go into the Circle Bar. And get in a fight there with one a the hillbillies in his sideburns and leather jacket that hangs out there and tries to take the foureyed chick home with him."

Both the women gasped, "Did the cops come?"

"If they did, they was late to the party. I grab this hillbilly by his leather jacket with my one arm—the strongest arm in this world—and throw him clean acrosst the room. And when his buddies come after me, I pound my chest like a figurin gorilla and make a figurin face at em, and they all of a sudden get their shirts up their necks and go back to listen to their hillbilly music. And I pick up the chick—she's laughin so hard she's chokin—and Elkins, white as a sheet out a the laundromat, after me, and away we go, and here we are."

"Yes, you fool, here you are!" shouted Deena. "Bringing that girl here in that condition! She'll start screaming her head off when she wakes up and sees you!"

"Go figure youself!" snorted Paley. "She was scared a me at first, and she tried to stay upwind a me. But she got to *likin* me. I could tell. And she got so she liked my smell, too. I knew she would. Don't all the broads? These False wimmen kin't say no once they get a whiff of us. Us Paleys got the gift in the blood."

Deena laughed and said. "You mean you have it in the head. Honest to God, when are you going to quit trying to force feed me with that bull? You're insane!"

Paley growled. "I tole you not never to call me nuts, not never!" and he slapped her across the cheek.

She reeled back and slumped against the wall, holding her face and crying, "You ugly stupid stinking ape, you hit me, the daughter of people whose boots you aren't fit to lick. *You* struck *me*!"

"Yeah, and ain't you glad I did," said Paley in tones like a complacent earthquake. He shuffled over to the cot and put his hand on the sleeping girl.

"Uh, feel that. No sag there, you two flabs."

"You beast!" screamed Deena. "Taking advantage of a helpless little girl!"

Like an alley cat, she leaped at him with claws out.

Laughing hoarsely, he grabbed one of her wrists and twisted it so she was forced to her knees and had to clench her teeth to keep from screaming with pain. Gummy cackled and handed Old Man a quart of beer. To take it, he had to free Deena. She rose, and all three, as if nothing had happened, sat down at the table and began drinking.

About dawn a deep animal snarl awoke the girl. She opened her eyes but could make out the trio only dimly and distortedly. Her hands, groping around for her glasses, failed to find them.

Old Man, whose snarl had shaken her from the high tree of sleep, growled again. "I'm tellin' you, Deena, I'm tellin' you, don't laugh at Old Man, don't laugh at Old Man, and I'm tellin' you again, three times, don't laugh at Old Man!"

His incredible bass rose to a high-pitched scream of rage.

"Whassa matta wi your figurin brain? I show you proof after proof, 'n you sit there in all your stupidity like a silly hen that sits down too hard on its eggs and breaks em but won't get up 'n admit she's squattin on a mess. I—I—Paley—Old Man Paley—kin prove I'm what I say I am, a Real Folker."

Suddenly, he propelled his hand across the table towards Deena.

"Feel them bones in my lower arm! Them two bones ain't straight and dainty like the arm bones a you False Folkers. They're thick as flagpoles, and they're curved out from each other like the backs a two tomcats outbluffing each other over a fishhead on a garbage can. They're built that way so's they kin be real strong anchors for my muscles, which is bigger'n False Folkers'. Go ahead, feel em.

"And look at them brow ridges. Like the tops a those shellrimmed spectacles all them intellekchooalls wear. Like the spectacles this collidge chick wears.

"And feel the shape a my skull. It ain't a ball like yours but a loaf a bread."

"Fossilized bread!" sneered Deena. "Hard as a rock, through and through."

Old Man roared on, "Feel my neck bones if you got the strength to feel through my muscles! They're bent forward, not—"

"Oh, I know you're an ape. You can't look overhead to see if that was a bird or just a drop of rain without breaking your back."

"Ape, hell! I'm a Real Man! Feel my heel bone! Is it like yours? No, it ain't! It's built different, and so's my whole foot!"

"Is that why you and Gummy and all those brats of yours have to walk like chimpanzees?"

"Laugh, laugh, laugh!"

"I am laughing, laughing, laughing. Just because you're a freak of nature, a monstrosity whose bones all went wrong in the womb, you've dreamed up this fantastic myth about being descended from the Neanderthals . . . "

"Neanderthals!" whispered Dorothy Singer. The walls whirled about her, looking twisted and ghostly in the half-light, like a room in Limbo.

" . . . all this stuff about the lost hat of Old King," continued Deena, "and how if you ever find it you can break the spell that keeps you so-called Neanderthals on the dumpheaps and in the alleys, is garbage, and not very appetizing . . . "

"And you," shouted Paley, "are headin for a beatin!"

"Thass wha she wants," mumbled Gummy. "Go ahead. Beat her. She'll get her jollies off, 'n quit needlin you. 'N we kin all git some shuteye. Besides, you're gonna wake up the chick."

"That chick is gonna get a wakin up like she never had before when Old Man gits his paws on her," rumbled Paley. "Guy In The Sky, ain't it somethin she should a met me and be in this house? Sure as an old shirt stinks, she ain't gonna be able to tear herself away from me.

"Hey, Gummy, maybe she'll have a kid for me, huh? We ain't had a brat around here for ten years. I kinda miss my kids. You gave me six that was Real Folkers, though I never was sure about that Jimmy, he looked too much like O'Brien. Now you're all dried up, dry as Deena always was, but you kin still raise em. How'd you like to raise the collidge chick's kid?"

Gummy grunted and swallowed beer from a chipped coffee mug. After belching loudly, she mumbled, "Don know. You're crazier'n even I think you are if you think this cute little Miss Foureyes'd have anything to do wi you. 'N even if she was out a her head nough to do it, what kind a life is this for a brat? Get raised in a dump? Have a ugly old maw 'n paw? Grow up so ugly nobody's have nothin to do wi him 'n smellin so strange all the dogs'd bite him?"

Suddenly, she began blubbering.

"It ain't only Neanderthals has to live on dumpheaps. It's the crippled 'n the stupid 'n the queer in the head that has to live here. 'N they become Neanderthals just as much as us Real Folk. No diff'rence, no diff'rence. We're all ugly 'n hopeless 'n rotten. We're all Neander . . . "

Old Man's fist slammed the table.

"Name me no names like that! That's a *G'Yaga* name for us Paleys—Real Folkers. Don't let me never hear that other name again! It don't mean a man; it means somethin like a high-class gorilla."

"Quit lookin in the the mirror!" shrieked Deena.

There was more squabbling and jeering and roaring and confusing and terrifying talk, but Dorothy Singer had closed her eyes and fallen asleep again.

Some time later, she awoke. She sat up, found her glasses on a little table beside her, put them on, and stared about her.

She was in a large shack built of odds and ends of wood. It had two rooms, each about ten feet square. In the corner of one room was a large kerosene-burning stove. Bacon was cooking in a huge skillet; the heat from the stove made sweat run from her forehead and over her glasses.

After drying them off with her handkerchief, she examined the furnishings of the shack. Most of it was what she had expected, but three things surprised her. The bookcase, the photograph on the wall, and the birdcage. The bookcase was tall and narrow and of some dark wood, badly scratched. It was crammed with comic books, Blue Books, and Argosies, some of which she supposed must be at least twenty years old. There were a few books whose ripped backs and waterstained covers indicated they'd been picked out of ash heaps. Haggard's *Allan and the Ice Gods, Wells's Outline of History,* Vol. I, and his *The Croquet Player*. Also *Gog and Magog, A Prophecy of Armageddon* by the Reverend Caleb G. Harris. Burroughs' *Tarzan the Terrible* and *In the Earth's Core*. Jack London's *Beyond Adam*.

The framed photo on the wall was that of a woman who looked much like Deena and must have been taken around 1890. It was very large, tinted in brown, and showed an aristocratic handsome woman of about thirty-five in a high-busted velvet dress with a highneckline. Her hair was drawn severely back to a knot on top of her head. A diadem of jewels was on her breast.

The strangest thing was the large parrot cage. It stood upon a tall support which had nails driven through its base to hold it to the floor. The cage itself was empty, but the door was locked with a long narrow bicycle lock.

Her speculation about it was interrupted by the two women calling to her from their place by the stove.

Deena said, "Good morning, Miss Singer, How do you feel?"

"Some Indian buried his hatchet in my head," Dorothy said. "And my tongue is molting. Could I have a drink of water, please?"

Deena took a pitcher of cold water out of the refrigerator, and from it filled up a tin cup.

"We don't have any running water. We have to get our water from the gas station down the road and bring it here in a bucket."

Dorothy looked dubious, but she closed her eyes and drank.

"I think I'm going to get sick," she said. "I'm sorry."

"I'll take you to the outhouse," said Deena, putting her arm around the girl's shoulder and heaving her up with surprising strength.

"Once I'm outside," said Dorothy faintly, "I'll be all right."

"Oh, I know," said Deena. "It's the odor. The fish, Gummy's cheap perfume, Old Man's sweat, the beer. I forgot how it first affected me. But it's no better outside."

Dorothy didn't reply, but when she stepped through the door, she murmured, "Ohh!"

"Yes, I know," said Deena. "It's awful, but it won't kill you . . . "

Ten minutes later, Deena and a pale and weak Dorothy came out of the ramshackle outhouse.

They returned to the shanty, and for the first time Dorothy noticed that Elkins was sprawled face up on the seat of the truck. His head hung over the end of the seat, and the flies buzzed around his open mouth.

"This is horrible," said Deena. "He'll be very angry when he wakes up and finds out where he is. He's such a respectable man."

"Let the heel sleep it off," said Dorothy. She walked into the shanty, and a moment later Paley clomped into the room, a smell of stale beer and very peculiar sweat advancing before him in a wave.

"How you feel?" he growled in a timbre so low the hairs on the back of her neck rose.

"Sick. I think I'll go home."

"Sure. Only try some a the hair."

He handed her a half-empty pint of whiskey. Dorothy reluctantly downed a large shot chased with cold water. After a brief revulsion, she began feeling better and took another shot. She then washed her face in a bowl of water and drank a third whiskey.

"I think I can go with you now," she said. "But I don't care for breakfast."

"I ate already," he said. "Let's go. It's ten-thirty according to the clock on the gas station. My alley's prob'ly been cleaned out by now. Them other ragpickers are always moochin in on my territory when they think I'm stayin home. But you kin bet they're scared out a their pants every time they see a shadow cause they're afraid it's Old Man and he'll catch em and squeeze their gut out and crack their ribs with this one good arm."

Laughing a laugh so hoarse and unhuman it seemed to come from some troll deep in the caverns of his bowels, he opened the refrigerator and took another beer.

"I need another to get me started, not to mention what I'll have to give that damn balky bitch, Fordiana."

As they stepped outside, the saw Elkins stumble towards the outhouse and then fall headlong through the open doorway. He lay motionless on the floor, his feet sticking out of the entrance. Alarmed, Dorothy wanted to go after him, but Paley shook his head.

"He'sa big boy; he kin take care a hisself. We got to git Fordiana up and goin."

Fordiana was the battered and rusty pick-up truck. It was parked outside Paley's bedroom window so he could look out at any time of the night and make sure no one was stealing parts or even the whole truck.

"Not that I ought a worry about her," grumbled Old Man. He drank three fourths of the quart in four mighty gulps, then uncapped the truck's radiator and poured the rest of the beer down it.

"She knows nobody else'll give her beer, so I think that if any a these robbin figurers that live on the dump or at the shacks aroun the bend was to try to steal anything off'n her, she'd honk and backfire and throw rods and oil all over the place so's her Old Man could wake up and punch the figurin shirt off a the thievin figurer. But maybe not. She's a female. And you can't trust a figurin female."

He poured the last drop down the radiator and roared, "There! Now don't you dare *not* turn over. You're robbin me a the good beer I could be havin! If you so much as backfire, Old Man'll beat hell out a you with a sledge hammer!"

Wide-eyed but silent, Dorothy climbed onto the ripped open front seat beside Paley. The starter whirred, and the motor sputtered.

"No more beer if you don't work!" shouted Paley.

There was a bang, a fizz, a sput, a *whop, whop, whop,* a clash of gears, a monstrous and triumphant showing of teeth of Old Man, and they were bumpbumping over the rough ruts.

"Old Man knows how to handle all them bitches, flesh or tin, twolegged, fourlegged, wheeled. I sweat beer and passion and promise em a kick in the tailpipe if they don't behave, and that gets em all. I'm so figurin ugly I turn their stomachs. But once they git a whiff a the out-a-this-world stink a me, they're done for, they fall prostrating at my big hairy feet. That's the way it's always been with us Paley men and the *G'yaga* wimmen. That's why their menfolks fear us, and why we got into so much trouble."

Dorothy did not say anything, and Paley fell silent as soon as the truck swung off the dump and onto U.S. Route 24. He seemed to fold up into himself, to be trying to make himself as inconspicuous as possible. During the three minutes it took the truck to get from the shanty to the city limits, he kept wiping his sweating palm against his blue workman's shirt.

But he did not try to release the tension with oaths. Instead, he muttered a string of what seemed to Dorothy nonsense rhymes.

"Eenie, meenie, minie, moe. Be a good Guy, help me go. Hoola boola, teenie weenie, ram em, damn em, figure em, duck em, watch me go, don't be a shmoe. Stop em, block em, sing a go go go."

Not until they had gone a mile into the city of Onaback and turned from 24 into an alley did he relax.

"Whew! That's torture, and I been doin it ever since I was sixteen, some years ago. Today seems worse'n ever, maybe cause you're along. *G'yaga* men don't like it if they see me with one a their wimmen, specially a cute chick like you."

Suddenly, he smiled and broke into a song about being covered all over "with sweet violets, sweeter than all the roses." He sang other songs, some of which made Dorothy turn red in the face, though at the same time she giggled. When they crossed a street to get from one alley to another, he cut off his singing, even in the middle of a phrase, and resumed it on the other side.

Reaching the west bluff, he slowed the truck to a crawl while his little blue eyes searched the ash heaps and garbage cans at the rears of the houses. Presently, he stopped the truck and climbed down to inspect his find.

"Guy In The Sky, we're off to a flyin start! Look!—some old grates from a coal furnace. And a pile a Coke and beer bottles, all redeemable. Get down, Dor'thy—if you want a know how us ragpickers make a livin, you gotta get in and and sweat and cuss with us. And if you come across any hats, be sure to tell me."

Dorothy smiled. But when she stepped down from the truck, she winced.

"What's the matter?"

"Headache."

"The sun'll boil it out. Here's how we do this collectin, see? The back end a the truck is boarded up into five sections. This section here is for the iron and the wood. This, for the paper. This, for the cardboard. You get a higher price for the cardboard. This, for rags. This, for bottles we can get a refund on. If you find any int'restin books or magazines, put em on the seat. I'll decide if I want to keep em or throw em in with the old paper."

They worked swiftly, and then drove on. About a block later, they were interrupted at another heap by a leaf of a woman, withered and blown by the winds of time. She hobbled out from the back porch of a large three-storied house with diamond-shaped panes in the windows and doors and cupolas at the corners. In a quaverying voice she explained that she was the widow of a wealthy lawyer who had died fifteen years ago. Not until today had she made up her mind to get rid of his collection of law books and legal papers. These were all neatly cased in cardboard boxes not too large to be handled.

Not even, she added, her pale watery eyes flickering from Paley to Dorothy, not even by a poor one-armed man and a young girl.

Old Man took off his homburg and bowed.

"Sure, ma'am, my daughter and myself'd be glad to help you out in your housecleanin."

"Your daughter?" croaked the old woman.

"She don't look like me a tall," he replied. "No wonder. She's my fosterdaughter, poor girl, she was orphaned when she was still fillin her diapers. My best friend was her father. He died savin my life, and as he laid gaspin his life away in my arms, he begged me to take care a her as if she was my own. And I kept my promise to my dyin friend, may his soul rest in peace. And even if I'm only a poor ragpicker, ma'am, I been doin my best to raise her to be a decent Godfearin obedient girl."

Dorothy had to run around to the other side of the truck where she could cover her mouth and writhe in an agony of attempting to smother her laughter. When she regained control, the old lady was telling Paley she'd show him where the books were. Then she started hobbling to the porch.

But Old Man instead of following her across the yard, stopped by the fence that separated the alley from the backyard. He turned around and gave Dorothy a look of extreme despair.

"What's the matter?" she said. "Why're you sweating so? And shaking? And you're so pale."

"You'd laugh if I told you, and I don't like to be laughed at."

"Tell me. I won't laugh."

He closed his eyes and began muttering, "Never mind, it's in the mind. Never mind, you're just fine." Opening his eyes, he shook himself like a dog just come from the water.

"I kin do it. I got the guts. All them books're a lotta beer money I'll lose if I don't go down into the bowels a hell and get em. Guy In The Sky, give me the guts a a goat and the nerve a a pork dealer in Palestine. You know Old Man ain't got a yellow streak. It's the wicked spell a the False Folkers workin on me. Come on, let's go, go, go."

And sucking in a deep breath, he stepped through the gateway. Head down, eyes on the grass at his feet, he shuffled towards the cellar door where the old lady stood peering at him.

Four steps away from the cellar entrance, he halted again. A small black spaniel had darted from around the corner of the house and begun yapyapping at him.

Old Man suddenly cocked his head to one side, crossed his eyes, and deliberately sneezed.

Yelping, the spaniel fled back around the corner, and Paley walked down the steps that led to the cool dark basement. As he did so, he muttered, "That puts the evil spell on em figurin dogs."

When they had piled all the books in the back of the truck, he took off his homburg and bowed again.

"Ma'am, my daughter and myself both thank you from the rockbottom a our poor but humble hearts for this treasure trove you give us. And if ever you've anythin else you don't want, and a strong back and a weak mind to carry it out . . . well, please remember we'll be down this alley every Blue Monday and Fish Friday about time the sun is three-quarters acrosst the sky. Providin it ain't rainin cause the Old Guy In The Sky is cryin in his beer over us poor mortals, what fools we be."

Then he put his hat on, and the two got into the truck and chugged off. They stopped by several other promising heaps before he announced that the truck was loaded enough. He felt like celebrating; perhaps they should stop off behind Mike's Tavern's and down a few quarts. She replied that perhaps she might manage a drink if she could have a whiskey. Beer wouldn't set well.

"I got some money," rumbled Old Man, unbuttoning with slow clumsy fingers his shirtpocket and pulling out a roll of worn tattered bills while the truck's wheels rolled straight in the alley ruts.

"You brought me luck, so Old Man's gonna pay today through the hose, I mean, nose, har, har, har!"

He stopped Fordiana behind a little neighborhood tavern. Dorothy, without being asked, took the two dollars he handed her and went into the building. She returned with a can opener, two quarts of beer, and a halfpint of V.O.

"I added some of my money. I can't stand cheap whiskey."

They sat on the running board of the truck, drinking, Old Man doing most of the talking. It wasn't long before he was telling her of the times when the Real Folk, the Paleys, had lived in Europe and Asia by the side of the wooly mammoths and the cave lion.

"We worshipped the Guy In The Sky who says what the thunder says and lives in the east on the tallest mountain in the world. We faced the skulls a our dead to the east so they could see the Old Guy when he came to take them to live with him in the mountain.

And we was doin fine for a long long time. Then, out a the east come them motherworshippin False Folk with their long straight legs and long straight necks and flat faces and thundermug round heads and their bows and arrows. They claimed they was sons a the goddess Mother Earth, who was a virgin. But we claimed the truth was that a crow with stomach trouble sat on a stump and when it left the hot sun hatched em out.

"Well, for a while we beat them hands-down because we was stronger Even one a our wimmen could tear their strongest man to bits. Still, they had that bow and arrow, they kept pickin us off, and movin in and movin in, and we kept movin back slowly, till pretty soon we was shoved with our backs against the ocean.

"Then one day a big chief among us got a bright idea. 'Why don't we make bows and arrows, too?' he said. And so we did, but we was clumsy at makin and shootin em cause our hands was so big, though we could draw a heavier bow'n em. So we kept gettin run out a the good huntin grounds.

"There was one thing might a been in our favor. That was, we bowled the wimmen a the Falsers over with our smell. Not that we smell good. We stink like a pig that's been making love to a billy goat on a manure pile. But, somehow, the wimmen folk a the Falsers was all mixed up in their chemistry, I guess you'd call it, cause they got all excited and developed roundheels when they caught a whiff a us. If we'd been left alone with em, we could a Don Juan'd them alsers right off a the face a the earth. We would a mixed our blood with theirs so much that after a while you coun't tell the difference. Specially since the kids lean to their pa's side in looks. Paley blood is so much stronger.

"But that made sure there would always be war tween us. Specially after our king, Old King Paley, made love to the daughter a the Falser king, King Raw Boy, and stole her away.

"Gawd, you shou'd a seen the fuss then! Raw Boy's daughter flipped over Old King Paley. And it was her give him the bright idea a calling in every able-bodied Paley that was left and organizin em into one big army. Kind a puttin all our eggs in one basket, but it seemed a good idea. Every man big enough to carry a club went out in the big mob on Operation False Folk Massacree. And we ganged up on every little town a them mother-worshippers we found. And kicked hell out a em. And roasted the men's hearts and ate em. And every now and then took a snack off the wimmen and kids, too.

"Then, all of a sudden, we come to a big plain. And there's a army a them False Folk, collected by Old King Raw Boy. They outnumber us, but we feel we kin lick the world. Specially since the magic strength a the *G'yaga* lies in their wimmen folk, cause they worship a woman god, the Old Woman In The Earth. And we've got their chief priestess Raw Boy's daughter.

"All our own personal power is collected in Old King Paley's hat—his magical headpiece. All a us Paleys believed that a man's strength and his soul was in his headpiece.

"We bed down the night before the big battle. At dawn there's a cry that'd wake up the dead. It still sends shivers down the necks a us Paleys fifty thousand years later. It's King Paley roarin and cryin. We ask him why. He says that that dirty little sneakin little hoor, Raw Boy's daughter, has stole his headpiece and run off with it to her father's camp.

"Our knees turn weak as nearbeer. Our manhood is in the hands a our enemies. But out we go to battle, our witch doctors out in front rattlin their gourds and whirlin their bullroarers and prayin. And here come the *G'yaga* medicine men doin the same. Only thing, their hearts is in their work cause they got Old King's headpiece stuck on the end a a spear.

"And for the first time they use dogs in war, too. Dogs never did like us any more'n we like em.

"And then we charge into each other. Bang! Wallop! Crash! Smash! Whack! Owwwrrroooo! And they kick hell out a us, do it to us. And we're never again the same, done forever. They had Old King's headpiece and with it our magic, cause we'd all put the soul a us Paleys in that hat.

"The spirit and power a us Paleys was prisoners cause that headpiece was. And life became too much for us Paleys. Them as wasn't slaughtered and eaten was glad to settle down on the garbage heaps a the conquerin Falsers and pick for a livin with the chickens, sometimes comin out second best.

"But we knew Old King's headpiece was hidden somewhere, and we organized a secret society and swore to keep alive his name and to search for the headpiece if it took us forever. Which it almost has, it's been so long.

"But even though we was doomed to live in shantytowns and stay off the streets and prowl the junkpiles in the alleys, we never gave up hope. And as time went on some a the no-counts a the *G'yaga* came down to live with us. And we and they had kids. Soon, most a us had disappeared into the bloodstream a the low class *G'yaga*. But there's always been a Paley family that tried to keep their blood pure. No man kin do no more, kin he?"

He glared at Dorothy. "What d'ya think a that?"

Weakly, she said, "Well, I've never heard anything like it."

"Gawdamighty!" snorted Old Man. "I give you a history longer'n a hoor's dream, more'n fifty thousand years a history, the secret story a a long lost race. And all you kin say is that you never heard nothin like it before."

He leaned towards her and clamped his huge hand over her thigh.

"Don't flinch from me!" he said fiercely. "Or turn you head away. Sure, I stink, and I offend your dainty figurin nostrils and upset your figurin delicate little guts. But what's a minute's whiff a me on your part compared to a lifetime on my part a havin all the stinkin garbage in the universe shoved up my nose, and my mouth filled with what you woun't say if your mouth was full a it? What do you say to that, huh?"

Coolly, she said, "Please take your hand off me."

"Sure, I din't mean nothin by it. I got carried away and forgot my place in society."

"Now, look here," she said earnestly. "That has nothing at all to do with your so-called social position. It's just that I don't allow anybody to take liberties with my body. Maybe I'm being ridiculously Victorian, but I want more than just sensuality. I want love, and—"

"O.K. I get the idea."

Dorothy stood up and said, "I'm only a block from my apartment. I think I'll walk on home. The liquor's given me a headache."

"Yeah," he growled. "You sure it's the liquor and not me?"

She looked steadily at him. "I'm going, but I'll see you tomorrow morning. Does that answer your question?"

"O.K.," he grunted. "See you. Maybe."

She walked away very fast.

Next morning, shortly after dawn, a sleepy-eyed Dorothy stopped her car before the Paley shanty. Deena was the only one home. Gummy had gone to the river to fish, and Old Man was in the outhouse. Dorothy took the opportunity to talk to Deena, and found her, as she had suspected, a woman of considerable education. However, although she was polite, she was reticent about her background. Dorothy, in an effort to keep the conversation going, mentioned that she had phoned her former anthropology professor and asked him about the chances of Old Man being a genuine Neanderthal. It was then that Deena broke her reserve and eagerly asked what the professor had thought.

"Well," said Dorothy, "he just laughed. He told me it was an absolute impossibility that a small group, even an inbred group isolated in the mountains, could have kept their cultural and genetic indentity for fifty thousand years.

"I argued with him. I told him Old Man insisted he and his kind had existed in the village of Paley in the mountains of the Pyrenees until Napoleon's men found them and tried to draft them. Then they fled to America, after a stay in England. And his groups was split up during the Civil War, driven out of the Great Smokies. He, as far as he knows, is the last purebreed, Gummy being a half or quarter-breed.

"The professor assured me that Gummy and Old Man were cases of glandular malfunctioning, of acromegaly. That they may have a superficial resemblance to the Neanderthal man, but a physical anthropologist could tell the difference at a glance. When I got a little angry and asked him if he wasn't taking an unscientific and prejudiced attitude, he became rather irritated. Our talk ended somewhat frostily.

"But I went down to the university library that night and read everything on what makes *Homo Neanderthalensis* different from *Homo Sapiens*."

"You almost sound as if you believe Old Man's private little myth is the truth," said Deena.

"The professor taught me to be convinced only by the facts and not to say anything is impossible," replied Dorothy. "If he's forgotten his own teachings, I haven't."

"Well, Old Man is a persuasive talker," said Deena. "He could sell the devil a harp and halo."

Old Man, wearing only pair of blue jeans, entered the shanty. For the first time Dorothy saw his naked chest, huge, covered with long redgold hairs so numerous they formed a matting almost as thick as an orangutang's. However, it was not his chest but his bare feet at which she looked most intently. Yes, the big toes were widely separated from the others, and he certainly tended to walk on the outside of his feet.

His arm, too, seemed abnormally short in proportion to his body.

Old Man grunted a good morning and didn't say much for a while. But after he had sweated and cursed and chanted his way through the streets of Onaback, and had arrived safely at the alleys of the west bluff, he relaxed. Perhaps he was helped by finding a large pile of papers and rags.

"Well, here we go to work, so don't you dare to shirk. Jump, Dor'thy! By the sweat a your brow, you'll earn your brew!"

When that load was on the truck, they drove off. Paley said, "How you like this life without no strife? Good, huh? You like alleys, huh?"

Dorothy nodded. "As a child, I liked alleys better than streets. And they still preserve something of their first charm for me. They were more fun to play in, so nice and cozy. The trees and bushes and fences leaned in at you and sometimes touched you as if they had hands and liked to feel your face to find out if you'd been there before, and they remembered you. You felt as if you were sharing a secret with the alleys and the things of the alleys. But streets, well, streets were always the same, and you had to watch out the cars didn't run over you, and the windows in the houses were full of faces and eyes, poking their noses into your business, if you can say that eyes had noses."

Old Man whooped and slapped his thigh so hard it would have broke if it had been Dorothy's.

"You must be a Paley! We feel that way, too! We ain't allowed allowed to hang around streets, so we make our alleys into little kingdoms. Tell me, do you sweat just crossin a street from one alley to the next?"

He put his hand on her knee. She looked down at it but said nothing, and he left it there while the truck putputted along, its wheels following the ruts of the alley.

"No, I don't feel that way at all."

"Yeah? Well, when you was a kid, you wasn't so ugly you hadda stay off the streets. But I still wasn't too happy in the alleys because a them figurin dogs. Forever and forever they was barkin and bitin at me. So I took to beatin the bejesus out a them with a big stick I always carried. But after a while I found I only had to look at em in a certain way. Yi, yi, yi, they'd run away yapping, like that old black spaniel did yesterday. Why? Cause they knew I was sneezin evil spirits at em. It was then I began to know I wasn't human. A course, my old man had been telling me that ever since I could talk.

"As I grew up I felt every day that the spell a the *G'yaga* was gettin stronger. I was gettin dirtier and dirtier looks from em on the streets. And when I went down the alleys, I felt like I really *belonged* there. Finally, the day came when I coun't cross a street without gettin sweaty hands and cold feet and a dry mouth and breathin hard. That was cause I was becomin a full-grown Paley, and the curse a the *G'yaga* gets more powerful as you get more hair on your chest."

"Curse?" said Dorothy. "Some people call it a neurosis."

"It's a curse."

Dorothy didn't answer. Again, she looked down at her knee, and this time he removed his hand. He would have had to do it, anyway, for they had come to a paved street.

On the way down to the junk dealer's, he continued the same theme. And when they got to the shanty, he elaborated upon it.

During the thousands of years the Paleys lived on the garbage piles of the *G'yaga*, they were closely watched. So, in the old days, it had been the custom for the priests and warriors of the False Folk to descend on the dumpheap dwellers whenever a strong and obstreperous Paley came to manhood. And they had gouged out an eye or cut off his hand or leg or some other member to ensure that he remembered what he was and where his place was.

"That's why I lost this arm," Old Man growled, waving the stump. "Fear a the *G'yaga* for the Paleys did this to me."

Deena howled with laughter and said, "Dorothy, the truth is that he got drunk one night and passed out on the railroad tracks, and a freight train ran over his arm."

"Sure, sure, that's the way it was. But it coun't a happened if the Falsers din't work through their evil black magic. Nowadays, stead a cripplin us openly, they use spells. They ain't got the guts anymore to do it themselves."

Deena laughed scornfully and said, "He got all those psychopathic ideas from reading those comics and weird tale magazines and those crackpot books and from watching that TV program, *Alley Oop and the Dinosaur*. I can point out every story from which he's stolen an idea."

"You're a liar!" thundered Old Man.

He struck Deena on the shoulder. She reeled away from the blow, then leaned back toward him as if into a strong wind. He struck her again, this time across her purple birthmark. Her eyes glowed, and she cursed him. And he hit her once more, hard enough to hurt but not to injure.

Dorothy opened her mouth as if to protest, but Gummy lay a fat sweaty hand on her shoulder and lifted her finger to her own lips.

Deena fell to the floor from a particularly violent blow. She did not stand up again. Instead, she got to her hands and knees and crawled toward the refuge behind the big iron stove. His naked foot shoved her rear so that she was sent sprawling on her face, moaning, her long stringy black hair falling over her face and birthmark.

Dorothy stepped forward and raised her hand to grab Old Man. Gummy stopped her, mumbling, " 'S all right. Leave em alone."

"Look a that figurin female being happy!" snorted Old Man. "You know why I *have* to beat the hell out a her, when all I want is peace and quiet? Cause I look like a figurin caveman, and they're suppose to beat their hoors silly. That's why she took up with me."

"You're an insane liar," said Deena softly from behind the stove, slowly and dreamily nursing her pain like the memory of a lover's caresses. "I came to live with you because I'd sunk so low you were the only man that'd have me."

"She's a retired high-society mainliner, Dor'thy," said Paley. "You never seen her without a longsleeved dress on. That's cause her arms're full a holes. It was me that kicked the monkey off a her back. I cursed her with the wisdom and magic a the Real Folk, where you coax the evil spirit out by talkin it out. And she's been living with me ever since. Can't get rid a her.

"Now, you take that toothless bag there. I ain't never hit her. That shows I ain't no womanbeatin bastard, right? I hit Deena cause she likes it, wants it, but I don't ever hit Gummy. . . . Hey, Gummy, that kind a medicine ain't what you want, is it?"

And he laughed his incredibly hoarse *hor, hor, hor*.

"You're a figurin liar," said Gummy, speaking over her shoulder because she was squatting down, fiddling with the TV controls. "You're the one knocked most a my teeth out."

"I knocked out a few rotten stumps you was gonna lose anyway. You had it comin cause you was running around with that O'Brien in his green shirt."

Gummy giggled and said, "Don't think for a minute I quit goin with that O'Brien in his green shirt just cause you slapped me around a little bit. I quite cause you was a better man 'n him."

Gummy giggled again. She rose and waddled across the room towards a shelf which held a bottle of her cheap perfume. Her enormous brass earrings swung, and her great hips swung back and forth.

"Look a that," said Old Man. "Like two bags a mush in a windstorm."

But his eyes followed them with kindling appreciation, and, on seeing her pour the reeking liquid over her pillowsized bosom, he hugged her and buried his huge nose in the valley of her breasts and sniffed rapturously.

"I feel like a dog that's found an old bone he buried and forgot till just now," he growled. "Arf, arf, arf!"

Deena snorted and said she had to get some fresh air or she'd lose her supper. She grabbed Dorothy's hand and insisted she take a walk with her. Dorothy, looking sick, went with her.

The following evening, as the four were drinking beer around the kitchen table, Old Man suddenly reached over and touched Dorothy affectionately. Gummy laughed, but Deena glared. However, she did not say anything to the girl but instead began accusing Paley of going too long without a bath. He called her a flatchested hophead and said that she was lying, because he had been taking a bath every day. Deena replied that, yes he had, ever since Dorothy had appeared on the scene. An argument raged. Finally, he rose from the table and turned the photograph of Deena's mother so it faced the wall.

Wailing, Deena tried to face it outward again. He pushed her away from it, refusing to hit her despite her insults—even when she howled at him that he wasn't fit to lick her mother's shoes, let alone blaspheme her portrait by touching it.

Tired of the argument, he abandoned his post by the photograph and shuffled to the refrigerator.

"If you dare turn her around till I give the word, I'll throw her in the creek. And you'll never see her again."

Deena shrieked and crawled onto her blanket behind the stove and there lay sobbing and cursing him softly.

Gummy chewed tobacco and laughed while a brown stream ran down her toothless jaws. "Deena pushed him too far that time."

"Ah, her and her figurin mother," snorted Paley. "Hey, Dor'thy, you know how she laughs at me cause I think Fordiana's got a soul. And I put the evil eye on them hounds? And cause I think the salvation a us Paleys'll be when we find out where Old King's hat's been hidden?

"Well, get a load a this. This here intellekshooal purple-faced dragon, this retired mainliner, this old broken-down nag for a monkey-jockey, she's the sooperstishus one. She thinks her mother's a god. And she prays to her and asks forgiveness and asks what's gonna happen in the future. And when she thinks nobody's around, she talks to her. Here she is, worshippin her mother like the Old Woman In The Earth, who's The Old Guy's enemy. And she knows that makes the Old Guy sore. Maybe that's the reason he ain't allowed me to find the longlost headpiece a Old King, though he knows I been lookin in every ash heap from here to godknowswhere, hopin some fool *G'yaga* would throw it away never realizin what it was.

"Well, by all that's holy, that pitcher stays with its ugly face to the wall. Aw, shut up, Deena, I wanna watch Alley Oop."

Shortly afterwards, Dorothy drove home. There she again phoned her sociology professor. Impatiently, he went into more detail. He said that one reason Old Man's story of the war between the Neanderthals and the invading *Homo Sapiens* was very unlikely was that there was evidence to indicate that *Homo Sapiens* might have been in Europe before the Neanderthals—it was very possible the *Homo Neanderthalensis* was the invader.

"Not invader in the modern sense," said the professor. "The influx of a new species of race or tribe into Europe during the Paleolithic would have been a sporadic migration of little groups, an immigration which might have taken a thousand to ten thousand years to complete.

"And it is more than likely that *Neanderthalensis* and *Sapiens* lived side by side for millennia with very little fighting between them because both were too busy struggling for a living. For one reason or another, probably because he was outnumbered, the Neanderthal was absorbed by the surrounding peoples. Some anthropologists have speculated that the Neanderthals were blonds and they they had passed their light hair directly to North Europeans.

"Whatever the guesses and surmises," concluded the professor, "it would be impossible for such a distinctly different minority to keep its special physical and cultural characteristics over a period of half a hundred millennia. Paley has concocted this personal myth to compensate for his extreme ugliness, his inferiority, his feelings of rejection. The elements of the myth came from the comic books and TV.

"However," concluded the professor, "in view of your youthful enthusiasm and naiveté, I will reconsider my judgment if you bring me some physical evidence of this Neandethaloid origin. Say you could show me that he had a taurodont tooth. I'd be flabbergasted, to say the least."

"But, professor," she pleaded, "why can't you give him a personal examination? One look at Old Man's foot would convince you, I'm sure."

"My dear, I am not addicted to wild goose chases. My time is valuable."

That was that. The next day, she asked Old Man if he had ever lost a molar tooth or had an X-ray made of one.

"No," he said, "I got more sound teeth than brains. And I ain't gonna lose them. Long as I keep my headpiece, I'll keep my teeth and my digestion and my manhood. What's more, I'll keep my good sense, too. The loosescrew tighteners at the State Hospital really gave me a good goin-over, fore and aft, up and down, in and out, all night long, don't never take a hotel room right by the elevator. And they proved I wasn't hatched in a cuckoo clock. Even though they tore their hair and said something must be wrong. Specially after we had that row about my hat. I woun't let them take my blood for a test, you know because I figured they was goin to mix it with—water—*G'yaga* magic—and turn my blood to water. Somehow, that Elkins got wise that I hadda wear my hat—cause I woun't take it off when I undressed for the physical, I guess—and he snatched my hat. And I was done for. Stealin it was stealin my soul; all Paleys wears their souls in their hats. I hadda get it back. So I ate humble pie; I let them poke and pry all over and take my blood."

There was a pause while Paley breathed in deeply to get power to launch another verbal rocket. Dorothy, who had been struck by an idea, said, "Speaking of hats, Old Man, what does this hat that the daughter of Raw Boy stole from King Paley look like? Would you recognize it if you saw it?"

Old Man stared at her with wide blue eyes for a moment before he exploded.

"Would I recognize it? Would the dog that sat by the railroad tracks recognize his tail after the locomotive cut it off? Would you recognize your own blood if somebody stuck you in the guts with a knife and if pumped out with every heartbeat? Certainly, I would recognize the hat a Old King Paley! Every Paley at his mother's knee gits a detailed description a it. You want a hear about the hat? Well, hang on, chick, and I'll describe every hair and bone a it."

Dorothy told herself more than once that she should not be doing this. If she was trusted by Old Man, she was, in one sense, a false friend. But, she reassured herself, in another sense she was helping him. Should he find the hat, he might blossom forth, actually tear himself loose from the taboos that bound him to the dumpheap, to the alleys, to fear of dogs, to the conviction he was an inferior and oppressed citizen. Moreover, Dorothy told herself, it would aid her scientific studies to record his reaction.

The taxidermist she hired to locate the necessary materials and fashion them into the desired shape was curious, but she told him it was for an anthropological exhibit in Chicago and that it was meant to represent the headpiece of the medicine man of an Indian secret society dedicated to phallic mysteries. The taxidermist sniggered and said he'd give his eyeteeth to see those ceremonies.

Dorothy's intentions were helped by the run of good luck Old Man had in his alleypicking while she rode with him. Exultant, he swore he was headed for some extraordinary find; he could feel his good fortune building up.

"It's gonna hit," he said, grinning with his huge widely-spaced gravestone teeth. "Like lightning."

Two days later, Dorothy rose even earlier than usual and drove to a place behind the house of a well-known doctor. She had read in the society column that he and his family were vacationing in Alaska, so she knew they wouldn't be wondering at finding a garbage can already filled with garbage and a big cardboard box full of cast-off clothes. Dorothy had brought the refuse from her own apartment to make it seem as if the house were occupied. The old garments, with one exception, she had purchased at a Salvation Army store.

About nine that morning, she and Old Man drove down the alley on their scheduled route.

Old Man was first off the truck; Dorothy hung back to let him make the discovery. Old Man picked the garments out of the box one by one.

"Here's a velvet dress Deena kin wear. She's been complainin she hasn't had a new dress in a long time. And here'a blouse and skirt big enough to wrap around an elephant. Gummy kin wear it. And here . . . ''

He lifted up a tall conical hat with a wide brim and two balls of felted horsemane attached to the band. It was a strange headpiece, fashioned of roan horsehide over a ribwork of split bones. It must have been the only one of its kind in the world, and it certainly looked out of place in the alley of a mid-Illinois city.

Old Man's eyes bugged out. Then they rolled up, and he fell to the ground as if shot. The hat, however, was still clutched in his hand.

Dorothy was terrified. She had expected any reaction but this. If he had suffered a heart-attack, it would, she thought, be her fault.

Fortunately, Old Man had only fainted. However, when he regained consciousness, he did not go into ecstasies as she had expected. Instead, he looked at her, his face grey, and said, ''It kin't be! It must be a trick the Old Woman In The Earth's playing on me so she kin have the last laugh on me. How could it be the hat a Old King Paley's? Woun't the *G'yaga* that been keepin it in their famley all these years know what it is?''

''Probably not,'' said Dorothy. ''After all, the *G'yaga*, as you call them, don't believe in magic any more. Or it might be that the present owner doesn't even know what it is.''

''Maybe. More likely it was thrown out by accident during housecleaning. You know how stupid them wimmen are. Anyway, let's take it and get going. The Old Guy In The Sky might a had a hand in fixing up this deal for me, and if he did, it's better not to ask questions. Let's go.''

Old Man seldom wore the hat. When he was home, he put it in the parrot cage and locked the cage door with the bicycle lock. At nights, the cage hung from the stand; days, it sat on the seat of the truck. Old Man wanted it always where he could see it.

Finding it had given him a tremendous optimism, a belief he could do anything. He sang and laughed even more than he had before, and he was even able to venture out onto the streets for several hours at a time before the sweat and shakings began.

Gummy, seeing the hat, merely grunted and made a lewd remark about its appearance. Deena smiled grimly and said, ''Why haven't the horsehide and bone rotted away long ago?''

''That's just the kind a question a *G'yaga* dummy like you'd ask,'' said Old Man, snorting. ''How kin the hat rot when there's a million Paley souls crowded into it, standing room only? There ain't even elbow room for germs. Besides, the horsehide and the bones're jampacked with the power and the glory a all the Paleys that died before our battle with Raw Boy, and all the souls that died since. It's seething with soul-energy, the lid held on it by the magic a the *G'yaga*.''

''Better watch out it don't blow up 'n wipe us all out,'' said Gummy, sniggering.

"Now you have the hat, what are you going to do with it?" asked Deena.

"I don't know. I'll have to sit down with a beer and study the situation."

Suddenly, Deena began laughing shrilly.

"My God, you've been thinking for fifty thousand years about this hat, and now you've got it, you don't know what to do about it! Well, I'll tell you what you'll do about it! You'll get to thinking big, a right! You'll conquer the world, rid it of all False Folk, all right! You fool! Even if your story isn't the raving of a lunatic, it would still be too late for you! You're alone! The last! One against two billion! Don't worry, World, this ragpicking Rameses, this alley Alexander, this junkyard Julius Caesar, he isn't going to conquer you! No, he's going to put on his hat, and he's going forth! To do what?

"To become a wrestler on TV, that's what! That's the height of his halfwit ambition—to be billed as the one-Armed Neanderthal, the Awful Apeman. That is the culmination of fifty thousand years, ha, ha, ha!"

The others looked apprehensively at Old Man, expecting him to strike Deena. Instead, he removed the hat from the cage, put it on, and sat down at the table with a quart of beer in his hand.

"Quit your cackling, you old hen," he said. "I got my thinking cap on."

The next day Paley, despite a hangover, was in a very good mood. He chattered all the way to the west bluff and once stopped the truck so he could walk back and forth on the street and show Dorothy he wasn't afraid.

Then, boasting he could lick the world, he drove the truck up an alley and halted it by the backyard of a huge but somewhat rundown mansion. Dorothy looked at him curiously. He pointed to the jungle-thick shrubbery that filled a corner of the yard.

"Looks like a rabbit coun't get in there, huh? But Old Man knows things the rabbit don't. Folly me."

Carrying the caged hat, he went to the shrubbery, dropped to all threes, and began inching his way through a very narrow passage. Dorothy stood looking dubiously into the tangle until a hoarse growl came from its depths.

"You scared? Or is your fanny too broad to get through here?"

"I'll try anything once," she announced cheerfully. In a short time she was crawling on her belly, then had come suddenly into a little clearing. Old Man was standing up. The cage was at his feet, and he was looking at a red rose in his hand.

She sucked in her breath. "Roses! Peonies! Violets!"

"Sure, Dor'thy," he said, swelling out his chest. "Paley's Garden a Eden, his secret hothouse. I found this place a couple a years ago, when I was looking for a place to hide if the cops was looking for me or I just wanted a place to be alone from everybody, including myself.

"I planted these rosebushes in here and these other flowers. I come here every now and then to check on em, spray them, prune them. I never take any home, even though I'd like to give Deena some. But Deena ain't no dummy, she'd know I wasn't getting them out a garbage pail. And I just din't want to tell her about this place. Or anybody."

He looked directly at her as if to catch every twitch of a muscle in her face, every repressed emotion.

"You're the only person besides myself knows about this place." He held out the rose to her. "Here. It's yours."

"Thank you. I am proud, really proud, that you've shown this place to me."

"Really are? That makes me feel good. In fact, great."

"It's amazing. This, this spot of beauty. And . . . and . . . and . . . "

"I'll finish it for you. You never thought the ugliest man in the world, a dumpheaper, a man that ain't even a man or a human bein, a—I hate that word—a Neanderthal, could appreciate the beauty of a rose. Right? Well, I growed these because I loved em.

"Look, Dor'thy. Look at this rose. It's round, not like a ball but a flattened roundness . . ."

"Oval."

"Sure. And look at the petals. How they fold in on one another, how they're arranged. Like one ring a red towers protectin the next ring a red towers. Protectin the gold cup on the inside, the precious source a life, the treasure. Or maybe that's the golden hair a the princess a the castle. Maybe. And look at the bright green leaves under the rose. Beautiful, huh? The Old Guy knew what he was doing when he made these. He was an artist then.

"But he must a been sufferin from a hangover when he shaped me, huh? His hands was shaky that day. And he gave up after a while and never bothered to finish me but went on down to the corner for some a the hair a the dog that bit him."

Suddenly, tears filled Dorothy's eyes.

"You shouldn't feel that way. You've got beauty, sensitivity, a genuine feeling, under . . . "

"Under this?" he said, pointing his finger at his face. "Sure. Forget it. Anyway, look at these green buds on these baby roses. Pretty, huh? Fresh with promise a the beauty to come. They're shaped like the breasts a young virgins."

He took a step towards her and put his arm around her shoulders.

"Dor'thy."

She put both her hands on his chest and gently tried to shove herself away.

"Please," she whispered, "please, don't. Not after you've shown me how fine you really can be."

"What do you mean?" he said, not releasing her. "Ain't what I want to do with you just as fine and beautiful a thing as this rose here? And if you really feel for me, you'd want to let your flesh say what your mind thinks. Like the flowers when they open up for the sun."

She shook her head. "No. It can't be. Please. I feel terrible because I can't say yes. But I can't. I—you—there's too much diff—"

"Sure, we're diff'runt. Goin in diff'runt directions and then, comin round the corner—bam!—we run into each other, and we wrap our arms around each other to keep from fallin."

He pulled her to him so her face was pressed against his chest.

"See!" he rumbled. "Like this. Now, breathe deep. Don't turn your head. Sniff away. Lock yourself to me, like we was glued and nothing could pull us apart. Breathe deep. I got my arm around you, like these trees round these flowers. I'm not hurtin you; I'm givin you life and protectin you. Right? Breathe deep."

"Please," she whimpered. "Don't hurt me. Gently . . ."

"Gently it is. I won't hurt you. Not too much. That's right, don't hold yourself stiff against me, like you're stone. That's right, melt like butter I'm not forcin you, Dor'thy, remember that. You want this, don't you?"

"Don't hurt me," she whispered. "You're so strong, oh my God, so strong."

For two days, Dorothy did not appear at the Paleys'. The third morning, in an effort to fire her courage, she downed two double shots of V.O. before breakfast. When she drove to the dumpheap, she told the two women that she had not been feeling well. But she had returned because she wanted to finish her study, as it was almost at an end and her superiors were anxious to get her report.

Paley, though he did not smile when he saw her, said nothing. However, he kept looking at her out of the corners of his eyes when he thought she was watching him. And though he took the hat in its cage with him, he sweated and shook as before while crossing the streets. Dorothy sat staring straight ahead, unresponding to the few remarks he did make. Finally, cursing under his breath, he abandoned his effort to work as usual and drove to the hidden garden.

"Here we are," he said. "Adam and Eve returnin to Eden."

He peered from beneath the bony ridges of his brows at the sky. "We better hurry in. Looks as if the Old Guy got up on the wrong side a the bed. There's gonna be a storm."

"I'm not going in there with you," said Dorothy. "Not now or ever."

"Even after what we did, even if you said you loved me, I still make you sick?" he said. "You din't act then like Old Ugly made you sick."

"I haven't been able to sleep for two nights," she said tonelessly. "I've asked myself a thousand times why I did it. And each time I could only tell myself I didn't know. Something seemed to leap from you to me and take me over. I was powerless."

"You certainly wasn't paralyzed," said Old Man, placing his hand on her knee. "And if you was powerless, it was because you wanted to be."

"It's no use talking," she said. "You'll never get a chance again. And take your hand off me. It makes my flesh crawl."

He dropped his hand.

"All right. Back to business. Back to pickin people's piles a junk. Let's get out a here. Fergit what I said. Fergit this garden, too. Fergit the secret I told you. Don't tell nobody. The dumpheapers'd laugh at me. Imagine Old Man Paley, the one-armed candidate for the puzzle factory, the fugitive from the Old Stone Age, growin peonies and roses! Big, laugh, huh?"

Dorothy did not reply. He started the truck, and as they emerged onto the alley, they saw the sun disappear behind the clouds. The rest of the day, it did not come out, and Old Man and Dorothy did not speak to each other.

As they were going down Route 24 after unloading at the junkdealer's, they were stopped by a patrolman. He ticketed Paley for not having a chauffeur's license and made Paley follow him downtown to court. There Old Man had to pay a fine of twenty-five dollars. This, to everybody's amazement, he produced from his pocket.

As if that weren't enough, he had to endure the jibes of the police and the courtroom loafers. Evidently he had appeared in the police station before and was known as *King Kong, Alley Oop,* or just plain Chimp. Old Man trembled, whther with suppressed rage or nervouness Dorothy could not tell. But later, as Dorothy drove him home, he almost frothed at the mouth in a tremendous outburst of rage. By the time they were within sight of his shanty, he was shouting that his life savings had been wiped out and that it was all a plot by the *G'yaga* to beat him down to starvation.

It was then that the truck's motor died. Cursing, Old Man jerked the hood open so savagely that one rusty hinge broke. Further enraged by this, he tore the hood completely off and threw it away into the ditch by the roadside. Unable to find the cause of the breakdown, he took a hammer from the tool-chest and began to beat the sides of the truck.

"I'll make her go, go, go!" he shouted. "Or she'll wish she had! Run, you bitch, purr, eat gasoline, rumble your damn belly and eat gasoline but run, run, run! Or your ex-lover, Old Man, sells you for junk, I swear it!"

Undaunted, Fordiana did not move.

Eventually, Paley and Dorothy had to leave the truck by the ditch and walk home. And as they crossed the heavily traveled highway to get to the dumpheap, Old Man was forced to jump to keep from getting hit by a car.

He shook his fist at the speeding auto.

"I know you're out to get me!" he howled. "But you won't! You been tryin for fifty thousand years, and you ain't made it yet! We're still fightin!"

At that moment, the black sagging bellies of the clouds overhead ruptured. The two were soaked before they could take four steps. Thunder bellowed, and lightning slammed into the earth on the other end of the dumpheap.

Old Man growled with fright, but seeing he was untouched, he raised his fist to the sky.

"O.K., O.K., so you got it in for me, too. I get it. O.K., OK!"

Dripping, the two entered the shanty, where he opened a quart of beer and began drinking. Deena took Dorothy behind a curtain and gave her a towel to dry herself with and one of her white terrycloth robes to put on. By the time Dorothy came out from behind the curtain, she found Old Man opening his third quart. He was accusing Deena of not frying the fish correctly, and when she answered him sharply, he began accusing her of every fault, big or small, real or imaginary, of which he could think. In fifteen minutes, he was nailing the portrait of her mother to the wall with its face inwards. And she was whimpering behind the stove and tenderly stroking the spots where he had struck her. Gummy protested, and he chased her out into the rain.

Dorothy at once put her wet clothes on and announced she was leaving. She'd walk the mile into town and catch the bus.

Old Man snarled, "Go! You're too snotty for us, anyway. We ain't your kind, and that's that."

"Don't go," pleaded Deena. "If you're not here to restrain him, he'll be terrible to us."

"I'm sorry," said Dorothy. "I should have gone home this morning."

"You sure should," he growled. And then he began weeping, his pushed-out lips fluttering like a bird's wings, his face twisted like a gargoyle's.

"Get out before I fergit myself and throw you out," he sobbed.

Dorothy, with pity on her face, shut the door gently behind her.

The following day was Sunday. That morning, her mother phoned her she was coming down from Waukegan to visit her. Could she take Monday off?

Dorothy said yes, and then, sighing, she called her supervisor. She told him she had all the data she needed for the Paley report and that she would begin typing it out.

Monday night, after seeing her mother off on the train, she decided to pay the Paleys a farewell visit. She could not endure another sleepless night filled with fighting the desire to get out of bed again and again, to scrub herself clean, and the pain of having to face Old Man and the two women in the morning. She felt that if she said goodbye to the Paleys, she could say farewell to those feelings, too, or at least, time would wash them away more quickly.

The sky had been clear, star-filled, when she left the railroad station. By the time she had reached the dumpheap clouds had swept out from the west, and a blinding rainstorm was deluging the city. Going over the bridge, she saw by the lights of her headlamps that the Kickapoo Creek had become a small river in the two days of heavy rains. Its muddy frothing current roared past the dump and down to the Illinois River, a half mile away.

So high had it risen that the waters lapped at the doorsteps of the shanties. The trucks and jaloppies parked outside them were piled high witha household goods, and their owners were ready to move at a minute's notice.

Dorothy parked her car a little off the road, because she did not want to get it stuck in the mire. By the time she had walked to the Paley shanty, she was in stinking mud up to her calves, and night had fallen.

In the light streaming from a window stood Fordiana, which Old Man had apparently succeeded in getting started. Unlike the other vehicles, it was not loaded.

Dorothy knocked on the door and was admitted by Deena. Paley was sitting in the ragged easy chair. He was clad only in a pair of faded and patched blue jeans. One eye was surrounded by a big black, blue, and green bruise. The horsehide hat of Old King was firmly jammed onto his head, and one hand clutched the neck of a quart of beer as if he were choking it to death.

Dorothy looked curiously at the black eye but did not comment on it. Instead, she asked him why he hadn't packed for a possible flood.

Old Man waved the naked stump of his arm at her.

"It's the doins a the Old Guy In The Sky. I prayed to the old idiot to stop the rain, but it rained harder'n ever. So I figure it's really the Old Woman In The Earth who's kickin up this rain. The Old Guy's too feeble to stop her. He needs strength. So . . . I thought about pouring out the blood a a virgin to him, so he kin lap it up and get his muscles back with that. But I give that up, cause there ain't no such thing any more, not within a hundred miles a here, anyway.

"So . . . I been thinkin about going outside and doin the next best thing, that is pourin a quart or two a beer out on the ground for him. What the Greeks call pourin a liberation to the Gods . . . "

"Don't let him drink none a that cheap beer," warned Gummy. "This rain fallin on us is bad enough. I don't want no god pukin all over the place."

He hurled the quart at her. It was empty, because he wasn't so far gone he'd waste a full or even half-full bottle. But it was smashed against wall, and since it was worth a nickel's refund, he accused Gummy of malicious waste.

"If you'd a held still, it woun't a broke."

Deena paid no attention to the scene. "I'm pleased to see you, child," she said. "But it might have been better if you had stayed home tonight."

She gestured at the picture of her mother, still nailed face inwards. "He's not come out of his evil mood yet."

"You kin say that again," mumbled Gummy. "He got a pistolwhippin from the young Limpy Doolan who lives in that packinbox house with the Jantzen bathing suit ad pasted on the side, when Limpy tried to grab Old King's hat off a Old Man's head jist for fun."

"Yeah, he tried to grab it," said Paley. "But I slapped his hand hard. Then he pulls a gun out a his coat pocket with the other hand and hit me in this eye with its butt. That don't stop me. He sees me comin at him like I'm late for work, and he says he'll shoot me if I touch him again. My old man din't raise no silly sons, so I don't charge him. But I'll get him sooner or later. And he'll be limpin in both legs, if he walks at all.

"But I don't know why I never had nothin but bad luck ever since I got this hat. It ain't supposed to be that way. It's supposed to be bringing me all the good luck the Paleys ever had."

He glared at Dorothy and said, "Do you know what? I had good luck until I showed you that place, you know, the flowers. And then, after you know what, everything went sour as old milk. What did you do, take the power out a me by doin what you did? Did the Old Woman In The Earth send you to me so you'd draw the muscle and luck and life out a me if I found the hat when Old Guy placed it in my path?"

He lurched up from the easy chair, clutched two quarts of beer from the refrigerator to his chest, and staggered towards the door.

"Kin't stand the smell in here. Talk about *my* smell. I'm sweet violets, compared to the fish a some a you. I'm goin out where the air's fresh. I'm goin out and talk to the Old Guy In The Sky, hear what the thunder has to say to me. He understand me; he don't give a damn if I'm a ugly ole man that's ha'f-ape."

Swiftly, Deena ran in front of him and held out her claws at him like a gaunt, enraged alley cat.

"So that's it! You've had the indencency to insult this young girl! You evil beast!"

Old Man halted, swayed, carefully deposited the two quarts on the floor. Then he shuffled to the picture of Deena's mother and ripped it from the wall. The nails screeched; so did Deena.

"What are you going to do?"

"Somethin I been wantin to do for a long long time. Only I felt sorry for you. Now I don't. I'm gonna throw this idol a yours into the creek. Know why? Cause I think she's a delegate a the Old Woman In The Earth, Old Guy's enemy. She's been sent here to watch on me and report to Old Woman on what I was doin. And you're the one brought her in this house."

"Over my dead body you'll throw that in the creek!" screamed Deena.

"Have it your own way," he growled, lurching forward and driving her to one side with his shoulder.

Deena grabbed at the frame of the picture he held in his hand, but he hit her over the knuckles with it. Then he lowered it to the floor, keeping it from falling over with his leg while he bent over and picked up the two quarts in his huge hand. Clutching them, he squatted until his stump was level with the top part of the frame. The stump clamped down over the upper part of the frame, he straightened, holding it tightly, lurched towards the door, and was gone into the driving rain and crashing lightning.

Deena stared into the darkness for a moment, then ran after him.

Stunned, Dorothy watched them go. Not until she heard Gummy mumbling, "They'll kill each other," was Dorothy able to move.

She ran to the door, looked out, turned back to Gummy.

"What's got into him?" she cried. "He's so cruel, yet I know he has a soft heart. Why must he be this way?"

"It's you," said Gummy. "He thought it din't matter how he looked, what he did, he was still a Paley. He thought his sweat would git you like it did all them chicks he was braggin about, no matter how uppity the sweet young thing was. 'N you hurt him when you din't dig him. Specially cause he thought more a you 'n anybody before.

"Why'd you think life's been so miserable for us since he found you? What the hell, a man's a man, he's always got the eye for the chicks, right? Deena din't see that. Deena hates Old Man. But Deena can't do without him, either . . . "

'I have to stop them," said Dorothy, and she plunged out into the black and white world.

Just outside the door, she halted, bewildered. Behind her, light streamed from the shanty, and to the north was a dim glow from the city of Onaback. But elsewhere was darkness. Darkness, except when the lightning burned away the night for a dazzling frightening second.

She ran around the shanty towards the Kickapoo, some fifty yards away—she was sure that they'd be somewhere by the bank of the creek. Halfway to the stream, another flash showed her a white figure by the bank.

It was Deena in her terrycloth robe, Deena now sitting up in the mud, bending forward, shaking with sobs.

"I got down on my knees," she moaned. "To him, to him. And I begged him to spare my mother. But he said I'd thank him later for freeing me from worshipping a false goddess. He said I'd kiss his hand."

Deena's voice rose to a scream. "And then he did it! He tore my blessed mother to bits! Threw her in the creek! I'll kill him! I'll kill him!"

Dorothy patted Deena's shoulder. "There, there. You'd better get back to the house and get dry. It's a bad thing he's done, but he's not in his right mind. Where'd he go?"

"Towards that clump of cottonwoods where the creek runs into the river."

"You go back," said Dorothy. "I'll handle him. I can do it."

Deena seized her hand.

"Stay away from him. He's hiding in the woods now. He's dangerous, dangerous as a wounded boar. Or as one of his ancestors when they were hurt and hunted by ours."

"Ours?" said Dorothy. "You mean you believe his story?"

"Not all of it. Just part. That tale of his about the mass invasion of Europe and King Paley's hat is nonsense. Or, at least it's been distorted through God only knows how many thousands of years. But it's true he's at least part Neanderthal. Listen! I've fallen low, I'm only a junkman's whore. Not even that, now—Old Man never touches me any more, except to hit me. And that's not his fault, really. I ask for it; I want it.

"But I'm not a moron. I got books from the library, read what they said about the Neanderthal. I studied Old Man carefully. And I *know* he must be what he says he is. Gummy too—she's at least a quarter-breed."

Dorothy pulled her hand out of Deena's grip.

"I have to go. I have to talk to Old Man, tell him I'm not seeing him any more."

"Stay away from him," pleaded Deena, again seizing Dorothy's hand. "You'll go to talk, and you'll stay to do what I did. What a score of others did. We let him make love to us because he isn't human. Yet, we found Old Man as human as any man, and some of us stayed after the lust was gone because love had come in."

Dorothy gently unwrapped Deena's fingers from her hand and began walking away.

Soon she came to the group of cottonwood trees by the bank where the creek and the river met and there she stopped.

"Old Man!" she called in a break between the rolls of thunder. "Old Man! It's Dorothy!"

A growl as of a bear disturbed in his cave answered her, and a figure like a tree trunk come to life stepped out of the inkiness between the cottonwoods.

"What you come for?" he said, approaching so close to her that his enormous nose almost touched hers. "You want me just as I am, Old Man Paley, descendant a the Real Folk—Paley, who loves you? Or you come to give the batty old junkman a tranquilizer so you kin take him by the hand like a lamb and lead him back to the slaughterhouse, the puzzle factory, where they'll stick a ice pack back a his eyeball and rip out what makes him a man and not an ox."

"I came . . ."

"Yeah?"

"For this!" she shouted, and she snatched off his hat and raced away from him, towards the river.

Behind her rose a bellow of agony so loud she could hear it even above the thunder. Feet splashed as he gave pursuit.

Suddenly, she slipped and sprawled face down in the mud. At the same time, her glasses fell off. Now it was her turn to feel despair, for in this halfworld she could see nothing without her glasses except the lightning flashes. She must find them. But if she delayed to hunt for them, she'd lose her headstart.

She cried out with joy, for her groping fingers found what they sought. But the breath was knocked out of her, and she dropped the glasses again as a heavy weight fell upon her back and half-stunned her. Vaguely, she was aware that the hat had been taken away from her. A moment later, as her senses came back into focus, she realized she was being raised into the air. Old Man was holding her in the crook of her arm, supporting part of her weight on his bulging belly.

"My glasses. Please, my glasses. I need them."

"You won't be needin em for a while. But don't worry about em. I got em in my pants pocket. Old Man's takin care a you."

His arm tightened around her so she cried out with pain.

Hoarsely, he said, "You was sent down by the *G'yaga* to get that hat, wasn't you? Well, it din't work cause the Old Guy's stridin the sky tonight, and he's protectin his own."

Dorothy bit her lip to keep from telling him that she had wanted to destroy the hat because she hoped that that act would also destroy the guilt of having made it in the first place. But she couldn't tell him that. If he knew she had made a false hat, he would kill her in his rage.

"No. Not again," she said. "Please. Don't. I'll scream. They'll come after you. They'll take you to the State Hospital and lock you up for life. I swear I'll scream."

"Who'll hear you? Only the Old Guy, and he'd get a kick out a seeing you in this fix cause you're a Falser and you took the stuffin right out a my hat and me with your Falser Magic. But I'm gettin back what's mine and his, the same way you took it from me. The door swings both ways."

He stopped walking and lowered her to a pile of wet leaves.

"Here we are. The forest like it was in the old days. Don't worry. Old Man'll protect you from the cave bear and the bull o' the woods. But who'll protect you from Old Man, huh?"

Lightning exploded so near that for a second they were blinded and speechless. The Paley shouted, "The Old Guy's whoopin it up tonight, just like he used to do! Blood and murder and wickedness're ridin the howlin night air!"

He pounded his immense chest with his huge fist.

"Let the Old Guy and the Old Woman fight it out tonight. They ain't going to stop us. Dor'thy. Not unless that hairy old god in the clouds is goin to fry me with his lightnin, jealous a me cause I'm havin what he can't."

Lightning rammed against the ground from the charged skies, and lightning leaped up to the clouds from the charged earth. The rain fell harder than before, as if it were being shot out of a great pipe from a mountain river and pouring directly over them. But for some time the flashes did not come close to the cottonwoods. Then, one ripped apart the night beside them, deafened and stunned them.

And Dorothy, looking over Old Man's shoulder, thought she would die of fright because there was a ghost standing over them. It was tall and white, and its shroud flapped in the wind, and its arms were raised in a gesture like a curse.

But it was a knife that it held in its hand.

Then, the fire that rose like a cross behind the figure was gone, and night rushed back in.

Dorothy screamed. Old Man grunted, as if something had knocked the breath from him.

He rose to his knees, gasped something unintelligible, and slowly got to his feet. He turned his back to Dorothy so he could face the thing in white. Lightning flashed again. Once more Dorothy screamed, for she saw the knife sticking out of his back.

Then the white figure had rushed towards Old Man. But instead of attacking him, it dropped to its knees and tried to kiss his hand and babbled for forgiveness.

No ghost. No man. Deena, in her white terrycloth robe.

"I did it because I love you!" screamed Deena.

Old Man, swaying back and forth, was silent.

"I went back to the shanty for a knife, and I came here because I knew what you'd be doing, and I didn't want Dorothy's life ruined because of you, and I hated you, and I wanted to kill you. But I don't really hate you."

Slowly, Paley reached behind him and gripped the handle of the knife. Lightning made everything white around him, and by its brief glare the women saw him jerk the blade free of his flesh.

Dorothy moaned, "It's terrible, terrible. All my fault, all my fault."

She groped through the mud until her fingers came across the old Man's jeans and its backpocket, which held her glasses. She put the glasses on, only to find that she could not see anything because of the darkness. Then, and not until then, she became concerned about locating her own clothes. On her hands and knees she searched through the wet leaves and grass. She was about to give up and go back to Old Man when another lightning flash showed the heap to her left. Giving a cry of joy, she began to crawl to it.

But another stroke of lightning showed her something else. She screamed and tried to stand up but instead slipped and fell forward on her face.

Old Man, knife in hand, was walking slowly towards her.

"Don't try to run away!" he bellowed. "You'll never get away! The Old Guy'll light things up for me so you kin't sneak away in the dark. Besides, your white skin shines in the night, like a rotten toadstool. You're done for. You snatched away my hat so you could get me out here defenseless, and then Deena could stab me in the back. You and her are Falser witches, I know damn well!"

"What do you think you're doing?" asked Dorothy. She tried to rise again but could not. It was as if the mud had fingers around her ankles and knees.

"The Old Guy's howlin for the blood a *G'yaga* wimmen. And he's gonna get all the blood he wants. It's only fair. Deena put the knife in me, and the Old Woman got some a my blood to drink. Now it's your turn to give the Old Guy some a yours."

"Don't!" screamed Deena. Dorothy had nothing to do with it! And you can't blame me, after what you were doing to her!"

"She's done everything to me. I'm gonna make the last sacrifice to Old Guy. Then they kin do what they want to me. I don't care. I'll have had one moment a bein a real Real Folker."

Deena and Dorothy both screamed. In the next second, lightning broke the darkness aroud them. Dorothy saw Deena hurl herself on Old Man's back and carry him downward. Then, night again.

There was a groan. Then, another blast of light. Old Man, bent almost double but not bent so far Dorothy could not see the handle of the knife that was in his chest.

"Oh, Christ!" wailed Deena. "When I pushed him, he must have fallen on the knife. I heard the bone in his chest break. Now he's dying!"

Paley moaned. "Yeah, you done it now, you sure paid me back didn't you? Paid me back for my taking the monkey off a your back and supportin you all these years."

"Oh, Old Man," sobbed Deena, "I didn't mean to do it. I was just trying to save Dorothy and save you from yourself. Please! Isn't there anything I can do for you?"

"Sure you kin. Stuff up the two big holes in my back and chest. My blood, my breath, my real soul's flowin out a me. Guy In The Sky, what a way to die! Kilt by a crazy woman!"

"Keep quiet," said Dorothy. "Save your strength. Deena, you run to the service station. It'll still be open. Call a doctor."

"Don't go, Deena," he said. "It's too late. I'm hanging on to my soul by its big toe now; in a minute, I'll have to let go, and it'll jump out a me like a beagle after a rabbit.

"Dor'thy, Dor'thy, was it the wickedness a the Old Woman put you up to this? I must a meant somethin to you . . . under the flowers . . . . . . maybe it's better . . . I felt like a god, then . . . not what I really am . . . a crazy old junkman . . . a alley man . . . Just think a it . . . fifty thousand years behint me . . . older'n Adam and Eve by far . . . now, this . . . "

Deena began weeping. He lifted his hand, and she seized it.

"Let loose," he said faintly. "I was gonna knock hell otta you for blubberin . . . just like a Falser bitch . . . kill me . . . then cry . . . you never did 'preciate me . . . like Dor'thy . . ."

"His hand's getting cold," murmured Deena.

"Deena, bury that damn hat with me . . . least you kin do . . . Hey, Deena who you goin to for help when you hear that monkey chitterin outside the door, huh? Who . . . ?"

Suddenly, before Dorothy and Deena could push him back down, he sat up. At the same time, lightning hammered into the earth nearby and it showed them his eyes, looking past them out into the night.

He spoke, and his voice was stronger, as if his life had drained back into him through the holes in his flesh.

"Old Guy's givin me a good send-off. Lightning and thunder. The works. Nothin cheap about him, huh? Why not? He knows this is the end a the trail fer me. The last a his worshippers . . . last a the Paleys . . ."

He choked on his own blood and sank back and spoke no more.

JOHN JAKES

The Sellers of the Dream

1

HIS GAUDY wristwatch showed thirty minutes past nine, sixth July. It was time. From here on it was do the job right or be ruined. If not physically, then professionally.

Finian Smith dug for tools in the pouches of his imitation stomach. The left eye of the watch's moon face gave a ludicrous wink to complete the time signal. Finian hated the watch. He'd got used to the confines of the camouflaged polymer leech clinging to the keel of the hydrofoiler. He'd got used to performing necessary bodily functions in intimate contact with the leech's servomechanisms for thirty-six hours. But the watch—never.

It was effete, like his clothes. Effeteness was big this year. Next year it would be hand-loomed woolens. But he wasn't being paid to inherit the soul of the man he was impersonating, after all. He applied the first of his meson torches to the thick hull. His long, pleasantly ugly face began to bead with perspiration.

He had precisely four minutes to cut through.

His face was half shadowed by the hull as he worked, half washed in flickering sunlight through anemone and brain coral. He defused a large U-shaped section and replaced the torch with a pistol unit fitted with a round cup at the muzzle. This cup he applied to the hull. A blue whine of power—he forced the hull inward far enough to accommodate entry to the fuel baffle chamber.

He set a small black box to blow the polymer leech off the hull in fifty seconds, glad that he'd spent a full twenty nights under the hypnolearner. The penetration plan was drummed so deeply into his skull he could operate like an automaton.

With a last tool he re-sealed the hull, touched a stud and watched the tool collapse to gritty pumice. Right now the leach should be quietly disintegrating, without so much as a murmur to disturb the TTIC spy radar. It took a lot of money to arrange this penetration, Finian thought. Knowing how much made him nervous.

Finian hurried up a lonely companionway. Before stepping to the yacht's deck he dusted his pleatless puce satin pantaloons and also made sure the precision camera, a combined effort of G/S dental technicians and optics men, was in place where his right front incisor had once been. The blade shutter's release was a knob on the tooth's inner surface, triggered by tongue pressure. Fake enamel would fly aside a micro-instant and TTIC secrets would be recorded for posterity, not to mention G/S market analysts.

On deck, Finian adjusted his identification badge.

Beneath his picture it said *Woodrow Howslip, Missoula, Mont., Upper North American Distributorship*. Finian hoped Woodrow Howslip was still lost in the Mojave Desert. If so, the only thing Finian had to worry over was his old enemy.

Every few yards along the deck armed TTIC security men stood at attention: TTIC seemed to have innumerable armed guards. So did G/S for that matter. Finian often wondered why. No one got angry any more, why have armed guards?

"Hi, there, I'm Woody Howslip."

"Morning, sir." The guard stared into the Pacific's cobalt swell.

"Say, fella. Last year when I came to see the new models innerduced, I ran into a hell of a swell person—Spool or Stool. Sure like to buy him a drink. Is he on board?"

"I don't believe so, sir."

"Oh, too bad. Maybe he'll show up. They always have the top dogs at these distributor shows. I hear Stool's a top dog. Chief of company spies or something."

The guard concealed irritation.

"*Sprool*, sir. Chief of industrial investigation."

Finian gigged the man's ribs. "Keeps those Goods/Services jerks hopping, huh? Well, sorry Sprool isn't around. Maybe later. See you in the videofunnies—"

Overdoing it, Finian thought as he hurried along. Still, it was reassuring to know the intelligence was correct: Sprool was in Bombay. Finian had run up against him most recently when TTIC tried to steal G/S designs for the mid-year hair-do changes during the 2004-5 season.

Finian joined a crowd of distributors hurrying into an auditorium beneath a banner reading:

WELCOME
Things to Come Incorporated
World Distributors
*"Last Year's Woman Is This
Year's Consumer"*

As he took a seat in the shadowy hall he listened to voices all around:

"It's rumored she's of the Grecian mode," said the European Common Market distributor.

"What? Copy the tripe G/S peddled two years ago?" That was the White/Blue Nile man.

The Chinese distributor protested: "Last year, too severe. Humble per cent of market drop severely. Five thousand years in fields, China women do not desire box haircut, woolen socks."

"Hope it's a real smasher this time," said the British Empire distributor, a seedy fellow wearing Cologne. One rundown warehouse in Jamaica comprised the Empire any more. TTIC or G/S could buy or sell the Empire a thousand times. Or any other country. Finian was sweating. No wonder the stakes were so high.

On an austere platform up front sat three men. One was a florid old gentleman with dewlaps and blue, vaguely crossed eyes. Another—a spindly type with a flower at each cuff—rose and was introduced by a loudspeaker as Corporate Director of Sales, Northcote Hastings.

"Thank you, thank you. I won't waste time, gentlemen. You've traveled thousands of miles in secrecy and we appreciate it. We trust you also appreciate why we must maintain the mobility of our personality design center. One never knows when the—ah—competition might infiltrate a permanent site. They can't match our sales in new personalities, so they try to outfight us with punches below the belt."

He fingered his, of ermine, to illustrate. Finian joined the laughter, but meant his.

"After luncheon, gentlemen, you're scheduled for individual sessions with our designers, psychiatrists, plastic surgeons and sociability co-ordinators, not to mention apparel teams and accessory experts."

Hastings glanced at the old gentleman with the vaguely crossed eyes.

"Before we proceed, however, I should like to introduce TTIC's beloved chairman of the board, Mr. Alvah Loudermilk. Stand up, Mr. Loudermilk." The sales manager was plainly annoyed by having to make the introduction. The old dodderer took a step towards the podium. Hastings let a tolerant smile be seen by the distributors but did not relinquish the mike.

"You can talk with Mr. Loudermilk personally later, gentlemen."

The florid old gentleman sat down again, as though no one appreciated him. Smoothly Hastings continued, "Let me get on by bringing forward the great design chief of Things to Come Incorporated—" He flung out a hand. "Dr. Gerhard Krumm."

The famed Krumm, an obese toad with the inevitable disarrayed look of the corporate intellectual, walked to the podium. His apricot slippers, pantaloons and bolero jacket seemed to have come from a dustbin. Behind Krumm stage blowers whirred. They were readying curtains and screen.

Finian slid his tongue near his tooth.

"Gentlemen," Krumm said, "first the bad news."

At the unhappy grumble he held up his hand. "Next year—I promise!—TTIC will absolutely and without qualification be ready to introduce the concept of the obsolescent male personality, exactly as we did in the female market ten years ago. I can only emphasize again the tremendous physical problems confronting us, and point to the lag in male fashion obsolescence that was not finally overcome until the late twentieth century, by the sheer weight of promotion. Men, unlike women, accept new decorative concepts slowly. TTIC has a lucrative share of the semi-annual male changeover, but we are years behind the female personality market. Next year we catch up.''

''May we see what you have for the girls, old chap?'' someone asked. ''Then we'll decide whether we're happy.''

''Very well.'' Krumm began to read from a promotion script: ''This year we steal a leaf from yesterday's—uh—scented album.'' The lights dimmed artfully. Perfume sprayed the chamber from hidden ducts. A stereo orchestra swelled. The curtains parted. Finian's upper lip was rolled back as far as possible.

A nostalgic solido view of New York when it was once populated by people flashed on the screen. Violins throbbed thrillingly.

''Remember the sweet, charming girl of yesteryear? We capture her for you—warm, uncomplicated, reveling in—uh, let's see—sunlight and outdoor sports.''

A series of solido slides, illustrating Krumm's points with shots of nuclear ski lifts or the Seine, merged one into another.

''Gone is the exaggerated IQ of this year, gone the modish clothing. A return of softness. A simple mind, clinging, sweet. The stuff of everyman's dreams. Gentlemen, I give you—''

Hidden kettledrums swelled. The name flashed on the screen:

DREAM DESIRE.

''Dream Desire! New Woman of the 2007-08 market year!''

Over enthusiastic applause Krumm continued: ''At our thirty thousand personality alteration centers over the world, every woman will be able to change her body and mind, by means of surgical and psychological techniques of which TTIC is the acknowledged master, to become Dream Desire. Backed by the most intensive promotion program in history, we promise that more women will become Dream Desire than have ever become one of our previous models. Because, gentlemen, no woman could possible resist becoming—this.''

Sitting forward with tooth ready to shoot, Finian was unprepared for the shock that awaited him.

On the screen slid the naked figure of a girl. Only her back was exposed. Nothing could be seen of her face. Her hair was yellow, that was all. The flesh itself was tanned, in sharp contrast to the pale library look currently being merchandised. The proportions of the girl's buttocks had been surgically worked out to be almost the apex of voluptuousness. But what shook Finian to the soles of his mink slippers was a star-shaped raspberry mark on the new model's left rear.

That isn't Dream Desire, he thought wildly. *That's—that's—*

"We begin with the, uh, rear elevation," said Krumm. "In that colorful mark you see TTIC marketing genius. That mark will stamp the woman who buys this new personality as a genuine Dream Desire, not a shoddy G/S counterfeit. To be frank, adoption of this unique—ah—signature, was not planned. When we sought a girl for our prototype, we discovered the girl we chose was blessed with such a mark. It inspired serendipity. But this is just the beginning. See what we have done with the face."

Only just in time did Finian remember to trigger his tooth and take a shot of the rear elevation before the front view flashed on. The girl, naked and coy on a divan, had pink cheeks, red lips, china blue doll eyes. Pretty, in a cuddlesome, vapid way.

Quickly he exposed two more frames. He was falling apart, muffing the job. Krumm's voice became a drone detailing the surgical and analytical procedures necessary for a woman to buy the appearance and personality of Dream Desire. Finian didn't hear a thing about price schedules or what lower-priced models were contemplated.

He photographed each slide mechanically, thinking of the raspberry mark.

It's not Dream Desire, he said to himself. *My God—it's Dolly Novotny*.

Not the face, not the breasts. But *there*, far down in the eyes. They weren't even brown any more. But colored contacts could change eyes so easily.

Never had he been more profoundly shocked. His own sweet lost Dolly!

A heavy hand seized his shoulder.

"Here he is!"

Finian was dragged from his seat. A searing light flashed in his face.

"Well, well. Finian Smith. When you took hold of that rail coming into the hall, you should have recalled we have sweat prints for all you G/S boys. Give me the camera and come along quietly," finished Sprool.

2

"I thought you were in Bombay," said Finian. "I got bum information."

Sprool smiled somewhere in the depths of his almost colorless eyes. His pale, saturnine face, however, was devoid of humor.

"Never trust Lyman Pushkyn for information, Fin. Since when is an advertising man qualified to supervise an industrial investigation program?"

"You're right. I tried to get them to give me the post once."

"Did you? I didn't realize that. When?"

"Right after I was cashiered by the DOCs and finished my first case for

G/S." He couldn't repress a smile. "The time I stole your men's change-over layouts by disguising myself as part of the lavatory wall. When you still had the design center on land, out in California."

Sprool chuckled flatly. "We've been friendly enemies quite a while, haven't we, Fin?"

"You never put one over on me like this, though."

"Shame you forgot sweat prints."

"My own damned fault." Finian thrust out his jaw. "I'll take what's coming. I was counting on this play to cut through all that stupid bureaucracy at the top of G/S and maybe net me the chief investigator's post." Finian scowled out of the office porthole to the heaving blue Pacific. Sprool smoothed thinning hair.

"Might as well give me the camera."

Finian made a show of dipping into his artificial paunch. He came up with a palm-sized micro 35 mm. and snapped open the case release. He pulled the leader on the cassette all the way out, exposing the film. Chuckling, Sprool picked up the cylinder.

"Very nice, Finian. May I now have the real camera?"

"Ah, you slick bastard," grumbled Finian. This time he took a piece of equipment from beneath his singlet. Sprool dropped it down a hissing disposal tube.

"You look positively vengeful, Fin."

"I could smash a few heads right now. That damn G/S Comptroller Central makes investigators do their own penetration work-ups. They're nickel-nursers besides. I *thought* of sweat prints. They said the corrective was too expensive. I wasn't positive you had the index on file, so—"

"Fin, please don't bristle. Remember we have telephotos on you at this very moment. In that bust of Loewy, for instance. His collar button is watching you. Don't fight me and you won't get hurt. TTIC is a business operation just like G/S. Firm but paternalistic. When we dispose of an irritant, we do it with flexibility and permanence, but no physical pain."

"That's nice to know, considering you'll probably ruin my career."

"Were you ever really cut out for business, Fin?"

"If I wasn't, *what* the hell was I cut out for? Not the DOCs."

Sprool raised a chiding finger. "See? That burst of temper is all too typical of you. People simply don't rock the boat these days, Fin. Why, if either G/S or TTIC went for more than a 50 percent share of the renewal personality market—plus or minus the 2 percent gain or loss as a result of spying, design leaks and so forth—the U.N. would have its economic cycle theorists down on us instantly."

"God, Sprool, I try and try. I guess I just wasn't meant to be a twenty-first-century man. I never had the proper education, like those reading primers written by the market boys from—where was it?—BBDO? I went to private school. On my Pop's knee."

"Then your attitudes are understandable. How can you expect to be anything but yourself when your father was a Galbraither? Perhaps the last of that persuasion allowed to teach economics in public universities? Your father was dead set against the kind of obsolescence practiced by the corporations we both represent. The two largest corporations in the world!"

"Pop wanted consumer money spent on libraries, schools, highways, pretty green roadside picnic parks."

"None of which contributes very much to keeping the world running at top output. None of which provides the millions of jobs needed to give black and yellow and white alike ample opportunity for the good life. If you'd only understand yourself, how you fit the scheme of things."

"I don't. That's the trouble. What the hell am I supposed to do, join the prisoners in New York? I keep quiet about what I think. I call it well enough to be an operative for the Department of Obsolescence Control. I was doing all right until—"

Memory clouded his brow. He wriggled deep down in the foam of his chair. He wished he were free of this hellish interview, free to think on the problem of Dream Desire who was not Dream Desire at all but Dolly.

"Until what? I never really knew."

"Until I rocked the boat, God damn it! I was chief of the Indiana bureau. I tried to stop a car-smash rally a week before the new models came out. The district supervisor was there, making a speech. I thought I saw a kid inside one of the levacars the crowd was pushing into the Wabash River. I went to see, hold back the crowd. The district supervisor told me to stop. I hit him. *I hit him*. You know what happens when you hit an executive."

Finian pinched the bridge of his nose to shut out the ugly memory. At length he added, "In case you never heard the rest of the story either, a wreck crew examined the levacar afterwards. There was no kid inside. Only a big mechanical doll somebody had forgotten to take out before the smash."

"Very touching," said Sprool emptily.

"Come on, Sprool. Let's get this over."

"Of course. But let me make one more point. Do you know why I'm here, not in Bombay?"

"The mental riot at the TTIC nylon plant was a fake."

"Not at all. The rioters were manning the controls of the motorized strike gangs day and night, from their homes. The moment TTIC cabled agreement to their demand for two extra holidays, before and after Nehru's birthday, they gave up all their other requests—for free anti-cigarette immunization and the like. People are soft, Fin. They co-operate. It must be so, or the plant would stop functioning. How many billions do G/S and TTIC employ? Put those people out of work—disaster! Hunger, pestilence, *real* rioting. The people also have another role to fill, as consumers. If they're unhappy, they respond less adequately to advertising. The plant slows down. Why, until TTIC conceived the idea of introducing new female personalities every year, not just new clothes but complete new mental patterns, the world was headed for ruin. We ran out of new gadgets long ago.''

''Don't kid me,'' Finian said cynically. ''Personality obsolescence was thought up by Old Man Pharoh of G/S. His granddad told him a story about the Kennedy lady's mushroom hair changing the style overnight and it started him thinking.''

''He had considerable help from Alvah Loudermilk.''

''Who cares? All I say is, it's a hell of a shame the Triple Play War didn't end in something besides a stalemate. We wouldn't have had everybody palsy-walsy, black and white and yellow. And this damned population problem—the first rockets rusting on the moon and nobody interested in following them in person. Everybody's a consumer and a worker and—and damn it, soft as jello. And it's a miserable mess from top to bottom.''

Sprool was genuinely shocked.

''Fin, are you seriously advancing periodic wars?''

Finian shielded his eyes from the sun falling through the port.

''Oh, no. I can't think of anything else, that's all. Fatness or fighting, fighting or fatness. In my book they're both lousy. I wish there were a third way. I can't think of one. Maybe if I were smart like you—'' Finian stopped, bitterly.

Sprool dialed a magenta visorphone. ''Really, Fin, this is becoming pointless temperament.'' Into the phone he said, ''We're ready, Doctor.'' To Finian again: ''Please don't try to reform our delicately balanced world, my friend. At least not until we scrub your mind clean of what you saw in the auditorium.''

A shiver crawled on Finian's spine.

''*Scrub—?*''

Too late. Pneumatic doors slid aside. Two unsavory specimens in white smocks bordered with lace wheeled a rubber-tired mechanism into the room. Before Finian could move they adjusted several wing nuts and lowered a bowl device over his head. He tried to stand up, cursing. He was quickly but painlessly pinioned by sleek tubular metal arms clasping him from the back of the chair.

''The worst damage you did was on film,'' Sprool said, striding back and forth, dry-washing his hands. ''I naturally assume that in your heightened nervous state, what you saw with your eyes didn't make much of an impression. But we'll be sure. Give him a mild jolt to start, boys.''

Several sinister cathode tubes began to hiss at various points on the machine. Finian felt a tingle on his scalp, similar to a healthful massage. He closed his eyes and tried to remember the rear elevation of Dream Desire.

He panicked.

Almost as though there were a mental vacuum cleaner in his head, certain synapses were blocked, certain memory receptors temporarily sucked dry. The technique was a portion of that employed in changing the female consumer's intelligence quotient from year to year to conform to the new personality design she purchased. It made Finian fume to think of them tampering with his skull. He was no rotten Metropolis wife merchandised into adopting the latest fashion trend. He writhed ferociously.

Try as he might, Finian could not remember what—*good lord!* He'd forgotten the name!

What did she look like? *What?*

He had a blurry recollection of colors on a screen, little else. The laboratory cretins unhooded him. The chair relaxed. Sprool assisted him to his feet.

"Feeling better? Free of unpleasant memories?"

"You've no business tampering—"

Dolly Novotny had a raspberry mark.

So did Dream Desire.

"Yeah, yeah, I'm okay."

It took all Finian's strength to keep from revealing that the mental dyke had just burst.

He wasn't really surprised. Dolly Novotny had once meant far more to him than assignment could. She would again, when he learned how and why she—

He laughed inwardly. Poor Sprool. He'd stolen a march. Two. Finian still had the tooth camera. And how could Sprool know Finian wanted to—*must*—remember Dolly Novotny, because she was the only creature he ever really loved?

Dolly was the girl to whom he'd been engaged, before her parents broke it off after he was cashiered from the DOCs. An ex-DOC who became an industrial investigator was little more than a low-life spy in their estimations. Finian had been away so much, on assignment. Dolly had tried to resist her parents, but they held the cash-box for a modelling career. She tried; she loved him. But one day when he came back to Bala Cynwyd she was gone. The whole family had moved.

Finian received one final letter. He thought from the words, or rather what was between them, really, that she still loved him. The words were obviously parentally ghosted.

Blinking at Sprool now, scratching his scalp to relieve the prickle, Finian realized anew the rather disheartening truth. He was a maverick. Pop had made him so, against his mother's shrill protests. So be it. Especially since someone—the system, maybe, he didn't know, cared less because a man couldn't really fight a system, not an ordinary man anyway—had corrupted the flesh he loved so well.

Finian was vaguely aware of Sprool, bland, pointing.

"Up that stairway, Fin. Directly to the vertijet takeoff stage. Spare you the embarrassment of going on deck." He extended his hand. "Luck, Fin. I hope the sacking isn't too bad."

Finian slipped the hand aside. He grinned. If you had to be a loony, why not enjoy it?

"Thanks for nothing, pal."

He marched defiantly up the stairs into the sunlight.

Who had Sprool been kidding about paternalism? Three hours later the vertijet hovered six inches from Lyman Pushkyn's green front door, the lawn of Panpublix on the outskirts of the Eastern metropolis. Finian was rudely pushed out. The vertijet climbed a white column of vapor into the sky.

Finian picked fresh-cut grass from his pantaloons. Oh, that kind, gentle Sprool. On his instructions the vertijet pilot had beamed an anonymous message on the Panpublix band, announcing that Finian Smith was being returned to continental U.S. by a TTIC skycraft. Still, Finian had one ace to stave off financial disaster.

Five minutes later he lost it.

A squad of G/S industrial guards boiled on to the lawn and hustled Finian to a cold tile room in the personnel wing. There, he discovered two astonishing things. One, the corporation was not quite so paternalistic as it masked itself to appear. The policemen roughed him as they stripped him. Two, the vast G/S industrial police force was not the harmless, aimless body it looked to be from outside. Apparently the guards were paid so well because they had to move savagely if a bubble boiled up the bland surface of the world stew.

In fact, their professionalism with the see-rays in the personnel lab relieved him, howling and kicking and pummeling, of the precious tooth-camera just before he was hustled to Pushkyn's floor.

3

Panpublix was the wholly owned internal advertising agency for G/S. The building loomed forty stories. Within its curtain-walls quite a few thousand communicators devoted themselves to the task of planning and executing campaigns to move the bodies, as the expression went. The fortieth, or solarium, floor belonged to the agency's executive officer, Pushkyn, into whose presence Finian was unceremoniously thrust.

"You miserable creep," Lyman said, as he shooed away his masseuse and beetled his thick Ukrainian brows. "You bumbler, you! We heard all about your incredible performance from Sprool's agents. You're fired. Blackballed. Eradicated. *Kapoosht*."

Finian had a hard light in his eyes. He sat down, tilted his feet to the chaise footrest and dialed the arm for a B-complex cocktail. "Lyman, those goonies of yours messed me up. I never knew they were more than window dressing. I didn't know they were supposed to fight."

Pudgy Pushkyn snapped the elastic of his old rose knickerbockers. His stomach, lumpy and white as the rest of him, hung out unglamorously.

"Rock the boat some more, creepnik. You'll find out how they can fight."

"Oh shut up. I delivered your pictures. Even if your men did take them by force."

Pushkyn turned his back. "Peddle it another place, jerk. You're through."

"You can't talk to me that way. If you hadn't chintzed about a lousy sweat-print job—"

Pushkyn squinted around. "So *that's* how. That Sprool, he's a regular fiend."

"Damn it, Lyman—"

Extending a trembling sausage finger Pushkyn breathed, "*You* we ought to have psyched, deep and permanent. What a fool I was to string along with you for years! A stumblebum private cop dignifying himself by calling himself an industrial investigator. Come in here storming, cursing—no wonder the DOCs kicked you out!"

Momentarily bewildered, Finian countered, "Lyman, your own guards—"

"Quiet! We'll get a nice fat rap in the public image when the investigator trade journals pick up the story of how G/S flopped."

Glowering, Finian stalked him. "Regardless of that, I delivered. I want my fee."

"I'll be damned if I—"

Conflict was temporarily forestalled by the arrival of a thin assistant art director, carrying a square item masked in grey silk. Finian stared moodily at the G/S model announcement layouts in the wall display racks. The tradename of the new G/S woman and her figure were greeked; but from the woodcut and steel-engraving technique of the gatefold and bleed comps, Finian suspected G/S was going to market a bit of nostalgia even older than the kind chosen by TTIC. Bustless, mandolins and stereopticons by gaslight? Finian had a prepossessing urge to throw up.

"Want to see this, chief?" said the assistant art director.

He whipped off the silk, revealing an oil painting in a platinum frame.

"What the rinkydink hell is that?" Pushkyn cried.

The art director blanched. "Why, chief, it's R.R. Pharoh III!"

"Of course, of course, jerkola. You think I don't know? I haven't seen the old smeller in three years maybe, but think I don't know the chairman of my own bread and butter? Why the fancy-fancy oil treatment? You do it?"

"Spare time, only, chief," trembled the art director. "Got a memo. Salinghams—you know, the audiotonal effects veep—memoized Pharoh. Wanted a personal portrait of his leader. Pharoh memoized me, okaying having his picture done. I patched together this little work from the descriptive PR biog. There aren't any good portraits extant."

"Why bring it to me?"

"But chief! You memoized me when I memoized you that—"

"I did! Oh, yeah. Well, I'm busy. Take it to Salinghams."

The art director veiled his creation and disappeared down the tube. Pushkyn was about to speak to Finian when he noted the grey sweat patina on Finian's face. He demanded to know whether Finian was ill.

"Nothing, nothing's wrong," said Finian, shivering, wildly curious.

The image in the portrait burned into Finian's skull. It was that of a florid old gentleman with dewlaps and blue, vaguely crossed eyes.

Tightening his nerves, Finian said, "Pushkyn, let me lay it out. I got to have the fee. I need it to find the prototype of the TTIC girl. I used to know her."

A visorphone glowed. Pushkyn slapped the command button. A pale man danced up and down on the screen.

"Chief, chief, it's a breakthrough, a breakthrough! We turned up the TTIC pilot plant just an hour ago. Molecular triangulation. My God, sir, it's a miracle of deception. Manhattan! The prison! An old rundown distillery company building in the worst stews of—" He consulted a paper. "Parkave, that's the place."

Listening transfixed, Pushkyn started, slid his gaze to Finian and snarled at the screen, "Oh, boy, is *your* fat in the fire. Call me back." He shut off and squinted at Finian, whose mind churned. "You were talking?"

Finian swallowed hard. "Pushkyn, I must find out what's happened to the girl they made into the TTIC prototype. If they've changed her they've done wrong. She was sweet and desirable. They've made her all soft and disgusting. Like marshmallow."

"The new TTIC broad? You were hot for her once, that it?"

"That's it. I was only holding back the camera so you'd pay me. Give me a chance!"

"Think we run a sniveling charity?" Pushkyn's sweeping gesture encompassed the heavens and the pulsing, overpopulated smog blanks beneath. "We gotta keep the plant running! Create demand every minute! Off with the old woman! On with the new! The old woman, she smells, she's out of date! We got a crusade here at Panpublix! We got a holy mission! You want the plant wheels to stop like they put sand in them? While we take care of your *personal* problems? Don't be a jerkola. Like to argue about the fee? I'll call up the guards again."

Something akin to a cool rush of air swept Finian's brain.

"Then I'll find her without the fee, Lyman."

"Hah-hah, sure. Big independent operator, big millionaire. Go get psyched and lose those hostile tendencies. Don't rock the world, she don't rock so good. Everybody's happy, you be happy. Go grub and be happy."

"I'm not happy. All of a sudden I'm not happy, if people like you make the only girl I ever fell in love with obsolete."

"Get out, chummo. I don't like you any more. You're dangerous."

Finian Smith nodded crisply. "I could very well be." And left.

As Finian left the Panpublix building he heard a menacing hiss. He tried to dodge the rainbow spray. Too late.

His clothing was soon soaked with a noxious admixture of water, special nitrites and phosphorus compounds shot into the air by the underground sprinkler system.

At the levacar station he finally controlled his anger. How petty they could be, to order the lawns sprinkled just then.

Waiting passengers moved away and made rude remarks about his smell. Finian found himself sole occupant of the front car on the ride down the Philadelphia spur.

The enforced loneliness gave him a chance to organize his muddled thoughts and decide what course of action he had to pursue concerning Dolly Novotny.

Two facts he possessed. What they meant, he didn't know.

A likely place to find her was the TTIC pilot plant on Manhattan, the prison island. Still, he was certain to have a rough time getting on to the island and into the plant after that. With few resources at his disposal it might be better to pursue the other thread a bit.

Its significance left him even more muddled. Alvah Loudermilk, TTIC chairman, had appeared at the dealer presentation, somewhat to the annoyance of his inferiors. And R. R. Pharoh, top G/S executive, hadn't been acting quite sensibly either when he permitted an oil portrait of himself to be painted. Finian had never seen a public photo of either man. Both executives were practically legendary.

Then why in the name of Galbraith did they look so much like each other?

When Finian thought on it, one cold, unpleasant word gnawed his head. *Conspiracy*.

A moment later his professional memory dredged up a source of proving or disproving his odd theory. What he intended to do with evidence, if any existed, he couldn't say. But he had a vague desire to be armed with a little more certainty before he sought Dolly.

An achingly musical name. *Dolly, Dolly—*

He remembered her so well, from summer evenings on the back porch before Bala Cynwyd, like the other suburbs, was swallowed in the fester of the metropolis.

Her dark hair. Her gentle eyes. Her animated mouth. And the raspberry mark, one night during an electrical storm.

She'd tentatively shared Finian's inherited ideas about their constantly obsolete world, ideas long suppressed in him and now flooding back under the double stimulus of Sprool's lecture and Pushkyn's vindictive parsimony.

Dolly hadn't exactly been sympathetic. The philosophy of enduring worth was too daring even then. (Today it was sheer lunacy.) But neither had she been as adamant as most citizens. As her parents, for example. They replaced their furniture monthly with the latest G/S fiberboard laminate imitation Finnish modern modes. Good consumers, both. Then came his dismissal from the DOCs, the enforced break-up—

The levacar slowed for Bala Cynwyd. In the abstract, remodeling a woman's mind to make her the pattern to which nearly all other women in the world could conform was acceptable to Finian. When it came to the specific of changing Dolly to the marshmallow-trumpery creature looming on the screen behind Krumm, that was too much.

As he stepped off at Bala Cynwyd, it began to rain. He hurried along beneath warped building fronts of chartreuse and electric blue extruded plastic. From a doorway a hapless bum in last year's pseudo-cotton sport clothes begged for three dollars for a tube of model cement to sniff. Finian shuddered and walked faster. He stopped at Abe Kane's Autosuiter, the last shop left open on the block, selected a few new clothes from the plastic catalogue sheets fastened to the walls, and fed his universal credit card into the slot after punching out his measurements.

A red lucite sign blinked on: *Credit N. G.*

Finian frowned, hit the cancel lever and tried again. The third time he tried his card was not returned.

Pushkyn! Damn the vindictive bastard.

He trudged on through the rain, never having felt so alone in his life. It was a queer sensation, the total absence of credit. Once, he remembered dimly, Pop had brought home a suit of clothes purchased with cash. It had caused a near-riot among Bala Cynwyd burghers.

Reaching his shabby apartment, Finian changed from the effete suit, scrubbed up as best he could, packed his few belongings into a satchel and walked back into the rain. He passed a crowd of workers from the local G/S visorphone plant. It specialized in treating receiver parts with reagents that would crack the plastic precisely eight months after installation.

A little smog had mixed with the rain, turning the street ghostly. At a corner booth Finian used his last few coins to make a toll call to the House of Sinatra in Los Angeles.

A sound truck rolled past, repeating over and over. *"Gee-ess, Gee-ess, don't guess, it's bess—Take free shuttle at Exit 5–6 to the G/S Plaza—Gee-ess, don't—"*

A dapper young man appeared on the screen, snapping his fingers. "Hiyah. What can this gasser of a full-service bank do for you, Clyde?"

Finian showed his bank identification card.

"I'd like to withdraw my balance."

The banker came back into view a moment later. "Get lost. Your balance is nonesville. Garnisheed at noon. Unperformance and non-fulfilling of verbal contract, with waiver of co-operation. You signed it, Charlie.''

''Damn it, I performed—'' Finian began.

The screen had already blacked.

He staggered into the drifting smog. So Pushkyn had gone that far. Just for the sake of meanness. Well, Finian Smith would show the whole rotten bunch. They had angered him now. He wasn't quite witless, not yet.

Gee-ess, Gee-ess, it's bess came a lonely bellow. The polluted smog made Finian cough. His eyes smarted as he turned his pockets inside out.

A dollar left. Enough for a cup of coffee. No transportation. Just a single walking man in a cloud of industrial fumes and a long, empty night for thinking of Dolly.

Resolutely Finian hefted his satchel and started out to walk to Missouri.

4

Thirty-six days later Finian staggered into the National Record Office in Rolla. Thirty-six frightening, alarming, eye-opening, solitary, transfiguring days they had been, too.

Days of dodging robot levacars whose spot-beams hunted him in the shadows beneath the elevated turnpikes, seeking to arrest him for pedestrianship.

Days of remembering his Pop. And nights too. Especially nights, thinking as he lay under a berry bush half-starved and chilly, how Pop had enjoyed prize-fights, antisocial, uncooperative prize-fights. How young Finian had been dragged to lonely boxcars or dim garages where furtive men watched the sport before it was finally stamped out in the name of bland humanity.

The world too was one bland custard, blandly happy. Except not really, as Finian, horrified, discovered.

No plant could function at total efficiency, at complete peak year after year. A low percentage of chronic unemployment had never been whipped by the cyclid theorists. Strange wild caravans of men and wives and children, human wolves almost passed Finian occasionally on red-leafed back-roads in Pennsylvania and Ohio. He almost fell into the hands of one such band. Thereupon he decided he must possess a weapon of self-defense at all costs. His belly he could protect by shoveling in wild berries and an occasional stolen chunk of honeycomb. But his life, against such a seething pack of wild creatures as he had fled from on that lonely road, needed more dependable protection.

Difficult problem. Under law, weapons were prohibited except under special occasions. What necessity for weapons when all was pleasant co-operation.

Yet the G/S guards carried weapons. So did the TTIC internal force. Finian was beginning to believe he knew why that might be so. Too early to tell, however. And the other problem pressed him to concentration upon it.

Weapon-devotees were even more suspect than pedestrians in the lonely country between metropolises. Occasionally Finian glimpsed a wire compound, acres and acres, against the sunburnt horizon. Manhattan Prison was too far for local DOCs to send recalcitrant Hoosier or Buckeye anti-obsols, so they were thrown into smaller country compounds, together with those few madmen who settled disputes with fists. Such compound inmates were described as juves, Finian remembered, passing one such wire enclosure on a white moonlit night and shuddering. He didn't recognize the term juve, but it obviously meant the middle-aged or geriatric specimens huddled within the cages, a few defiantly wearing ancient gaudy jackets with mottoes stitched on them, forgotten anarchist slogans like Pfluger's Idle Hour Pin Barons.

On the outskirts of South Bend, Finian luckily came upon an obsolescence carnival.

Several thousand people swarmed across a treeless terrain in a housing project smash. Motorized workgangs stood at the development's fringe, waiting to set up new prefab Moorish Manors to replace obsolete Five-Bedroom Geneva Chateaux.

Finian infiltrated the wild carnival crowd, ripping draperies and smashing furniture with feigned laughter ringing from his lips. When the carnival wore itself out near dawn and the workgangs rolled in through clouds of soy-fuel smoke, Finian filched a shiny flick-blade knife from a Boy Scout chopping up a last slab of plastic plaster and lath.

The Scout shrieked for the DOCs on duty. Finian was away and running through a hydroponic cornfield before he could be caught.

Now, dressed in his only presentable suit, last year's G/S Nubby Oppenheimer, he flashed his personal identification card before the computer grid in the empty green marble rotunda of the National Record Office. Personal identity was one quantity Pushkyn couldn't revoke.

Finian felt his fingers tingle as the grid scanned the card.

"Investigator Smith, Bond Number PA-5006, you are recognized."

"Permission to examine ownership statements for corporations over one billion, please."

"What year?" buzzed the mechanical voice.

"Not certain," Finian replied. "Could be as far back as 1980 or even 1970."

"Second tier from lowest level. Tube nine, your left."

It gave Finian a weird sensation, plummeting in the air-tube and realizing he was dropping eighty stories into the depths of the nation's largest insane asylum. But legal transactions had proliferated so in the past decades, as had neurotic behavior, that only a combined institution and record office was feasible for saving space and offering a less-than-fatal end for hopeless maniacs.

The reading room below ground smelled of mold. Grey block walls heightened the unpleasant mood. Finian sat at the call-out console. He manipulated the controls and spoke into the unit:

"Let me have the volume covering Goods/Services corporation for—ah—1974, please."

Several minutes passed. A door slid aside. A white male, perhaps seventy, with yellow-rimmed lack-luster eyes and a lantern jaw, shuffled in and waited with docile manner. The creature wore a seedy twill uniform, anciently cut.

"What do you have on any asset transfers for Goods/Services, please?" Finian asked.

The elderly gentleman did not so much as blink. He hesitated only a moment as the index system in his sick skull, instilled by hypnolearning, turned over record after invisible record. Finally he said vacantly, "No asset transfers."

"Nothing in the way of stock, even?"

"No asset transfers, no asset transfers."

"Thank you, that's all."

But the man had already departed, needing no thanks. Finian turned to the console again wondering whether he could endure as many days at it might take:

"Let me have the volume covering Goods/Services corporation for 1975."

A total of eighteen hours went by, relieved only by three short naps above ground, Finian sleeping in a magnolia bush on Rolla's outskirts, before he found what he wanted.

He'd worked through Goods/Services from its 1969 inception to 1997, interviewing assorted madmen and women who shuffled in, reeled off figures and names or lack of them, then shuffled back out. Asset transfers exhausted itself as a lead. He tried register of directorship as well as deposition of tangible real-estate sale. Useless, useless. Only then did it slip back.

In some dim time in the past—Pushkyn had mentioned it once—public stock of G/S had been called off the market.

Once more he began with a different set of volumes, working his way down the years. In 1992, he located it: All certificates redeemed.

The scent overpowered the must of the underground box like the smell of blood. He called out the volume covering Things to Come Incorporated for the same year. It was a naturalized Japanese weighing close to three hundred pounds.

One month after the G/S redemption came a callback by the board of TTIC. Finian almost wished the poor Japanese could appreciate tea. He'd have bought him a bucket, had he the money.

Tensely his fingers flew to the console.

"Two volumes, please. For 1992 and 1993. Covering Flotations without tangible assets."

When 1992 arrived (a mulatto with his face fixed in a perpetual grin) Finian was disappointed. Nothing. The volume for 1993 (a strikingly voluptuous red-haired girl who had eyes that made him think hauntingly of Dolly) was another case entirely. Finian trembled:

"Give me what you have on holding companies, please."

The third was it, the redhead staring through him:

"Holders Limited. Ten thousand shares privately issued."

Finian was on his feet, sweating, his empty belly a-churn. "Officers, please."

"Chairman of the board, Alvah Pharoh."

"There must be some mistake. Uh—re-check, please. What is the name?"

"Full legal name Alvah Robert Loudermilk Pharoh."

A florid old gentleman with dewlaps and blue, vaguely crossed—by heaven!

Finian almost forgot to return the volume to its detention cell after he got the names of the other registered corporate executives, which meant nothing to him. But Alvah Robert Loudermilk Pharoh most certainly did.

Finian wondered, as he left the National Record building and turned his face east again, what had possessed the old man to think it safe to occasionally appear as head of both companies. Not that he appeared often, mind you. The painting *must* have been a slip. So too the appearance on the hydrofoiler, displeasing his underlings.

Senility? Senility and a strength that had refused to completely drain away, as the dewlaps lengthened?

Hungry and tattered though he was, Finian felt renewed as he threw himself into the weary tramp back to Manhattan. The flick-blade knife armed him. So did the knowledge that even the most mighty, even those who kept the plant running at all costs, including the cost of sloth, could occasionally slip.

And they still had Dolly.

5

Ahead in the gloomy purple twilight, giant rats were squealing after blood.

Quickening his step, Finian unshipped the flick-knife. Making headway was hard. This particular section of the Hudson Bluffs National Dump was a miniature mountain range of discarded but eminently serviceable—except for the usual engineered-to-fail tubes and cracked cabinets—solido sets. To the east behind the rubble the towers of Manhattan Prison thrust into the darkening sky.

Finian walked rapidly away from the squee-squee of the rats. He'd glimpsed a pack of them earlier, down by the Tunnel at the far end of the hundred-thousand-acre junk tract. They were nearly three feet long from drinking the waste spewed out by the pharmaceutical factories upriver. Hoping to avoid a meeting with needly fangs, Finian was suddenly arrested by a fresh sound.

A human voice, in fright.

He doubled back in his tracks, cold sweat all over him. The vitaminized beasts were attacking a real person!

Finian rounded a solido heap. A little wisp-haired balloon of a man in a ragged grey smock was backed against a trash peak, trying vainly to swing at three of the rats, armed only with a plastic leg broken from a solido console. The man's left trouser leg was shredded, black-shining with blood. The blood maddened the rats. They danced and snapped and squee-squeed and made the little man even more pale.

Finian snatched up a solido cabinet and heaved. One of the rats yipped, turned and scuttled at Finian like a small furry tank. Shaking, Finian stood his ground. He tried to dodge the creature's leap but was not agile enough. Hellish teeth sank into his arm.

Finian jammed his flick-knife into the smelly hair at the base of the rat's brain. Squirting blood like a fountain, the rat flipped over in the air and gave a death-squee. Its comrades received solid whacks between the eyes from the other man. They turned tail and vanished.

"Let me see that arm," said the man, a filthy specter with moist, disappointed eyes. "Oh, not good at all. Come along. I'm a doctor. Humphrey Cove."

Finian gaped as he was led along the bluff. "A doctor? In the National Dump?"

"I live here. Never mind, I'll explain later. I have a shack. Hurry, we don't want those rat toxins to run through you. I think I have immunization. Oh, I was really done for until you came along."

The small doctor giggled as he hustled Finian along. Finian was not too sure he approved of his would-be savior. In spite of Dr. Cove's rather pitiful mien, there was a certain unsteadiness in his wet eyes. He clucked and talked to himself as he led the way to a ramshackle structure nearly the size of a small private dwelling, constructed solely of panels from solido consoles jerry-rigged together with wire and other scrap materials.

"No one comes here. No humans. Only the littersweep convoys from up and down the coast, all mech-driven. The only people I ever talk with are the poor juves in the prison. What's your name? What are you doing here?"

At the hovel entrance Cove suddenly halted, stared at Finian and turned pale.

"Did you come to arrest—?"

Finian shook his head. "I came to get into Manhattan."

"Via the Dumps?" Cove blinked suspiciously. "There's the Tunnel."

"To use the Tunnel, you have to be a priest going in for last rites. Or a coroner or a psychiatry student. Or have a DOC pass. I watched the Tunnel three hours." Suddenly Finian had an impulse to trust this odd little person: "I have no pass. I'll be entering the prison illegally."

"Well, then! Come inside, do come inside!"

Names were exchanged again. Cove having forgotten he'd given his. From behind a triple stack of ancient medical texts Cove said he'd rescued from dump piles, the doctor produced a frowsy leather-plas diagnostic kit. He clamped the analyzer to Finian's upper arm and switched on the battery. A whir. A moment later the proper medication had been pressure-sprayed through Finian's epidermal cells.

Cove watched with proud glowing eyes, saying as he unstrapped the unit:

"A miracle I found this kit, I'll tell you. Three years ago. The only persons who use it are the poor juves. No regular medical help for them, I'm afraid. So I've a skiff. Actually an old levacar inverted. I paddle across once a month after dark." He giggled. "The DOCs at the Tunnel post would psych me if I got caught. But I feel I'm doing my bit to keep the anti-obsols content in their unhappiness."

Through a rift in the wall Cove's moist eyes sought the darkening towers. His voice was quickly vengeful.

"I'd like to see those buildings fall to ash. Margarita, ah poor Margarita." He whipped his head around, eyes almost as vicious as those of the rats. "Who are you? If this is all a clever trap to smoke me out—"

"No trap," Finian assured him. "I'll tell you about it. But do you have any food?"

Cove nodded and fetched a brown gallon pharmaceutical bottle, instructing Finian to drink.

"Protein and vitamins. Distill it myself from the drug sludge in the river. After you drink I may or may not give you one of the soy bars I get from the juves. When their wives bear children, it's the only way they can pay, you know. They're very proud, always pay."

Cove squatted with difficulty, an oddly savage little man in the fading light.

"Whether I let you have a soy bar depends on your story. If you're an enemy, I can run away and leave you to wander the Dumps at night. You won't last long with the rats, being a stranger."

"There's a woman over on that island I have to find," said Finian and launched out.

As he recounted his tale, careful not to become too emotional about it, he noticed a growing excitement in Cove's damp eyes. Finally, when he had concluded, Cove leaped up.

"Capital, Smith, that's capital. Let me help. Let me ferry you across."

Finian smiled grudgingly. "Okay. I was prepared to swim it."

"The sludge would poison you before you got halfway."

"What's your stake in this, Cove? I mean, this food pays me back for the rats."

Cove's little eyes were miserable.

"Margarita. My wife. She died over there."

Painfully the story came out, dredged from an unhappy past:

Cove had been a plastic surgeon by specialty, in the employ of TTIC at its Bangor Personality Salon. But a quirk in his nature made him rebel against his work, permitted him to fall prey to dangerous Galbraither notions. His wife had informed on him.

Cove discovered it before the TTIC police could arrest him. He fled to the outskirts of Bangor, hiding there in the woods while a few reluctant friends supplied him with food. TTIC industrial police combed the woods with talk-horns, threatening to psych his wife into anti-obsol attitudes if he didn't surrender.

"The filth!" Cove rocked on his haunches. "I thought it was a trick, a lever. I ran away. Margarita, poor thing, was on their side. She couldn't help what she did. She came of a respected family. TTIC middle management. But a year later I found out. They did it anyway. Oh, they smile and smile and treat the mob kindly. But underneath, when they're opposed—I learned Margarita had been sentenced to Manhattan. It took me another nine months to get here and find means of crossing. By that time she'd died of pneumonia. No antibiotics allowed the juves, you see. Juves are worthless. She died." Cove rocked and rocked, wild-eyed. "Died, died."

"Doctor Cove, will you help me get across?"

Of course, of course. But to hunt that pilot plant, a knife won't be much good. The moment you're discovered they'll set on you like wild dogs."

"Then I'll need something else."

Finian's brain ran rapidly with his career with G/S. He recalled Leveranz, an unfortunate operative charged with a dangerous penetration of the TTIC Marketing Office in Beirut.

"I knew a man once who was bombed. Is there anything here—?" Finian's gesture swept the shack and dump beyond. "Do you remember enough, even if we could find an explosive source, to bomb me?"

The moist eyes of Cove widened with malicious delight. "Blow them up?"

Now Finian himself felt hard and cold.

"I just might, if they've hurt her."

"Possibly we could use the charger pack from an old solido." Cove was warming to the challenge. "Yes, we very well might. Extremely miniaturized. I'd have to check the formula but I think I have a chem text in that pile. And a military medicine volume, too.'' He began to tear through the books. ''No anesthesia, or precious little. Perhaps I could knock you out.''

''What for a trigger?'' Finian questioned. He showed his mouth. ''I have this empty socket where I carried a camera once.''

Chortling, Cove scuffled among his belongings and produced a cardboard carton full of ivory chips of all sizes.

''Why, that ought to work, Smith. The miserable juves aren't fluoridated either. I do quite a few extractions. Imagine a plasic surgeon doing extractions! Let's see, give me a minute to find the chem text . . .''

Dr. Humphrey Cove unearthed the text in two minutes. The rest took four days.

Finian suffered excruciatingly, especially during the operation. Cove kept smacking him on the head with a solido leg when the pain grew too hideous. Finian dug his nails into his palms and thought of murmurous summer evenings on the back porch in Bala Cynwyd, and vowed in his pain-streaked mind the hurt was worth it if only he had a means to strike at them if they'd hurt Dolly, his own Dolly.

When he was ready to enter the prison, his left foot flesh carried a small capsule that would detonate an explosive force when the yellowing tooth in his dead socket was turned a proper one-half turn in its clumsily hand-chiseled housing.

An old trick, bombing. A relic of the Triple Play War. But it gave Finian a little more courage to go hunting death.

In an unpleasant mist-clammy midnight, Dr. Cove paddled the improvised skiff through the sticky penicillin waste forming a crust on the Hudson, to the dilapidated pier that once belonged to the Cunard division of G/S. Off down black, ruined streets distant reddish lights pulsed. Cove shook his hand fervently. ''I hope you kill them. I hope you don't co-operate and kill them all.''

Then the skiff slithered away into the smelly broth. Finian shivered and walked.

They hissed and backed a terrified Finian against a polybrick wall. The leader of the juve pack, an oldster of eighty in tapered blue denim trousers and an antiquarian jacket spangled with fake platinum stars and buckles swaggered up and down, thumbs hooked in a six-inch belt.

''Sending DOCs into the streets these days, are they, sonny?''

''I'm no DOC.'' Finian searched the hostile eyes for succor. There was none.

''We eat DOCs alive in the prison. They step off the guard post, we swallow 'em up and chew 'em to pieces, sonnyboy.''

''A DOC stew tonight! Oh, wunnerful!'' piped a seven-year-old.

''Scream a little for us, will you please?'' said the ageing juve with a smile, shuffling forward.

Finian thought of the flick-knife and whipped it out. Another sibilant hiss ran from mouth to mouth as the blade caught the distant red glow.

"Look, don't kill me. See this? It's a knife, a real knife. You people can recognize a genuine useful antique twentieth-century artifact, can't you? Non-obsolescent. Non-obsolescent, see? Still works?"

A touched stud and the blade retracted. Another touch and it sprang out.

"Would I be a DOC and carry this?"

The juve leader had an almost religious expression on his face. His hand shook as he extended it.

"Uh—could you—leave me see?"

Finian thrust it into his hand.

"Yours. Listen, take it." A dark, malicious streak forced out the next words. "Could you make more? Why don't you try? Now you have a pattern. Then you wouldn't have to wait for the DOCs to leave the guard post. Then a lot of you could pay them a visit."

Whispering over their icon, the juves melted into the night.

6

Keeping to back streets, Finian crossed Bway several blocks above a strange complex of glittering red lights. Cove had told him it was the prison recreation area, a kind of open plaza known, unpronounceably, as Timesq. Hurrying on, he reached Parkave.

Several blocks south he saw a white chain working its way across the ruined thoroughfare. Approaching in the cover of shadows, he gazed up at a glistening glass structure with windows painted over. Then he looked down to the street again.

The white chain came apart into individual females, double-timing along between a cordon of TTIC industrial guards. One chain rushed west, another east, vanishing into the building. Finian skulked, grinning mirthlessly, estimating the time to be somewhere in the neighborhood of eleven at night. Protected, the pilot plant nursing staff was changing shift. Cove had told Finian about the nurses, and also what might be done. He hurried back towards Bway.

The recreation area was curiously deserted of juves at this hour. Finian wondered whether the flick-knife was really that much of a talisman. It must be, since he'd seen no juves after the first encounter. Cove said there were several hundred thousand on the island. Perhaps they'd gone underground to the ruined transportation tubes.

Timesq featured open shops subsidized out of national taxes as a sop to the theory of rehabilitation . . . antiques, genuine meatburgers, bizarre novelty stores where articles were actually displayed on open counters instead of behind automated windows. But the shops were actually intended to pander to the vices of the juves. Else why would Finian have been able to slip so easily into a deserted costumer's?

Half starved, his shanks frozen by wind whistling under the ancient white uniform and the musty grey wig prickling his ears, Finian dozed the daylight hours away in an alley, blearily on the alert for juves. He saw one large pack passing a block away, several hundred on the run. They didn't see him. Otherwise he was undisturbed until night fell again.

Midway between the hotel which apparently served as nurses' quarters and the ruined liquor building, Finian ducked into one of the double-timing white chains as the eleven o'clock shift changed. He hoped his male shoes wouldn't be too noticeable. But the street was dark. The hundred or so nurses were on dangerous extra-pay duty from the way they rushed along between the guard cordons, not speaking, intent only on gaining the safety of the pilot plant.

As in all hospitals, lights burned low in the marble mausoleum of a lobby as the nurses fanned out to the various tube banks. Finian spied a rest room next to a boarded-up newsstand, slipped inside and waited half an hour out of sight.

Then he returned to the lobby. A late nurse was hurrying to the tubes. Outside, the TTIC guard cordons were no more. Finian ran up behind the nurse, thinking smugly that it had been easy so far. He'd remembered to touch no doors, in case there was a sweat-print check.

The nurse gave a frightened *kkk* sound as Finian looped his elbow around her neck.

"Where's the prototype kept, lady? Tell me or I'll crack you in half."

"Tw'twelve," came the panicky answer. "I can't breathe!"

"You won't ever again unless you take me up there."

"It's not my floor—"

"With lights out who'll know? There's the tube. Inside! Don't speak to anyone. Don't even raise an eyebrow, or I'll throttle you."

In the deserted tube the alarmed woman, elderly, eyed Finian's wig, all too obvious in the full illumination.

"What are you, some kind of degenerate?"

"Yes, but not the kind you think."

Finian laughed, feeling frightened and brave all at once.

On twelve, isolated pools of radiance interspersed vast islands of aseptic black. Three nurses clustered at a floor desk to the right. Finian's terrified victim led him to the left.

Double doors loomed at the far corridor end. Why was it so easy? Finian felt vague alarm as he shoved the old lady through the doors. The isolation, that must be it, he reasoned. The improbable isolation here on Manhattan where no investigator would dream of looking for a pilot plant.

Still, Pushkyn's people had discovered it by molecular-triangulation sonics. Were they penetrating even now?

In the chamber a white blur stretched naked in the warm, purified air. Finian held tight to the old nurse's arm and approached the dreaming girl. The raspberry mark stood out black in the faint gleam from the half-open door of an attached dispensary. There encephalographs and other equipment winked, chromed and cold.

"Dolly?" Finian's lips felt like shreds of paper, crinkled dry. "Dolly, hear me?"

A vacuous mewing sound came from the girl. She twisted deeper in silk coverlets. "Wake her," Finian ordered.

"You're a madman! I don't know how, I'm on six, neurosearch."

He shoved her rudely. "There must a chart in the dispensary."

Finian had to threaten to cuff her several times before she tremblingly translated the medical Latin in the last twelve thick casebooks on the dispensary shelf. From the section marked *Emergency Antidotal Procedures* she read out the correct mix of ampoules from the wall-wide freezer.

Finian was acutely conscious of the silence of the great dark room, the whisper of Dolly's breathing from the bed, the rush of controlled air in and out of blowers. Time was moving inexorably. What he would do when and if he wakened Dolly he was not precisely sure. All he could tell was that he must talk to her. Talking to her once was what he had worked and tramped and almost died for.

The pressuredermic barrel gleamed in the light. Finian snatched it from the nurse.

"If you've tricked me—I don't take to hurting women, but I will!"

"I swear to Loudermilk I didn't. Only please don't hurt me."

"In there," Finian instructed. He latched the dispensary door behind her. There was no visorphone inside. He would be safe a moment longer.

With shaking hands he pressed the instilling cup near the raspberry mark, and plunged.

Slowly, slowly, the naked girl rolled over, lids fluttering drowsily. Finian crouched by the bed. His hand knotted up in the silken sheets. He'd turned up a rheostat to provide a gleam for judging her eyes. Doll-blue, they flew open—

Blank, unknowing.

"Why, hello there." The voice tormented him. It was so speaking, so silly. "Whatever are you doing in Dream's bedroo— Dream's bed—"

Like a broken mechanism the voice ran down. One of her voluptuous hands crept tentatively towards his. *"Finian?"*

"Oh, my God, my God, Dolly."

He buried his head on her shoulder, almost crying.

When he had controlled himself sufficiently to talk, he asked her what it was like.

"Not too terrible." Dolly's voice now, not her body but for the mark, only her voice trying painfully to re-form old associations. "When we moved . . . Well, it was luck and a little moral compromise that snared me a chance to be the prototype."

"Do you remember anything? I mean, when you're under?"

"A little. A very little. Far down in my head, like the bottom of a well. I won't in a week or two, so they say."

"It's wrong, Dolly! It's wrong for them to change you!"

She laughed tolerantly, not a little sadly.

"Those wild old ideas of yours again."

"I love you, Dolly. I want you the way you were."

"Impossible, Fin. My body's changed." One hand lifted the hem of the sheet. "It's part of the price for being the prototype. I nearly died when my parents made us move. I wasn't strong. I'm not much stronger now. This"—a gesture to the room—"when they're finished with me, in a week or two, I'll never be able to go back. The prototype can't. Other women can, the change isn't so deep when it's purchased. But in return I'll receive more money than most women ever see. I wish you hadn't come here, Fin. I'd nearly got over you."

"Take out the contacts, Dolly. Then tell me it's all over."

"Fin, I can't. They're permanent." She clutched his arm. "If you're caught here—"

Rapidly he told her of what he'd learned at the National Record Office. "Some kind of conspiracy, Dolly. Awful, awful. Hell, I'm not bright enough to fathom what it means. Maybe Pop could have. I'm just certain I want you out before this crazy doublecross blows right up."

Dolly hesitated. "I'm not sure. My mind's full of someone else—"

"Don't let him frighten you," said a voice. "He's done anyway."

Caught, heartbeat wild and racing, Finian turned as all the lights blazed up in the room. Dolly shrieked and burrowed under the sheet.

Outside the panel Finian glimpsed a phalanx of armed TTIC police. The three men inside moved swiftly towards him. Sprool and Pushkyn shoulder to shoulder, and shuffling behind, Alvah Robert Loudermilk Pharoh with his dewlaps jiggling and his blue, vaguely crossed eyes filled with fright.

"We should of killed the jerko," Pushkyn offered.

"Be quiet." Sprool breathed tightly, thinking hard.

"No one listens to me," Alvah Robert Loudermilk Pharoh whined. "No one listens any more even though I'm the chief executive of Holders."

"You simpleton!" Sprool spun on him, barely able to control his fury. "You incredible wreck! I wish Pushkyn and I had retired you to a senility farm long ago. If your addled brain could have understood it wasn't safe for you to go around making public appearances! Having your portrait painted!"

"Holders is my firm!"

"It *was*. Before your brains turned to mashed potatoes," said Pushkyn.

"You wouldn't have penetrated the pilot plant, would you, Pushkyn?" Finian was suddenly enraged, and beginning to understand. "Even though you knew where it was."

Pushkyn sneered. "Whaddya think, put sand in the wheels? Always the funny finko, huh? If it wasn't for me, Sprool and a few others on both sides, running the show while the old bonebag sits on the Holders board—"

"He means to say," Sprool put in, somewhat sadly, "we have done our best to keep the plant running. You, Fin, have done your best to stop it."

"How did you find me?" Finian demanded.

Sprool shrugged. "See-ray."

"I never touched a doorknob anyplace!"

"There is a false socket in your head. Every person entering or leaving this plant is rayed for dental coding. Yours failed to check. It took a few minutes to collect Pushkyn. And the old man. I want him to see the fruits of his senility. We vertijetted."

"Ah, damn," said Finian, impotently.

"I very nearly admire you," Sprool told him. "In proper circumstances you might have filled a responsible position with Holders. Do you realize what a difficult and exciting enterprise it is to run this world, Fin?"

"I realize you sold everybody a bill of goods, kept them soft, sucked their guts out."

"Would you rather have howling millions out of work and rioting?"

"Yes! Yes. I mean, no. I don't want people to starve, but this way—I'd rather have some guts in life. Trouble and guts."

"Trouble we have, Finian," Sprool returned with a sigh. "Do you know what we saw as we came over the Tunnel in the vertijet? The DOC post in ruins. The juves are breaking out, Fin, actually breaking out. Most of them are dead, of course, But several hundred escaped. There's a pitched battle going on in Jersey this minute. The juves will die as soon as I give the mobilization order. A few may get away and start in other cities, inciting riot, pulling down what we've built so carefully to insure everyone a decent life. Both TTIC and G/S are alerting industrial guards trained for trouble such as this. We'll also have to apply considerable pressure for the DOCs to move. But we'll win. We gave up war long ago, Fin. We won't permit another to start."

"The creeps had knives!" Pushkyn bellowed. "Real knives! You stupid, did you—?"

"I think so," Finian looked up. "I hope so."

Again Sprool sighed, almost sympathetically.

"Fin, Fin. You seem to think we're evil men. We're not. We're *businessmen*. We didn't begin the system. We only inherited it. But you've never understood, have you? Always, I think, you resented us as a result of what your father taught you." Sprool was white now, impassioned. "We had no choice! Either we maintained calm or—"

"You changed Dolly! I don't understand your theories beyond that!"

Sprool outshouted him: "The alternative to a rocked boat is *chaos!*"

"There's got to be another way."

"Go to the guard post! See the mangled bodies and then say that."

"I don't *care*, Sprool! I'm taking Dolly off the island."

"Creep, you won't set one foot from here."

Finian peeled his lips back.

"Look at the tooth, Lyman. You know what was there before." He waggled his left foot. "I'm bombed. The tooth will set it off. Either instantaneously or on timed delay. Stop me from walking out with Dolly and find out."

"Salinghams wanted my portrait—" the florid old gentleman began.

"Bluffer! Lousy, rotten bluffer!" Screaming, Pushkyn rushed forward.

Sprool's hand flew up.

"*Don't!* I believe him."

For the first time Finian Smith saw Sprool perspiring.

"He's the kind to do it, Pushkyn. I don't want slaughter here, too. So you keep quiet and remember who's senior troubleshooter."

Cold, shrewd lights glittered in Sprool's eyes. "Fin, what guarantee can you offer if we release this woman to you, allow her to go with you under duress?"

"No."

Heads swung, startled. Dolly went on slowly:

"I think—I want—"

A disgusted sigh came from Sprool's lips. He controlled himself. "Very well, Fin. If we permit you to leave, what guarantees do you offer that you'll cause no further trouble? We'll have our hands full quelling the disturbances the juves will start. It hasn't got too far out of hand yet. But if I don't give the mobilization order, it could go nationwide. Even to other countries. I have to be around to stop it. It can be done, even though I don't much like removing the velvet glove."

"Guarantees?" said Finian. "My word. That's all."

Sprool walked quickly to the door and opened it. The threatening knot of industrial police still waited in the shadows. Finian bundled Dolly into the bedclothes and moved her towards the entrance as Sprool said, "Let him pass."

"I won't stand for it!" Pushkyn leaped forward and landed a solid one that rocked Finian on his heels. Then Sprool snapped his fingers. The TTIC police carried the foam-lipped Pushkyn into the dispensary.

Trembling, suddenly cold and trembling clear through, Finian made an effort to keep his face an inflexible mask as he guided Dolly through the aisle between the guards. He hoped she wouldn't question him, wouldn't relent until they were free. Sick fear engulfed him as he touched the tip of his tongue gingerly to the fake tooth while the tube shot down.

Dolly leaned on his shoulder, her hair warm. She made frightened mewing sounds. Finian shepherded her into the night, began the long, terrible walk to the Tunnel, hoping she wouldn't come to her senses until they reached the opposite shore. In time she'd be herself again. That much he could give her even if his search had been all for nothing.

The DOC post at the Tunnel entrance was afire. Juve corpses sprawled everywhere.

Midway along the empty tunnel Finian halted. A figure capered towards them.

"Capital, oh, marvelous!" Humphrey Cove trilled, stepping over a dead DOC's open-mouthed head. "Three hundred of them got out, running for their lives. I think it will spread this time. The local camps, the jobless—full-scale! There are so many really lovely pockets of resistance!"

"Shut up and walk." Finian pushed Cove back towards the Jersey side.

"What in heaven's name is wrong with you, Smith?"

"Armed." Finian whispered it so Dolly couldn't hear. "A guy hit me, I'm armed. Can't have more than half an hour before I blow. Cove, don't you say anything. When we're outside, you take care of this girl, understand? Watch out for her until she recovers. She's free of them, I bought her that much."

They passed a shrilling visorphone in a lighted kiosk at the far Tunnel mouth. A DOC alert was being scheduled for Philadelphia. Juve gangs were forming in the streets there, hand-made knives were appearing. The mask was off. Full mobilization of combined TTIC and G/S industrial police was being ordered by Sprool. Cove clapped his hands.

Rain was falling as Finian led Dolly out of the Tunnel. Three DOC vertijets from the south were homing on Manhattan, agleam with emergency lights. Dolly murmured. Finian lifted her chin and stared into the doll-blue eyes a moment, conscious of the bomb working, working towards detonation in the flesh of his foot. He couldn't even feel the death seed. Wasn't that a joke?

"Cove'll take care of you," Finian said. He kissed her. Bewildered, Dolly called for him as he turned and walked rapidly away, not seeing the rain or the littered bodies.

He had gone but a dozen steps when something felled him and brought the dark.

Pain, incredible pain was his first sensation.

Then a warmth of flesh. Dolly bending over him. Through a slatted section of solido panel he saw vertijets winking over Manhattan. Finian wriggled, then struggled up, screaming:

"My leg . . . *what happened?*"

Crying, Dolly pressed him down.

"Cove did it. Cove operated. He hates them, Fin. He hates TTIC. Something about his wife. He said you ought to live, even with—I wish my mind would straighten out. I can't say things all right yet."

Finian fought the terror, the dull-fire agony. ''Where is he?''

Dolly shuddered. ''He packed it in a valise and ran for the Tunnel.''

In a burst of fire the center of Manhattan Prison blew up.

When the reverberations and Dolly's screams had stopped, the two of them clung together, listening to the hysterical automatic sirens at both ends of the island wailing as they hadn't wailed since the Triple Play War. Confused, hurting, glad of life, guilty and fearsomely glad and yet sickened by the suddenly swarming sky full of vertijets, their flaring emergency lights promising violence across the land, violence maybe everywhere. Finian clutched the girl to his shoulder and stared at the inferno of the prison island.

''My God, I think I started a war, Dolly. Sprool said—I didn't mean to start—''

The words tore out of him, almost animal: *''Is this the only way?''*

Dolly sobbed. There wasn't any other answer, except the sirens multiplying all around in the disrupted night.

DONALD KINGSBURY

*The Moon Goddess and the Son**

1

DIANA'S AMBITION to get a job on the moon really started the day she found out that her namesake was the moon goddess. She was six and she crawled out her bedroom window onto the porch roof so she could stare at the full moon in the sky where she belonged. Her father caught her. He was furious because she could have fallen off and hurt herself, so he stripped her and tied her to the bed and beat her bleeding with his belt.

The pain blotted out this man, blotted out even the pain itself. She saw a wild boar and she cast an arrow into his heart from her perch safe behind the shield of the moon. But in time the trauma evaporated, leaving only the pain of being touched by a bloodstained bed in Ohio that refused to stop torturing her body with its prodding fingers. When the moon rose so high that her round eyes could no longer see it through the window, she felt abandoned.

On her seventh birthday a high school boy showed her his portable tracking telescope. The cratered mountains of the moon stunned her with their beauty—*her* mountains, *her* craters, *her* plains, *her* rills and streamers. Meticulously she located each of the old Apollo landing sites. In a moment of astral travel she imagined herself in a crater full of trees with lots of nymphs to take care of.

He showed her Jupiter and the Pleieades. Another evening they followed the bright thread of the half-built spaceport as it arrowed through the southern sky in those few minutes before it faded into the Earth's shadow. When it was gone he explained that they could see the spaceport this far north only because it hadn't yet been towed into equatorial orbit.

At eight Diana had a temper tantrum and stoically endured five beatings until her mother papered her wall with a photomontage of the moon's surface. At nine she took up archery in school and worked at it until she became the regional champ for her age. When she was ten she ran away from home to visit a space museum but the police brought her back. After the police were gone her father beat her until even her mother cried. At twelve she ran away from home with her arm in a cast, broken by her father

---

*This is the original short novel that was the basis for a full-length book of the same name, also by Donald Kingsbury.

when he found her collection of newspaper stories about families who murdered their children in the night.

She fixed her hair like the March cover girl of *Viva Magazine* and she wore one of her mother's bras stuffed with an extra pair of socks. People gave her rides. She told them she was going to visit her mother in California because her father was out of work.

The best ride she got was from a truck driver whom she targeted at a diesel station in Newton, Iowa, mainly because his rig carried a Washington license plate and she knew vaguely that spaceships were built in Washington. He wasn't supposed to take passengers but she flaunted her spare socks and he broke down and got to liking her over the steak he bought her. She chattered to him about a historical novel called *Diana's Temple*.

An endless ride later, through farmland and broken hills and over decaying interstate highways, they pulled into a rest stop near Elk Mountain to sleep in the cab for the night. Diana tried to seduce her driver because she thought girls were supposed to reward nice men. The cast on her arm got in the way and a sock fell out of her bra.

He laughed, holding her by the chin in a vise grip between thumb and fingers. "Diana was a virgin."

"Yeah, I know." She cringed out of the vise to a position back against the door of the cab.

He didn't want to hurt her feelings. He reached out and pulled her shoulders into his large arm tenderly. "Your virginity is the most valuable thing you have right now. Hang onto it. Grow up a little bit and when you throw it away make sure he's the nicest guy in the world."

"How do you tell the nice guys from the mean ones?"

"Did you ever have any trouble with that?"

"My father always beat me. For *nothing*!"

"Then you know what the bad ones are like."

"What are the good ones like?"

"Me," he laughed.

For a year Diana stayed in a small town near Seattle where they assembled feeder spacecraft for the spaceport as well as cruise missiles for the military. The tiny nine-meter-long automatic lighters rocketed to the spaceport from an equatorial base and flew back on stubby delta wings. Diana was excited at first. She did housework and cared for the children of one of the foremen whose wife was recovering from an auto accident. But this sleepy Earth town was just as far away from the moon as Ohio.

She stole some money and caught a bus for L.A. It was scary panhandling in Hollywood. She got picked up by a pimp she didn't know was a pimp and had to crawl out a window in the middle of the night and sleep under a car like a cat. After three days alone she found a family of runaways and slept on the floor. They were all into stealing and hustling and one of them was into heroin, but she found a job as a waitress from which she got fired because she didn't have any papers.

Twilight was panhandling time. Afterwards she took her addict friend to a crowded basement dive so she could have company being depressed. The smoke coiled through the dim light, choking at life. She sat there crazying and suddenly darted toward the ladies' room where she knew they had a little open window where she could breathe for a minute, alone.

A large hand clamped on her shoulder. "You got holes in your head, spending time with that buzzhead? He'll take you for everything you've got."

She whirled on the scruffy young man who had a 1950 hairdo. "What have I got to take? I haven't even got a job."

"Lots of jobs around."

"I don't want to be a whore, smartass."

He smiled sardonically. "A waitress, then?"

"I got fired as a waitress because I don't have any papers."

"How about that!" He shook her hand. "I'm a forger." He escorted her into the ladies' room and, after locking the door, hung his head through the window. "What name you want to be known by?"

"I can change my name?"

"Yeah and you get a birth certificate and a L.A. high school record and a social security number. I figure if we stretched it a bit you could pass for eighteen."

"What do you get out of it?" she asked cynically.

"A girl to ferret around records offices who doesn't arouse suspicion. I need new faces all the time." He laughed. "I'm square. My side lady would kill me if I didn't give every thirteen-year-old an integrity deal."

"Could I get a job on the moon with your papers?"

2

Charlie McDougall was an only child with thickly lashed eyes. He first learned to roll his eyes at his parents when he was thirteen—behind their backs. His whole memory of life was of two giants giving him orders that had to be executed on some strict schedule if he didn't want to be driven crazy by shouting directed into his eardrum.

Mama wanted him to become the world's greatest violinist or maybe a dancer who would wow them in Moscow. Papa wanted him to become the greatest space engineer who ever lived, the cutting edge of the Last Hope of Mankind.

During those crucial years when most babies discover the first spark of individuality by playing with the power of the word "no," Charlie had been broken. He learned to obey. He hated the violin and he hated dancing and he hated space, but he hated screaming parents even more. Obeying was the only peace he had.

Still, while he became a fine violinist, his strings had a perpetual habit of snapping. He was invariably the best dancer in his class but he was always being thrown out because of his incurable habit of peeking into the girls' dressing room.

For his father he devised even more diabolical tortures. Though he slaved dutifully over his physics and chemistry and math and model building, he refused to read science fiction. On his fifteenth birthday his father tried to seduce him with a luxury hardbound copy of *Dune* with a facsimile Frank Herbert signature.

"You'll love it."

"Hey Papa, that's a great gift. This evening I have some spare time and maybe I'll take a crack at it." When his father went out for a beer, he rolled his eyes.

That evening the old man peeked into his room on tiptoes to see how the first chapter of *Dune* was going, just as Charlie knew he would. Charlie was engrossed in the eighth chapter of Robert's *Differential Equations* setting up the ninth problem.

"Have you had a chance to look at *Dune*?"

"Tomorrow. I got myself hung up on the breaking mode of long cylinders and I don't want to sleep on it."

The coup had kept Charlie happy for weeks. *Dune* was still on his shelf, unopened.

It was only when he was seventeen that he discovered the perfect shelter from his parents, digital music. Electronic instruments frightened his mother. She had a Ph.D. in musicology from Mills but couldn't tell a Fourier compact series from a quartet concert series; a resistor had something to do with the draft, and a chip was what an uncouth person carried on his shoulder. As for Charlie's father, who polished off textbooks like most slow readers polished off light novels, engineered music was in the same category as purple smells or painted cooking.

Waves, repetitions, pulsations, rumblings, the rise of a violin taking off can all be described by a Fourier series—an amalgamation of sine and cosine waves of different frequencies and amplitudes. A frequency is a number. An amplitude is a number. Charlie composed by choosing those numbers and deciding when they were to change. His computer executed the commands.

He created his own computer language for simulating instruments. It was a simple matter for him to write a subroutine for oboe or violin or harmonica. He had ten violins on file, four of them matching in sound the finest violins ever crafted, the other six of a haunting timbre that could never come from a material violin, wood lacking the proper resonant qualities. He doodled up new instruments in pensive moments and gave them frivolous names like the pooh and the eeyore and the kanga.

By using his world of numbers as an open sesame to the trance underground, he burrowed assiduously into this dark world his parents couldn't understand. Once when he was twenty and deliriously celebrating the end of his junior year by smashing out in the popular Boston Trance Hall where the show was continuous and the waitresses sported silver pantsuits with cutout buttocks, all seven of his friends became dazzled by the nubility of the singer. She was wearing a golden necklace from which her dress flowed, cupric green, so slashed in a thousand ribbons that one saw both all and some of her body as she sang.

Charlie noted the ordinary voice—slightly brassy with a tendency to slurring—and rashly bet his friends she would date him. Gleefully they put $200 in the pot, impelling him to keep pace by taking her hand as she left the stage.

"You have a zorchy voice—a lot could be done with it."

She smiled coolly and let him hold her fingers just long enough to appear unrude. It gave him time to press his card into that hand, a hand so cold his must have seemed tropical.

ELECTRONIC MADMAN
DIGITALIZED MUSIC

Her eyes widened slightly when she read it—DM was a controversial thing on the pop music scene; one loved or hated its sounds and argued endlessly about the awesome scope of its territory. DM projected mystery and resentment. Few musicians could handle its technical demands. But an ambitious woman with an ordinary voice would know what a DM magician could do for her.

She sat down and the cupric cloth rippled, sometimes revealing, sometimes hiding, always teasing. "What do you hear in my voice?"

"You'll have to come to my place and listen. It's beautiful."

"It's not. I don't think my mouth is the right shape."

"But you don't hear what I hear."

"Do you do real time or augmented?"

"Both. I can feed your mike right into the shoebox if that's what you want."

She took his palm and read it silently. Then she looked into his face with the eyes of a judge. "What sign are you?"

"Aquarius."

Her face broke into a smile of relief.

"Fantastic!" And she wouldn't let his hand go. Charlie's friends, conceding, shoved a money-filled envelope into the other hand.

Betty worked with him. He showed her many versions of her voice. He washed her car. He rushed her clothes out for dry cleaning to give her extra sleep. When she had a new gig, he set up for her. He worked late into many nights decoding the structure of her voice until he was able to customize a shoebox that transformed her into a siren at the wave of a mike.

Charlie's new life thrilled him. He spent all his time thinking about seducing Betty. Devious plans grew out of dreams and finally he convinced

Betty to let him move into her place in what had once been the maid's room back in the century when Irish labor was plentiful. He promised to cook and do the dishes and not molest her. His theory was that the way to a girl's heart was through her stomach and after a month of being taken care of by a man who loved her, she would melt.

In a mailgram that gave him great pleasure to write he told his father that he was not returning to MIT. Within a week his father arrived in Boston from orbit and charmed Betty off to Mexico City for a vacation. She sent him a card from Xicotencatl wishing he was there. The card was forwarded to New Hampshire, where his mother had taken him by the ear, screaming at him all the time, insisting that if he wasn't going to continue his engineering he had to sign up for the Berlin Conservatory. In self-defense he re-registered at MIT, all the while plotting perfect murders.

It took him only two months to utterly crush his mother. He digitalized a secret recording of one of her screaming rages. Slowly he added harmonicas. He mushed the words until their content was lost against a pure emotion. Here he amplified the rage, there he added piteous undertones. Violins played at dramatic moments. Sobbing children filled the silences. He had the tape cut and sold the pressing to a company that pushed it up to thirty-second place on the hit parade.

Charlie figured it would take longer to crush his father. His father was tough. He would have to bide his time and strike at an unexpected moment with overwhelming force.

3

It was a nice name. *Diana Grove*. She could go anywhere and do anything with it. Mostly she went to Texas and Arizona because John the Forger's main business was manufacturing new identities for Mexicans. When she became too well known he let her go and she became a waitress.

Rooming with older girls taught Diana how to imitate adult behavior. Her manners became flirtatious. She was a sassy summertime flower to the bees, little caring whether the men she attracted were young or old or handsome or married—but she never dated the same man twice. She had a perfect excuse whenever an admirer wanted a second date.

"But that's the day I'm seeing Larry."

"How about Saturday then?"

"I always go out with George on Saturday."

When too many people wanted her, she changed jobs or roommates. Eventually she began to move up the coast, carefully picking only the most expensive and popular restaurants. Once in Coos Bay, Oregon, a drunk whacked her around and that so frightened her she flew to San Francisco the very next day.

Not having a job was unimportant. At the airport she bought a paper and answered a classified ad demanding an exceptionally attractive and experienced waitress to work at Namala in the Pacific. Diana was a long-time space buff and knew very well that Namala was one of the equatorial stations that supplied the orbiting spaceport.

The secretary of Ling Enterprises smiled and Diana reciprocated. It helped her nervousness that the secretary was sitting down and she was standing. She could pretend that she was just earning a five-dollar tip.

The speaker beside the video camera spoke in a gentle voice. "Send her in. She's expected."

Diana instantly turned her smile on the camera. It was President Ling speaking. That was very suspicious. Presidents of restaurant chains did *not* interview waitresses. She felt faint and, what was worse, she felt fifteen years old.

When she peered around Mr. Ling's door she found him to be Chinese and ancient. His office was Contemporary American except for the paintings—a battle between Earthmen and beastoid in a jungle under a large red sun, the other a desolate landscape somewhere in the galaxy near a star cluster. The fear went out of her.

"You're another space cookie," she said relieved, all her poise back.

"It's a comfortable disease."

"Do you remember when they landed on the moon?"

He laughed. "I'm so old I remember when they thought landing on the moon was impossible."

"Do you own a restaurant on the moon?"

"No, but when they build one, I'll be running it."

She loved him already. She was his slave. She sat down on the couch and couldn't take her eyes off his face, lined and old and frail and the most fascinating face she'd ever seen.

He moved closer to her, sitting on the desk top. "Are you wondering why a president is interviewing waitresses?"

"Yes," she grinned. "I'm ready to run out the door screaming."

"I have six space-related restaurants and I take a personal interest in them. The frustrated astronaut in me."

"What's Namala like?"

"Hard work for you. Too many men."

"I'm a good girl and surprisingly self-reliant."

"Sometimes you'll need advice. Madam Lilly, who runs my Namala franchise, has large skirts for hiding behind when it is necessary."

"I never need help," said Diana defiantly.

"An unwise consideration."

They talked. He found out all he needed to know and she found out all she needed to know. He offered her the job. She accepted. There was nothing more to say but she didn't want to leave just yet.

He watched her silence as she moved her fingers and played with a ring. "Ah, I've finally caught you when you're not smiling."

"I'm hungry and I want to invite you for lunch," she said with frogs' legs in her throat.

He smiled a thousand wrinkles.

"Would your wife mind?" she then asked awkwardly.

"I'm a widower."

"We could go to the Calchas. I've worked there. It's beautiful and I miss their food."

She made him talk about himself over too much wine. He was the rebel in his family. His father wanted him to take over the restaurant business and he wanted to be an engineer. He had edited a science fiction fanzine called *Betelgeuse* which went to fourteen issues, but when he became engaged to his illustrator who was a Caucasian, his family disowned him. He didn't do well enough in school to get a scholarship and ended up as a city bureaucrat, married, with three lovely mongrel children while he tried to write at night.

Finally his father died and his brothers expanded and took the family fortune into a close brush with disaster and he made a pact with his mother to run the family business. He was good at it. Later he made his breakthrough by discovering how to franchise variety in a world of McDonald's, Johnson's, and Colonel's.

Diana had fun. They ran up quite a bill at Mr. Ling's insistence (he thought he was paying) and she had the best fight of her life taking the bill away from him. To make up for it he bought her beautiful luggage. She sighed and told him she had nothing to put in it, so he bought her clothes. She sighed and told him she had no place to take them because she hadn't rented a hotel room yet, so he gave her the key to his place.

She cooked Mr. Ling a gourmet dinner in his kitchen after making many phone calls to the office to find out what he liked and when he would be in. They spent the whole meal and three liqueurs discussing the history of Jerusalem. She discovered his wicked sense of humor. He convinced her that there had been a whole order of Chinese Knights who fought in the crusades.

"Don't laugh so hard!" she complained. "You're just lucky I didn't bake a lemon meringue pie for supper or you'd get it right in your kisser!"

Ten o'clock was his bedtime. He excused himself gracefully and escorted her all the way to the guest room where he put an arm around her shoulder and thanked her for a lovely evening before he left her.

Diana peeked. She waited until the light went out under his door and then, dressed only in a candle flame, entered his room. "I've come to kiss you goodnight." It was easy to pretend you were twenty years old when you were nude.

His smile in the candlelight was wistful. "Goddess Diana, I am much too old for such escapades."

"That makes us even. I'm much too young for such escapades." She blew out the candle and slipped under the sheets with him. "Don't die of a heart attack just yet. I want my job on the moon." She snuggled up beside him, deciding that she liked to sleep with men. It was the sleep of innocence.

The next day a great aircraft flew her over the ocean to the equator.

4

The rocket-supplied lunar base was an improbable cluster of forms on Mare Imbrium which had lately grown a spiderweb rectenna farm to receive microwaves from a small twenty-five-megawatt solar power station that had been built in low Earth orbit and towed up to the Lagrange 1 position 58,000 km above the moon. Each new addition was part of a single-minded plan. The sole purpose of the base was to build an electromagnetic landing track so that access to the moon might be made cheap. This deep out in space, rockets fueled from Earth were not cheap.

When Byron McDougall took the assignment to construct the initial lunar base he was given one-fourth of the money originally allocated for that task. He was a military man from a military family. He thought like a soldier who could still fight when his supply lines had been cut. McDougall's base had shafts without elevators. He used cast basalt instead of aluminum. Eighty percent of the parts by weight of all imported machines were made of lunar metals and glasses. All food was raised locally. The lunar day was given over to energy-intensive tasks such as metals production. The lunar night was given over to effort-intensive tasks such as design work and machining.

From his tiny office Byron called Louise. "Sweetheart, do you have a bottle of champagne tucked away?" He knew she didn't.

"Champagne? You're mad. All I have is a liter of Ralph's turnip rotgut."

"Too bad. How can we celebrate on that? Any last-minute hassles with the SPS?"

"No. We should have power exactly on time."

"Good."

"Your son has been trying to reach you. We'll have the connection set up in fifteen minutes. Do you want to take it there or here?"

"I'm hopping right up to the control room."

Byron switched off, smiling slyly. He took out a half bottle of champagne he had hidden, all he could afford to smuggle in by rocket, but enough to give them a taste of victory. It wasn't really victory: getting the SPS power so they weren't energy starved at night was just another milestone, but one certainly worth celebrating.

Maybe there never would be a final victory. Byron sometimes despaired. Maybe in two years this effort might be a ghost town in spite of all the billions that had been invested in it. Risk funding was so damned erratic.

Support waxed and waned in Congress. It had been waning now for years, even though thc pay-off was a certainty.

He slipped out of his office, soared up the shaft, caught himself, and made his slow leap into the control room with the bottle high in his hand. "Who's got strong thumbs?"

"How did you get that!" Louise's nature lent itself to exclamations.

"False-bottomed suitcase."

One of the men turned to Byron from the console display with a smile. "The SPS is powered and checking through beautifully. We should get the first beam down soon."

"Is your son as handsome as you?" asked Louise dreamily.

"Why should you care?"

"Braithwaite was telling me he's coming up here to work on the track as soon as he graduates from MIT."

"No, I'm much better looking than my son. You should try older men once in a while."

"Not a chance. You see through all of my tricks. I *might* get away with batting my eyes at your son. He's six years younger than I am."

"Actually you might have a chance. When he gets here I'll set you up. He chases older women—but I've never seen him chase one as bright as you. I once took a girl friend of his off to Mexico City. She was a great lady, but I was bored to death with her chatter."

"Byron! You stole your son's girl friend? How could you be so cruel? And I always thought you were such a *nice* man!"

"I did him a favor. She was using him," he said bitterly.

"He probably needed her!"

That stung Byron's anger. "Like hell he needed her. She didn't have enough sense to send him back to school when he quit to take care of her. For that I could have killed the bitch. I shipped her off to Paris with enough bread to keep her amused."

Louise was grinning. "What was your wife saying about all this?"

"She divorced me."

"Byron!"

He laughed. "Something else to celebrate."

The phone rang. Louise took it and chatted with the operator. "Byron. It's your son."

"Hi, Papa."

"Charlie!"

Two-second pause.

"I'm calling you up to congratulate you. I hear you're not going to need candles at night anymore. Hey, pretty soon you'll have hot running water in the trenches."

"It's pretty good. We'll be powered except for six hours once a month at eclipse."

Two-second pause.

"I just got your comments on my last batch of homework. You're two days faster than my profs. I'm glad I'm getting clever enough with my mistakes so even you can't see them."

"While you're on the line I want you to talk with Braithwaite. You'll be working with him on the lunar track. He's anxious to get you after all he's heard about you."

Byron motioned frantically for Braithwaite to come over while his voice traveled to Earth and his son's came back.

"You still want me to get involved in that thing, eh?"

"You bet. When we get it built this place is going to start to pay for itself. She'll mushroom. We've been tooling up for the track and now that we have the power, we're ready to roll."

The lunar track was an electromagnetic cushion to take fifteen-ton ships in for a horizontal landing at lunar circular velocity. Or shoot them off.

"Say Papa, I'm calling to tell you not to bother to come back to Earth for my graduation."

"But of course I'm coming. I need the vacation."

Two-second pause.

"Yeah, but I just quit school."

"You're at the top of your class!"

Two-second pause.

"I don't want your job. I just want to play around and listen to the birds sing. Why put myself in the position where I need a vacation when I can have one all the time?"

Byron thought frantically. "It's the chance of your lifetime! It will make your career! From this job you can go anywhere!"

Two-second pause. There was no real way to argue over this distance. He had caught a barracuda and the line was too light.

"I never liked engineering. Good luck in your log cabin. I'm hanging up, now."

The line went dead. Byron waited for two seconds, stunned, then he smashed his bottle against the bulkhead wall. Gracefully, the champagne foamed as it arced in a slow-motion spatter.

"She's ready," said the operations man, as calmly as if he had witnessed a christening. "There she goes. The grid is powered."

Louise was rushing over to Byron. "It's all right."

Byron was frozen, his hand outstretched where it had grasped sudden defeat from victory. "No," he said in pain.

"Are you going back to Earth to talk to him?"

"No." Byron paused for two thoughtful seconds, his hand slowly sinking. "I had to push him and push him and push him, the little bastard. He did so well, I couldn't resist. If I didn't push him, he didn't move. So I pushed him. God, how I wanted him here under my thumb where I could make a man out of him." He shrugged bitterly. "It's no use. If you have to push a man, he's not going to move anywhere."

"He'll settle out."

"Yeah, he'll settle out. He'll settle out as a third-rate musician."

5

Namala was the tropical sea, blue water and a sometimes billowy clouded sky and green islands that, to Diana's airborne eyes, seemed to sleep in the vast moat of the Pacific like a drowsy crocodile. She arrived at sunset while the water was deepening to purple. Never in her life had she been so exhilarated. She was here—part of a base that was shipping goods to the moon to make a home for her that would be there when she found a way to go.

While she waited on the airfield terrace for Madam Lilly, the drowsy crocodile awoke. A barrage of delta winged lighters began to lift in roaring flame from the launch area. Then Diana saw to the west the silver thread of the spaceport rising majestically out of the ocean. At first it was only a small thread, a wavering glimmer. On the horizon the spaceport's 150-kilometer length was foreshortened to hardly more than a degree of sky, but, within minutes, as it rose to the thunder of the lighter launches, it grew to stretch its gossamer strand over almost a sixth of the sky—before vanishing into the shadow of the Earth, leaving only stars. She remembered a spider riding a filament of web over the cornfields of Ohio.

Soon another fleet of lighters, electromagnetically ejected from the spaceport as it passed overhead, began a screaming drop out of the blackness, swooping into the floodlamps of the lagoon to be received with the efficiency of a squadron returning to the deck of its aircraft carrier. Some of the lighters were laden with goods manufactured in the factory pods that lined the spaceport's length like factories had once sprung up along a railway spur line. Some of the lighters came down empty.

The ground crews ran a standard maintenance check on each vehicle, inserting a new 500-kilogram payload module, pumping kerosene and oxygen into the tanks, recooling the superconducting coils that would electromagnetically accelerate the lighter once it had been swallowed by the spaceport's electromagnetic interstine on its next spaceward trip.

Finally the fresh-readied lighter was rolled to the launch site and pointed at the sky on its own gantry, there to await the return of the spaceport. Every ninety minutes, day and night, this cycle repeated at all of the equatorial stations.

Madam Lilly was standing behind Diana, unwilling to intrude on the girl's rapture. She turned out to be a hard taskmaster. Her restaurant carried the Ling symbol, but like all Ling restaurants it supported its own name, the *Kaleidoscope*, which meant that it was constantly changing its atmosphere.

Madam Lilly was a theater person. She could do miracles with a few props and backdrops and screens, but her main focus was on the girls. She costumed them perfectly and taught them gesture and emotion and expression and dialogue.

When Diana arrived they were doing World War II. There was a Rosie the Riveter in slacks and a Sultry Pinup in black negligee. Diana served the veranda in shorts with a tray over her head as a Hep Carhop. Sometimes she chewed gum and she always said "swell" to the customers. The music was "Deep in the heart of Texas . . ." or "Kiss me once . . ."

Namala was a paradise for a girl scared of men. The ratio of single men to women was four to one and she had so many dates that she could easily play one against the other for safety. If that failed, Diana pleaded work. She had to rehearse the movements of a Burmese dancer, or walk like a Persian lady, or catch the subtle way a geisha presented a plate of raw fish. You could find her laughing with her arms around two men, or alone on the beach in the moonlight watching the fireworks supply the spaceport.

The beach could be fun. During the *Kaleidoscope*'s twenties' stint Madam Lilly strictly forbade her girls to wear their monokinis and instead had them splashing about in the latest daring flapper bathing suit that exposed the knees. It caused a riot and was very good for business.

Time and the smallness of the Namala community was her enemy. She met a boy named Jack in her martial arts class. He always spoke to her; she consistently ignored him. Their Japanese instructor repeated that the greatest perfection was to defeat an opponent with the minimum of force. Diana was having none of that. She was there to learn how to *demolish* men with the thrust of her heel or the back of her hand. She believed in a safety factor of ten. Break their skulls and then ask questions.

But Jack survived. Smitten, he arranged a surprise birthday party. There were twenty-one candles on the cake even though she was only turning sixteen. She had a fabulous time hugging everyone for their gifts and singing and fooling around. She successfully avoided Jack for three hours, knowing how dangerous a man in love can be.

Her fatal mistake was to need a Kleenex. Jack kept some in his study, which had remained off limits to the party because of the delicate model of the lunar base he kept there. She caught a glimpse of its detail and fell heels over head. Long after the revelry had died she was still in the study, her arms wrapped around Jack, kissing his nose and asking him questions about the lunar electromagnetic landing track.

The affair lasted two weeks, a miracle of involvement for Diana. She went everywhere with him. She haunted the launch site when he was at work. He spent all his money at the *Kaleidoscope*. They went surfing together and kissed at every opportunity. He hinted that he wanted to sleep with her. She hinted that she wanted to wait but to herself decided that he was the nicest guy in the world and she was going to throw her virginity away on him and live happily ever after.

In time they found themselves alone. Unhurriedly, gently he began to undress her. Diana only noticed that he was between her and the door. Since she had been a small girl she had learned to keep herself always between her father and a door. For awhile she tried to suppress her silly need, but the anxiety didn't go away—it became worse. It became imperative. Smiling at her insanity she took Jack in her arms hoping to roll him away from the door, toward the wall, without having to say anything. He chose that moment to be assertive.

Suddenly panicked, Diana threw him off the bed. When he looked up in anger, still commanding the doorway, she was so terrified that she struck him with a reflex karate kick to the head, and ran, not remembering that she ran. The next day he apologized when he found her. She turned away without speaking.

He flew in flowers from the States. He sent her letters. He papered love declarations on the corridor walls of her apartment. He slept on her steps. His intensity frightened her. She stayed awake with images of him murdering her. When he came to the *Kaleidoscope*, the other girls waited on him. Madam Lilly soothed her and told her that it was normal for men to go crazy, that it was nothing to worry about, but Diana worried. Jack persisted. He even sent one of the female mechanics he worked with to talk to her. Diana became so upset that she wrote to Mr. Ling a mailgram pleading for a transfer.

The reply bounced back via satellite and was printed up immediately. "Spend a week with me. Ling."

6

At the emergency meeting in the main control room of the lunar base Zimmerman told a joke about a congressman that ended with the punch line: "I got no luck at all, nohow. Jist as I was gettin' my ass trained to work without eatin', she has to up and die on me!"

It wasn't a funny joke when you were the ass. They poked at the budget cut and they went over their own expenses from five different angles. No sane way of handling the cut emerged.

During the next shift out on the lunar plain, Byron chewed over his anger in one of the construction trucks along the half-built track. His mind kept wandering off to Earth, that goddess of inconsistency.

One year you had Congress convinced that what you were doing was in the economic self-interest of the United States. You'd ask them if they were *sure* because you wanted them to be *sure* before you went ahead. Yes, they were sure. They backed you to the hilt. They made laws. But the next year they were convinced of something else, riding some new fad.

Back at the base Byron took dinner in his room. He cut off the intercom and tended his climbing vines, still seeking a solution to this latest sudden change in the rules. Adam Smith was wrong; men were not motivated by self-interest—they were too myopic to perceive self-interest farther than an inch away. A man would grab for that cigarette because the pleasure was immediate; the surgeon's knife cutting out his cancerous lung lay an unreal fifteen years in the future.

Byron's eyes blurred and for a moment he beheld a religious vision. A luminous hand was reaching out of the stars and that hand was a mosaic of little men held together by little hands in the pockets of the men above. Each little man was complaining about somebody else's greed. The conquest of space was not, at the moment, a gloriously cooperative venture. It was a war of pickpockets. But war gave him an edge. He smiled. Byron was an old fighter pilot.

His fingers switched off the lights so that he was in total darkness, the bed easy under his body. What did a soldier do when he was cornered? He remembered one of the favorite maxims of his father. "There is no such thing as losing," said that very stern man. It was an absurd maxim, parochially American, but one his father could imbue with a peculiar vitality.

As a ten-year-old Byron had been no fool. "That's what Hitler said at Stalingrad," he argued hotly.

"Ah, but Hitler confused winning with being on the offensive. You and I would have retreated and won."

"We retreated all over the place in Vietnam and lost!"

"Son, recall that you and I were in Germany during that disgraceful affair. Real soldiers aren't so clumsy as to defend something by destroying it."

"What's a real soldier?"

"An ordinary soldier fights well when he is grandly equipped. A *real* soldier can still fight after his supply lines have been cut. A real soldier doesn't even need any help from Congress!"

Once on a 300-kilometer hike with his father he had crumpled, refusing to go farther. The pain was overwhelming.

"A man inured to hell cannot lose."

"He can die," Byron remembered himself whining.

His son-of-a-bitch father had then lifted him up by the hair. "No. You forget. Death comes first. Then hell. Get moving. McDougalls are tough enough to walk out of hell. You're that tough. We make camp in two hours."

Byron walked out of his father's hell into an Air Force recruiting office on his eighteenth birthday. The Air Force groomed him, disciplined him, toughened him, and then sent him to Saudi Arabia to train Bedouins to fly the F-15. It was hell. He found himself drawing upon his father's wisdom and coping with hells because it was all he had. He used that empty time in the desert like a good commander might use a lull in the fighting—to build up his striking power. He sweated out an engineering education by correspondence course.

In those days few Americans cared about space, not even Byron. NASA's program had collapsed to a dismal four-shuttle fleet with no solid funding in sight. Russian space ventures began to show signs of life again and Congress frantically authorized the building of the spaceport, giving Rockwell a contract for 70 modified space shuttles. Byron found himself flying one of them above the Earth, above a vision that shattered his isolation.

He resigned from the Air Force and transferred easily into a spaceport construction crew, engineering with love where no men had built before, 275 kilometers above the silly wars in Africa and Afghanistan and Argentina. That was a boom time. Today it was bust.

Yes, it is like war, he thought there in the dark. This was a battle to take the high ground. You won some and you lost some. The battle up the slope always cost more than you wanted to pay. Sometimes the home front got tired of the war. Still you kept on fighting your way higher in the hope that once you reached the peak you could dig in and hold it cheaply.

The first low orbital spaceport had to be built on the money of incredibly expensive orbital rockets, but once in place the 150-kilometer-long, double-barreled spaceport could swallow and electromagnetically accelerate cheap suborbital rocket freighters and spew the unloaded freighters back down again to maintain momentum equilibrium. But that wasn't the end of the battle. That was only a ridge, a defense line, a trench.

The 275 kilometers wasn't high enough. As long as more mass was rising than falling, momentum balancing of the spaceport required a net energy input into the spaceport's mass drivers. That assumed an expensive auxiliary orbiting power plant which tended to limit spaceport capacity. And so the astronautical strategists began to covet the really high ground, the moon. If lunar mass could be delivered to Earth through the spaceport, momentum balancing of the spaceport would cease to depend upon auxiliary power. Capacity would go way up and costs down. If more mass was going down than coming up, the spaceport would generate a net surplus of power. A kilogram of moon delivered to the Earth contains eight times as much energy as a kilogram of the most powerful chemical rocket propellant.

The dust at the bottom of a minor lunar crater holds more energy reserves than in the whole of the Arabian peninsula. The potential energy of the moon is enough to power the wildest space program for millions of years. Damn the cost! Capture the high ground! Economics demanded it!

And so the war went on. Byron McDougall was chief field engineer when the second spaceport was built parallel to the first. It was designed to accelerate vehicles to high orbit beyond the Van Allen belts and to receive the vehicles back from high orbit. He did the job in three years.

By then congressional support was disintegrating. The Russian tortoise had fallen behind again. Wars are not fought on the battlefield alone. They are backed up by a whole support structure. And a loot-hungry populace is impatient with long sieges.

His father had something to say about long wars. "When the enemy's line is solid, endure, survive, and observe. Do not expect a break to appear at an enemy strong point. The breaks appear where *no one* expects trouble. When they appear victory goes to the swiftest. A place which has no strategic importance may achieve importance simply because it is not being defended."

7

Every civilization contains eddies of its past, sometimes within walking distance of its major centers. An eddy of the nineteenth century lay tucked away between two mountains of the California Coast Range, below the grasslands where the topography traps enough ocean fog to water a redwood stand. A Chinese family has long owned a log cabin there beside a dammed stream. There is no electricity. The road is dirt. Legend has it that every time a land developer comes this way, the wood nymphs call up a fog from the sea to sift through the redwood forest until it becomes invisible.

When Diana was with her Chinese friend she was all woman. At night she lay cozy with him under heavy blanket, by day she cooked over wood for her sage—flapjacks with sweet fried tomato syrup, and eggs and beans and bacon, even bread from flour and yeast. She kissed him and swam with him behind the dam and massaged him and flattered him.

But when she was by herself she reverted to girl. Deep in the forest she built a shrine out of stone to the goddess of moon and glade so that Diana might properly be worshipped. She tracked animals but they got away. She practiced archery for hours. Once she saw a deer and they both stood frozen, staring at each other in awe in that cathedral of trees.

On their last day she splashed in the cold pool behind the dam and toweled herself sassily in front of her boss because she knew he liked to look at her body even if he couldn't do anything with it. A wondrous evening light sneaked through the redwood needles.

"I have a job for you," he said, lighting the coals for a barbecue.

"You just sit down," she smiled. "I'll take care of everything. What do you want me to cook?"

"I meant a job *opening*. One of my places needs a new girl."

"Are you ever nice to me. Where?"

"You might not want it. It's a costume place. It involves playing up to some crazy men."

"What other kind is there?"

"Put this on," he said, giving her a shining package.

She held it out. "Brass bras!" she hooted. "*Mr. Ling*, I didn't know you ran a skin dive."

"Try it on."

Modestly she held it in front of herself. "I'll show through."

"You'll look beautiful, if slightly kinky."

So she stepped into what there was of it. Her hair spilled out of the helmet, a simple brass band around her forehead that supported oval headpieces which might or might not have been earphones. Her breasts spilled out of their immodest cups and her hips spilled out of their hardly adequate metallic banding. "Where do you get your outrageous ideas?"

He took her by the hand into the cabin and pulled his old copies of *Planet Stories* from a shelf. "Treat them like gold. They are from the forties and early fifties and fragile."

Diana shrieked at the cover of an issue he handed her. "That's me! Brass bras and all! And if that monster goes with the job, I'm quitting yesterday! Where is this restaurant?"

"On the spaceport."

Her heart jumped. "How high is that thing?"

"One hundred sixty-five miles."

"In kilometers! I didn't go to school in the dark ages like you."

"Two hundred seventy-five."

"And how high is the moon?"

"Too high for the restaurant business at the moment. They have to make do with a cafeteria."

"Damn," she said. "Don't forget me when you get your first lunar franchise. I'm going to send you vitamin pills every week. I want to make sure that you'll live that long."

"You haven't said yes to the spaceport yet."

She squeezed his hand. "When have I ever said no to you? I'm so thrilled I'm speechless. What's the name of your restaurant?"

"*Planet Stories*."

8

For sixty kilometers the raised track swept across the surface of the Imbrian plain. Since the lunar horizon was only three kilometers away, the track stabbed to the edge of the universe like God's knife separating the light from the darkness.

If they were allowed to finish it, within four months graceful ships would be skimming in tangentially at orbital velocity, to be picked up by a traveling platform equipped with superconducting coils, and braked on the maglev track. Right now Byron's staff was installing auxiliary systems, a series of flywheels near the track to soak up the energy of a landing, or feed out energy in the case of a take-off. A fifteen-ton ship moving at 1680 m/sec and decelerating at two Earth gravities generates 500 megawatts of electricity which has to go somewhere.

The flywheels were housed in huts which could be pressurized during construction and maintenance and evacuated during operation. They rotated on magnetic bearings in a vacuum. Their basic frame was built on Earth but the bulk mass for the wheel was made of lunar laminates. It was those laminates that were giving trouble.

Byron was with one of the flywheel crews when he got a call from the main base. ''McDougall. Braithwaite here. Louise hasn't been able to find you. She has an urgent call from Earth.''

''Goddamn that phone! I've got enough to do seeing if you and Anne are on schedule and under budget without having to listen to every gripe from Earth.''

''Louise said it was a panicky message from Seattle. You're going to be recalled.''

''I just got back! Oh for Christ's sake. I suppose they aren't satisfied with the deal I made in Washington. I know damn well it was a stopgap, but it was the best I could do. It has *got* to do for the next four months.''

''I think the call was about the crisis,'' said Braithwaite.

''Which crisis? An old one or a new one?''

''You vac-head. *The revolution.*''

''What revolution?''

''In Saudi Arabia.''

''Yeah, yeah, Saudi Arabia is going to revolt when hell freezes over. I know those sand eaters. I know Abdul Zamani, the defense minister. I taught him how to fly the F-15.''

''Abdul Zamani is dead. The last I heard the refinery complex at Dhahran was in flames. And God alone knows if the new leaders will continue to sell us oil. We don't yet know which freak Marxist heresy they belong to. Old Poker Face raced in from Camp David and seems to be trying to gather support to send in the marines—but hell, it's already way too late. The Royalists who were yelling for help are already dead.''

''You're kidding me?''

''You didn't scan the news this morning? We saw rows of Royal Bodies hanging headless by their feet from the lampposts in Riyadh. The King was murdered three hours ago.''

''My God! And you didn't tell me!''

''I automatically assume you know everything.''

''I'm coming in. Sweet Jesus!''

Back in the huts of the main base Byron replayed the late news on his console screen. It had been a stunning coup. The battle was over before the

Pentagon had even received orders to organize an airlift. And the CIA had heard the news via CBS. Modern Arab coups evidently weren't the clumsy affairs of yesterday.

Swat, just like that.

He felt disoriented, remembering the tough men he had trained. Those Saudi fighter pilots had been Royalist to the core. He couldn't imagine them siding with the Palestinians and the Pakistanis and the other immigrants who chafed under Royal rule. But he didn't let his disorientation stop him from sensing that here was an extraordinary battlefield situation to be exploited *immediately*.

Zimmerman came into his office with a worried look. "That's bad news. You heard the news?"

"Yeah. I still don't believe it."

"Look, no American should try already to understand an Arab intrigue."

"You sound upset."

"The House of Saud supported *moderate* terrorists. Me, I'm thinking the new government will maybe support *extreme* terrorists."

"I have a simple philosophy about terrorists—shaved ones and unshaved ones," said Byron. "Give any one of them a buck to do in your blood enemies, and they'll use it to buy a gun to do you in for the *rest* of your money. Bankrolling hatred is a risky line of work."

"You think the terrorists are behind the coup?"

"Zimmerman, I haven't got a clue. Money is power and power is a double-edged sword, that's all I know. There is no denying that the Royalists have been feeding murderers. Maybe that money was used to kill Jews, maybe it turned into graft, maybe it flowed backwards to water the plots in Jidda. Who will ever know? Whatever the basis for the coup, somebody just lost a queen in a big chess game. The USA is up the creek. And we on the moon have been dealt an ace." Byron glanced at his watch. "Hungry?"

"It's cucumber salad today," said Zimmerman disconsolately.

"I'm going to have to crack that whip to get that landing track finished so we can ship in some beef."

"With whose money?"

"You think money will be a problem after today?"

"I see a depression," Zimmerman said gloomily.

Byron was grinning as they drifted off toward the cafeteria. "I see gas rationing in the States, and I'm dying laughing. I'm seeing the pipes bursting in the middle of winter and I'm rolling in the aisles. I'm seeing the Russians trading weapons for Saudi oil and I'm grinning from ear to ear."

"That bad you see it?"

"I used to like Americans," said Byron with amused savagery. "I'm an American. It used to feel great to go to them and say, 'Here's a solution to a problem that hasn't happened yet.' So how do they react? They sniff daisies. Even my son. Zimmerman, if an American jumps out of an airplane, you can't sell him a parachute until *after* he hits the ground. I don't even flap about it anymore. Americans are manic freaks who slack off suicidally between crises and then work their asses to a bone to meet a crisis *after* it has bashed them in the face—all the time bitching bitterly that no one ever told them that the fist was on the way. Well, *I* told them. *I* was on my knees begging them, for Christ's sake. That's the whole story. It's a mania that will kill us all dead one day, and our Constitution besides, that one last crisis too many, but in the meantime it is no use yammering to deaf ears about how to prevent a coming crisis, you just have to be cool and work quietly until you know exactly what to tell them to do *after* the crisis has them screaming in pain—and hope to God they can get their silly asses in gear as fast as they always have before. Don't have the parachutes ready! Know all about splints!''

''Well done!'' exclaimed Zimmerman. ''I haven't heard you rant that well for three days.''

Braithwaite appeared from behind the potted plants and joined them at their table. ''Have you phoned Seattle yet?''

''Why should I call Seattle? I know what they are going to say. They're going to send me back to D.C. to try to sell Congress on putting up the risk capital to set up a production line that will crank out one ten-begawatt solar power satellite per month. I'll go; I'll make salvation noises, and our politicians will stand there with their knees shaking, those Georges who have cut us colonials down to the bone, and they'll kiss my ass and they'll buy it. Eight years ago I would have kissed *their* asses.''

''You're so happy it depresses me,'' moped Zimmerman. ''The State Department is having a morbid nightmare, and you're happy.''

''Give us a smile, Zim.''

''How can I give you a smile? My son is in Israel. I'm worried.''

''Arabs are killing each other and he's worried. Give us a smile. This is the break we've been praying for. Now the bureaucrats need us in a bad way.''

''You really think D.C. is going to buy anything? With our luck they'll revoke our return tickets and turn off the air. We'll starve. Here, maybe have some cucumber salad before it is gone already.''

9

The pods were attached all along the sides of the spaceport. Floating down the central corridor of Pod 43, a customer faced the logo of *Planet Stories* set into a glass rectangle above liquid crystal credits for the waitresses such as:

MOON CRAWLERS
by Diana Grove

Framed by this layout was the control room of a 1940s class rocketship battle cruiser. The busy "captain" could be seen in free fall, perhaps with his hand on the Pressor Beam Rheostat mixing a whisky sour. Beyond him was a porthole and an awesome view of the Earth filling half the sky.

Beside the porthole sat a surly Bug Eyed Monster deep in his cups. He was so lifelike that the unwary frequently approached him to see if they couldn't detect a defect left by the artist and got the shock of their lives. The BEM turned with a cat's suppleness, bared his teeth and snarled at people who came too close. His electronic innards were, of course, made on the spaceport.

Diana was late for work, the first time in many weeks. It wasn't her fault. There had been a minor malfunction on the maglev transport line that carried passengers and freight and empty lighters along the 150-km length of the spaceport. Her apartment, which she shared with another girl employed in large-scale integrated microelectronics, was 20 km from *Planet Stories*.

She popped through the airlock entrance—a real emergency airlock—whispered hurried words to the "captain" and scooted to the ladies' room where she slipped into her brass scanties and emerged ready to serve. Serving in free fall was freaky but she already knew how to do it with grace.

"Diana!"

She turned. A man with pepper hair and blue eyes was smiling lazily at her. He wore lunar togs. He had a strong aura about him and she thought she saw in his face a gentle fondness for women. That strange heady feeling of love at first sight struck. She let the emotion tingle through her mainly because he was an older man and that made him safe. Three other men hovered with him at a service booth. She glided over, her willingness to serve at a level above and beyond the call of duty.

"What's a Moon Crawler?" he asked.

"How do you know I'm Diana?"

"I've kissed all the other bylines."

"And they rejected your clever pass so you're trying me as a last resort?"

"Byron," said one of the others, "she's armed."

"And beautiful arms they are," said Byron, undiscouraged.

"A Moon Crawler," replied Diana, "is a slimy worm from outer space who telepathically poses as an irresistible woman. All that's left of the man in the morning is his toenails."

"Ouch," said Byron. "Let's hug and make up."

"You wouldn't survive. Now what do you want to order?"

He was amused. "I'm rich and charming and experienced, a classic winner. What did I do to deserve you?"

At the first opportunity Diana asked the "captain" in his Tri-planet

Rocketforce uniform, "Who is that distinguished one with those accountant types? He's a regular here, isn't he?"

"McDougall."

"Thanks. That tells me a lot."

"He has a few interesting stories to tell. He's an old fighter pilot. He's an old Rockwell shuttle pilot. He built half of this bird we're flying on. I think he is a close friend of Arnold." Arnold had designed the spaceport. "He's top dog of the moon base construction crew."

"He's really been to the moon?" Her eyes darted to the corner.

"He *commutes* to the moon."

She leaned conspiratorially over the battle cruiser weapons' control array. "Is he married?"

"Divorced."

She shivered at that news. "He likes me, did you notice?"

"Diana sweetheart, listen to me. You have a superlative bod. He's a make-em and leave-em man. He's out of your class."

"What do *you* know about trapping men!" she flared and left with their dinners.

One thing she liked about her job, the girls were supposed to entertain intellectually as well as serve and be sexy. Ling never sent a woman to *Planet Stories* who wasn't a good conversationalist. It was easy to wedge into this group and dominate the chat. She made her points by touching them lightly with excited hands—except McDougall. She let the men fondle her body—except McDougall. But while his companions caressed her brass armor, she flirted with those flecked blue eyes.

Duties called her away, yet she made special trips back to *his* corner. Only as they finished their after-dinner drinks did she tousle Byron's hair and whisper in his ear. "I'm off at 2 A.M. Why don't you pick me up then?" She was trembling with embarrassment.

He smiled. "Too bad I'm not on vacation. This Saudi mess has a stake up all our asses." He scribbled something and handed her a note. "Drop by when you get off. You may have to watch me work."

Diana didn't look at the note until he was gone. It was his Hilton hotel room, the executive suite. She had a flash of anger. *I won't go.* He wanted her to chase him. It was humiliating. *I'll go home and chain myself to the hammock.*

She stared at the wall. On it hung an original *Planet Stories* illustration of the Princess of Io, wearing a World War II hairdo and burlesque costume, racing between the moons of Jupiter on her rocket sled and being pursued. *Some women have all the luck!*

It was a long ride to the Hilton on the maglev. If you were close to the tubes, you could hear the lighters coming in or being shot out, a kind of humming swoosh that came through your feet, but in the maglev bus, suspended in vacuum, you could hear nothing. She did catch an occasional glimpse of an unloaded lighter, its delta wings retracted, moving along the central transport line in electromagnetic suspension where it was being taken to maintenance or loading or to the ejection breech at the leading edge of the spaceport.

Tremulously, at two-thirty, she was at McDougall's door, knocking. He opened. He seemed confused to see her. Behind him papers were mag-locked to the walls and the combination info-computer console that went with the executive suite was alive with readout.

"Didn't you invite me?" She clutched his note, unsure of herself on his territory.

He shook himself. "I wasn't expecting you."

"I thought you invited me."

He eased her inside. "And I thought you were pulling my leg. You pulled my leg all evening. So I pulled yours. If I'd known you were serious I would have been after you with roses. I hate being stood up."

Slightly mollified she said, "Where would you get roses in space?"

"There are ways, my little Moon Crawler."

She watched the tension lift from his face. A lined face could not hide tension as easily as a young face. *He's happy to have me.* He took her in his arms and held her warmly. She let him. *What am I doing here? He's going to try to lay me. I've got to get out of here.* "Did I interrupt something?"

"You most certainly did."

"I'm sorry. I won't bother you. I'll just watch. I love to watch men work. They're so involved."

"Give me another hour or so. I'm making up a presentation for a congressional committee. Looking at energy alternatives with Saudi oil knocked out."

"I thought we weren't importing as much oil from Saudi Arabia as we used to." Always get a man to talk about his work.

"We're not. But try turning off 30 percent of your oil supply when you're all geared up for it. That new crew of camel-smelling sister-beaters are throwing out their American oil men and importing Soviet technicians to put their oil fields back in production. They killed more than 20,000 of their own American-trained men in the battle. And we can't do a damn thing about it.

Her eyes were glowing. "Will they have to build solar power satellites now?"

"There's a good chance."

"They'll just dig more coal," she said disdainfully.

"Where I used to live in Ohio, everything was done with coal."

He snorted. "Coal has been having problems for a long time. Do you know how many billions of dollars the government spends on coal-related disabilities every year? I could buy a lunar colony for that budget." He called up a display on the screen. "And look at that. Hydrogen fusion is still 3000 times as expensive as fission. That leaves breeder reactors and solar power satellites. And *we* are clean. It will take a mix of both. It is a pain in the ass figuring out the trade-offs. Time is the factor now. We've got to move *fast* and that changes the trade-offs."

"Is there anything I can do? Sort papers or something?"

"Diana," he said warmly, "you've had a hard day. You've done a whole shift, for God's sake. Get to bed. I'll join you later."

"I'd rather watch." With a cringing fascination she watched the terror that was beginning to rise in her.

"And I'd rather see some rosy cheeks in the morning." He took her behind the room screen and pulled out the bed netting and casually began to undress her.

She froze.

He backed off. "We've made different postulates?"

She was panicky. She didn't know how to explain. "I have to be between you and the door. I'm crazy."

He changed position with her, careful not to touch her, instantly willing to put her at ease. "Is that better?"

He was puzzled, and half amused.

She nodded.

"Have you ever made love in space?"

"No."

"You'll enjoy it."

"I'm getting out of here."

"Stay." It was a command. He did not raise his hands.

She stared at those blue eyes which held her, knowing that he would let her go if she had the strength to leave. "I can undress myself." She did so, swiftly, awkwardly, and slipped into the net. "Kiss me goodnight."

Quietly, at six in the morning, he woke her. His body was comfortably warm. That part was like Mr. Ling and she enjoyed it. But Byron's fingers were hungry. That part confused her. She tried to be like the girls in the movies. It didn't work. It was like trying to take control of a runaway horse.

He stopped. "How old did you say you were?"

"Twenty-one."

"You're a virgin."

"Is that bad?"

"Holy Jesus."

"I'm sorry. It's not my fault. I was born that way."

"I'm rattled. You aren't in the space I thought you were in, and I'm astonished that I missed it."

"You don't want me?" She was ready to cry.

He didn't stop making love to her, but he was slower and carefully gentle, less intense, more propitiative, and he took contraceptive precautions because he didn't trust her innocence. The pleasure of it astonished her and she clung to him and wouldn't let him go.

"My father used to beat me. I've had a hard time liking men. You're a good lover."

"How would you know? I'm a lousy lover."

"You're so delicious that all that's going to be left of you is toenails."

"Maybe it is just space. The first time you try it on Earth, you'll be shocked—especially if you are stuck with a 200-pound man like me."

"I'm never going back to Earth!"

"I am. In three days."

She began to cry. "Are you going to marry me?"

"Sweet Jesus. I could be your father."

"It doesn't matter. I love you. I remember everything you said. In *Planet Stories* you said you'd never met a woman who could love both you and space. Well, I love you and I love space and I want to settle down on the moon just like you do."

"Wench, we will discuss this later when you are sober."

Diana called up one of the other girls and arranged an exchange of days off. She did her best not to let Byron out of her sight. He didn't seem to mind. She let Byron work. She helped him when she could. But the minute he showed signs of relaxing, she seduced him with every wile she knew. Sex, for two whole days, was her entire universe.

The door slid open. Byron's eyes blazed with blue fire. "Get dressed!" Terrified she slipped into her blouse but his anger couldn't wait and he gathered the collar of the blouse in his fist and shoved her against the wall. "You lied to me!"

"There is no Diana Grove." He shook her like a dog shakes a rat. "Your name is Osborne and you are sixteen years old. You are jailbait!" He let her go. "Do you realize how much trouble you could get me into?"

"Don't hit me. Don't hit me!" She was cringing.

"You slipped up in some of your stories. I got to thinking. And the company has ways of checking up on people. We can't tolerate fools in space. Sixteen. My God. Sixteen! You should be home with your parents!"

"My father beats me," she said piteously. "That's why I ran away when I was twelve."

Byron remained angry. "Kids always blame their fathers. A favorite sport. Fathers happen to be nice guys. Maybe you just never understood what your father was saying. Maybe you are headstrong and willful and don't see the dangers a father sees. You're young. Fathers know, kid. They *know*."

Her face twisted into agony. "You don't love me anymore."

A single tear rolled out of his eye. "Jesus, what a damn fool I am. Yes, I love you. And I'm responsible for you. I'm leaving tomorrow and you're coming with me."

Sometimes the sun breaks through the clouds. "You're going to marry me?"

"I'm going to take you home to your family."

The sun can disappear again behind a thundercloud. "I *hate* my father!"

He took Diana in his arms and soothed her. "Can you remember something nice about him?"

"Why should I?"

"For me."

She paused, wanting to please Byron. "He bought me a rug when I wanted one."

"Did you like the rug?"

"Yeah."

"Remember something else nice.'

She thought a long time, her eyes staring off in the direction of Arcturus. "He always made lemon and honey for my mother when she was sick."

"See. He's a nice man. It's been a long time. Our minds don't remember some things well because we are committed to proving that our decisions were right. You'll like him. You'll see."

"Mr. Ling will never forgive me," she said petulantly.

"I'm buying your contract."

"You can't make me go!"

"Oh yes I can," he said grimly.

10

The snow in Ohio was dirty with coal dust. Coal smells were on the air because the wind blew from that direction. Diana was surprised to see her father smiling, surprised to see him contrite, surprised at the warmth of the welcome he gave to the distinguished Mr. McDougall whose power awed him.

She arrived back in her familiar rat warren of factories and dry cleaning stores and chunky houses on tiny lots with potholes in the streets, a prisoner of the man she loved, determined to be emotionless—instead she cried with her mother. Both her parents lavished her with affection.

It was weird to go back to school with kids who hadn't changed since they were twelve because they hadn't done anything since they were twelve. The boys giggled when they said "boobs" and the girls were all virgins who thought SPS was a new thing to put in face cream to keep your pores clean.

Diana introverted into thoughts of Byron, suppressing all the evidence that might tell her she had been abandoned. He had hairs on his chest like Samson and she had some of them in an old perfume bottle. He was a hero angel who built stairways to the stars for men who were as yet too savage to understand. His fingers were pleasure, his eyes an ultimate beauty.

In her loneliness she began a letter to him. She wasn't sure she was going to mail it but the poetry of her love ached on her tongue. "Dearest Byron, I had a dream that there was nothing left of you but toenails and woke up in my bed nude (and beautiful as you well know) and imagined sweet touches. . . ." She redrafted the letter again and again, hiding it under the leather blotter on her desk.

One day when she came home from an errand to buy milk, her father chased her up the stairs raging against the depraved McDougall and against his daughter's dirty pornographic mind. He cornered her in her room, crumpling the letter in his fist.

Karate habits told her to take a defensive posture. She found herself cringing instead but when his arm lashed out to hit, her reflexes took over. A precisely placed foot smashed into his elbow, breaking it. She never looked back. She grabbed her Diana Grove papers from hiding and leaped through the window onto the porch roof and down onto the ground, rebounding in a run, unprotected against the winter cold.

A man and his wife found her on the highway, half frozen to death, thumbing a ride. They wrapped her in a car blanket and turned up the heat. She told them she was trying to go to her mother in New Hampshire. Only after she said New Hampshire did she remember that Byron's home was there.

The couple were active Christians and though they gave her endless advice about God and finding Jesus they were also practical. They insisted on taking her home, feeding her and finding winter clothes for her from their friends. They insisted on paying her bus fare and when she protested, they merely smiled and told her she could pay them back by helping someone else someday.

On the bus she prepared the scathing lecture with which she intended to axe-murder Byron.

(1) You are a monster!

(2) You seduced me and, not content with just rejecting me, you ruthlessly destroyed the whole wonderful life that I was building up for myself.

(3) And once you smashed my life, you weren't satisfied; you had to deliver me to a sadist for safekeeping, just so you could walk away without any burden.

(4) How am I ever going to get a job like that spaceport job again?

(5) It's not my fault that I had to pretend to be five years older than I really am. The government is stupid. They won't let me work and they won't take care of me.

I'll strangle him. He better give me some money. He better give me a job on the moon.

Halfway to New Hampshire she realized she didn't have a mark on her body and she wouldn't have a story to tell Byron that he would believe. At one of the hour-long rest stops she went out to a brick wall and bashed her head against it until it was bloody and swollen. When some friendly passengers tried to ask her what had happened she queered them by talking up the joys of head pounding.

Looking like an accident victim and in a state of confusion, she stepped off the bus, penniless, at a roadside terminal in a little New Hampshire town. It was madness to think that Byron would be home. He would be in D.C. or Seattle or anywhere but New Hampshire. She was going to a shuttered home buried in snow. His ex-wife, she knew, was in Florida.

She had a cry in the ladies' room before she went over to the post office and asked about Mr. McDougall. The woman told her he wasn't home, but that his son was, and a no-good drifter he had for a son. Diana panhandled a quarter for a phone call and when she heard the son's voice, hung up without saying a word. She walked in the snow, ten kilometers, until she reached the McDougall place.

A dark-haired young man with Byron's blue eyes answered the door. "You've been walking. Your car is stuck? I have a truck."

"No. I'm your father's mistress."

He tried to say seven things in reply and only a squeak came out. She walked past him, hugging herself. He rushed after her. "Hey, you're cold."

"Take me to your radiator."

"You've had an accident."

She touched her face. "The swelling is down. The black eye is pretty awful, isn't it? My old man beat me up for sleeping with your old man."

"My father abandoned you?"

"Yeah."

"Didn't he give you a free year in Paris?"

"He gave me a free year in an Ohio coal town."

"You could have asked for more."

"You don't ask for things when you're in love."

"You're too young for him."

"I *don't* think *that* is *any* of your *business*!"

"Are you pregnant?"

"*No*, I'm *not* pregnant," she said through gritted teeth.

"I'll have some hot tea ready in a minute."

She sat down in the kitchen by the radiator and took her boots off. Her feet were white and numb. "Where is he?"

"I just got a check from Houston, but that was a week ago."

"A lot of good that does me." She started to cry.

"Aw, hey now. It can't be that bad."

"If you come over here with your big blue eyes and try to comfort me, I'll slug you!"

11

Diana sulked in the master bedroom except for meals. Across the veranda she had a view of snowed-in farmlands, the kind of rolling landscape rich people purchase when they are bored by the city. The room had a handcrafted look with walnut trim and carved walnut doors. It was wholly a woman's room. Perfume bottles were on display, but things like heavy brass hairbrushes were neatly placed in drawers. Two portraits hung over the bed: a woman lit by sun reflected from spring leaves and a man glooming beneath some autumnal overcast in a fighter pilot uniform. The portrait of Mrs. McDougall, Diana hid under the bed. *His* portrait she launched upon the bed, a raft for a lonely girl to cling to in a king-sized ocean of softness.

Sulking made Diana restless. She had never tried it before and didn't like it. After three days she took a couple of hours off to bake a chicken casserole and that was such a relief she began trying on Mrs. McDougall's clothes, modifying the ones she liked on the sewing machine. A timid knock interrupted her concentration sometime during her fourth day of sewing.

"Like to come to the village? I'm going for groceries."

"Thank God! Did Byron finally send you more money?"

"Naw. I did some electrical work at the Hodge farm."

"You worked?" she exclaimed incredulously.

"Yeah, you're eating me out of house and home."

"And here I thought I was starving!"

"So today we'll have steak. I figured that if my father can keep *my* girlfriend in Paris, I can at least buy *his* girlfriend a steak."

In the village she noticed that the highway restaurant needed a waitress and she went in and took the job. It was a drag to live with a wastrel like Charlie who ate macaroni every night, sweet as he was. She was used to money.

Sometimes she hitchhiked home after work. Sometimes Charlie was waiting for her if she paid for the gas. Once he arrived to pick her up and found her being hassled by three toughs who wanted to give her a ride. The leader blew smoke in his face.

"You being bothered by these lung disease cases?" he asked.

"Stay out of this, Charlie. I know karate."

"It's not a job for a lady." He assumed the stance of a battle-tried colonel. "Leave!"

They left.

"How did you do that?" She was amazed.

He laughed. "Ordering men around and saving women and children runs in the family. Old military tradition. I'm considered the sissy of the McDougalls."

Diana decided to become independent of Charlie and bought a fifty-dollar car and pay-by-the-week insurance policy after she had wangled some gas ration tickets. The car got her halfway home.

"Charlie," said a plaintive voice over the phone. "I'm stuck on the Stonefield road at the hairpin. Would it be too much trouble for you to come and get me? Bring a chain."

"A chain?"

"To pull my car."

"Your car!"

"I bought a car."

"How much did you pay?"

She muttered an answer.

"Good God! You can't buy an unrusty hubcap for that!"

"It made noises and quit. Can you fix it?"

He sighed. "Maybe it's the spark plugs. I'll be right down."

The engine had seized. "How much does a new engine cost?" she whined.

"Oh, maybe a thousand dollars."

She cried all the way home. He tried to console her by telling her he could get something for the tires, and maybe sell a few other parts, but she was inconsolable. He began to feel so sorry for her that the next day he towed the car off to a friend's garage and spent all day doing an engine job. That evening he picked her up.

"Where's the truck?"

"I brought the car."

"I didn't know you could fix cars."

"I can't but I used to repair obsolete jet engines at MIT."

"Where did you get the money for parts?"

Charlie grinned like a man who has just won somebody else's gambling money. "My father is a millionaire. I have a kind of credit around here. He grumbles like hell, but he pays the bills."

"I don't understand you. Why do you loaf around when you could get a job as a mechanic?"

"Diana! That's work! I only did it for you."

"You're my nice sweetie pie. How can I sacrifice myself for you?"

"Entertain me in bed."

"I belong to your father!" she said indignantly.

"What kind of garbage is that?" he snarled.

"A girl belongs to the man who took her virginity."

He groaned. "You believe that drivel?"

"I certainly do!"

"You sound like my grandfather."

"Are you in love with me?" she asked warily.

"An inch, going on an inch and a quarter."

As they were thrown around the hairpin turn on Stonefield Road she kissed him. "If I hadn't met your father first, I'd love you an inch and a quarter, too." She kissed him again.

"Watch that stuff. You'll get dirty. I couldn't wash all the grease off."

"I don't care. I want to be nice to you. What was the nicest thing that ever happened to you—besides sex?"

"When Betty let me give her a bath."

Diana screeched. "I'll give you a bath!"

She sudsed him carefully, in no hurry to finish caressing away the black grease. It made her lonely to touch him, and happy at the same time. He tried to convince her to join him in the tub but she refused. When she was toweling him afterwards, he tried to kiss her and she hit him and they had a fight. She ran to the master bedroom and locked the door but hugging Byron's angular portrait proved to be no way to go to sleep. She kept thinking about crazy Charlie.

At four in the morning she wrapped a sheet around her body and shuffled to the kitchen for a glass of milk. She returned by way of Charlie's study, curiosity driving her to rifle through his papers. It was mostly schoolwork—equations, printouts, drawings, projects, experiments.

Charlie appeared at the door in his pajamas. "You're not asleep." He paused. "I'm sorry."

"I'm not mad at you. What are all those things?"

"I used to go to MIT."

"What are you?"

"A lunar engineer. It's not that really; I didn't specialize in lunar construction problems until my last year."

"Is that what these diagrams are?"

"Yeah."

"You never told me."

"It's not important to me."

Like a dash of hot Tabasco the old excitement was in her body as it sauced her blood with adrenaline and a pinch of lust. "Did you flunk?"

"I was the top of my class."

"Why aren't you building houses on the moon? It would be fun."

"Fun? It would be like New Hampshire in January with the air missing. Why take the moon when the worst that can happen to you on Earth is to be staked to an anthill in Nevada."

"But you could go if you wanted?"

"My father would love it. Staking me to an anthill isn't good enough for him."

A small adjustment of her shoulders let one curious nipple peek over the sheet at his blue eyes. "And what's all that electronic junk?"

"My music."

"Is that the weird stuff I hear once in a while?"

"No, the weird stuff is when I'm composing. That's just experiments and subthemes. Sometimes it's a foundation sound on which I'm going to build." Then he added shyly, "I've been composing a piece for you."

"Oh, you *are* in love with me!" she teased. "May I hear it?"

"You sing this wild stuff in the shower. I built it on that. You'll have to forgive me for bugging your shower."

"But I have a slug's voice!"

"Ah, but it's all filtered through my electronic ears and I hear the most beautiful things when I listen to you."

"If you weren't so lazy you could work as a queen's flatterer."

"It's called 'Diana in the Rain.'"

Nothing larval was left in the voice he had transformed with his silken touch. Mostly it wasn't even human. Perhaps a nymph bathing in a mountain waterfall would sing that way. The sound folded and unfolded wings of joy so startling even she failed to recognize herself as the music gripped her with her own emotion. Background instruments fluted in tonal patterns no wooden instrument had ever emitted. Her mind, captured by his net, remembered mythical worlds she had never seen.

He stood breathless, anxious, watching her reaction. Slowly becoming aware of what his metamorphic magic had done to her, she worked out of her percale cocoon with little jerking cries of pleased embarrassment.

"Golly."

He was drugged with happiness, just watching her.

"Don't stare at me like that or I'll turn you into a stag and your own hounds will hunt you down!"

Gently he carried her off to bed but, when responding to his memory of her earlier anger, he withdrew, she would not let him go. What is true one hour is false the next.

"Stay with me and cuddle. As long as I get the door side of the bed. You can make love to me in the morning."

When she woke she found him staring at her with his blue eyes. She rubbed noses with him. "Hi," he said. "Is it morning yet?"

Their sexing was an awkward disaster. The gravity threw her off and he was a virgin. Alternately they swore at each other and laughed. Finally they decided that at least they knew how to hug.

"It reminds me of a story that my grandfather loves to tell," he sighed. "Once upon a time there was a new recruit for the 43rd Cavalry Regiment and the commanding officer asked him, 'Have you ever ridden before, my boy?' 'No, sir,' said the boy. 'Hmm,' replied the colonel, 'I have just the horse for you; she's never been ridden before, either.'"

"Let's have breakfast and try it again," she said.

For three days Diana ran around in a daze, baking, washing his clothes, laughing at his jokes, buying him presents with her tip money and hugging him every time she met him. The second time she found herself scrubbing the kitchen floor in one week, she frowned. Did sex always make a woman feel this way? Byron had given her goosebumps, too. Were men similarly affected? She peeked out the kitchen window and saw Charlie freezing his fingers off changing a bearing on her right front wheel and that was reassuring.

By Friday she was enough in control of her emotions to begin the Great Plan. (1) Get Charlie a job. (2) Get him to finish school. (3) Get him a job on the moon. (4) Marry him. (5) Have children. She wasn't going to do it by nagging. She hated nagging a man. She'd rather leave a man than nag him. She was going to do it by worshipping him when he moved in the right direction and with patience and humor.

A driver's mother died and he trucked potatoes for three days; Diana let him make love to her for three evenings and three mornings. A neighbor's pipes froze and he joined the plumbing crew; she cooked him a four-course meal. Slyly she began to encourage him to be more ambitious. He took a weekend gig in Concord with his music. But spring came and he was still only doing odd jobs. Happiness gave her patience. They went walking in the woods when the buds sprouted. They splashed nude in the ice-cold brook.

She began to read to him from the papers about the big new push into space. Money was flooding into the effort. Overnight the high frontier had become a business almost half as big as the American cigarette, dope, and cosmetics trade. Charlie was never interested. She hid her hurt.

The Saudi Arabian situation improved. Escaped Royalists had money in America and Europe with which to influence politics at home. Intrigues prospered. Assassinations were frequent. The new leaders found it easier to conquer than to rule, and found some appeasement of the western capitalists necessary. Still the oil situation was grim and as reserves were depleted the United States imposed draconian gasoline rationing. Syntigas plants were pushed to full capacity in spite of a coal strike, suppressed by the Army. But sabotage continued to decimate coal tonnage.

Red tape was cut so that breeder reactors could be put on line in four years but nuisance protests continued to mount. A new tar sands plant was financed for Alberta. Hydrogen fusion power was brought down to $100 per kilowatt hour. A new gas field was discovered at great depth in the Gulf of Mexico. Mainly the economy was gearing up for solar power satellite production.

She read to Charlie the fabulous job offers in the *New York Times*. He wasn't interested. She sulked.

One day like a bolt from Jupiter the father called and Diana listened on the upstairs phone, tears rolling out of her eyes. *There* was a man. He could build. He could fight. His very voice called forth loyalty. He was on the cover of *Time* magazine. He could even be tender to virgins. His kind forged the glory of man. She ached to hold him. Could a woman ever forget her first man?

That noon Diana cooked pies and a mouth-watering lasagna. She made a fresh spring salad of new asparagus tips. She adjusted Charlie's collar. She teased him and in all ways was free and easy with her love. When she went to work she left a note in the truck's windshield wiper. "I have a job on the moon." Which wasn't true. "I'll *always* love you." Which was true for the moment. "Keep in touch."

She stopped at the restaurant only long enough to collect her pay and buy a packet of black-market stamps which got her as far as Montana. In Butte she abandoned the car and took a bus to Seattle, curled over two seats with her head pressed against her wadded jacket, dreaming that she was asleep next to Byron's facial stubble.

12

For three hours a nervous girl waited in the hotel lobby where that flighty secretary said he was staying. It stunned her when he sailed by, his weathered eyes scanning over her like a reef to be avoided, his wake washing away the hello in her throat. She buttoned the décolleté she had arranged to remind him of her womanhood, and followed him into the waiting elevator, ignoring him while they touched shoulders.

He left the elevator. She followed silently. He stopped and took out his key card. She waited.

"Diana! For the love of God!"

"So you finally noticed," she said petulantly.

"I had you pegged as one of the convention girls," he apologized, somewhat untactfully, switching on the light and walking over to the telephone. "What'll I order for you?"

"Poison darts!"

He spoke into the phone. "A double whisky for room 412. Also an extra glass, a bucket of ice and three bottles of ginger ale." Carefully he cradled the receiver. "So you ran away again?"

"He beat me up the minute you left! I mistook myself for a gong. I escaped by jumping two stories into the snow. A couple of good samaritans found me frozen to death at the end of a trail of blood. I learned about fathers what I already knew."

He was gazing at her with quizzical amusement. "Any scars?"

"No sir!" She snapped her heels. "Regrouped, resupplied, rested, and ready for active duty, you son-of-a-bitch, sir!" A clipped salute finished her report.

"*Now* I remember you," he said amiably. "And how have you been spending your AWOL?"

"Living with your son."

His face crumpled like a piece of paper being prepared for a bureaucrat's wastebasket. "You've seen Charlie?"

"We're lovers."

"Did he send you here for money?"

"Oh Byron! I heard your voice last week on the phone. I became nostalgic. I came here to marry you. We're going to have three children and live on the moon."

"A minute ago you were ready to kill me with poison darts."

"That was a minute ago. I'd be a good wife."

"I'm tempted," he said.

"Yeah?" She unbuttoned her décolleté.

"But my good sense remains. I'll give you a choice. I'll argue with you or I'll send you to an orphan asylum."

"Argue with me."

"You laid Charlie, eh?"

"What's it to you! The last I heard from you, just before you abandoned me to that prick father of mine, you wanted me to live in the coal dust and be virtuous."

Byron was trying to visualize being married to her. "I was thinking that you are young, even for Charlie."

"Yaah! Charlie's young, even for me."

"It wouldn't work between you and me," he said decisively.

"Why not!"

"I'm more than thirty years older than you are. I'm dying. You are beginning to flower."

She undid another button and rummaged around under the bed for his dirty socks which she angrily threw into a plastic bag. "Corpses make good fertilizer for flowers. Your power and my youth; it's a fair exchange. Jesus, Byron," she turned to him with regret, "I swooned when I saw you on *Time*. I was horny for a day."

"You'd tire of an old man."

"But it's *men* who are fickle. Women aren't like that. They're faithful. When they love a man, they *love* him. I'd be faithful to you. I'd forgive you anything."

He was settling into his decision. "That's what they all say when they are seventeen. When they are twenty-seven it's a different story."

"Already you're complaining about ten glorious years?" she stormed. "I'll bet you think you deserve fifty!"

There was a polite knock on the door.

"Young girls tend to bore experienced men," he reminded her.

She flung open the door and took the double whisky from the bellhop's cart before he had fully entered the room. She set the glass on the dresser, imperiously tipped the man, and poured Byron a ginger ale. "For your liver, old man. So I bore you, do I?"

"You started me thinking about those fifty years."

She half finished the whisky in one slurp.

"Can't I even have a sip of my whisky?" he complained.

"I've decided to blackmail you instead of marry you," she answered calmly.

"Blackmail me!" She had his attention. "We're not even married yet and you're being a bitch. I hope your lawyers are cheaper than my lawyers! You've stolen my whisky. What else do you want?"

"A job on the moon."

His humor left him. "No. That's final. What's your countermove?"

"You damn fool!" she flared. "Your son is in love with me! He'll follow me to the moon! That's where you want him!"

"And do you love Charlie?"

"No! I can't *stand* drifters. Yes. He's very kind."

Byron gripped her arms in the iron curl of his fingers. "Diana. He *won't* follow you to the moon."

"Yes."

"*No*. I know my son."

"You've seen him lately with my legs around him?" she lilted sarcastically, not even trying to escape his crushing hold. "I've watched him butter my toast. I've watched him scatter men who were trying to molest me. I've seen his eyes in the morning. You know *nothing* about your son. You're a dried-up old man, remember, who has forgotten what it's like to be driven by his juices. Charlie would follow me to hell. I planned it that way." She started to cry. "At least he will if we move fast enough before he has time to sober up and get another girl."

"He could follow you and refuse to work."

"Then I'd let him die. No man of mine is a suck." She smiled through her tears. "But for me he'd work. He's a sweet guy, Byron."

He began to march around the room, shaking ice from the ginger ale glass he had exchanged for her arm. "And you think I give a *damn* whether he goes to space? I don't give a *damn* anymore. I used to care. Now I'd be happy if he did anything. *Anything*. Wash cars even. How is his *damned* music going?"

"Like his engineering. He piddles at it."

"Is he healthy?"

"He's fine. I took good care of him. He's probably very unhappy right now."

"Suffering, eh?" Byron was smiling again. "A couple of months in the trenches will do him good. Finish your whisky and let's go. You've earned a dinner in Seattle's only real French restaurant."

At dinner he refused to gossip about his son. He ordered the best meal on the menu, the third most expensive. "It's good to eat like this again. For awhile I didn't even have an expense account."

"I'm on your expense account?"

"You're goddamned right. This year the Saudi Arabian Royal family lucked out and I'm enjoying every minute of their agony. We're tripling the size of the lunar colony. I wouldn't have believed that last year. And you should see the assembly line we're setting up for the solar power satellites; subcontracts all over the nation. It is going to be a boom year for the economy even though oil is short."

Her eyes were grinning. "I heard rumors that next year hydrogen fusion prices will drop to one cent a kilowatt hour."

Byron almost didn't laugh. "How could I let my son marry a girl with such a macabre sense of humor?"

He took her walking along the night beach, barefoot, sometimes on the sand, sometimes over the great driftwood trees, his shoes tied by the shoelaces over his shoulder and hers stuffed in his jacket pockets. The Pacific wind was cold and she sheltered herself behind his body, wondering at his silence that lasted for miles, not daring to invade his thoughts. The waves came and broke and went. Their feet were alternately drowned by foam and then free to make wet tracks in the moonlit sand.

"I'm not sure you'd like it up there. There is no moon in the sky for lovers."

"We can make poems about the Earth."

"You still have your Diana Grove papers?"

"Sure."

"They need to be made more solid. I'll spend some money."

She hugged his arm, thanking him silently, the glory and the triumph rising in her bosom to shout down the Pacific wind.

"I'm shipping out in two weeks. I'll take you with me. Not because of Charlie. Charlie can go to hell. For you. If Charlie follows, well, there'll be a job for him. We're building a second electromagnetic track to separate the take-offs from the landings."

Blackmail works! She was amazed. "What will I be doing?"

"Who knows."

"May I stay with you tonight?"

"No!"

"My hotel by the bus station has cockroaches!"

They were halfway back along the beach before he answered. "Zimmerman tells this story about some New York cockroaches that followed him to the moon. He claims to have spaced them and that they didn't die but are running around the crater Aristarchus to this day."

13

Rockets were still used to carry passengers and large freight to orbit. The electromagnetic interaction of a vehicle and the spaceport involved momentum transfer and large lighters would have required a more massive spaceport. Since the material of the original spaceport had to be carried to orbit by rocket, cost demanded that, once built, it would be supplied by a swarm of midget freighters which were intrinsically unsuitable for passenger transport.

Diana felt like a veteran. A mere year ago she had first been thrown into space by a rattletrap Rockwell Mark VI transport, a much modified version of the original Rockwell shuttle but still launched essentially by the means pioneered during the 1980s. Today she was aboard a modern impact rocket fresh from the factory at San Diego, its very design younger than her "Grove" identity. Even the upholstery smelled clean.

"How do you like this imp?" asked Byron, cramped beside her, not a patch of their bodies unsupported. Imp was the name by which impact rockets had become known.

"It's super."

"You're not scared?"

"I'm going to heaven!"

"I'm scared to death. I get nervous out of the cockpit."

There were no stewardesses. A robot seat monitored each passenger, checking that regulations were complied with during the countdown. ". . . three . . . two . . . one . . ."

Blastoff crushed them. The imp was, among other things, an oxygen-hydrogen rocket of mass ratio four, carrying enough propellant to reach slightly more than half orbital velocity. The roar cut off. A button tumbled in free fall in front of Diana. Then, as the imp found the apogee of its orbit among the blaze of stars, they met the spaceport, an express to hell passing under them so fast that its linear bulk was already perspective lines piercing infinity at the very moment the four-gravity acceleration hit them.

The imp's magnetically suspended arms had reached down and were receiving oxygen from precision valved nozzles set into a perfectly straight feed pipe laid along the spaceport. The oxygen was hurtling at circular velocity as it entered the imp's ducts. The gas suffered an almost elastic collision against the vehicle, swinging through the ducts, around and out the rear jets with its relative velocity reversed—thus violently thrusting the ship forward without affecting the momentum of the spaceport at all. As the imp began to catch up with the spaceport the impacting oxygen became less and less effective. Then the imp began to inject hydrogen into the reaction chamber, adding fire to the recoil.

Ten percent of the oxygen used by this impact system was already being supplied by the moon. Eventually all of it would be. In the meantime oxygen was imported from the Earth via the hybrid lighters.

"Poor little Byron, you can relax now. We're here."

"Whew! The old shuttle was a piece of cake compared with this sobering ride. I feel like I've just been put up in front of a firing squad and asked to gently kiss a machine gun burst."

"You're such a stick-in-the-mud. You're too old for me."

They ate at the *Planet Stories* with leisurely gusto. Diana got drunk for the first time in her life. She told shaggy-dog stories and, when she had the attention of five booths, tried to dance on the tabletop. If you've ever seen a drunk try to dance on a tabletop in null gravity you may understand the extent to which laughing tears convulsed her audience. When she passed out, Byron towed her back to the Hilton.

The next day they caught a ferry to geosynchronous orbit at the construction site of the first ten-begawatt solar power satellite. For eleven hours the five passengers played poker while the captain distributed sandwiches and made coffee.

There was some more ship maneuvering. When they went into a parking orbit, the captain called Diana into the cockpit. "Take a look." The matchstick framework of the SPS angled away into the star-laden blackness. "It's hard to comprehend how immense it is. Look, see that crane over there? It's a whopping big crane. See the little dot? That's the cabin for two men."

"Wow."

"I'll give you the grand picture. That thing is going to be as big as Manhattan Island. What you see is only five of the eight modules. What's out there would reach from Battery Park to 110th Street at the end of Central Park. The next module, the one that would contain Columbia University off in one corner if it was a piece of New York City, is being assembled in low orbit right now. They bring them up here by pushing hydrogen through porous electrically heated tungsten to get it through the Van Allen belts quickly, and then the rest of the way with ion jets."

McDougall was laughing behind them. "Tell her how to get from the A train to the Seventh Avenue line."

Within the hour they docked with a lunar lander and exchanged lunar oxygen for terran hydrogen. The captain of the lunar lander stuck his head through the hatch, mainly to get a chance to razz McDougall. Byron didn't introduce him to Diana until the visit was over.

"Maltby and I used to fly in Saudi Arabia under the same command. He'll be taking care of you from here in. But don't depend on him. He's a rascal. Take care of yourself. Write Charlie. And don't let them send your bags to Mexico City. Ciao."

Maltby took her back through the tunnel.

"You sit copilot with me."

"Where's your copilot?"

"He's too fat. I left him home. Where would I put you if he was here? This ain't no taxicab. This here boat is a freighter. You want to fly the beast?"

"You're scaring me."

"It seems complicated to you? Shucks, you just say 'giddiap' and the beast goes. She has a brain of her own. She knows where home is. The smell of oats."

"Giddiap," said Diana. Nothing happened.

Maltby did a few quick things with his fingers and the ship swung around. Then he yelled "Giddiap!" with an ear-piercing Texas drawl and the ship roared to life.

This trip, instead of poker, she learned how to play chess. He gave her a two-pawn-and-a-rook handicap and she won one out of five games in the next three days.

The ship faced backwards for the horizontal landing, its rockets firing in tiny vernier adjustments. Lazily the barren moon flowed by, slowly rising to meet them. Only when they were skimming the plain at crater-rim height did their speed become evident. A mile every second. Nearby features ran together in a watercolor blur. Suddenly the track appeared beneath them and she saw, for a split second, the rocket-catching cradle racing up the track toward them. She remembered the spaniel who used to gallop from the neighbor's house to chase her bicycle. The cradle positioned itself underneath them, grabbing with gentle jaws until their ship and the maglev vehicle became one.

Maltby was yelling "Whoa!" at the bloodcurdling top of his Texas voice. Electromagnetic fields cut in to convert fifteen tons of mass flow into an electron flood. Force hit then, two gravities that slowly built to five. The blur beyond the windows resolved into the majesty of the lunar desert, and finally they were moving sedately along a shunt line towards a shed. Maltby was fondly patting the control panel, smiling. "Atta girl."

I'm here, she thought and wonder was all within her.

She was assigned to the hydroponic gardens under a scowling beak-nosed boss who went through his chambers constantly tasting tomatoes and carrots and broccoli like a Punch making passes at lady puppets.

"Now that's a strawberry," he cackled. "I have the little buggers fooled that they are living on the slopes of a British Columbian mountain. Taste is everything. To hell with yield. Yield we can leave to the Californians." Slowly his grin grew, showing his upper gums above his jagged teeth.

She decided that her boss was crazy—not that what he *said* was crazy, but he had papered the wall of the small strawberry room with a fantastic view of a British Columbian valley. It didn't take her long to find out that everyone else was crazy, too. In the cafeteria with the construction workers she listened curiously to a conversation beside her. Billy was sick. He'd been anemic for months. His leaves were drying around the edges. *His leaves?*

Byron's friend, Zimmerman, dropped around after work to play scrabble. Diana asked him, "What kind of fruitcake would name a lemon tree Billy?"

Zimmerman nodded. "I hear Billy is pretty sick about it, too. My tree, I named Hershel Ostropolier and he's never been sick a day in his life."

Then there was the tiny cook who had a redwood tree called Paul Bunyan. Weird. But he was into Bonsai so Diana supposed it might be all right. When she bought her own baby orange tree she decided it was *not* going to have a name; however, one evening in a humorous mood when the conversation came around to the Celtic worship of trees, she toasted her tree with a local version of Irish Mist. "To my true Irish friend!" Henceforth her orange tree was invariably referred to as "the Irishman."

It wasn't easy living on the moon. The corridors were cramped. The rooms were small. There was no place to go. She missed Charlie and hiking through the New Hampshire woods.

Worse, an enormous sense of loss began to plague her. She had no direction, no purpose to her life, which had always known a fierce purpose. It was awful. It was like being a compass that had smashed its way through to the north magnetic pole and was now spinning, aimless. One night she dreamed about the truck driver who had taken her to Washington when she was twelve. In the dream he said with an ironic smile, "Better be careful what you want, kid—you may get it!"

Somehow the most important thing in her life became the study of plants. She was going to become a genius and bring life to the moon. She borrowed botany books and began to memorize all the names. She began to read biology books and agricultural texts and every hydroponic book in the library of her boss. Studying became an urgent compulsion. There wasn't even time to socialize, and finally no time to sleep.

One afternoon, looking for a scrabble game, Zimmerman found her wandering around the landing track control room trying to explain a theory of hers that no one could understand.

14

Every time she woke up and tried to get out of bed so she could go back to work, they held her down and shot her full of drugs again. Once she escaped and turned up for work in her pajamas. They brought her back and put her to sleep. This time she was going to be more cunning. She'd pretend to be asleep until the drugs were all worn off and *then* she'd get up and go to work.

She peeked.

"Ah, you're awake," said Charlie.

She opened her eyes in wide disbelief. "Charlie! What are you doing here?"

"The old man called me up. He told me to get off my ass and take care of you. It was like listening to a wire brush cleaning out the hole between my ears."

"Are you on *their* side?"

"I don't know from nothing. I got here an hour ago. Tomorrow I'm out working on the new track. The old man got me a job as a laborer, the rat."

"Get me out of here, Charlie. I have to go back to work."

"You're on a paid vacation and you're complaining?"

"They'll fire me." She was terrified.

"Nobody is going to fire you with my old man backing you."

"What happened to me? They won't tell me."

"You were wandering around passionately trying to convince people that milkweed was going to save the moon. The flowers are edible or something."

"I wasn't! I don't believe you!" She hid under the covers in shame.

"Yeah, you were really around the bend."

"I don't understand," she said through the covers.

"Neither does the doctor. But I do. You ought to see the loonies wandering around MIT during final exam time."

"You'll take care of me?"

"Do you think I'll let you out of my sight again? You gave me the shock of my life. For a week I thought I was strong enough to dismiss you. Then a funny thing began to happen. The sweet flowered fields of New Hampshire dissolved away into the flowered fields of hell. And the moon up there in the sky began to take on a heavenly beauty."

"Can I go back to work? I could finish the afternoon shift if I started now."

"Maybe tomorrow. We have to settle things between us. Like who is this Irishman you're living with?"

"That's not my Irishman! That's my orange tree!"

"I'm competing with an orange tree? Do you think I have a chance?"

She laughed as Charlie tried to walk her home. He needed low-gravity locomotion lessons. Once he collided with one of the awkwardly placed potted trees. "Charlie! Excuse yourself to Jezebel." He looked at her askance as she patted the pear tree. "There, there, Jezebel. Everything is going to be all right." Then she burst into tears.

Select friends gave Diana a homecoming party. Her boss arrived with a bowl of strawberries so delicious they needed neither sugar nor cream. Zimmerman leaned against the wall stealing more than his share. Louise was there and Maltby brought his guitar and his regular copilot. The Irishman moved into one corner to make room for them all.

Later Charlie explained to her the profounder truths of the universe as he saw them. "Some unsolved problem starts to push you. A couple of weeks without sleep and the borderline between the real world and imagination begins to fuzz. You fall asleep on your feet. You begin to treat real people as if they were the ghosts of your dreams and that's when the guys in the white coats come after you. Happens all the time at MIT in May. So if you get eight hours of sleep, I'll let you go to work. Otherwise, no."

"Make love to me. That'll put me to sleep."

"Thanks."

"Is that what happened to you at MIT?"

"Naw. I was pushing to get my father's ass. Sweet revenge. Haven't you ever wanted to strangle your father?"

"Oh yes!" she said brightly.

"I was going to get 100 percent in every course my last year just to rub that martinet's nose in the robot he'd made out of me. But no matter how much I strove I just couldn't make it as a robot. I couldn't get past 98 percent. It drove me crazy. It was like continually jumping in front of my father's Buick to prove to him what a bad driver he was and always coming out between the wheels without a scratch."

"You're crazier than I am!"

"I owe it all to my father." He was smiling.

"I like Byron!"

"That's because you're a girl." He sighed. "Maybe one of these days I'll make my peace with the old prick."

"You could have finished school. It was in your own best interest."

He shrugged. "I wasn't doing it for me."

"Why didn't you do more with your music?"

"My music was something they *didn't* want, so it was a reaction, too, I guess."

"What *do* you want then?"

"You."

"Oh Charlie! That's not enough and you know it!"

"Maybe it is. Men are more romantic than women. Women only pretend to be romantic because they know men like it."

Are you calling me a fake?" she bridled.

"No. You made it very clear that what you wanted to do was sit on a peak 380,000 kilometers high and look down on the rest of us."

"Screw you!" She strode to the furthest corner of the room, which wasn't very far away, and sat with her arms crossed, confronting him belligerently.

"Don't you think it's romantic that I climbed a peak that high just to ask you to marry me?"

She smiled mischievously, still with her arms crossed. "You haven't passed the other tests yet. You have to learn how to work first. Then *maybe* I'll marry you."

Within two years Charlie worked his way to assistant chief construction engineer. He was known with awe as the 100 percent man; the man who got the job perfect the first time. He lived with Diana and refused to take an SPS construction job because it would take him away from her.

Diana began to write papers on taste in high yield crops. For a lark she sent some tomatoes to a California fair and won first prize. She had seven projects going at once. Some people suspected that she never slept. Then, when necessity moved the command center out of the original Spartan diggings into much larger quarters, Diana made some frantic calls to Byron before someone else could find a use for the space. Charlie did the conversion design work. Zimmerman did the politicking. Ling, her old friend Ling, put up the money.

The place is called *Diana's Grove*. There are trees everywhere, not big trees, but what they lack in size they make up for in lushness. Some of them bear fruit—lemons and oranges and figs. There are vines and bamboo stands, even a brook that flows in too dreamlike a manner to gurgle. The benches are real wood. The food is the best in the solar system—just don't ask for beef. Nymphs with names like Callisto serve the tables wearing Roman hairdos and wispy gowns.

Diana, when she comes, makes her appearance in a white tunic with quiver over her shoulder. She knows everyone. Often she has a dinner party in one of the alcoves and brings people together who should be together, sometimes for major or minor politicking, sometimes because she delights in the clash of disparate views, sometimes because she is a secret matchmaker, sometimes for trivial reasons—an old professor of Charlie's needs company or one of her friends needs to discuss curtains. She is fiercely protective of the girls who work for her.

If you've ever heard the music at *Diana's Grove* you know that Charlie has risen into the league of the greatest. He claims it is just a hobby. The compositions from somewhere beyond the leaves—a heron's cry, a sightseeing flock southbound, a lone warbler—or it can be a conversation stopping argument between the gods.

Infrequently Charlie still proposes to Diana. She smiles her teasing smile, even though they already have one child, and writes him out a new contract in a flourishing script that promises she will be faithful to him for at least the next fortnight. He grumbles that living with her is like being an untenured professor.

The solar power satellites are winking on all around the equator, half of their mass coming from the moon now. All of the oxygen used by the space fleet is manufactured on the moon. America is prosperous, doing what it has always done best, selling high technology to the rest of the world. Her economy has achieved power independence and resource independence. The investment is considerable but it is, as yet, not well defended. Both McDougalls belong to an unofficial defense ministry which considers problems that Pentagon thinking is too archaic to handle. Serious decisions have to be made to secure the high ground in the face of a Russian resurgence into space. Such duties take Charlie back to the homeworld once a year.

Diana never goes with him. She is a minor Earth deity who worked hard for her promotion to moon goddess and she is well content with her position.

BARRY LONGYEAR

Enemy Mine

THE DRACON'S three-fingered hands flexed. In the thing's yellow eyes I could read the desire to either have those fingers around a weapon or my throat. As I flexed my own fingers, I knew it read the same in my eyes.

"*Irkmaan!*" the thing spat.

"You piece of Drac slime." I brought my hands up in front of my chest and waved the thing on. "Come on, Drac; come and get it."

"*Irkmaan vaa, koruum su!*"

"Are you going to talk or fight? Come on!" I could feel the spray from the sea behind me—a boiling madhouse of whitecapped breakers that threatened to swallow me as it had my fighter. I had ridden my ship in. The Drac had ejected when its own fighter had caught one in the upper atmosphere, but not before crippling my power plant. I was exhausted from swimming to the gray, rocky beach, and pulling myself to safety. Behind the Drac, among the rocks on the otherwise barren hill, I could see its ejection capsule. Far above us, its people and mine were still at it, slugging out the possession of an uninhabited corner of nowhere. The Drac just stood there and I went over the phrase taught us in training—a phrase calculated to drive any Drac into a frenzy. "*Kiz da yuomeen, Shizumaat!*" Meaning: Shizumaat, the most revered Drac philosopher, eats Kiz excrement. Something on the level of stuffing a Moslem full of pork.

The Drac opened its mouth in horror, then closed it as black anger literally changed its color from yellow to reddish-brown. "Irkmaan, yaa stupid Mickey Mouse is!"

I had taken an oath to fight and die over many things, but that venerable rodent didn't happen to be one of them. I laughed, and continued laughing until the guffaws in combination with my exhaustion forced me to my knees. I forced open my eyes to keep track of my enemy. The Drac was running toward the high ground, away from me and the sea. I half-turned toward the sea and caught a glimpse of a million tons of water just before they fell on me, knocking me unconscious.

"*Kiz da yuomeen, Irkmaan, ne?*"

My eyes were gritty with sand and stung with salt, but some part of my awareness pointed out "Hey, you're alive." I reached to wipe the sand from my eyes and found my hands bound. A straight metal rod had been run through my sleeves and my wrists tied to it. As my tears cleared the sand from my eyes, I could see the Drac sitting on a smooth black boulder looking at me. It must have pulled me out of the drink. "Thanks, toadface. What's with the bondage?"

"*Ess?*"

I tried waving my arms and wound up giving an impression of an atmospheric fighter dipping its wings. "Untie me, you Drac slime!" I was seated on the sand, my back against a rock.

The Drac smiled, exposing the upper and lower mandibles that looked human, except instead of separate teeth they were solid. "*Eh, ne, Irkmaan.*" It stood, walked over to me and checked my bonds.

"Untie me!"

The smile disappeared. "*Ne!*" It pointed at me with a yellow finger. "*Kos son va?*"

"I don't speak Drac, toadface. You speak Esper or English?"

The Drac delivered a very human-looking shrug, then pointed at its own chest. "*Kos va son Jeriba Shigan.*" It pointed again at me. "*Kos son va?*"

"Davidge. My name is Willis E. Davidge."

"*Ess?*"

I tried my tongue on the unfamiliar syllables. "*Kos va son Willis Davidge.*"

"*Eh.*" Jeriba Shigan nodded, then motioned with its fingers. "*Dasu, Davidge.*"

"Same to you, Jerry."

"*Dasu, dasu!*" Jeriba began sounding a little impatient. I shrugged as best I could. The Drac bent over and grabbed the front of my jump suit with both hands and pulled me to my feet. "*Dasu, dasu, kizlode!*"

"All right! So *dasu* is 'get up.' What's a *kizlode?*"

Jerry laughed. "*Gavey 'kiz'?*"

"Yeah, I *gavey.*"

Jerry pointed at its head. "*Lode.*" It pointed at my head. "*Kizlode, gavey?*"

I got it, then swung my arms around, catching Jerry upside its head with the metal rod. The Drac stumbled back against a rock looking surprised. It raised a hand to its head and withdrew it covered with that pale pus that Dracs think is blood. It looked at me with murder in its eyes. "*Gefh! Nu Gefh, Davidge!*"

"Come and get it, Jerry, you *kizlode* sonofabitch!"

Jerry dived at me and I tried to catch it again with the rod, but the Drac caught my right wrist in both hands and, using the momentum of my swing, whirled me around, slamming my back against another rock. Just as I was getting back my breath, Jerry picked up a small boulder and came at me with every intention of turning my melon into pulp. With my back against the rock, I lifted a foot and kicked the Drac in the midsection, knocking it to the sand. I ran up, ready to stomp Jerry's melon, but he pointed behind me. I turned and saw another tidal wave gathering steam, and heading our way. "*Kiz!*" Jerry got to its feet and scampered for the high ground with me following close behind.

With the roar of the wave at our backs, we weaved in and out of the black water-and-sand-ground boulders, until we reached Jerry's ejection capsule. The Drac stopped, put its shoulder to the egg-shaped contraption, and began rolling it uphill. I could see Jerry's point. The capsule contained all of the survival equipment and food either of us knew about. "Jerry!" I shouted above the rumble of the fast-approaching wave. "Pull out this damn rod and I'll help!" The Drac frowned at me. "The rod, *kizlode*, pull it out!" I cocked my head toward my outstretched arm.

Jerry placed a rock beneath the capsule to keep it from rolling back, then quickly untied my wrists and pulled out the rod. Both of us put our shoulders to the capsule, and we quickly rolled it to higher ground. The wave hit and climbed rapidly up the slope until it came up to our chests. The capsule bobbed like a cork, and it was all we could do to keep control of the thing until the water receded, wedging the capsule between three big boulders. I stood there, puffing.

Jerry dropped to the sand, its back against one of the boulders, and watched the water rush back out to sea. "*Magasienna!*"

"You said it, brother." I sank down next to the Drac, we agreed by eye to a temporary truce, and promptly passed out.

My eyes opened on a sky boiling with blacks and grays. Letting my head loll over on my left shoulder, I checked out the Drac. It was still out. First, I thought that this would be the perfect time to get the drop on Jerry. Second, I thought about how silly our insignificant scrap seemed compared to the insanity of the sea that surrounded us. Why hadn't the rescue team come? Did the Dracon fleet wipe us out? Why hadn't the Dracs come to pick up Jerry? Did they wipe out each other? I didn't even know where I was. An island. I had seen that much coming in, but where and in relation to what? Fyrine IV; the planet didn't even rate a name, but was important enough to die over.

With an effort, I struggled to my feet. Jerry opened its eyes and quickly pushed itself to a defensive crouching position. I waved my hand and shook my head. "Ease off, Jerry. I'm just going to look around." I turned my back on it and trudged off between the boulders. I walked uphill for a few minutes until I reached level ground.

It was an island, all right, and not a very big one. By eyeball estimation, height from sea level was only eighty meters, while the island itself was about two kilometers long and less than half that wide. The wind whipping my jump suit against my body was at least drying it out, but as I looked around at the smooth ground boulders on top of the rise, I realized that Jerry and I could expect bigger waves then the few puny ones we had seen.

A rock clattered behind me and I turned to see Jerry climbing up the slope. When it reached the top, the Drac looked around. I squatted next to one of the boulders and passed my hand over it to indicate the smoothness, then I pointed toward the sea. Jerry nodded. "*Ae. Gavey.*" It pointed downhill toward the capsule, then to where we stood. "*Echey masu, nasesay.*"

I frowned, then pointed at the capsule. "*Nasesay?* The capsule?"

"*Ae,* capsule *nasesay. Echey masu.*" Jerry pointed at its feet.

I shook my head. "Jerry, if you *gavey* how these rocks got smooth," I pointed at one, "then you *gavey* that *masuing* the *nasesay* up here isn't going to do a damned bit of good." I made a sweeping up-and-down movement with my hands. "Waves." I pointed at the sea below. "Waves, up here," I pointed to where we stood. "Waves, *echey.*"

"*Ae, gavey.*" Jerry looked around the top of the rise, then rubbed the side of its face. The Drac squatted next to some small rocks and began piling one on top of another. "*Viga, Davidge.*"

I squatted next to it and watched while its nimble fingers constructed a circle of stones that quickly grew into a doll-house-sized arena. Jerry stuck one of its fingers in the center of the circle. "*Echey, nasesay.*"

The days on Fyrine IV seemed to be three times longer than any I had seen on any other habitable planet. I use the designation "habitable" with reservations. It took us most of the first day to painfully roll Jerry's *nasesay* up to the top of the rise. The night was too black to work, and was bone-cracking cold. We removed the couch from the capsule which made just enough room for both of us to fit inside. The body heat warmed things up a bit, and we killed time between sleeping, nibbling on Jerry's supply of ration bars (they taste a bit like fish mixed with cheddar cheese) and trying to come to some agreement about language.

"Eye."

"*Thuyo.*"

"Finger."

"*Zurath.*"

"Head."

The Drac laughed. "*Lode.*"

"Ho, ho, very funny."

"*Ho, ho.*"

At dawn on the second day, we rolled and pushed the capsule into the center of the rise and wedged it between two large rocks, one of which had an overhang that we hoped would hold down the capsule when one of those big soakers hit. Around the rocks and capsule, we laid a foundation of large stones and filled in the cracks with smaller stones. By the time the wall was knee high, we discovered that building with those smooth, round stones and no mortar wasn't going to work. After some experimentation, we figured out how to bust the stones to give us flat sides with which to work. It's done by picking up one stone and slamming it down on top of another. We took turns, one slamming and one building. The stone was almost a volcanic glass, and we also took turns extracting rock splinters from each other. It took nine of those endless days and nights to complete the walls, during which waves came close many times, and once washed up ankle deep. For six of those nine days, it rained. The capsule's survival equipment included a plastic blanket, and that became our roof. It sagged in at the center, and the hole we put in it there allowed the water to run out, keeping us almost dry and with a supply of fresh water. If a wave of any determination came along, we could kiss the roof good-bye, but we both had confidence in the walls, which were almost two meters thick at the bottom and at least a meter thick at the top.

After we finished, we sat inside and admired our work for about an hour, until it dawned on us that we had just worked ourselves out of jobs. "What now, Jerry?"

"*Ess?*"

"What do we do now?"

"Now wait, we." The Drac shrugged. "Else what, *ne*?"

I nodded. "*Gavey.*" I got to my feet and walked to the passageway we had built. With no wood for a door, where the walls would have met, we bent one out and extended it about three meters around the other wall with the opening away from the prevailing winds. The never-ending winds were still at it, but the rain had stopped. The shack wasn't much to look at, but looking at it stuck there in the center of that life-deserted island made me feel good. As Shizumaat observed: "Intelligent life making its stand against the universe." Or, at least, that's the sense I could make out of Jerry's hamburger of English. I shrugged and picked up a sharp splinter of stone and made another mark in the large standing rock that served as my log. Ten scratches in all, and under the seventh, a small "x" to indicate the big wave that just covered the top of the island.

I threw down the splinter. "Damn, I hate this place!"

"*Ess?*" Jerry's head poked around the edge of the opening. "Who talking at, Davidge?"

I glared at the Drac, then waved my hand at it. "Nobody."

"*Ess va*, 'nobody'?"

"Nobody. Nothing."

"*Ne gavey*, Davidge."

I poked at my chest with my finger. "Me! I'm talking to myself! You *gavey* that stuff, toadface!"

Jerry shook its head. "Davidge, now I sleep. Talk not so much nobody, *ne*?" It disappeared back into the opening.

"And so's your mother!" I turned and walked down the slope. *Except, strictly speaking, toadface, you don't have a mother—or father. "If you had your choice, who would you like to be trapped on a desert island with?*'' I wondered if anyone ever picked a wet, freezing corner of Hell shacked up with a hermaphrodite.

Half of the way down the slope, I followed the path I had marked with rocks until I came to my tidal pool, that I had named ''Rancho Sluggo.'' Around the pool were many of the water-worn rocks, and underneath those rocks below the pool's waterline lived the fattest orange slugs either of us had ever seen. I made the discovery during a break from house-building and showed them to Jerry.

Jerry shrugged. ''And so?''

''And so what? Look, Jerry, those ration bars aren't going to last forever. What are we going to eat when they're all gone?''

''Eat?'' Jerry looked at the wriggling pocket of insect life and grimaced. ''*Ne*, Davidge. Before then pickup. Search us find, then pickup.''

''What if they don't find us? What then?''

Jerry grimaced again and turned back to the half-completed house. ''Water we drink, then until pickup.'' He had muttered something about kiz excrement and my tastebuds, then walked out of sight.

Since then I had built up the pool's walls, hoping the increased protection from the harsh environment would increase the herd. I looked under several rocks,but no increase was apparent. And, again, I couldn't bring myself to swallow one of the things. I replaced the rock I was looking under, stood and looked out to the sea. Although the eternal cloud cover still denied the surface the drying rays of Fyrine, there was no rain and the usual haze had lifted.

In the direction past where I had pulled myself up on the beach, the sea continued to the horizon. In the spaces between the whitecaps, the water was as gray as a loan officer's heart. Parallel lines of rollers formed approximately five kilometers from the island. The center, from where I was standing, would smash on the island, while the remainder steamed on. To my right, in line with the breakers, I could just make out another small island, perhaps ten kilometers away. Following the path of the rollers, I looked far to my right, and where the gray-white of the sea should have met the lighter gray of the sky,there was a black line on the horizon.

The harder I tried to remember the briefing charts on Fyrine IV's land masses, the less clear it became. Jerry couldn't remember anything either—at least nothing it would tell me. Why should we? The battle was supposed to be in space, each one trying to deny the other an orbital staging area in the Fyrine system. Neither side wanted to set foot on Fyrine, much less fight a battle there. Still, whatever it was called, it was land and considerably larger than the sand and rock bar we were occupying.

How to get there was the problem. Without wood, fire, leaves or animal skins, Jerry and I were destitute compared to the average poverty-stricken caveman. The only thing we had that would float was the *nasesay*. The capsule. Why not? The only real problem to overcome was getting Jerry to go along with it.

That evening, while the grayness made its slow transition to black, Jerry and I sat outside the shack nibbling our quarter-portions of ration bars. The Drac's yellow eyes studied the dark line on the horizon, then it shook its head. "*Ne,* Davidge. Dangerous is."

I popped the rest of my ration bar into my mouth and talked around it. "Any more dangerous than staying here?"

"Soon pickup, *ne*?"

I studied those yellow eyes. "Jerry, you don't believe that any more than I do," I leaned forward on the rock and held out my hands. "Look, our chances will be a lot better on a larger land mass. Protection from the big waves, maybe food. . . ."

"Not maybe, *ne*?" Jerry pointed at the water. "How *nasesay* steer, Davidge? In that, how steer? *Ess eh* soakers, waves, beyond land take, *gavey*? *Bresha*," Jerry's hands slapped together. "*Ess eh bresha* rocks on, *ne*? Then we death."

I scratched my head. "The waves are going in that direction from here, and so is the wind. If the land mass is large enough, we won't have to steer, *gavey*?"

Jerry snorted. "*Ne* large enough; then?"

"I didn't say it was a sure thing."

"*Ess?*"

"A sure thing; certain, *gavey*?" Jerry nodded. "And for smashing up on the rocks, it probably has a beach like this one."

"Sure thing, *ne*?"

I shrugged. "No, it's not a sure thing, but what about staying here? We don't know how big those waves can get. What if one just comes along and washes us off the island? What then?"

Jerry looked at me, its eyes narrowed. "What there, Davidge? *Irkmaan* base, *ne*?"

I laughed. "I told you, we don't have any bases on Fyrine IV."

"Why want go, then?"

"Just what I said, Jerry. I think our chances would be better."

"Ummm." The Drac folded its arms. "*Viga*, Davidge, *nasesay* stay. I know."

"Know what?"

Jerry smirked, then stood and went into the shack. After a moment it returned and threw a two-meter-long metal rod at my feet. It was the one the Drac had used to bind my arms. "Davidge, I know."

I raised my eyebrows and shrugged. "What are you talking about? Didn't that come from your capsule?"

"*Ne, Irkmaan.*"

I bent down and picked up the rod. Its surface was uncorroded and at one end were arabic numerals—a part number. For a moment a flood of hope washed over me, but it drained away when I realized it was a civilian part number. I threw the rod on the sand. "There's no telling how long that's been here, Jerry. It's a civilian part number and no civilian missions have been in this part of the galaxy since the war. Might be left over from an old seeding operation or exploratory mission. . . .''

The Drac nudged it with the toe of his boot. ''New, *gavey*?''

I looked up at it. ''You *gavey* stainless steel?''

Jerry snorted and turned back toward the shack. ''I stay, *nasesay* stay; where you want, you go, Davidge!''

With the black of the long night firmly bolted down on us, the wind picked up, shrieking and whistling in and through the holes in the walls. The plastic roof flapped, pushed in and sucked out with such violence it threatened to either tear or sail off into the night. Jerry sat on the sand floor, its back leaning against the *nasesay* as if to make clear that both Drac and capsule were staying put, although the way the sea was picking up seemed to weaken Jerry's argument.

''Sea rough now is, Davidge, *ne*?''

''It's too dark to see, but with this wind. . . .'' I shrugged more for my own benefit than the Drac's, since the only thing visible inside the shack was the pale light coming through the roof. Any minute we could be washed off that sandbar. ''Jerry, you're being silly about that rod. You know that?''

''*Surda*.'' The Drac sounded contrite if not altogether miserable.

''*Ess?*''

''*Ess eh 'Surda'?*''

''*Ae*.''

Jerry remained silent for a moment. ''Davidge, *gavey* 'not certain not is'?''

I sorted out the negatives. ''You mean 'possible,' 'maybe,' 'perhaps'?''

''*Ae*, possiblemaybeperhaps. Dracon fleet Irkmaan ships have. Before war buy; after war capture. Rod possiblemaybeperhaps Dracon is.''

''So, if there's a secret base on the big island, *surda* it's a Dracon base?''

''Possiblemaybeperhaps, Davidge.''

''Jerry, does that mean you want to try it? The *nasesay*?''

''*Ne*.''

''*Ne*? Why, Jerry? If it might be a Drac base—''

''*Ne*! *Ne* talk!'' The Drac seemed to choke on the words.

''Jerry, we talk, and you better *believe* we talk! If I'm going to death it on this island, I have a right to know why.''

The Drac was quiet for a long time. ''Davidge.''

''*Ess?*''

''*Nasesay*, you take. Half ration bars you leave. I stay.''

I shook my head to clear it. ''You want me to take the capsule alone?''

''What you want is, *ne*?''

''*Ae*, but why? You must realize by now there won't be any pickup.''

''Possiblemaybeperhaps.''

''*Surda*, nothing. You know there isn't going to be a pickup. What is it? You afraid of the water? If that's it, we have a better chance—''

"Davidge, up your mouth shut. *Nasesay* you have. Me *ne* you need, *gavey*?"

I nodded in the dark. The capsule was mine for the taking; what did I need a grumpy Drac along for—especially since our truce could expire at any moment? The answer made me feel a little silly—human. Perhaps it's the same thing. The Drac was all that stood between me and utter aloneness. Still, there was the small matter of staying alive. "We should go together, Jerry."

"Why?"

I felt myself blush. If humans have this need for companionship, why are they also ashamed to admit it? "We just should. Our chances would be better."

"Alone your chances better are, Davidge. Your enemy I am."

I nodded again and grimaced in the dark. "Jerry, you *gavey* 'loneliness'?"

"*Ne gavey.*"

"Lonely. Being alone, by myself."

"*Gavey* you alone. Take *nasesay*; I stay."

"That's it . . . See, *viga*, I don't want to."

"You want together go?" A low, dirty chuckle came from the other side of the shack. "You Dracon like? You me death, Irkmaan." Jerry chuckled some more. "*Irkmaan poorzhab* in head, *poorzhab*."

"Forget it!" I slid down from the wall, smoothed out the sand and curled up with my back toward the Drac. The wind seemed to die down a bit and I closed my eyes to try and sleep. In a bit, the snap-crack of the plastic roof blended in with the background of shrieks and whistles and I felt myself drifting off, when my eyes opened wide at the sound of footsteps in the sand. I tensed, ready to spring.

"Davidge?" Jerry's voice was very quiet.

"What?"

I heard the Drac sit on the sand next to me. "You loneliness, Davidge. About it hard you talk, *ne*?"

"So what?" The Drac mumbled something that was lost in the wind. "What?" I turned over and saw Jerry looking through a hole in the wall.

"Why I stay. Now, you I tell, *ne*?"

I shrugged. "Okay; why not?"

Jerry seemed to struggle with the words, then opened its mouth to speak. Its eyes opened wide. "*Magasienna!*"

I sat up. "*Ess?*"

Jerry pointed at the hole. "Soaker!"

I pushed it out of the way and looked through the hole. Steaming toward our island was an insane mountainous fury of whitecapped rollers. It was hard to tell in the dark, but the one in front looked taller than the one that had wet our feet a few days before. The ones following it were bigger. Jerry put a hand on my shoulder and I looked into the Drac's eyes. We broke and ran for the capsule. We heard the first wave rumbling up the slope as we felt around in the dark for the recessed doorlatch. I just got my finger on it when the wave smashed against the shack, collapsing the roof. In half a second we were underwater, the currents inside the shack agitating us like socks in a washing machine.

The water receded, and as I cleared my eyes, I saw that the windward wall of the shack had caved in. "Jerry!"

Through the collapsed wall, I saw the Drac staggering around outside. "Irkmaan?" Behind him I could see the second roller gathering speed.

"*Kizlode*, what'n the Hell you doing out there? Get in here!"

I turned to the capsule, still lodged firmly between the two rocks, and found the handle. As I opened the door, Jerry stumbled through the missing wall and fell against me. "Davidge . . . forever soakers go on! Forever!"

"Get in!" I helped the Drac through the door and didn't wait for it to get out of the way. I piled in on top of Jerry and latched the door just as the second wave hit. I could feel the capsule lift a bit and rattle against the overhang of the one rock.

"Davidge, we float?"

"No. The rocks are holding us. We'll be all right once the breakers stop."

"Over you move."

"Oh." I got off Jerry's chest and braced myself against one end of the capsule. After a bit, the capsule came to rest and we waited for the next one. "Jerry?"

"*Ess?*"

"What was it that you were about to say?"

"Why I stay?"

"Yeah."

"About it hard me talk, *gavey*?"

"I know, I know."

The next breaker hit and I could feel the capsule rise and rattle against the rock. "Davidge, *gavey 'vi nessa'*?"

"*Ne gavey.*"

"*Vi nessa* . . . little me, *gavey*?"

The capsule bumped down the rock and came to rest. "What about little you?"

"Little me . . . little Drac. From me, *gavey*?"

"Are you telling me you're *pregnant*?"

"Possiblemaybeperhaps."

I shook my head. "Hold on, Jerry. I don't want any misunderstandings. Pregnant . . . are you going to be a parent?"

"*Ae*, parent, two-zero-zero in line, very important is, *ne*?"

"Terrific. What's this got to do with you not wanting to go to the other island?"

"Before *vi nessa, gavey*? *Tean* death."

"Your child, it died?"

"*Ae!*" The Drac's sob was torn from the lips of the universal mother. "I in fall hurt. *Tean* death. *Nasesay* in sea us bang. *Tean* hurt, *gavey*?"

"*Ae*, I *gavey*." So, Jerry was afraid of losing another child. It was almost certain that the capsule trip would bang us around a lot, but staying on the sandbar didn't appear to be improving our chances. The capsule had been at rest for quite a while, and I decided to risk a peek outside. The small canopy windows seemed to be covered with sand, and I opened the door. I looked around, and all of the walls had been smashed flat. I looked toward the sea, but could see nothing. "It looks safe, Jerry. . . ." I looked up, toward the blackish sky, and above me towered the white plume of a descending breaker. "Maga damn sienna!" I slammed the hatch door.

"*Ess*, Davidge?"

"Hang on, Jerry!"

The sound of the water hitting the capsule was beyond hearing. We banged once, twice against the rock, then we could feel ourselves twisting, shooting upward. I made a grab to hang on, but missed as the capsule took a sickening lurch downward. I fell into Jerry then was flung to the opposite wall where I struck my head. Before I went blank, I heard Jerry cry "*Tean! Vi tean!*"

. . . the lieutenant pressed his hand control and a figure—tall, humanoid, yellow—appeared on the screen.

"Dracslime!" shouted the auditorium of seated recruits.

The lieutenant faced the recruits. "Correct. This is a Drac. Note that the Drac race is uniform as to color; they are all yellow." The recruits chuckled politely. The officer preened a bit, then with a light wand began pointing out various features. "The three-fingered hands are distinctive, of course, as is the almost noseless face, which gives the Drac a toad-like appearance. On average, eyesight is slightly better than human, hearing about the same, and smell. . . ." The lieutenant paused. "The smell is terrible!" The officer beamed at the uproar from the recruits. When the auditorium quieted down, he pointed his light wand at a fold in the figure's belly. "This is where the Drac keeps its family jewels—all of them." Another chuckle. "That's right, Dracs are hermaphrodites, with both male and female reproductive organs contained in the same individual." The lieutenant faced the recruits. 'You go tell a Drac to go boff himself, then watch out, because he can!" The laughter died down and the lieutenant held out a hand toward the screen. "You see one of these things, what do you do?"

"KILL IT. . . ."

. . . I cleared the screen and computer-sighted on the next Drac fighter, looking like a double 'x' in the screen's display. The Drac shifted hard to the left, then right again. I felt the autopilot pull my ship after the fighter, sorting out and ignoring the false images, trying to lock its electronic crosshairs on the Drac. "Come on, toadface . . . a little bit to the left. . . ."

The double cross-image moved into the ranging rings on the display and I felt the missile attached to the belly of my fighter take off. "Gotcha!" Through my canopy I saw the flash as the missile detonated. My screen showed the Drac fighter out of control, spinning toward Fyrine IV's cloud-shrouded surface. I dived after it to confirm the kill . . . skin temperature increasing as my ship brushed the upper atmosphere. "Come on, damn it, blow!" I shifted the ship's systems over for atmospheric flight when it became obvious that I'd have to follow the Drac right to the ground. Still above the clouds, the Drac stopped spinning and turned. I hit the auto override and pulled the stick into my lap. The fighter wallowed as it tried to pull up. Everyone knows the Drac ships work better in atmosphere. . . . Heading toward me on an interception course. . . . Why doesn't the slime fire? . . . . Just before the collision, the Drac ejects. . . . Power gone; have to deadstick it in. I track the capsule as it falls through the muck, intending to find that Dracslime and finish the job. . . .

It could have been for seconds or years that I groped into the darkness around me. I felt touching, but the parts of me being touched seemed far, far away. First chills, then fever, then chills again, my head being cooled by a gentle hand. I opened my eyes to narrow slits and saw Jerry hovering over me, blotting my forehead with something cool. I managed a whisper. "Jerry."

The Drac looked into my eyes and smiled. "Good is, Davidge. Good is."

The light on Jerry's face flickered and I smelled smoke. "Fire."

Jerry got out of the way and pointed toward the center of the room's sandy floor. I let my head roll over and realized that I was lying on a bed of soft, springy branches. Opposite my bed was another bed, and between them crackled a cheery campfire. "Fire now we have, Davidge. And wood." Jerry pointed toward the roof made of wooden poles thatched with broad leaves.

I turned and looked around, then let my throbbing head sink down and closed my eyes. "Where are we?"

"Big island, Davidge. Soaker off sandbar us washed. Wind and waves us here took. Right you were."

"I . . . I don't understand; *ne gavey*. It'd take days to get to the big island from the sandbar."

Jerry nodded and dropped what looked like a sponge into a shell of some sort filled with water. "Nine days. You I strap to *nasesay*, then here on beach we land."

"Nine days? I've been out for nine days?"

Jerry shook his head. "Seventeen. Here we land eight days. . . ." The Drac waved its hand behind itself.

"Ago . . . eight days ago."

"*Ae.*"

Seventeen days on Fyrine IV was better than a month on Earth. I opened my eyes again and looked at Jerry. The Drac was almost bubbling with excitement. "What about *tean*, your child."

Jerry patted its swollen middle. "Good is, Davidge. You more *nasesay* hurt."

I overcame an urge to nod. "I'm happy for you." I closed my eyes and turned my face toward the wall, a combination of wood poles and leaves. "Jerry?"

"*Ess?*"

"You saved my life."

"*Ae.*"

"Why?"

Jerry sat quietly for a long time. "Davidge. On sandbar you talk. Loneliness now *gavey.*" The Drac shook my arm. "Here, now you eat."

I turned and looked into a shell filled with a steaming liquid. "What is it; chicken soup?"

"*Ess?*"

"*Ess va?*" I pointed at the bowl, realizing for the first time how weak I was.

Jerry frowned. "Like slug, but long."

"An eel?"

"*Ae*, but eel on land, *gavey*?"

"You mean 'snake'?"

"Possiblemaybeperhaps."

I nodded and put my lips to the edge of the shell. I sipped some of the broth, swallowed and let the broth's healing warmth seep through my body. "Good."

"You *custa* want?"

"*Ess?*"

"*Custa.*" Jerry reached next to the fire and picked up a squareish chunk of clear rock. I looked at it, scratched it with my thumbnail, then touched it with my tongue.

"Halite! Salt!"

Jerry smiled. "*Custa* you want?"

I laughed. "All the comforts. By all means, let's have *custa*."

Jerry took the halite, knocked off a corner with a small stone, then used the stone to grind the pieces against another stone. He held out the palm of his hand with a tiny mountain of white granules in the center. I took two pinches, dropped them into my snake soup and stirred it with my finger. Then I took a long swallow of the delicious broth. I smacked my lips. "Fantastic."

"Good, *ne*?"

"Better than good, fantastic." I took another swallow making a big show of smacking my lips and rolling my eyes.

"Fantastic, Davidge, *ne*?"

"*Ae.*" I nodded at the Drac. "I think that's enough. I want to sleep."

"*Ae*, Davidge, *gavey*." Jerry took the bowl and put it beside the fire. The

Drac stood, walked to the door and turned back. Its yellow eyes studied me for an instant, then it nodded, turned and went outside. I closed my eyes and let the heat from the campfire coax the sleep over me.

In two days I was up in the shack trying my legs, and in two more days Jerry helped me outside. The shack was located at the top of a long, gentle rise in a scrub forest; none of the trees any taller than five or six meters. At the bottom of the slope, better then eight kilometers from the shack, was the still-rolling sea. The Drac had carried me. Our trusty *nasesay* had filled with water and had been dragged back into the sea soon after Jerry pulled me to dry land. With it went the remainder of the ration bars. Dracs are very fussy about what they eat, but hunger finally drove Jerry to sample some of the local flora and fauna—hunger and the human lump that was rapidly drifting away from lack of nourishment. The Drac had settled on a bland, starchy type of root, a green bushberry that when dried made an acceptable tea, and snakemeat. Exploring, Jerry had found a partly eroded salt dome. In the days that followed, I grew stronger, and added to our diet with several types of sea mollusk and a fruit resembling a cross between a pear and a plum.

As the days grew colder, the Drac and I were forced to realize that Fyrine IV had a winter. Given that, we had to face the possibility that the winter would be severe enough to prevent the gathering of food—and wood. When dried next to the fire, the berrybush and roots kept well, and we tried both salting and smoking snakemeat. With strips of fiber from the berrybush for thread, Jerry and I pieced together the snake skins for winter clothing. The design we settled on involved two layers of skins with the down from berrybush seed pods stuffed between and then held in place by quilting the layers.

We agreed that the house would never do. It took three days of searching to find our first cave, and another three days before we found one that suited us. The mouth opened onto a view of the eternally tormented sea, but was set in the face of a low cliff well above sea level. Around the cave's entrance we found great quantities of dead wood and loose stone. The wood we gathered for heat and the stone we used to wall up the entrance, leaving only space enough for a hinged door. The hinges were made of snake leather and the door of wooden poles tied together with berrybush fiber. The first night after completing the door, the sea winds blew it to pieces, and we decided to go back to the original door design we had used on the sandbar.

Deep inside the cave, we made our living quarters in a chamber with a wide, sandy floor. Still deeper, the cave had natural pools of water, which were fine for drinking but too cold for bathing. We used the pool chamber for our supply room. We lined the walls of our living quarters with piles of wood and made new beds out of snakeskins and seed-pod down. In the center of the chamber we built a respectable fireplace with a large flatstone over the coals for a griddle. The first night we spent in our new home, I discovered that, for the first time since ditching on that damned planet, I couldn't hear the wind.

During the long nights, we would sit at the fireplace making things—gloves, hats, pack bags—out of snake leather, and we would talk. To break the monotony, we alternated days between speaking Drac and English, and by the time the winter hit with its first ice storm, each of us was comfortable in the other's language.

We talked of Jerry's coming child:

"What are you going to name it, Jerry?"

"It already has a name. See, the Jeriba line has five names. My name is Shigan; before me came my parent, Gothig; before Gothig was Haesni; before Haesni was Ty, and before Ty was Zammis. The child is named Jeriba Zammis."

"Why only the five names? A human child can have just about any name its parents pick for it. In fact, once a human becomes an adult, he or she can pick any name he or she wants."

The Drac looked at me, its eyes filled with pity. "Davidge, how lost you must feel. You humans—how lost you must feel."

"Lost?"

Jerry nodded. "Where do you come from, Davidge?"

"You mean my parents?"

"Yes."

I shrugged. "I remember my parents."

"And their parents?"

"I remember my mother's father. When I was young we used to visit him."

"Davidge, what do you know about this grandparent?"

I rubbed my chin. "It's kind of vague . . . I think he was in some kind of agriculture—I don't know."

"And his parents?"

I shook my head. "The only thing I remember is that somewhere along the line, English and Germans figured. *Gavey* Germans and English?"

Jerry nodded. "Davidge, I can recite the history of my line back to the founding of my planet by Jeriba Ty, one of the original settlers, one hundred and ninety-nine generations ago. At our line's archives on Draco, there are the records that trace the line across space to the race-home planet, Sindie, and there back seventy generations to Jeriba Ty, the founder of the Jeriba line."

"How does one become a founder?"

"Only the firstborn carries the line. Products of second, third or fourth births must found their own lines."

I nodded, impressed. "Why only the five names? Just to make it easier to remember them?"

Jerry shook its head. "No. The names are things to which we add distinction; they are the same, commonplace five so that they do not overshadow the events that distinguish their bearers. The name I carry, Shigan, has been served by great soldiers, scholars, students of philosophy and several priests. The name my child will carry has been served by scientists, teachers and explorers."

"You remember all of your ancestor's occupations?"

Jerry nodded. "Yes, and what they each did and where they did it. You must recite your line before the line's archives to be admitted into adulthood, as I was twenty-two of my years ago. Zammis will do the same, except the child must begin it recitation . . ."—Jerry smiled—"with my name, Jeriba Shigan."

"You can recite almost two hundred biographies from memory?'

"Yes."

I went over to my bed and stretched out. As I stared up at the smoke being sucked through the crack in the chamber's ceiling, I began to understand what Jerry meant by feeling lost. A Drac with several dozens of generations under its belt knew who it was and what it had to live up to. "Jerry?"

"Yes, Davidge?"

"Will you recite them for me?" I turned my head and looked at the Drac in time to see an expression of utter surprise melt into joy. It was only after many months had passed that I learned I had done Jerry a great honor in requesting his line. Among the Dracs, it is a rare expression of respect, not only of the individual but of the line.

Jerry placed the hat he was sewing on the sand, stood and began.

"Before you here I stand, Shigan of the line of Jeriba, born of Gothig, the teacher of music. A musician of high merit, the students of Gothig included Datzizh of the Nem line, Perravane of the Tuscor line and many lesser musicians. Trained in music at the Shimuram, Gothig stood before the archives in the year 12,051 and spoke of its parent Haesni, the manufacturer of ships. . . ."

As I listened to Jerry's singsong of formal Dracon, the backward biographies—beginning with death and ending with adulthood—I experienced a sense of time-bending, of being able to know and touch the past. Battles, empires built and destroyed, discoveries made, great things done—a tour through twelve thousand years of history, but perceived as a well-defined, living continuum.

Against this: I Willis of the Davidge line stand before you, born of Sybil the housewife and Nathan the second-rate civil engineer, one of them born of Grandpop, who probably had something to do with agriculture, born of nobody in particular. . . . Hell, I wasn't even that! My older brother carried the line; not me. I listened and made up my mind to memorize the line of Jeriban.

We talked of war:

"That was a pretty neat trick, suckering me into the atmosphere, then ramming me."

Jerry shrugged. "Dracon fleet pilots are best; this is well known."

I raised my eyebrows. "That's why I shot your tail feathers off, huh?"

"Lucky shot."

"And ramming my ship with a crippled fighter at five times the speed of sound with no pilot wasn't a lucky shot, is that it?"

Jerry shrugged, frowned and continued sewing on the scraps of snake leather. "Why do the Earthmen invade this part of the galaxy, Davidge? We had thousands of years of peace before you came."

"Hah! Why do the Dracs invade? We were at peace, too. What are you doing here?"

"We settle these planets. It is the Drac tradition. We are explorers and founders."

"Well, toadface, what do you think we are, a bunch of homebodies? Humans have had space travel for less than a hundred years, but we've settled almost twice as many planets as the Dracs—"

Jerry held up a finger. "Exactly! You humans spread like a disease. Enough! We don't want you here!"

"Well, we're here, and here to stay. Now, what are you going to do about it?"

"You see what we do, *Irkmaan*, we fight!"

"Phooey! You call that little scrap we were in a fight? Hell, Jerry, we were kicking you junk jocks out of the sky—"

"Haw, Davidge! That's why you sit here sucking on smoked snake-meat!"

I pulled the little rascal out of my mouth and pointed it at the Drac. "I notice your breath has a snake flavor too, Drac!"

Jerry snorted and turned away from the fire. I felt stupid, first because we weren't going to settle an argument that had plagued a hundred worlds for almost a century. Second, I wanted to have Jerry check my recitation. I had over a hundred generations memorized. The Drac's side was toward the fire, leaving enough light falling on its lap to see its sewing.

"Jerry, what are you working on?"

"We have nothing to talk about, Davidge."

"Come on, what is it?"

Jerry turned its head toward me, then looked back into its lap and picked up a tiny snakeskin suit. "For Zammis." Jerry smiled and I shook my head, then laughed.

We talked of philosophy:

"You studied Shizumaat, Jerry, why won't you tell me about its teachings?"

Jerry frowned. "No, Davidge."

"Are Shizumaat's teachings secret or something?"

Jerry shook his head. "No. But we honor Shizumaat too much for talk."

I rubbed my chin. "Do you mean too much to talk about it, or to talk about it with a human?"

"Not with humans, Davidge; just not with you."

"Why?"

Jerry lifted its head and narrowed its yellow eyes. "You know what you said . . . on the sandbar."

I scratched my head and vaguely recalled the curse I laid on the Drac about Shizumaat eating it. I held out my hands. "But, Jerry, I was mad, angry. You can't hold me accountable for what I said then."

"I do."

"Will it change anything if I apologize?"

"Not a thing."

I stopped myself from saying something nasty and thought back to that moment when Jerry and I stood ready to strangle each other. I remembered something about that meeting and screwed the corners of my mouth in place to keep from smiling. "Will you tell me Shizumaat's teachings if I forgive you . . . for what you said about Mickey Mouse?" I bowed my head in an appearance of reverence, although its chief purpose was to suppress a cackle.

Jerry looked up at me, its face pained with guilt. "I have felt bad about that, Davidge. If you forgive me, I will talk about Shizumaat."

"Then, I forgive you, Jerry."

"One more thing."

"What?"

"You must tell me of the teachings of Mickey Mouse."

"I'll . . . uh, do my best."

We talked of Zammis:

"Jerry, what do you want little Zammy to be?"

The Drac shrugged. "Zammis must live up to its own name. I want it to do that with honor. If Zammis does that, it is all I can ask."

"Zammy will pick its own trade?"

"Yes."

"Isn't there anything special you want, though?"

Jerry nodded. "Yes, there is."

"What's that?"

"That Zammis will, one day, find itself off this miserable planet."

I nodded. "Amen."

"Amen."

The winter dragged on until Jerry and I began wondering if we had gotten in on the beginning of an ice age. Outside the cave, everything was coated with a thick layer of ice, and the low temperature combined with the steady winds made venturing outside a temptation of death by falls or freezing. Still, by mutual agreement, we both went outside to relieve ourselves. There were several isolated chambers deep in the cave, but we feared polluting our water supply, not to mention the air inside the cave. The main risk outside was dropping one's drawers at a wind-chill factor that froze breath vapor before it could be blown through the thin face muffs we had made out of our flight suits. We learned not to dawdle.

One morning, Jerry was outside answering the call while I stayed by the fire, mashing up dried roots with water for griddle cakes. I heard Jerry call from the mouth of the cave. "Davidge!"

"What?"

"Davidge, come quick!"

A ship! It had to be! I put the shell bowl on the sand, put on my hat and gloves and ran through the passage. As I came close to the door, I untied the muff from around my neck and tied it over my mouth and nose to protect my lungs. Jerry, its head bundled in a similar manner, was looking through the door, waving me on. "What is it?"

Jerry stepped away from the door to let me through. "Come, look!"

Sunlight. Blue sky and sunlight. In the distance over the sea, new clouds were piling up, but above us the sky was clear. Neither of us could look at the sun directly, but we turned our faces to it and felt the rays of Fyrine on our skins. The light glared and sparkled off the ice-covered rocks and trees. "Beautiful."

"Yes." Jerry grabbed my sleeve with a gloved hand. "Davidge, you know what this means?"

"What?"

"Signal fires at night. On a clear night, a large fire could be seen from orbit, *ne*?"

I looked at Jerry, then back at the sky. "I don't know. If the fire were big enough, and we get a clear night, and if anybody picks that moment to look. . . ." I let my head hang down. "That's always supposing there's someone in orbit up there to do the looking." I felt the pain begin in my fingers. "We better go back in."

"Davidge, it's a chance!"

"What are we going to use for wood, Jerry?" I held out an arm toward the trees above and around the cave. "Everything that can burn has at least fifteen centimeters of ice on it."

"In the cave—"

"Our firewood?" I shook my head. "How long is this winter going to last? Can you be sure that we have enough wood to waste on signal fires?"

"It's a chance, Davidge. It's a chance!"

Our survival riding on a toss of the dice. I shrugged. "Why not?"

We spent the next few hours hauling a quarter of our carefully gathered firewood and dumping it outside the mouth of the cave. By the time we were finished, and long before night came, the sky was again a solid blanket of gray. Several times each night we would check the sky, waiting for stars to appear. During the days, we would frequently have to spend several hours beating the ice off the woodpile. Still, it gave both of us hope, until the wood in the cave ran out and we had to start borrowing from the signal pile.

That night, for the first time, the Drac looked absolutely defeated. Jerry sat at the fireplace, staring at the flames. Its hand reached inside its snakeskin jacket through the neck and pulled out a small golden cube suspended on a chain. Jerry held the cube clasped in both hands, shut its eyes and began mumbling in Drac. I watched from my bed until Jerry finished. The Drac sighed, nodded and replaced the object within its jacket.

"What's that thing?"

Jerry looked up at me, frowned, then touched the front of its jacket. "This? It is my *Talman*—what you call a Bible."

"A Bible is a book. You know, with pages that you read."

Jerry pulled the thing from its jacket, mumbled a phrase in Drac, then worked a small catch. Another gold cube dropped from the first and the Drac held it out to me. "Be very careful with it, Davidge."

I sat up, took the object and examined it in the light of the fire. Three hinged pieces of the golden metal formed the binding of a book two and half centimeters on an edge. I opened the book in the middle and looked over the double columns of dots, lines and squiggles. "It's in Drac."

"Of course."

"But I can't read it."

Jerry's eyebrows went up. "You speak Drac so well, I didn't remember. . . . Would you like me to teach you?"

"To read this?"

"Why not? You have an appointment you have to keep?"

I shrugged. "No." I touched my finger to the book and tried to turn one of the tiny pages. Perhaps fifty pages went at once. "I can't separate the pages."

Jerry pointed at a small bump at the top of the spine. "Pull out the pin. It's for turning the pages."

I pulled out the short needle, touched it against a page and it slide loose of its companion and flipped. "Who wrote your *Talman*, Jerry?"

"Many. All great teachers."

"Shizumaat?"

Jerry nodded. "Shizumaat is one of them."

I closed the book and held it in the palm of my hand. "Jerry, why did you bring this out now?"

"I needed its comfort." The Drac held out its arms. "This place. Maybe we will grow old here and die. Maybe we will never be found. I see this today as we brought in the signal firewood." Jerry placed its hands on its belly. "Zammis will be born here. The *Talman* helps me to accept what I cannot change."

"Zammis; how much longer?"

Jerry smiled. "Soon."

I looked at the tiny book. "I would like you to teach me to read this, Jerry."

The Drac took the chain and case from around its neck and handed it to me. "You must keep the *Talman* in this."

I held it for a moment, then shook my head. "I can't keep this, Jerry. It's obviously of great value to you. What if I lost it?"

"You won't. Keep it while you learn. The student must do this."

I put the chain around my neck. "This is quite an honor you do me."

Jerry shrugged. "Much less than the honor you do me by memorizing the Jeriban line. Your recitations have been accurate, and moving." Jerry took some charcoal from the fire, stood and walked to the wall of the chamber. That night I learned the thirty-one letters and sounds of the Drac alphabet, as well as the additional nine sounds and letters used in formal Drac writings.

The wood eventually ran out. Jerry was very heavy and very, very sick as Zammis prepared to make its appearance, and it was all the Drac could do to waddle outside with my help to relieve itself. Hence, wood-gathering, which involved taking our remaining stick and beating ice off the dead standing trees, fell to me, as did cooking.

On a particularly blustery day, I noticed that the ice on the trees was thinner. Somewhere we had turned winter's corner and were heading for spring. I spent my ice-pounding time feeling great at the thought of spring, and I knew Jerry would pick up some at the news. The winter was really getting the Drac down. I was working the woods above the cave, taking armloads of gathered wood and dropping them down below, when I heard a scream. I froze, then looked around. I could see nothing but the sea and the ice around me. Then, the scream again. "Davidge!" It was Jerry. I dropped the load I was carrying and ran to the cleft in the cliff's face that served as a path to the upper woods. Jerry screamed again, and I slipped, then rolled until I came to the shelf level with the cave's mouth. I rushed through the entrance, down the passageway, until I came to the chamber. Jerry writhed on its bed, digging its fingers into the sand.

I dropped on my knees next to the Drac. "I'm here, Jerry. What is it? What's wrong?"

"Davidge!" The Drac rolled its eyes, seeing nothing, its mouth worked silently, then exploded with another scream.

"Jerry, it's me!" I shook the Drac's shoulder. "It's me, Jerry. Davidge!"

Jerry turned its head toward me, grimaced, then clasped the fingers of one hand around my left wrist with the strength of pain. "Davidge! Zammis . . . something's gone wrong!"

"What? What can I do?"

Jerry screamed again, then its head fell back to the bed in a half-faint. The Drac fought back to consciousness and pulled my head down to its lips. "Davidge, you must swear."

"What, Jerry? Swear what?"

"Zammis . . . on Draco. To stand before the line's archives. Do this."

"What do you mean? You talk like you're dying."

"I am, Davidge. Zammis two hundredth generation . . . very important. Present my child, Davidge. Swear!"

I wiped the sweat from my face with my free hand. "You're not going to die, Jerry. Hang on!"

"Enough! . . . face truth, Davidge! I die! You must teach the line of Jeriba to Zammis . . . and the book, the *Talman, gavey*?"

"Stop it!" Panic stood over me almost as a physical presence. "Stop talking like that! You aren't going to die, Jerry. Come on; fight, you *kizlode* sonofabitch. . . ."

Jerry screamed. Its breathing was weak and the Drac drifted in and out of consciousness. "Davidge."

"What?" I realized I was sobbing like a kid.

"Davidge, you must help Zammis come out."

"What . . . how? What in the Hell are you talking about?"

Jerry turned its face to the wall of the cave. "Lift my jacket."

"What?"

"Lift my jacket, Davidge. Now!"

I pulled up the snakeskin jacket exposing Jerry's swollen belly. The fold down the center was bright red and seeping a clear liquid. "What . . . what should I do?"

Jerry breathed rapidly, then held its breath. "Tear it open! You must tear it open, Davidge!"

"No!"

"Do it! Do it, or Zammis dies!"

"What do I care about your goddamn child, Jerry? What do I have to do to save you?"

"Tear it open. . . ." whispered the Drac. "Take care of my child, *Irkmaan*. Present Zammis before the Jeriba archives. Swear this to me."

"Oh, Jerry. . . ."

"Swear this!"

I nodded, hot, fat tears dribbling down my cheeks. "I swear it. . . ." Jerry relaxed its grip on my wrist and closed its eyes. I knelt next to the Drac, stunned. "No. No, no, no, no."

Tear it open! You must tear it open, Davidge!

I reached up a hand and gingerly touched the fold on Jerry's belly. I could feel life struggling beneath it, trying to escape the airless confines of the Drac's womb. I hated it; I hated the damned thing as I never hated anything before. Its struggles grew weaker, then stopped.

Present Zammis before the Jeriban archives. Swear this to me. . . .

"I swear it. . . ."

I lifted my other hand and inserted my thumbs into the fold and tugged gently. I increased the amount of force, then tore at Jerry's belly like a madman. The fold burst open, soaking the front of my jacket with the clear fluid. Holding the fold open, I could see the still form of Zammis huddled in a well of the fluid, motionless.

I vomited. When I had nothing more to throw up, I reached into the fluid and put my hands under the Drac infant. I lifted it, wiped my mouth on my upper left sleeve, and closed my mouth over Zammis' and pulled the child's mouth open with my right hand. Three times, four times, I inflated the child's lungs, then it coughed. Then it cried. I tied off the two umbilicals with berrybush fiber, then cut them. Jeriba Zammis was freed of the dead flesh of its parent.

I held the rock over my head, then brought it down with all of my force upon the ice. Shards splashed away from the point of impact exposing the dark green beneath. Again, I lifted the rock and brought it down, knocking loose another rock. I picked it up, stood and carried it to the half-covered corpse of the Drac. "The Drac," I whispered. *Good. Just call it 'the Drac.' Toadface. Dragger. The enemy. Call it anything to insulate those feelings against the pain.*

I looked at the pile of rocks I had gathered, decided it was sufficient to finish the job, then knelt next to the grave. As I placed the rocks on the pile unmindful of the gale-blown sleet freezing on my snakeskins, I fought back the tears.

I smacked my hands together to help restore the circulation. Spring was coming, but it was still dangerous to stay outside too long. And I had been a long time building the Drac's grave. I picked up another rock and placed it into position. As the rock's weight leaned against the snakeskin mattress cover, I realized that the Drac was already frozen. I quickly placed the remainder of the rocks, then stood.

The wind rocked me and I almost lost my footing on the ice next to the grave. I looked toward the boiling sea, pulled my snakeskins around myself more tightly, then looked down at the pile of rocks. *There should be words. You don't just cover up the dead, then go to dinner. There should be words.* But what words? I was no religionist, and neither was the Drac. Its formal philosophy on the matter of death was the same as my informal rejection of Islamic delights, pagan Valhallas, and Judeo-Christian pies in the sky. Death is death; *finis*; the end; the worms crawl in, the worms crawl out. . . . *Still, there should be words.*

I reached beneath my snakeskins and clasped my gloved hand around the golden cube of the *Talman*. I felt the sharp corners of the cube through my glove, closed my eyes and ran through the words of the great Drac philosophers. But there was nothing they had written for this moment.

The *Talman* was a book on life. *Talma* means life, and this occupies Drac philosophy. They spare nothing for death. Death is a fact; the end of life. The *Talman* had no words for me to say. The wind knifed through me, causing me to shiver. Already my fingers were numb and pains were beginning in my feet. Still, there should be words. But, the only words I could think of would open the gate, flooding my being with pain—with the realization that the Drac was gone. *Still . . . still, there should be words.*

"Jerry, I. . . ." I had no words. I turned from the grave, my tears mixing with the sleet.

With the warmth and silence of the cave around me, I sat on my mattress, my back against the wall of the cave. I tried to lose myself in the shadows and flickers of light cast on the opposite wall by the fire. Images would half form, then dance away before I could move my mind to see something in them. As a child I used to watch clouds, and in them see faces, castles, animals, dragons and giants. It was a world of escape—fantasy; something to inject wonder and adventure into the mundane, regulated life of a middle-class boy leading a middle-class life. All I could see on the wall of the cave was a representation of Hell; flames licking at twisted, grotesque representations of condemned souls. I laughed at the thought. We think of Hell as fire, supervised by a cackling sadist in a red union suit. Fyrine IV taught me that much: Hell is loneliness, hunger and endless cold.

I heard a whimper, and I looked into the shadows toward the small mattress at the back of the cave. Jerry had made the snakeskin sack filled with seed-pod down for Zammis. It whimpered again, and I leaned forward, wondering if there was something it needed. A pang of fear tickled my guts. What does a Drac infant eat? Dracs aren't mammals. All they ever taught us in training was how to recognize Dracs—that, and how to kill them. Then real fear began working on me. "What in the Hell am I going to use for diapers?"

It whimpered again. I pushed myself to my feet, walked to the sandy floor to the infant's side,then knelt beside it. Out of the bundle that was Jerry's old flight suit, two chubby, three-fingered arms waved. I picked up the bundle, carried it next to the fire, and sat on a rock. Balancing the bundle on my lap, I carefully unwrapped it. I could see the yellow glitter of Zammis' eyes beneath yellow, sleep-heavy lids. From the almost noseless face and solid teeth to its deep yellow color, Zammis was every bit a miniature of Jerry, except for the fat. Zammis fairly wallowed in rolls of fat. I looked, and was grateful to find that there was no mess.

I looked into Zammis' face. "You want something to eat?"

"Guh."

Its jaws were ready for business, and I assumed that Dracs must chew solid food from day one. I reached over the fire and picked up a twist of dried snake, then touched it against the infant's lips. Zammis turned its head. "C'mon, eat. You're not going to find anything better around here."

I pushed the snake against its lips again, and Zammis pulled back a chubby arm and pushed it away. I shrugged. "Well, whenever you get hungry enough, it's there."

"Guh meh!" Its head rocked back and forth on my lap, a tiny three-fingered hand closed around my finger, and it whimpered again.

"You don't want to eat, you don't need to be cleaned up, so what do you want? *Kos va nu*?"

Zammis' face wrinkled, and its hand pulled at my finger. Its other hand waved in the direction of my chest. I picked Zammis up to arrange the flight suit, and the tiny hands reached out, grasped the front of my snakeskins, and held on as the chubby arms pulled the child next to my chest. I held it close, it placed its cheek against my chest and promptly fell asleep. "Well . . . I'll be damned."

Until the Drac was gone, I never realized how closely I had stood near the edge of madness. My loneliness was a cancer—a growth that I fed with hate: hate for the planet with its endless cold, endless winds and endless isolation; hate for the helpless yellow child with its clawing need for care, food and an affection that I couldn't give; and hate for myself. I found myself doing things that frightened and disgusted me. To break my solid wall of being alone, I would talk, shout and sing to myself—uttering curses, nonsense, or meaningless croaks.

Its eyes were open and it waved a chubby arm and cooed. I picked up a large rock, staggered over to the child's side and held the weight over the tiny body. "I could drop this thing, kid. Where would you be then?" I felt laughter coming from my lips. I threw the rock aside. "Why should I mess up the cave? Outside. Put you outside for a minute, and you die! You hear me? Die!"

The child worked its three-fingered hands at the empty air, shut its eyes and cried. "Why don't you eat? Why don't you crap? Why don't you do anything right, but cry?" The child cried more loudly. "Bah! I ought to pick up that rock and finish it! That's what I ought. . . ." A wave of revulsion stopped my words and I went to my mattress, picked up my cap, gloves and muff, then headed outside.

Before I came to the rocked-in entrance to the cave, I felt the bite of the wind. Outside, I stopped and looked at the sea and sky—a roiling panorama in glorious black and white, gray and gray. A gust of wind slapped against me, rocking me back toward the entrance. I regained my balance, walked to the edge of the cliff and shook my fist at the sea. "Go ahead! Go ahead and blow, you *kizlode* sonofabitch! You haven't killed me yet!"

I squeezed the windburned lids of my eyes shut, then opened them and looked down. A forty-meter drop to the next ledge, but if I took a running jump I could clear it. Then it would be a hundred and fifty meters to the rocks below. *Jump*. I backed away from the cliff's edge. "Jump! Sure, jump!" I shook my head at the sea. "I'm not going to do your job for you! You want me dead, you're going to have to do it yourself!"

I looked back and up, above the entrance to the cave. The sky was darkening, and in a few hours night would shroud the landscape. I turned toward the cleft in the rock that led to the scrub forest above the cave.

I squatted next to the Drac's grave and studied the rocks I had placed there, already fused together with a layer of ice. "Jerry. What am I going to do?"

The Drac would sit by the fire, both of us sewing. And we talked.

"You know, Jerry, all this,"—I held up the Talman—*"I've heard it all before. I expected something different."*

The Drac lowered its sewing to its lap and studied me for an instant. Then it shook its head and resumed its sewing. "You are not a terribly profound creature, Davidge."

"What's that supposed to mean?"

Jerry held out a three-fingered hand. "A universe, Davidge—there is a universe out there, a universe of life, objects and events. There are differences, but it is all the same universe, and we all must obey the same universal laws. Did you ever think of that?"

"No."

"That is what I mean, Davidge. Not terribly profound."

I snorted. "I told you, I'd heard this stuff before. So, I imagine that shows humans to be just as profound as Dracs."

Jerry laughed. "You always insist on making something racial out of my observations. What I said applied to you, not to the race of humans. . . ."

I spat on the frozen ground. "You Dracs think you're so damned smart." The wind picked up, and I could taste the sea salt in it. One of the big blows was coming. The sky was changing to that curious darkness that tricked me into thinking it was midnight blue rather than black. A trickle of ice found its way under my collar.

"What's wrong with me just being me? Everybody in the universe doesn't have to be a damned philosopher, toadface!" There were millions—billions—like me. More, maybe. "What difference does it make to anything whether I ponder existence or not? It's here; that's all I have to know."

"Davidge, you don't even know your family line beyond your parents, and now you say you refuse to know that of your universe that you can know. How will you know your place in this existence, Davidge? Where are you? Who are you?"

I shook my head and stared at the grave, then I turned and faced the sea. In another hour, or less, it would be too dark to see the whitecaps. "I'm me, that's who." But, was *that* "me" who held the rock over Zammis, threatening a helpless infant with death? I felt my guts curdle as the loneliness I thought I felt grew claws and fangs and began gnawing and slashing at the remains of my sanity. I turned back to the grave, closed my eyes, then opened them. "I'm a fighter pilot, Jerry. Isn't that something?"

"That is what you do, Davidge; that is not who nor what you are."

I knelt next to the grave and clawed at the ice-sheathed rocks with my hands. "You don't talk to me now, Drac! *You're dead!*" I stopped, realizing that the words I had heard were from the *Talman*, processed into my own context. I slumped against the rocks, felt the wind, then pushed myself to my feet. "Jerry, Zammis won't eat. It's been three days. What do I do? Why didn't you tell me anything about Drac brats before you? . . . ." I held my hands to my face. "Steady, boy. Keep it up, and they'll stick you in a home." The wind pressed against my back, I lowered my hands, then walked from the grave.

I sat in the cave, staring at the fire. I couldn't hear the wind through the rock and the wood was dry, making the fire hot and quiet. I tapped my fingers against my knees, then began humming. Noise, any kind, helped to drive off the oppressing loneliness. "Sonofabitch." I laughed and nodded. "Yea, verily, and *kizlode va nu, dutshaat*." I chuckled, trying to think of all the curses and obscenities in Drac that I had learned from Jerry. There were quite a few. My toe tapped against the sand and my humming started up again. I stopped, frowned, then remembered the song.

"Highty tighty Christ Almighty,
Who the Hell are we?
Zim zam, Gawd damn,
We're in Squadron B."

I leaned back against the wall of the cave, trying to remember another verse. *A pilot's got a rotten life/No crumpets with our tea/We have to service the general's wife/And pick fleas from her knee*. "Damn!" I slapped my knee, trying to see the faces of the other pilots in the squadron lounge. I could almost feel the whiskey fumes tickling the inside of my nose. Vadik, Wooster, Arnold . . . the one with the broken nose—Demerest, Kadiz. I hummed again, swinging an imaginary mug of issue grog by its imaginary handle.

"And if he doesn't like it,
I'll tell you what we'll do:
We'll fill his ass with broken glass,
And seal it up with glue."

The cave echoed with the song. I stood, threw up my arms and screamed. "Yaaaaahoooooo!"

Zammis began crying. I bit my lip and walked over to the bundle on the mattress. "Well? You ready to eat?"

"Unh, unh, weh." The infant rocked its head back and forth. I went to the fire, picked up a twist of snake, then returned. I knelt next to Zammis and held the snake to its lips. Again the child pushed it away. "Come on, you. You have to eat." I tried again with the same results. I took the wraps off the child and looked at its body. I could tell it was losing weight, although Zammis didn't appear to be getting weak. I shrugged, wrapped it up again, stood and began walking back to my mattress.

"Guh, weh."

I turned. "What?"

"Ah, guh, guh."

I went back, stooped over and picked the child up. Its eyes were open and it looked into my face, then smiled.

"What're you laughing at, ugly? You should get a load of your own face."

Zammis barked out a short laugh, then gurgled. I went to my mattress, sat down and arranged Zammis in my lap. "Gumma, buh, buh." Its hand grabbed a loose flap of snakeskin on my shirt and pulled on it.

"Gumma buh buh to you, too. So, what do we do now? How about I start teaching you the line of Jeriba? You're going to have to learn it sometime, and it might as well be now." I looked into Zammis' eyes. "When I bring you to stand before the Jeriba archives, you will say this: 'Before you here I stand, Zammis of the line of Jeriba, born of Shigan, the fighter pilot.'" I smiled, thinking of the upraised yellow brows if Zammis continued: *"And by damn, Shigan was a helluva good pilot, too. Why, I was once told he took a smart round in his tail feathers, then pulled around and rammed the* kizlode *sonofabitch, known to one and all as Willis E. Davidge. . . .* I shook my head. "You're not going to get your wings by doing the line in English, Zammis." I began again:

"Naatha nu enta va Zammis zea dos Jeriba, estay va Shigan, asaam naa denvadar. . . ."

For eight of those long days and nights, I feared the child would die. I tried everything—roots, dried berries, dried plumfruit, snakemeat dried, boiled, chewed and ground. Zammis refused it all. I checked frequently, but each time I looked through the child's wraps, they were as clean as when I had put them on. Zammis lost weight, but seemed to grow stronger. By the ninth day it was crawling the floor of the cave. Even with the fire, the cave wasn't really warm. I feared that the kid would get sick crawling around naked, and I dressed it in the tiny snakeskin suit and cap Jerry had made for it. After dressing it, I stood Zammis up and looked at it. The kid had already developed a smile full of mischief that, combined with the twinkle in its yellow eyes, suit and cap, made it look like a elf. I was holding Zammis up in a standing position. The kid seemed pretty steady on its legs, and I let go. Zammis smiled, waved its thinning arms about, then the child laughed and took a faltering step toward me. I caught it as it fell, and the little Drac squealed.

In two more days Zammis was walking and getting into everything that could be gotten into. I spent many an anxious moment searching the chambers at the back of the cave for the kid after coming in from outside. Finally, when I caught him at the mouth of the cave heading full steam for the outside, I had had enough. I made a harness out of snakeskin, attached it to a snake-leather leash, and tied the other end to a projection of rock above my head. Zammis still got into everything, but at least I could find it.

Four days after it learned to walk, it wanted to eat. Drac babies are probably the most convenient and considerate infants in the universe. They live off their fat for about three or four Earth weeks, and don't make a mess the entire time. After they learn to walk, and can therefore make it to a mutually agree-upon spot, then they want food and begin discharging wastes. I showed the kid once how to use the litter box I had made, and never had to again. After five or six lessons, Zammis was handling its own drawers. Watching the little Drac learn and grow, I began to understand those pilots in my squadron who used to bore each other—and everyone else—with countless pictures of ugly children, accompanied by thirty-minute narratives for each snapshot. Before the ice melted, Zammis was talking. I taught it to call me "Uncle."

For lack of a better term, I called the ice-melting season "spring." It would be a long time before the scrub forest showed any green, or the snakes would venture forth from their icy holes. The sky maintained its eternal cover of dark, angry clouds, and still the sleet would come and coat everything with a hard, slippery glaze. But the next day the glaze would melt, and the warmer air would push another millimeter into the soil.

I realized that this was the time to be gathering wood. Before the winter hit, Jerry and I working together hadn't gathered enough wood. The short summer would have to be spent putting up food for the next winter. I was hoping to build a tighter door over the mouth of the cave, and I swore that I would figure out some kind of indoor plumbing. Dropping your drawers outside in the middle of winter was dangerous. My mind was full of these things as I stretched out on my mattress watching the smoke curl through a crack in the roof of the cave. Zammis was off in the back of the cave playing with some rocks that it had found, and I must have fallen asleep. I awoke with the kid shaking my arm.

"Uncle?"

"Huh? Zammis?"

"Uncle. Look."

I rolled over on my left side and faced the Drac. Zammis was holding up his right hand, fingers spread out. "What is it, Zammis?"

"Look." It pointed at each of its three fingers in turn. "One, two, three."

"So?"

"Look." Zammis grabbed my right hand and spread out the fingers. "One, two, three, *four, five*!"

I nodded. "So, you can count to five."

The Drac frowned and made an impatient gesture with its tiny fists. "Look." It took my outstretched hand and placed its own on top of it. With its other hand, Zammis pointed first at one of its own fingers, then at one of mine. "One, one." The child's yellow eyes studied me to see if I understood.

"Yes."

The child pointed again. "Two, two." It looked at me, then looked back at my hand and pointed. "Three, three." Then he grabbed my two remaining fingers. *"Four, Five!"* It dropped my hand, then pointed to the side of its own hand. "Four, five?"

I shook my head. Zammis, at less than four Earth months old, had detected part of the difference between Dracs and humans. A human child would be—what?—five, six or seven years old before asking questions like that. I sighed. "Zammis."

"Yes, Uncle?"

"Zammis, you are a Drac. Dracs only have three fingers on a hand." I held up my right hand and wiggled the fingers. "I'm a human. I have five."

I swear that tears welled in the child's eyes. Zammis held out its hands, looked at them, then shook its head. "Grow four, five?"

I sat up and faced the kid. Zammis was wondering where its other four fingers had gone. "Look, Zammis. You and I are different . . . different kinds of beings, understand?"

Zammis shook his head. "Grow four, five?"

"You won't. You're a Drac." I pointed at my chest. "I'm human." This was getting me nowhere. "Your parent, where you came from was a Drac. Do you understand?"

Zammis frowned. "Drac. What Drac?"

The urge to resort to the timeless standby of "you'll understand when you get older" pounded at the back of my mind. I shook my head. "Dracs have three fingers on each hand. Your parent had three fingers on each hand." I rubbed my beard. "My parent was a human and had five fingers on each hand. That's why I have five fingers on each hand."

Zammis knelt on the sand and studied its fingers. It looked up at me, back to its hands, then back at me. "What parent?"

I studied the kid. It must be having an identity crisis of some kind. I was the only person it had ever seen, and I had five fingers per hand. "A parent is . . . the thing. . . ." I scratched my beard again. "Look . . . we all come from someplace. I had a mother and father—two different kinds of humans—that gave me life, that made me. Understand?" Zammis gave me a look that could be interpreted as "Mac, you are full of it." I shrugged. "I don't know if I can explain it."

Zammis pointed at its own chest. "My mother? My father?"

I held out my hands, dropped them into my lap, pursed my lips, scratched my beard and generally stalled for time. Zammis held an unblinking gaze on me the entire time. "Look, Zammis. You don't have a mother and a father. I'm a human, so I have them; you're a Drac. You have a parent—just one, see?"

Zammis shook its head. It looked at me, then pointed at its own chest. "Drac."

"Right."

Zammis pointed at my chest. "Human."

"Right again."

Zammis removed its hand and dropped it in its lap. "Where Drac come from?"

Sweet Jesus! Trying to explain hermaphroditic reproduction to a kid who shouldn't even be crawling yet? "Zammis. . . ." I held up my hands, then dropped them into my lap. "Look. You see how much bigger I am than you?"

"Yes, Uncle."

"Good." I ran my fingers through my hair, fighting for time and inspiration. "Your parent was big, like me. Its name was . . . Jeriba Shigan." Funny how just saying the name was painful. "Jeriba Shigan was like you. It only had three fingers on each hand. It grew you in its tummy." I poked Zammis' middle. "Understand?"

Zammis giggled and held its hands over its stomach. "Uncle, how Dracs grow there?"

I lifted my legs onto the mattress and stretched out. Where do little Dracs come from? I looked over to Zammis and saw the child hanging upon my every word. I grimaced and told the truth. "Damned if I know, Zammis. Damned if I know." Thirty seconds later, Zammis was back playing with its rocks.

Summer, and I taught Zammis how to capture and skin the long gray snakes, and then how to smoke the meat. The child would squat on the shallow bank above a mudpool, its yellow eyes fixed on the snake holes in the bank, waiting for one of the occupants to poke out its head. The wind would blow, but Zammis wouldn't move. Then a flat, triangular head set with tiny blue eyes would appear. The snake would check the pool, turn and check the bank, then check the sky. It would advance out of the hole a bit, then check it all again. Often the snakes would look directly at Zammis, but the Drac could have been carved from rock. Zammis wouldn't move until the snake was too far out of the hole to pull itself back in tail first. Then Zammis would strike, grabbing the snake with both hands just behind the head. The snakes had no fangs and weren't poisonous, but they were lively enough to toss Zammis into the mudpool on occasion.

The skins were spread and wrapped around tree trunks and pegged in place to dry. The tree trunks were kept in an open place near the entrance to the cave, but under an overhang that faced away from the ocean. About two-thirds of the skins put up in this manner cured; the remaining third would rot.

Beyond the skin room was the smokehouse, a rock-walled chamber that we would hang with rows of snakemeat. A greenwood fire would be set in a pit in the chamber's floor, then we would fill in the small opening with rocks and dirt.

"Uncle, why doesn't the meat rot after it's smoked?"

I thought upon it. "I'm not sure; I just know it doesn't."

"Why do you know?"

I shrugged. "I just do. I read about it probably."

"What's read?"

"Reading. Like when I sit down and read the *Talman*."

"Does the *Talman* say why the meat doesn't rot?"

"No. I meant that I probably read it in another book."

"Do we have more books?"

I shook my head. "I meant before I came to this planet."

"Why did you come to this planet?"

"I told you. Your parent and I were stranded here during the battle."

"Why do the humans and Dracs fight?"

"It's very complicated." I waved my hands about for a bit. The human line was that the Dracs were aggressors invading our space. The Drac line was that the humans were aggressors invading their space. The truth? "Zammis, it has to do with the colonization of new planets. Both races are expanding and both races have a tradition of exploring and colonizing new planets. I guess we just expanded into each other. Understand?"

Zammis nodded, then became mercifully silent as it fell into deep thought. The main thing I learned from the Drac child was all of the questions I didn't have answers to. I was feeling very smug, however, at having gotten Zammis to understand about the war, thereby avoiding my ignorance on the subject of preserving meat. "Uncle?"

"Yes, Zammis?"

"What's a planet?"

As the cold, wet summer came to an end, we had the cave jammed with firewood and preserved food. With that out of the way, I concentrated my efforts on making some kind of indoor plumbing out of the natural pools in the chambers deep within the cave. The bathtup was no problem. By dropping heated rocks into one of the pools, the water could be brought up to a bearable—even comfortable—temperature. After bathing, the hollow stems of a bamboo-like plant could be used to siphon out the dirty water. The tub could then be refilled from the pool above. The problem was where to siphon the water. Several of the chambers had holes in their floors. The first three holes we tried drained into our main chamber, wetting the low edge near the entrance. The previous winter, Jerry and I had considered using one of those holes for a toilet that we would flush with water from the pools. Since we didn't know where the goodies would come out, we decided against it.

The fourth hole Zammis and I tried drained out below the entrance to the cave in the face of the cliff. Not ideal, but better than answering the call of nature in the middle of a combination ice storm and blizzard. We rigged up the hole as a drain for both the tub and toilet. As Zammis and I prepared to enjoy our first hot bath, I removed my snakeskins, tested the water with my toe, then stepped in. "Great!" I turned to Zammis, the child still half-dressed. "Come on in, Zammis. The water's fine." Zammis was staring at me, its mouth hanging open, "What's the matter?"

The child stared wide-eyed, then pointed at me with a three-fingered hand. "Uncle . . . what's that?"

I looked down. "Oh." I shook my head, then looked up at the child. "Zammis, I explained all that, remember? I'm a human."

"But, what's it *for*?"

I sat down in the warm water, removing the object of discussion from sight. "It's for the elimination of liquid wastes . . . among other things. Now, hop in and get washed."

Zammis shucked its snakeskins, looked down at its own smooth-surfaced, combined system, then climbed into the tub. The child settled into the water up to its neck, its yellow eyes studying me. "Uncle?"

"Yes?"

"What *other things*?"

Well, I told Zammis. For the first time, the Drac appeared to be trying to decide whether my response was truthful or not, rather than its usual acceptance of my every assertion. In fact, I was convinced that Zammis thought I was lying—probably because I was.

Winter began with a sprinkle of snowflakes carried on a gentle breeze. I took Zammis above the cave to the scrub forest. I held the child's hand as we stood before the pile of rocks that served as Jerry's grave. Zammis pulled its snakeskins against the wind, bowed its head, then turned and looked up into my face. "Uncle, this is the grave of my parent?"

I nodded. "Yes."

Zammis turned back to the grave, then shook its head. "Uncle, how should I feel?"

"I don't understand, Zammis."

The child nodded at the grave. "I can see that you are sad being here. I think you want me to feel the same. Do you?"

I frowned, then shook my head. "No. I don't want you to be sad. I just wanted you to know where it is."

"May I go now?"

"Sure. Are you certain you know the way back to the cave?"

"Yes. I just want to make sure my soap doesn't burn again."

I watched as the child turned and scurried off into the naked trees, then I turned back to the grave. "Well, Jerry, what do you think of your kid? Zammis was using wood ashes to clean the grease off the shells, then it put a shell back on the fire and put water in it to boil off the burnt-on food. Fat and ashes. The next thing, Jerry, we were making soap. Zammis' first batch almost took the hide off us, but the kid's getting better. . . ."

I looked up at the clouds, then brought my glance down to the sea. In the distance, low, dark clouds were building up. "See that? You know what that means, don't you? Ice storm number one." The wind picked up and I squatted next to the grave to replace a rock that had rolled from the pile. "Zammis is a good kid, Jerry. I wanted to hate it . . . after you died. I wanted to hate it." I replaced the rock, then looked back toward the sea.

"I don't know how we're going to make it off planet, Jerry." I caught a flash of movement out of the corner of my vision. I turned to the right and looked over the tops of the trees. Against the gray sky, a black speck streaked away. I followed it with my eyes until it went above the clouds.

I listened, hoping to hear an exhaust roar, but my heart was pounding so hard all I could hear was the wind. Was it a ship? I stood, took a few steps in the direction the speck was going, then stopped. Turning my head, I saw that the rocks on Jerry's grave were already capped with thin layers of fine snow. I shrugged and headed for the cave. "Probably just a bird."

Zammis sat on its mattress, stabbing several pieces of snakeskin with a bone needle. I stretched out on my own mattress and watched the smoke curl up toward the crack in the ceiling. Was it a bird? Or was it a ship? Damn, but it worked on me. Escape from the planet had been out of my thoughts, had been buried, hidden for all that summer. But again, it twisted at me. To walk where a sun shined, to wear cloth again, experience central heating, eat food prepared by a chef, to be among . . . people again.

I rolled over on my right side and stared at the wall next to my mattress. People. Human people. I closed my eyes and swallowed. Girl human people. Female persons. Images drifted before my eyes—faces, bodies, laughing couples, the dance after flight training. . . . What was her name? Dolora? Dora?

I shook my head, rolled over and sat up, facing the fire. Why did I have to see whatever it was? All those things I had been able to bury—to forget—boiling over.

"Uncle?"

I looked up at Zammis. Yellow skin, yellow eyes, noseless toadface. I shook my head. "What?"

"Is something wrong?"

Is something wrong, hah. "No. I just thought I saw something today. It probably wasn't anything." I reached to the fire and took a piece of dried snake from the griddle. I blew on it, then gnawed on the stringy strip.

"What did it look like?"

"I don't know. The way it moved, I thought it might be a ship. It went away so fast, I couldn't be sure. Might have been a bird."

"Bird?"

I studied Zammis. It'd never seen a bird; neither had I on Fyrine IV. "An animal that flies."

Zammis nodded. "Uncle, when we were gathering wood up in the scrub forest, I saw something fly."

"What? Why didn't you tell me?"

"I meant to, but I forgot."

"Forgot!" I frowned. "In which direction was it going?"

Zammis pointed to the back of the cave. "That way. Away from the sea." Zammis put down its sewing. "Can we go see where it went?"

I shook my head. "The winter is just beginning. You don't know what it's like. We'd die in only a few days."

Zammis went back to poking holes in the snakeskin. The winter would kill us. But spring would be something else. We could survive with double-layered snakeskins stuffed with seed-pod down, and a tent. We had to have a tent. Zammis and I could spend the winter making it, and packs. Boots. We'd need sturdy walking boots. Have to think on that. . . .

It's strange how a spark of hope can ignite, and spread, until all desperation is consumed. Was it a ship? I didn't know. If it was, was it taking off, or landing? I didn't know. If it was taking off, we'd be heading in the wrong direction. But, the opposite direction meant crossing the sea. Whatever. Come spring we would head beyond the scrub forest and see what was there.

The winter seemed to pass quickly, with Zammis occupied with the tent and my time devoted to rediscovering the art of boot-making. I made tracings of both of our feet on snakeskin, and after some experimentation I found that boiling the snake leather with plumfruit made it soft and gummy. By taking several of the gummy layers, weighting them, then setting them aside to dry. the result was a tough, flexible sole. By the time I finished Zammis' boots, the Drac needed a new pair.

"They're too small, Uncle."

"Waddaya mean, too small?"

Zammis pointed down. "They hurt. My toes are all crippled up."

I squatted down and felt the tops over the child's toes. "I don't understand. It's only been twenty, twenty-five days since I made the tracings. You sure you didn't move when I made them?"

Zammis shook its head. "I didn't move."

I frowned, then stood. "Stand up, Zammis." The Drac stood and I moved next to it. The top of Zammis' head came to the middle of my chest. Another sixty centimeters and it'd be as tall as Jerry. "Take them off, Zammis. I'll make a bigger pair. Try not to grow so fast."

Zammis pitched the tent inside the cave, put glowing coals inside, then rubbed fat into the leather to waterproof it. It had grown taller, and I had held off making the Drac's boots until I could be sure of the size it would need. I tried to do a projection by measuring Zammis' feet every ten days, then extending the curve into spring. According to my fingers, the kid would have been resembling a pair of attack transports by the time the snow melted. By spring, Zammis would be full-grown. Jerry's old flight boots had fallen apart before Zammis had been born, but I had saved the pieces. I used the soles to make my tracings and hoped for the best.

I was busy with the new boots and Zammis was keeping an eye on the tent treatment. The Drac looked back at me.

"Uncle?"

"What?"

"Existence is the first given?"

I shrugged. "That's what Shizumaat says; I'll buy it."

"But, Uncle, how do we *know* that existence is real?"

I lowered my work, looked at Zammis, shook my head, then resumed stitching the boots. "Take my word for it."

The Drac grimaced. "But, Uncle, that is not knowledge; that is faith."

I sighed, thinking back to my sophomore year at the University of Nations—a bunch of adolescents lounging around a cheap flat experimenting with booze, powders and philosophy. At a little more than one Earth year old, Zammis was developing into an intellectual bore. "So, what's wrong with faith?"

Zammis snickered. "Come now, Uncle. *Faith*?"

"It helps some of us along this drizzle-soaked coil."

"Coil?"

I scratched my head. "This mortal coil; life. Shakespeare, I think."

Zammis frowned. "It is not in the *Talman*."

"He, not it. Shakespeare was a human."

Zammis stood, walked to the fire and sat across from me. "Was he a philosopher, like Mistan or Shizumaat?"

"No. He wrote plays—like stories, acted out."

Zammis rubbed its chin. "Do you remember any of Shakespeare?"

I held up a finger. "'To be, or not to be; that is the question.'"

The Drac's mouth dropped open, then it nodded its head. "Yes. Yes! To be or not to be; that *is* the question!" Zammis held out its hands. "How do we *know* the wind blows outside the cave when we are not there to see it? Does the sea still boil if we are not there to feel it?"

I nodded. "Yes."

"But, Uncle, how do we *know*?"

I squinted at the Drac. "Zammis, I have a question for you. Is the following statement true or false?: What I am saying right now is false."

Zammis blinked. "If it is false, then the statement is true. But . . . if it's true . . . the statement is false, but. . . ." Zammis blinked again, then turned and went back to rubbing fat into the tent. "I'll think upon it, Uncle."

"You do that, Zammis."

The Drac thought upon it for about ten minutes, then turned back. "The statement is false."

I smiled. "But that's what the statement said, hence it is true, but. . . ." I let the puzzle trail off. Oh, smugness, thou temptest even saints.

"No, Uncle. The statement is meaningless in its present context." I shrugged. "You see, Uncle, the statement assumes the existence of truth values that can comment upon themselves devoid of any other reference. I think Lurrvena's logic in the *Talman* is clear on this, and if meaninglessness is equated with falsehood. . . ."

I sighed. ''Yeah, well—''

''You see, Uncle, you must, first, establish a context in which your statement has meaning.''

I leaned forward, frowned and scratched my beard. ''I see. You mean I was putting Descartes before the horse?''

Zammis looked at me strangely, and even more so when I collapsed on my mattress cackling like a fool.

''Uncle, why does the line of Jeriba have only five names? You say that human lines have many names.''

I nodded. ''The five names of the Jeriba line are things to which their bearers must add deeds. The deeds are important—not the names.''

''Gothig is Shigan's parent as Shigan is my parent.''

''Of course. You know that from your recitations.''

Zammis frowned. ''Then, I *must* name my child Ty when I become a parent?''

''Yes. And Ty must name its child Haesni. Do you see something wrong with that?''

''I would like to name my child Davidge, after you.''

I smiled and shook my head. ''The Ty name has been served by great bankers, merchants, inventors and—well, you know your recitation. The name Davidge hasn't been served by much. Think of what Ty would miss by not being Ty.''

Zammis thought awhile, then nodded. ''Uncle, do you think Gothig is alive?''

''As far as I know.''

''What is Gothig like?''

I thought back to Jerry talking about its parent, Gothig. ''It taught music, and is very strong. Jerry . . . Shigan said that its parent could bend metal bars with its fingers. Gothig is also very dignified. I imagine that right now Gothig is also very sad. Gothig must think that the line of Jeriba has ended.''

Zammis frowned and its yellow brow furrowed. ''Uncle, we must make it to Draco. We must tell Gothig the line continues.''

''We will.''

The winter's ice began thinning, and boots, tent and packs were ready. We were putting the finishing touches on our new insulated suits. As Jerry had given the *Talman* to me to learn, the golden cube now hung around Zammis' neck. The Drac would drop the tiny golden book from the cube and study it for hours at a time.

''Uncle?''

''What?''

''Why do Dracs speak and write in one language and the humans in another?''

I laughed. ''Zammis, the humans speak and write in many languages. English is just one of them.''

"How do the humans speak among themselves?"

I shrugged. "They don't always; when they do, they use interpreters—people who can speak both languages."

"You and I speak both English and Drac; does that make us interpreters?"

"I suppose we could be, if you could ever find a human and a Drac who want to talk to each other. Remember, there's a war going on."

"How will the war stop if they do not talk?"

"I suppose they will talk, eventually."

Zammis smiled. "I think I would like to be an interpreter and help end the war." The Drac put its sewing aside and stretched out on its new mattress. Zammis had outgrown even its old mattress, which it now used for a pillow. "Uncle, do you think that we will find anybody beyond the scrub forest?"

"I hope so."

"If we do, will you go with me to Draco?"

"I promised your parent that I would."

"I mean after. After I make my recitation, what will you do?"

I stared at the fire. "I don't know." I shrugged. "The war might keep us from getting to Draco for a long time."

"After that, what?"

"I suppose I'll go back into the service."

Zammis propped itself up on an elbow. "Go back to being a fighter pilot?"

"Sure. That's about all I know how to do."

"And kill Dracs?"

I put my own sewing down and studied the Drac. Things had changed since Jerry and I had slugged it out—more things than I had realized. I shook my head. "No. I probably won't be a pilot—not a service one. Maybe I can land a job flying commercial ships." I shrugged. "Maybe the service won't give me any choice."

Zammis sat up, was still for a moment, then it stood, walked over to my mattress and knelt before me on the sand. "Uncle, I don't want to leave you."

"Don't be silly. You'll have your own kind around you. Your grandparent, Gothig, Shigan's siblings, their children—you'll forget all about me."

"Will you forget about me?"

I looked into those yellow eyes, then reached out my hand and touched Zammis' cheek. "No. I won't forget about you. But remember this, Zammis: you're a Drac and I'm a human, and that's how this part of the universe is divided."

Zammis took my hand from his cheek, spread the fingers and studied them. "Whatever happens, Uncle, I will never forget you."

The ice was gone, and the Drac and I stood in the windblown drizzle, packs on our backs, before the grave. Zammis was as tall as I was, which made it a little taller than Jerry. To my relief, the boots fit. Zammis hefted its pack up higher on its shoulders, then turned from the grave and looked out at the sea. I followed Zammis' glance and watched the rollers steam in and smash on the rocks. I looked at the Drac. "What are you thinking about?"

Zammis looked down, then turned toward me. "Uncle, I didn't think of it before, but . . . I will miss this place."

I laughed. "Nonsense! This place?" I slapped the Drac on the shoulder. "Why would you miss this place?"

Zammis looked back out to sea. "I have learned many things here. You have taught me many things here, Uncle. My life happened here."

"Only the beginning, Zammis. You have a life ahead of you." I nodded my head at the grave. "Say good-bye."

Zammis turned toward the grave, stood over it, then knelt to one side and began removing the rocks. After a few moments, it had exposed the hand of a skeleton with three fingers. Zammis nodded, then wept. "I am sorry, Uncle, but I had to do that. This has been nothing but a pile of rocks to me. Now it is more." Zammis replaced the rocks, then stood.

I cocked my head toward the scrub forest. "Go on ahead. I'll catch up in a minute."

"Yes, Uncle."

Zammis moved off toward the naked trees, and I looked down at the grave. "What do you think of Zammis, Jerry? It's bigger than you were. I guess snake agrees with the kid." I squatted next to the grave, picked up a small rock and added it to the pile. "I guess this is it. We're either going to make it to Draco, or die trying." I stood and looked at the sea. "Yeah, I guess I learned a few things here. I'll miss it, in a way." I turned back to the grave and hefted my pack up. "*Ehdevva sahn, Jeriba Shigan*. So long, Jerry."

I turned and followed Zammis into the forest.

The days that followed were full of wonder for Zammis. For me, the sky was still the same, dull gray, and the few variations in plant and animal life that we found were nothing remarkable. Once we got beyond the scrub forest, we climbed a gentle rise for a day, and then found ourselves on a wide, flat, endless plain. It was ankle deep in a purple weed that stained our boots the same color. The nights were still too cold for hiking, and we would hole up in the tent. Both the greased tent and suits worked well, keeping out the almost constant rain.

We had been out perhaps two of Fyrine IV's long weeks, when we saw it. It screamed overhead, then disappeared over the horizon before either of us could say a word. I had no doubt that the craft I had seen was in landing attitude.

"Uncle! Did it see us?"

I shook my head. "No. I doubt it. But it was landing. Do you hear? It was landing somewhere ahead."

"Uncle?"

"Let's get moving! What is it?"

"Was it a Drac ship, or a human ship?"

I cooled in my tracks. I had never stopped to think about it. I waved my hand. "Come on. It doesn't matter. Either way, you go to Draco. You're a noncombatant, so the USE forces couldn't do anything, and if they're Dracs you're home free."

We began walking. "But, Uncle, if it's a Drac ship what will happen to you?"

I shrugged. "Prisoner of war. The Dracs say they abide by the interplanetary war accords, so I should be all right." *Fat chance,* said the back of my head to the front of my head. The big question was whether I preferred being a Drac POW or a permanent resident of Fyrine IV. I had figured out that long ago. "Come on, let's pick up the pace. We don't know how long it will take to get there, or how long it will be on the ground."

Pick 'em up; put 'em down. Except for a few breaks, we didn't stop—even when night came. Our exertion kept us warm. The horizon never seemed to grow nearer. The longer we slogged at it, the duller my mind grew. It must have been days, my mind as numb as my feet, when I fell through the purple weed into a hole. Immediately, everything grew dark, and I felt a pain in my right leg. I felt the blackout coming, and I welcomed its warmth, its rest, its peace.

"Uncle? Uncle? Wake up! Please wake up!"

I felt slapping against my face, although my face was somehow detached. Agony thundered into my brain, bringing me wide awake. Damned if I didn't break my leg. I looked up and saw the weedy edges of the hole. My rear end was seated in a trickle of water. Zammis squatted next to me. "What happened?"

Zammis nodded up. "This hole was only covered by a thin crust of dirt and plants. The water must have taken the ground away. Are you all right?"

"My leg. I think I broke it." I leaned my back against the muddy wall. "Zammis, you're going to have to go on by yourself."

"I can't leave you, Uncle!"

"Look, if you find anyone, you can send them back for me."

"What if the water in here comes up?" Zammis felt along my leg until I winced. "I must carry you out of here. What must I do for the leg?"

The kid had a point. Drowning wasn't in my schedule. "We need something stiff. Bind the leg so it doesn't move."

Zammis pulled off its pack, and kneeling in the water and mud the Drac went through its pack, then through the tent roll. Using the tent poles, he wrapped my leg with snakeskins torn from the tent. Then, using more snakeskins, Zammis made two loops, slipped one over each of my legs, then propped me up and slipped the loops over its shoulders. It lifted, and I blacked out.

On the ground, covered with the remains of the tent, Zammis shaking my arm. "Uncle? Uncle?"

"Yes?" I whispered.

"Uncle, I'm ready to go." I pointed to my side. "Your food is here, and when it rains just pull the tent over your face. I'll mark the trail I make so I can find my way back."

I nodded. "Take care of yourself."

Zammis shook its head. "Uncle, I can carry you. We shouldn't separate."

I weakly shook my head. "Give me a break, kid. I couldn't make it. Find somebody and bring 'em back." I felt my stomach flip, and cold sweat drenched my snakeskins. "Go on; get going."

Zammis reached out, grabbed its pack and stood. The pack shouldered, Zammis turned and began running in the direction that the craft had been going. I watched until I couldn't see it. I faced up and looked at the clouds. "You almost got me that time, you *kizlode* sonofabitch, but you didn't figure on the Drac. . . . You keep forgetting . . . there's two of us. . . ." I drifted in and out of consciousness, felt rain on my face, then pulled up the tent and covered my head. In seconds, the blackout returned.

"Davidge? Lieutenant Davidge?"

I opened my eyes and saw something I hadn't seen for four Earth years: a human face. "Who are you?"

The face, young, long and capped by short blond hair, smiled. "I'm Captain Steerman, the medical officer. How do you feel?"

I pondered the question and smiled. "Like I've been shot full of very high-grade junk."

"You have. You were in pretty bad shape by the time the survey team brought you in."

"Survey team?"

"I guess you don't know. The United States of Earth and the Dracon Chamber have established a joint commission to supervise the colonization of new planets. The war is over."

"Over?"

"Yes."

Something heavy lifted from chest. "Where's Zammis?"

"Who?"

"Jeriba Zammis; the Drac that I was with."

The doctor shrugged. "I don't know anything about it, but I suppose the Draggers are taking care of it."

Draggers. I'd once used the term myself. As I listened to it coming out of Steerman's mouth, it seemed foreign, alien, repulsive. "Zammis is a Drac, not a Dragger."

The doctor's brows furrowed, then he shrugged. "Of course. Whatever you say. Just you get some rest, and I'll check back on you in a few hours."

"May I see Zammis?"

The doctor smiled. "Dear, no. You're on your way back to the Delphi USEB. The . . . Drac is probably on its way to Draco." He nodded, then turned and left. God, I felt lost. I looked around and saw that I was in the ward of a ship's sick bay. The beds on either side of me were occupied. The man on my right shook his head and went back to reading a magazine. The one on my left looked angry.

"You damned dragger suck!" He turned on his left side and presented me his back.

Alien Earth. As I stepped down the ramp onto the USE field in Orleans, those were the first two words that popped into my head. Alien Earth. I looked at the crowds of USE Force personnel bustling around like so many ants, inhaled the smell of industrial man, then spat on the ramp.

"How you like, put in stockade time?"

I looked down and saw a white-capped Force Police private glaring up at me. I continued down the ramp. "Get bent."

"*Quoi?*" The FP marched over and met me at the end of the ramp.

"Get bent." I pulled my discharge papers from my breast pocket and waved them. "*Gavey* shorttimer, *kizlode*?"

The FP took my papers, frowned at them, then pointed at a long, low building at the edge of the field. "*Continuez tout droit.*"

I smiled, turned and headed across the field, thinking of Zammis asking about how humans talk together. And where was Zammis? I shook my head, then entered the building. Most of the poeple inside the low building were crowding the in-processing or transportation-exchange aisles. I saw two bored officials behind two long tables and figured that they were the local customs clerks. A multilingual sign above their stations confirmed the hunch. I stopped in front of one of them. She glanced up at me, then held out her hand. "*Vôtre passeport?*"

I pulled out the blue and white booklet, handed it over, then stood holding my hands as I waited. I could feel the muscles at the back of my neck knot as I observed an old anti-Drac propaganda poster on the wall behind her. It showed two yellow, clawed hands holding a miniature Earth before a fanged mouth. Fangs and claws. The caption read: "They would call this victory" in seven languages.

"*Avez-vous quelque chose à déclarer?*"

I frowned at her. "*Ess?*"

She frowned back. "*Avez-vous quelque chose à déclarer?*"

I felt a tap on my back. "Do you speak English?"

I turned and saw the other customs clerk. My upper lip curled. "*Surda; ne surda. Adze Dracon?*"

His eyebrows went up as he mouthed the word "Drac." He turned to the other clerk, took my passport from her, then looked back at me. He tapped the booklet against his fingertips, then opened it, read the ident page, and looked back at me. "Come with me, Mister Davidge. We must have a talk.'' He turned and headed into a small office. I shrugged and followed. When I entered, he pointed toward a chair. As I lowered myself into it, he sat down behind a desk. ''Why do you pretend not to speak English?''

''Why do you have that poster on the wall? The war is over.''

The customs clerk clasped his hands, rested them on the desk, then shook his head. ''The fighting is over, Mister Davidge, but for many the war is not. The Draggers killed many humans.''

I cocked my head to one side. ''A few Dracs died, too.'' I stood up. ''May I go now?''

The customs clerk leaned back in his chair. ''That chip on your shoulder you will find to be a considerable weight to bear on this planet.''

''I'm the one who has to carry it.''

The customs clerk shrugged, then nodded toward the door. ''You may go. And good luck, Mister Davidge. You'll need it.''

''Dragger suck.'' As an invective the term had all the impact of several historical terms—Quisling, heretic, fag, nigger-lover, all rolled into one. Ex-Force pilots were a drag on the employment market, with no commercial positions open, especially not to a pilot who hadn't flown in four years, who had a gimpy leg, and who was a Dragger suck. Transportation to North America, and after a period of lonely wandering, to Dallas. Mistan's eight-hundred-year-old words from the *Talman* would haunt me: *Misnurram va siddeth*; Your thought is loneliness. Loneliness is a thing one does to oneself. *Jerry shook his head that one time, then pointed a yellow finger at me as the words it wanted to say came together. ''Davidge . . . to me loneliness is a discomfort—unpleasant, and a thing to be avoided, but not a thing to be feared. I think you would prefer death to being alone with yourself.''*

Mistan observed: ''If you are alone with yourself, you will forever be alone with others.'' A contradiction? The test of reality proves it true. I was out of place on my own planet, and it was more than a hate that I didn't share or a love that, to others, seemed impossible—perverse. Deep inside of myself, I had no use for the creature called ''Davidge.'' Before Fyrine IV there had been other reasons—reasons that I could not identify; but now, my reason was known. My fault or not, I had betrayed an ugly, yellow thing called Zammis, as well as the creature's parent. *''Present Zammis before the Jeriba archives. Swear this to me.''*

Oh, Jerry. . . .

Swear this!

I swear it. . . .

I had forty-eight thousand credits in back pay, and so money wasn't a problem. The problem was what to do with myself. Finally, in Dallas, I landed a job in a small book house translating manuscripts into Drac. It seemed that there was a craving among Dracs for westerns: ''Stick 'em up, *naagusaat*!''

"*Nu geph*, lawman!" Thang! Thang! The guns flashed and another *kizlode shaddsaat* bit the dust.

I quit.

I finally called my parents. *Why didn't you call before, Willy? We've been worried sick. . . . Had a few things I had to straighten out, Dad. . . . No, not really. . . . Well, we understand, son . . . it must have been awful. . . . Dad, I'd like to come home for awhile. . . .*

Even before I put down the money on the used Dearman Electric, I knew I was making a mistake going home. I felt the need of a home, but the one I had left at the age of eighteen wasn't it. But, I headed there because there was nowhere else to go.

I drove alone in the dark, using only the old roads, the quiet hum of the Dearman's motor the only sound. The December midnight was clear, and I could see the stars through the car's bubble canopy. Fyrine IV drifted into my thoughts, the raging ocean, the endless winds. I pulled off the road onto the shoulder and killed the lights. In a few minutes, my eyes adjusted to the dark and I stepped outside and shut the door. Kansas has a big sky, and the stars seemed close enough to touch. Snow crunched under my feet as I looked up, trying to pick Fyrine out of the thousands of visible stars.

Fyrine is in the constellation Pegasus, but my eyes were not practiced enough to pick the winged horse out from the surrounding stars. I shrugged, felt a chill, and decided to get back in the car. As I put my hand on the doorlatch, I saw a constellation that I did recognize, north, hanging just above the horizon: Draco. The Dragon, its tail twisted around Ursa Minor, hung upside down in the sky. Eltanin, the Dragon's nose, is the homestar of the Dracs. Its second planet, Draco, was Zammis' home.

Headlights from an approaching car blinded me, and I turned toward the car as it pulled to a stop. The window on the driver's side opened and someone spoke from the darkness.

"You need some help?"

I shook my head. "No, thank you." I held up a hand. "I was just looking at the stars."

"Quite a night, isn't it?"

"Sure is."

"Sure you don't need any help?"

I shook my head. "Thanks. . . . Wait. Where is the nearest commercial spaceport?"

"About an hour ahead in Salina."

"Thanks." I saw a hand wave from the window, then the other car pulled away. I took another look at Eltanin, then got back in my car.

Nine weeks later I stood before the little gray man who ran Lone Star Publishing, Inc. He looked up at me and frowned. "So, what do you want? I thought you quit."

I threw a thousand-page manuscript on his desk. "This."

He poked it with a finger. "What is it?"

"The Drac bible; it's called the *Talman*."

"So what?"

"So it's the only book translated from Drac into English; so it's the explanation for how every Drac conducts itself; so it'll make you a bundle of credits."

He leaned forward, scanned several pages, then looked up at me. "You know, Davidge, I don't like you worth a damn."

I shrugged. "I don't like you either."

He returned to the manuscript. "Why now?"

"Now is when I need money."

He shrugged. "The best I can offer would be around eight or ten thousand. This is untried stuff."

"I need twenty-four thousand. You want to go for less than that, I'll take it to someone else."

He looked at me and frowned. "What makes you think that anyone else would be interested?"

"Let's quit playing around. There are a lot of survivors of the war—both military and civilian—who would like to understand what happened." I leaned forward and tapped the manuscript. "That's what's in there."

"Twenty-four thousand is a lot for a first manuscript."

I gathered up the pages. "I'll find someone who has some coin to invest in a sure thing."

He placed his hand on the manuscript. "Hold on, Davidge." He frowned. "Twenty-four thousand?"

"Not a quarter-note less."

He pursed his lips, then glanced at me. "I suppose you'll be Hell on wheels regarding final approval."

I shook my head. "All I want is the money. You can do whatever you want with the manuscript."

He leaned back in his chair, looked at the manuscript, then back at me. "The money. What're you going to do with it?"

"None of your business."

He leaned forward, then leafed through a few more pages. His eyebrows notched up, then he looked back at me. "You aren't picky about the contract?"

"As long as I get the money, you can turn that into *Mein Kampf* if you want to."

He leafed through a few more pages. "This is some pretty radical stuff."

"It sure is. And you can find the same stuff in Plato, Aristotle, Augustine, James, Freud, Szasz, Nortmyer, and the Declaration of Independence."

He leaned back in his chair. "What does this mean to you?"

"Twenty-four thousand credits."

He leafed through a few more pages, then a few more. In twelve hours I had purchased passage to Draco.

Six months later, I stood in front of an ancient cut-stone gate wondering what in the Hell I was doing. The trip to Draco, with nothing but Dracs as companions on the last leg, showed me the truth in Namvaac's words: "Peace is often only war without fighting." The accords, on paper, gave me the right to travel to the planet, but the Drac bureaucrats and their paperwork wizards had perfected the big stall long before the first human step into space. It took threats, bribes, and long days of filling out forms, being checked, and rechecked for disease, contraband, reason for visit, filling out more forms, refilling out the forms I had already filled out, more bribes, waiting, waiting, waiting. . . .

On the ship, I spent most of my time in my cabin, but since the Drac stewards refused to serve me, I went to the ship's lounge for my meals. I sat alone, listening to the comments about me from other booths. I figured the path of least resistance was to pretend I didn't understand what they were saying. It is always assumed that humans do not speak Drac.

"Must we eat in the same compartment with the *Ikrmaan* slime?"

"Look at it, how its pale skin blotches—and that evil-smelling thatch on top. Feh! The smell!"

I would grind my teeth a little and keep my glance riveted to my plate.

"It defies the *Talman* that the universe's laws could be so corrupt as to produce a creature such as that."

I turned and faced the three Dracs sitting in the booth across the aisle from mine. In Drac, I replied: "If your line's elders had seen fit to teach the village *kiz* to use contraceptives, you wouldn't even exist." I returned to my food while the two Dracs struggled to hold the third Drac down.

On Draco, it was no problem finding the Jeriba estate. The problem was getting in. A high stone wall enclosed the property, and from the gate I could see the huge stone mansion that Jerry had described to me. I told the guard at the gate that I wanted to see Jeriba Zammis. The guard stared at me, then went into an alcove behind the gate. In a few moments, another Drac emerged from the mansion and walked quickly across the wide lawn to the gate. The Drac nodded at the guard, then stopped and faced me. It was a dead ringer for Jerry.

"You are the *Irkmaan* that asked to see Jeriba Zammis?"

I nodded. "Yes. Zammis must have told you about me. I'm Willis Davidge."

The Drac studied me. "I am Estone Nev, Jeriba Shigan's sibling. My parent, Jeriba Gothig, wishes to see you." The Drac turned abruptly and walked back to the mansion. I followed, feeling heady at the thought of seeing Zammis again. I paid little attention to my surroundings until I was ushered into a large room with a vaulted stone ceiling. Jerry had told me that the house was four thousand years old. I believed it. As I entered, another Drac stood and walked over to me. It was old, but I knew who it was.

"You are Gothig, Shigan's parent."

The yellow eyes studied me. "Who are you, *Irkmaan*?" It held out a wrinkled, three-fingered hand. "What do you know of Jeriba Zammis, and why do you speak the Drac tongue with the style and accent of my child Shigan? What are you here for?"

"I speak Drac in this manner because that is the way Jeriban Shigan taught me to speak it."

The old Drac cocked its head to one side and narrowed its yellow eyes. "You knew my child? How?"

"Didn't the survey commission tell you?"

"It was reported to me that my child, Shigan, was killed in the battle of Fyrine IV. That was over six of our years ago. What is your game, *Irkmaan*?"

I turned from Gothig to Nev. The younger Drac was examining me with the same look of suspicion. I turned back to Gothig. "Shigan wasn't killed in the battle. We were stranded together on the surface of Fyrine IV and lived there for a year. Shigan died giving birth to Jeriba Zammis. A year later the joint survey commission found us and—"

"Enough! Enough of this, *Irkmaan*! Are you here for money, to use my influence for trade concessions—what?"

I frowned. "Where is Zammis?"

Tears of anger came to the old Drac's eyes. "There is no Zammis, *Ikrmaan*! The Jeriban line ended with the death of Shigan!"

My eyes grew wide as I shook my head. "That's not true. I know. I took care of Zammis—you heard nothing from the commission?"

"Get to the point of your scheme, *Irkmaan*. I haven't all day."

I studied Gothig. The old Drac had heard nothing from the commission. The Drac authorities took Zammis, and the child had evaporated. Gothig had been told nothing. Why? "I was with Shigan, Gothig. That is how I learned your language. When Shigan died giving birth to Zammis, I—"

"*Irkmaan*, if you cannot get to your scheme, I will have to ask Nev to throw you out. Shigan died in the battle of Fyrine IV. The Drac Fleet notified us only days later."

I nodded. "Then, Gothig, tell me how I came to know the line of Jeriba? Do you wish me to recite it for you?"

Gothig snorted. "You say you know the Jeriba line?"

"Yes."

Gothig flipped a hand at me. "Then recite."

I took a breath, then began. By the time I had reached the hundred and seventy-third generation, Gothig had knelt on the stone floor next to Nev. The Dracs remained that way for the three hours of the recital. When I concluded, Gothig bowed its head and wept. "Yes, *Irkmaan*, yes. You must have known Shigan. Yes." The old Drac looked up into my face, its eyes wide with hope. "And, you say Shigan continued the line—that Zammis was born?"

I nodded. "I don't know why the commission didn't notify you."

Gothig got to its feet and frowned. "We will find out, *Irkmaan*—what is your name?"

"Davidge. Willis Davidge."

"We will find out, Davidge."

Gothig arranged quarters for me in its house, which was fortunate, since I had little more than eleven hundred credits left. After making a host of inquiries, Gothig sent Nev and I to the Chamber Center in Sendievu, Draco's capital city. The Jeriba line, I found, was influential, and the big stall was held down to a minimum. Eventually, we were directed to the Joint Survey Commission representative, a Drac named Jozzdn Vrule. It looked up from the letter Gothig had given me and frowned. "Where did you get this, *Irkmaan*?"

"I believe the signature is on it."

The Drac looked at the paper, then back at me. "The Jeriba line is one of the most respected on Draco. You say that Jeriba Gothig gave you this?"

"I felt certain I said that; I could feel my lips moving—"

Nev stepped in. "You have the dates and the information concerning the Fyrine IV survey mission. We want to know what happed to Jeriba Zammis."

Jozzdn Vrule frowned and looked back at the paper. "Estone Nev, you are the founder of your line, is this not true?"

"It is true."

"Would you found your line in shame? Why do I see you with this *Irkmaan*?"

Nev curled its upper lip and folded its arms. "Jozzdn Vrule, if you contemplate walking this planet in the forseeable future as a free being, it would be to your profit to stop working your mouth and to start finding Jeriba Zammis."

Jozzdn Vrule looked down and studied its fingers, then returned its glance to Nev. "Very well, Estone Nev. You threaten me if I fail to hand you the truth. I think you will find the truth the greater threat." The Drac scribbled on a piece of paper, then handed it to Nev. "You will find Jeriba Zammis at this address, and you will curse the day that I gave you this."

We entered the retard colony feeling sick. All around us, Dracs stared with vacant eyes, or screamed, or foamed at the mouth, or behaved as lower-order creatures. After we had arrived, Gothig joined us. The Drac director of the colony frowned at me and shook its head at Gothig. "Turn back now, while it is still possible, Jeriba Gothig. Beyond this room lies nothing but pain and sorrow."

Gothig grabbed the director by the front of its wraps. "Hear me, insect: If Jeriba Zammis is within these walls, bring my grandchild forth! Else, I shall bring the might of the Jeriban line down upon your pointed head!"

The director lifted its head, twitched its lips, then nodded. "Very well. Very well, you pompous *Kazzmidth*! We tried to protect the Jeriba reputation. We tried! But now you shall see." The director nodded and pursed its lips. "Yes, you overwealthy fashion follower, now you shall see." The director scribbled on a piece of paper, then handed it to Nev. "By giving you that, I will lose my position, but take it! Yes, take it! See this being you call Jeriba Zammis. See it, and weep!"

Among trees and grass, Jeriba Zammis sat upon a stone bench, staring at the ground. Its eyes never blinked, its hands never moved. Gothig frowned at me, but I could spare nothing for Shigan's parent. I walked to Zammis. "Zammis, do you know me?"

The Drac retrieved its thoughts from a million warrens and raised its yellow eyes to me. I saw no sign of recognition. "Who are you?"

I squatted down, placed my hands on its arms and shook them. "Damn it, Zammis, don't you know me? I'm your Uncle. Remember that? Uncle Davidge?"

The Drac weaved on the bench, then shook its head. It lifted an arm and waved to an orderly. "I want to go to my room. Please, let me go to my room."

I stood and grabbed Zammis by the front of its hospital gown. "Zammis, it's me!"

The yellow eyes, dull and lifeless, stared back at me. The orderly placed a yellow hand upon my shoulder. "Let it go, *Irkmaan*."

"Zammis!" I turned to Nev and Gothig. "Say something!"

The Drac orderly pulled a sap from its pocket, then slapped it suggestively against the palm of its hand. "Let it go, *Irkmaan*."

Gothig stepped forward. "Explain this!"

The orderly looked at Gothig, Nev, me, and then Zammis. "This one—this creature—came to us professing a love, a *love*, mind you, of humans! This is no small perversion, Jeriba Gothig. The government would protect you from this scandal. Would you wish the line of Jeriba dragged into this?"

I looked at Zammis. "What have you done to Zammis, you *kizlode* sonofabitch? A little shock? A little drug? Rot out its mind?"

The orderly sneered at me, then shook its head. "You, *Irkmaan*, do not understand. This one would not be happy as an *Irkmaan vul*—a human lover. We are making it possible for this one to function in Drac society. You think this is wrong?"

I looked at Zammis and shook my head. I remembered too well my treatment at the hands of my fellow humans. "No. I don't think it's wrong . . . I just don't know."

The orderly turned to Gothig. "Please understand, Jeriba Gothig. We could not subject the Jeriba line to this disgrace. Your grandchild is almost well and will soon enter a reeducation program. In no more than two years, you will have a grandchild worthy of carrying on the Jeriba line. Is this wrong?"

Gothig only shook its head. I squatted down in front of Zammis and looked up into its yellow eyes. I reached up and took its right hand in both of mine. "Zammis?"

Zammis looked down, moved its left hand over and picked up my left hand and spread the fingers. One at a time Zammis pointed at the fingers of my hand, then it looked into my eyes, then examined the hand again. "Yes. . . ." Zammis pointed again. "One, two, three, *four, five*!" Zammis looked into my eyes. "Four, five!"

I nodded. "Yes. Yes."

Zammis pulled my hand to its cheek and held it close. "Uncle . . . Uncle. I told you I'd never forget you."

I never counted the years that passed. Mistaan had words for those who count time as though their recognition of its passing marked their place in the Universe. Mornings, the weather as clear as weather gets on Fyrine IV, I would visit my friend's grave. Next to it, Estone Nev, Zammis, Ty and I buried Gothig. Shigan's parent had taken the healing Zammis, liquidated the Jeriba line's estate, then moved the whole shebang to Fyrine IV. When told the story, it was Ty who named the planet "Friendship."

One blustery day I knelt between the graves, replaced some rocks, then added a few more. I pulled my snakeskins tight against the wind, then sat down and looked out to sea. Still the rollers steamed in under the gray-black cover of clouds. Soon the ice would come. I looked at my scarred, wrinkled hands, then at the grave.

"I couldn't stay in the colony with them, Jerry. Don't get me wrong: it's nice. Damned nice. But, I kept looking out my window, seeing the ocean, thinking of the cave. I'm alone, in a way. But it's good. I know what and who I am, Jerry, and that's all there is to it, right?"

I heard a noise. I crouched over, placed my hands upon my withered knees and pushed myself to my feet. The Drac was coming from the colony compound, a child in its arms.

I rubbed my beard. "Eh, Ty, so that is your first child?"

The Drac nodded. "I would be pleased, Uncle, if you would teach it what it must be taught: the line, the *Talman*, and about life on Friendship."

I took the bundle into my arms. Chubby three-fingered arms waved at the air, then grasped my snakeskins. "Yes, Ty, this one is a Jeriban." I looked up at Ty. "And how is your parent, Zammis?"

Ty shrugged. "It is as well as can be expected. My parent wishes you well."

I nodded. "And the same to it, Ty. Zammis ought to get out of that air-conditioned capsule and come back to live in the cave. It'll do it good."

Ty grinned and nodded its head. "I will tell my parent, Uncle."

I stabbed my thumb into my chest. "Look at me! You don't see me sick, do you?"

"No, Uncle."

"You tell Zammis to kick that doctor out of there and to come back to the cave, hear?"

"Yes, Uncle." Ty smiled. "Is there anything you need?"

I nodded and scratched the back of my neck. "Toilet paper. Just a couple of packs. Maybe a couple of bottles of whiskey—no, forget the whiskey. I'll wait until Haesni, here, puts in its first year. Just the toilet paper."

Ty bowed. "Yes, Uncle, and may the many mornings find you well."

I waved my hand impatiently. "They will, they will. Just don't forget the toilet paper."

Ty bowed again. "I won't, Uncle."

Ty turned and walked through the scrub forest back to the colony. I lived with them for a year, but I moved out and went back to the cave. I gathered the wood, smoked the snake, and withstood the winter. Zammis gave me the young Ty to rear in the cave, and now Ty had handed me Haesni. I nodded at the child. "Your child will be called Gothig, and then. . . ." I looked at the sky and felt the tears drying on my face. ". . . And then, Gothig's child will be called Shigan." I nodded and headed for the cleft that would bring us down to the level of the cave.

LARRY NIVEN

Flash Crowd

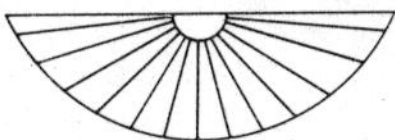

1

FROM EDGE to edge and for all of its length, from Central Los Angeles through Beverly Hills and West Los Angeles and Santa Monica to the sea, Wilshire Boulevard was a walkway.

Once there had been white lines on concrete, and raised curbs to stop the people from interfering with the cars. Now the lines were gone, and much of the concrete was covered with soil and grass. There were even a few trees. Concrete strips had been left for bicycles, and wider places for helicopters carrying cargo too big for the displacement booths.

Wilshire was wide for a walkway. People seemed to hug the edges, even those on bikes and motor skates. A boulevard built for cars was too big for mere people.

Outlines of the street still showed through. Ridges in the grass marked where curbs had been, with breaks where there had been driveways. Some stretches in Westwood had a concrete center divider. The freeway ramps were unchanged and unused. Someday the city would do something about them.

Jerryberry Jansen lived in what had been a seaside motel halfway between Bakersfield and San Francisco. On long-ago summer nights the Shady Rest had been packed with transients at ten dollars a head. Now it made a dandy apartment house, with swimming pool and everything, including a displacement booth outside the manager's office.

There was a girl in the booth when Jerryberry left his apartment. He glimpsed long, wavy brown hair and the shape of her back in the instant before she disappeared. Janice Wolfe. Too bad she hadn't waited . . . but she hadn't even seen him.

Nobody was ever around the booths long enough to say hello to. You could meet someone by hovering outside the booths, but what would they think?

Meeting people was for the clubs.

A displacement booth was a glass cylinder with a rounded top. The machinery that made the magic was invisible, buried beneath the booth. Coin slots and a telephone dial were set into the glass at sternum level.

Jerryberry inserted his C.B.A. credit card below the coin slots. He dialed by punching numbered buttons. Withdrawing the credit card closed a circuit. An eye blink later he was in an office in the Central Broadcasting Association building in downtown Los Angeles.

The office was big and empty. Only once in an aeon was all that empty space ever used, though several score of newstapers saw it for a few seconds each day. One wall was lined with displacement booths. A curved desk down at the end was occupied by Jerryberry's boss.

George Bailey was fat from too much sitting and darkly tanned by the Nevada sun. He commuted to work every morning via the long-distance booths at Los Angeles International. Today he waved at Jerryberry without speaking. Routine, then. Jerryberry chose one of several cameras and slung the padded strap over his shoulder. He studied several lists of numbers posted over the table before picking one.

He turned and moved to avoid three more newstapers stepping out of booths. They nodded; he nodded; they passed. As he reached for a booth door, a woman flicked in in front of him. Rush hour. He smiled at her and stepped over to the next booth, consulted the list, dialed, and was gone.

He had not spoken to anyone that morning.

The east end of Wilshire Boulevard was a most ordinary T-intersection between high, blocky buldings. Jerryberry looked around even as he was dialing. Nothing newsworthy? No. He was two blocks away and dialing.

He punched the numbered buttons with a ballpoint pen when he remembered. Nonetheless, his index finger was calloused.

The streets of the inner city were empty, this early. In a minute or so Jerryberry was in sight of the freeway. He stepped out of the booth to watch trucks and bulldozers covering this part of the Pasadena-Harbor Freeway with topsoil. Old machines find new use—but others were covering the event. He moved on.

The booths were all identical. He might have been in a full-vision theater, watching scenes flick around him. He was used to the way things jerked about. He flicked west on Wilshire, waiting for something to happen.

It was a cheap, effective way to gather news. At a chocolate dollar per jump per man, C.B.A. could afford to support a score of wandering newstapers in addition to the regular staff. They earned low salaries, plus a bonus for each news item, plus a higher bonus per item used. The turnover was high. It had been higher before C.B.A. learned not to jumble the numbers at random. An orderly progression down a single street was easier on the mind and nerves.

Jerryberry Jansen knew every foot of Wilshire. At twenty-eight he was old enough to remember cars and trucks and traffic lights. When the city changed, it was the streets that had changed most.

He watched Wilshire change as he dialed.

At the old hat-shaped Brown Derby they were converting the parking lot into a miniature golf course. About time they did something with all that wasted space. He queried Bailey, but Bailey wasn't interested.

The Miracle Mile was a landscaped section. Suddenly there were people: throngs of shoppers, so thick that many preferred to walk a block instead of waiting for a booth. They seemed stratified, with the older people hugging the curbs and the teens taking the middle of the street. Jerryberry had noticed it before. As a child he'd been trained to cross only in the cross-walks, with the light. Sometimes his training came back, and he found himself looking both ways before he could step out from the curb.

He moved on, west, following the list of numbers that was his beat.

The mall had been a walkway when displacement booths were no more than a theorem in quantum mechanics. Dips in the walk showed where streets had crossed, but the Santa Monica Mall had always been a sanctuary for pedestrians and windowshoppers. Here were several blocks of shops and restaurants and theaters, low buildings that did not block the sky.

Displacement booths were thick here. People swarmed constantly around and in and out of them. Some travelers carried fold-up bicycles. Many wore change purses. From noon onward there was always the tension of too many people trying to use the same space for the same purpose.

The argument started outside Penney's Department Store. At the time one could see only that the police officer was being firm and the woman—middle-aged, big, and brawny—was screaming at the top of her lungs. A crowd grew, not because anyone gave a damn but because the two were blocking the walkway. People had to stream around them.

Some of them stopped to see what was happening. Many later remembered hearing the policeman repeating, "Madam, I place you under arrest on suspicion of shoplifting. Anything you say—" in a voice that simply did not carry. If the officer had used his shockstick then, nothing more would have happened. Maybe. Then again, he might have been mobbed. Already the crowd blocked the entire mall, and too many of them were shouting—genial or sarcastic suggestions, random insults, and a thousand variations of "Get out of my way!" and "I can't, you idiot!"—for any to be heard at all.

At 12:55 Jerryberry Jansen flicked in and looked quickly about him while his hands were reinserting his credit card. His eyes registered the ancient shops at the end of the mall and lingered a moment on the entrance to Romanoff's. Anyone newsworthy? Sometimes they came, the big names, for the cuisine or the publicity. No?—passed on, jumped to the crowd in front of Penney's two blocks down.

There were booths nearer, but he didn't know the numbers offhand. Jerryberry picked up his card and stepped out of the booth. He signaled the studio but didn't bother to report. Circumstantial details he could give later. But he turned on his camera, and the event was now . . . real.

He jogged the two blocks. Whatever was happening might end without him.

A young, bemused face turned at Jerryberry's hail. "Excuse me, sir. Can you tell me how this started?"

"Nope. Sorry. I just got here," said the young man, and he strolled off. He would be edited from the tape. But other heads were turning, noticing the arrival of—

A lean young man with an open, curious, friendly face, topped by red-blond hair curly as cotton. A tiny mike at his lips, a small plug in one ear, a coin purse at his belt. In his hands, a heavy gyrostabilized teevee camera equipped with a directional mike.

A newstaper. One pair of eyes turned for an instant too long. The woman swung her purse. The policeman's arm came up too late to block the purse, which bounced solidly off his head. Something heavy in that purse.

The policeman dropped.

Things happened very fast.

Jerryberry talked rapidly to himself while he panned the camera. Occasional questions in his earpiece did not interrupt the flow of his report, though they guided it. The gyrostabilized camera felt like a living thing in his hands. It followed the woman with the heavy purse as she pushed her way through the crowd, shot Jerryberry a venomous look, and ran for a displacement booth. It watched someone break a jeweler's window, snatch up a handful of random jewelry, and run. The directional mike picked up the scream of an alarm.

The police officer was still down.

Jerryberry went to help him. It occurred to him that of those present, the policeman was most likely to know what had been going on. The voice in his earpiece told him that others were on their way, even as his eye found them leaving the booths: faces he knew on men carrying cameras like his own. He knelt beside the policeman.

"Officer, can you tell me what happened?"

The uniformed man looked up with hurt, bewildered eyes. He said something that the directional mike picked up, but Jerryberry's ears lost it in the crowd noise. He heard it later on the news. "Where's my hat?"

Jerryberry repeated, "What happened here?" while a dozen C.B.A. men around him were interviewing the crowd, and police were pouring out of the displacement booths. The flow of blue uniforms looked like far more than they were. They had to use their shock-sticks to get through the crowd.

Some of the spectators-shoppers-strollers had decided to leave. A wise decision, but impractical. The nearest booths could not be used at all. They held passengers cased in glass, each trying to get his door open against the press of the mob. Every few seconds one would give up and flick out, and another trapped passenger would be pushing at the door.

For blocks around, there was no way to get into a displacement booth. As fast as anyone left a booth, someone else would flick in. Most were nondescript citizens who came to gape. A few carried big cardboard rectangles carelessly printed in fluorescent colors, often with the paint still wet. A different few, nondescript otherwise, had rocks in their pockets.

For Jerryberry, kneeling above the felled policeman and trying to get audible sense out of him, it all seemed to explode. He looked up, and it was a riot.

"It's a riot," he said, awed. The directional mike picked it up.

The crowd surged, and he was moving. He looked back, trying to see if the policeman had gained his feet. If he hadn't, he could be hurt . . . but the crowd surged away. In this mob there was no conservation of matter; there were sources and sinks in it, and today all the sinks were sources. The flow had to go somewhere.

A young woman pushed herself close to Jerryberry. Her eyes were wide; her hair was wild. A kind of rage, a kind of joy, made her face a battlefield. "Legalize direct-current stimulus!" she screamed at him. She lunged and caught the snout of Jerryberry's camera and mike and pulled it around to face her. *"Legalize wireheading!"*

Jerryberry wrenched the camera free. He turned it toward the big display window in Penney's. The glass was gone. Men crawled in the display window, looting. Jerryberry held the camera high, taking pictures of them over the bobbing heads. He had the scene for a moment—and then three signs shot up in front of the camera. One said ""TANSTAAFL," and one bore a mushroom cloud and the words "POWER CORRUPTS!" and Jerryberry never read the third because the crowd surged again and he had to scramble to keep his feet. There were men and women and children being trampled here. He could be one of them.

How had it happened? He'd seen it all, but he didn't understand.

He tried to keep the camera over his head. He got a big brawny hairy type carrying a stack of teevees under his arm, half a dozen twenty-inch sets almost an inch thick. The thief saw the camera facing him and the solemn face beneath, and he roared and lunged toward Jerryberry.

Jerryberry abruptly realized that there were people here who would not want to be photographed. The big man had dropped his teevees and was plowing toward him with murder on his face. Jerryberry had to drop his camera to get away. When he looked back, the big man was smashing the camera against a lamp post.

Idiot. The scene was on tape now, in the C.B.A. buildings in Los Angeles and in Denver.

The riot splashed outward. Jerryberry perforce went with it. He concentrated on keeping his feet.

2

The explosive growth of the mall riot has taken enforcement agencies by surprise. Police have managed to hold the perimeter and are letting people through the lines, but necessarily in small numbers. . . .

The screen showed people being filtered through a police blockade, one at a time. They looked tired, stunned. One had two pockets full of stolen wristwatches. He did not protest when they confiscated the watches and led him away. A blank-eyed girl maintained a death grip on a rough wooden stick glued to a cardboard rectangle. The cardboard was crumpled and torn, the Day-Glo colors smeared.

Meanwhile all displacement booths in the area have been shut down from outside. The enclosed area includes fourteen city blocks. Viewers are warned away from the following areas. . . . These scenes were taken by C.B.A. helicopter. . . .

Most of the street lights were out. Those left cast monstrous shadows through the mall. Orange flames flickered in the windows of a furniture store. Diminutive figures, angered by spotlights in the helicopter, pointed and shouted silently into the camera viewpoint. The deep, earnest voice went on: *We are getting no transmissions from inside the affected area. A dozen C.B.A. newsmen and an undisclosed number of police in the area have not been heard from. . . .*

Many of the rioters are armed. A C.B.A. helicopter was shot down early today but was able to crash-land beyond the perimeter. Close shot of a helicopter smashed against a brick wall. Two men being carried out on stretchers, in obvious haste. *The source of weapons is not known. Police conjecture that they may have been looted from Kerr's Sport Shop, which has a branch in the mall. . . .*

How did it all start?

The square brown face looking out of the tridee screen was known throughout the English-speaking world. When news was good, that wide mouth would smile enormously, the filter cigarette in the middle of it smoldering delicately between white front teeth. It was not smiling now. That expression was more earnest; it was shaken.

Jerryberry Jansen looked back with no expression at all.

He had thrown away his camera and seen it destroyed. He had dropped his coin purse and ear mike into a trash can. Not being a newsman was a good idea during the mall riot. Now, an hour after the police had let him through, he was still wandering aimlessly. He had no goal. Almost, he had thrown away his identity.

He stood in front of an appliance-store window, watching teevee. The deep, precise voice of Wash Evans was audible through the glass—barely.

How did it all start?

Evans vanished, and Jerryberry watched scenes taken by his own camera. A milling crowd, mostly trying to get past a disturbance . . . a blue-uniformed man, a brawny woman with a heavy purse. . . . *The officer was trying to arrest a suspected shoplifter, who has not been identified, when this man appeared on the scene. . . .*

Picture of Jerryberry Jansen, camera held high, caught in the view of another C.B.A. camera.

Barry Jerome Jansen, a roving newstaper. It was he who reported the disturbance (The woman swung her purse. The policeman went down, his arms half-raised as if to hide his head.) *and reported it as a riot, to this man.* Bailey, at his desk in the C.B.A. building. Jerryberry twitched. Sooner or later he would have to report to Bailey. And explain where his camera had gone.

He'd picked up some good footage, and it was being used. A string of bonuses waiting for him . . . unless Bailey docked him for the cost of the camera. . . .

George Lincoln Bailey sent in a crew to cover the disturbance. He also put the report on teevee, practically live, editing it as it came. At this point anyone with a teevee, anywhere in the United States, could see the violence being filmed by a dozen veteran C.B.A. newstapers.

The square dark face returned. *And then it all blew up. The population of the mall expanded catastrophically, and they all started breaking things. Why?* Wash Evans flashed a white grin with a cigarette in it. *Well, it seems that there are people who like riots.*

Jerryberry cocked his head. He had never heard it put quite like that.

Now, that seems silly. Who would want to be caught in a riot? Wash Evans had long, expressive fingers with pink nails. He began ticking off items on his fingers. *First, more police, to stop what's being reported as a riot. Second, more newstapers. Third, anyone who wants publicity.* On the screen behind Wash Evans signs shot out of a sea of moving heads. A girl's face swelled enormously, so close she seemed all mouth, and shrieked, "Legalize wireheading!"

Anyone with a cause. Anyone who wants the ear of the public. There are newsmen here, man! And cameras! And publicity!

Behind Evans the scene jumped. That was Angela Monk coming out of a displacement booth! Angela Monk, the semi-porno movie actress, very beautiful in a dress of loose-mesh net made from white braided yarn, very self-possessed in the split second before she saw what she'd flicked into. She tried to dodge back inside and to hell with the free coverage. A yell went up; hands pulled the door open before she could dial again; other hands pulled her out.

Then there are people who have never seen a riot in person. A lot of them came. What they think about it now is something else again.

Now, all of these might not be a big fat percentage of the public. How many people would be dumb enough to come watch a riot? But that little percentage, they all came at once, from all over the United States and some other places, too. And the more there were, the bigger the crowd got, the louder it got—the better it looked to the looters. Evans folded down his remaining finger. *And the looters came from everywhere, too. These days you can get from anywhere to anywhere in three flicks.*

Scenes shifted in Evans's background. Store windows being smashed, a subdued wail of sirens. A C.B.A. helicopter thrashing bout in midair. An ape of a man carrying stolen tridees under one arm. Evans looked soberly out at his audience. *So there you have it. An unidentified shoplifting suspect, a roving newsman who reported a minor disturbance as a riot—*

"Good God!" Jerryberry Jansen was jolted completely awake. "They're blaming me!"

"They're blaming me, too,' said George Bailey. He ran his hands through his hair, glossy shoulder-length white hair that grew in a fringe around a dome of suntanned scalp. "You're second in the chain. I'm tired. If only they could find the woman who hit the cop!"

" They haven't?"

"Not a sign of her. Jansen, you look like hell."

"I should have changed suits. This one's been through a riot." Jerryberry's laugh sounded forced, and was. "I'm glad you waited. It must be way past your quitting time."

"Oh, no. We've been in conference all night. We only broke up about twenty minutes ago. Damn Wash Evans anyway! Have you heard—"

"I heard some of it."

"A couple of the directors want to fire him. Not unlike the ancient technique of using gasoline to put out a fire. There were some even wilder suggestions. . . . Have you seen a doctor?"

"I'm not hurt. Just bruised . . . and tired, and hungry, come to think of it. I lost my camera."

"You're lucky you got out alive."

"I know."

George Bailey seemed to brace himself. "I hate to be the one to tell you. We're going to have to let you go, Jansen."

"What? You mean fire me?"

"Yah. Public pressure. I won't make it pretty for you. Wash Evans's instant documentary has sort of torn things open. It seems you caused the mall riot. It would be nice if we could say we fired you for it."

"But—but I *didn't!*"

"Yes, you did. Think about it." Bailey wasn't looking at him. "So did I. C.B.A. may have to fire me too."

"Now—" Jerryberry stopped and started over—"now wait a minute. If you're saying what I think you're saying. . . . but what about freedom of the press?"

"We talked about that, too."

"I didn't exaggerate what was happening. I reported a—a *disturbance*. When it turned into a riot, I called it a riot. Did I lie about anything? *Anything?*"

"Oh, in a way," Bailey said in a tired voice. "You've got your choice about where to point that camera. You pointed it where there was fighting, didn't you? And I picked out the most exciting scenes. When we both finished, it looked like a small riot. Fighting everywhere! Then everyone who wanted to be in the middle of a small riot came flicking in, just like Evans said, and in thirty seconds we had a large riot.

"You know what somebody suggested? A time limit on news. A law against reporting anything until twenty-four hours after it happens. Can you imagine anything sillier? For ten thousand years the human race has been working to send news farther and faster, and now. . . . Oh, hell, Jansen, *I* don't know about freedom of the press. But the riot's still going on, and everyone's blaming you. You're fired."

"Thanks." Jerryberry surged out of his chair on what felt like the last of his strength. Bailey moved just as fast, but by the time he got around the desk, Jerryberry was inside a booth, dialing.

He stepped out into a warm black night. He felt sick and miserable and very tired. It was two in the morning. His paper suit was torn and crumpled and clammy.

George Bailey stepped out of the booth behind him.

"Thought so. Now, Jansen, let's talk sense."

"How did you know I'd be here?"

"I had to guess you'd come straight home. Jansen, you won't suffer for this. You may make money on it. C.B.A. wants an exclusive interview on the riot, your viewpoint. Thirty-five hundred bucks."

"Screw that."

"In addition, there's two weeks' severance pay and a stack of bonuses. We used a lot of your tape. And when this blows over, I'm sure we'll want you back."

"Blows over, huh?"

"Oh, it will. News gets stale awfully fast these days. I know. Jansen, why don't you want thirty-five hundred bucks?"

"You'd play me up as the man who started the mall riot. Make me more valuable. . . . Wait a minute. Who have you got in mind for the interview?"

"Who else?"

"Wash Evans!"

"He's fair. You'd get your say." Bailey considered him. "Let me know if you change your mind. You'd have a chance to defend yourself, and you'd get paid besides."

"No chance."

"All right." Bailey went.

3

For Eric Jansen and his family, displacement booths came as a disaster.

At first he didn't see it that way. He was twenty-eight (and Barry Jerome Jansen was three) when JumpShift, Inc., demonstrated the augmented tunnel diode effect on a lead brick. He watched it on television. He found the prospects exciting.

Eric Jansen had never worked for a salary. He wrote. Poetry and articles and a few short stories, highly polished, admired by a small circle of readers, sold at infrequent intervals to low-paying markets that he regarded as prestigious. His money came from inherited stocks. If he had invested in JumpShift then—but millions could tell that sad story. It was too risky then.

He was thirty-one when commercial displacement booths began to be sold for cargo transport. He was not caught napping. Many did not believe that the magic could work until suddenly the phenomenon was changing their world. But Eric Jansen looked into the phenomenon very carefully.

He found that there was an inherent limitation on the augmented tunnel diode effect. Teleportation over a difference in altitude made for drastic temperature changes: a drop of seven degrees Fahrenheit for every mile upward, and vice versa, due to conservation of energy. Conservation of momentum, plus the rotation of the Earth, put a distance limit on lateral travel. A passenger flicking east would find himself kicked upward by the difference between his velocity and the Earth's. Flicking west, he would be slapped down. North and south, he would be kicked sideways.

Cargo and passenger displacement booths were springing up in every city in America, but Eric Jansen knew that they would always be restricted to short distances. Even a ten-mile jump would be bumpy. A passenger flicking halfway around the equator would have to land running—at half a mile per second.

JumpShift stock was sky-high. Eric Jansen decided it must be overpriced.

He considered carefully, then made his move.

He sold all of his General Telephone stock. If anyone wanted to talk to someone, he would just *go*, wouldn't he? A displacement booth took no longer than a phone call.

He tried to sell his General Motors, wisely, but everyone else wisely made the same decision, and the price fell like a dead bird. At least he got something back on the stock he owned in motorcycle and motorscooter companies. Later he regretted that. It developed that people rode motorcycles and scooters for fun. Now, with the streets virtually empty, they were buying more than ever.

Still, he had fluid cash—and the opportunity to make a killing.

Airline stock had dropped with other forms of transportation. Before the general public could realize its mistake, Eric Jansen invested every dime in airlines and aircraft companies. The first displacement booths in any city were links to the airport. That lousy half-hour drive from the center of town, the heavy taxi fare in, were gone forever. And the booths couldn't compete with the airlines themselves!

Of course you still had to check in early—and the planes took off only at specified times. . . .

What it amounted to was that plane travel was made easier, but short-distance travel via displacement booth was infinitely easier (infinitely—try dividing any ten-minute drive by zero). And planes still crashed. Cassettes had copped the entertainment market, so that television was mostly news these days; you didn't have to *go* anywhere to find out what was happening. Just turn on the TV.

A plane flight wasn't worth the hassle.

As for the telephone stock, people still made long-distance calls. They tended to phone first before they went visiting. They would give out a phone-booth number, whereas they would not give out a displacement-booth number.

The airlines survived, somehow, but they paid rock-bottom dividends. Barry Jerome Jansen grew up poor in the midst of a boom period. His father hated the displacement booths but used them, because there was nothing else.

Jerryberry accepted that irrational hatred as part of his father's personality. He did not share it. He hardly noticed the displacement booths. They were part of the background. The displacement booths were the most important part of a newstaper's life, and still he hardly noticed their existence.

Until the day they turned on him.

4

In the morning there were messages stored in his phone. He heard them out over breakfast.

Half a dozen news services and tapezines wanted exclusives on the riot. One call was from Bailey at C.B.A. The price had gone up to four thousand. The others did not mention price, but one was from *Playboy*.

That gave him furiously to think. *Playboy* paid high, and they liked unpopular causes.

Three people wanted to murder him. On two of them the teevee was blanked. The third was a graying dowdy woman, all fat and hate and disappointed hopes, who showed him a kitchen knife and started to tell him what she wanted to do with it. Jerryberry cut her off, shuddering. He wondered if any of them could possibly get hold of his displacement-booth number.

There was a check in the mail. Severance pay and bonuses from C.B.A. So that was that.

He was setting the dishes in the dishwasher when the phone rang. He hesitated, then decided to answer.

It was Janice Wolfe—a pretty oval face, brown eyes, a crown of long, wavy, soft brown hair—and not an anonymous killer. She lost her smile as she saw him. "You look grim. Could you use some cheering up?"

"Yes!" Jerryberry said fervently. "Come on over. Apartment six, booth number—"

"I live here, remember?"

He laughed. He'd forgotten. You got used to people living anywhere and everywhere. George Bailey lived in Nevada; he commuted to work every morning in three flicks, using the long-distance displacement booths at Las Vegas and Los Angeles International Airports.

Those long-distance booths had saved the airlines—after his father had dribbled away most of his stocks to feed his family. They had been operating only two years. And come to think of it—

Doorbell.

Over coffee he told Janice about the riot. She listened sympathetically, asking occasional questions to draw him out. At first Jerryberry tried to talk entertainingly, until he realized, first, that she wasn't indulging in a spectator sport, and second, that she knew all about the riot already.

She knew he'd been fired, too. "That's why I called. They put it on the morning news," she told him.

"It figures."

"What are you going to do now?"

"Get drunk. Alone if I have to. Would you like to spend a lost weekend with me?"

She hesitated. "You'll be bitter."

"Yah, I probably will. Not fit to live with. . . . Hey, Janice. Do you know anything about how the long-distance displacement booths work?"

"No. Should I?"

"The mall riot couldn't have happened without the long-distance booths. That damn Wash Evans might at least have mentioned the fact . . . except that I only just thought of it myself. Funny. There hasn't *ever* been a riot that happened that quick."

"I'll come with you," Janice decided.

"What? *Good.*"

"You don't start drinking this early in the morning, do you?"

"I guess not. Are you free today?"

"Every day, during summer. I teach school."

"Oh. So what'll we do? San Diego Zoo?" he suggested at random.

"Sounds like fun."

They made no move to get up. It felt peaceful in Jerryberry's tiny kitchen nook. There was still coffee.

"You could get a bad opinion of me this way. I feel like tearing things up."

"Go ahead."

"I mean it."

"Me, too," she said serenely. "You need to tear things up. Fine, go ahead. After that you can try to put your life back together."

"Just what kind of school do you teach?"

Janice laughed. "Fifth grade."

There was quiet.

"You know what the punch line is? Wash Evans wants to interview me! After that speech he made!"

"That sounds like a good idea," she said surprisingly. "Gives you a chance to give your side of the story. You didn't *really* cause the mall riot, did you?"

"No! . . . No. Janice, he's just too damn good. He'd make mincemeat of me. By the time he got through I'd be The Man Who Caused the Mall Riot in every English-speaking country in the world, and some others, too, because he gets translations—"

"He's just a *commentator*."

Jerryberry started to laugh.

"He makes it look so easy," he said. "A hundred million eyes out there, watching him, and he knows it. Have you ever seen him self-conscious? Have you ever heard him at a loss for words? My dad used to say it about writing, but it's true for Wash Evans. The hardest trick in the world is to make it look easy, so easy that any clod thinks he can do it just as well.

"Hell, *I* know what caused the mall riot. The news program, yes. He's right, there. But the long-distance displacement booth did it, too. Control those, and we could stop that kind of riot from ever happening again. . . . But what could I tell Wash Evans about it? What do I know about displacement booths?"

"Well, what *do* you know?"

Jerryberry Jansen looked into his coffee cup for a long time. Presently he said, "I know how to find out things. I know how to find out who knows most about what and then go ask. Legwork. They *hammered* at it in the journalism classes. I know legwork."

He looked up and met her eyes. Then he lunged across the table to reach the phone.

"Hello? Oh, hi, Jansen. Changed your mind?"

"Yes, but—"

"Good, good! I'll put you through to—"

"*Yes, but!*"

"Oh. Okay, go ahead."

"I want some time to do some research."

"Now, damn it, Jensen, you know that time is just what we don't have! Old news is no news. What kind of research?"

"Displacement booths."

"Why that? Never mind; it's your business. How much time?"

"How much can you afford?"

"Damn little."

"Bailey, C.B.A. upped my price to four thousand this morning. How come?"

"You didn't see it? It's on every screen in the country. The rioters broke through the police line. They've got a good section of Venice now, and there are about twice as many of them, because the police didn't shut down the displacement booths in the area until about twenty minutes too late. Twenty minutes!" Bailey seemed actually to be grinding his teeth. "We held off reporting the breakthrough until they could do it. *We* did. A.B.S. reported it live on all stations. *That's* where all the new rioters came from."

"Then . . . it looks like the mall riot is going to last a little longer."

"That it does. And you want more time. Things are working out, aren't they?" Then, "Sorry. Those A.B.S. bastards. How much time do you want?"

"As much as I can get. A week."

"You've *got* to be kidding. You maybe can get twenty-four hours, only I can't make the decision. Why don't you talk to Evans himself?"

"Fine. Put him on."

The teevee went on hold. Pale-blue flow patterns floated upward in what had become a twenty-inch Kalliroscope. Waiting, Jerryberry said, "If this riot gets any bigger, I could be more famous than Hitler."

Janice set his coffee beside him. She said, "Or Mrs. O'Leary's cow."

The screen came on. "Jansen, can you get over here right now? Wash Evans wants to talk to you in person."

"Okay." Jerryberry clicked off. He felt a thrumming inside him . . . as if he felt the motion of the world, and the world were spinning faster and faster. Surely things were happening fast. . . .

Janice said, "No lost weekend."

"Not yet, love. Have you any idea what you've let me in for? I may not sleep for days. I'll have to find out what teleportation is, what it does. . . . where do I start?"

"Wash Evans. You'd better get moving."

"Right." He bolted his coffee in three swift gulps. "Thanks. Thanks for coming over, thanks for jarring me off the dime. We'll see how it works out." He went, pulling on a coat.

Wash Evans was five feet four inches tall. People sometimes forgot that size was invisible in a teevee close-up. In the middle of a televised interview, when the camera was flashing back and forth between two angry faces, then the deep, sure voice and the dark, mobile, expressive face of Wash Evans could be devastatingly convincing.

Wash Evans looked up at Jerryberry Jansen and said, "I've been wondering if I owe you an apology."

"Take your time," said Jerryberry. He finished buttoning his coat.

"I don't. Fact is, I psyched out the mall riot as best I knew how, and I think I did it right. I didn't tell the great unwashed public you caused it all. I just told it like it happened."

"You left some things out."

"All right, now we've got something to talk about. Sit down."

They sat. Their faces were level now. Jerryberry said, "This present conversation is not for publication and is not to be considered an interview. I have an interview to sell. I don't want to undercut myself."

"I accept your terms on behalf of the network. We'll give you a tape of this conversation."

"I'm making my own." Jerryberry tapped his inside pocket, which clicked.

Wash Evans grinned. "Of course you are, my child. Now, what did I miss?"

"Displacement booths."

"Well, *sure*. If the booths had been cut off earlier—"

"If the booths didn't exist."

"You're kidding. No, you're not. Jansen, that's a wishing horse. Displacement booths are here to stay."

"I know. But think about this. Newstapers have been around longer than displacement booths. Roving newstapers, like me—we've been using the booths since they were invented."

"So?"

"Why didn't the mall riot happen earlier?"

"I see what you mean. Hmm. The airport booths?"

"Yah."

"Jansen, are you actually going to face the great unwashed teevee public and tell them to give up long-distance displacement booths?"

"No. I . . . don't know just what I have in mind. That's why I want some time. I want to know more."

"Uh-huh," said Evans, and waited.

Jerryberry said, "Turn it around. Are you going to try to talk the public into giving up news programs?"

"No. Maybe to put some restrictions on newstaping practices. We're *too* fast these days. A machine won't work without friction. Neither does a civilization. . . . But we'd ruin the networks, wouldn't we?"

"You'd cut your own throat."

"Oh, *I'd* be out." Evans mashed out a cigarette. "Take away the news broadcasts, and they wouldn't have anything left to sell but educational teevee. Nothing to sell but toys and breakfast cereal. Jansen, I don't know."

"Good," said Jerryberry.

"You question my dispassionate judgment?" Evans chuckled in his throat. "I'm on *both* sides. Suppose we do an interview live, at ten tonight. That'll give you twelve hours—"

"Twelve hours!"

"That's enough, isn't it? You want to research teleportation. I want to get this in while people are still interested in the riot. Not just for the ratings,but because we both have something to say." Jerryberry tried to interrupt, but Evans overrode him. "We'll advance you a thousand, and three more if we do the interview. Nothing if we don't. That'll get you back on time."

Jerryberry accepted it. "One thing. Can you make Bailey forget to cancel my C.B.A. card for a while? I may have to do a lot of traveling."

"I'll tell him. I don't know if he'll do it."

5

He flicked in at Los Angeles International, off-center in a long curved row of displacement booths: upright glass cylinders with rounded tops, no different from the booths on any street corner. On the opposite wall, a good distance away, large red letters said "TWA." He stood a moment, thinking. Then he dialed again.

He was home, at the Shady Rest. He dialed again.

He was near the end of the row—a different row, with no curve to it. And the opposite wall bore the emblem of United.

The terminal was empty except for one man in a blue uniform who was waxing the floor.

Jerryberry stepped out. For upwards of a minute he watched the line of booths. People flicked in at random. Generally they did not even look up. They would dial a long string of digits—sometimes making a mistake, snarling something, and starting over—and be gone. There were so many that the booths themselves seemed to be flickering.

He took several seconds of it on the Minox.

Beneath the United emblem was a long, long row of empty counters with scales between them, for luggage. The terminal was spotless—and empty, unused. Haunted by a constant flow of ghosts.

A voice behind him said, "You want something?"

"Is there a manager's office?"

The uniformed man pointed down an enormous length of corridor. "The maintenance section's down that way, where the boarding area used to be. I'll call ahead, let them know you're coming."

The corridor was long, unnecessarily long, and it echoed. The walk was eating up valuable time . . . and then an open cart came from the other end and silently pulled up alongside him. A straight-backed old man in a one-button business lounger said, "Hello. Want a ride?"

"Thanks." Jerryberry climbed aboard. He handed over his C.B.A. credit card. "I'm doing some research for a—a documentary of sorts. What can you tell me about the long-distance booths?"

"Anything you like. I'm Nils Kjerulf. I helped install these booths, and I've been working on them ever since."

"How do they work?"

"Where do I start? Do you know how a normal booth works?"

"Sure. The load isn't supposed to exist at all between the two end points. Like the electron in a tunnel diode." An answer right out of the science section of any tapezine. Beyond that he could fake it.

This Nils Kjerulf was lean and ancient, with deep smile wrinkles around his eyes and mouth. His hair was thick and white. He said, "They had to give up that theory. When you're sending a load to Mars, say, you have to assume that *something* exists in the ten minutes or so it takes the load to make the trip. Conservation of energy."

"All right. What is it?"

"For ten minutes it's a kind of superneutrino. That's what they tell me. I'm not a physicist. I was in business administration in college. A few years ago they gave me a year of retraining so I could handle long-distance displacement machinery. If you're really interested in theory, you ought to ask someone at Cape Canaveral. Here we are."

Two escalators, one going up, one motionless. They rode up. Jerryberry asked, "Why didn't they build closer? Think of all the walking we'd save."

"You never heard a 707 taking off?"

"No."

"Sound is only part of it. If a plane ever crashed here, nobody would want it hitting all the main buildings at once."

The escalator led to two semicircular chambers. One was empty but for a maze of chairs and couches and low partitions, all done in old chrome and fading orange. In the other the couches had been ripped out and replaced with instrument consoles. Jerryberry counted half a dozen men supervising the displays.

A dim snoring sound began somewhere, like an electric razor going in the next-door apartment. Jerryberry turned his head, seeking. It was outside. Outside, behind a wall of windows, a tiny single-engine plane taxied down a runway.

"Yes, we still function as an airport," said Nils Kjerulf. "Skydiving, sport flying, gliding. I fly some myself. The jumbo-jet pilots used to hate us; we use up just as much landing time as a 747. Now we've got the runways to ourselves."

"I gather you were a manager somewhere."

"Right here. I ran this terminal before anyone had heard of teleportation. I watched it ruin us. Thirty years, Mr. Jansen."

"With no offense intended whatever, why did they train a professional administrator in quantum displacement physics? Why not the other way around?"

"There *weren't* any experts where the long-distance booths were concerned, Mr. Jansen. They're *new*."

"What have you learned in two years? Do you still get many breakdowns?"

"We still do. Every two weeks or so, something goes out of synch. Then we go out of service for however long it takes to find it and fix it—usually about an hour."

"And what happens to the passenger?"

Kjerulf looked surprised. "Nothing. He stays where he started—or rather, that giant neutrino we were talking about is reflected back to the transmitter if the receiver can't pick it up. The worst thing that can happen is that the link to the velocity damper could be lost, in which case—but we've developed safeguards against that.

"No, the passengers just stop coming in, and we go out of service, and the other companies take the overflow. There isn't any real competition between the companies anymore. What's the point? T.W.A. and United and Eastern and the rest used to advertise that they had better meals in flight, more comfortable seats, prettier hostesses . . . like that. How long do you *spend* in a displacement booth? So when we converted over, we set the dialing system up so you just dial Los Angeles International or whatever, and the companies get customers at random. Everyone saves a fortune in advertising."

"An antitrust suit—"

"Would have us dead to rights. Nobody's done it, because there's no point. It works, the way we run it. Each company has its own velocity shift damper. We couldn't all get knocked out at once. In an emergency I think any of the companies could handle all of the long-distance traffic."

"Mr. Kjerulf, what is a velocity shift damper?"

Kjerulf looked startled. Jerryberry said, "I took journalism."

"Ah."

"It's not just curiosity. My dad lost a fortune on airline stock—"

"So did I," said Kjerulf, half-smiling with old pain.

"Oh?"

"Sometimes I feel I've sold out. The booths couldn't possibly compete with the airlines, could they? They wouldn't send far enough. Yet they ruined us."

"My dad figured the same way."

"And now the booths *do* send that far, and I'm working for them, or they're working for me. There wasn't all that much reason to build the long-distance systems at airports. Lots of room here, of course, and an organization already set up . . . but they really did it to save the airline companies."

"A little late."

"Perhaps. Some day they'll turn us into a public utility." Kjerulf looked about the room, then called to a man seated near the flat wall of the semicircle. "Dan!"

"Yo!" the man boomed without looking up.

"Can you spare me twenty minutes for a public-relations job?"

The man stood up, then climbed up on his chair. He looked slowly about the room. Jerryberry guessed that he could see every instrument board from where he was standing. He called, "Sure. No sweat."

They took the cart back to the terminal. They entered a booth. Jerryberry inserted his C.B.A. credit card, then waited while Kjerulf dialed.

They were in a concrete building. Beyond large square windows a sunlit sea of blue water heaved and splashed, almost at floor level. Men looked around curiously, recognized Nils Kjerulf, and turned back to their work.

"Lake Michigan. And out there—" Kjerulf pointed. Jerryberry saw a tremendous white mass, a flattened dome, very regular. A great softly rounded island. "—is the United Air Lines velocity damper. All of the dampers look about like that, but they float in different lakes or oceans. Aeroflot uses the Caspian Sea. The T.W.A. damper is in the Gulf of Mexico."

"Just what is it?"

"Essentially it's a hell of a lot of soft iron surronded by a hell of a lot more foam plastic, enough to float it, plus a displacement-booth receiver feeding into the iron. Look, see it surge?"

The island rose several feet, slowly, then fell back as slowly. Ripples moved outward and became waves as they reached the station.

"That must have been a big load. Now, here's how it works. You know that the rotation of the Earth puts a limit on how far you can send a load. If you were to shift from here to Rio de Janeiro, say, you'd flick in moving up and sideways—mainly up, because Rio and L.A. are almost the same distance from the equator.

"But with the long-distance booths, the receiver picks up the kinetic energy and shunts it to the United Air Lines velocity damper. That big mass of iron surges up or down or sideways until the water stops it—or someone flicks in from Rio and the damping body stops cold."

Jerryberry thought about it. "What about conservation of rotation? It sounds like you're slowing down the Earth."

"We are. There's nothing sacred about conservation of rotation, except that the energy has to go somewhere. There are pumps to send water through the damper bodies if they get too hot."

Jerryberry pulled out the Minox. "Mind if I take some pictures?"

"No, go ahead."

The Minox was a movie camera, but it would not have the resolution of a press camera. No matter. If he had the time he could come back . . . not that he thought he would. He took shots of the men at work in the station, of Nils Kjerulf with his back to the windows. He shot almost a minute of the great white island itself. He was hoping it would surge; and presently it did, sinking sideways, surging up again. Waves beat at the station. A jet of white steam sprayed from the top of the great white mass.

"Good," he said briskly to himself. He folded the spidery tripod legs and dropped the camera in his pocket. He turned to Kjerulf, who had been watching the proceedings with some amusement. "Mr. Kjerulf, can you tell me anything about traffic control? Is there any?"

"How do you mean? Customs?"

"Not exactly . . . but tell me about customs."

"The customs terminal in Los Angeles is at T.W.A. You haven't been out of the country recently? No? Well, any big-city airport has a customs terminal. In a small country there's likely to be just one. If you dial a number outside the country, *any* country, you wind up in somebody's customs terminal. The booths there don't have dials, you see. You have to cross the customs line to dial out."

"Clever. Are there any restrictions on traffic within the United States?"

"No, you just drop your chocolate dollars in and dial. Unless it's a police matter. If the police know that someone's trying to leave the city they may set up a watch in the terminals. We can put a delay on the terminals to give a detective time to look at a passenger's face and see if he's who they want."

"But nothing to stop passengers from coming in."

"No, except that it's possible to . . . " Kjerulf trailed off oddly, then finished, " . . . turn off any booth by remote control, from the nearest JumpShift maintenance system. What are you thinking of, the mall riot?"

"Yah."

There was no more to say. He left Nils Kjerulf in the United terminal in Los Angeles. He dialed for customs.

For several minutes Jerryberry watched them flicking in. There were two types:

The tourists came in couples, sometimes with a child or two. They flicked in looking interested and harried and a little frightened. Their clothing was outlandish and extraordinary. Before they left the booths, they would look about them mistrustfully. Sometimes they formed larger groups.

The businessmen traveled alone. They wore conservative or old-fashioned clothing and carried one suitcase: large or small, but one. They were older than the tourists. They moved with authority, walking straight out of the booths the moment they appeared.

At the barrier: four men in identical dark suits with shield-shaped shoulder patches. Jerryberry was on the wrong side of the barrier to command their attention. He was thinking of dialing himself to Mexico and back when one of them noticed him and pegged him as a newstaper.

His name was Gregory Scheffer. Small and round and middle-aged, he perched on the wooden barrier and clasped one knee in both hands. "Sure, I can talk awhile. This isn't one of the busy days. The only time these booths really get a workout is Christmas and New Year and Bastille Day and like that. Look around you," he said, waving a pudgy hand expansively.

"About four times as many incoming as there was six months ago. I used to want to search every bag that came through, just to be doing something. If we keep getting more and more of them this way, we'll need twice as many customs people next year."

"Why do you suppose—"

"Did you know that the long-distance booths have been operating for *two solid years?* It's only in the last six months or so that we've started to get so many passengers. They had to get used to traveling again. Look around you; look at all this space. It used to be *full* before JumpShift came along. People have got out of the habit of traveling, that's all there is to it. For twenty solid years. They have to get back into it."

"Guess so." Jerryberry tried to remember why he was here. "Mr. Scheffer—"

"Greg."

"Jerryberry. Customs' main job is to stop smuggling, isn't it?"

"Well . . . it used to be. Now we only slow it down, and not very damn much. Nobody in his right mind would smuggle anything through customs. There are safer ways."

"Oh?"

"Diamonds, for instance. Diamonds are practically indestructible. You could rig a cargo booth in Kansas to receive from . . . oh, there's a point in the South Pacific to match anyplace in the United States: same longitude, opposite latitude. You don't need a velocity damper if you put the boat in the right place. Diamonds? You could ship in Swiss watches that way. Though that's pretty finicky. You'd want to pad them."

"Good grief. You could smuggle anything you pleased, anywhere."

"Just about. You don't need the ocean trick. Say you rig a booth a mile south of the Canadian border, and another booth a mile north. That's not much of a jump. You can flick further than that just in L.A. I think we're obsolete," said Scheffer. "I think smuggling laws are obsolete. You won't publish this?"

"I won't use your name."

"I guess that's okay."

"Can you get me over to the incoming booths? I want to take some pictures."

"What for?"

"I'm not sure yet."

"Let's see some ID." Gregory Scheffer didn't trust evasive answers. The incoming booths were in his jurisdiction. He studied the C.B.A. card for a few seconds and suddenly said, "Jansen! Mall riot!"

"Right!"

"What was it like?"

Jerryberry invested half a minute telling him. "So now I'm trying to find out how it got started. If there were some way to stop all of those people from pouring in like that—"

"You won't find it here. Look, a dozen passengers and we're almost busy. A thousand people suddenly pour through those booths, and what would we do? Hide under something, that's what we'd do."

"I still want to see the incoming booths."

Scheffer thought it over, shrugged, and let him through. He stood at Jerryberry's shoulder while Jerryberry used his eye and his camera.

The booth was just like a street-corner booth, except for the blank metal face where a dial would be. "I don't know what's underneath," Scheffer told him. "For all of me, it's just like any other booth. How much work would it be to leave off the dial?"

Which made sense. But it was no help at all.

6

They tape the *Tonight Show* at two in the afternoon.

Twenty minutes into it, the first guest is lolling at his ease, just rapping, talking off the top of his head, ignoring the probable hundred million eyes behind the cameras. This is a valuable knack, and rare. *Tonight's* first guest is a series hero in a science-fiction tapezine.

He is saying, "Have you ever seen a red tide? It's *thick* down at Hermosa Beach. I was there this weekend. In the daytime it's just dirty water, muddy-looking, and it smells. But at *night* . . ."

This enthusiasm that can reach through a teevee screen to touch fifty million minds, this enthusiasm is in no way artificial. He means it. He only expresses it better than most men. He leans forward in his chair; his eyes blaze; there is harsh tension in his voice. "The breakers glow like churning blue fire! Those plankton are fluorescent. And they're all through the wet sand. Walk across it, it flashes blue light under your feet! Kick it, scuff your feet through it, it lights up. Throw a handful of sand, it flashes where it hits! This light isn't just on the surface. Stamp your foot, you can see the structure of the sand by the way it flares. You've got to see it to believe it," he says.

They will run the tape starting at eight thirty tonight.

7

Standard booths: how standardized?

Who makes them besides JumpShift? Monopoly? How extensive?

Skip spaceflight?

Space exploration depended utterly on teleportation. But the subject was likely to be very technical and not very useful. He could gain time by skipping it entirely. Jerryberry considered, then turned the question mark into an exclamation point.

His twelve hours had become nine.

Of the half-dozen key clubs to which he belonged, the Cave des Roys was the quietest. A place of stone and wood, a good place to sit and think. The wall behind the bar was several hundred wine bottles in a cement matrix. Jerryberry looked into the strange lights in the glass, sipped occasionally at a silver fizz, and jotted down whatever occurred to him.

Sociology. What has teleportation done to society?

Cars.

Oil companies. Oil stocks. See back issues Wall Street Journal.

Watts riot? Chicago riot? He crossed that last one out. The Chicago riot had been political, hadn't it? Then he couldn't remember any other riots. They were too far in the past. He wrote:

Riot control. Police procedure.

Crime? The crime rate should have soared after displacement booths provided the instant getaway. Had it?

Sooner or later he was going to have to drop in at police headquarters. He'd hate that, but he might learn something. Likewise the library, for several hours of dull research. Then?

He certainly wasn't going to persuade everybody to give up displacement booths:

He wrote: *OBJECTIVE: Demonstrate that displacement booths imply instant riot. It's a social problem. Solve it on that basis.* For the sake of honesty he added, *Get 'em off my back. CROWDS.* In minutes the mall had become a milling mass of men. But he'd seen crowds form almost as fast. It might happen regularly in certain places. After a moment's thought he wrote. *Tahiti. Jerusalem. Mecca. Easter Island. Stonehenge. Olduvai Gorge.*

He stood up. Start with the phone calls.

"Doctor Robin Whyte," Jerryberry said to the phone screen. "Please."

The receptionist at Seven Sixes was no sex symbol. She was old enough to be Jerryberry's aunt, and handsome rather than beautiful. She heard him out with a noncommittal dignity that, he sensed, could turn glacial in an instant.

"Barry Jerome Jansen," he said carefully.

He waited on hold, watching dark-red patterns flow upward in the phone screen.

Key clubs were neither new nor rare. Some were small and local; others were chains, existing in a dozen or a hundred locations. Everyone belonged to a club; most people belonged to several.

But Seven Sixes was something else. Its telephone number was known universally. Its membership, large in absolute terms, was small for an organization so worldwide. It included presidents, kings, winners of various brands of Nobel prize. Its location was—unknown. Somewhere in Earth's temperate zones. Jerryberry had never heard of its displacement-booth number being leaked to anyone.

It took a special kind of gall for one of Jerryberry's social standing to dial 666-6666. He had learned that gall in journalism class. *Go to the source*—no matter how highly placed; be polite, be prepared to wait, but keep trying, and never, never worry about wasting the great man's time.

Funny: They still called it journalism, though newspapers had died. And the Constitution that had protected newspapers still protected "the press." For a while. But laws could change. . . .

The screen cleared.

Robin Whyte the physicist had been a mature man of formidable reputation back when JumpShift first demonstrated teleportation. Today, twenty-five years later, he was the last living member of the team that had formed JumpShift. His scalp was pink and bare. His face was round and soft, almost without wrinkles, but slack, as if the muscles were tired. He looked like somebody's favorite grandfather.

He looked Jerryberry Jansen up and down very thoroughly. He said, "I wanted to see what you looked like." He reached for the cutoff switch.

"I didn't do it," Jerryberry said quickly.

Whyte stopped with his finger on the cutoff. "No?"

"I am not responsible for the mall riot. I hope to prove it."

The old man thought it over. "And you propose to involve *me*? How?"

Jerryberry took a chance. "I think I can demonstrate that displacement booths and the mall riot are intimately connected. My problem is that I don't know enough about displacement-booth technology."

"And you want *my* help?"

"You invented the displacement booths practically single-handed," Jerryberry said straight-faced. "Instant riots, instant getaways, instant smuggling. Are you going to just walk away from the problem?"

Robin Whyte laughed in a high-pitched voice, his head thrown way back, his teeth white and perfect and clearly false. Jerryberry waited, wondering if it would work.

"All right," Whyte said. "Come on over. Wait a minute, what am I thinking? *You* can't come to Seven Sixes. I'll meet you somewhere. L'Orangerie, New York City. At the bar."

The screen cleared before Jerryberry could answer. *That was quick,* he thought. And, *Move, idiot. Get there before he changes his mind.*

In New York it was just approaching cocktail hour. L'Orangerie was polished wood and dim lighting and chafing dishes of Swedish meatballs on toothpicks. Jerryberry captured a few to go with his drink. He had not had lunch yet.

Robin Whyte wore a long-sleeved gray one-piece with a collar that draped into a short cape, and the cape was all the shifting rainbow colors of an oil film. The height of fashion, except that it should have been skin-tight. It was loose all over, bagging where Whyte bagged, and it looked very comfortable. Whyte sipped at a glass of milk.

"One by one I give up my sins," he said. "Drinking was the last, and I haven't really turned loose of it yet. But almost. That's why your reverse salesmanship hooked me in. I'll talk to anyone. What do I call you?"

"Barry Jerome Jansen."

"Let me put it this way. I'm Robbie. What do I call you?"

"Oh. Jerryberry."

Whyte laughed. "I can't call anyone Jerryberry. Make it Barry."

"God bless you, sir."

"What do you want to know?"

"How big is JumpShift?"

"Ooohhh, pretty big. What's your standard of measurement?"

Jerryberry, who had wondered if he was being laughed at, stopped wondering. "How many kinds of booth do you make?"

"Hard to say. Three, for general use. Maybe a dozen more for the space industry. Those are still experimental. We lose money on the space industry. We'd make it back if we could start producing drop-ships in quantity. We've got a ship on the drawing boards that would transmit itself to any drop-ship receiver."

Jerryberry prompted him. "And three for general use, you said."

"Yes. We've made over three hundred million passenger booths in the past twenty years. Then there's a general-use cargo booth. The third model is a tremendous portable booth for shipping really big, fragile cargoes. Like a prefab house or a rocket booster or a live sperm whale. You can set the thing in place almost anywhere, using three strap-on helicopter setups. I didn't believe it when I saw it." Whyte sipped at his milk. "You've got to remember that I'm not in the business anymore. I'm still chairman of the board, but a bunch of younger people give most of the orders, and I hardly ever get into the factories."

"Does JumpShift have a monopoly on displacement booths?"

He saw the *Newstaper!* reaction, a tightening at Whyte's eyes and lips. "Wrong word," Jerryberry said quickly. "Sorry. What I meant was, who makes displacement booths? I'm sure you make most of the passenger booths in the United States."

"All of them. It's not a question of monopoly. Anyone could make his own booths. Any community could. But it would be hideously expensive. The cost doesn't drop until you're making millions of them. So suppose . . . Chile, for instance. Chile has less than a million passenger booths, all JumpShift model. Suppose they *had* gone ahead and made their own. They'd have only their own network, unless they built a direct copy of some other model. All the booths in a network have to have the same volume."

"Naturally."

"In practice there are about ten networks worldwide. The U.S.S.R. network is the biggest by far. I think the smallest is Brazil—"

"What happens to the air in a receiver?"

Whyte burst out laughing. "I *knew* that was coming! It never fails." He sobered. "We tried a lot of things. It turns out the only practical solution is to send the air in the receiver back to the transmitter, which means that every transmitter has to be a receiver, too."

"Then you could get a free ride if you knew who was about to flick in from where, when."

"Of course you could, but would you want to bet on it?"

"I might, if I had something to smuggle past customs."

"How do you mean?"

"I'm just playing with ideas. The incoming booths at customs are incoming because there's no way to dial out—"

"I remember. Type I's with the dials removed."

"Okay. Say you wanted to smuggle something into the country. You flick to customs in Argentina. Then a friend flicks from California to Argentina, into your booth. You wind up in his booth, in California, and *not* behind the customs barrier."

"Brilliant," said Whyte. "Unfortunately there's a fail-safe to stop anyone from flicking into an occupied booth."

"Damn."

"Sorry," Whyte said, grinning. "What do you care? There are easier ways to smuggle. Too many. I'm not really sorry. I'm a laissez-faire man myself."

"I wondered if you could do something with dials to stop another mall riot."

Whyte thought about it. "Not by taking the dials off. If you wanted to stop a riot, you'd have to stop people from coming *in*. Counters on the booths, maybe."

"Mmm."

"What was it like, Barry?"

"Crowded. Like a dam broke. The law did shut the booths down from outside, but not fast enough. Maybe that's the answer. Cut out the booths at the first sign of trouble."

"We'd get a lot of people mad at us."

"You would, wouldn't you?"

"Like the power brownouts in the seventies and eighties. Or like obscene telephone calls. You couldn't do anything about them, except get more and more uptight . . . readier to smash things. . . . That's why riots happen, Barry. People who are a little bit angry all the time."

"Oh?"

"All the riots I remember." Whyte smiled. "There haven't been any for a long time. Give JumpShift some credit for that. We stopped some of the things that kept everyone a little bit angry all the time. Smog. Traffic jams. Slow mail. Slum landlords; you don't *have* to live near your job or your welfare office or whatever. Job hunting. Crowding. Have you ever been in a traffic jam?''

''Maybe when I was a little boy.''

''Friend of mine was a college professor for a while. His problem was he lived in the wrong place. Five days a week he would spend an hour driving to work—you don't believe me?—and an hour and a quarter driving home, because traffic was heavier then. Eventually he gave it up to be a writer.''

''Gawd, I should hope so!''

''It wasn't even that rare,'' Whyte said seriously. ''It was rough if you owned a car, and rougher if you didn't. JumpShift didn't cause riots; we *cured* them.''

And he seemed to wait for Jerryberry's agreement.

Silence stretched long enough to become embarrassing . . . yet the only thing Jerryberry might have said to break it was ''But what about the mall riot?'' He held his peace.

''Drain that thing,'' Whyte said abruptly. ''I'll *show* you.''

''Show me?''

''Finish that drink. We're going places.'' Whyte drank half a glass of milk in three gulps, his Adam's apple bobbing. He lowered the glass. ''Well?''

''Ready.''

On Madison Avenue the sunset shadows ran almost horizontally along the glass faces of buildings. Robin Whyte stepped out of L'Orangerie and turned right. Four feet away, a displacement booth.

In the booth he blocked the hand Jerryberry would have used to insert his C.B.A. card. ''My treat. This was my idea. . . . Anyway, some of these numbers are secret.'' He inserted his own card and dialed three numbers.

Twice they saw rows of long-distance booths. Then it was bright sunlight and sea breeze. Far out beyond a sandy beach and white waves, a great cylinder with a rounded top rose high out of the water. Orange letters on the curved metal flank read: ''JUMPSHIFT FRESHWATER TRANSPORT.''

''I could take you out in a boat,'' said Whyte. ''But it would be a waste of time. You wouldn't see much. Nothing but vacuum inside. You know how it works?''

''Sure.''

''Teleportation was like laser technology. One big breakthrough and then a thousand ways to follow up on it. We spent *twelve solid years* building continuous teleport pumps for various municipalities to ship fresh water in various directions. When all the time the real problem was *getting* the fresh water, not moving it.

''Do you know how we developed this gimmick? My secretary dreamed it up one night at an office party. She was about half smashed, but she wrote it down, and the next morning we all took turns trying to read her handwriting. . . . Well, never mind. It's a simple idea. You build a tank more than thirty-four feet above sea level, open at the bottom, airtight, and you put the teleport pump in the top. You teleport the air out. When the air goes, the seawater boils. From then on you're teleporting cold water-vapor. It condenses wherever you ship it, and you get fresh water. Want to take pictures?''

''No.''

''Then let's look at the results,'' Whyte said, and dialed.

Now it was even brighter. The booth was backed up against a long wooden building. Far away was a white glare of salt flats, backed by blue ghosts of mountains. Jerryberry blinked and squinted. Whyte opened the door.

Jerryberry said, ''Whoooff!''

''Death Valley. Hot, isn't it?''

''Words fail me at a time like this, but I suggest you look up the dictionary definition of *blast furnace*.'' Jerryberry felt perspiration start as a rippling itch all over him. ''I'm going to pretend I'm in a sauna. Why doesn't anyone ever put displacement booths inside?''

''They did for a while. There were too many burglaries. Let's go around back.''

They walked around the dry wooden building . . .

. . . and into an oasis. Jerryberry was jarred. On one side of the building, the austere beauty of a barren desert. On the other was a manicured forest: rows and rows of trees.

''We can grow damn near anything out here. We started with date palms, went to orange and grapefuit trees, pineapples, a *lot* of rice paddies, mangoes—anything that grows in tropic climates will grow here, as long as you give it enough water.''

Jerryberry had already noticed the water tower. It looked just like the transmitter. He said, ''And the right soil.''

''Well, yes. Soil isn't that good in Death Valley. We have to haul in too much fertilizer.'' Rivulets of perspiration ran down Whyte's cheeks. His soft face looked almost stern. ''But the principle holds. With teleportation, men can live practically anywhere. We gave people room. A man can work in Manhattan or Central Los Angeles or Central Anywhere and live in—in—''

''Nevada.''

''Or Hawaii! Or the Grand Canyon! Crowding caused riots. We've eliminated crowding—for a while, anyway. At the rate we're going we'll still wind up shoulder to shoulder, but not until you and I are both dead.''

Jerryberry considered keeping his mouth shut but decided he didn't have the willpower. ''What about pollution?''

''What?''

''Death Valley used to have an ecology as unique as its climate. What's your unlimited water doing to that?''

''Ruining it, I guess.''

''Hawaii, you said. Grand Canyon. There are laws against putting up apartment buildings in national monuments, thank God. Hawaii probably has the population density of New York by now. Your displacement booths can put men anywhere, right? Even places they don't belong.''

''Well, maybe they can,'' Whyte said slowly. ''Pollution. Hmm. What do you know about Death Valley?''

''It's hot.'' Jerryberry was wet through.

''Death Valley used to be an inland sea. A salt sea. Then the climate changed, and all the water went away. What did *that* do to the ecology?''

Jerryberry scratched his head. ''A *sea*?''

''Yes, a sea! And drying it up ruined one ecology and started another, just like we're doing. But never mind that. I want to show you some things. Pollution, huh?'' Whyte's grip on Jerryberry's arm was stronger than it had any right to be.

Whyte was angry. In the booth he froze, with his brow furrowed and his forefinger extended. Trying to remember a number. Then he dialed in trembling haste.

He dialed two sequences. Jerryberry saw the interior of an airline terminal, then—dark.

''Oh, damn. I forgot it would be night here.''

''Where are we?''

''Sahara Desert. Rudolph Hill Reclamation Project. No, don't go out there; there's nothing to see at night. Do you know anything about the project?''

''You're trying to grow a forest in the middle of the Sahara: trees, leaf-eating molds, animals, the whole ecology.'' Jerryberry tried to see out through the glass. Nothing. ''How's it working?''

''Well enough. If we can keep it going another thirty years, this part of the Sahara should stay a forest. Do you think we're wiping out another ecology?''

''Well, it's probably *worth* it *here*.''

''The Sahara used to be a lush, green land. It was men who turned it into a desert, over thousands of years, mainly through overgrazing. We're trying to put it back.''

''Okay,'' said Jerryberry. He heard Whyte dialing. Through the glass he could now see stars and a horizon etched with treetop shadows.

He squinted against airport-terminal lights. He asked, ''How did we get through customs?''

''Oh, the Hill project is officially United States territory.'' Whyte swung the local directory out from the wall and leafed through it before dialing a second time. ''Some day you'll make *any* journey by dialing two numbers,'' he was saying. ''Why should you have to dial your local airport first? Just dial a long-distance booth near your destination. Of course the change-over will cost us considerable. Here we are.''

Bright sunlight, sandy beach, blue sea stretching to infinity. The booth was backed up against a seaside hotel. Jerryberry followed Whyte, whose careful, determined stride took him straight toward the water.

They stopped at the edge. Tiny waves brushed just to the tips of their shoes.

"Carpinteria. They advertise this beach as the safest beach in the world. It's also the dullest, of course. No waves. Remember anything about Carpinteria, Barry?"

"I don't think so."

"Oil-slick disaster. A tanker broke up out there, opposite Santa Barbara, which is up the coast a little. All of these beaches were black with oil. I was one of the volunteers working here to save the birds, to get the oil off their feathers. They died anyway. Almost fifty years ago, Barry."

Part of a history lesson floated to the top of his mind. "I thought that happened in England."

"There were several oil-slick disasters. Almost I might say, there were many. These days we ship oil by displacement booths, and we don't use anything like as *much* oil."

"No cars."

"No oil wells, practically."

They shifted.

From an underwater dome they gazed out at an artificial reef made from old car bodies. The shapes seemed to blend, their outlines obscured by mud and time and swarming fish. Bent and twisted metal bodies had long since rusted away, but their outlines remained, held by shellfish living and dead. Ghosts of cars, the dashboards and upholstery showing through. An occasional fiber-glass wreck showed as if it had been placed yesterday.

The reef went on and on, disappearing into gray distance.

All those cars.

"People used to joke about the East River catching fire and burning to the ground. It was that dirty," said Whyte. "Now look at it."

Things floated by: wide patches of scum, with plastic and metal objects embedded in them. Jerryberry said, "It's pretty grubby."

"Maybe, but it's not an open sewer. Teleportation made it easier to get rid of garbage."

"I guess my trouble is I never saw anything as dirty as you claim it was. Oil slicks. Lake Michigan. The Mississippi." *Maybe you're exaggerating.* "Just what has teleportation done for garbage collection?"

"There are records. Pictures."

"But even with your wonderful bottomless garbage cans, it must be easier just to dump it in the river."

"Ahh, I guess so."

"And you still have to *put* the gupp somewhere after you collect it."

Whyte was looking at him oddly. "Very shrewd, Barry. Let me show you the next step."

* * *

Whyte kept his hand covered as he dialed. "Secret," he said. "Jump-Shift experimental laboratory. We don't need a lot of room, because experiments with teleportation aren't particularly dangerous. . . . "

. . . but there was room, lots of it. The building was a huge inflated Quonset hut. Through the transparent panels Jerryberry could see other buildings, set wide apart on bare dirt. The sun was 45 degrees up. If he had known which way was north, he could have guessed longitude and latitude.

A very tall, very black woman in a lab smock greeted Whyte with glad cries. Whyte introduced her as "Gemini Jones, Phud."

"Gem, where do you handle disposal of radioactive waste?"

"Building Four." The physicist's hair exploded around her head like a black dandelion, adding unnecessary inches to her height. She looked down at Jerryberry with genial curiosity. "Newstaper?"

"Yah."

"Don't ever try to fool anyone. The eyes give you away."

They took the booth to Building Four. Presently they were looking down through several densities of leaded glass into a cylindrical metal chamber.

"We get a package every twenty minutes or so," said Gem Jones. "There's a transmitter linked to this receiver in every major power plant in the United States. We keep the receiver on all the time. If a package gets reflected back, we have to find out what's wrong, and that can get hairy, because it's usually wrong at the drop-ship."

Jerryberry said, "Drop-ship?"

Gemini Jones showed surprise at his ignorance. Whyte said, "Back up a bit, Barry. What's the most dangerous garbage ever?"

"Give me a hint."

"Radioactive wastes from nuclear power plants. Most dangerous per pound, anyway. They send those wastes here, and we send them to a drop-ship. You've *got* to know what a drop-ship is."

"Of *course* I—"

"A drop-ship is a moving teleport receiver with one end open. Generally it's attached to a space probe. The payload flicks in with a velocity different from that of the drop-ship. Of course it's supposed to come tearing out the open end, which means somebody has to keep it turned right. And of course the drop-ship only operates in vacuum."

"Package," Gem Jones said softly. Something had appeared in the metal chamber below. It was gone before Jerryberry could quite see what it was.

"Just where is your drop-ship?"

"Circling Venus," said Whyte. "Originally it was part of the second Venus expedition. You can send anything through a drop-ship: fuel, oxygen, food, water, even small vehicles. There are drop-ships circling every planet in the solar system, except Neptune.

"When the Venus expedition came home, they left the drop-ship in orbit. We thought at first that we might send another expedition through it, but—face it, Venus just isn't worth it. We're using the planet as a garbage dump, which is about all it's good for.

"Now, there's no theoretical reason we can't send unlimited garbage through the Venus drop-ship, as long as we keep the drop-ship oriented right. Many transmitters, one receiver. The payload doesn't stay in the receiver more than a fraction of a second. If it did get overloaded, why, some of the garbage would be reflected back to the transmitter, and we'd send it again. No problem."

"What about cost?"

"Stupendous. Horrible. Too high for any kind of garbage less dangerous than this radioactive stuff. But maybe we can bring it down someday." Whyte stopped; he looked puzzled. "Mind if I sit down?"

There were fold-up chairs around a card table with empty pop bulbs on it. Whyte sat down rather disturbingly hard, even with Gem Jones trying to support his weight. She asked, "Can I get Doctor Janesko?"

"No, Gem, just tired. Is there a pop machine?"

Jerryberry found the pop machine. He paid a chocolate dollar for a clear plastic bulb of cola. He turned and almost bumped into Gemini Jones.

She spoke low, but there was harsh intensity in her voice. "You're running him ragged. Will you lay off of him?"

"He's been running *me*!" Jerryberry whispered.

"I believe it. Well, don't let him run you so fast. Remember, he's an old man."

Whyte pulled the cola bulb open and drank. "Better." He sighed . . . and was back in high gear. "Now, you see? We're *cleaning up* the world. *We* aren't polluters."

"Right."

"Thank you."

"I never should have raised the subject. What have you got for the mall riot?"

Whyte looked confused.

"The mall riot is still going on, and they're still blaming me."

"And you still blame JumpShift."

"It's a matter of access," Jerryberry said patiently. "Even if only . . . ten men in a million, say, would loot a store, given the opportunity, that's still about four thousand people in the United States. And all four thousand can get to the Santa Monica Mall in the time it takes to dial twenty-one digits."

When Whyte spoke again, he sounded bitter. "What are we supposed to do, stop inventing things?"

"No, of course not." Jerryberry pulled open another bulb of cola.

"What, then?"

"I don't know. Just . . . keep working things out." He drank. "There's always another problem behind the one you just solved. Does that mean you should stop solving problems?"

"Well, let's solve this one."

They sat sipping cola. It was good to sit down. *The old man's running me ragged,* thought Jerryberry.

"Crowds," he said.

"Right."

"You can make one receiver for many transmitters. In fact . . . every booth in a city receives from any other booth. Can you make a booth that transmits only?"

Whyte looked up. "Sure. Give it an unlisted number. Potentially it would still be a receiver, of course."

"Because you have to flick the air back to the transmitter."

"How's this sound? You can put an E on the booth number. The only dials with E's in them are at police stations and fire stations. E for Emergency."

"All *right*. Now, you put a lot of these escape booths wherever a crowd might gather—"

"That could be anywhere. You said so yourself."

"Yah."

"We'd have to double the number of booths in the country . . . or cut the number of incoming booths in half. You'd have to walk twice as far to get where you're going from any given booth. Would it be worth it?"

"I don't think this is the last riot," said Jerryberry. "It's growing. Like tourism. Your short-hop booths cut tourism way down. The long-distance booths are bringing it back, but slowly. Would you believe a permanent floating riot? A mob that travels from crowd to crowd, carrying coin purses, looting where they can."

"I *hate* that idea."

Jerryberry put his hand on the old man's shoulder. "Don't worry about it. You're a hero. You made a miracle. What people do with it isn't your fault. Maybe you even saved the world. The pollution was getting very rough before JumpShift came along."

"By God, it was."

"I've got to be going. There are things I want to see before I run out of time."

8

Tahiti. Jerusalem. Mecca. Easter Island. Stonehenge. The famous places of the world. Places a man might dial almost on impulse. Names that came unbidden to the mind.

Mecca. Vast numbers of Muslims (a number he could look up later) bowed toward Mecca five times a day. The Koran called for every Muslim to make a pilgrimage to Mecca at least once in a lifetime. The city's only industry was the making of religious articles. And you could get there just by dialing. . . .

Jerusalem. Sacred to three major religions. Jews still toasted each other at Passover: "Next year in Jerusalem." Still a forming ground of history after thousands of years. And you could get there just by dialing. . . .

Stonehenge. An ancient mystery. What race erected those stones, and when and why? These would never be known with certainty. From the avenue at the northeast entrance a path forked and ran up a hill between burial mounds . . . and there was a long-distance displacement booth on the hill.

It would be eleven at night in Stonehenge. One in the morning in Mecca and Jerusalem. No action there. Jerryberry crossed them out.

Eiffel Tower, the pyramids, the Sphinx, the Vatican . . . dammit, the most memorable places on Earth were all in the same general area. What could he see at midnight?

Well—

Tahiti. Say "tropical paradise," and every stranger in earshot will murmur, "Tahiti." Once Hawaii had had the same reputation, but Hawaii was too close to civilization. Hawaii had been civilized. Tahiti, isolated in the southern hemisphere, might have escaped that fate.

Everything lurched as he finished dialing. Jerryberry stumbled against the booth wall. Briefly he was terrified. But he'd be dead if the velocity transfer had failed. It must be a little out of synch.

He knew too much, that was all.

There were six booths of different makes this side of customs. The single official had a hopeless look. He waved through a constant stream of passengers without seeming to see them.

Jerryberry moved with the stream.

They were mostly men. Many had cameras; few had luggage. English, American, French, German, some Spanish and U.S.S.R. Most were dressed lightly—and poorly, in cheap clothes ready to come apart. They swarmed toward the outgoing booths, the rectangular Common Market booths with one glass side. Jerryberry saw unease and dismay on many faces. Perhaps it was the new, clean, modern building that bothered them. This was an island paradise? Air conditioning. Fluorescent lighting.

Jerryberry stood in line for the phone. Then he found that it wouldn't take his coin or his credit card. On his way to the change counter he thought to examine the displacement booths. They took only French money. He bought a heavy double handful of coins, then got back in line for the phone.

They have to get used to traveling again. Right on.

The computerized directory spoke English. He used it to get a string of booth numbers in downtown Papeete.

* * *

He was a roving newstaper again. Dial, watch the scene flick over, look around while inserting a coin and dialing. The coin slot was in the wrong place, and the coins felt wrong—too big, too thin—and the dial was a disk with holes in it. A little practice had him in the routine.

There was beach front lined with partly built hotels in crazily original shapes. Of all the crowds he saw in Papeete, the thickest were on the beaches and in the water. Later he could not remember the color of the sand; he hadn't seen enough of it.

Downtown he found huge blocks of buildings faced in glass, some completed, some half built. He found old slums and old mansions. But wherever the streets ran, past mansions or slums or new skyscrapers, he found tents and leantos and board shacks hastily nailed together. They filled the streets, leaving small clear areas around displacement booths and public rest rooms and far more basic portable toilets. An open-air market ran for several blocks and was closed at both ends by crowds of tents. The only way in or out was by booth.

They're ahead of us, thought Jerryberry. *When you've got booths, who needs streets?* He was not amused. He was appalled.

There were beggars. At first he was moving too fast; he didn't realize what they were doing. But wherever he flicked in, one or two habitants immediately came toward his booth. He stopped under a vertical glass cliff of a building, where the tents of the squatters ran just to the bottommost of a flight of stone steps, and waited.

Beggars. Some were natives, men and women and children, uniform in their dark-bronze color and in their dress and their speech and the way they moved. They were a thin minority. Most were men and white and foreign. They came with their hands out, mournful or smiling; they spoke rapidly in what they guessed to be his language, and were right about half the time.

He tried several other numbers. They were everywhere.

Tahiti was a white man's daydream.

Suddenly he'd had enough. On his list of jotted numbers was one that would take him out of the city. Jerryberry dialed it.

Air puffed out of the booth when he opened the door. Jerryberry opened his jaws wide to pop his ears.

The view! He was near the peak of a granite mountain. Other mountains marched away before him, and the valleys between were green and lush. Greens and yellows and white clouds, the blue-gray of distant peaks, and beyond everything else, the sea.

It was a bus terminal. An ancient Greyhound was just pulling out. The driver stopped alongside him and shouted something amiable in French. Jerryberry smiled and shook his head violently. The driver shrugged and pulled away.

This could not have been the original terminal. Before displacement booths it could have been reached only after hours of driving. In moving the terminal up here, the touring company had saved the best for first and last.

The bus had looked full. Business was good.

Jerryberry stood for a long time, drinking in the view. This was the beauty that had made Tahiti famous. It was good to know that Tahiti's population explosion had left something intact.

In good time he remembered that he was running on a time limit. He walked around to the ticket window.

The young man in the booth laid a paperback book face down. He smiled agreeably. "Yes?"

"Do you speak English?"

"Certainly." He wore a kind of uniform, but his features and color were those of a Tahitian. His English was good, the accent not quite French. "Would you like to buy a tour ticket?"

"No, thanks. I'd like to talk, if you have a minute."

"What would you like to talk about?"

"Tahiti. I'm a newstaper."

The man's smile drooped a bit. "And you wish to give us free publicity."

"Something like that."

The smile was gone. "You may return to your country and tell them that Tahiti is full."

"I noticed that. I have just come from Papeete."

"I have the honor to own a house in Papeete, a good property. We, my family and myself, we have been forced to move out! There was no—no *paysage*—" he was too angry to talk as fast as he wanted—"no passage from the house to anyplace. We were surrounded by the tents of the—" He used a word Jerryberry did not recognize. "We could not buy an instant-motion booth for the house. I had not the money. We could not have moved the booth to the house because the—"that word again—"blocked the streets. The police can do nothing. Nothing."

"Why not?"

"There are too many. We are not monsters; we cannot simply shoot them. It would be the only way to stop them. They come without money or clothing or a place to stay. And they are not the worst. You will tell them this when you return?"

"I'm recording," said Jerryberry.

"Tell them that the worst are those with much money, those who build hotels. They would turn our island into an enormous hotel! See!" He pointed where Jerryberry could not have seen himself, down the slope of the mountain. "The Playboy Club builds a new hotel below us."

Jerryberry looked down to temporary buildings and a great steel box with helicopter rotors on it. He filmed it on the Minox, then filmed a panoramic sweep of the mountains beyond, and finished with the scowling man in the ticket booth.

"Squatters," the ticket-taker said suddenly. "The word I wanted. The squatters are in my house now, I am sure of it, in my house since we moved out. Tell them we want no more squatters.''

''I'll tell them,'' said Jerryberry.

Before he left, he took one more long look about him. Green valleys, gray-blue mountains, distant line of sea . . . but his eyes kept dropping to the endless stream of supplies that poured from the Playboy Club's Type III cargo booth.

Easter Island. Tremendous, long-faced, solemn stone statues with top-knots of red volcanic tuff. Cartoons of the statues were even more common than pictures (''Shut up until those archaeologists leave,'' one statue whispers to another), and even pictures can only hint at their massive solemnity. But you could get there just by dialing. . . .

Except that the directory wouldn't give him a booth number for Easter Island.

Surely there must be booth travel to Easter Island. Mustn't there? But how eager would the Peruvian government be to see a million tourists on Easter Island?

The other side of the coin. Displacement booths made any place infinitely accessible, but only if you moved a booth in. Jerryberry was grinning with delight as he dialed Los Angeles International. There *was* a defense.

9

At the police station on Purdue Avenue he couldn't get anyone to talk to him.

The patience of a newstaper was unique in a world of instant transportation. He kept at it. Eventually a desk man stopped long enough to tell him, ''Look, we don't have *time*. Everybody's out cleaning up the mall riot.''

''Cleaning up? Is it over?''

''Just about. We had to move in old riot vehicles from Chicago. I guess we'll have to start building them again. But it's over.''

''Good!''

''Too right. I don't mean to say we *got* them all. Some looters managed to jury-rig a cargo booth in the basement of Penney's. They moved their loot out that way and then got out that way themselves. We're going to hate it the next time they show up. They've got guns now.''

''A permanent floating riot?''

''Something like that. Look, I don't have time to talk.'' And he was back on the phone.

The next man Jerryberry stopped recognized him at once. ''You're the man who started it all! Will you get out of my way?''

Jerryberry left.

* * *

Sunset on a summer evening. It was cocktail hour again . . . three and a half hours later.

Jerryberry felt unaccountably dizzy outside the police station. He rested against the wall. Too much change. Over and over again he had changed place and time and climate. From evening in New York to a humid seacoast to the dry furnace of Death Valley to night in the Sahara. It was hard to remember where he was. He had lost direction.

When he felt better, he shifted to the Cave des Roys.

For each human being there is an optimum ratio between change and stasis. Too little change, he grows bored. Too little stability, he panics and loses his ability to adapt. One who marries six times in ten years will not change jobs. One who moves often to serve his company will maintain a stable marriage. A woman chained to one home and family may redecorate frantically or take a lover or go to many costume parties.

Displacement booths make novelty easy. Stability comes hard. For many the clubs were an element of stability. Many key clubs were chains; a man could leave his home in Wyoming and find his club again in Denver. Members tended to resemble one another. A man changing roles would change clubs.

Clubs were places to meet people, as buses and airports and even neighborhoods no longer were. Some clubs were good for pickups ("This card gets me laid"), others for heavy conversation. At the Beach Club you could always find a paddle-tennis game.

The Cave was for quiet and stability. A quick drink and the cool darkness of the Cave's bar were just what Jerryberry needed. He looked into the lights in the wall of bottles and tried to remember a name. When it came, he jotted it down, then finished his drink at leisure.

Harry McCord had been police chief in Los Angeles for twelve years and had been on the force for far longer. He had retired only last year. The computer-directory took some time to find him. He was living in Oregon.

He was living in a small house in the middle of a pine forest. From McCord's porch Jerryberry could see the dirt road that joined him to civilization. It seemed to be fading away in weeds. But the displacement booth was new.

They drank beer on the porch. "Crime is a pretty general subject," said Harry McCord.

"Crime *and* displacement booths," said Jerryberry. "I want to know how your job was affected by the instant getaway."

"Ah."

Jerryberry waited.

"Pretty drastically, I guess. The booths came in . . . when? Nineteen ninety? But they came slowly. We had a chance to get used to them. Let's see; there were people who put displacement booths in their living rooms, and when they got robbed, they blamed us. . . . " McCord talked haltingly at first, then gaining speed. He had always been something of a public figure. He talked well.

Burglary: The honors were even there. If the house or apartment had an alarm, the police could be on the scene almost instantly. If the burglar moved fast enough to get away, he certainly wouldn't have time to rob his target.

There were sophisticated alarms now that would lock the displacement-booth door from the inside. Often that held the burglar up just long enough for the police to shift in. At opposite extremes of professionalism, there were men who could get through an alarm system without setting it off—in which case there wasn't a hope in hell of catching them after they'd left—and men who had been caught robbing apartment houses because they'd forgotten to take coins for the booth in the lobby.

"Then there was Lon Willis. His MO was to prop the booth door open before he went to work on the house. If he set the alarm off, he'd run next door and use that booth. Worked pretty well—it slowed us up just enough that we never did catch him. But one night he set off an alarm, and when he ran next door, the next-door neighbor blew a small but adequate hole in him."

Murder: The alibi was an extinct species. A man attending a party in Hawaii could shoot a man in Paris in the time it would take him to use the bathroom. "Like George Clayton Larkin did. Except that he used his credit card, and we got him," said McCord, "and we got Lucille Downey because she ran out of coins and had to ask at the magazine stand for change. With blood all over her sleeves!"

Pickpockets: "Do you have a lock pocket?"

"Sure," said Jerryberry. It was an inside pocket lined with tough plastic. The zipper lock took two hands to open. "They're tough to get into, but not impossible."

"What's in it? Credit cards?"

"Right."

"And you can cancel them in three minutes. Picking pockets isn't profitable any more. If it was, they would have *mobbed* the mall riot."

Smuggling: Nobody even tried to stop it.

Drugs: "There's no way to keep them from getting in. Anyone who wants drugs can get them. We make arrests where we can, and so what? Me, I'm betting on Darwin."

"How do you mean?"

"The next generation won't use drugs because they'll be descended from people who had better sense. I'd legalize wireheading if it were up to me. With a wire in your pleasure center, you're getting what all the drugs are supposed to give you, and no dope peddler can hold out on you."

Riots: The mall riot was the first *successful* riot in twenty years. "The police can get to a riot before it's a riot," said McCord. "We call them *flash crowds,* and we watch for them. We've been doing it ever since . . . well, ever since it became possible." He hesitated and evidently decided to go on. "See, the coin booths usually went into the shopping centers first and then the residential areas. It wasn't till JumpShift put them in the slum areas that we stopped having riots."

"Makes sense."

McCord laughed. "Even that's a half-truth. When the booths went into the slums, we pretty near stopped having slums. Everyone moved out. They'd commute."

"Why do you think the police didn't stop the mall riot?"

"That's a funny one, isn't it? I was there this afternoon. Did you get a chance to look at the cargo booth in Penney's basement?"

"No."

"It's a professional job. Whoever rigged it knew exactly what he was doing. No slips. He probably had a model to practice on. We traced it to a cargo receiver in downtown L.A., but we don't know where it was sending to, because someone stayed behind and wrecked it and then shifted out. Real professional. Some gang has decided to make a profession of riots."

"You think this is their first job?"

"I'd guess. They must have seen the mall-type riots coming. Which is pretty shrewd, because a flash crowd couldn't have formed that fast before long-distance displacement booths. It's a new crime. Makes me almost sorry I retired."

"How would you redesign the booths to make life easier for the police?"

But McCord wouldn't touch the subject. He didn't know anything about displacement-booth design.

Seven o'clock. The interview with Evans was at ten.

Jerryberry shifted back to the Cave. He was beginning to get nervous. The Cave, and a good dinner, should help ease his stage fright.

He turned down a couple of invitations to join small groups. With the interview hanging over his head, he'd be poor company. He sat alone and continued to jot during dinner.

Escape booths. Send anywhere, receive only from police and fire departments.

Police can shut down all booths in an area. Except escape booths? No, that would let the looters escape, too. But there might be no way to stop that. At least it would get the innocent bystanders out of a riot area.

Hah! *Escape booths send only to police station!!!*

He crossed that out and wrote, *All booths send only to police station!!!* He crossed that out, too, to write an expanded version:

1. Riot signal from police station.

2. All booths in area stop receiving.

3. All booths in area send only to police station.

He went back to eating. Moments later he stopped with his fork half raised, put it down, and wrote:

4. A million rioters stomp police station to rubble, from inside.

And it had seemed like such a good idea.

* * *

He was dawdling over coffee when the rest of it dropped into place. He went to a phone.

The secretary at Seven Sixes promised to have Dr. Whyte call as soon as he checked in. Jerryberry put a time limit on it, which seemed to please her.

McCord wasn't home.

Jerryberry went back to his coffee. He was feeling twitchy now. He had to know if this was possible. Otherwise he would be talking through his hat—in front of a big audience.

Twenty minutes later, as he was about to get up and call again, the headwaiter came to tell him that Dr. Robin Whyte was on the phone.

"It's a design problem," said Jerryberry. "Let me tell you how I'd like it to work, and then you can tell me if it's possible, okay?"

"Go ahead."

"First step is the police get word of a flash crowd, a mall riot-type crowd. They throw emergency switches at headquarters. Each switch affects the displacement booths in a small area."

"That's the way it works now."

"*Now* those switches *turn off* the booths. I'd like them to do something more complex. Set them so they can only receive from police and fire departments and can only transmit to a police station."

"We can do that." Whyte half-closed his eyes to think. "Good. Then the police could release the innocent bystanders, send the injured to a hospital, hold the obvious looters, get everybody's names . . . right. Brilliant. You'd put the receiver at the top of a greased slide and a big cell at the bottom."

"Maybe. At least the receiver would be behind bars."

"You could issue override cards to the police and other authorities to let them shift in through a blockade."

"Good."

Whyte stopped suddenly and frowned. "There's a hole in it. A really big crowd would either wreck the station or smother, depending on how strong the cell was. Did you think of that?"

"I'd like to use more than one police station."

"How many? There's a distance limit. . . . Barry, what are you thinking?"

"As it stands now, a long-distance passenger has to dial three numbers to get anywhere. You said you could cut that to two. Can you cut it to one?"

"I don't know."

"It's poetic justice," said Jerryberry. "Our whole problem is that rioters can converge on one point from all over the United States. If we could use *police stations* all over the United States, we wouldn't have a problem. As soon as a cell was full here, we'd switch to police stations in San Diego or Oregon!"

Whyte was laughing. "If you could see your face! Barry, you're a dreamer."

"You can't do it."

"No, of course we can't do it. Wait a minute." Whyte pursed his lips. "There's a way. We could do it if there was a long-distance receiver at the police station. Hook the network to a velocity damper! I told you, there's no reason you shouldn't be able to dial to a long-distance receiver from *any* booth."

"It would work, then!"

"You'd have to talk the public into paying for it. Design wouldn't be much of a problem. We could cover the country with an emergency network in a couple of years."

"Can I quote you?"

"Of course. We sell displacement booths. That's our business."

10

Talk shows are one of the few remaining pure entertainment features on teevee. With cassettes the viewer buys a package; with a talk show he never knows just what he's getting. It is a different product. It is cheap to produce. It can compete.

The *Tonight Show* shows at 8:30 P.M., prime time.

Around nine they start flicking in, pouring out of the coin booths that line the street above the last row of houses. They mill about, searching out the narrow walks that lead down to the strand. They pour over the low stone wall that guards the sand from the houses. They pause, awed.

Breakers roll in from the black sea, flashing electric-blue.

Within minutes Hermosa Beach is aswarm with people: men, women, children, in couples and family groups. They hold hands and look out to sea. They stamp the packed wet sand, dancing like savages, and whoop with delight to see blue light flash beneath their feet. High up on the dry sand are piles of discarded clothing. Swimmers are thick in the water, splashing blue fire at each other.

Many were drunk or high on this or that when the *Tonight Show* led them here. Those who came were happy to start with. They came to do a happy thing. Some carry six-packs or pouches of pot.

The line of them stretches around the curve of the shore to the north, beyond Hermosa Pier to the south, bunching around the pier. More are shifting in all the time, trickling down to join the others.

Jerryberry Jansen flicked in almost an hour early for the interview.

The station was an ant's nest, a swarm of furious disorganization. Jerryberry was looking for Wash Evans when Wash Evans came running past him from behind, glanced back, and came to a jarring halt.

" 'Lo," said Jerryberry. "Is there anything we need to go over before we go on?"

Evans seemed at a loss. "Yah," he said, and caught his breath a little. "You're not news anymore, Jansen. We may not even be doing the interview."

Jerryberry said a dirty word. "I *heard* they'd cleared up the riot—"

"More than that. They caught the lady shoplifter."

"Good!"

"If you say so. One out of a thousand people that recognized your pictures of her turned out to be right. Woman name of Irma Hennessey, lives in Jersey City but commutes all over the country. She says she's never hit the same store twice. She's a kick, Jansen. A newstaper's dream. No offense intended, but I wish they'd let her out of jail tonight. I'd interview *her*."

"So I didn't cause the mall riot anymore, now you've got Irma Hennessey. Well, *good*. I didn't like being a celebrity. Anything else?"

He was thinking, *All that jumping around, all the things I learned today, all wasted. Unless I can get a tapezine lecture out of it. . . .*

Evans said, "Yah, there's a new mall riot going on at Hermosa Beach."

"What the hell?"

"Craziest damn thing." Wash Evans lit a cigarette and talked around it. "You know Gordon Lundt, the 'zine star? He was on the *Tonight Show*, and he happened to mention the red tide down at Hermosa Beach. He said it was pretty. The next thing anyone knows, every man, woman, and child in the country has decided he wants to see the red tide at Hermosa Beach."

"How bad is it?"

"Well, nobody's been hurt, last I heard. And they aren't breaking things. It's not that kind of crowd, and there's nothing to steal but sand, anyway. It's a happy riot, Jansen. There's just a bitch of a lot of people."

"Another flash crowd. It figures," said Jerryberry. "You can get a flash crowd anywhere there are displacement booths."

"Can you?"

"They've been around a long time. It's just that they happen faster with the long-distance booths. Some places are permanent floating flash crowds. Like Tahiti. . . . what's wrong?"

Wash Evans had a funny look. "It just hit me that we don't really have anything to replace you with. You've been doing your homework, have you?"

"All day." Jerryberry dug out the Minox. "I've been everywhere I could think of. Some of this goes with taped interviews." He produced the tape recorder. "Of course there isn't much time to sort it out—"

"No. Gimme." Evans took the camera and the recorder. "We can follow up on these later. Maybe they'll make a special. Right now the news is at Hermosa Beach. And you sound like you know how it happened and what to do about it. Do you still want to do that interview?"

"I—sure."

"Go get a C.B.A. camera from George Bailey. Let's see, it's—nine fifteen, dammit. Spend half an hour, see as much as you can, then get back here. Find out what you can about the—flash crowd at Hermosa Beach. That's what we'll be talking about."

George Bailey looked up as Jerryberry arrived. He pointed emphatically at the single camera remaining on the table, finger-combed the hair back out of his eyes, and went back to monitoring half a dozen teevee screens.

The camera came satisfyingly to life in Jerryberry's hands. He picked up a list of Hermosa Beach numbers and turned to the displacement booths. Too much coffee sloshed in his belly. He stopped suddenly, thinking:

One big riot-control center would do it. You wouldn't need a police network—just one long-distance receiver to serve the whole country, and a building the size of Yankee Stadium, big enough to handle any riot. A federal police force on permanent guard. Rioting was an interstate crime now anyway. You could build such a center faster and cheaper than any network.

Not now. Back to work. He stepped into a booth, dialed, and was gone.

FREDERIK POHL
In the Problem Pit

DAVID

BEFORE I left the apartment to meet my draft call I had packed up the last of Lara. She had left herself all over our home: perfumes, books, eye shadow, Tampax, ivory animals she had forgotten to take and letters from him that she had probably meant for me to read. I didn't read them. I packed up the whole schmear and sent it off to her in Djakarta, with longing and hatred.

Since I was traveling at government expense, I took the hyperjet and then a STOL to the nearest city and a cab from there. I paid for the whole thing with travel vouchers, even the cab, which enormously annoyed the driver; I didn't tip him. He bounced off down the road muttering in Spanish, racing his motor and double-clutching on the switchbacks, and there I was in front of the pit facility, and I didn't want to go on in. I wasn't ready to talk to anybody about any problems, especially mine.

There was an explosion of horns and gunned motors from down the road. Somebody else was arriving, and the drivers were fighting about which of them would pull over to let the other pass. I made up my mind to slope off. So I looked for a cubbyhole to hide my pack and sleeping bag in and found it behind a rock, and I left the stuff there and was gone before the next cab arrived. I didn't know where I was going, exactly. I just wanted to walk up the trails around the mountains in the warm afternoon rain.

It was late afternoon, which meant it was, I calculated, oh, something like six in the morning in Djakarta. I could visualize Lara sound asleep in the heat, sprawled with the covers kicked off, making that little ladylike whistle that served her in place of a snore. (I could not visualize the other half of the bed.)

I was hurting. Lara and I had been married for six years, counting two separations. And the way trouble always does, it had screwed up my work. I'd had this commission from the library in St. Paul, a big, complicated piece for over the front foyer. Well, it hadn't gone well, being more Brancusi and interior-decorator art than me, but still it had been a lot of work and just about finished. And then when I had it in the vacuum chamber and was floating the aluminum plating onto it, I'd let the pressure go up, and air got in, and of course the whole thing burned.

So partly I was thinking about whether Lara would come back and partly whether there was any chance I could do a whole new sculpture and plate it and deliver it before the library purchasing commission got around to canceling my contract, and partly I wasn't thinking at all, just huffing and puffing up those trails in the muggy mist. I could see morning glories growing. I picked up a couple and put them in my pocket. The long muscles in my thighs were beginning to burn, and I was fighting my breathing. So I slowed down, spending my concentration on pacing my steps and my breathing so that I could keep my head away from where the real pain was. And then I found myself almost tripping over a rusted, bent old sign that said *Pericoloso* in one language and *Danger* in another.

The sign spoke truth.

In front of me was a cliff and a catwalk stretching out over what looked like a quarter of a mile of space.

I had blundered on to the old telescope. I could see the bowl way down below, all grown over with bushes and trees. And hanging in the air in front of me, suspended from three cables, was a thing like a rusty trolley car, with spikes sticking out of the lower part of it.

No one was around; I guess they don't use the telescope any more. I couldn't go any farther unless I wanted to go out on the catwalk, which I didn't, and so I sat down and breathed hard. As I began to get caught up on my oxygen debt, I began to think again; and since I didn't want to do that, I pulled the crushed morning glories out of my pocket and chewed on a few seeds.

Well, I had forgotten where I was. In Minneapolis you grow them in a window box. You have to pound them and crush them and soak them and squeeze them, hundreds of seeds at a time, before you get anything. But these had grown in a tropical climate.

I wasn't stoned or tripping, really. But I was—oh, I guess the word is "anesthetized." Nothing hurt any more. It wasn't just an absence of hurting, it was a positive *not* hurting, like when you've broken a tooth and you've finally got to the dentist's office and he's squirted in the novocaine and you can feel that not-hurting spread like a golden glow across your jaw, blotting up the ache as it goes.

I don't know how long I sat there, but by the time I remembered I was supposed to report in at the pit the shadows were getting long.

So I missed dinner, I missed signing in properly, I got there just in time for the VISTA guard to snap at me, "Why the hell can't you be on time, Charlie?" and I was the last one down the elevators and into the pit. Everybody else was gathered there already in a big room that looked like it had been chopped out of rock, which I guess it had, with foam cushions scattered around the floor and, I guess, 12 or 14 people scattered around on the cushions, all with their bodies pointed toward an old lady in black slacks and a black turtleneck, but their faces pointed toward me.

I flung down my sleeping bag and sat on it and said, "Sorry."

She said, rather nicely, "Actually, we were just beginning." And everybody looked at me begrudgingly, as though they had no choice but to wait while I blew my nose or built myself a nest out of straws or whatever I was going to do to delay them all still further, but I just sat there, trying not to look stoned, and after a while she began to talk.

TINA'S TALK

Hello. My name is Tina Wattridge, and I'm one of your resource people.

I'm not the leader of this group. There isn't any leader. If the group ever decides it has to have a leader, well, it can pick one. Or if you want to be a leader, you can pick yourself. See if anybody follows. But I'm not it, I'm only here to be available for answering questions or giving information.

First, I will tell you what you already know. The reason you are all here is to solve problems.

(She paused for a moment, scratching her nose and smiling, and then went on.)

Thank you. A lot of groups start complaining and making jokes right there, and you didn't. That's nice, because I didn't organize this group, and although I must say I think the groups work out well, it isn't my fault that you're here. And I appreciate your not blaming it on me.

Still, you are here, and we are expected to state some problems and solve them, and we will stay right here until we do that, or enough of it so that whoever's watching us is satisfied enough to let us go. That might be a couple of weeks. I had a group once that got out in 72 hours, but don't expect that. Anyway, you won't know how long it is. The reason we are in these caves is to minimize contact with the external world, including all sorts of times cues. And if any of you have managed to smuggle watches past the VISTA people, please give them to me now. They're not allowed here.

I saw some of you look interested when I talked about who is watching us, and so I ought to say right now I don't know how they watch or when, and I don't care. They do watch. But they don't interfere. The first word we will get from them is when the VISTA duty people unlock the elevator and come down and tell us we can go home.

Food. You can eat whenever you want to, on demand. If you want to establish meal hours, any group of you can do so. If you want to eat singly, whenever you want to, fine. Either way you simply sign in in the dining room—"sign in" means you type your names on the monitor; they'll know who you are; just the last name will do—and order what you want to eat. Your choices are four: "Breakfast," "snack," "light meal" and "full meal." It doesn't matter what order you eat them in or when you want them. When you put in your order, they make them and put them in the dumbwaiter. Dirty dishes go back in the dumbwaiter except for the disposable ones, which go in the trash chute. You can ask for certain special dishes—the way you want your eggs, for instance—but in general you take what they give you. It's all explained on the menu.

Sleep. You sleep when you want to, where you want to. In these three rooms—this one, the problem pit and the eating room, as well as the pool and showers—the lights are permanently on. In the two small rooms out past the bathrooms and laundry the lights can be controlled, and whoever is in the room can turn them on or off any way you like. If you can't agree, you'll just have to work it out.

(She could see them building walls between themselves and her, and quickly she tried to reduce them.)

Listen, it's not as bad as it sounds. I always hate this part because it sounds like I'm giving you orders, but I'm not; those are just the ground rules and they bind me too. And, honestly, you won't all hate it, or not all of it. I've done this 15 times now, and I look forward to coming back!

All right, let's see. Showers, toilets and all are over there. Washer-dryers are next to them. I assume you all did what you were told and brought wash-and-wear clothes, as well as sleeping bags and so on; if you didn't, you'll have to figure out what to do about it yourselves. When you want to wash your clothes, put your stuff in one of the net bags and put it in the machine. If there's something already in the machine, just take it out and leave it on the table. The owner will pick it up when he wants it, no doubt. You can do three or four people's wash in a single cycle without any trouble. They're big machines. And there's plenty of water—you people who come from the Southwest and the Plains States don't have to worry. Incidentally, the sequenced water-supply system that you use there to conserve potable water was figured out right in this cave. The research and development people had to work it over hard, to get the fluidic controls responsive enough, but the basic idea came from here; so, you see, there's a point to all this.

(She lit a cigarette and looked cheerfully around at the group, pleased that they were not resisting, less pleased that they were passive. She was a tall and elderly red-headed woman, who usually managed to look cheerful without smiling.)

That brings me to computation facilities, for those of you who want to work on something that needs mathematical analysis or data access. I will do a certain amount of keyboarding for you, and I'll be there to help—that's basically my job, I guess. There are two terminals in the pit room. They are on-line, real-time, shared-time programs, and those of you who are familiar with ALGOL, COBOL, and so on can use them direct. If you can't write a program in computer language, you can either bring it to me—up to a point—or you can just type out what you want in clear. First, you type the words HELP ME; then you say what you want; then you type THAT'S

ALL. The message will be relayed to a programmer, and he will help you if I can't, or if you don't want me to. You can blind-type your queries if you don't want me looking over your shoulder. And sign your last name to everything. And, as always, if more of you want to use the terminals than we have terminals, you'll have to work it out among you. I don't care how.

Incidentally, the problem pit is there because some groups like to sit face to face in formal surroundings. Sometimes it helps. Use it or not, as you like. You can solve problems anywhere in these chambers. Or outside, if you want to go outside. You can't leave through the elevator, of course, because that's locked now. Where you can go is into the rest of the cave system. But if you do that, it's entirely your own responsibility. These caves run for at least 80 miles and maybe more, right down under the sea. We're at least ten miles by the shortest route from the public ones where the tourists come. I doubt you could find your way there. They aren't lighted, and you can very easily get lost. And there are no, repeat no, communications facilities or food available there. Three people have got lost and died in the past year, although most people do manage to find their way back—or are found. But don't count on being found. No one will even start looking for you until we're all released, and then it can take a long time.

My personal advice—no, I'm sorry. I was going to say that my personal advice is to stay here with the rest of us, but it is, as I say, your decision to make, and if you want to go out you'll find two doors that are unlocked.

Now, there are two other resource people here. The rest of you are either draftees or volunteers. You all know which you are, and for any purposes I can think of it doesn't matter.

I'll introduce the two other pros. Jerry Fein is a doctor. Stand up, will you, Jerry? If any of you get into anything you can't handle, he'll help if he can.

And Marge Klapper over there is a physiotherapist. She's here to help, not to order you around, but—advice and personal opinion again, not a rule—I think you'll benefit from letting her help you. The rest of you can introduce yourselves when we get into our first session. Right now I'll turn you over to—what? Oh, thanks, Marge. Sorry.

The pool. It's available for any of you, any time, as many of you as want to use it. It's kept at 78 degrees, which is two degrees warmer than air temperature. It's a good place to have fun and get the knots out, but, again, you can use it for any purpose you like. Some groups have had active, formal problem-solving sessions in it, and that's all right too.

Now I think that's it, so I'll turn you over to Marge.

MARGE INTERACTING

Marge Klapper was 24 years old, pretty, married but separated, slightly pregnant but not by her husband, and a veteran of eight problem-group marathons.

She would have challenged every part of the description of her, except the first and the last, on the grounds that each item defined her in terms of her relationship to men. She did not even like to be called "pretty." She wasn't in any doubt that she was sexually attractive, of course. She simply didn't accept the presumption that it was only her physical appearance that made her so. The men she found sexually attractive came in all shapes and sizes, one because he was so butchy, one because of his sense of humor, one because he wrote poems that turned into bars of music at the end. She didn't much like being called a physiotherapist, either; it was her job classification, true, but she was going for her master's in Gestalt psychology and was of half a mind to become an M.D. Or else to have the baby that was just beginning to grow inside her; she had not yet reached a decision about that.

"Let's get the blood flowing," she said to all of them, standing up and throwing off her shorty terry-cloth robe. Under it she wore a swimsuit with a narrow bikini bottom and a halter top. She would have preferred to be nude, but her breasts were too full for unsupported calisthenics. She thought the way they flopped around was unaesthetic, and at times it could be actively painful. Also, some of the group were likely to be shy about nudity, she knew from experience. She liked to let them come to it at their own pace.

Getting them moving was the hard part. She had got to the pit early and chatted with some of them ahead of time, learning some of the names, picking out the ones who would work right away, identifying the difficult ones. One of the difficult ones was the little dark Italian man who was "in construction," he had said, whatever that meant; she had sat down next to him on purpose, and now she pulled him up next to her and said:

"All right. Let's start nice and slow and get some of the fug out of our heads. This is easy: we'll just reach."

She lifted her arms over her head, up on tiptoe, fingers upstretched. "High as you can go," she said. "Look up. Let's close our eyes and feel for the roof."

But what Marge was feeling for was the tension and needs of the group. She could almost taste, almost smell, their feelings. What Ben Ittri, next to her, was feeling was embarrassment and fear. The shaggy man who had come in late: a sort of numb pain, so much pain that it had drowned out his receptors. The fat girl, Dolores: anger. Marge could identify with that anger; it was man-directed anger.

She put the group through some simple bending energetics, or at least did with those who would cooperate. She had already taken a census of her mind. Not counting the three professionals, there were five in the group who were really with the kinetics. She supposed they were the volunteers, and probably they had had experience of previous sessions. The other eight, the ones she assumed were draftees, were a spectrum of all the colors of disengagement. The fat girl simply did not seem physically able to stand on tiptoes, though her anger carried her through most of the bending and turning; it was like a sack of cement bending, Marge thought, but she could sense the bones moving under the fat. The bent old black man who sat obstinately on the floor, regarding the creases on his trousers, was a different kind of problem; Marge had not been able to see how to deal with him.

She began moving around the room, calling out instructions. "Now bend sidewise from the waist, You can do it with your hands up like this, or you might be more comfortable with your hands on your hips. But see how far you can go. Left. Right. Left—"

They were actually responding rather well, considering. She stopped in front of a slight black youth in a one-piece Che Guevara overall. "It's fun if we do it together," she said, reaching out for his hands. He flinched away, then apologetically allowed her to take his hands and bend with him. "It's like a dance," she said, smiling, but feeling the tension in his arms and upper torso as he allowed himself unwillingly to turn with her. Marge was not used to that sort of response from males, except from homosexuals, or occasionally the very old ones who had been brought up under the Protestant ethic. He didn't seem to be either of those. "You know my name," she said softly. "It's Marge."

"Rufous," he said, looking away from her. He was acutely uncomfortable; reluctantly she let him go and moved on. She felt an old annoyance that these sessions would not allow her to probe really deeply into the hangups she uncovered, but of course that was not their basic purpose; she could only do that if the people themselves elected to work on that problem.

The other black man, the one who was so obdurately sitting on the floor, had not moved; Marge confronted him and said, "Will you get up and do something with me?"

For a moment she thought he was going to refuse. But then, with dignity, he stood up, took her hands and bent with her, bending left, bending right. He was as light as a leaf but strong, wire rather than straw. "Thank you," she said, and dropped his hands, pleased. "Now," she said to the group, "we're going to be together for quite a while, so let's get to know each other, please. Let's make a circle and put our arms around each other. Right up close! Close as you can get! All of us. Please?"

It was working out nicely, and Marge was very satisfied. Even the old black man was now in the circle, his arms looped around the shoulders of the fat girl on one side and a middle-aged man who looked like an Irish tenor on the other. The group was so responsive, at least compared to most groups in the first hour of their existence as groups, that for a moment Marge considered going right into the pool, or nonverbal communication—but no, she thought, that's imposing my will on them; I won't push it.

"All right, that's wonderful," she said. "Thank you all."

Tina said, "From here on, it's all up to you. All of you. There's tea and coffee and munch over there if anyone wants anything. Marge, thank you; that was fun."

"Anytime," called Marge, stretching her legs against the wall. "I mean that. If any of you ever want to work out with me, just say. Or if you see me doing anything and want to join in, please do.''

''Now,'' said Tina, ''if anybody wants to start introducing himself or talking about a problem, I, for one, would like to listen.''

INTRODUCTIONS

The hardest thing to learn to do was wait.

Tina Wattridge worked at doing it. She pushed a throw pillow over to the floor next to the corner of a couch and sat on it, cross-legged, her back against the couch. Tina's opinion of Marge Klapper was colored by the fact that she had a graddaughter only seven or eight years younger than Marge, which, Tina was aware, led her to think of the therapist as immature; nevertheless, there was something in the notion that the state of the body controlled the state of the mind, and Tina let her consciousness seep into her toes, the tendons on the soles of her feet, her ankles, her knees, all the way up her body, feeling what they felt and letting them relax. It was good in itself, and it kept her from saying anything. If she waited long enough, someone would speak . . .

''Well, does anybody mind if I go first?''

Tina recognized the voice, was surprised and looked up. It was Jerry Fein. It was not against the rules for one of the pros to start, because there were no rules, exactly. But it was unusual. Tina looked at him doubtfully. She had never worked with him before. He was the plumpish kind of young man who looks older than he is; he looked about forty, and for some reason Tina was aware that she didn't like him.

''The thing is,'' said Dr. Fein, haunching himself backward on the floor so that he could see everyone in the group at once, ''I do have a problem. It's a two-part problem. The first part isn't really a problem, except in personal terms, for me. I got a dose from a dear friend two months ago.'' He shrugged comically. ''Like shoemaker's children that never have shoes, you know? I think we doctors get the idea somewhere in med school that when we get into practice we'll be exempt from diseases, they're only things that happen to patients. Well, anyway, it turned out to be syphilis, and so I had to get the shots and all. It's not too bad a thing, you know, but it isn't a lot of fun because there are these resistant strains of spirochetes around, and I had one of the toughest of them, Mary-Bet 13 it's called—so it didn't clear up overnight. But it is cleared up,'' he added reassuringly. ''I mention this in case any of you should be worrying. I mean about maybe using the same drinking glass or something.

''But the part of the problem I want to throw in front of you is, why should anybody get syphilis in the first place? I mean, if there are any diseases in the world we could wipe out in thirty days from a standing start, syphilis and gonorrhea are the ones. But we don't. And I've been thinking about it. The trouble is people won't report themselves. They won't report their contacts even more positively. And they never, *never* think of getting an examination until they're already pretty sure they've got a dose. So if any of you can help me with this public health problem that's on my mind, I'd like to hear."

It was like talking into a tape recorder in an empty room; the group soaked up the words, but nothing changed in their faces or attitudes. Tina closed her eyes, half hoping that someone would respond to the doctor, half that someone else would say something. But the silence grew. After a moment the doctor got up and poured himself a cup of coffee, and when he sat down again his face was as blank as the others.

The man next to Tina stirred and looked around. He was young and extremely good-looking, with the fair hair and sharp-featured face of a Hitler Youth. His name was Stanwyck. Tina had negative feelings toward him, too, for some reason she could not identify; one of the things she didn't like about Jerry Fein was his sloppiness—he was wearing two shirts, one over the other, like a Sicilian peasant. One of the things she didn't like about Stanwyck was his excessive neatness; like the old black man, Bob Sanger, he was wearing a pressed business suit.

But Stanwyck didn't speak.

The fat girl got up, fixed herself a cup of tea with sugar and milk, took a handful of raisins out of a bowl and went back to her place on the floor.

"I think I might as well talk," said somebody at last. (Tina exhaled, which made her realize she had been holding her breath.)

It was the elderly black man, Sanger. He was sitting, hugging his knees to himself, and he stayed that way all the time he was talking. He did not look up but addressed his words to his knees, but his voice was controlled and carrying. "I am a volunteer for this group," he said, "and I think you should know that I asked to join because I am desperate. I am seventy-one years old. For more than forty years I have been the owner and manager of a dental-supply manufacturing company, Sanger Hygiene Products, of Fresno, California. I do not have any response to make to what was said by the gentleman before me, nor am I very sympathetic to him. I am satisfied that God's Word is clear on the wages of sin. Those who transgress against His commandments must expect the consequences, and I have no desire to make their foulness less painful for them. But mine is, in a sense, also a public health problem; so perhaps it is not inappropriate for me to propose it to you now."

"Name?" Tina murmured.

He did not look up at her, but he said, "Yes, Mrs. Wattridge, of course. My name is Bob Sanger. My problem is that halidated sugar and tooth-bud transplants have effectively depleted the market for my products. As you all may be aware, there simply is not a great demand for dental therapy any more. What work is done is preventive and does not require the bridges and caps and plates we make in any great volume. So we are in difficulties such that, at the present projection, my company will have crossed the illiquidity level in at most twelve months, more likely as little as four; and my problem is to avoid bankruptcy.''

He rubbed his nose reflectively against one knife-creased knee and added, ''More than three hundred people will be out of work if I close the plant. If you would not care to help me for my sake, perhaps you will for theirs.''

''Oh, Bob, cut the crap,'' cried the fat girl, getting up for more raisins. ''You don't have to blackmail us!''

He did not look at her or respond in any way. She stood by the coffee table with a handful of raisins for a moment, looking around, and then grinned and said:

''You know, I have the feeling I just volunteered to go next.''

She waited for someone to contradict her, or even to agree with her. No one did, but after a moment she went on. ''Well, why not? My name is Dolores Belli. That's bell-*eye*, not bell-*ee*. I've already heard all the jokes and they're not too funny; I know I'm fat, so what else is new? I'm not sensitive about it,'' she explained. ''But I *am* kind of tired of the subject. Okay. Now about problems. I'll help any way I can, and I do want to think about what both of you have said, Jerry and Bob. Nothing occurs to me right now, but I'll see if I can make something occur, and then I'll be back. I don't have any particular problem of my own to offer, I'm afraid. In fact, I wouldn't be here if I hadn't been drafted. Or truthfully,'' she said, smiling, ''I do have a problem. I missed dinner. I'd like to see what the food is like here. Is that all right?''

When no one volunteered an answer, she said sharply, ''Tina? Is it all right?''

''It's up to you, Dolores,'' said Tina gently.

''Sure it is. Well, let's get our feet wet. Anybody want to join me?''

A couple of the others got up, and then a third, all looking somewhat belligerent about it. They paused at the door, and one of them, a man with long hair and a Zapata mustache, said, ''I'll be back, but I really am starving. My name is David Jaretski. I do have a problem on my mind. It's personal. I don't seem to be able to keep my marriage together, although maybe that's because I don't seem to be able to keep my life together. I'll talk about it later.'' He thought of adding something else but decided against it; he was still feeling a little stoned and not yet ready either to hear someone else's troubles or trust the group with his own.

The man next to him was good-looking in the solid, self-assured way of a middle-aged Irish tenor. He said, in a comfortable, carrying voice, ''I'm Bill Murtagh. I ran for Congress last year and got my tail whipped, and I guess that's what I'll be hoping to talk to you folks about later on.''

He did not seem disposed to add to that, and so the other woman who had stood up spoke. Her blond schoolgirl hair did not match the coffee-and-cream color of her skin or the splayed shape of her nose, but she was strikingly attractive in a short jacket and flared pants. "My name's Barbara Devereux," she said. "I'm a draftee. I haven't figured out a problem yet." She started to leave with the others, then turned back. "I don't like this whole deal much," she said thoughtfully. "I'm not sure I'm coming back. I might prefer going into the caves."

THE CAST OF CHARACTERS

In Terre Haute, Indiana, at the Headquarters of SAD, the Social Affairs Department, in the building called the Heptagon, Group 95-114 had been put together with the usual care. The total number was 16, of whom three were professional resource people, five were volunteers and the remainder selectees. Nine were male, seven female. The youngest had just turned 18; the oldest 71. Their homes were in eight of the 54 states; and they represented a permissible balance of religions, national origins, educational backgrounds and declared political affiliations.

These were the people who made up the 114th group of the year:

BELLI, Dolores. 19. White female, unmarried. Volunteer (who regretted it and pretended she had been drafted; the only one who knew this was untrue was Tina Wattridge, but actually none of the others really cared). As a small child her father had called her Dolly-Belly because she was so cutely plump. She wanted very much to be loved. The men who appealed to her were all-American jocks, and none of them had ever shown the slightest interest in her.

DEL LA GARZA, Caspar. 51. White male. Widower, no surviving children. Draftee. In Harlingen, Texas, where he had lived most of his life, he was assistant manager of an A&P supermarket, a volunteer fireman and a member of the Methodist Church. He had few close friends, but everyone liked him.

DEVEREUX, Barbara. 31. Black female, unmarried. Draftee. Although she had been trained as an architect and had for a time been employed as a fashion artist, she was currently working for a life insurance agent in Elgin, Illinois, processing premiums. With any luck she would have had seven years of marriage and at least one child by now, but the man she loved had been killed serving with the National Guard during the pollution riots of the '80s.

FEIN, Gerald, M.D. 38. White male. Professional resource person, now in his third problem marathon. Jerry Fein was either separated or partially married, depending on how you looked at it; he and his wife had opted for an open marriage, but for more than a year they had not actually lived in the same house. Still, they had never discussed any formal change in the relationship. His wife, Aline, was also a doctor—they had met in medical school—and he often spoke complimentarily of her success, which was much more rapid and impressive than his own.

GALIFINIAKIS, Rose. 44. White female, married, no children. She had been into the Christ Reborn movement in her twenties, New Maoism in her thirties and excursions into commune living, Scientology and transcendental meditation since then, through all of which she had maintained a decorous home and conventional social life for her husband, who was an accountant in the income tax department of the state of New Mexico. She had volunteered for the problem marathon in the hope that it would be something productive and exciting to do.

ITTRI, Benjamin. 32. White male. Draftee. Ittri was a carpenter, but so was Jesus of Nazareth. He thought about that a lot on the job.

JARETSKI, David. 33. White male, listed as married but de facto wifeless, since Lara had run off with a man who traveled in information for the government. Draftee. David was a sculptor, computer programmer and former acid head.

JEFFERSON, Rufous, III. 18. Black male, unmarried, Draftee. Rufous was studying for the priesthood in the Catholic Church in an old-rite seminary which retained the vows of celibacy and poverty and conducted its masses in Latin.

KLAPPER, Marjorie, B.A., Mem. Am. Guild Ther. 24. White female, separated. Professional resource person. Five weeks earlier, sailing after dark with a man she did not know well but really liked, Marge Klapper had decided not to bother with anything and see if she happened to get pregnant. She had, and was now faced with the problem of deciding what to do about it, including what to say to her husband, who thought they had agreed to avoid any relationship with anybody, including each other, until they worked things out.

LIM, Felice. 30. White female, married, one child. Technically a draftee, but she had waived exemption (on grounds of dependent child at home—her husband had vacation time coming and had offered to take care of the baby). Felice Lim had quite a nice natural soprano voice and had wanted to be an opera singer, but either she had a bad voice teacher or the voice simply would not develop. It was sweet and true, but she could not fill a hall, and so she got married.

MENCHEK, Philip. 48. White male, married, no children. Draftee. Menchek was an associate professor of English Literature in a girl's college in South Carolina and rather liked the idea of the problem marathon. If he hadn't been drafted, he might have volunteered, but this way there was less chance of a disagreement with his wife.

MURTAGH, William. 45. White male, married (third time), five children (aggregate of all marriages). Volunteer. Murtagh, when a young college dropout who called himself Wee Willie Wu, had been a section leader in the Marin County Cultural Revolution. It was the best time of his life. His original True Maoists had occupied a nine-bedroom mansion on the top of a mountain in Belvedere, overlooking the Bay, with a private swimming pool they used for struggling with political opponents and a squash court for mass meetings. But they were only able to stay on Golden Gate Avenue for a month. Then they were defeated and disbanded as counterrevolutionaries by the successful East Is Red Cooperative Mao Philosophical Commune, who had helicopters and armored cars. Expelled and homeless, Murtagh had dropped out of the revolutionary movement and back into school, got his degree at San Jose State and became an attorney.

SANGER, Robert, B.Sc., M.A. 71. Black male. Wife deceased, one child (male, also deceased), two grandchildren. Volunteer. Bob Sanger's father, a successful orthodontic dentist in Parsippany, New Jersey, celebrated his son's birth, which happened to occur on the day Calvin Coolidge was elected to his own full term as President, by buying a bottle of bootleg champagne. It was a cold day for November, and Dr. Sanger slipped on the ice. He dropped the bottle. It shattered. A week later the family learned that everyone drinking champagne out of that batch had gone blind, since it had been cooked up out of wood alcohol, ethylene glycol, Seven-Up and grape squeezings. They nicknamed the baby "Lucky Bob" to celebrate. Lucky Bob was, in fact, lucky. He got his master's degree just when the civil rights boom in opportunities for black executives was at its peak. He had accumulated seed capital just when President Nixon's Black Capitalism program was spewing out huge hunks of investment cash. He was used to being lucky, and the death of his industry, coming at the end of his own long life, threw him more than it might have otherwise.

STANWYCK, Devon. 26. White male, unmarried. Volunteer. Stanwyck was the third generation to manage the family real estate agency, a member of three country clubs and a leading social figure in Bucks County, Pennsylvania. When he met Ben Ittri, he said, "I didn't know carpenters would be at this marathon." His grandfather had brought his father up convinced that he could never do anything well enough to earn the old man's respect; and the father, skills sharpened by thirty years of pain, did the same to his son.

TEITLEBAUM, Khanya. 32. White female, divorced, no children. Draftee. Khanya Teitlebaum was a loving, big Malemute of a woman, six feet four inches tall and stronger than any man she had ever known. She was an assistant personnel manager for a General Motors auto-assembly plant in an industrial park near Baton Rouge, Louisiana, where she kept putting cards through the sorter, looking for a man who was six feet or more and unmarried.

WATTRIDGE, Albertina. 62. White, female, married, one child, one grandchild. Professional resource person. A curious thing about Tina, who had achieved a career of more than thirty years as a group therapist and psychiatric counselor for undergraduates at several universities before joining the SAD problem-marathon staff, was that she had been 28 years old and married for almost four before she realized that every human being had a navel. Somehow, the subject had never come up in conversation, and she had always been shy of physical exposure. At first she had thought her belly button a unique and personal physical disfigurement. After marriage she had regarded it as a wondrous and fearful coincidence that her husband bore the same blemish. It was not until her daughter was born that she discovered what it was for.

DAVID AGAIN

It was weird never knowing what time it was. It didn't take long to lose all connection with night and day; I think it happened almost when I got off the elevator. Although that may have been because of the morning glory seeds.

It was sort of like a six-day bash, you know, between exams and when you get your grades, when no one bothers to go to classes but no one can afford to leave for home yet. I would be in the pool with the girls, maybe. We'd get out, and get something to eat, and talk for a while, and then Barbie would yawn, and look at the bare place on her wrist the way she did, and say, "Well, how about if we get a little sleep?" So we'd go into one of the sleeping rooms and straighten out our bags and get in. And just about then somebody else would sit up and stretch and yawn, and poke the person next to him. And they'd get up. And a couple of others would get up. And pretty soon you'd smell bacon and eggs coming down the dumbwaiter, and then they'd all be jumping and turning with Marge Klapper just as you were dropping off.

Barbie and Dolly-Belly and I stayed tight with each other for a long time. We hadn't picked each other out, it just happened that way. I felt very self-conscious that first night in the common room, still flying a little and expecting everybody could see what I was doing. It wasn't that they were so sexually alluring to me. There were other women in the group who, actually, were more my type, a girl from New Mexico who had that long-haired, folk-singer look, a lot like Lara. Even Tina. I couldn't figure her age very well. She might easily have been fifty or more. But she had a gorgeous teenage kind of figure and marvelous skin. But I wasn't motivated to go after them, and they didn't show any special interest in me.

Barbie was really very good-looking, but I'd never made it with a black girl. Some kind of leftover race prejudice, which may come from being born in Minnesota among all those fair-haired WASPs, I suppose. Whatever it was, I didn't think of her that way right at first, and then after that there were the three of us together almost every minute. We kept our sleeping bags in the same corner, but we each stayed in our own.

And Dolly-Belly herself could have been quite pretty, in a way, if all that fat didn't turn you off. She easily weighed two hundred pounds. There was a funny thing about that. I had inside my head an unpleasant feeling about both fat women and black women, that they would smell different in a repulsive way. Well, it wasn't true. We could smell each other very well almost all the time, not only because our sleeping bags were so close together but holding each other, or doing nonverbal things, or just sitting back to back, me in the middle and one of the girls propped on each side of me, in group, and all I ever smelled from either of them was Tigress from Barbie and Aphrodisia from Dolly-Belly. And yet in my head I still had the feeling.

There was no time, and there was no place outside the group. Just the sixteen of us experiencing each other and ourselves. Every once in a while somebody would say something about the outside world. Willie Murtagh would wonder out loud what the Rams had done. Or Dev Stanwyck would come by with Tina and say, "What do you think about building underground condominium homes in abandoned strip mines, and then covering them over with landscaping?" We didn't see television; we didn't know if it was raining or hot or the world had come to an end. We hadn't heard if the manned Grand Tour fly-by had anything to say about the rings of Saturn, which it was about due to be approaching, or whether Donny Osmond had announced his candidacy for the presidency. We, or at least the three of us, were living in and with each other, and about anything else we just didn't want to know.

Fortunately for the group, most of the others were more responsible than we were. Tina and Dev would almost always be in the problem pit, hashing over everybody's problems all the time. So would Bob Sanger, sitting by himself in one of the top rows, silent unless somebody spoke to him directly, or to his problem, or rarely when he had a constructive and well-thought-out comment to offer. So would Jerry Fein and that big hairy bird, Khanya. Almost everybody would be working hard a lot of the time, except for Willie Murtagh, who did God knows what by himself but was almost never in sight after the three of us decided we didn't like him very much, that first night, and the young black kid, Rufous, who spent a lot of his time in what looked like meditation but I later found out was prayer. And the three of us.

I don't mean we copped out entirely. Sometimes we would look in on them. Almost any hour there would be four or five of them in the big pit, with the chairs arranged in concentric circles facing in so that no matter where you sat you were practically looking right in the face of everyone else. We even took part. Now and then we did. Sometimes we'd even offer problems. Barbie got the idea of making them up, like, "I'm worried," she said once, "that the Moon will fall on us. Could we build some kind of a big net and hang it between mountains, like?" That didn't go over a bit. Then Dolly tried a sort of complicated joke about how the CIA should react if Amazonia intervened in the Ecuadorian elections, with the USIS parachuting disc jockeys into the Brazilian bulge to drive them crazy with concentrated-rock music. I didn't like that a bit; the USIS part made me think of Lara's boy friend, which made me remember to hurt. I didn't want to hurt.

I guess that's why we all three of us stayed with made-up problems, and other people's problems: because we didn't want to hurt. But I didn't think of that at the time.

"Of course," Dolly-Belly said one time, when she and I were rocking Barbie in the pool, "we're not going to get out of here until Joe Good up there in the Heptagon marks our papers and says we pass."

I concentrated on sliding Barbie headward, slowing her down, sliding her back. The long blond hair streamed out behind her when she was going one way, wrapped itself around her face when she was going the other. She looked beautiful in the soft pool light, although it was clear, if it had needed to be clear, that she was a natural blond. "So?" I said.

Barbie caught the change in rhythm or something, opened her eyes, lifted one ear out of the water to hear what we were saying.

"So what's the smart thing for us to do, my David? Get down to work and get out faster? Or go on the way we're going?"

Barbie wriggled off our hands and stood up. "Why are we worrying? They'll let the whole group go at the same time anyway," she said.

Dolly-Belly said sadly, "You know, I think that's what's worrying me. I kind of like it here. Hey! Now you two swing me!"

PRELIMINARY REPORTS

The one part of the job that Tina didn't like was filing interim reports with the control monitors up at the old radio-telescope computation center. It seemed to her sneaky. The whole thing about the group was that it built up trust within itself, and the trust made it possible for the people to speak without penalty. And every time Tina found the computer terminals unoccupied and dashed in to file a report she was violating that trust.

However, rules were rules. Still dripping from the pool, where nearly all the group were passing each other hand to hand down a chain, she sat before the console, pulled the hood over her fingers, set the machine for blind-typing and began to type. Nothing appeared on the paper before her, but the impulses went out to the above-ground monitors. Of course, with no one else nearby that much secrecy was not really essential, but Tina had trained herself to be a methodical person. She checked her watch, pinned inside her bra—another deceit—and logged in:

Day 4, hour 0352. WATTRIDGE reporting. INTERACTION good, CONSENSUALITY satisfactory. No incapacitating illnesses or defections.

Seven individuals have stated problem areas of general interest, as follows:

DE LA GARZA. Early detection of home fires. Based on experience as a volunteer fireman (eight years), he believes damage could be reduced "anyway half" if the average time of reporting could be made ten minutes earlier. GROUP proposed training in fire detection and diagnosis for householders.

(That had been only a few hours before, when most of the group were lying around after a session with Marge's energetics. The little man had really come to life then. "See, most people, they think a fire is what happens to somebody else; so when they smell smoke, or the lights go out because wires have melted and a fuse blows, or whatever, they spend 20 minutes looking for cigarettes burning in the ashtrays, or putting new fuses in. And then half the time they run down to the kitchen and get a pan of water and try to put it out themselves. So by the time we get there it's got a good start, and there's three, four thousand dollars just in water damage getting it out, even if we can save the house.")

FEIN. National or world campaign to wipe out VD. States that failure to report disease and contacts is only barrier to complete control of syphilis and gonorrhea. GROUP proposal for free examinations every month, medallion in the form of bracelet or necklace charm to be issued to all persons disease-free or accepting treatment.

(That one had started as a joke. That big girl, Khanya, said "What you really need is a sort of kosher stamp that everybody has to wear." And then the group had got interested, and the idea of issuing medallions had come out of it.)

LIM. Part-time professional assistance for amateur theater and music groups. States that there are many talented musicians who cannot compete for major engagements but would be useful as backup for school, community or other music productions. Could be financed by government salaries repaid from share of admissions.

MURTAGH. Failure of electorate to respond to real issues in voting. Statement of problem as yet unclear; no GROUP proposals have emerged.

SANGER. Loss of market of dental supplies. GROUP currently considering solutions.

STANWYCK. Better utilization of prime real estate by combining function. GROUP has proposed siting new homes underground, and/or building development homes with flat joined roofs with landscaping on top. Interaction continuing.

(Tina wanted to go on with Dev Stanwyck's problem, because she was becoming aware that she cared a great deal about solving problems for him, but her discipline was too good to let her impose her personal feelings in the report. And anyway, Tina did not believe that the problem Dev stated was anywhere near the real problems he felt.)

TEITLEBAUM. Stated problem as unsatisfactory existing solitaire games. (Note: There is a personality problem here presumably due to unsatisfactory relationships with other sex.) GROUP proposed telephone links to computer chess-, checker, or card-playing programs, perhaps to be furnished as a commercial service of phone company.

PERSONALITY PROBLEMS exhibited by nine group members, mostly marital, career or parental conflicts. Some resolution apparent.

TRANSMISSION ENDS.

No one had disturbed Tina, and she pushed the hood away from the keyboard and clicked off the machine without rising. She sat there for a moment, staring at the wall. The group was making real progress in solving problems, but it seemed to her strange that it also appeared to have generated one in herself. All therapists had blind spots about their own behavior. But even a blind person could see that Tina Wattridge was working herself in pretty deep with a boy not much too old to be her grandchild, Devon Stanwyck.

DAVID CATHECTING THE LEADER

One time when we were just getting ready to go to sleep, we went into the room we liked—not that there was much difference between them, but this one they had left the walls pretty natural, and there were nice, transparent, waterfally rock formations that looked good with the lights low—and Tina and Dev Stanwyck were sitting by themselves in a corner. It seemed as though Dev was crying. We didn't pay much attention, because a lot of people cried, now and then, and after a while they went out without saying anything, and we got to sleep. And then, later on, Barbie and I were eating some of the frozen steaks and sort of kidding Dolly-Belly about her fruit and salads, and we heard a noise in the shower, and I went in, and there were Tina and Dev again. Only this time it looked as though Tina was crying. When I came back I told the girls about it. It struck me as odd: Tina letting Devon cry was one thing, Devon holding Tina while she was crying was another.

"I think they're in love," said Dolly-Belly.

"She's twice as old as he is," I said.

"More than that, for God's sake. She's pushing sixty."

"And what has that got to do with it, you two Nosy Parkers? How does it hurt you?"

"Peace, Barbie," I said. "I only think it's trouble. You'd have to be blind not to see she's working herself in pretty deep."

"You've got something against being in love?" Barbie demanded, her brown eyes looking very black.

I got up and threw the rest of my "light meal, steak" away. I wasn't hungry any more. I said, "I just don't want them to get hurt."

After a while Dolly said, "David. Why do you assume being in love is the same as being hurt?"

"Oh, cut it out, Dolly-Belly! She's too old for him, that's all."

Barbie said, "Who wants to go in the pool?"

We had just come out of the pool.

Dolly said, "David, dear. What kind of a person was your wife?"

I sat down and said, "Has one of you got a cigarette?" Barbie did, and gave it to me. "Well," I said, "she looked kind of like Felice. A little younger. Blue eyes. We were married six years, and then she just didn't want to live with me any more."

I wasn't really listening to what I was saying, I was listening to myself, inside. Trying to diagnose what I was feeling. But I was having trouble. See, for a couple of weeks I'd always known what I felt about Lara, because I hurt. It was almost like an ache, as though somebody were squeezing me around the chest. It was a kind of wriggly feeling in my testicles, as though they were gathering themselves up out of harm's way, getting ready for a fight. It was as if I was five years old and somebody had stolen my tricycle. All of those things. And the thing was that I could feel them all, every one, but I suddenly realized I hadn't *been* feeling them. I had forgotten to hurt at all, a lot of the time.

I had not expected that would happen.

Along about that time, I do not know if there was a casual relationship, I became aware of the fact that I was feeling pretty chipper pretty much of the time, and I began to like it. Only sometimes when I was trying to get to sleep, or when I happened to think about going back to Minnesota and remembered there was nobody there to go back to, I hurt. But I could handle it because I knew it would go away again. The cure for Lara was Barbie and Dolly-Belly, even though I had not even kissed either of them, except in a friendly good-night way.

Time wore on, we could only tell how much by guessing from things like the fact that we all ran out of cigarettes. Dolly's were the last to go. She shared with us, and then she complained that Barbie was smoking them twice as fast as she was, and I was hitting them harder than that; she'd smoke two or three cigarettes, and I'd have finished the pack. It was our mixed-up time sense, maybe? Then Rufous came and shared a meal with us once and heard us talking about it, and later he took me aside and offered to trade me a carton for a couple of bananas. I grabbed the offer, ordered bananas, picked them off the dumbwaiter, handed them to Rufous, took the cigarettes and was smoking one before it occurred to me that he could have ordered bananas for himself if he'd wanted them. Barbie said he knew that, he just wanted to give me something, but he didn't want me to feel obligated.

We were all running out of everything we'd brought in with us. There wasn't any dope. Dolly-Belly had brought in some grass, and I guess some of the others had too, but it was gone. Dolly smoked hers up all by herself the first night, or anyway the first time between when we decided we were sleepy and when we got to sleep finally, before we were really close enough to share.

We were all running out, except Willie the Weeper. He had cigarettes. I saw them. But he didn't smoke them. He also had a pocket flask that he kept nipping out of. And he kept ordering fruit off the dumbwaiter, which surprised me when I thought about it because I didn't see him eating any. "He's making cave drippings somewhere," Dolly told me.

"What's cave drippings?"

"It's like when you make homemade wine. Only you drink it as soon as it ferments. Any kind of fruit will do, they say."

"How do you know so much about it if you've never been here before?"

"Oh, screw you, David, are you calling me a liar?"

"No. Honestly not, Dolly-Belly. Get back to cave drippings."

"Well. It's kind of the stuff you made when you're in the Peace Corps in the jungle and you've run out of beer and hash. I bet you a thousand dollars Willie's got some stewing away somewhere. Only I don't smell it." And she splashed out of the pool and went sniffing around the connecting caves, still bare. There was a lot of Dolly-Belly to be bare, and quite a few of the people didn't care much for group nudity even then. But she didn't care.

Out of all the people in our group, 16 of us altogether, Willie was about the only one I didn't really care for. I mean, I didn't like him. He was one of those guys my father used to bring home for dinner when I was little. So very tolerant of kids, so very sure we'd change. So very different in what they did from the face they showed the world. Willie was always bragging about his revolutionary youth and his commitment to Goodness and Truth, one of those fake nine-percenters that, if you could see his income tax form, wasn't pledging a penny behind what he had to give. Even when he came in with us that first night and as much as asked us for help, you couldn't believe him. He wasn't asking what he did wrong, he was asking why the voters in his district were such perverse fools that they voted for his opponent.

Some of the others were strange, in their ways. But we got along. Little Rufous stayed to himself, praying mostly. That big broad Khanya would drive you crazy with how she had poltergeists in her house if you'd let her. Dev Stanwyck was a grade-A snob, but he was tight with Tina most of the time, and he couldn't have been all lousy, because she was all right. I guess the hardest to get along with was the old black millionaire, or ex-millionaire, or maybe-about-to-be-ex-millionaire, Bob Sanger. He didn't seem to like any part of us or the marathon. But he was always polite, and I never saw anybody ask him for anything that he didn't try to give. And so everybody tried to help him.

SOME SOLUTIONS FOR SANGER

After several days, only Tina knew exactly how many, the group found itself united in a desire to deal with the problems of Bob Sanger, and so a marathon brainstorming took place in the problem pit. Every chair was occupied at one time or another. Some 61 proposals were written down by Rose Galifiniakis, who appointed herself recorder because she had a pencil.

The principal solutions proposed were the following:

1. Reconvert to the manufacture of medical and surgical equipment, specifically noble-metal joints for prostheses, spare parts for cyborgs, surgical instruments "of very high quality" and "self-warming jiggers that they stick in you when you have your Pap test, that are always so goddamn cold you scream and jump right out of the stirrups."

2. Take all the money out of the company treasury and spend it on advertising to get kids crazy about cotton candy.

3. Hire a promoter and start a national fad for the hobby of collecting false teeth, bridges, etc., "which you can then sell by mail and save all the dealers' commissions."

4. Reconvert to making microminiaturized parts for guided missiles "in case somebody invents a penetration device to get through everybody's antimissile screens."

5. Hire a lobbyist and get the government to stockpile dental supplies in case there is another Cultural Revolution with riots and consequently lots of broken teeth.

6. Start a saturation advertising campaign pitched to the sado-maso trade about "getting sexual jollies out of home dentistry."

7. Start a fashion for wearing different-colored teeth to match dresses for formal wear. "You could make caps, sort of, out of that plastic kind of stuff you used to make the pink parts of sets of false choppers out of."

8. Move the factory to the Greater Los Angeles area in order to qualify for government loans, subsidies, and tax exemptions under the Aid to Impoverished Areas bill.

9. Get into veterinarian dentistry, particularly for free clinics for the millions of cats roaming the streets of depopulated cities "that some old lady might leave you a million dollars to take care of."

10. Revive the code duello, with fistfights instead of swords.

There were 51 others that were unanimously adjudged too dumb to be worth even writing down, and Rose obediently crossed them out. Bob Sanger did not say that. He listened patiently and aloofly to all of them, even the most stupid of them. The only effect he showed as the marathon wore on was that he went on looking thinner and blacker and smaller all the time.

Of the ten which survived the initial rounds, Numbers 2, 3, 6, 7, and 10 were ruled out for lack of time to develop their impact. Bob thanked the group for them, but pointed out that advertising campaigns took time, maybe years, and he had only weeks. "Especially when they involve basic changes in folkways," agreed Willie Murtagh. "Anyway, seriously. Those are pretty crazy to begin with. You need something real and tangible and immediate, like the idea I threw into the hopper about the Aid to Impoverished Areas funding."

"I do appreciate your helpfulness," said Bob. "It is a matter of capital and, again, time. I have not the funds to relocate the entire plant."

"Surely a government loan—"

"Oh, drop it, Willie," said Marge Klapper. "Time, remember? How fast are you going to get SAD to move? No, Bob, I understand what you're saying. What about the idea of the cats? I was in Newark once and there were like thousands of them."

"I regret to inform you that many of my competitors have anticipated you in this, at least insofar as the emphasis of veterinary dentistry is concerned," said Bob politely. "As to the notion of getting some wealthy person to establish a foundation, I know of no such person. Also the matter of stockpiling supplies has been anticipated. It is this that has kept us going since '92."

Rufous Jefferson looked up from his worry beads long enough to say, "I don't like that idea of making missiles, Mr. Sanger."

"It wouldn't work," said Willie the Weeper positively. "I know. You couldn't switch over *and* get the government back in the missile business in time anyway."

"Besides," said Dolly-Belly, "everybody's got plenty of missiles put away already. No, forget it, fellows, we've bombed out except for one thing. It's your only chance, Bob. You've got to go for that surgical stuff. *And* that self-warming jigger. You don't know, Bob, you're not a woman, but I swear to God every time I go to my gynecologist I leap right up the wall when he touches me with that thing. Brrr!"

"Dumb," said Tina affectionately. "Dolores, dear, I bet you go to a man gynecologist."

"Well, sure," said Dolly defensively. "It's kind of a sex thing with me, I don't like to have women messing me around there."

"All right, but if you went to a woman doctor she'd know what it feels like. How could a man know? *He* never gets that kind of an examination."

Bob Sanger uncrossed his legs and recrossed them the other way. "Excuse me," he said with a certain amount of pain in his voice. "I am afraid I'm not quite following what you are saying."

Tina said with tact, "It's for vaginal examination, Bob. In order to make a proper examination they use a dilator, which is kept sterile, of course, so it has to be metal. And it's cold. *My* doctor keeps the sterile dilators in a little jar next to an electric light so they're warm . . . but she's a woman. She knows what it feels like. Long ago, when I was pregnant, I went to a male obstetrician, and it's just like they say, Bob. You jump. You really do. A self-warming dilator would make a million dollars."

Sanger averted his eyes. His face seemed darker than usual; perhaps he was blushing. "It is an interesting idea," he said, and then added reluctantly, "but I'm afraid there are some difficulties. I can't quite see a place for it in our product line. Self-warming, you say? That would make them quite expensive, and perhaps hard to sterilize, as well. Let me think. I can envision perhaps marketing some sort of little cup containing a sterile solution maintained at body temperature by a thermostat. But would doctors buy it? Assuming we were able to persuade them of the importance of it—and I accept your word, ladies,'' he added hastily. ''Even so. Why wouldn't a doctor just keep them by an electric light, as Tina's does?''

''Come on, Bob. Don't you have a research department?'' Willie demanded.

''I do, yes. What I don't have is time. Still it could have been a useful addition to our line, under other circumstances, I am sure,'' Bob said politely, once again addressing the crease in his trousers.

Then nobody said anything for a while until Tina took a deep breath, let go of Dev Stanwyck's hand and stood up. ''Sorry, Bob,'' she said gently. ''We'll try more later. Now how about the pool?''

And the group dispersed, some yelling and stripping off their clothes, and slapping and laughing as they headed for the pool chamber, one or two to eat, Bob Sanger remaining behind, tossing a dumbbell from hand to hand and looking angrily at his kneecap, left alone.

DAVID CATHECTING THE GROUP

They keep the pool at blood temperature, just like one of Tina's thingamabobs. As, in spite of everything, the walls stay cold—I suppose because of the cold miles and miles of rock behind them—it stays all steamy and dewy in there. And the walls are unfinished, pretty much the way God left them when he poked the caves out of the Puerto Rican rock. Some places they look like dirty green mud, like the bottom of a creek. Some places they look like diamonds. There is one place that is like a frozen waterfall, and one like icicles melting off the roof; and when they built the pool and lighted it, they put colored lights behind the rocks in some places, and you can switch them to go on and off at random. We liked that a lot. We went racing in, and Dolly-Belly pushed me in right on top of Barbie and went to turn on the lights, and then she came leaping like a landslide into the pool almost on top of both of us. Half the water in the pool came surging out, it looked like. But it all drains right back and gets churned around some way to kill the bugs and fungi, and so we jumped and splashed most of it out again and yelled and dived and then settled down to just holding each other, half drowsing, until the pool got too crowded and we felt ourselves being pushed into a corner and decided to get out.

We put some clothes on and sort of stood in the corridor, between the pool and the showers, trying to make up our minds what to do.

''Want to get some sleep?'' Barbie asked, but not very urgently. Neither of us said yes.

''How about eating something?'' I offered.

Dolly-Belly said politely, ''No thanks. I'm not hungry now.'' I found one of Rufous the Third's cigarettes and we passed it around, trying to keep it dry although the girls' hair kept dripping on it, and then we noticed that we were in front of the door that opens into the empty caves. And we realized we had all been looking at it, and then at each other, and then at the door again.

So Dolly tried the knob, and it turned. I pushed on the door, and it opened. And Barbie stepped through, and we followed.

It closed behind us.

We were alone in the solid dark and cold of the caves. A little line of light ran around three sides of the door we had just come through; and if we listened closely, we could hear, very faintly, an occasional word or sound from the people behind it. That was all. Outside of that, nothing.

Barbie took one of my hands. I reached out and took Dolly's with the other.

We stood silently for a moment, waiting to see if our eyes would become dark-adapted, but it was no use. The darkness was too complete. Dolly-Belly was twisting around at the end of our extended arms' length, and after a moment she said, "I can feel along a wall here. There's a kind of rope. Watch where you step."

Someone had put duckboards down sometime. Although we couldn't see a thing, we could feel what we were doing. I had socks on; the girls were barefoot. Since I had one hand in the hand of each of them, I couldn't guide myself by the rope or the wall, as Barbie and Dolly could, but we went very slowly.

We had done a sensitivity thing a while earlier, two sleeps and about 11 meals earlier, I think, blindfolding each of us in turn and letting ourselves be led around to smell and hear and touch things. It was like that. In the same way, none of us wanted to talk. We were extending our other senses, listening, and feeling, and smelling.

Then Dolly-Belly stopped and said, "End of the rope." She disengaged her fingers and bent down. Barbie came up beside me, and I slipped my hand free of hers and around her waist.

Dolly said, "I think there are some steps going down. Be careful, hear? It's scary."

I let go of Barbie, passed myself in front of Dolly, felt with my toes, knelt down and explored with my fingertips. It was queasy, all right. I felt as though I were falling over forward, not being able to see where I might be falling. There were wooden steps there, all right. But how far down they went and what was at the end of them and how long they had been rotting away there and what shape they were in, I could not tell.

So we juggled ourselves around cautiously and sat on the top step, which was just wide enough for the three of us, even Dolly-Belly. We listened to the silence and looked at the emptiness, until Barbie said suddenly:

"I hear something."

And Dolly said, "I smell something. What do you hear?"

"What do you smell?"

"Sort of like vinegar."

"What I hear is sort of like somebody breathing."

And a light flared up at us from the bottom of the stairs, blinding us by its abruptness although it was only a tiny light, and the voice of Willie the Weeper said, "Great balls o' fahr, effen 'tain't the Revenooers come to bust up mah li'l ol' still!"

I flung my head away from the light and yelled, "Willie, for Christ's sake! What are you doing here?"

"Dumb question, my David," said Barbie beside me. "Don't you remember about cave drippings? Willie's got himself a supply of home brew out here."

"Right," said Willie benevolently. "Thought I recognized your voice, my two-toned sepia queen. Say, how are your roots doing?"

Barbie didn't say a word, and neither did any of the rest of us. After a moment Willie may have felt a little ashamed of himself, because he flicked off his light. "I've only got the one battery," he explained apologetically from the darkness. "Oh, wait a minute. Take a look." And he turned on the little penlight again, shined it at arm's length on himself, and then against the wall, where he had four fruit bowls covered by dinner plates and a bunch of paper cups. "I thought you might like to see my little popskull plant," he said pridefully, turning the light off again. "Care for a shot?"

"Why not?" said Barbie, and we all three eased ourselves down to the lower steps and accepted a paper cup of the stuff, sharing it among us.

"Straining it was the hard part," said Willie. "You may notice a certain indefinable piquancy to the bouquet. I had to use my underwear."

Barbie, just swallowing, coughed and giggled. "Not bad, Willie. Here, try it, David. It's a little bit like Dutch gin."

To me it tasted like the liquid that accumulates in the bottom of the vegetable bins in a refrigerator, and I said so.

"Right, that's what I mean. My compliments to the vintner, Willie. Do you come here a lot?"

"No. Oh, well, maybe, I guess so. I don't like being hassled around in there." I couldn't see his face in the darkness, but I could imagine it: angry and defensive. So, to make it worse, I said,

"I thought you volunteered for this."

"Hell! I didn't know it would be like this."

"What did you think it would be like, Willie?" Barbie asked. But her voice wasn't mocking.

He said, with pauses, "I suppose, in a way . . . I suppose I thought it would be kind of like the revolution. I don't suppose you remember. You're probably too young, and anyway it was mostly on the West Coast. But we were all together then, you know . . . I mean, even the ones we were fighting and struggling were part of it. Chaos, chaos, and out of it came some good things. We struggled with the chief of police of San Francisco in the middle of Market Street, and afterwards he was all bruised and bleeding, but he thanked me."

We didn't say anything. He was right, we were too young to have been involved except watching it on TV, where it seemed like another entertainment.

"And then," said Willie, "nothing ever went right." And he didn't say anything more for a long time, until Dolly-Belly said:

"Can I have another shot of drippings?"

And then we just sat for a while, thinking about Willie, and finally not thinking about anything much. I didn't feel blind any more, even with the light off. Just that bit from Willie's flash had given me some sense of domain. I could remember the glimpse I had got: the flat, unreflective black wall off to my right, just past Dolly-Belly, the wooden steps down (there had been nine of them), the duckboards along the rough shelf above us, the faint occasional drip of water from the bumps in the cave roof over us, the emptiness off to the left past where the light from Willie's penlamp did any good, Willie's booze factory down below. With a girl on either side of me I didn't even feel cold, except for my feet, and after a while Willie put his hand on one of them. It felt warm and I liked it, but I heard myself saying, "You've got the wrong foot, Willie. Barbie's on my left, Dolly's on my right."

After a moment he said, "I knew it was yours. I'm already holding one of Dolly's." But he took it away.

Barbie said thoughtfully, "If you'd been a voter in your district, Willie, who would you have voted for?"

"Do you think I haven't asked myself that?" he demanded. "You're right. I would have voted for Tom Gdansk."

Dolly said, "It's time for a refill, Willie friend." And we all churned around getting our paper cups topped off and readjusting ourselves and when Willie prudently turned the penlight off again, we were all sitting together against the wall, touching and drinking, and talking. Willie was doing most of the talking. I didn't say much. I wasn't holding back; it was just that I had had the perception that it was more important for Willie to talk than for me to respond. I let the talk wash over me. Time slowed and shuddered to a stop.

It came to me that we four were sitting there because it was meant from the beginning of time that we should be sitting there, and that sitting there was the thing and the only thing that we were ordained to do. My spattered statue for the library? It didn't matter. It was in a different part of reality. Not the part we four were in just then. Willie's worries about being not-loved? It mattered that he was telling us about it (he was back to his third birthday, when his older brother's whooping cough had canceled Willie's party), but it didn't matter that it had happened. Dolly's fatness? *N'importe*. Barbie's fitful soft weeping, over she never said what? *De nada*. Lara leaving me for the USIS goon? *Machts nicht* . . . well, no. That did amount to something real and external. I could feel it working inside me.

But I was not prepared to let it interfere with the groupness of our group, which was a real and immanent thing in itself. After a while, Dolly began to hum to herself. She had a bad, reedy voice, but she wasn't pushing it, and it fitted in nicely behind Willie's talking and Barbie's weeping. We eased each other, all four of us. It must have been in some part Willie's terrible foul brew, but it could not have been all that; it was weak stuff and tasted so awful you could drink it only one round at a time. It was, in some ways, the finest time of my life.

"Time," I said wonderingly. "And time, and time, and all of the kinds of time." I don't suppose it meant anything, but it seemed to at that—yes. At that time. And for a time we talked timelessly about time, which, in my perception, had the quality of a mobile or a medallion or a coffee-table book, in that it was something one discussed for its pleasant virtues but not something that constrained one.

Except that there too there was some sort of inner activity, like stomach rumblings, going on all the time.

While we were there, what was happening in those external worlds we had left? In the world in the caves behind us? Had the group been judged and passed and discharged while we were gone? If it had, how would we ever know?

But Barbie said (and I had not known I had asked her, or spoken out loud) that that was unlikely because, as far as she could see, our group had done damn-all about solving any problems, especially its own, and if we were to be excused only after performance, we had all the performance yet to perform. Everybody knew the numbers. Most groups got out in some three weeks. But what was three weeks? Twenty-one sleeps? But we slept when we chose, and no two of us had exactly the same number. Sixty-three meals? Dolly had stopped eating almost entirely. How could you tell? Only by the solutions of problems, maybe. If you knew what standards were applied, and who the judges were. But I could see little of that happening, like Barbie, like all of us, I was still trapped in my own internal problems that, even there, came funneling in by some undetectable pipeline from that larger external world beyond the caves. And I had solved no part of them. Lara was still gone and would still be gone. Whatever time it was in Djakarta, she was there. Whatever was appropriate to that time, she was doing, with her USIS man and not with me, for I was not any part of her life and never would be again. She probably never thought of me, even. Or if she did, only with anger. "I feel bad about the anger," I said out loud, only then realizing I had been talking out loud for some time, "because I earned it richly and truly. I own it and acknowledge it as mine."

"So do you want to do anything about it?" asked somebody, Dolly I think, or maybe Willie.

I considered that for a timeless stretch. "Only to tell her about it," I said finally, "to tell her what's true, that I earned it."

"Do you want her back?" asked Willie. (Or Barbie.)

I considered that for a long time. I don't know whether I ever answered the question, or what I said. But I began to see what the answer was, at least. Really I didn't want her back. Not exactly. At least, I didn't want the familiar obligatory one-to-oneness with Lara, the getting up with Lara in the morning, the making the coffee for Lara, the sharing the toast with Lara, the following Lara to the bus twenty minutes after, the calling Lara at her office from my office, wondering who Lara was seeing for lunch, being home before Lara and waiting for Lara to come in, sharing a strained dinner with Lara, watching TV with Lara, fighting with Lara, swallowing resentments against Lara; I didn't even want going to bed with Lara or those few moments, so brief and in recollection so illusory, when Lara and I were peacefully at one or pleasuring each other with some discovery or joy. Drowsily I began to feel that I wanted nothing from Lara except the privilege of letting go of her without anger or pain; letting go of all pain, maybe, so that I did not have to have it eating at me.

But how much of this I said, or heard, I do not know, I only remember bits and tableaux. I remember Willie the Weeper actually weeping, softly and easingly like Barbie. I remember that there was a point when there was no more of the cave drippings left except some little bit that had just begun to work. I remember kissing Dolly, who was crying in quite a different and more painful way, and then I only remember waking up.

At first I was not sure where I was. For a moment I thought we had all got ourselves dead drunk and wandering, and perhaps had gone out into the cave and got ourselves lost in some deadly, foolish way. It scared me. How could we ever get back?

But it wasn't that way, as I perceived as soon as I saw that we were huddled in a corner of one of the sleeping rooms. I was not alone in my sleeping bag; Barbie was there with me, her arms around me and her face beautiful and slack. There was a weight across our feet which I thought was Dolly.

But it wasn't. It was Willie Murtagh, wrapped in his own bag, stretched flat and snoring, and Dolly was not anywhere around.

ASPECTS OF EXTERNAL REALITY

Geology. About a hundred million years before the birth of Christ, during the period called the Upper Cretaceous when the Gulf of Mexico swelled to drown huge parts of the Southern United States, a series of volcanic eruptions racked the sea that would become the Caribbean. The chains of islands called the Greater and Lesser Antilles were born.

As the molten rock boiled forth and the pressure dropped, great bubbles of trapped gas evolved, some bursting free into the air, others remaining imprisoned as the cooling and hardening of the lava raced against the steady upward crawl of the gas. In time the rock cooled and became agelessly hard. The rains drenched it, the seas tore at it, the winds scoured it, and all of them brought donations: waveborne insects, small animals floating on bits of vegetation or sturdily swimming, air-borne dust, bird-borne seeds. After a time the islands became densely overgrown with reeds and grasses, orchids and morning-glories, bamboo, palm, cedar, ebony, calabash, whitewood; it was a place of karst topography, so wrinkled and seamed that it was like a continent's worth of landscaping crammed into a single island, and overgrown everywhere.

Under the rock the bubbles remained; and as the peaks weathered, some of the bubbles thinned and balded at the top, opened, and collapsed, leaving great, round, open valleys like craters. When astronomers wanted to build the biggest damned radio telescope the world had ever seen, they found one of these opened-out bubbles. They trimmed it and smoothed it and drained it and inlaid it with wire mesh to become the thousand-foot dish of the Arecibo Observatory. Countless other bubbles remained. Those that had been farther under the surface remained under the surface and were hidden until animals found them, then natives, then pirates, then geologists and spelunkers, who explored them and declared them to be perhaps the biggest chain of connected caverns ever found in the earth. Tourists gaped. Geologists plumbed. Astronomers peered, in their leisure hours. And then, when all radio telescopy was driven to the far side of the Moon by a thousand too many radio-dispatched taxicabs and a million too many radar ovens, the observatory no longer served a function and was abandoned.

But the caves remained.

Physical Description. After examining nearly all of the Puerto Rican cave system, a group of four linked caverns was selected and suitably modified. By blasting and hammering they were shaped and squared. Concrete flowed into the lower parts of the flooring to make them level. Wiring reached out to the generators of the old observatory, and then there were lighting, power, and communications facilities. In a separate cavern near the surface, almost burst through to the air, rack upon rack of salt crystals were stored; in the endless Puerto Rican sun the salt accepted heat, and when warmth was needed below, air was pumped through the salt. Decorators furnished and painted the chambers. Plumbers and masons installed fixtures and the pool. Water? There was endless water from the inexhaustible natural springs in the mountains. Drainage? The underground rivers that flowed off to the sea carried everything away. (When the astronomers came to build their telescope, they found that the valley had become a stagnant lake; its natural drain, through underground channels to the sea, had become blocked. Divers opened it, and the water swept sweetly away.) Two short elevator shafts, one for use and one for backup, completed the construction program. The result was an isolation pit exempt from the diurnal swing and the seasonal shift, without time or external stimuli, without distraction.

Support facilities. Maintenance, care and supervision of the problem pits is provided by a detachment of 50 VISTA volunteers, working out their substitute for military service. They tended the pumps, kept the machinery in repair, and did the housekeeping for the inmates. Their duties were quite light. The climate was humid but pleasant, especially in the northern hemisphere's winter months. Except for the long jackknifing drive to the city of Arecibo on the coast, for beer and company, the VISTA detachment was well pleased to be where they were. The principal everyday task was cooking, and that was no problem; it was all TV dinners, basically, prefabricated and prefrozen. All the duty chefs had to do was take the orders, pull them out of the freezers, pop them in the microwave ovens, and put them on the dumbwaiter. Plus, of course, something like scrambling eggs and buttering toast from time to time. There were seldom problems of any importance. The attempt of the United Brotherhood of Government Employees, in 1993, to organize the paramilitary services was the most traumatic event in the detachment's history. There had been a strike. Twenty-two persons, comprising the ongoing group of problem personnel, were temporarily marooned in the caves. For 18 days they were without food, light or communications, except for a few dumbwaiter loads of field rations smuggled down by one of the strikers. The inconvenience was considerable, but there were no deaths.

Monitoring and evaluation. Technical supervision is carried on by administratively separate personnel. There are two main areas of technical project control.

The first, employing sophisticated equipment originally designed for observatory use but substantially modified, is based near the old thousand-foot dish in the former administration and technical headquarters. Full information retrieval and communications capabilities exist, with on-line microwave links to the Heptagon, in Terre Haute, Indiana, via synchronous satellite. This is the top headquarters and decision-making station, and the work there is carried on by an autonomous division of SAD with full independent departmental status. The personnel of both technical supervision installations are interchangeable, and generally rotate duty from Indiana to Puerto Rico, six months or a year at a time.

The personnel of the technical project control centers are primarily professionals, including graduate students in social sciences and a large number of career civil service scientists in many disciplines. While stationed in Puerto Rico, most of these live along the coast with their families and commute to the observatory center by car or short-line STOL flight. They do not ordinarily associate with the VISTA crews, and only exceptionally have any firsthand contact with the members of the problem-solving groups, even the professional resource people included. This was not the original policy. At first the professionals actually participating in the groups were drawn by rota from the administrative personnel. It was found that the group identity was weakened by identification with the outside world, and so after the third year of operation the group-active personnel were kept separate, both administratively and physically. When off duty the group-active professionals are encouraged to return to their own homes and engage in activities unrelated to the work of the problem pits.

The problem pits were originally sponsored by a consortium consisting of the Rand Corporation, the Hudson Institute, Cornell University, the New York Academy of Sciences, and the Puerto Rican Chamber of Commerce, under a matched-funds grant shared by SAD and the Rockefeller Foundation. In 1994 it was decided that they could and should be self-financing, and so a semipublic stock corporation similar to COMSAT and the fusion-power corporations was set up. All royalties and licensing fees are paid to the corporation, which by law distributes 35 percent of income as dividends to its stockholders, 11 percent to the State of Puerto Rico, and 4 percent to the federal government, reinvesting the balance in research-and-development exploitation.

Results to date. The present practice of consensual labor arbitration, the so-called "Nine Percent" income tax act, eight commercially developed board games, some 125 therapeutic personality measures, 51 distinct educational programs (including the technique of teaching elementary schoolchildren foreign languages through folksinging), and more than 1,800 other useful discoveries or systems have come directly from the problem-solving sessions in the Arecibo caves and elsewhere and from research along lines suggested by these sessions.

Here are two examples:

The Nine Percent Law. After the California riots, priority was assigned to social studies concerning "involvement," as the phrase of the day put it. Students, hereditarily unemployed aerospace workers, old people, and other disadvantaged groups who had united and overthrown civil government along most of the Pacific Coast for more than 18 months, were found to be suffering from the condition called *anomie*, characterized by a feeling that they were not related to the persons or institutions in their environment and had no means of control or participation in the events of the day. In a series of problem-pit sessions the plan was proposed which ultimately was adopted as the Kennedy-Moody Act of 1993, sometimes called "The Nine Percent Law." Under this act taxpayers are permitted to direct a proportion of their income tax to a specific function of government, e.g., national defense, subsidization of scientific research, education, highways, etc. A premium of 1 percent of the total tax payable is charged for each 10 percent which is allocated in this way, up to a limit of 9 percent of the base tax (which means allocating 90 percent of the tax payable). The consequences of this law are well known, particularly as to the essential disbanding of the DoD.

The militia draft. After the 1991 suspension of Selective Service had caused severe economic dislocation because of the lack of employment for youths not serving under the draft, a problem-pit session proposed resuming the draft and using up to 60 percent of draftees, on a volunteer basis, as adjuncts to local police forces all over the nation. It had been observed that law enforcement typically attracted rigid and often punitive psychological types, with consequent damage to the police-civilian relations, particularly with minority groups. The original proposal was that all police forces cease recruiting and that all vacancies be filled with national militia draftees. However, the increasing professionalization of police work made that impractical, and the present system of assigning militia in equal numbers to every police force was adopted. The success of the program may be judged from the number of other nations which have since come to imitate it.

In recent years some procedural changes have been made, notably in giving preference to nongoal-oriented problem-solving sessions, in which all participants are urged to generate problems as well as solutions. A complex scoring system, conducted in Terre Haute, gives credits for elapsed time, for definition of problems, for intensity of application and for (estimated) value of proposals made. As the group activity inevitably impinges on personality problems, a separate score is given to useful or beneficial personality changes which occur among the participants. When the score reaches a given numerical value (the exact value of which has never been made public), the group is discharged and a new one convened.

The procedures used in the problem pits are formative, eclectic and heuristic. Among the standard procedures are sensitivity training, encounter, brainstorming, and head-cloning. More elaborate forms of problem-solving and decision-making, such as Delphi, relevance-tree construction, and the calculus of statement, have been used experimentally from time to time. At present they are not considered to be of great value in the basic pit sessions, although each of them retains a place in the later R&D work carried on by professional teams, either in Terre Haute or, through subcontracting, in many research institutions around the country.

Selection procedures. Any citizen is eligible to volunteer and, upon passing a simple series of physical and psychological tests designed to determine fitness for the isolation experience, may be called as openings occur. Nearly all volunteers are accepted and actually participate in a pit session within 10 months to one year after application, although in periods when the number of volunteers is high, some proportion are used in sessions in other places than Arecibo, under slightly different ground rules.

In order to maintain a suitable ethnic, professional, religious, sexual, and personality mix, and as part of a randomizing procedure, about one half of all participants are selectees. These are chosen through Selective Service channels in the first instance, comprising all citizens who have not otherwise discharged their military obligation. Of course, the number thus provided is far in excess of need, and so a secondary lottery is then held. Those persons thus chosen are given the battery of tests required of volunteers, and those who pass remain subject to call for the remainder of their lives. As a matter of policy, many of the youngest age groups are given automatic deferments for a period of years, to provide a proper age mix for each working group.

Summary and future plans. The problem-pit sessions have proven so productive that there have been many attempts to expand them to larger formats, e.g., the so-called "Universal Town Meeting." These have achieved considerable success in special areas, but at the cost of limiting spontaneity and interpersonal interaction. Some studies have criticized the therapeutic aspects of pit sessions as distractive and irrelevant to their central purpose. Yet experimental sessions conducted on a purely problem-solving basis have been uniformly less productive, perhaps due to the emergence of a professionalist elite group who dominate such sessions; as their expertise is acquired through professional exposure over a period of time, their contributions are often too conventional and thus limited. The fresh, if uninformed, thoughts of nonexperts give the pit sessions their special qualities of innovation and daring. Most observers feel that the interpersonal quality of the sessions cannot be achieved on a mass scale except with the concomitant danger of violence, personal danger and property destruction, as in the California Cultural Revolution. However, studies are still being pursued with the end in view of enlarging the scope and effectiveness of the sessions.

In conclusion, we can only agree with the oft-quoted extemporaneous rhyme offered by Sen. Moody at the ceremonies attendant on the tenth anniversary of the establishment of the problem pits:

The pits are quirky,
Perfection they're not.
The best you can say's
They're the best we've got.

THE STATEMENT OF TINA'S PROBLEM

In Tina Wattridge's head lived a dozen people, all of whom were her and all of whom fought like tigers for sole ownership. Pit Leader Tina moved among the group, offering encouragement here, advice there, bringing one person to interact with another. Mother Tina remembered, after a third of a century, the costive agony of childbirth and the inexpressible love that drowned her when they first laid her daughter in her arms. Tina the Spy eavesdropped and snooped, and furtively slipped into the communications room to type out her reports on group progress. Homemaker Tina loathed the cockroach yellow paint on the walls of the main social room and composed unsent demands to the control authorities for new mats for the pool chamber, where the dank and the hard use had eaten them into disgraceful tatters. And all the Tinas were Tina Wattridge, and when they battled among themselves for her, she felt fragmented and paralyzed. When she felt worst was when one of the long-silent Tina's came arrogantly to the fore and drove her in a direction she had long forgotten. It was happening now. She knew what a spectacle she must seem to everyone present, most of all to the other parts of herself, but she could not help herself; she was in love; could not possibly be in love; was.

And while she was numb to everything but the external love and the interior pain of reproach, her group was exploding in a dozen directions. She couldn't cope; somehow she did cope, moment by moment, but always at the cost of feeling that there she had spent the last erg of energy, the last moiety of will and had nothing left—until another demand came. And they came every minute, it seemed. Bob Sanger shouting and trembling, demanding that the group be terminated and he be let to get back to his collapsing business. David Jaretski and Barbara Devereux screaming that their friend Dolores had blundered off into the caves to die. Marge Klapper (who should have known better!) whispering that she wanted to get out now, right now, to have the other man's baby pumped out of her so she could go back to the man she was married to. And back and forth to the teletypes, sneaking in reports; and worrying about every person there; and most of the time, all of the time, with her mind full of Dev Stanwyck and their utterly preposterous, utterly overpowering love.

She could not sleep. She would lie down exhausted, more often than not with Dev beside her, and sometimes there would be sex, fast and total, and sometimes there would be his passionate attempt to explain and justify all of his life. Sometimes nothing but exhaustion alone; she would feel herself falling away into sleep and hear Dev's breathing deepen beside her. And then some voice from the other room, or some memory, or some discomfort from the fold of the sleeping bag would come. Not much. Enough. Enough to pull her back from sleep, fighting angrily against it, and in a minute she would be wide awake with her mind furiously circling into a kind of panic.

Then she would get up, trying not to disturb Dev, trying to avoid the rest of the group, and head for the only place in the caves where she could have privacy, the toilets. And with the door locked, in the end stall, she would reach behind the flush tank and slide one piece of molding over another and take out the rough copies of her reports, trying to force her mind back onto her job.

Day 1, hour 2300. WATTRIDGE reporting. FEIN introduced VD epidemiology problem; no group uptake. SANGER states problem of approaching bankruptcy in dental findings industry; n.g.u. JEFFERSON made no overt statement but indicates sexual inadequacy problem. JARETSKI marital situation; wife has left him. ITTRI despondent career status; attributes lack of education. MURTAGH states criticism of Congressional election procedure; n.g.u. GROUP interaction in weak normal range.

They had all been strangers then. Dev Stanwyck's name did not even appear in that first report!

Day 4, hour 2220. WATTRIDGE reporting. KLAPPER and BELLI hostility; fought with bats without resolution. GROUP effective in bioenergetics and immersion therapy. Some preliminary diagnoses: DEVEREUX passive-aggressive, deep frustration feelings. BELLI compulsive and anal-retentive. STANWYCK latent homosexual father-dominated. (Note: I have personal feelings toward STANWYCK. I think of him as a son.)

She flipped hastily through the pages of the notebook, trying to ignore the fact that somebody was silently moving around outside the toilet door, apparently listening. Then she found the page she was looking for:

Day 13, hour 2330. WATTRIDGE reporting. Clique formation: BELLI-DEVEREUX-JARETSKI: semisexual triad, some bonding to rest of group. STANWYCK-ITTRI, bivalent pairing, sociopersonal conflict vs. joint hostility to rest of group, little interaction. FEIN-KLAPPER-SANGER, weak professional communality of interest in medical areas; unstable bond, with individual links to other group members. No overt sexual interaction observed. Problem solving: SANGER received full group brainstorm but did not consider any proposal satisfactory; forwarded for analysis. FEIN received approximately 30 minutes intensive discussion, no formal proposals but interaction taking place. ITTRI: Has become able to perceive own failure to make use of adult-education and other resources, accepts suggestions for courses and new career orientation. (Note: BELLI noticed in the pool that I was wearing my watch. I tried to persuade her that it was only an ornament and did not keep time. However, she told some of the others. STANWYCK in particular has been observing me closely, making these transmissions difficult even with blind-typing.)

And there it was, an absolute fraud! It hadn't happened that way at all. It had been Dev Stanwyck who had noticed it first, Dolly Belli only a day later; and Tina remembered cringingly with what anger and passion she had blown up at Dolly's half-joking question. It had stopped the questioning, all right; Dolly climbed out of the pool without another word, and her friends followed her. What else had it stopped: How close had Dolly been to opening up to the group at large?

And where had the anger come from? It was only when Tina had realized that the anger was all out of proportion to the stimulus that she had plumbed in her mind for another source and found it transferred from her own feelings about Dev Stanwyck.

Slowly she turned to a blank page and began her latest report:

Day 17, hour 2300. WATTRIDGE reporting. BELLI still missing. Tensions peaking. GROUP interaction maintaining plateau in high normal range. Sexual pairing marked: JARETSKI-DEVEREUX, KLAPPER-FEIN (temporary and apparently discontinued), ITTRI-TEITLEBAUM. Also WATTRIDGE-STANWYCK. (Note: I find this professionally disconcerting and am attempting to disengage. I am too old for him!)

She put down the pencil and wrinkled her eyes; repentance oft I swore, yes, but was I sober when I swore? How could she disengage herself from someone a third her age who found that she turned him on? And how could she not?

The breathing outside stopped for a moment, and then Dev's voice said, "Tina, is that you in there?"

She could not answer; some maiden shyness kept her from speaking while sitting on a toilet, or else she simply did not know what to say to Dev.

"I think you better come out," he went on. "Something's happening."

HASSLING WILLIE

In the main social room Marge Klapper was facing Willie Murtagh across a mat. Both were tense and angry, which troubled Marge more than Willie because she did not like to be professionally inept. The one-night stand with Jerry Fein had left her upset, especially as Jerry didn't want to let it stay a one-night stand; she was angry; she wanted to get out to get rid of her souvenir of one other one-night stand; she wanted to go back to her husband and find out if the marriage could be made to work; and, most difficult of all, she wanted to do all those things while retaining her self-image as a competent professional intact. So she reached out for Willie:

"Do you want to fight?"

He stood angrily mute and shook his head.

She dropped the soft, inflated plastic bats and put a professional smile on her face. "Shall we push? Would you like to go in the pool?"

"No." He wasn't helping at all. He was uptight and souring the whole group with his tensions and giving her nothing to work on—nothing, she realized, except that intensity with which he was looking at her, as though hoping the next word out of her mouth would be what he wanted. So she tried again. She stepped up on the edge of the mat and said sweetly to Willie, "Would you like to try something with me? Let's jump."

Willie said, "Oh, Christ."

"Go on," Jerry Fein put in helpfully. "Shake the tensions out."

"Stay out of this, Jerry!" Marge snapped. And then forced herself to relax. "Like this, Willie," she said, jumping, coming down, jumping again. "Try it."

He glowered, looked around the room and gave a half-hearted hop.

"Great!" cried Marge. "Higher!"

He shrugged and jumped a mighty leap, twice as high as hers. Then another. "Beautiful, Willie," said Marge breathlessly. "Keep it up!" It was like an invisible seesaw, first Marge in the air, then Willie, Marge again; he began to move his feet like a Russian dancer, coming down with one knee half bent, then the other, turning his body from side to side. "Make a noise, Willie!" Marge yelled triumphantly, and demonstrated: "Yow! Whee! Hoooo!"

The whole group was joining in—anyway, that part of it that was in the room, all yelling with Willie. Marge felt triumphant and fulfilled; and then Tina had to come in and spoil it all.

"Sorry, Marge," she called from the doorway. "Listen, everybody. Does anybody know where Barbie and David are?"

"In the pool?" somebody guessed helpfully.

"No. I looked everywhere."

Marge panted angrily. "Tina, do you have to take attendance now?"

"I'm sorry, Marge. But I'm afraid they've gone into the caves after Dolly. Is anyone else missing?"

The group looked around at itself. "Rufous!" cried Jerry Fein. "Where's he?"

Dev Stanwyck, as always tagging along after Tina, said in his superior way, "We've already checked the sleeping rooms. Rufous is there. Anybody else?"

No answer for a moment, and then three or four people at once: "Bob Sanger!"

Tina looked around, then nodded grimly. "Thanks." And she disappeared, Stanwyck hurrying after.

Nevertheless, the interruption had wrecked Marge's mood. And hadn't done any good for Willie, either; he was collapsed on the floor, staring into space.

"Well," said Marge heartily, "want to get back to it, Willie?"

He looked up and said, "I know where they are. It's kind of my fault." He straightened up and said, "Hell, it's *exactly* my fault. I was trying to get with that colored girl, and I said something I shouldn't have. Dolly took it the wrong way and split for the caves, and I—well, I told David it was his fault, so he went after her. I didn't actually think he'd take Barbie with him."

"Or Sanger," said someone.

"I don't know anything about Sanger. But I know where they are. They're wandering."

Tina said from the entrance, "No, not in the caves, they aren't." All at once she looked every year of her age. "They're outside," she said. "I just heard from the VISTA crew; they identified four persons leaving the caves about a quarter of a mile from here, one alone, then three more about an hour ago."

"At least they're outside," said Willie thankfully.

"Oh, yes," said Tina, "they're outside. In the dark. Wandering around. Did you look at the terrain when you came in, Willie?" She absent-mindedly pressed her hands against her face. It smeared her make-up, but she was no longer aware she had it on. "One other thing," she said. "You can all go home now. The word just came down over the teletype; our group is discharged with thanks and, how did they say it?—oh, yes. 'Tell them it was a good job well done,' " she said.

RUNNING HOME

I didn't really believe Willie even when it was clearly to his advantage to tell the truth, but it was the way he said: follow the piece of string he had laid out, exploring the caves to keep from exploring his own head, and you came to a rock slope, very steep but with places where somebody had once cut handholds into it, and at the end of the handholds you found yourself out in the fresh air. When we got out we were all beat. Bob Sanger was the worst off of us, which was easy to figure when you considered he was a pretty old guy who hadn't done anything athletic for about as long as Barbie and I had been alive. But he was right with us. "I'll leave you now," he said. "I do appreciate your help."

"Cut it out, Bob," wheezed Barbie. "Where do you think you're going?"

It had turned out to be night, and a very dark night with a feeble tepid rain coming down, too—perhaps they had no other kinds around there. I couldn't see his face, but I could imagine his expression, very remote and contented with whatever interior decisions he had reached. "I'll make my own way, thank you," he said politely. "It is only a matter of finding a road, and then following it downhill, I imagine."

"Then what?" I demanded. "We're AWOL, you know."

"That's why I have attorneys, Mr. Jaretski," he said cheerfully.

"Sitting on the bottom of the hill waiting for you?"

"Of course not. Really, you should not worry about me. I took the precaution of retaining my money belt when we checked our valuables. U.S. currency will get me to Ponce, and from there there are plenty of flights to the mainland. I'll be in California in no more than eight or nine hours, I should think."

"Listen, Bob!" I exploded—but stopped; Barbie squeezed my shoulder.

"Bob," she said, in a tone quite different from mine, "it isn't just that we're worried about you. We're worried about Dolly. Please help us find her."

Silence. I wished I could have seen his face. Then he said, "Please believe me, I am not ungrateful. But consider these facts. First, as I explained to all of you when we started this affair, it is of considerable importance to me to keep my company solvent. I believe that I have reasoned out a way to do so, and *I have no spare time*. I have no idea how much time we've wasted, and it may already be too late. Second, this is a big island. It is quite hopeless to search it for one girl with a long start, with no lights and no idea of where she has gone. I would help you if I could. I can't."

I said, trying to crawl down from my anger, "We don't have any other way to do it, Bob. I think I know where she is; anyway, that's where I want to look. But three of us can look fifty percent better than two."

"Call the VISTA crew," he said.

"I don't know where they are."

"Anyway, you're assuming she may be in some kind of danger. She is quite capable of taking care of herself."

"Capable, yes. Motivated, no. She's jealous and angry, Bob. Barbie and I were shacked up and it—" I hesitated; I didn't know exactly how to say it. "It spoiled things for her," I said. "I think she might do something crazy."

Sanger spluttered, "Your f-fornications are your own business, Mr. Jaretski! I must go. I—"

He hesitated and became, for him, confidential. "I believe that the discussion of my problem has in fact borne fruit. The, ah, gynecological instruments are an area in which I had little knowledge."

"You've invented a warmer for the thingy?" Barbie asked, interestedly.

"For the speculum, yes. A warmer, no. It isn't necessary. Metal conducts heat so rapidly that if it isn't warm it feels cold. Plastic such as our K-14A is as strong as metal, as poreless and thus readily sterilized as metal and has a very low thermal conductivity. I think—well. The remainder of what I think is properly my own business, Miss Devereux, and I want to get back to my own business to implement it before it is too late."

"Jesus, Bob," I said, really angry, "don't you feel anything at all? You got something good out of the group. Don't you want to help?"

I could hear him walking away. "Not in the least," he said.

"Won't you at least come over to the radio mirror with us to look? There's a road there. . . ."

But he didn't even answer.

And we had wasted enough time, more than enough time. I took Barbie's hand, and we started off to where the faint sky glow suggested there were buildings. There was nothing much else in these hills; it had to be either the administration buildings around the radio dish or the cave entrance, and either way I could find my way from there. Of course, Dolly might not have gone to the dish. But where else would she go? Down the hill to civilization, maybe, but in that case she would be all right. But if she had gone to the dish, if she had been listening when I told her about the slippery catwalk and the five-hundred-foot drop—no, there was not much more time to waste.

There was no road near the outcropping with the crevice through which we had come. People had been there before. There was a sort of bruised part of the undergrowth that might have been a kind of path. It didn't help much. We bulldozed our way through the brush, with wet branches slapping at us and wet vines and bushes wrapping themselves around our legs; a little of that was plenty, on the up-and-down hillsides, but after half an hour or so we did hit a road. Something like a road, anyway; two parallel ruts that presumably were used from time to time, because the vegetation had not quite obliterated it. It circled a hill, and from the far side of it I could see not one but two glowing spots in the cloud. The nearer and brighter one looked like the entrance to the pit. Ergo, the other was where we wanted to go.

I think it took us a couple of hours to get there, and we didn't have the breath for much talking. We were lower down than I had been before. The suspended thing that looked like an old trolley car slung from wires was now higher up than we were; the rain had stopped, and the clouds were beginning to lighten with dawn coming. I stopped, gasping, and Barbie leaned against me, and the two of us stared around the great round bowl.

"I don't see her," Barbie said.

I didn't see her either. That was not all bad. The good part was that I didn't see her body spread out over the rusting wire mesh at the bottom of the bowl. "Maybe she didn't come here after all," I said.

"Where else would she go?"

"She could have got lost." Or she could have blundered down the mountains looking for a road. Or she could have found another cliff to jump off.

But I didn't think so, and then Barbie said, very softly, "Oh, look up there, my David. What's that that's moving?"

I looked. It was still gray and I could not be sure; but, yes, there was something moving.

It was actually in the big metal instrument cage, whatever it was.

I said, "I don't know, Barb. Let's go find out."

It was easy to say that, hard to do; the catwalk started out from the side of a hill but unfortunately not the hill we were on; we had to skirt one and circle around another before we reached the end of the catwalk. That was twenty minutes or so, I guess; and by then the day was brighter. And that was not all good. The bad part was that I could see the catwalk very clearly. It had not been used much for, I would guess, ten or fifteen years. Maybe more. It had a plank floor with spaces between the planks and spaces where planks seemed to have rotted out and fallen off. It had a wire-net side-barrier: rusty. The cables themselves, the overhead ones from which it was slung and the smaller ones that bound it to them, looked sturdy enough, but what good would that do us if the boards split under us and we fell through?

There were, however, only two alternatives, and neither of them was any good. The tangible alternative was a sort of bucket car that rose from the administration buildings to the machine cage, but to get to that meant going halfway around the bowl, and who could know if it would be working? The intangible alternative was to turn away. So in effect we had no alternatives, and I took Barbie's hand and led her out onto the catwalk. By the time we were ten yards along it, we became aware of wind (we had not felt it before) and the rain (which slammed into us from the side). And we became aware that the whole suspended walk was swaying, and making creaking, testy, failing sounds as it swayed. We walked as lightly as we could. . . .

I was almost surprised when we discovered that we were at the machine cage. Down between our feet was a whole lot of emptiness, with the wire mesh and the greenery poking through at the end. Over us was the machinery. And I didn't know what to do next.

Barbie did; she called, "Dolly dear, are you up there?"

There was no answer.

I tried: "Dolly, please come down! We want you."

No answer, except what might have been the wind blowing, and might have been a sob.

Barbie looked at me. "Do you want to go up and look around?"

I shook my head. There was a metal ladder, but it went into a hatch and the hatch was shut. I really didn't like the idea of climbing those few extra feet, but most of all I didn't like the idea of driving Dolly farther and farther away, until I drove her maybe out of some window. I yelled, "Dolly, we didn't come all this way just to say good-bye. We want you with us, Dolly!" I hadn't asked Barbie if that was true; it didn't matter.

Silence that prolonged itself, and then there was a grating sound and the hatch opened. Dolly peered down at us, looking cross but otherwise not unusual. "Crap," she said. "Okay, you've soothed your consciences. Now go back to bed."

Barbie, holding on to the ladder—the whole structure was vibrating now—looked up at her and said, "Dolly, are you mad because David and I went to bed?"

With dignity Dolly said, "I have nothing to be angry about. Not to mention I'm used to it."

"Because it wasn't that big a deal, Dolly," Barbie went on. "It just happened that way. It could have been you and David, and I wouldn't have been mad."

"You're not me," said Dolly, and added, very carefully and precisely, "you're not a girl that's always been fifty pounds too fat, that everybody laughs at, that buys the kind of clothes you wear all the time and tries them on in front of a mirror, and then throws them out and cries herself to sleep."

She stopped there. Neither Barbie nor I said anything for a moment. Then I started, "Dolly dear—" But Barbie put her hand on my shoulder and stopped me.

She gathered her thoughts and then said, "Dolly, that's right, I'm not you. I'm me, but maybe you don't know what it's like to be me, either. Would you like me to tell you who I am? I'm a girl who really looked forward to this group, which took all the guts I had, because it meant letting myself hope for something, and then ran out of courage and never asked anybody for the help I wanted. I'm a black girl, Dolly, and that may not seem like much of a bad thing to you, but I happen to be a black girl who's going to die of it. Or to put it another way, Dolly dear, you're a girl who can make plans for Christmas, and I'm a girl who won't be here then."

You hear words like that, and for a minute you don't know what it is you've heard. I stood there, one hand holding on to the ladder, looking at Barbie with the expression of polite interest you give someone who is telling you a complicated story of which you have not yet seen the point. I couldn't make that expression go off my face. I couldn't find the right expression to replace it with.

Dolly said, "What the hell are you talking about?" And her voice was suddenly shrill.

"What I say," said Barbie. "It's what they call sickle-cell anemia. You white folks don't get it much, but us black folks, we get it. You know. All God's chillun got hemoglobin, but where your hemoglobin has something they call glutamic acid, my hemoglobin has something they call valine. Sounds like nothing much? Yeah, Dolly, but we die of it. Used to be we died before we grew up, most of the time, but they do things better now. I'm thirty-one, and they say I've got, oh, easily another five or six months."

Dolly's face pulled back out of the hatch, and her voice, muffled, yelled, "Wait a minute," and Dolly's legs and bottom appeared as she lowered herself down the ladder. When she got there, all she said was Barbie's name, and put her arms around both of us.

I don't know how long we stayed like that, but it was a long time. And might have been longer if we hadn't heard voices and looked up and saw people coming toward us along the catwalk. A hell of a lot of people, a dozen or so, and we looked again, and it was Bob Sanger leading all the rest.

"Why, son of a bitch," said Barbie in deep surprise. "You know what he did? He went and got the group to see if we needed help."

And Dolly said, "And you know what? We do. We all do." And then she said, "Dear Barbie. We could all be dead before Christmas. If David will have us, let's stick together a while. I mean—a while. As long as we want to." And before Barbie could say anything, she went on. "You know, I volunteered for this group. I didn't exactly ever say what I wanted, but I can tell you two. I guess I could tell all of them, and maybe I will." She took a deep breath. "What I wanted," she said, "was to find out how to be loved."

And I said, "You are."

THE WRAP-UP

Tina Wattridge Final Report. Attached are the analysis sheets, work-ups, recommendations, and SR-4 situation cards.

There is one omission. I left out Jerry Fein's solution to his own problem. If you refer to D6H2140, you will find the problem stated (epidemiological control measures for VD). He ultimately provided his own solution, quote his words from my notes: "Suppose we make a monthly check for VD for the whole population. Everybody who shows up and is clear on the tests gets a little button to wear, like in the shape of a heart, with a date. You know, like the inspection sticker in a car. It could be like a charm bracelet for girls, maybe love beads for men. And if you don't pass the test that month, or start treatment if you fail, you don't get to wear the emblem." The reason I did not forward it was not that I thought it a bad idea; actually, I thought it kind of cute, and with the proper promotion it might work. What I did think, in fact what I was sure of, was that it was a setup. Jerry planted the problem and had the solution in his head when he came in, I guess to get brownie points. Maybe he wants my job. Maybe he just wanted to end the session sooner. Anyway he was playing games, and the reason I'm passing it on now is that I've come to the conclusion that I don't really care if he was playing games. It's still not a bad idea and is forwarded for R&D consideration.

One final personal note: Dev Stanwyck kissed me sweetly and weepily good-bye and took off for Louisiana with the Teitlebaum girl. I hated it, but there it is, and anyway—Well, I don't mind his being young enough to be my youngest son, but I was beginning to kind of mind being his mother. When I was a little girl, I saw an old George Arliss movie on TV; he played an Indian rajah who had tried to abduct an English girl for his harem, and after his plot was foiled, at the end of the picture, he said something that I identify with right now. He looked into the camera and lit a cigarette and said, "Ah, well. She would have been a damn nuisance anyhow."

All in all, it was a good group. I'm taking two weeks accumulated leave effective tomorrow. Then I'll be ready for the next one.

ROBERT SILVERBERG

The Desert of Stolen Dreams

SO THE legend of Arioc has obscured the truth of him, Hissune sees now, as legend has obscured truth in so many other ways. For in the distortions of time Arioc has come to seem grotesque, whimsical, a clown of sudden instability; and yet if the testimony of Lord Calintane means anything, it was not that way at all. A suffering man sought freedom and chose an outlandish way to attain it: no clown, no madman at all. Hissune, himself trapped in the Labyrinth and longing to taste the fresh air without, finds the Pontifex Arioc an unexpectedly congenial figure—his brother in spirit across the thousands of years.

For a long while thereafter Hissune does not go to the Register of Souls. The impact of those illicit journeys into the past has been too powerful; his head buzzes with stray strands out of the souls of Thesme and Calintane and Sinnabor Lavon and Group Captain Eremoil, so that when all of them set up a clamor at once he has difficulty locating Hissune, and that is dismaying. Besides, he has other things to do. After a year and a half he has finished with the tax documents, and by then he has established himself so thoroughly in the House of Records that another assignment is waiting for him, a survey of the distribution of aboriginal population groups in present-day Majipoor. He knows that Lord Valentine has had some problems with Metamorphs—that in fact it was a conspiracy of the Shapeshifter folk that tumbled him from his throne in that weird event of a few years back—and he remembers from what he had overheard among the great ones on Castle Mount during his visit there that it is Lord Valentine's plan to integrate them more fully into the life of the planet, if that can be done. So Hissune suspects that these statistics he has been asked to compile have some function in the grand strategy of the Coronal, and that gives him a private pleasure.

It gives him, too, occasion for ironic smiles. For he is shrewd enough to see what is happening to the street-boy Hissune. That agile and cunning urchin who caught the Coronal's eye seven years ago is now an adolescent bureaucrat, transformed, tamed, civil, sedate. So be it, he thinks: one does not remain fourteen years old forever, and a time comes to leave the streets and become a useful member of society. Even so he feels some regret for the loss of the boy he had been. Some of that boy's mischief still bubbles in him; only some, but enough. He finds himself thinking weighty thoughts about the nature of society on Majipoor, the organic interrelationship of the political forces, the concept that power implies responsibility, that all beings are held together in harmonious union by a sense of reciprocal obligation. The four great Powers of the realm—the Pontifex, the Coronal, the Lady of the Isle, the King of Dreams—how, Hissune wonders, have they been able to work so well together? Even in this profoundly conservative society, where over thousands of years so little has changed, the harmony of the Powers seems miraculous, a balance of forces that must be divinely inspired. Hissune has had no formal education; there is no one to whom he can turn for knowledge of such things; but nevertheless, there is the Register of Souls, with all the teeming life of Majipoor's past held in a wondrous suspension, ready to release its passionate vitality at a command. It is folly not to explore that pool of knowledge now that such questions trouble his mind. So once again Hissune forges the documents; once again he slides himself glibly past the slow-witted guardians of the archives; once again he punches the keys, seeking now not only amusement and the joy of the forbidden but also an understanding of the evolution of his planet's political institutions. What a serious young man you are becoming, he tells himself, as the dazzling lights of many colors throb in his mind and the dark, intense presence of another human being, long dead but forever timeless, invades his soul.

1

Suvrael lay like a glowing sword across the southern horizon—an iron band of dull red light, sending shimmering heat-pulsations into the air. Dekkeret, standing at the bow of the freighter on which he had made the long dreary sea journey, felt a quickening of the pulse. Suvrael at last! That dreadful place, that abomination of a continent, that useless and miserable land, now just a few days away, and who knew what horrors would befall him there? But he was prepared. Whatever happens, Dekkeret believed, happens for the best, in Suvrael as on Castle Mount. He was in his twentieth year, a big burly man with a short neck and enormously broad shoulders. This was the second summer of Lord Prestimion's glorious reign under the great Pontifex Confalume.

It was as an act of penance that Dekkeret had undertaken the voyage to the burning wastes of barren Suvrael. He had committed a shameful deed—certainly not intending it, at first barely realizing the shame of it—while hunting in the Khyntor Marches of the far northland, and some sort of expiation seemed necessary to him. That was in a way a romantic and flamboyant gesture, he knew, but he could forgive himself that. If he did not make romantic and flamboyant gestures at twenty, then when? Surely not ten or fifteen years from now, when he was bound to the wheel of his destinies and had settled snugly in for the inevitable bland easy career in Lord Prestimion's entourage. This was the moment, if ever. So, then, to Suvrael to purge his soul, no matter the consequences.

His friend and mentor and hunting companion in Khyntor, Akbalik, had not been able to understand. But of course Akbalik was no romantic, and a long way beyond twenty, besides. One night in early spring, over a few flasks of hot golden wine in a rough mountain tabern, Dekkeret had announced his intention and Akbalik's response had been a blunt snorting laugh. "Suvrael?" he had cried. "You judge yourself too harshly. There's no sin so foul that it merits a jaunt in Suvrael."

And Dekkeret, stung, feeling patronized, had slowly shaken his head. "Wrongness lies on me like a stain. I'll burn it from my soul under the hotland sun."

"Make the pilgrimage to the Isle instead, if you think you need to do something. Let the blessed Lady heal your spirit."

"No. Suvrael."

"Why?"

"To suffer," said Dekkeret. "To take myself far from the delights of Castle Mount, to the least pleasant place on Majipoor, to a dismal desert of fiery winds and loathsome dangers. To mortify the flesh, Akbalik, and show my contrition. To lay upon myself the discipline of discomfort and even pain—*pain*, do you know what that is?—until I can forgive myself. All right?"

Akbalik, grinning, dug his fingers into the thick robe of heavy black Khyntor furs that Dekkeret wore. "All right. But if you must mortify, mortify thoroughly. I assume you'll not take this from your body all the while you're under the Suvraelu sun."

Dekkeret chuckled. "There are limits," he said, "to my need for discomfort." He reached for the wine. Akbalik was nearly twice Dekkeret's age, and doubtless found his earnestness funny. So did Dekkeret, to a degree; but that did not swerve him.

"May I try once more to dissuade you?"

"Pointless."

"Consider the waste," said Akbalik anyway. "You have a career to look after. Your name is frequently heard at the Castle now. Lord Prestimion has said high things of you. A promising young man, due to climb far, great strength of character, all that kind of noise. Prestimion's young; he'll rule a long while; those who are young in his early days will rise as he rises. And here you are, deep in the wilds of Khyntor playing when you should be at court, and already planning another and more reckless trip. Forget this

Suvrael nonsense, Dekkeret, and retun to the Mount with me. Do the Coronal's bidding, impress the great ones with your worth, and build for the future. These are wonderful times on Majipoor, and it will be splendid to be among the wielders of power as things unfold. Eh? Eh? Why throw yourself away in Suvrael? No one knows of this—ah—*sin* of yours, this one little lapse from grace—"

"*I* know."

"Then promise never to do it again, and absolve yourself."

"It's not so simple," Dekkeret said.

"To squander a year or two of your life, or perhaps lose your life entirely, on a meaningless, useless journey to—"

"Not meaningless. Not useless."

"Except on a purely personal level it is."

"Not so, Akbalik. I've been in touch with the people of the Pontificate and I've wangled on official appointment. I'm a mission of inquiry. Doesn't that sound grand? Suvrael isn't exporting its quota of meat and livestock and the Pontifex wants to know why. You see? I continue to further my career even while going off on what seems to you a wholly private adventure."

"So you've already made arrangements."

"I leave on Fourday next." Dekkeret reached his hand toward his friend. "It'll be at least two years. We'll meet again on the Mount. What do you say, Akbalik, the games at High Morpin, two years from Winterday?"

Akbalik's calm gray eyes fastened intently on Dekkeret's. "I will be there," he said slowly. "I pray that you'll be too."

That conversation lay only some months in the past; but to Dekkeret now, feeling the throbbing heat of the southern continent reaching toward him over the pale green water of the Inner Sea, it seemed incredibly long ago, and the voyage infinitely long. The first part of the journey had been pleasing enough—down out of the mountains to the grand metropolis of Ni-moya, and then by riverboat down the Zimr to the port of Piliplok on the eastern coast. There he had boarded a freighter, the cheapest transport he could find, bound for the Suvraelu city of Tolaghai, and then it had been south and south and south all summer long, in a ghastly little cabin just downwind from a hold stuffed with bales of dried baby sea-dragons, and as the ship crossed into the tropics the days presented a heat unlike anything he had ever known, and the nights were little better; and the crew, mostly a bunch of shaggy Skandars, laughed at his discomfort and told him that he had better enjoy the cool weather while he could, for real heat was waiting for him in Suvrael. Well, he had wanted to suffer, and his wish was being amply granted already, and worse to come. He did not complain. He felt no regret. But his comfortable life among the young knights of Castle Mount had not prepared him for sleepless nights with the reek of sea-dragon in his nostrils like stilettos, nor for the stifling heat that engulfed the ship a few weeks out of Piliplok, nor for the intense boredom of the unchanging seascape. The planet was so impossibly *huge*, that was the trouble. It took forever to get from anywhere to anywhere. Crossing from his native continent of Alhanroel to the western land of Zimroel had been a big enough project, by riverboat to Alaisor from the Mount, then by sea to Piliplok and up the river into the moutain marches, but he had had Akbalik with him to lighten the time, and there had been the excitement of his first major journey, the strangeness of new places, new foods, new accents. And he had had the hunting expedition to look forward to. But this? This imprisonment aboard a dirty creaking ship stuffed with parched meat of evil odor? This interminable round of empty days without friends, without duties, without conversation? If only some monstrous sea-dragon would heave into view, he thought, and enliven the journey with a bit of peril; but no, no, the dragons in their migrations were elsewhere, one great herd said to be in western waters out by Narabal just now and another midway between Piliplok and the Rodamaunt Archipelago, and Dekkeret saw none of the vast beasts, not even a few stragglers. What made the boredom worse was that it did not seem to have any value as catharsis. He was suffering, true, and suffering was what he imagined would heal him of his wound, but yet the awareness of the terrible thing he had done in the mountains did not seem to diminish at all. He was hot and bored and restless, and guilt still clawed at him, and still he tormented himself with the ironic knowledge that he was being praised by no less than the Coronal Lord Prestimion for great strength of character while he could find only weakness and cowardice and foolishness in himself. Perhaps it takes more than humidity and boredom and foul odors to cure one's soul, Dekkeret decided. At any rate he had had more than enough of the process of getting to Suvrael, and he was ready to begin the next phase of his pilgrimage into the unknown.

2

Every journey ends, even an endless one. The hot wind out of the south intensified day after day until the deck was too hot to walk and the barefoot Skandars had to swab it down every few hours; and then suddenly the burning mass of sullen darkness on the horizon resolved itself into a shoreline and the jaws of a harbor. They had reached Tolaghai at last.

All of Suvrael was tropical; most of its interior was desert, oppressed perpetually by a colossal weight of dry dead air around the periphery of which searing cyclones whirled; but the fringes of the continent were more or less habitable, and there were five major cities along the coasts, of which Tolaghai was the largest and the one most closely linked by commerce to the rest of Majipoor. As the freighter entered the broad harbor Dekkeret was struck by the strangeness of the place. In his brief time he had seen a great many of the giant world's cities—a dozen of the fifty on the flanks of Castle Mount, and towering windswept Alaisor, and the vast astounding white-walled Ni-moya, and magnificent Piliplok, and many others—and never had he beheld a city with the harsh, mysterious, forbidding look of this one. Tolaghai clung like a crab to a low ridge along the sea. Its buildings were flat, squat things of sun-dried orange brick, with mere slits for windows, and there were only sparse plantings around them, dismaying angular palms, mainly, that were all bare trunk with tiny feathery crowns far overhead. Here at midday the streets were almost deserted. The hot wind blew sprays of sand over the cracked paving-stones. To Dekkeret the city seemed like some sort of prison outpost, brutal and ugly, or perhaps a city out of time, belonging to some prehistoric folk of a regimented and authoritarian race. Why had anyone chosen to build a place so hideous? Doubtless it was out of mere efficiency, ugliness like this being the best way to cope with the climate of the land, but still, still, Dekkeret thought, the challenges of heat and drought might surely have called forth some less repellent architecture.

In his innocence Dekkeret thought he could simply go ashore at once, but that was not how things worked here. The ship lay at anchor for more than an hour before the port officials, three glum-looking Hjorts, came aboard. Then followed a lengthy business with sanitary inspections and cargo manifests and haggling over docking fees; and finally the dozen or so passengers were cleared for landing. A porter of the Ghayrog race seized Dekkeret's luggage and asked the name of his hotel. He replied that he had not booked one, and the reptilian-looking creature, tongue flickering and black fleshy hair writhing like a mass of serpents, gave him an icy mocking look and said, "What will you pay? Are you rich?"

"Not very. What can I get for three crowns a night?"

"Little. Bed of straw. Vermin on the walls."

"Take me there," said Dekkeret.

The Ghayrog looked as startled as a Ghayrog is capable of looking. "You will not be happy there, fine sir. You have the bearing of lordship about you."

"Perhaps so, but I have a poor man's purse. I'll take my chances with the vermin."

Actually the inn turned out to be not as bad as he feared: ancient, squalid, and depressing, yes, but so was everything else in sight, and the room he received seemed almost palatial after his lodgings on the ship. Nor was there the reek of sea-dragon flesh here, only the arid piercing flavor of Suvraelu air, like the stuff within a flask that had been sealed a thousand years. He gave the Ghayrog a half-crown piece, for which he had no thanks, and unpacked his few belongings.

In late afternoon Dekkeret went out. The stifling heat had dropped not at all, but the thin cutting wind seemed less fierce now, and there were more people in the streets. All the same the city felt grim. This was the right sort of place for doing a penance. He loathed the blank-faced brick buildings, he hated the withered look of the landscape, and he missed the soft sweet air of his native city of Normork on the lower slopes of Castle Mount. Why, he wondered, would anyone choose to live here, when there was opportunity aplenty on the gentler continents? What starkness of the soul drove some millions of his fellow citizens to scourge themselves in the daily severities of life on Suvrael?

The representatives of the Pontificate had their offices on the great blank plaza fronting the harbor. Dekkeret's instructions called upon him to present himself there, and despite the lateness of the hour he found the place open, for in the searing heat all citizens of Tolaghai observed a midday closing and transacted business well into evening. He was left to wait a while in an antechamber decorated with huge white ceramic portraits of the reigning monarchs, the Pontifex Confalume shown in full face with a look of benign but overwhelming grandeur, and young Lord Prestimion the Coronal in profile, eyes aglitter with intelligence and dynamic energy. Majipoor was fortunate in her rulers, Dekkeret thought. When he was a boy he had seen Confalume, then Coronal, holding court in the wondrous city of Bombifale high up the Mount, and he had wanted to cry out from sheer joy at the man's calmness and radiant strength. A few years later Lord Confalume succeeded to the Pontificate and went to dwell in the subterranean recesses of the Labyrinth, and Prestimion had been made Coronal—a very different man, equally impressive but all dash and vigor and impulsive power. It was while Lord Prestimion was making the grand processional through the cities of the Mount that he had spied the young Dekkeret in Normork and had chosen him, in his random unpredictable way, to join the knights in training in the High Cities. Which seemed an epoch ago, such great changes having occurred in Dekkeret's life since then. At eighteen he had allowed himself fantasies of ascending the Coronal's throne himself one day; but then had come his ill-starred holiday in the mountains of Zimroel, and now, scarcely past twenty, fidgeting in a dusty outer office in this drab city of cheerless Suvrael, he felt he had no future at all, only a barren stretch of meaningless years to use up.

A pudgy sour-faced Hjort appeared and announced, "The Archiregimand Golator Lasgia will see you now."

That was a resonant title; but its owner proved to be a slender dark-skinned woman not greatly older than Dekkeret, who gave him careful scrutiny out of large glossy solemn eyes. In a perfunctory way she offered him greeting with the hand-symbol of the Pontificate and took the document of his credentials from him. "The Initiate Dekkeret," she murmured. "Mission of inquiry, under commission of the Khyntor provincial superstrate. I don't understand, Initiate Dekkeret. Do you serve the Coronal or the Pontifex?"

Uncomfortably Dekkeret said, "I am of Lord Prestimion's staff, a very low echelon. But while I was in Khyntor Province a need arose at the office of the Pontificate for an investigation of certain things in Suvrael, and when the local officials discovered that I was bound for Suvrael anyway, they asked me in the interests of economy to take on the job even though I was not in the employ of the Pontifex. And—''

Tapping Dekkeret's papers thoughtfully against her desktop, Golator Lasgia said, ''You were bound for Suvrael anyway? May I ask why?''

Dekkeret flushed. ''A personal matter, if you please.''

She let it pass. ''And what affairs of Suvrael can be of such compelling interest to my Pontifical brothers of Khyntor, or is my curiosity on that subject also misplaced?''

Dekkeret's discomfort grew. 'It has to do with an imbalance of trade,'' he answered, barely able to meet her cool penetrating gaze. ''Khyntor is a manufacturing center; it exchanges goods for the livestock of Suvrael; for the past two years the export of blaves and mounts out of Suvrael has declined steadily, and now strains are developing in the Khyntor economy. The manufacturers are encountering difficulty in carrying so much Suvraelu credit.''

''None of this is news to me.''

''I've been asked to inspect the rangelands here,'' said Dekkeret, ''in order to determine whether an upturn in livestock production can soon be expected.''

''Will you have some wine?'' Golator Lasgia asked unexpectedly.

Dekkeret, adrift, considered the proprieties. While he faltered she produced two flasks of golden, deftly snapped their seals, and passed one to him. He took it with a grateful smile. The wine was cold, sweet, with a faint sparkle.

''Wine of Khyntor,'' she said. ''Thus we contribute to the Suvraelu trade deficit. The answer, Initiate Dekkeret, is that in the final year of the Pontifex Prankipin a terrible drought struck Suvrael—you may ask, Initiate, how we can tell the difference here between a year of drought and a year of normal rainfall, but there is a difference, Initiate, there is a significant difference—and the grazing districts suffered. There was no way of feeding our cattle, so we butchered as many as the market could hold, and sold much of the remaining stock to ranchers in western Zimroel. Not long after Confalume succeeded to the Labyrinth, the rains returned and the grass began to grow in our savannas. But it takes several years to rebuild the herds. Therefore the trade imbalance will continue a time longer, and then will be cured.'' She smiled without warmth. ''There. I have spared you the inconvenience of an uninteresting journey to the interior.''

Dekkeret found himself perspiring heavily. ''Nevertheless I must make it, Archiregimand Golator Lasgia.''

''You'll learn nothing more than I've just told you.''

''I mean no disrespect. But my commission specifically requires me to see with my own eyes—''

She closed hers a moment. ''To reach the rangelands just now will involve you in great difficulties, extreme physical discomfort, perhaps considerable personal danger. If I were you, I'd remain in Tolaghai, sampling such pleasures as are available here, and dealing with whatever personal business brought you to Suvrael; and after a proper interval, write your report in consultation with my office and take yourself back to Khyntor."

Immediate suspicions blossomed in Dekkeret. The branch of the government she served was not always cooperative with the Coronal's people; she seemed quite transparently trying to conceal something that was going on in Suvrael; and, although his mission of inquiry was only the pretext for his voyage to this place and not his central task, all the same he had his career to consider, and if he allowed a Pontifical Archiregimand to bamboozle him too easily here it would go badly for him later. He wished he had not accepted the wine from her. But to cover his confusion he allowed himself a series of suave sips, and at length said, "My sense of honor would not permit me to follow such an easy course."

"How old are you, Initiate Dekkeret?"

"I was born in the twelfth year of Lord Confalume."

"Yes, your sense of honor would still prick you, then. Come, look at this map with me." She rose briskly. She was taller than he expected, nearly his own height, which gave her a fragile appearance. Her dark, tightly coiled hair emitted a surprising fragrance, even over the aroma of the strong wine. Golator Lasgia touched the wall and a map of Suvrael in brilliant ochre and auburn hues sprang into view. "This is Tolaghai," she said, tapping the northwest corner of the continent. "The grazing lands are here." She indicated a band that began six or seven hundred miles inland and ran in a rough circle surrounding the desert at the heart of Suvrael. "From Tolaghai," she went on, "there are three main routes to the cattle country. This is one. At present it is ravaged by sandstorms and no traffic can safely use it. This is the second route: we are experiencing certain difficulties with Shapeshifter bandits there, and it is also closed to travelers. The third way lies here, by Khulag Pass, but that road has fallen into disuse of late, and an arm of the great desert has begun to encroach on it. Do you see the problems?"

As gently as he could Dekkeret said, "But if it is the business of Suvrael to raise cattle for export, and all the routes between the grazing lands and the chief port are blocked, is it correct to say that a lack of pasture is the true cause of the recent shortfalls of cattle exports?"

She smiled. "There are other ports from which we ship our produce in this current situation."

"Well, then, if I go to one of those, I should find an open highway to the cattle country."

Again she tapped the map. "Since last winter the port of Natu Gorvinu has been the center of the cattle trade. This is it, in the east, under the coast of Alhanroel, about six thousand miles from here."

"Six thousand—"

"There is little reason for commerce between Tolaghai and Natu Gorvinu. Perhaps once a year a ship goes from one to the other. Overland the situation is worse, for the roads out of Tolaghai are not maintained east of Kangheez—" she indicated a city perhaps a thousand miles away—"and beyond that, who knows? This is not a heavily settled continent."

"Then there's no way to reach Natu Gorvinu?" Dekkeret said, stunned.

"One. By ship from Tolaghai to Stoien on Alhanroel, and from Stoien to Natu Gorvinu. It should take you only a little over a year. By the time you reach Suvrael again and penetrate the interior, of course, the crisis that you've come to investigate will probably be over. Another flask of the golden, Initiate Dekkeret?"

Numbly he accepted the wine. The distances stupefied him. Another horrendous voyage across the Inner Sea, all the way back to his native continent of Alhanroel, only to turn around and cross the water a third time, sailing now to the far side of Suvrael, and then to find, probably, that the ways to the interior had meanwhile been closed out there, and—no. No. There was such a thing as carrying a penance too far. Better to abandon the mission altogether than subject himself to such absurdities.

While he hesitated Golator Lasgia said, "The hour is late and your problems need longer consideration. Have you plans for dinner, Initiate Dekkeret?"

Suddenly, astoundingly, her somber eyes gleamed with mischief of a familiar kind.

3

In the company of the Archiregimand Golator Lasgia, Dekkeret discovered that life in Tolaghai was not necessarily as bleak as first superficial inspection had indicated. By floater she returned him to his hotel—he could see her distaste at the look of the place—and instructed him to rest and cleanse himself and be ready in an hour. A coppery twilight had descended, and by the time the hour had elapsed the sky was utterly black, with only a few alien constellations cutting jagged tracks across it, and the crescent hint of one or two moons down near the horizon. She called for him punctually. In place of her stark official tunic she wore now something of clinging mesh, almost absurdly seductive. Dekkeret was puzzled by all this. He had had his share of success with women, yes, but so far as he knew he had given her no sign of interest, nothing but the most formal of respect; and yet she clearly was assuming a night of intimacy. Why? Certainly not his irresistible sophistication and physical appeal, nor any political advantage he could confer on her, nor any other rational motive. Except one, that this was a foul backwater outpost where life was stale and uncomfortable, and he was a youthful stranger who might provide a woman herself still young with a night's amusement. He felt used by that, but otherwise he could see no great harm in it. And after months at sea he was willing to run a little risk in the name of pleasure.

They dined at a private club on the outskirts of town, in a garden elegantly decorated with the famous creature-plants of Stoienzar and other flowering wonders that had Dekkeret calculating how much of Tolaghai's modest water supply was diverted toward keeping this one spot flourishing. At other tables, widely separated, were Suvraelinu in handsome costume, and Golator Lasgia nodded to this one and that, but no one approached her, nor did they stare unduly at Dekkeret. From within the building blew a cool refreshing breeze, the first he had felt in weeks as though some miraculous machine of the ancients, some cousin to the ones that generated the delicious atmosphere of Castle Mount, were at work in there. Dinner was a magnificent affair of lightly fermented fruits and tender juicy slabs of a pale green-fleshed fish, accompanied by a fine dry wine of Amblemorn, no less, the very fringes of Castle Mount. She drank freely, as did he; they grew bright-eyed and animated; the chilly formality of the interview in her office dropped away. He learned that she was nine years his senior, that she was a native of moist lush Narabal on the western continent, that she had entered the service of the Pontifex when still a girl, and had been stationed in Suvrael for the past ten years, rising upon Confalume's accession to the Pontificate to her present high administrative post in Tolaghai.

"Do you *like* it here?" he asked.

She shrugged. "One gets accustomed to it."

"I doubt that I would. To me Suvrael is merely a place of torment, a kind of purgatory."

Golator Lasgia nodded. "Exactly."

There was a flash from her eyes to his. He did not dare ask for amplification; but something told him that they had much in common.

He filled their glasses once again and permitted himself the perils of a calm, knowing smile.

She said, "Is it purgatory you seek here?"

"Yes."

She indicated the lavish gardents, the empty wine-flasks, the costly dishes, the half-eaten delicacies. "You have made a poor start, then."

"Milady, dinner with you was no part of my plan."

"Nor mine. But the Divine provides, and we accept. Yes? Yes?" She leaned close. "What will you do now? The voyage to Natu Gorvinu?"

"It seems too heavy an enterprise."

"Then do as I say. Stay in Tolaghai until you grow weary of it; then return and file your report. No one will be the wiser in Khyntor."

"No. I must go inland."

Her expression grew mocking. "Such dedication! But how will you do it? The roads from here are closed."

"You mentioned the one by Khulag Pass, that had fallen into disuse. Mere disuse doesn't seem as serious as deadly sandstorms, or Shapeshifter bandits. Perhaps I can hire a caravan leader to take me that way."

"Into the desert?"

"If needs be."

"The desert is haunted," said Golator Lasgia casually. "You should forget that idea. Call the waiter over: we need more wine."

"I think I've had enough, milady."

"Come, then. We'll go elsewhere."

Stepping from the breeze-cooled garden to the dry hot night air of the street was a shock; but quickly they were in her floater, and not long after they were in a second garden, this one in the courtyard of her official residence, surrounding a pool. There were no weather-machines here to ease the heat, but the Archiregimand had another way, dropping her gown and going to the pool. Her lean, supple body gleamed a moment in the starlight; then she dived, sliding nearly without a splash beneath the surface. She beckoned to him and quickly he joined her.

Afterward they embraced on a bed of close-cropped thick-bladed grass. It was almost as much like wrestling as lovemaking, for she clasped him with her long muscular legs, tried to pinion his arms, rolled over and over with him, laughing, and he was amazed at the strength of her, the playful ferocity of her movements. But when they were through testing one another they moved with more harmony, and it was a night of little sleep and much exertion.

Dawn was an amazement: without warning, the sun was in the sky like a trumpet-blast, roasting the surrounding hills with shafts of hot light.

They lay limp, exhausted. Dekkeret turned to her—by cruel morning light she looked less girlish than she had under the stars—and said abruptly. "Tell me about this haunted desert. What spirits will I meet there?"

"How persistent you are!"

"Tell me."

"There are ghosts there that can enter your dreams and steal them. They rob your soul of joy and leave fears in its place. By day they sing in the distance, confusing you, leading you from the path with their clatter and their music."

"Am I supposed to believe this?"

"In recent years many who have entered that desert have perished there."

"Of dream-stealing ghosts."

"So it is said."

"It will make a good tale to tell when I return to Castle Mount, then."

"*If* you return," she said.

"You say that not everyone who has gone into that desert has died of it. Obviously not, for someone has come out to tell the tale. Then I will hire a guide, and take my chances among the ghosts."

"No one will accompany you."

"Then I'll go alone."

"And certainly die." She stroked his powerful arms and made a little purring sound. "Are you so interested in dying, so soon? Dying has no value. It confers no benefits. Whatever peace you seek, the peace of the grave is not it. Forget the desert journey. Stay here with me."

"We'll go together."

She laughed. "I think not."

It was, Dekkeret realized, madness. He had doubts of her tales of ghosts and dream-stealers, unless what went on in that desert was some trickery of the rebellious Shapeshifter aborigines, and even then he doubted it. Perhaps all her tales of danger were only ruses to keep him longer in Tolaghai. Flattering if true, but of no help in his quest. And she was right about death being a useless form of purgation. If his adventures in Suvrael were to have meaning, he must succeed in surviving them.

Golator Lasgia drew him to his feet. They bathed briefly in the pool; then she led him within, to the most handsomely appointed dwelling he had seen this side of Castle Mount, and gave him a breakfast of fruits and dried fish.

Suddenly in mid-morning she said, "*Must* you go into the interior?"

"An inner need drives me in that direction."

"Very well. We have in Tolaghai a certain scoundrel who often ventures inland by way of Khulag Pass, or so he claims, and seems to survive it. For a purse full of royals he'll no doubt guide you there. His name is Barjazid; and if you insist, I'll summon him and ask him to assist you."

4

"Scoundrel" seemed the proper word for Barjazid. He was a lean and disreputable-looking little man, shabbily dressed in an old brown robe and worn leather sandals, with an ancient necklace of mismatched sea-dragon bones at his throat. His lips were thin, his eyes had a feverish glaze, his skin was burned almost black by the desert sun. He stared at Dekkeret as though weighing the contents of his purse.

"If I take you," said Barjazid in a voice altogether lacking in resonance but yet not weak, "you will first sign a quitclaim absolving me of any responsibility to your heirs, in the event of your death."

"I have no heirs," Dekkeret replied.

"Kinfolk, then. I won't be hauled into the Pontifical courts by your father or your elder sister because you've perished in the desert."

"Have you perished in the desert yet?"

Barjazid looked baffled. "An absurd question."

"You go into that desert," Dekkeret persisted, "and you return alive.

Yes? Well then, if you know your trade, you'll come out alive again this time, and so will I. I'll do what you do and go where you go. If you live, I live. If I perish, you'll have perished too, and my family will have no lien."

"I can withstand the power of the stealers of dreams," said Barjazid. "This I know from ample tests. How do you know you'll prevail over them as readily?"

Dekkeret helped himself to a new serving of Barjazid's tea, a rich infusion brewed from some potent shrub of the sandhills. The two men squatted on mounds of haigus-hide blankets in the musty backroom of a shop belonging to Barjazid's brother's son: it was evidently a large clan. Dekkeret sipped the sharp, bitter tea reflectively and said, after a moment, "Who are these dream-stealers?"

"I cannot say."

"Shapeshifters, perhaps?"

Barjazid shrugged. "They have not bothered to tell me their pedigree. Shapeshifters, Ghayrogs, Vroons, ordinary humans—how would I know? In dreams all voices are alike. Certainly there are tribes of Shapeshifters loose in the desert, and some of them are angry folk given to mischief, and perhaps they have the skill of touching minds along with the skill of altering their bodies. Or perhaps not."

"If the Shapeshifters have closed two of the three routes out of Tolaghai, the Coronal's forces have work to do here."

"This is no affair of mine."

"The Shapeshifters are a subjugated race. They must not be allowed to disrupt the daily flow of life on Majipoor."

"It was you who suggested that the dream-stealers were Shapeshifters," Barjazid pointed out acidly. "I myself have no such theory. And who the dream-stealers are is not important. What is important is that they make the lands beyond Khulag Pass dangerous for travelers."

"Why do you go there, then?"

"I am not likely ever to answer a question that begins with *why*," said Barjazid. "I go there because I have reason to go there. Unlike others, I seem to return alive."

"Does everyone else who crosses the pass die?"

"I doubt it. I have no idea. Beyond question many have perished since the dream-stealers first were heard from. At the best of times that desert has been perilous." Barjazid stirred his tea. He began to appear restless. "If you accompany me, I'll protect you as best I can. But I make no guarantees for your safety. Which is why I demand that you give me legal absolution from responsibility."

Dekkeret said, "If I sign such a paper it would be signing a death warrant. What would keep you from murdering me ten miles beyond the pass, robbing my corpse, and blaming it all on the dream-stealers?"

"By the Lady, I am no murderer! I am not even a thief."

"But to give you a paper saying that if I die on the journey you are not to be blamed—might that not tempt even an honest man beyond all limits?"

Barjazid's eyes blazed with fury. He gestured as though to bring the interview to an end. "What goes beyond limits is your audacity," he said, rising and tossing his cup aside. "Find another guide, if you fear me so much."

Dekkeret, remaining seated, said quietly, "I regret the suggestion. I ask you only to see my position: a stranger and a young man in a remote and difficult land, forced to seek the aid of those he does not know to take him into places where improbable things happen. I must be cautious."

"Be even more cautious, then. Take the next ship for Stoien and return to the easy life of Castle Mount."

"I ask you again to guide me. For a good price, and nothing more about signing a quitclaim to my life. How much is your fee?"

"Thirty royals," Barjazid said.

Dekkeret grunted as though he had been struck below the ribs. It had cost him less than that to sail from Piliplok to Tolaghai. Thirty royals was a year's wage for someone like Barjazid; to pay it would require Dekkeret to draw on an expensive letter of credit. His impulse was to respond with knightly scorn, and offer ten; but he realized that he had forfeited his bargaining strength by objecting to the quitclaim. If he haggled now over the price as well, Barjazid would simply terminate the negotiations.

He said at length, "So be it. But no quitclaim."

Barjazid gave him a sour look. "Very well. No quitclaim, as you insist."

"How is the money to be paid?"

"Half now, half on the morning of departure."

"Ten now," said Dekkeret, "and ten on the morning of departure, and ten on the day of my return to Tolaghai."

"That makes a third of my fee conditional on your surviving the trip. Remember that I make no guarantee of that."

"Perhaps my survival becomes more likely if I hold back a third of the fee until the end."

"One expects a certain haughtiness from one of the Coronal's knights, and one learns to ignore it as a mere mannerism, up to a point. But I think you have passed the point." Once again Barjazid made a gesture of dismissal. "There is too little trust between us. It would be a poor idea for us to travel together."

"I meant no disrespect," said Dekkeret.

"But you ask me to leave myself to the mercies of your kinfolk if you perish, and you seem to regard me as an ordinary cutthroat or at best a brigand, and you feel it necessary to arrange my fee so that I will have less motivation to murder you." Barjazid spat. "The other face of haughtiness is courtesy, young knight. A Skandar dragon-hunter would have shown me more courtesy. I did not seek your employ, bear in mind. I will not humiliate myself to aid you. If you please—"

"Wait."

"I have other business this morning."

"Fifteen royals now," said Dekkeret, "and fifteen when we set forth, as you say. Yes?"

"Even though you think I'll murder you in the desert?"

"I became too suspicious because I didn't want to appear too innocent," said Dekkeret. "It was tactless for me to have said the things I said. I ask you to hire yourself to me on the terms agreed."

Barjazid was silent.

From his purse Dekkeret drew three five-royal coins. Two were pieces of the old coinage, showing the Pontifex Prankipin with Lord Confalume. The third was a brilliant newly minted one, bearing Confalume as Pontifex and the image of Lord Prestimion on the reverse. He extended them toward Barjazid, who selected the new coin and examined it with great curiosity.

"I have not seen one of these before," he said. "Shall we call in my brother's son for an opinion of its authenticity?"

It was too much. "Do you take me for a passer of false money?" Dekkeret roared, leaping to his feet and looming ferociously over the small man. Rage throbbed in him; he came close to striking Barjazid.

But he perceived that the other was altogether fearless and unmoving in the face of his wrath. Barjazid actually smiled, and took the other two coins from Dekkeret's trembling hand.

"So you too have little liking for groundless accusations, eh, young knight?" Barjazid laughed. "Let us have a treaty, then. You'll not expect me to assassinate you beyond Khulag Pass, and I'll not send your coins out to the money changer's for an appraisal, eh? Well? Is it agreed?"

Dekkeret nodded wearily.

"Nevertheless this is a risky journey," said Barjazid, "and I would not have you too confident of a safe return. Much depends on your own strength when the time of testing comes."

"So be it. When do we leave?"

"Fiveday, at the sunset hour. We depart the city from Pinitor Gate. Is that place known to you?"

"I'll find it," Dekkeret said. "Till Fiveday, at sunset." He offered the little man his hand.

5

Fiveday was three days hence. Dekkeret did not regret the delay, for that gave him three more nights with the Archiregimand Golator Lasgia; or so he thought, but in fact it happened otherwise. She was not at her office by the waterfront on the evening of Dekkeret's meeting with Barjazid, nor would her aides transmit a message to her. He wandered the torrid city disconsolately until long after dark, finding no companionship at all, and ultimately ate a drab and gritty meal at his hotel, still hoping that Golator Lasgia would miraculously appear and whisk him away. She did not, and he slept fitfully and uneasily, his mind obsessed by the memories of her smooth flanks, her small firm breasts, her hungry, aggressive mouth. Toward dawn came a dream, vague and unreadable, in which she and Barjazid and some Hjorts and Vroons performed a complex dance in a roofless sandswept stone ruin, and afterward he fell into a sound sleep, not awakening until midday on Seaday. The entire city appeared to be in hiding then, but when the cooler hours came he went round to the Archiregimand's office once again, once again not seeing her, and then spent the evening in the same purposeless fashion as the night before. As he gave himself up to sleep he prayed fervently to the Lady of the Isle to send Golator Lasgia to him. But it was not the function of the Lady to do such things, and all that did reach him in the night was a bland and cheering dream, perhaps a gift of the blessed Lady but probably not, in which he dwelled in a thatched hut on the shores of the Great Sea by Til-omon and nibbled on sweet purplish fruits that squirted juice to stain his cheeks. When he awakened he found a Hjort of the Archiregimand's staff waiting outside his room, to summon him to the presence of Golator Lasgia.

That evening they dined together late, and went to her villa again, for a night of lovemaking that made their other one seem like a month of chastity. Dekkeret did not ask her at any time why she had refused him these two nights past, but as they breakfasted on spiced gihornaskin and golden wine, both he and she vigorous and fresh after having had no sleep whatever, she said, "I wish I had had more time with you this week, but at least we were able to share your final night. Now you'll go to the Desert of Stolen Dreams with my taste on your lips. Have I made you forget all other women?"

"You know the answer."

"Good. Good. You may never embrace a woman again; but the last was the best, and few are so lucky as that."

"Were you so certain I'll die in the desert, then?"

"Few travelers return," she said. "The chances of my seeing you again are slight."

Dekkeret shivered faintly—not out of fear, but in recognition of Golator Lasgia's inner motive. Some morbidity in her evidently had led her to snub him those two nights, so that the third would be all the more intense, for she must believe that he would be a dead man shortly after and she wanted the special pleasure of being his last woman. That chilled him. If he were going to die before long, Dekkeret would just as soon have had the other two nights with her as well; but apparently the subtleties of her mind went beyond such crass notions. He bade her a courtly farewell, not knowing if they would meet again or even if he wished it, for all her beauty and voluptuary skills. Too much that was mysterious and dangerously capricious lay coiled within her.

Not long before sunset he presented himself at Pinitor Gate on the city's southeastern flank. It would not have surprised him if Barjazid had reneged on their agreement, but no, a floater was waiting just outside the pitted sandstone arch of the old gate, and the little man stood leaning against the vehicle's side. With him were three companions: a Vroon, a Skandar, and a slender, hard-eyed young man who was obviously Barjazid's son.

At a nod from Barjazid the giant four-armed Skandar took hold of Dekkeret's two sturdy bags and stowed them with a casual flip in the floater's keep. "Her name," said Barjazid, "is Khaymak Gran. She is unable to speak, but far from stupid. She has served me many years, since I found her tongueless and more than half dead in the desert. The Vroon is Serifain Reinaulion, who often speaks too much, but knows the desert tracks better than anyone of this city." Dekkeret exchanged brusque salutes with the small tentacular being. "And my son, Dinitak, will also accompany us," Barjazid said. "Are you well rested, Initiate?"

"Well enough," Dekkeret answered. He had slept most of the day, after his unsleeping night.

"We travel mainly by darkness, and camp in heat of day. My understanding is that I am to take you through Khulag Pass, across the wasteland known as the Desert of Stolen Dreams, and to the edge of the grazing lands around Ghyzyn Kor, where you have certain inquiries to make among the herdsmen. And then back to Tolaghai. Is this so?"

"Exactly," Dekkeret said.

Barjazid made no move to enter the floater. Dekkeret frowned; and then he understood. From his purse he produced three more five-royal pieces, two of them old ones of the Prankipin coinage, the third a shining coin of Lord Prestimion. These he handed to Barjazid, who plucked forth the Prestimion coin and tossed it to his son. The boy eyed the bright coin suspiciously. "The new Coronal," said Barjazid. "Make yourself familiar with his face. We'll be seeing it often."

"He will have a glorious reign," said Dekkeret. "He will surpass even Lord Confalume in grandeur. Already a wave of new prosperity sweeps the northern continents, and they were prosperous enough before. Lord Prestimion is a man of vigor and decisiveness, and his plans are ambitious."

Barjazid said, with a shrug, "Events on the northern continents carry very little weight here, and somehow prosperity on Alhanroel or Zimroel has a way of mattering hardly at all to Suvrael. But we rejoice that the Divine has blessed us with another splendid Coronal. May he remember, occasionally, that there is a southern land also, and citizens of his realm dwelling in it. Come, now: time to be traveling."

6

The Pinitor Gate marked an absolute boundary between city and desert. To one side there was a district of low sprawling villas, walled and faceless;

to the other was only barren waste beyond the city's perimeter. Nothing broke the emptiness of the desert but the highway, a broad cobbled track that wound slowly upward toward the crest of the ridge that encircled Tolaghai.

The heat was intolerable. By night the desert was perceptibly cooler than by day, but scorching all the same. Though the great blazing eye of the sun was gone, the orange sands, radiating the stored heat of the day toward the sky, shimmered and sizzled with the intensity of a banked furnace. A strong wind was blowing—with the coming of the darkness, Dekkeret had noticed, the flow of the wind reversed, blowing now from the heart of the continent toward the sea—but it made no difference: shore-wind or sea-wind, both were oppressive streams of dry baking air that offered no mercies.

In the clear arid atmosphere the light of the stars and moons was unusually bright, and there was an earthly glow as well, a strange ghostly greenish radiance that rose in irregular patches from the slopes flanking the highway. Dekkeret asked about it. "From certain plants," said the Vroon. "They shine with an inner light in the darkness. To touch such a plant is always painful and often fatal."

"How am I to know them by daylight?"

"They look like pieces of old string, weathered and worn, sprouting in bunches from clefts in the rock. Not all the plants of such a form are dangerous, but you would do well to avoid any of them."

"And any other," Barjazid put in. "In this desert the plants are well defended, sometimes in surprising ways. Each year our garden teaches us some ugly new secret."

Dekkeret nodded. He did not plan to stroll about out there, but if he did, he would make it his rule to touch nothing.

The floater was old and slow, the grade of the highway steep. Through the broiling night the car labored unhurriedly onward. There was little conversation within. The Skandar drove, with the Vroon beside her, and occasionally Serifain Reinaulion made some comment on the condition of the road; in the rear compartment the two Barjazids sat silently, leaving Dekkeret alone to stare with growing dismay at the infernal landscape. Under the merciless hammers of the sun the ground had a beaten, broken look. Such moisture as winter had brought this land had long ago been sucked forth, leaving gaunt, angular fissures. The surface of the ground was pockmarked where the unceasing winds had strafed it with sand particles, and the plants, low and sparsely growing things, were of many varieties but all appeared twisted, tortured, gnarled, and knobby. To the heat Dekkeret gradually found himself growing accustomed: it was simply there, like one's skin, and after a time one came to accept it. But the deathly ugliness of all that he beheld, the dry rough spiky uncaring bleakness of everything, numbed his soul. A landscape that was hateful was a new concept to him, almost an inconceivable one. Wherever he had gone on Majipoor he had known only beauty. He thought of his home city of Normork spread along the crags of the Mount, with its winding boulevards and its wondrous stone wall and its gentle midnight rains. He thought of the giant city of Stee higher on the Mount, where once he had walked at dawn in a garden of trees no taller than his ankle, with leaves of a green hue that dazzled his eyes. He thought of High Morpin, that glimmering miracle of a city devoted wholly to pleasure, that lay almost in the shadow of the Coronal's awesome castle atop the Mount. And the rugged forested wilds of Khyntor, and the brilliant white towers of Ni-moya, and the sweet meadows of the Glayge Valley—how beautiful a world this is, Dekkeret thought, and what marvels it holds, and how terrible this place I find myself in now!

He told himself that he must alter his values and strive to discover the beauties of this desert, or else it would paralyze his spirit. Let there be beauty in utter dryness, he thought, and beauty in menacing angularity, and beauty in pockmarks, and beauty in ragged plants that shine with a pale green glow by night. Let spiky be beautiful, let bleak be beautiful, let harsh be beautiful. For what is beauty, Dekkeret asked himself, if not a learned response to things beheld? Why is a meadow intrinsically more beautiful than a pebbled desert? Beauty, they say, is in the eye of the beholder; therefore re-educate your eye, Dekkeret, lest the ungliness of this land kill you.

He tried to make himself love the desert. He pulled such words as "bleak" and "dismal" and "repellent" from his mind as though pulling fangs from a wild beast, and instructed himself to see this landscape as tender and comforting. He made himself admire the contorted strata of the exposed rock faces and the great gouges of the dry washes. He found aspects of delight in the bedraggled beaten shrubs. He discovered things to esteem in the small toothy nocturnal creatures that occasionally scuttered across the road. And as the night wore on, the desert did become less hateful to him, and then neutral, and at last he believed he actually could see some beauty in it; and by the hour before dawn he had ceased to think about it at all.

Morning came suddenly: a shaft of orange flame breaking against the mountain wall to the west, a limb of bright red fire rising over the opposite rim of the range, and then the sun, its yellow face tinged more with bronzy-green than in the northern latitudes, bursting into the sky like an untethered balloon. In this moment of apocalyptic sunrise Dekkeret was startled to find himself thinking in sharp pain of the Archiregimand Golator Lasgia, wondering whether she was watching the dawn, and with whom; he savored the pain a little, and then, banishing the thought, said to Barjazid, "It was a night without phantoms. Is this desert not supposed to be haunted?"

"Beyond the pass is where the real trouble begins," the little man replied.

They rode onward through the early hours of the day. Dinitak served a rough breakfast, dry bread and sour wine. Looking back, Dekkeret saw a mighty view, the land sloping off below him like a great tawny apron, all folds and cracks and wrinkles, and the city of Tolaghai barely visible as a huddled clutter at the bottom end, with the vastness of the sea to the north rolling on to the horizon. The sky was without clouds, and the blue of it was so enhanced by the terra-cotta hue of the land that it seemed almost to be a second sea above him. Already the heat was rising. By mid-morning it was all but unendurable, and still the Skandar driver moved impassively up the breast of the mountain. Dekkeret dozed occasionally, but in the cramped vehicle sleep was impossible. Were they going to drive all night and then all day too? He asked no questions. But just as weariness and discomfort were reaching intolerable levels in him, Khaymak Gran abruptly swung the floater to the left, down a short spur of the road, and brought it to a halt.

"Our first day's camp," Barjazid announced.

Where the spur ended, a high flange of rock reared out of the desert floor, forming an overarching shelter. In front of it, protected by shadows at this time of day, was a wide shady area that had obviously been used many times as a campsite. At the base of the rock formation Dekkeret saw a dark spot where water mysteriously seeped from the ground, not exactly a gushing spring but useful and welcome enough to parched travelers in this terrible desert. The place was ideal. And plainly the entire first day's journey had been timed to bring them here before the worst of the heat descended.

The Skandar and young Barjazid pulled straw mats from some compartment of the floater and scattered them on the sand; the midday meal was offered, chunks of dried meat, a bit of tart fruit, and warm Skandar mead; then, without a word, the two Barjazids and the Vroon and the Skandar sprawled out on their mats and dropped instantly into sleep. Dekkeret stood alone, probing between his teeth for a bit of meat caught there. Now that he could sleep, he was not at all sleepy. He wandered the edge of the campsite, staring into the sun-blasted wastes just outside the area in shadow. Not a creature could be seen, and even the plants, poor shabby things, seemed to be trying to pull themselves into the ground. The mountains rose steeply above him to the south; the pass could not be far off. And then? And then?

He tried to sleep. Unwanted images plagued him. Golator Lasgia hovered above his mat, so close that he felt he could seize her and draw her down to him, but she bobbed away and was lost in the heat-haze. For the thousandth time he saw himself in that forest in the Khyntor Marches, pursuing his prey, aiming, suddenly trembling. He shook that off and found himself scrambling along the great wall at Normork, with cool delectable air in his lungs. But these were not dreams, only idle fantasies and fugitive memories; sleep would not come for a long time, and when it did, it was deep and dreamless and brief.

Strange sounds awakened him: humming, singing, musical instruments in the distance, the faint but distinct noises of a caravan of many travelers. He thought he heard the tinkle of bells, the booming of drums. For a time he lay still, listening, trying to understand. Then he sat up, blinked, looked around. Twilight had come. He had slept away the hottest part of the day, and the shadows now encroached from the other side. His four companions were up and packing the mats. Dekkeret cocked an ear, seeking the source of the sounds. But they seemed to come from everywhere, or from nowhere. He remembered Golator Lasgia's tale of the ghosts of the desert that sing by day, confusing travelers, leading them from the true path with their clatter and their music.

To Barjazid he said, "What are those sounds?"

"Sounds?"

"You don't hear them? Voices, bells, footfalls, the humming of many travelers?"

Barjazid looked amused. "You mean the desert-songs."

"Ghost-songs?"

"They could be that. Or merely the sounds of wayfarers coming down the mountain, rattling chains, striking gongs. Which is more probable?"

"Neither is probable," said Dekkeret gloomily. "There are no ghosts in the world I inhabit. But there are no wayfarers on this road except ourselves."

"Are you sure, Initiate?"

"That there are no wayfarers, or no ghosts?"

"Either."

Dinitak Barjazid, who had been standing to one side taking in this interchange, approached Dekkeret and said, "Are you frightened?"

"The unknown is always disturbing. But at this point I feel more curiosity than fear."

"I will gratify your curiosity, then. As the heat of the day diminishes, the rocky cliffs and the sands give up their warmth, and in cooling they contract and release sounds. Those are the drums and bells you hear. There are no ghosts in this place," the boy said.

The elder Barjazid made a brusque gesture. Serenely the boy moved away.

"You didn't want him to tell me that, did you?" Dekkeret asked. "You prefer me to think that there are ghosts all about me."

Smiling, Barjazid said, "It makes no difference to me. Believe whichever explanation you find more cheering. You will meet a sufficiency of ghosts, I assure you, on the far side of the pass."

7

All Starday evening they climbed the winding road up the face of the mountain, and near midnight came to Khulag Pass. Here the air was cooler, for they were thousands of feet above sea level and warring winds brought some relief from the swelter. The pass was a broad notch in the mountain wall, surprisingly deep; it was early Sunday morning before they completed its traversal and began their descent into the greater desert of the interior.

Dekkeret was stunned by what lay before him. By bright moonlight he beheld a scene of unparelleled bleakness, that made the lands on the cityward side of the pass look like gardens. That other desert was a rocky one, but this was sandy, an ocean of dunes broken here and there by open patches of hard pebble-strewn ground. There was scarcely any vegetation, none at all in the duned places and the merest of sorry scraggles elsewhere. And the heat! Upward out of the dark bowl ahead there came currents of stupefying hot blasts, air that seemed stripped of all nourishment, air that had been baked to death. It astounded him that somewhere in that furnace there could be grazing lands. He tried to remember the map in the Archiregimand's office: the cattle country was a belt that flanked the continent's innermost zone of desert, but here below Khulag Pass an arm of the central wastes had somehow encroached—that was it. On the far side of this band of formidable sterility lay a green zone of grass and browsing beasts, or so he prayed.

Through the early morning hours they headed down the inner face of the mountains and onto the great central plateau. By first light Dekkeret noticed an odd feature far downslope, an oval patch of inky darkness sharply outlined against the buff breast of the desert, and as they drew nearer he saw that it was an oasis of sorts, the dark patch resolving itself into a grove of slender long-limbed trees with tiny violet-flushed leaves. This place was the second day's campsite. Tracks in the sand showed where other parties had camped; there was scattered debris under the trees; in a clearing at the heart of the grove were half a dozen crude shelters made of heaped-up rocks topped with old dried boughs. Just beyond, a brackish stream wound between the trees and terminated in a small stagnant pool, green with algae. And a little way beyond that was a second pool, apparently fed by a stream that ran wholly underground, the waters of which were pure. Between the two pools Dekkeret saw a curious construction, seven round-topped stone columns as high as his waist, arranged in a double arc. He inspected them.

"Shapeshifter work," Barjazid told him.

"A Metamorph altar?"

"So we think. We know the Shapeshifters often visit this oasis. We find little Piurivar souvenirs here—prayer sticks, bits of feathers, small clever wickerwork cups."

Dekkeret stared about uneasily at the trees as if he expected them to transform themselves momentarily into a part of savage aborigines. He had had little contact with the native race of Majipoor, those defeated and displaced indigenes of the forests, and what he knew of them was mainly rumor and fantasy, born of fear, ignorance, and guilt. They once had had great cities, that much was certain—Alhanroel was strewn with the ruins of them, and in school Dekkeret had seen views of the most famous of all, vast stone Velalisier not far from the Labyrinth of the Pontifex; but those cities had died thousands of years ago, and with the coming of the human and other races to Majipoor the native Piurivars had been forced back into the darker places of the planet, mainly a great wooded reservation in Zimroel somewhere southeast of Khyntor. To his knowledge Dekkeret had seen actual Metamorphs only two or three times, frail greenish folk with strange blank-featured faces, but of course they slid from one form to another in mimicry of a marvelously easy kind and for all he knew this little Vroon here was a secret Shapeshifter, or Barjazid himself.

He said, "How can Shapeshifters or anyone else survive in this desert?"

"They're resourceful people. They adapt."

"Are there many of them here?"

"Who can know? I've encountered a few scattered bands, fifty, seventy-five all told. Probably there are others. Or perhaps I keep meeting the same ones over and over again in different guises, eh?"

"A strange people," Dekkeret said, rubbing his hand idly over the smooth stone dome atop the nearest of the altar-columns. With astonishing speed Barjazid grasped Dekkeret's wrist and pulled it back.

"Don't touch those!"

"Why not?" said Dekkeret, amazed.

"Those stones are holy."

"To you?"

"To those who erected them," said Barjazid dourly. "We respect them. We honor the magic that may be in them. And in this land one never casually invites the vengeance of one's neighbors."

Dekkeret stared in astonishment at the little man, at the columns, at the two pools, the graceful sharp-leaved trees that surrounded them. Even in the heat he shivered. He looked out, beyond the borders of the little oasis, to the swaybacked dunes all around, to the dusty ribbon of road that disappeared southward into the land of mysteries. The sun was climbing quickly now and its warmth was like a terrible flail pounding the sky, the land, the few vulnerable travelers wandering in this awful place. He glanced back, to the mountains he had just passed through, a huge and ominous wall cutting him off from what passed for civilization on this torrid continent. He felt frighteningly alone here, weak, lost.

Dinitak Barjazid appeared, tottering under a great load of flasks that he dropped almost at Dekkeret's feet. Dekkeret helped the boy fill them from the pure pool, a task that took an unexpectedly long while. He sampled the water himself: cool, clear, with a strange metallic taste, not displeasing, that Dinitak said came from dissolved minerals. It took a dozen trips to carry all the flasks to the floater. There would be no more sources of fresh water, Dinitak explained, for several days.

They lunched on the usual rough provisions and afterward, as the heat rose toward its overwhelming midday peak, they settled on the straw mats to sleep. This was the third day that Dekkeret had slept by day and by now his body was growing attuned to the change; he closed his eyes, commended his soul to the beloved Lady of the Isle, Lord Prestimion's holy mother, and tumbled almost instantly into heavy slumber.

This time dreams came.

He had not dreamed properly for more days than he cared to remember. To Dekkeret as to all other folk of Majipoor dreams were a central part of existence, nightly providing comfort, reassurance, instruction, clarification, guidance and reprimands, and much else. From childhood one was trained to make one's mind receptive to the messengers of sleep, to observe and record one's dreams, to carry them with one through the night and into the waking hours beyond. And always there was the benevolent omnipresent figure of the Lady of the Isle of Sleep hovering over one, helping one explore the working of one's spirit and through her sendings offering direct communication to each of the billions of souls that dwelled on vast Majipoor.

Dekkeret now saw himself walking on a mountain ridge that he perceived to be the crest of the range they had lately crossed. He was by himself and the sun was impossibly great, filling half the sky; yet the heat was not troublesome. So steep was the slope that he could look straight down over the edge, down and down and down for what seemed hundreds of miles, and he beheld a roaring smoking cauldron beneath him, a surging volcanic crater in which red magma bubbled and churned. That immense vortex of subterranean power did not frighten him; indeed it exerted a strange pull, a blatant appeal, so that he yearned to plunge himself into it, to dive to its depths and swim in its molten heart. He began to descend, running and skipping, often leaving the ground and floating, drifting, flying down the immense hillside, and as he drew nearer he thought he saw faces in the throbbing lava, Lord Prestimion, and the Pontifex, and Barjazid's face, and Golator Lasgia's—and were those Metamorphs, those strange sly half-visible images near the periphery? The core of the volcano was a stew of potent figures. Dekkeret ran toward them in love, thinking, Take me into you, here I am, here I come; and when he perceived, behind all the others, a great white disk that he understood to be the loving countenance of the Lady of the Isle, a deep and powerful bliss invaded his soul, for he knew this now to be a sending, and it was many months since last the kind Lady had touched his sleeping mind.

Sleeping but aware, watching the Dekkeret within the dream, he awaited the consummation, the joining of dream-Dekkeret to dream-Lady, the immolation in the volcano that would bring some revelation of truth, some instant of knowledge leading to joy. But then a strangeness crossed the dream like some spreading veil. The colors faded; the faces dimmed; he continued to run down the side of the mountain wall, but now he stumbled often, he tripped and sprawled, he abraded his hands and knees against hot desert rocks, and he was losing the path entirely, moving sideways instead of downward, unable to progress. He had been on the verge of a moment of delight, and somehow it was out of reach now and he felt only distress, uneasiness, shock. The ecstasy that seemed to be the promise of the dream was draining from it. The brilliant colors yielded to an all-encompassing gray, and all motion ceased: he stood frozen on the mountain face, staring rigidly down at a dead crater, and the sight of it made him tremble and pull his knees to his chest, and he lay there sobbing until he woke.

He blinked and sat up. His head pounded and his eyes felt raw, and there was a dismal tension in his chest and shoulders. This was not what dreams, even the most terrifying of dreams, were supposed to provide: such a gritty residue of malaise, confusion, fear. It was early afternoon and the blinding sun hung high above the treetops. Nearby him lay Khaymak Gran and the Vroon, Serifain Reinaulion; a bit farther away was Dinitak Barjazid. They seemed sound asleep. The elder Barjazid was nowhere in view. Dekkeret rolled over and pressed his cheeks into the warm sand beside his mat and attempted to let the tension ease from him. Something had gone wrong in his sleep, he knew; some dark force had meddled in his dream, had stolen the virtue from it and given him pain in exchange. So this was what they meant by the haunting of the desert? This was dream-stealing? He drew himself together in a knotted ball. He felt soiled, used, invaded. He wondered if it would be like this every sleep-period now, as they penetrated deeper into this awful desert; he wondered whether it might get even worse.

After a time Dekkeret returned to sleep. More dreams came, stray blurred scraps without rhythm or design. He ignored them. When he woke, the day was ending and the desert-sounds, the ghost-sounds, were nibbling at his ears, tinklings and murmurings and far-off laughter. He felt more weary than if he had not slept at all.

8

The others showed no sign of having been disturbed as they slept. They greeted Dekkeret upon rising in their usual manners—the huge taciturn Skandar woman not at all, the little Vroon with amiable buzzing chirps and much coiling and interlacing of tentacles, the two Barjazids with curt nods—and if they were aware that one member of their party had been visited with torments in his dreams, they said nothing of it. After breakfast the elder Barjazid held a brief conference with Serifain Reinaulion concerning the roads they were to travel that night, and then they were off into the moonlit darkness once again.

I will pretend that nothing out of the ordinary happened, Dekkeret resolved. I will not let them know that I am vulnerable to these phantoms.

But it was a short-lived resolution. As the floater was passing through a region of dry lakebeds out of which odd gray-green stony humps projected by the thousands, Barjazid turned to him suddenly and said, breaking a long silence, "Did you dream well?"

Dekkeret knew he could not conceal his fatigue. "I have had better rest," he muttered.

Barjazid's glossy eyes were fixed inexorably on his. "My son says you moaned in your sleep, that you rolled over many times and clutched your knees. Did you feel the touch of the dream-stealers, Initiate?"

"I felt the presence of a troubling power in my dreams. Whether this was the touch of the dream-stealers I have no way of knowing."

"Will you describe the sensations?"

"Are you a dream-speaker then, Barjazid?" Dekkeret snapped in sudden anger. "Why should I let you probe and poke in my mind? My dreams are my own!"

"Peace, peace, good knight. I meant no intrusion."

"Let me be, then."

"Your safety is my responsibility. If the demons of this wasteland have begun to reach your spirit, it is in your own interest to inform me."

"Demons, are they?"

"Demons, ghosts, phantoms, disaffected Shapeshifters, whatever they are," Barjazid said impatiently. "The beings that prey on sleeping travelers. Did they come to you or did they not?"

"My dreams were not pleasing."

"I ask you to tell me in what way."

Dekkeret let his breath out slowly. "I felt I was having a sending from the Lady, a dream of peace and joy. And gradually it changed its nature, do you see? It darkened and became chaotic, and all the joy was taken from it, and I ended the dream worse than when I entered it."

Nodding earnestly, Barjazid said, "Yes, yes, those are the symptoms. A touch on the mind, an invasion of the dream, a disturbing overlay, a taking of energy."

"A kind of vampirism?" Dekkeret suggested. "Creatures that lie in wait in this wasteland and tap the life-force from unwary travelers?"

Barjazid smiled. "You insist on speculations. I make no hypotheses of any kind, Initiate."

"Have you felt their touch in your own sleep?"

The small man stared at Dekkeret strangely. "No. No, never."

"Never? Are you immune?"

"Seemingly so."

"And your boy?"

"It has befallen him several times. It happens to him only rarely out here, one time out of fifty, perhaps. But the immunity is not hereditary, it appears."

"And the Skandar? And the Vroon?"

"They too have been touched," said Barjazid. "On infrequent occassions. They find it bothersome but not intolerable."

"Yet others have died from the dream-stealers' touch."

"More hypothesis," said Barjazid. "Most travelers passing this way in recent years have reported experiencing strange dreams. Some of them have lost their way and have failed to return. How can we know whether there is a connection between the disturbing dreams and the losing of the way?"

"You are a very cautious man," Dekkeret said. "You leap to no conclusions."

"And I have survived to a fair old age, while many who were more rash have returned to the Source."

"Is mere survival the highest achievement you think one can attain?"

Barjazid laughed. "Spoken like a true knight of the Castle! No, Initiate, I think there's more to living than mere avoidance of death. But survival helps, eh, Initiate? Survival's a good basic requirement for those who go on to do high deeds. The dead don't achieve a thing."

Dekkeret did not care to pursue that theme. The code of values of a knight-initiate and of such a one as Barjazid were hardly comparable; and, besides, there was something wily and mercurial about Barjazid's style of argument that made Dekkeret feel slow and stolid and hulking, and he disliked exposing himself to that feeling. He was silent a moment. Then he said, "Do the dreams get worse as one gets deeper into the desert?"

"So I am given to understand," said Barjazid.

Yet as the night waned and the time for making camp arrived, Dekkeret found himself ready and even eager to contend once more with the phantoms of sleep. They had camped this day far out on the bowl of the desert, in a low-lying area where much of the sand had been swept aside by scouring winds, and the underlying rock shield showed through. The dry air had a weird crackle to it, a kind of wind-borne buzz, as if the force of the sun were stripping the particles of matter bare in this place. It was only an hour before midday by the time they were ready for sleep. Dekkeret settled calmly on his mat of straw and, without fear, offered his soul on the verge of slumber to whatever might come. In his order of knighthood he had been trained in the customary notions of courage, naturally, and was expected to meet challenges without fear, but he had been little tested thus far. On placid Majipoor one must work hard to find such challenges, going into the untamed parts of the world, for in the settled regions life is orderly and courteous; therefore Dekkeret had gone abroad, but he had not done well by his first major trial, in the forests of the Khyntor Marches. Here he had another chance. These foul dreams held forth to him, in a way, the promise of redemption.

He gave himself up to sleep.

And quickly dreamed. He was back in Tolaghai, but a Tolaghai curiously transformed, a city of smooth-faced alabaster villas and dense green gardens, though the heat was still of tropical intensity. He wandered up one boulevard and down the next, admiring the elegance of the architecture and the splendor of the shrubbery. His clothing was the traditional green and gold of the Coronal's entourage, and as he encountered the citizens of Tolaghai making their twilight promenades he bowed gracefully to them, and exchanged with them the starburst finger-symbol that acknowledged the Coronal's authority. To him now came the slender figure of the lovely Archiregimand Golator Lasgia. She smiled, she took him by the hand, she led him to a place of cascading fountains where cool spray drifted through the air, and there they put their clothing aside and bathed, and rose naked from the sweet-scented pool, and strolled, feet barely touching the ground, into a garden of plants with arching stems and great glistening many-lobed leaves. Without words she encouraged him onward, along shadowy avenues bordered by rows of close-planted trees. Golator Lasgia moved just ahead of him, an elusive and tantalizing figure, floating only inches out of his reach and then gradually widening the distance to feet and yards. At first it seemed hardly a difficult task to overtake her, but he made no headway at it, and had to move faster and faster to keep within sight of her. Her rich olive-hued skin gleamed by early moonlight, and she glanced back often, smiling brilliantly, tossing her head to urge him to keep up. But he could not. She was nearly an entire length of the garden ahead of him now. With growing desperation he impelled himself toward her, but she was dwindling, disappearing, so far ahead of him now that he could barely see the play of muscles beneath her glowing bare skin, and as he rushed from one pathway of the garden to the next he became aware of an increase in the temperature, a sudden and steady change in the air, for somehow the sun was rising here in the night and its full force was striking his shoulders. The trees were wilting and drooping. Leaves were falling. He struggled to remain upright. Golator Lasgia was only a dot on the horizon now, still beckoning to him, still smiling, still tossing her head, but she grew smaller and smaller, and the sun was still climbing, growing stronger, searing, incinerating, withering everything within its reach. Now the garden was a place of gaunt bare branches and rough cracked arid soil. A dreadful thirst had come over him, but there was no water here, and when he saw figures lurking behind the blistered and blackened trees—Metamorphs, they were, subtle tricky creatures that would not hold their shapes still, but flickered and flowed in a maddening way—he called out to them for something to drink, and was given only light tinkling laughter to ease his dryness. He staggered on. The fierce pulsing light in the heavens was beginning to roast him; he felt his skin hardening, crackling, crisping, splitting. Another moment of this and he would be charred. What had become of Golator Lasgia? Where were the smiling, bowing, starburst-making townspeople? He saw no garden now. He was in the desert, lurching and stumbling through a torrid baking wasteland where even shadows burned. Now real terror rose in him, for even as he dreamed he felt the pain of the heat, and the part of his soul that was observing all this grew alarmed, thinking that the power of the dream might well be so great as to reach up to injure his physical self. There were tales of such things, people who had perished in their sleep of dreams that had overwhelming force. Although it went against his training to terminate a dream prematurely, although he knew he must ordinarily see even the worst of horrors through to its ultimate revelation, Dekkeret considered awakening himself for safety's sake, and nearly did; but then he saw that as a species of cowardice and vowed to remain in the dream even it if cost him his life. He was down on his knees now, groveling in the fiery sands, staring with strange clarity at mysterious tiny golden-bodied insects that were marching in single file across the rims of the dunes toward him: ants, they were, with ugly swollen jaws, and each in turn clambered up his body and took a tiny nip, the merest bit, and clung and held on, so that within moments thousands of the minute creatures were covering his skin. He brushed at them but could not dislodge them. Their pincers held and their heads came loose from their bodies: the sand about him was black now with headless ants, but they spread over his skin like a cloak, and he brushed and brushed with greater vigor while still more ants mounted him and dug their jaws in. He grew weary of brushing at them. It was actually cooler in this cloak of ants, he thought. They shielded him from the worst force of the sun, although they too stung and burned him, but not as painfully as did the sun's rays. Would the dream never end? He attempted to take control of it himself, to turn the stream of onrushing ants into a rivulet of cool pure water, but that did not work, and he let himself slip back into the nightmare and went crawling wearily onward over the sands.

And gradually Dekkeret became aware that he was no longer dreaming.

There was no boundary between sleep and wakefulness that he could detect, except that eventually he realized that his eyes were open and that his two centers of consciousness, the dreamer who observed and the dream-Dekkeret who suffered, had merged into one. But he was still in the desert, under the terrible midday sun. He was naked. His skin felt raw and blistered. And there were ants crawling on him, up his legs as far as his knees, minute pale ants that indeed were nipping their tiny pincers into his flesh. Bewildered, he wondered if he had tumbled into some layer of dream beneath dream, but no, so far as he could tell this was the waking world, this was the authentic desert and he was out in the midst of it. He stood up, brushing the ants away—and as in the dream they gripped him even at the cost of their heads—and looked about for the campsite.

He could not see it. In his sleep he had wandered out onto the bare scorching anvil of the open desert and he was lost. Let this be a dream still, he thought fiercely, and let me awaken from it in the shade of Barjazid's floater. But there was no awakening. Dekkeret understood now how lives were lost in the Desert of Stolen Dreams.

"Barjazid?" he called. "*Barjazid!*"

9

Echoes came back to him from the distant hills. He called again, two, three times, and listened to the reverberations of his own voice, but heard no reply. How long could he survive out here? An hour? Two? He had no water, no shelter, not even a scrap of clothing. His head was bare to the sun's great blazing eye. It was the hottest part of the day. The landscape looked the same in all directions, flat, a shallow bowl swept by hot winds. He searched for his own footprints, but the trail gave out within yards, for the ground was hard and rocky here and he had left no imprint. The camp might lie anywhere about, hidden from him by the slightest of rises in the terrain. He called out again for help and again heard only echoes. Perhaps if he could find a dune he would bury himself to his neck, and wait out the heat that way, and by darkness he might locate the camp by its campfire; but he saw no dunes. If there were a high place here that would give him a sweeping view, he would mount it and search the horizon for the camp. But he saw no hillocks. What would Lord Stiamot do in such a situation, he wondered, or Lord Thimin, or one of the other great warriors of the past? What is Dekkeret going to do? This was a foolish way to die, he thought, a useless, nasty, ugly death. He turned and turned and turned again, scanning every way. No clues; no point in walking at all, not knowing where he was going. He shrugged and crouched in a place where there were no ants. There was no dazzlingly clever ploy that he could use to save himself. There was no inner resource that would bring him, against all the odds, to safety. He had lost himself in his sleep, and he would die just as Golator Lasgia had said he would, and that was all there was to it. Only one thing remained to him, and that was strength of character: he would die quietly and calmly, without tears or anger, without raging against the forces of fate. Perhaps it would take an hour. Perhaps less. The important thing was to die honorably, for when death is inevitable there's no sense making a botch of it.

He waited for it to come.

What came instead—ten minutes later, half an hour, an hour, he had no way of knowing—was Serafain Reinaulion. The Vroon appeared like a mirage out of the east, trudging slowly toward Dekkeret struggling under the weight of two flasks of water, and when he was within a hundred yards or so he waved two of his tentacles and called, "Are you alive?"

"More or less. Are you real?"

"Real enough. And we've been searching for you half the afternoon." In a flurry of rubbery limbs the small creature pushed one of the flasks upward into Dekkeret's hands. "Here. Sip it. Don't gulp. *Don't gulp*. You're so dehydrated you'll drown if you're too greedy."

Dekkeret fought the impulse to drain the flask in one long pull. The Vroon was right; sip, sip, be moderate, or harm will come. He let the water trickle into his mouth, swished it around, soaked his swollen tongue in it, finally let it down his throat. *Ah*. Another cautious sip. Another, then a fair swallow. He grew a little dizzy. Serifain Reinuaulion beckoned for the flask. Dekkeret shook him off, drank again, rubbed a little of the water against his cheeks and lips.

"How far are we from the camp?" he asked finally.

"Ten minutes. Are you strong enough to walk, or shall I go back for the others?"

"I can walk."

"Let's get started, then."

Dekkeret nodded. "One more little sip—"

"Carry the flask. Drink whenever you like. If you get weak, tell me and we'll rest. Remember, I can't carry you."

The Vroon headed off slowly toward a low sandy ridge perhaps five hundred yards to the east. Feeling wobbly and lightheaded, Dekkeret followed, and was surprised to see the ground trending upward; the ridge was not all that low, he realized, but some trick of the glare had made him think otherwise. In fact it rose to two or three times his own height, high enough to conceal two lesser ridges on the far side. The floater was parked in the shadow of the farther one.

Barjazid was the only person at the camp. He glanced up at Dekkeret with what looked like contempt or annoyance in this eyes and said, "Went for a stroll, did you? At noontime?"

"Sleepwalking. The dream-stealers had me. It was like being under a spell." Dekkeret was shivering as the sunburn began to disrupt his body's heat-shedding systems. He dropped down alongside the floater and huddled under a light robe. "When I woke I couldn't see camp. I was sure that I would die."

"Half an hour more and you would have. You must be two-thirds fried as it is. Lucky for you my boy woke up and saw that you had disappeared."

Dekkeret pulled the robe tighter around him. "Is that how they die out here? By sleepwalking at midday?"

"One of the ways, yes."

"I owe you my life."

"You've owed me your life since we crossed Khulag Pass. Going on your own you'd have been dead fifty times already. But thank the Vroon, if you have to thank anyone. He did the real work of finding you."

Dekkeret nodded. "Where's your son? And Khaymak Gran? Out looking for me also?"

"On their way back," said Barjazid. And indeed the Skandar and the boy appeared only moments later. Without a glance at him the Skandar flung herself down on her sleeping-mat; Dinitak Barjazid grinned slyly at Dekkeret and said, "Had a pleasant walk?"

"Not very. I regret the inconvenience I caused you."

"As do we."

"Perhaps I should sleep tied down from now on."

"Or with a heavy weight sitting on your chest," Dinitak suggested. He yawned. "Try to stay put until sundown, at least. Will you?"

"So I intend," said Dekkeret.

But it was impossible for him to fall asleep. His skin itched in a thousand places from the bites of the insects, and the sunburn, despite a cooling ointment that Serifain Reinaulion gave him, made him miserable. There was a dry, dusty feeling in his throat that no amount of water seemed to cure, and his eyes throbbed painfully. As though probing an irritating sore he ran through his memories of his desert ordeal again and again—the dream, the heat, the ants, the thirst, the awareness of imminent death. Rigorously he searched for moments of cowardice and found none. Dismay, yes, and anger, and discomfort, but he had no recollection of panic or fear. Good. Good. The worst part of the experience, he decided, had not been the heat and thirst and peril but the dream, the dark and disturbing dream, the dream that had once again begun in joy and midway had undergone a somber metamorphosis. To be denied the solace of healthy dreams is a kind of death-in-life, he thought, far worse than perishing in a desert, for dying occupies only a single moment but dreaming affects all of one's time to come. And what knowledge was it that these bleak Suvraelu dreams were imparting? Dekkeret knew that when dreams came from the Lady they must be studied intently, if necessary with the aid of one who practices the art of dream-speaking, for they contain information vital to the proper conduct of one's life; but these dreams were hardly of the Lady, seeming rather to emanate from some other dark Power, some sinister and oppressive force more adept at taking than giving. Shapeshifters? It could be. What if some tribe of them had, through deceit, obtained one of the devices by which the Lady of the Isle is able to reach the minds of her flock, and lurked here in the hot heartland of Suvrael preying on unwary travelers, stealing from their souls, draining their vitality, imposing an unknown and unfathomable revenge one by one upon those who had stolen their world?

As the afternoon shadows lengthened he found himself at last slipping back into sleep. He fought it, fearing the touch of the invisible intruders on his soul once again. Desperately he held his eyes open, staring across the darkening wasteland and listening to the eerie hum and buzz of the desert-sounds; but it was impossible to fend off exhaustion longer. He drifted into a light, uneasy slumber, broken from time to time by dreams that he sensed came neither from the Lady nor from any other external force, but merely floated randomly through the strata of his weary mind, bits of patternless incident and stray incomprehensible images. And then someone was shaking him awake—the Vroon, he realized. Dekkeret's mind was foggy and slow. He felt numbed. His lips were cracked, his back was sore. Night had fallen, and his companions were already at work closing down their camp.

Serifain Reinaulion offered Dekkeret a cup of some sweet thick blue-green juice, and he drank it in a single draught.

"Come," the Vroon said. "Time to be going onward."

10

Now the desert changed again and the landscape grew violent and rough. Evidently there had been great earthquakes here, and more than one, for the land lay fractured and upheaved, with mighty blocks of the desert floor piled at unlikely angles against others, and huge sprawls of talus at the feet of the low shattered cliffs. Through this chaotic zone of turbulence and disruption there was only a single passable route—the wide, gently curving bed of a long-extinct river whose sandy floor swerved in long easy bends between the cracked and sundered rock-heaps. The large moon was full and there was almost a daylight brilliance to the grotesque scene. After some hours of passing through a terrain so much the same from one mile to the next that it seemed almost as though the floater were not moving at all, Dekkeret turned to Barjazid and said, "And how long will it be before we reach Ghyzyn Kor?"

"This valley marks the boundary between desert and grazing lands." Barjazid pointed toward the southwest, where the riverbed vanished between two towering craggy peaks that rose like daggers from the desert floor. "Beyond that place—Munnerak Notch—the climate is altogether different. On the far side of the mountain wall sea-fogs enter by night from the west, and the land is green and fit for grazing. We will camp halfway to the Notch tomorrow, and pass through it the day after. By Seaday at the latest you'll be at your lodgings in Ghyzyn Kor."

"And you?" Dekkeret asked.

"My son and I have business elsewhere in the area. We'll return to Ghyzyn Kor for you after—three days? Five?"

"Five should be sufficient."

"Yes. And then the return journey."

"By the same route?"

"There is no other," said Barjazid. "They explained to you in Tolaghai, did they not, that access to the rangelands was cut off, except by way of this desert? But why should you fear this route? The dreams aren't so awful, are they? And so long as you do no more roaming in your sleep, you'll not be in any danger here."

It sounded simple enough. Indeed he felt sure he could survive the trip; but yesterday's dream had been sufficient torment, and he looked without cheer upon what might yet come. When they made camp the next morning Dekkeret found himself again uneasy about entrusting himself to sleep at all. For the first hour of the rest-period he kept himself awake, listening to the metallic clangor of the bare tumbled rocks as they stretched and quivered in the midday heat, until at last sleep came up over his mind like a dense black cloud and took him unawares.

And in time a dream possessed him, and it was, he knew at its outset, going to be the most terrible of all.

Pain came first—an ache, a twinge, a pang, then without warning a racking explosion of dazzling light against the walls of his skull, making him grunt and clutch his head. The agonizing spasm passed swiftly, though, and he felt the soft sleep presence of Golator Lasgia about him, soothing him, cradling him against her breasts. She rocked him and murmured to him and eased him until he opened his eyes and sat up and looked around and saw that he was out of the desert, free of Suvrael itself. He and Golator Lasgia were in some cool forest glade where giant trees with perfectly straight yellow-barked trunks rose to incomprehensible heights, and a swiftly flowing stream, studded with rocky outcroppings, tumbled and roared wildly past almost at their feet. Beyond the stream the land dropped sharply away, revealing a distant valley, and, on the far side of it, a great gray saw-toothed snow-capped mountain which Dekkeret recognized instantly as one of the nine vast peaks of the Khyntor Marches.

"No," he said. "This is not where I want to be."

Golator Lasgia laughed, and the pretty tinkling sound of it was somehow sinister in his ears, like the delicate sounds the desert made at twilight. "But this is a dream, good friend! You must take what comes, in dreams!"

"I will direct my dream. I have no wish to return to the Khyntor Marches. Look: the scene changes. We are on the Zimr, approaching the river's great bend. See? See? The city of Ni-moya sparkling there before us?"

Indeed he saw the huge city, white against the green backdrop of forested hills. But Golator Lasgia shook her head.

"There is no city here, my love. There is only the northern forest. Feel the wind? Listen to the song of the stream. Here—kneel, scoop up the fallen needles on the ground. Ni-moya is far away, and we are here to hunt."

"I beg you, let us be in Ni-moya."

"Another time," said Golator Lasgia.

He could not prevail. The magical towers of Ni-moya wavered and grew transparent and were gone, and there remained only the yellow-boled trees, the chilly breezes, the sounds of the forest. Dekkeret trembled. He was the prisoner of this dream and there was no escape.

And now five hunters in rough black haigus-hide robes appeared and made perfunctory gestures of deference and held forth weapons to him, the blunt dull tube of an energy-thrower and a short sparkling poniard and a blade of a longer kind with a hooked tip. He shook his head, and one of the hunters came close and grinned mockingly at him, a gap-toothed grin out of a wide mouth stinking from dried fish. Dekkeret recognized her face, and looked away in shame, for she was the hunter who had died on that other day in the Khyntor Marches a thousand thousand years ago. If only she were not here now, he thought, the dream might be bearable. But this was diabolical torture, to force him to live through all this once again.

Golator Lasgia said, "Take the weapons from her. The steetmoy are running and we must be after them."

"I have no wish to—"

"What folly, to think that dreams respect wishes! The dream *is* your wish. Take the weapons."

Dekkeret understood. With chilled fingers he accepted the blades and the energy-thrower and stowed them in the proper place on his belt. The hunters smiled and grunted things at him in the thick harsh dialect of the north. Then they began to run along the bank of the stream, moving in easy loping bounds, touching the ground no more than one stride out of five; and willy-nilly Dekkeret ran with them, clumsily at first, then with much the same floating grace. Golator Lasgia, by his side, kept pace easily, her dark hair fluttering about her face, her eyes bright with excitement. They turned left, into the heart of the forest, and fanned out in a crescent formation that widened and curved inward to confront the prey.

The prey! Dekkeret could see three white-furred steetmoy gleaming like lanterns deep in the forest. The beasts prowled uneasily, growling, aware of intruders but still unwilling to abandon their territory—big creatures, possibly the most dangerous wild animals on Majipoor, quick and powerful and cunning, the terrors of the northlands. Dekkeret drew his poniard. Killing steetmoy with energy-throwers was no sport, and might damage too much of their valuable fur besides: one was supposed to get to close range and kill them with one's blade, preferably the poniard, if necessary the hooked machete.

The hunters looked to him. Pick one, they were saying, choose your quarry. Dekkeret nodded. The middle one, he indicated. They were smiling coldly. What did they know that they were not telling him? It had been like this that other time, too, the barely concealed scorn of the mountainfolk for the pampered lordlings who were seeking deadly amusements in their forests; and that outing had ended badly. Dekkert hefted his poniard. The dream-steetmoy that moved nervously beyond those trees were implausibly enormous, great heavy-haunched immensities that clearly could not be slain by one man alone, wielding only hand-weapons, but here there was no turning back, for he knew himself to be bound upon whatever destiny the dream offered him. Now with hunting-horns and hand-clapping the hired hunters commenced to stampede the prey; the steetmoy, angered and baffled by the sudden blaring strident sounds, rose high, whirled, raked trees with their claws, swung around, and more in disgust than fear began to run.

The chase was on.

Dekkeret knew that the hunters were separating the animals, driving the two rejected ones away to allow him a clear chance at the one he had chosen. But he looked neither to the right nor the left. Accompanied by

Golator Lasgia and one of the hunters, he rushed forward, giving pursuit as the steetmoy in the center went rumbling and crashing through the forest. This was the worst part, for although humans were faster, steetmoy were better able to break through barriers of underbrush, and he might well lose his quarry altogether in the confusions of the run. The forest here was fairly open; but the steetmoy was heading for cover, and soon Dekkeret found himself struggling past saplings and vines and low brush, barely able to keep the retreating white phantom in view. With singleminded intensity he ran and hacked with the machete and clambered through thickets. It was all so terribly familiar, so much of an old story, especially when he realized that the steetmoy was doubling back, was looping through the trampled part of the forest as if planning a counterattack—

The moment would soon be at hand, the dreaming Dekkeret knew, when the maddened animal would blunder upon the gap-toothed hunter, would seize the mountain woman and hurl her against a tree, and Dekkeret, unwilling or unable to halt, would go plunging onward, continuing the chase, leaving the woman where she lay, so that when the squat thick-snouted scavenging beast emerged from its hole and began to rip her belly apart there would be no one to defend her, and only later, when things were more quiet and there was time to go back for the injured hunter, would he begin to regret the callous uncaring focus of concentration that had allowed him to ignore his fallen companion for the sake of keeping sight of his prey. And afterward the shame, the guilt, the unending self-accusations—yes, he would go through all that again as he lay here asleep in the stifling heat of the Suvraelu desert, would he not?

No.

No, it was not that simple at all, for the language of dreams is complex, and in the thick mists that suddenly enfolded the forest Dekkeret saw the steetmoy swing around and lash the gap-toothed woman and knock her flat, but the woman rose and spat out a few bloody teeth and laughed, and the chase continued, or rather it twisted back on itself to the same point, the steetmoy bursting forth unexpectedly from the darkest part of the woods and striking at Dekkeret himself, knocking his poniard and his machete from his hands, rearing high overhead for the death-blow, but not delivering it, for the image changed and it was Golator Lasgia who lay beneath the plunging claws while Dekkeret wandered aimlessly nearby, unable to move in any useful direction, and then it was the huntswoman who was the victim once more, and Dekkeret again, and suddenly and improbably old pinch-faced Barjazid, and then Golator Lasgia. As Dekkeret watched, a voice at his elbow said, "What does it matter? We each owe the Divine a death. Perhaps it was more important for you then to follow your prey." Dekkeret stared. The voice was the voice of the gap-toothed hunter. The sound of it left him dazed and shaking. The dream was becoming bewildering. He struggled to penetrate its mysteries.

Now he saw Barjazid standing at his side in the dark cool forest glade. The steetmoy once more was savaging the mountain woman.

"Is this the way it truly was?" Barjazid asked.

"I suppose so. I didn't see it."

"What did you do?"

"Kept on going. I didn't want to lose the animal."

"You killed it?"

"Yes."

"And then?"

"Came back. And found her. Like that—"

Dekkeret pointed. The snuffling scavenger was astride the woman. Golator Lasgia stood nearby, arms folded, smiling.

"And then?"

"The others came. They buried their companion. We skinned the steetmoy and rode back to camp."

"And then? And then? And then?"

"Who are you? Why are you asking me this?"

Dekkeret had a flashing view of himself beneath the scavenger's fanged snout.

Barjazid said, "You were ashamed?"

"Of course. I put the pleasures of my sport ahead of a human life."

"You had no way of knowing she was injured."

"I sensed it. I saw it, but I didn't *let* myself see it, do you understand? I knew she was hurt. I kept on going."

"Who cared?"

"I cared."

"Did her tribesmen seem to care?"

"I cared."

"And so? And so? And so?"

"It mattered to me. Other things matter to them."

"You felt guilty?"

"Of course."

"You *are* guilty. Of youth, of foolishness, of naïveté."

"And are you my judge?"

"Of course I am," said Barjazid. "See my face?" He tugged at his seamed weatherbeaten jowls, pulled and twisted until his leathery desert-tanned skin began to split, and the face ripped away like a mask, revealing another face beneath, a hideous ironic distorted face twisted with convulsive mocking laughter, and the other face was Dekkeret's own.

11

In that moment Dekkeret experienced a sensation as of a bright needle of piercing light driving downward through the roof of his skull. It was the most intense pain he had ever known, a sudden intolerable spike of racking anguish that burned through his brain with monstrous force. It lit a flare in his consciousness by whose baleful light he saw himself grimly illuminated, fool, romantic, boy, sole inventor of a drama about which no one else cared, inventing a tragedy that had an audience of one, seeking purgation for a sin without context, which was no sin at all except perhaps the sin of self-indulgence. In the midst of his agony Dekkeret heard a great gong tolling far away and the dry rasping sound of Barjazid's demonic laughter; then with a sudden wrenching twist he pulled free of sleep and rolled over, quivering, shaken, still afflicted by the lancing thrust of the pain, although it was beginning to fade as the last bonds of sleep dropped from him.

He struggled to rise and found himself enveloped in thick musky fur, as if the steetmoy had seized him and was crushing him against its breast. Powerful arms gripped him—*four* arms, he realized, and as Dekkeret completed the journey up out of dreams he understood that he was in the embrace of the giant Skandar woman, Khaymak Gran. Probably he had been crying out in his sleep, thrashing and flailing about, and as he scrambled to his feet she had decided he was off on another sleepwalking excursion and was determined to prevent him from going. She was hugging him with rib-cracking force.

"It's all right," he muttered, tight against her heavy gray pelt. "I'm awake! I'm not going anywhere!"

Still she clung to him.

"You're—hurting—me—"

He fought for breath. In her great awkward solicitousness she was apt to kill him with motherly kindness. Dekkeret pushed, even kicked, twisted, hammered at her with his head. Somehow as he wriggled in her grasp he threw her off balance, and they toppled together, she beneath him; at the last moment her arms opened, allowing Dekkeret to spin away. He landed on both knees and crouched where he fell, aching in a dozen places and befuddled by all that had happened in the last few moments. But not so befuddled that when he stood up he failed to see Barjazid, on the far side of the floater, hastily removing some sort of mechanism from his forehead, some slender crownlike circlet, and attempting to conceal it in a compartment of the floater.

"What was that?" Dekkeret demanded.

Barjazid looked uncharacteristically flustered. "Nothing. A toy, only."

"Let me see."

Barjazid seemed to signal. Out of the corner of his eye Dekkeret saw Khaymak Gran getting to her feet and beginning to reach for him again, but before the ponderous Skandar could manage it Dekkeret had skipped out of the way and darted around the floater to Barjazid's side. The little man was still busy with his intricate bit of machinery. Dekkeret, looming over him as the Skandar had loomed over Dekkeret, swiftly caught Barjazid's hand and yanked it up behind his back. Then he plucked the mechanism from its storage case and examined it.

Everyone was awake now. The Vroon stared goggle-eyed at what was going on; and young Dinitak, producing a knife that was not much unlike the one in Dekkeret's dream, glared up at him and said, "Let go of my father."

Dekkeret swung Barjazid around to serve as a shield.

"Tell your son to put that blade away," he said.

Barjazid was silent.

Dekkeret said, "He drops the blade or I smash this thing in my hand. Which?"

Barjazid gave the order in a low growling tone. Dinitak pitched the knife into the sand almost at Dekkeret's feet, and Dekkeret, taking one step forward, pulled it to him and kicked it behind him. He dangled the mechanism in Barjazid's face: a thing of gold and crystal and ivory, elaborately fashioned, with mysterious wires and connections.

"What is this?" Dekkeret said.

"I told you. A toy. Please—give it to me, before you break it."

"What is the function of this toy?"

"It amuses me while I sleep," said Barjazid hoarsely.

"In what way?"

"It enhances my dreams and makes them more interesting."

Dekkeret took a closer look at it. "If I put it on, will it enhance my dreams?"

"It will only harm you, Initiate."

"Tell me what it does for you."

"That is very hard to describe," Barjazid said.

"Work at it. Strive to find the words. How did you become a figure in my dream, Barjazid? You had no business being in that particular dream."

The little man shrugged. He said uncomfortably, "Was I in your dream? How would I know what was happening in your dream? Anyone can be in anybody's dream."

"I think this machine may have helped put you there. And may have helped you know what I was dreaming."

Barjazid responded only with glum silence.

Dekkeret said, "Describe the workings of this machine, or I'll grind it to scrap in my hand."

"Please—"

Dekkeret's thick strong fingers closed on one of the most fragile-looking parts of the device. Barjazid sucked in his breath; his body went taut in Dekkeret's grip.

"Well?" Dekkeret said.

"Your guess is right. It—it lets me enter sleeping minds."

"Truly? Where did you get such a thing?"

"My own invention. A notion that I have been perfecting over a number of years."

"Like the machines of the Lady of the Isle?"

"Different. More powerful. She can only speak to minds; I can read dreams, control the shape of them, take command of a person's sleeping mind to a great degree."

"And this device is entirely of your own making. Not stolen from the Isle."

"Mine alone," Barjazid murmured.

A torrent of rage surged through Dekkeret. For an instant he wanted to crush Barjazid's machine in one quick squeeze and then to grind Barjazid himself to pulp. Remembering all of Barjazid's half-truths and evasions and outright lies, thinking of the way Barjazid had meddled in his dreams, how he had wantonly distorted and transformed the healing rest Dekkeret so sorely needed, how he had interposed layers of fears and torments and uncertainties into that Lady-sent gift, his own true blissful rest, Dekkeret felt an almost murderous fury at having been invaded and manipulated in this fashion. His heart pounded, his throat went dry, his vision blurred. His hand tightened on Barjazid's bent arm until the small man whimpered and mewed. Harder—harder—break it off—

No.

Dekkeret reached some inner peak of anger and held himself there a moment, and then let himself descend the farther slope toward tranquillity. Gradually, he regained his steadiness, caught his breath, eased the drumming in his chest. He held tight to Barjazid until he felt altogether calm. Then he released the little man and shoved him forward against the floater. Barjazid staggered and clung to the vehicle's curving side. All color seemed to have drained from his face. Tenderly he rubbed his bruised arm, and glanced up at Dekkeret with an expression that seemed to be compounded equally of terror and pain and resentment.

With care Dekkeret studied the curious instrument, gently rubbing the tips of his fingers over its elegant and complicated parts. Then he moved as if to put it on his own forehead.

Barjazid gasped. "Don't!"

"What will happen? Will I damage it?"

"You will. And yourself as well."

Dekkeret nodded. He doubted that Barjazid was bluffing, but he did not care to find out.

After a moment he said, "There are no Shapeshifter dream-stealers hiding in this desert, is that right?"

"That is so," Barjazid whispered.

"Only you, secretly experimenting on the minds of other travelers. Yes?"

"Yes."

"And causing them to die."

"No," Barjazid said. "I intended no deaths. If they died, it was because they became alarmed, became confused, because they panicked and ran off into dangerous places—because they began to wander in their sleep, as you did—"

"But they died because you had meddled in their minds."

"Who can be sure of that? Some died, some did not. I had no desire to have anyone perish. Remember, when *you* wandered away, we searched diligently for you."

"I had hired you to guide and protect me," said Dekkeret. "The others were innocent strangers whom you preyed on from afar, is that not so?"

Barjazid was silent.

"You knew that people were dying as a direct result of your experiments, and you went on experimenting."

Barjazid shrugged.

"How long were you doing this?"

"Several years."

"And for what reason?"

Barjazid looked toward the side. "I told you once, I would never answer a question of that sort."

"And if I break your machine?"

"You will break it anyway."

"Not so," Dekkeret replied. "Here. Take it."

"What?"

Dekkeret extended his hand, with the dream-machine resting on his palm. "Go on. Take it. Put it away. I don't want the thing."

"You're not going to kill me?" Barjazid said in wonder.

"Am I your judge? If I catch you using that device on me again, I'll kill you sure enough. But otherwise, no. Killing is not my sport. I have one sin on my soul as it is. And I need you to get me back to Tolaghai, or have you forgotten that?"

"Of course. of course." Barjazid looked astounded at Dekkeret's mercy.

Dekkeret said, "Why would I want to kill you?"

"For entering your mind—for interfering with your dreams—"

"Ah."

"For putting your life at risk on the desert."

"That too."

"And yet you aren't eager for vengeance?"

Dekkeret shook his head. "You took great liberties with my soul, and that angered me, but the anger is past and done with. I won't punish you. We've had a transaction, you and I, and I've had my money's worth from you, and this thing of yours has been of value to me." He leaned close and said in a low, earnest voice, "I came to Suvrael full of doubt and confusion and guilt, looking to purge myself through physical suffering. That was foolishness. Physical suffering makes the body uncomfortable and strengthens the will, but it does little for the wounded spirit. You gave me something else, you and your mind-meddling toy. You tormented me in dreams and held up a mirror to my soul, and I saw myself clearly. How much of that last dream were you really able to read, Barjazid?"

"You were in a forest—in the north—"

"Yes."

"Hunting. One of your comanions was injured by an animal, yes? Is that it?"

" Go on."

"And you ignored her. You continued the chase. And afterward, when you went back to see about her, it was too late, and you blamed yourself for her death. I sensed the great guilt in you. I felt the power of it radiating from you."

"Yes," Dekkeret said. "Guilt that I'll bear forever. But there's nothing that can be done for her now, is there?" An astonishing calmness had spread through him. He was not altogether sure what had happened, except that in his dream he had confronted the events of the Khyntor forest at last, and had faced the truth of what he had done there and what he had not done, had understood, in a way that he could not define in words, that it was folly to flagellate himself for all his lifetime over a single act of carelessness and unfeeling stupidity, that the moment had come to put aside all self-accusation and get on with the business of his life. The process of forgiving himself was under way. He had come to Suvrael to be purged and somehow he had accomplished that. And he owed Barjazid thanks for that favor. To Barjazid he said, "I might have saved her, or maybe not; but my mind was elsewhere, and in my foolishness I passed her by to make my kill. But wallowing in guilt is no useful means of atonement, eh, Barjazid? The dead are dead. My services must be offered to the living. Come: turn this floater and let's begin heading back toward Tolaghai."

"And what about your visit to the rangelands? What about Ghyzyn Kor?"

"A silly mission. It no longer matters, these questions of meat shortages and trade imbalances. Those problems are already solved. Take me to Tolaghai."

"And then?"

"You will come with me to Castle Mount. To demonstrate your toy before the Coronal."

"No!" Barjazid cried in horror. He looked genuinely frightened for the first time since Dekkeret had known him. "I beg you—"

"Father?" said Dinitak.

Under the midday sun the boy seemed ablaze with light. There was a wild and fiery look of pride on his face.

"Father, go with him to Castle Mount. Let him show his masters what we have here."

Barjazid moistened his lips. "I fear—"

"Fear nothing. Our time is now beginning."

Dekkeret looked from one to the other, from the suddenly timid and shrunken old man to the transfigured and glowing boy. He sensed that historic things were happening, that mighty forces were shifting out of balance and into a new configuration, and this he barely comprehended, except to know that his destinies and those of these desertfolk were tied in some way together; and the dream-reading machine that Barjazid had created was the thread that bound their lives.

Barjazid said huskily, "What will happen to me on Castle Mount, then?"

"I have no idea," said Dekkeret. "Perhaps they'll take your head and mount it atop Lord Siminave's Tower. Or perhaps you'll find youself set up on high as a Power of Majipoor. Anything might happen. How would I know?" He realized that he did not care, that he was indifferent to Barjazid's fate, that he felt no anger at all toward this seedy little tinkerer with minds, but only a kind of perverse abstract gratitude for Barjazid's having helped rid him of his own demons. "These matters are in the Coronal's hands. But one thing is certain, that you will go with me to the Mount, and this machine of yours with us. Come, now, turn the floater, take me to Tolaghai."

"It is still daytime," Barjazid muttered. "The heart of the day rages at its highest."

"We'll manage. Come: get us moving, and fast! We have a ship to catch in Tolaghai, and there's a woman in that city I want to see again, before we set sail!"

12

These events happened in the young manhood of him who was to become the Coronal Lord Dekkeret in the Pontificate of Prestimion. And it was the boy Dinitak Barjazid who would be the first to rule in Suvrael over the minds of all the sleepers of Majipoor, with the title of King of Dreams.